Samuel Patrick

# Terence`s Comedies

Samuel Patrick

**Terence`s Comedies**

ISBN/EAN: 9783744792660

Printed in Europe, USA, Canada, Australia, Japan

Cover: Foto ©Andreas Hilbeck / pixelio.de

More available books at **www.hansebooks.com**

# _TERENCE's_ COMEDIES,

Translated into English Prose,
As near as the Propriety of the Two Languages will admit.

Together with the

_Original Latin_ from the Best Editions.

WHEREIN

The Words of the Latin Text are ranged in their Grammatical Order; the Ellipses carefully supplied; the Observations of the most Valuable Commentators, both antient and modern, represented; and the Beauties of the Original explained in a new and concise Manner.

With Notes pointing out the Connexion of the several Scenes, and an Index Critical and Phraseological.

The Whole adapted to the Capacities of Youth at School, as well as of Private Gentlemen.

In TWO VOLUMES.

By _S. PATRICK_, LL.D.
Editor of Ainsworth's Dictionary, and Hedericus's Lexicon.

The THIRD EDITION.

VOL. II.

To which is prefixed the Life of _TERENCE_, with some Account of the Dramatic Poetry of the Antients.

LONDON:
Printed for Edward and Charles Dilly in the Poultry.

M,DCC,LXVI.

# PUBLII TERENTII ADELPHI.

# THE ADELPHI OF *TERENCE.*

# THE ADELPHI OF TERENCE.

## The TITLE.

THIS PLAY WAS EXHIBITED AT THE FUNERAL GAMES, GIVEN IN HONOUR OF L. ÆMILIUS PAULUS, BY QUINTUS FABIUS MAXIMUS AND P. CORNELIUS AFRICANUS. IT WAS ACTED BY THE COMPANIES OF L. ATILIUS PRÆNESTINUS, AND MINUCIUS PROTIMUS. FLACCUS, THE FREED-MAN OF CLAUDIUS, COMPOSED THE MUSIC, WHICH WAS PERFORMED ON TYRIAN FLUTES. IT IS COPIED FROM THE GREEK OF MENANDER, AND WAS FIRST ACTED UNDER THE CONSULSHIP OF L. ANICIUS, AND M. CORNELIUS.

## ANNOTATIONS.

[1] *L. Æmilii Pau'i.* — This is the same, *Æmilius Paulus* so famous for his Victory over *Perseus* King of *Macedonia*. He died in the Year of the City 593.

[2] *Quos fecere Q. Fabius Maximus, P. Cornelius Africanus.* — This reading is the Correction of *Muretus*, from an ancient MS. he saw at *Venice*. In former Editions we find *Q. Fabio Maximo, P. Cornelio Africano, Ædilibus Curulibus.* — This, as *Scaliger* and others have observed, must be erroneous. For not the *Curule Ædiles*, but the Childrens and the Relations of the Deceas'd, had the Care of the Funeral-Games. It is, moreover, certain, that *Scipio Africanus* was not at this time *Curule Ædile*: For we are told by *Aurelius Victor*, that the same Year he sued for the Ædileship, he was created Consul, before he had arrived at the Age required by Law; and this we know did not happen till the Year of the City 606, thirteen Years after the Death of his Father, and the Representation of this Piece; *Scipio* being even at this time only in his thirty sixth Year, at which Age, and not before, it was permitted to stand Candidate for the Ædileship. The two Persons here mentioned as giving these Games to the People, were both the Sons of *Æmilius Paulus*. The first is here called *Q. Fabius Maximus*, because he had been adopted by *Q. Fabius Maximus*; and the other *P. Cornelius Scipio*, as having been adopted by the Son of the first *Scipio Africanus*. He too afterwards, when in the third Punic War he had destroyed *Carthage*, obtained also the Name of *Africanus*. The *Curule Ædiles* of this Year were *Q. Fulvius Nobilior* and *L. Marcius*.

[3] *Tibiis Sarranis.* — *Tyre* was anciently called *Sor* by the *Phœnicians*. The *Carthaginians*, who were a Colony of that People, instead of *Sor* pronounced it *Sar*; from *Sar* it came to be called *Sarra. Sarranus* therefore is *Tyrian*, or of *Tyre*; as in *Virgil*, *Sarrano dormiat ostro;* "Let him sleep on Purple of *Tyre*." — *Sarranis Tibiis* therefore is, as we have translated it, on Tyrian

# P. TERENTII
# ADELPHI.

## TITULUS seu DIDASCALIA.

ACTA LUDIS FUNEBRIBUS L. ÆMILII PAULI, QUOS FECERE Q. FABIUS MAXIMUS, P. CORNELIUS AFRICANUS. EGERE L. ATTILIUS PRÆNESTINUS, MINUCIUS PROTIMUS. MODOS FECIT FLACCUS CLAUDII TIBIIS SARRANIS. FACTA E GRÆCA MENANDRU. L. ANICIO, M. CORNELIO COSS.

nandru; L. Anicio, M. Cornelio Consulibus.

ORDO.

HÆC comedia fuit acta ludis funebribus L. Æmilii Pauli; quos ludos Q. Fabius Maximus, P. Cornelius Africanus fecere. L. Attilius Prænestinus, Minucius Protimus egere. Flaccus Libertus Claudii fecit modos, tibiis Sarranis. Est facta è Græca Me-

## ANNOTATIONS.

*Tyrian Flutes*; that is, on equal left-handed Flutes, because they were in Imitation of the Music of *Tyre*. But here, as Madam *Dacier* observes, a great Difficulty arises: These *Tyrian* or left-handed Flutes had a great Number of Holes, and gave a shrill sharp Sound. They were employed always on Occasions of Mirth and Joy, because their Music was brisk and airy. How is it possible therefore, that the Sons of *Æmilius Paulus* should employ this kind of Music in the Representation of a Piece exhibited at the Funeral Games given in honour of their Father? This can never with any Reason be supposed. The Title therefore, as that learned Lady observes, has not only been corrupted, but considerably changed, as might easily be made appear. She therefore thinks we ought to read thus: *Acta primum tibiis Lydiis, deinde tibiis Sarranis. The Music at its first Representation was performed on Lydian Flutes, and afterwards on Tyrian.* Two equal right-handed Flutes were called *Lydian*, as being an Imitation of the Music of that Country. They had but a few Holes, and sounded a deep Base, and were on that account made use of on Occasions of Grief and Mourning, because their Music was grave and solemn. After the first Representation, it was played with left-handed Flutes, doubtless because acted upon some Occasions less mournful than this. Moreover, that she may not be accused of having proposed this Emendation without any apparent Ground for her Conjecture, she quotes the following passage from *Donatus* in his Preface to this Piece: *Modulata est autem tibiis dextris, id est, Lydiis, ob seriam gravitatem, qua fere in omnibus comœdiis utitur hic poeta. Sæpe tamen mutatis per scenam modis, cantica mutavit; quod significat titulus scenæ, habens subjectas personis literis M. M. C.* "The Music which "accompanied it in the Representation "was performed on right-handed Flutes, "or *Lydian*, on account of the Gravity "of the Subject, which prevails very much "in all our Poet's Plays. *Terence* how"ever afterwards changed the Music, as "we learn from the Title, at the Foot of "which, after the Names of the Persons, "we see these three Letters, *M. M. C. i. e.* "*Mutatis medis cantici.*" These three Letters which *Donatus* tells us were in the Titles of this Play in his Time, are not now to be found, which is a yet farther Proof that the Title is not entire.

*4 L. Anicio, M. Cornelio Coss.* Under the Consulship of *L. Anicius Gallus,* and *M. Cornelius Cethegus,* in the Year of the City 593, and 165 Years before the Birth of Christ.

MICIO *and* Demea *were two Brothers, very unlike in their Tempers: Demea followed a Country Life, the other lived in the City: this last lived single, the other had married.* Micio *was naturally mild and gentle,* Demea *severe: the first behaved with great Meekness even to Strangers, the other was rough to his own Family:* Micio *retained his Mildness even in Anger;* Demea, *at all times, looked stern.* Demea *had two Sons, the elder of whom,* Æschinus, Micio, *had adopted, and kept him with him in the City, giving him a very indulgent and liberal Education. The younger,* Ctesipho, *lived in the Country with his Father, under great Restrictions and Confinement.* Æschinus *had been in love with several Courtesans, one after another, his adopted Father winking at all; frequently gave Entertainments, and in fine gave into all the Extravagancies of Life, not only freely, but even to a degree of Licentiousness. At last he proceeded so far, that meeting one Night, when he was drunk, a young Virgin,* Pamphila *by Name, poor indeed, but virtuous, and of a good Family, whom her Mother* Sostrata, *a Widow, educated chastely, and with all the Care she could; he offered Violence to her, and got her with Child. Afterwards he came to her Mother, begging Forgiveness, and promising to take the Girl he had abused to Wife. In Consideration of this Engagement, she pardoned his Offence, and kept it secret.* Ctesipho, *as he came sometimes to the City, chanced to fall in love with a certain Music-Girl.* Æschinus, *to prevent this matter's taking Air, or coming to the Ears of his Father* Demea, *transfers the whole upon himself. But at length, when the Cock-bawd, who had the Disposal of this Girl, demanded that the Sum, at which he valued her, should be immediately told down, or threatned to sell her to another;* Ctesipho, *reduced to the highest Despair, was deliberating with himself about leaving his Country; when* Æschinus, *whom neither fear nor shame held in awe, understanding the matter, he forcibly entered the Cock-bawd's House, and, after beating and abusing him and his Family, carries off the Girl, and gives her to his Brother. The Noise of this Accident soon runs through the City;* Demea *comes to Town, accuses his Brother, exclaims and appeals to Gods and Men, that it was wholly through* Micio's *fault that* Æschinus *was become so dissolute, intemperate, given to Wine and Women, and in a word, had abandoned himself to every thing that was bad. He thanked the Gods, that he, at least, who lived in the Country with him, was temperate and frugal, minded both his Fortune and Reputation, and never so much as thought of those Excesses; so great was the difference between his Manner of training up his Son and his Brother's.* Micio *endeavours all he can to pacify him, and had actually accomplished it, when another Accident fell out, which raised yet greater Disturbances. The Story of the Music-Girl, whom* Æschinus *had carried off by Force, is brought to the Mother of* Pamphila, *who was so far gone with Child, that she was at this very time in Labour.*

*What*

# *M. Antonii Mureti* ARGUMENTUM.

*MICIO, et Demea, duo diffimillimo fratres ingenio fuere: ille urbanam vitam fecutus eft; hic rufticam? ille cœlebs vixit; hic uxorem duxit: ille ingenio leniffimo; hic afperrimo: ille mitis etiam in alienos; hic fævus etiam in fuos: ille etiam in irà placidus; hic etiam citra iram ferox. Erant Demeæ filii duo: ex quibus natu majorem Æfchinum fibi adoptavit Micio, eumque fecum in urbe liberaliffime indulgentiffimeque educavit. Minorem Ctefiphonem ruri fecum fevere imprimis ac reftricte habuit pater. Æfchinus multas meretrices, patre ad omnia connivente, adamavit: multa convivia celebravit; quæ denique juventus fert, ea omnia, non libere modo, fed etiam licenter exercuit. Poftremo ufque eo progreffus eft: in virginem pauperculam quidem, fed bonam, bonis prognatam, Pamphilam nomine, quam mater Softrata vidua fancte fecum et pudice, ut poterat, educabat, noctu temulentus quum incidiffet, vim ei attulit, gravidamque fecit. Venit poftea ad matrem illius, veniam petens, pollicenfque fe puellam uxorem ducturum. Ea fide data, et ignotum eft, et tacitum. Ctefipho, cum in urbem interdum ventitaret, ipfe quoque cithariftriæ cujufdam amore correptus eft. Totam ejus rei famam, ne qua emanaret, ac perveniret ad Demeam, in fefe Æfchinus transferebat. Tandem, quum leno, puellæ dominus, aut pecuniam fibi, quanti ea erat, vellet in manum dari, aut fe eam alii venditurum minitaretur, adductus in fummam defperationem Ctefipho, jam de relinquenda patria cogitabat: quum Æfchinus, re intellecta, qui nullo neque pudore teneretur, neque metu, domum lenonis per vim ingreffus eft, et ipfum et familiam contudit pugnis, puellamque per vim abreptam tradidit fratri. Spargitur tota urbe rumor, venit Demea, Micionem objurgat, inclamat, teftatur deos atque homines, quod diffolutus, quod intemperans, quod vinofus, quod fcortator, quod nullius bonæ rei Æfchinus foret, omnem in Micione una hærere culpam. Diis gratias agere, quod ille faltem, quem ipfe ruri haberet, frugi ac temperans effet; rei ftuderet, et famæ; illarum rerum nihil ne cogitaret quidem: tantum videlicet intereffe inter fuam & fratris difciplinam. Placat hominem, quantum in fe eft, Micio; jamque fe ab eo expediverat, quum fupervenit aliud, quod majores etiam tumultus excitaret. Raptam ab Æfchino cithariftriam, perfertur ad matrem Pamphilæ; quæ quidem Pamphila ita erat ad pariendum vicina, ut jam e dolore laboraret. Quid faceret mifera? mutatum Æfchini*



*animum,*

What could the wretched Mother do?—She imagined that Æschinus's
Mind was changed, and she and her Daughter perfidiously abandoned.
She sends Geta, a Servant, who alone supported, in the best manner he
could, that distressed Family, to Hegio, a Relation of Pamphila's, and
orders him to lay the Case before him as it really was. Mean time,
Demea had heard that his own Ctesipho too was present at this Rape;
and now he was all in a ferment, when Syrus a Slave of great Cunning,
contrives a Tale to bring him to Temper: That Ctesipho indeed had come
from the Country, but with a design to reproach Æschinus; that he
had said a great many severe Things to him in the public Forum, and
afterwards returned to the Country, to mind his Employment there.
Demea could scarce refrain from Tears, and congratulated himself, that
he had one Son, at least, who was an Example of his Father's Strictness.
In his return to the Country he chances to meet with Hegio, by whom
he is informed of the Rape committed upon Pamphila by Æschinus.
Again being put into a Rage, while he is in quest of his Brother, upon
whom he might vent all his ill Humour, he meets with one coming from the
Country, of whom inquiring concerning his Son, he learns that he was not
at home. He returns to Syrus, by whom a new Fiction is formed to
stop his mouth. He then asks where he is most likely to find his Brother;
and receives such an Answer, that the unfortunate old Man, giving too
much Credit to him, in vain hunts after him over all the City. Mean
time, Micio informed of every thing by Hegio, had himself gone to the
Women, soothed their Affliction, removed their Tears, and put an end to
all their Griefs, by promising that he would confirm the Marriage between Pamphila and Æschinus. Demea comes, when nothing but
Noise, Chiding, and Reproches are to be heard. Even before him too,
one of the Slaves unawares names Ctesipho. When rushing suddenly
into the House, he finds him, whom he believed minding his Business, in
the Country, sitting and drinking with his Mistress. This makes him
perfectly furious. When he exclaimed till he was wearied, at length, by
a peaceable and mild Speech of Micio, he is so far softened, that laying aside his wonted Severity, he thinks of becoming courteous, affable,
and calm. Therefore, not only by his Permission, but even at his Desire,
Pamphila is carried home, the Nuptials are celebrated, and the
Cock-bawd receives the Price of his Music-Girl: Micio himself takes
to Wife Sostrata; Hegio has a Competency assigned him to live on; and
Syrus with his Wife Phrygia are made free. When Micio, and all
the rest, but especially Micio, were admiring at this sudden and unexpected Change; Demea concludes the Play with a grave and affecting Speech: That if they had a mind to throw away their Fortunes, or
waste their whole Substance in Banqueting, Whoredom, and Debauchery;
that less concerned him than others, as he had probably a shorter time to
live: but if they would submit to be corrected in time, or would bear with
gentle Admonitions, and moderate Restraints, he was probably the Man
best qualified for that Province. At present, he indulges them in the
Enjoyment of all their Desires; and thus the Fable concludes.

P E R-

animum, se vero, filiamque suam proditas per summam perfidiam, ac de-
sertas putabat. Getam servulum, qui pauperem familiam solus, ut poterat, alebat, mittit ad Hegionem, puellæ cognatum, jubetque ei rem, ut
erat, exponere. - Interea audierat Demea, suum quoque Ctesiphonem in
raptione adfuisse: jamque totus in fermento, ut aiunt, erat: quum
Syrus, servus vaferrimus, mendaciolum adspergit; venisse quidem rure
Ctesiphonem, sed venisse objurgatum Æschinum; multa ei medio foro mala dixisse, deinde rediisse rus in præfecturam suam; lacrimare gaudio
Demea, et gratulari sibi, quod unum saltem haberet in quo extaret paternæ severitatis exemplum. Dum rus redit, incidit in Hegionem, a quo
de constuprata per vim ab Æschino Pamphila intelligit. Denuo commotus, dum fratrem, ut in eum iram evomeret, quærit, obvium habuit
mercenarium a villa; ex quo sciscitatus de filio, accipit, non esse ruri
Redit ad Syrum, a quo ei rursus novum mendacium, velut offa in os,
ne latraret, objicitur: quærit, ubi fratrem reperire possit: id vero ita
indicavit Syrus, ut infelix senex, dum illius verbis fidem habet, nequid-
quam omne oppidum perreptaverit. Interea Micio omnium ab Hegione
certior factus, ipsemet ad mulieres profectus, jacentes jam et afflictas
erexerat, labantes et dubias confirmaverat, tristitia ac mærore confe-
ctas recreaverat, pollicitus, se Æschino Pamphilam uxorem daturum.
Venit Demea, clamor, jurgium, convicia. Etiam eo præsente, servulus quidam Ctesiphonem per imprudentiam nominat. Ille quum subito per
vim in ædes irrupisset, quem jampridem putabat ruri fodere, aut ara-
re, aut aliquid ferre denique, eum accubantem cum amica, et suaviter
potitantem deprehendit. Ibi vero tanta iracundia incitatus est, ut ar-
deret. Satis diu vociferatus quum esset; tandem placita et composita
Micionis oratione eo perducitur, ut deposita vetere sævitia, benignus, affabilis, lepidus esse meditetur. Itaque ipso non permittente tantum, sed
etiam jubente, puerpera domum traducitur: fiunt nuptiæ: lenoni nume-
ratur argentum. Micio ipse Sostratam ducit uxorem; Hegioni datur,
unde vivat: Syrus una cum Phrygia uxore manumittitur. Quum Micio, cæterique omnes, sed tamen præcipue Micio, illam tantam, tam
insperatam, tam subitam mutationem admiraretur, gravi & cordata oratione claudit fabulam Demea. Si omnia profundere, si in omni libidine
ac nequitia vivere, si totam rem helluationibus, scortationibus, largitioni-
bus consumere libeat, nihilo id sua magis, aliquanto etiam minus, quo
sibi minus ætatis supersit, quam aliorum interesse: sin corrigi se in loco
et judice coerceri atque admoneri velint, eum esse se, qui id præstare
possit. Permittuntur ei omnia, ita fabula concluditur.

# PERSONS *of the* PLAY.

The Speaker of the PROLOGUE.

MICIO, an old Man, Brother to *Demea*, and Father by Adoption to *Æschinus*.

DEMEA, an old Man, Brother to *Micio*, and Father to *Æschinus* and *Ctesipho*.

ÆSCHINUS, a Youth, the Son of *Demea*, and adopted by his Uncle *Micio*.

CTESIPHO, a Youth, Brother to *Æschinus*.

SOSTRATA Mother to *Pamphila*.

PAMPHILA, the Daughter of *Sostrata*, *Æschinus*'s Miftrefs.

CANTHARA *Pamphila*'s Nurfe.

HEGIO, an old Man, *Pamphila*'s Kinfman.

GETA, Servant to *Sostrata*.

SANNIO, a Cock-bawd.

DROMO, Servant to *Micio*.

SYRUS, Servant to *Æschinus*.


# MUTES.

BABYLO.

PARMENO, a Servant.

STORAX, a Servant.

A MUSIC-GIRL, *Ctesipho*'s Miftrefs.


# SCENE, *ATHENS*.

PRO.

# The PROLOGUE.

WHEN the Poet found that his Writings were like to be attack'd by malicious Critics, and that his adversaries did all in their power to discredit the Play we are now going to act; he resolved himself to make an Appeal to you, and leave it to your Judgment, whether what they reproach him with, is worthy Praise or Blame.

The *Synapothnescontes* is a Comedy writ by *Diphilus*. *Plautus* has rendered it into *Latin*, and call'd it *Commorientes*. In the *Greek* of *Diphilus* there is a Youth, who, in the Beginning of the Play, takes a Girl by force from a Cock-bawd. This *Plautus* has left untouched, and our Poet has transferred it Word for Word into his *Adelphi*, a new Play that we are this Day to act before you. Judge, therefore, whether this ought to be call'd a Theft, or if it is not rather recovering what another's Negligence had overlook'd. For as to what these envious Men alledge, that some of our great Men assist him, and write daily in concert with him; this, which they look upon as a mighty Reproach, he regards as his greatest Praise, that he has it in his Power to please those, with whom you, and the whole People of *Rome* are so much pleased; and whose Services in War, in Peace, and even in your private Affairs, have been ever with so much Frankness offered and accepted. As to what remains, don't expect now to

## ANNOTATIONS.

6 *Synapothnescontes Diphili comœdia est.* *Synapothnescontes* was the original Title of the Play. It is a *Greek* Word of the same Signification as the *Latin Commorientes*; *Dying together.* It is not known what was the Subject of this Play, or how the Poet had conducted it. We only gather from the Title, that there were some Persons in it who were united in their Deaths. *Diphilus*, the Author of it, flourished about the times of *Menander*. *Vell. Paterculus* gives the following Account of him. *Lib. I. sub fin.* "Una, neque multorum annorum spatio di-" visa, ætas, per divini spiritus vires Æschy-" lum, Sophoclem, Euripidem, illustravit " tragœdias: una priscam illam et vete-" rem Cratino, Aristophane, et Eupolide " comœdiam; at novam comicam Menan-" drus, æqualesque ejus ætatis magis, quam " operis, Philemon ac Diphilus, et invenere " intra paucissimos annos, neque imitan-" da reliquere."

7 *Commorientes.* *Plautus* we are told, translated this Play, and intitled it *Commorientes*; which is the *Latin* Name corresponding to that of the original *Synapothnescontes*. *Varro* tells us that the Comedy of this name was not done by *Plautus*. But either he speaks of some other Piece which bore the same Title, or in his Time the Learned were divided in their Sentiments; some ascribing it to *Plautus*, others to *Aquilius*. However that was, the Authority of *Terence* ought to go a great way. The Play itself is now lost.

9 *In prima fabula.* We ought to observe the Manner of Expression here used, *in prima fabula*, which, as *Donatus* rightly observes, stands for *in prima fabulæ parte*. This is a Liberty very frequently taken by the *Latin* Writers, and of which innumerable Examples might be given. *Cic. pro Rosc. Amer.* 44. *In extrema oratione nostra, judices, audietis.* And *Epist. ad Att.* 5. 16. *Appius, ut audivit nos vehire, in ultimam provinciam se conjecit.*

10 *Eum hic locum sumsit sibi in Adelphos.* We are to observe here, that the *Adelphi* of *Terence* is not a Translation of the *Synapothnescontes* of *Diphilus*, but that the Part of it here mentioned, which *Plautus* had omitted in his Translation, had been inserted by our Poet in this Play; which is translated from one of *Menander*'s call'd the *Adelphoi*,

a *Greek*

# PROLOGUS.

POSTQUAM poeta ſenſit ſcripturam ſuam
Ab iniquis obſervari, & adverſarios
Rapere in pejorem partem, quam acturi ſu-
    mus;
Indicio de ſe ipſe erit: vos eritis judices,
Laudine an vitio duci factum id oporteat.    5
Synapothneſcontes Diphili comœdia eſt:
Eam Commorientes Plautus fecit fabulam.
In Græcâ adoleſcens eſt, qui lenoni eripit
Meretricem, in primâ fabulâ. eum Plautus locum
Reliquit integrum: cum hic locum ſumſit ſibi    10
In Adelphos: verbum de verbo expreſſum extulit.
Eam nos acturi ſumus novam: pernoſcite,
Furtumne factum exiſtumetis, an locum
Reprehenſum, qui præteritus negligentiâ eſt.
Nam quod iſti dicunt malevoli, homines nobiles    15
Eum adjutare, aſſiduéque unâ ſcribere:
Quod illi maledictum vehemens eſſe exiſtumant,
Eam laudem hic ducit maxumam, cùm illis placet,
Qui vobis univerſis, & populo placent;
Quorum operâ in bello, in otio, in negotio,    20
Suo quiſque tempore uſu' eſt ſine ſuperbiâ.
Dehinc ne exſpectetis argumentum fabulæ:

*POſtquam poeta ſenſit ſcripturam obſervari ab iniquis, et adverſarios rapere in pejorem partem comœdiam, quam ſumus acturi; ipſe erit indicio de ſe; vos eritis judices, oportetne id factum duci illi laudi an vitio. Synapothneſcontes eſt comœdia Diphili: Plautus fecit eam fabulam Commorientes. In Græca comœdia eſt adoleſcens, qui in prima fabula eripit meretricem lenoni. Plautus reliquit eum locum integrum. Hic noſter poeta ſumſit eum locum ſibi in Adelphos: et extulit verbum expreſſum de verbo. Nos ſumus acturi eam comœdiam novam: pernoſcite, exiſtimetiſne furtum eſſe factum, an locum reprehenſum, qui eſt præteritus negligentia Plauti. Nam quod iſti malevoli dicunt, homines nobiles adjutare eum, aſſidueque ſcribere una: Quod illi exiſtimant eſſe vehemens maledictum, hic ducit eam maximam laudem, cum placet illis, qui placent nobis univerſis, et populo. Quorum opera quiſque eſt uſus ſuo tempore in bello, in otio, in negotio, ſine ſuperbia. Dehinc ne expectetis argumentum fabulæ:*

## ANNOTATIONS.

a *Greek Name*, ſignifying the *Brothers*.

14 *Homines nobiles. Scipio, Lælius*, and *Furius Publius*. See the Life of the Poet.

18 *Eam laudem hic ducis maxumam.* Terence does not here deny the Charge brought againſt him, that theſe great Men aſſiſted him in writing his Comedies: It was a Charge that did him great Honour. For my own part, ſays Madam *Dacier*, I am perſuaded that *Terence*'s Modeſty on this Occaſion did not proceed either from the Honour which he imagined was done him, or a Deſire of pleaſing and flattering his Friends, but from the mere Force of Truth. For it is highly probable that theſe great Men, diſtinguiſhed alſo for their Politeneſs, were concerned in the Compoſition of theſe Plays. It is likely that a *Carthaginian* ſhould, in ſo ſhort a time, become ſuch a Maſter of all the Graces and Beauties of ſo difficult a Language, as to have remained always unrival'd in this Point, even by the native Writers themſelves?

20 *In bello, in otio, in negotio.* Commentators tell us, that *in bello* regards *Scipio*, who was a renown'd Captain; *in otio*, *Furius Publius*, a great Politician; *in negotio*, *Lælius*, who was accounted one of the wiſeſt Men in the Republic, and to whom almoſt all the City applied for his advice in their private Affairs.

21 *Sine ſuperbia.* I confeſs I am at a loſs what to make of this *ſine ſuperbia*; nor do I ſee how it can come in with any ſort of Propriety. *Eugraphius* paraphraſes it: *Quorum opera unuſquiſque uſus eſt in ſuis neceſſitatibus, ſine*

hear from me the Subject of the Play; the two Old Men, who come firſt, will let you into it in part, and the reſt will gradually appear in the Repreſentation. Do you, by a candid and impartial Attention, encourage the Poet to Induſtry in writing.

## ANNOTATIONS.

ſine aliqua eorum ſuperbia. In the ſame ſenſe has Madam *Dacier* too tranſlated it: "And who in Peace and in War, and alſo "in your private Concerns, have rendred "to the Republic in general, and to every "one in particular, the moſt conſiderable "Services, without becoming on that ac- "count the more haughty or overbearing." This is perhaps the only Turn that can be given to the Words, and yet after all it ap pears to me to be extremely flat.

25 *Facite, æquanimitas poetæ ad ſcriben- dum augeat induſtriam.* *Veſtra*, ſays *Dona- tus*, is wanting here to complete the Senſe: *facite, ut veſtra æquanimitas augeat induſtri- am poetæ ad ſcribendum.* But Dr. *Bentley* thinks that not a ſingle Word only, but a whole Verſe is here wanting, which he thus reſtores:

——*Fa-*

ACT

Senes qui primi venient, hi partem aperient :
In agendo partem oftendent. Facite, æquanimitas
Poetæ ad fcribendum augeat induftriam.          25

*Facite, ut veftra æquanimitas augeat induftriam poetæ ad agendum.*

bi ſenes, qui primi
venient, aperient
partem : oftendent
partem in agenda,

## ANNOTATIONS.

———*Facite, æquanimitas*
*Bonitaſque veftra, adjutrix noftræ in-*
*duftriæ,*
*Poetæ ad ſcribendum augeant induftriam.*

Thus in the *Phormio*, 35.

*Bonitaſque veftra adjutans, atque æquani-*
*mitas.*

And Prologue to the *Hecyra* 24.

——— *Veftra intelligentia*
*Sedabit, fi erit adjutrix noftræ induftria.*

It is a known Practice of *Terence*, in writing Prologues, to borrow from himfelf. Thus we find three fucceffive Verſes in the Prologue to the *Heautontimorumenos*, repeated in that of the *Hecyra*. But though all this may be, the Senſe is complete without this interpolated Verſe; and it is evident that the Doctor, without any Foundation for his Conjecture, has collected it himfelf from the other Prologues, and adapted it to chime in here.

ACTUS

## ACT I. SCENE I.

### ARGUMENT.

*Micio discovers a great deal of Solicitude for his adopted Son Æschinus, because he had not returned from a Supper he had been at the Night before. From this Scene too we may learn how Children are to be trained up, in which he thinks Gentleness of far greater service than Harshness and Severity.*

#### MICIO.

STORAX——*Æschinus*, I find, did not return last Night from Supper, nor any of the Servants who went to see for him. It is, indeed, a true Saying: If you are absent any where, or chance to stay longer than ordinary, better those things happen to you, which your Wife says, or fancies in her resentment, than what tender Parents are apt to suspect. Your Wife, if you are out late, fancies you have picked up a Girl, or a Girl you, or that you are at the Tavern, or in some party of Pleasure, and that you make yourself quite happy, while she is uneasy and pines at home. But for me now, what Apprehensions am I under, because my Son is not return'd; How anxious, lest peradventure he may have catched Cold, or had a Fall, or broke some Limb? Good Gods! that a Man should set his mind so much upon any thing, or admit it so far, as to become dearer to him than he is to himself! Nor is this Boy, indeed, my Son, but my Brother's: one, who is of a Temper very different from mine. Even from my Youth, I have courted Ease, and the quiet Enjoyments of a Town-

### ANNOTATIONS.

We are to suppose, that at the opening of this Scene, *Micio* was seen coming out pretty early in the Morning, and turning about calls upon *Storax*, who not answering, he thence concludes, that *Æschinus* had been abroad all Night. This leads him to a Train of Reflections, which the Poet has with great Judgment so contrived, that they flow naturally from the Circumstances in which we must suppose *Micio*, an indulgent tender-hearted Father to be; and at the same time let the Spectators into so much of the Plot as was necessary to enable them to understand the Design and Intention of the several Scenes, as they succeeded one another. For, first, he begins with expressing the Uneasiness he felt at his Son's not having returned home. This naturally leads him to wonder how Men should so far concern themselves for others, as in a manner to put their Happiness in their power. The Case was still more particular with him, as this *Æschinus*, who gave him so much Trouble, was his

only by Adoption, but in reality his Brother's Son. This of course introduces the Mention of that Brother; he observes his particular Temper, how contrary to his own, and of consequence in how different a manner they trained up the two Youths that were under their several Care. Thus the Reader is let insensibly into the whole Scheme of the Play.

¹ *Storax——non rediit, hâc nocte â cœna Æschinus.* This Verse, as *Donatus* observes, is by some mark'd with a Point of Interrogation. Did *Æschinus* return last Night from Supper, *Storax?* But this, however it may be defended, is not the Turn which Commentators generally choose to give the Words. *Micio,* coming out of his house pretty early in the Morning, calls upon *Storax,* one of the Servants who had been sent the Night before to wait upon *Æschinus* home: and finding that nobody answered him, he judges by that, that none of them had yet returned, neither Master nor Servants. Hence

# ACTUS I. SCENA I.

### ARGUMENTUM.

*Micio ostendit se admodum esse solicitum de Æschino adoptivo, quod nondum de cœna hesterna redierat. Tum ex hac cœna ratio educandi liberos peti potest, quos lenitate potius quàm asperitate aut vi instruendos præscribit.*

### MICIO.

STORAX. non rediit hac nocte à cœna Æschi-
nus,
　Neque servulorum quisquam, qui advorsum
ierant!
Profecto hoc verè dicunt: Si absis uspiam,
Aut ibi si cesses, evenire ea satius est,
Quæ in te uxor dicit, & quæ in animo cogitat　5
Irata, quàm illa, quæ parentes propitii.
Uxor, si cesses, aut te amare cogitat,
Aut tete amari, aut potare, aut animo obsequi,
Et tibi bene esse soli, cùm sibi sit malè.
Ego, quia non rediit filius, quæ cogito?　10
Quibu' nunc solicitor rebus? ne aut ille alserit,
Aut uspiam ceciderit, aut perfregerit　[stituere, aut
Aliquid: vah, quenquamne hominem in animum in-
Parare, quòd sit carius, quàm ipse est sibi!　14
Atque ex me hic natus non est, sed ex fratre. is adeò
Dissimili studio est. jam inde ab adolescentiâ

*cogito? Quibus rebus nunc solicitor? Ne aut ille alserit, aut ceciderit uspiam, aut perfregerit aliquid. Vah, quemquamne hominem instituere in animum, aut parare id, quod sit carius sibi, quam ipse est sibi! Atque hic non est natus ex me, sed ex fratre. Is adeo est studio dissimili. Ego jam inde ab adolescentia*

**ORDO.**

*STorax. Æschi-*
*nus non rediit*
*à cœna hac nocte,*
*nec quisquam ser-*
*vulorum, qui ierant*
*adversum! Pro-*
*fecto dicunt hoc*
*vere: Si absis us-*
*piam, aut si cessi-*
*ibi, satius est re-*
*evenire tibi, quæ*
*uxor dicit in te,*
*et quæ irata cogi-*
*tat in animo, quam*
*illa, quæ parentes*
*propitii cogitant. Si*
*cesset, uxor cogitat,*
*aut te amari, aut*
*tete amari, aut te*
*potare, aut obsequi*
*animo, et esse bene*
*tibi solis, cum sit*
*male sibi. Ego, quia*
*filius non rediit, quæ*
*am, aut perfregerit*
*quod sit carius sibi,*
*est studio dissimili.*

## ANNOTATIONS.

Hence he says to himself, *non rediit*, &c. *Æschinus*, I find, did not return last Night.

2 *Advorsum ierant.* To defend their Masters, and wait upon them home. The Servants to whom this Office was assigned were termed properly *Adversitores.*

12 *Aut perfregerit aliquid.* This is the reading we constantly find in all Manuscripts, nor is there any Necessity for altering it, as some have rashly pretended to do, since it is a manner of speaking patronized by the best Authors. *Liv. Lib.* 22. 20. *Naves omnes, quæ non aut perfregerant proras, littore illisas, aut carinas fixerant vadis, religatas puppibus in altum extraxere.* And Cicero *de Oratore,* 2. 62. *Ut in illum Titium, qui cùm studiosè pila luderet, et idem signa sacra noctu frangere putaretur, gregalesque cum in templum non venisse requirerem, extu-*savit Vespa Terentius, quod eum brachium fregisse diceret. *Phæd.* 5. 7, 8.

——*Sinistram fregit tibiam.*

We have here, as *Donatus* observes, an Example of Tenderness and Affection carried to excess. *Micio* dreads for his Son, though now advanc'd to Manhood, Accidents that are wont only to befal Children.

13 *Quenquamne hominem in animum instituere, aut parare.* The disjunctive Particle *aut* makes it evident, that the Poet means here to express two distinct things: *In animum instituere*, to receive into such a Degree of Favour, or, as Madam *Dacier* expresses it, *placer dans son cœur.* *Parare* again, to receive into his House. The Word was often used in Matters of Commerce, and was of the same Import as *emere.* So *Cic. ad Att.* 12. 13. *Cogis interdum todry*

*Tiberim*

a Town-Life, and, what Men of Pleasure count a Happiness, have always lived single. He again is quite the reverse of all this. Has lived in the Country, being always sparing and laborious, married, and had two Sons. Of these, I have adopted the eldest: bred him up from a Child, kept him with me; and loved him as my own; he is now my whole delight, and what alone I hold dear: and I do all I can too, that I may be equally dear to him. I give, I overlook things, I don't think it necessary to exert my Authority on every occasion. In fine, I have accustomed my Son not to conceal from me those little Extravagancies natural to Youth, which others are at so much pains to hide from their Parents. For he who once dares to lie to, or deceive his Father, will much more do so by others. And I think it the more prudent way, to hold Children to their Duty by the Ties of Modesty and Honour, than the Restraints of Fear. In this my Brother and I differ widely, nor is he at all pleased with my Manner. He often comes to me, loudly exclaiming, " What are you about, *Micio?* " Why do you thus ruin the Youth? Why does he drink? And why " do you supply him in all these extravagant Expences? You indulge " him too much in fine dress: you're quite silly in doing so." Why truly, he himself is much too severe, beyond what is either just or reasonable. And, in my Judgment, he deceives himself greatly, to imagine that an Authority established by force should be more lasting, or of greater weight than that which is founded on Friendship. For in this manner do I reason, and thus persuade myself to believe: He that does his Duty thro' mere Motives of Fear, will be upon his Guard no longer than while he thinks there is Danger of his being discovered. But if he can hope to escape Notice, he returns to his natural

ANNOTATIONS.

*Tiberim, hortos aliquos parare.* Hence the Word very aptly expresses one received into a House or Family, by Adoption, as that Ceremony carried in it some Resemblance of an Act of buying.

17 *Ego hanc clementem vitam urbanam.* The Expression here appears to me remarkable: *Vita clemens* instead of *vita quieta, otiosa, tranquilla.* Plautus uses the word *clementer* in the same Sense. *Stichus* 4.1.26.

*Hodiene exoneramus navem, frater?* PA. Clementer volo.

" Do we unload the Ship to-day, Brother? PA. With all my heart. *Dacier.*

18 *Et, quod fortunatum isti putant.* These Words are of *ambiguous* Signification, and accordingly have been explained differently. Some by *isti* understand those of a contrary Character to *Micio*, those of *Demea's* Disposition and Turn. If so, the Sentence must run thus: *Uxorem nunquam habui, quod* (scilicet uxorem habere) *isti fortunatum putant: isti, qui mei dissimiles studio & mo-*ribus sunt, qui uxorem ducunt cum magna dote, qui liberis dant operam, qui posteritati inserviunt.* Others, with more Reason, connect *isti* with the Verse immediately preceding *isti urbani,* thus: *et nunquam habui uxorem, quod isti urbani putant fortunatum.* The Sense, according to this, is complete without any Strain, and exactly agreeable to *Micio's* own Notions: " And, what " those of my Way of Life, who love Ease " and the Town, think a Happiness, I have " never married." It seems incongruous, to suppose *Micio* here making the Opposition between his own and his Brother's Sentiments, when he begins it expresly and formally in the next Sentence, and mentions this very Article:

—— *Ille contra, hæc omnia:*
*Ruri agere vitam, semper parce ac duriter*
*Se habere: uxorem duxit.*

26 *Non necesse habeo omnia pro meo jure agere.* Donatus here takes occasion to distinguish between *jus* and *æquitas. Jus,* says he,

Ego hanc clementem vitam urbanam atque otium
Secutus sum : &, quod fortunatum isti putant,
Uxorem nunquam habui. ille contrà, hæc omnia :
Ruri agere vitam, semper parcè ac duriter                20
Se habere : uxorem duxit : nati filii
Duo. inde ego hunc majorem adoptavi mihi :
Eduxi à parvulo, habui, amavi pro meo :
In eo me oblecto : solum id est carum mihi.
Ille ut item contrà me habeat, facio sedulo :            25
Do, prætermitto, non necesse habeo omnia
Pro meo jure agere : postremò, alii clanculum
Patres quæ faciunt, quæ fert adolescentia,
Ea ne me celet, consuefeci filium :
Nam qui mentiri, aut fallere insuérit patrem, aut  30
Audebit, tanto magis audebit cæteros.
Pudore & liberalitate liberos
Retinere, satius esse credo, quàm metu.
Hæc fratri mecum non conveniunt, neque placent.
Venit ad me sæpe clamitans, Quid agis, Micio?      35
Cur perdis adolescentem nobis? cur amat?
Cur potat? cur tu his rebus sumtum suggeris?
Vestitu nimio indulges : nimiùm ineptus es.
Nimiùm ipse est durus, præter æquumque & bonum :
Et errat longè, mea quidem sententiâ,                    40
Qui imperium credat gravius esse aut stabilius,
Vi quod fit, quàm illud, quod amicitiâ adjungitur.
Mea sic est ratio, & sic animum induco meum :
Malo coactus qui suum officium facit,
Dum id rescitum iri credit, tantisper cavet :           45
Si speret fore clàm, rursum ad ingenium redit.

sum secutus hanc clementem vitam urbanam, atque otium : et, quod ipsi putant fortunatum, nunquam habui uxorem. Ille contra, maluit hæc omnia : agere vitam ruri, semper habere se parce ac duriter : duxit uxorem : duo filii nati sunt illi. Inde ego adoptavi mihi hunc majorem : eduxi a parvulo, habui, amavi pro meo : oblecto me in eo : id solum est carum mihi. Facio sedulo, ut ille contra habeat me item carum sibi. Do, prætermitto, non habeo necesse agere omnia. pro meo jure : postremo, consuefeci filium, ne celet me ea, quæ adolescentia fert : et quæ alii filii faciunt clanculum patres. Nam qui insueverit aut audebit mentiri, aut fallere patrem, tanto magis audebit fallere cæteros. Credo esse satius retinere liberos pudore et liberalitate, quam metu. Hæc non conveniunt neque placent fratri mecum. Sæpe venit ad me clamitans, Quid agis, Micio? Cur perdis adolescentem nobis? Cur amat? Cur potat? Cur tu suggeris sumtum his rebus? Indulges nimium vestitui, nimium ineptus es. Equidem ipse est nimium durus præter æquumque et bonum; et quidem meâ sententiâ errat longe, qui credat imperium esse gravius aut stabilius, quod fit vi, quam illud, quod adjungitur amicitiâ : Ratio mea est sic, et sic induco meum animum credere : Qui facit suum officium coactus mala, tantisper cavet, dum credit id iri rescitum : si sperat fore clam, redit rursum ad ingenium.

## ANNOTATIONS.

he, "est quod omnia recta et inflexibilia "exigit: æquitas est quæ de jure multum "remittit: ergo hic sensus; non necesse est, "etiam si liceat, sævum esse partem. Et "mire ostendit jus summum; nisi necessi-"tate, non esse servandum."

27 *Postremo alii clanculum.* Not *alii patres,* but *alii adolescentes clanculum patres suos. Clanculum* has here all the Force of the Preposition, as if *clam patres.*

32 *Pudore et liberalitate. Pudor* here respects the Children. We are to inspire them with such Notions as will make them ashamed of Vice, and look upon it as something mean, base, and contemptible. *Liberalitas* regards Parents, and is equivalent to *Mildness, Gentleness, Affability,* the true Method of forming free Spirits, born to enjoy and defend Liberty.

41 *Qui imperium credat gravius esse, vi quod fit, quam quod amicitia adjungitur.* Nothing can be more just, useful, and instructive, than what *Micio* says here with regard to the Education of Youth. Indulgence, it is true, ought not to be carried too far, but Softness and Gentleness are always to be preferred to Harshness and Severity. For in the Management of Youth, it is

natural Bent: but where one is gained by Kindness, he acts from Inclination, strives to make a due Return, and present or absent will be the same. This, indeed, is the part of a Father, to accustom his Son to what is right, more from his own Choice, than any outward Fear; and here chiefly lies the Difference between a Father, and a Master. He that can't do this, let him own that he knows not how to train up Children. But is not this the very Man of whom I was speaking? 'Tis the same: he seems vex'd too, I can't think why. I believe, according to custom, we shall have a Quarrel. Demea, I am glad to see you so well.

*ANNOTATIONS.*

no otherwise than in the government of a Kingdom. Terror and Awe are but frail Bonds of Obedience; but the Affections and good Will of the People are what may be with safety relied on, as never-failing Resources in every Exigence. This is a Reflection frequently to be met with in ancient Authors. *Sall. Jugurth.* 10. *Non exercitus, neque*

---

# ACT I.   SCENE II.

### ARGUMENT.

Demea, *a Man rough and severe in his Disposition, complains heavily to* Micio *of* Æschinus, *as froward, debauch'd, and mischievous.* Micio *excuses him rather with too much Softness and Indulgence.*

DEMEA, MICIO.

*Demea.* OH! well met: you're the very Man I was looking for.
    *Mic.* What makes you look so vex'd?

*Dem.* Can you ask why? when we have got such a Son as Æschinus?

· *Mic.* (*To himself.*) Didn't I say it would be so? (*to* Demea.) What has he done?

*Dem.* What has he done? one, who is ashamed of nothing, nor fears any one, nor imagines that any law can control him. For, not to speak of things past, but just now what a Project has he been upon?

    *Mic.* What is it?                      *Dem.*

*ANNOTATIONS.*

In this Scene we are let more particularly into the different Characters of the two Brothers. *Demea* hearing that *Æschinus* had broke into the House of a Cock bawd, and taken thence by force a Musick Girl, comes to reproach his Brother *Micio* with it. This was his usual way. For as he knew *Micio* to be of an easy indulgent Temper, and that he was not severe in checking these youthful Sallies of his Son, he judged that it would be in vain for him to chide the young man himself, so long as his Brother overlooked his Follies, and even granted him whatever he wanted to support them. He therefore carries his first Complaints to *Micio*, and accuses him as the cause of all these Irregularities. The other endeavours to defend his Conduct, as agreeable to Reason and good Sense, which provokes *Demea* so much, that they are near coming to a downright Quarrel.

¹ *Ehem, opportunè. Demea's* Churlishness and Rusticity appears in his very first Address. He neglects his Brother's Salutation, as impatient to vent his Spleen against him.

² *Rogas me, ubi nobis Æschinus sit?* These words

Quem beneficio adjungas, ille ex animo facit:
Studet par referre, præsens absensque idem erit.
Hoc patrium est, potius consuefacere filium
Suâ sponte rectè facere, quàm alieno metu.          50
Hoc pater, ac dominus intereſt: hoc qui nequit,
Fateatur nescire imperare liberis.
Sed estne hic ipsus, de quo agebam? & certè is est.
Nescio quid tristem video. credo jam, ut solet,
Jurgabit. Salvum te advenire, Demea,          55
Gaudemus.

*Ille, quem adjungas bentficio, facit ex animo. Studet referre par, præsens absensque erit idem. Hoc est patrium potius consuefacere filium facere rectè suâ sponte, quam alieno metu. Hoc interest pater ac dominus. Qui nequit hoc, fateatur se nescire imperare*

*liberis. Sed estne hic ipsus frater, de quo agebam? et certe est is. Nescio propter quid video eum tristem. Credo jam jurgabit, ut solet. Demea, gaudemus te advenire salvum.*

ANNOTATIONS.

*neque thesauri,* præsidia regni sunt, verum *amici,* quos neque armis cogere, neque auro parare queas: officio & fide pariuntur. The Words of *Micipsa,* King of *Numidia,* to *Jugurtha.* And *Cicero, Off.* 2. 7. *Rerum autem omnium nec aptius est quidquam ad opes tuendas & tenendas, quam dirigi: nec alienius, quam timeri.*

---

## ACTUS I. SCENA II.

### ARGUMENTUM.

*Demea, homo durus & asper, graviter cum Micione expostulat de Æschini absentis petulantia, cupiditatibus, & injuriis: excusat eundem Micio, plus nimis indulgens pater.*

DEMEA, MICIO          ORDO.

EHEM, opportunè: teipsum quærito.
  MI. Quid tristis es? DE. rogas me, ubi nobis Æschinus
Siet, quid tristis ego sim? MI. dixin' hoc fore?
Quid fecit? DE. quid ille fecerit? quem neque pudet
Quidquam, nec metuit quenquam, neque legem putat
Tenere se ullam. nam illa, quæ antehac facta sunt, 6
Omitto: modò quid designavit? MI. quidnam id est?

*DE. Ehem, opportunè: quærito teipsum. MI. Quid es tristis? DE. Rogas me, quid ego sim tristis, ubi Æschinus sit nobis? MI. Dixine hoc fore? Quid fecit? DE. Quid ille fecerit?*

*Quem neque quidquam pudet, nec metuit quenquam, neque putat ullam legem tenere se. Nam omitto illa, quæ sunt facta antehac: quid designavit modo? MI. Quidnam id est?*

ANNOTATIONS.

words will admit of different Meanings, and accordingly have been differently explain'd by Commentators. Some will have It; *Can you put that Question to me, who have got such a Son as* Æschinus? This is Eugraphius's Opinion; whose Words are, *Interrogas, quid ego tristis sim, cum Æschinum filium habeamus?* But Madam *Dacier* contends that we ought to understand *ubi, apud quem. Tune rogas me quid ego sim tristis, tu apud quem* Æschinus *sit.*

7 *Modo quid designavit? Designare* is a word taken sometimes in a good, sometimes in a bad Sense, and properly denotes the doing any thing new or extraordinary. We

find that among the *Romans,* they who had the care of Funeral Games, were call'd *Designatores;* probably for this Reason, that, in exhibiting them, they were generally at a great deal of pains to find out things new and wonderful, such as might both please and surprize the people. Hence *Donatus* conjectures, that *Designatio* was a collecting or drawing together the People into a Body. This happened when a Man, by any remarkable Exploit, drew the Eyes of the Populace upon him, and held them, expecting how he would acquit himself, as the *Designatores,* by the several Shews exhibited in funeral Games retained the admiring Multitude.

———*Dem.* He has broke open another's Door, rush'd into his House, beat the Master and his whole Family almost to death, and carried away a Wench he had taken a liking to by force. All the Town exclaim against it as a vile thing. How many told me of it, as I was coming to you, *Micio?* It's in every body's mouth. In fine, would he but take example, does he not see his Brother, industrious, contented to live in the Country, frugal and sober, not guilty of any of these mad tricks? But *Micio*, when I thus blame *Æschinus*, I blame you too, for you are the cause of his Ruin.

*Mic.* There is nothing more unreasonable than a Man without Experience of the World, who will allow nothing right, but what he does himself.

*Dem.* What means this?

*Mic.* Because, *Demea*, you judge wrong of these matters. It is not, believe me, any mighty Crime in a young Man to wench or drink; it is not indeed, or to break open a Door. If neither you nor I did so in our younger Days, it was because Poverty check'd us; and you would now make a Merit of what was owing to downright Necessity. 'Tis unfair: for had we had wherewithal to do it, we should have been just like others: and it would be wise in you to allow the same Liberty to that other Son of yours, while he is of an Age fit for it, rather than that after getting rid of you, a thing long wish'd for with Impatience; he should yet give into these Follies at an Age when they will less become him.

*Dem.* O *Jupiter!* the Man will drive me to Distraction! Is it no Crime in a young Man to do these things?

*Mic.* Oh! only hear what I have to say, and don't for ever teaze
me

*ANNOTATIONS.*

1 *In ædas irruit alienas.* The Poet takes care to make every one speak agreeably to his Character, and the Designs he may have in view. *Demea* here wants to represent this late Attempt of *Æschinus* in the worst Light, that by making him appear highly blameable; he may the more irritate his Brother against him. For this reason he suppresses part of the Truth, and in telling *Micio* what he had done, says, in *ædes irruit alienas*, which makes the offence appear very heinous; whereas, had he told it plainly as it was, *in ædes irruit lenonis*, he knew his Brother would have laughed at it as a trifle. We are to observe here farther, the idea which the Poet gives of the Manners of those Times. It was the Custom then, as well as now, for young Rakes, if refused Admittance to their Mistresses, to assault the House violently, and raise Disturbances. *Horace*, in one of his Odes, speaks of some Instruments wherewith young Men were provided for this very purpose; and that it was common for them, arm'd with these, to range the Streets all Night, and engage in such like Adventures. Nay, so far did they carry this, that the Courtezans themselves were proud to have their Doors and Windows frequently battered by the young Fellows; and we find him objecting it as a Reproach to one of them, who had disobliged him, that she was now become so despicable, as to be no longer disturbed by these nightly Visits. *Odarum Lib. I. 25. 1.*

*Parcius junctas quatiunt fenestras*
*Ictibus crebris juvenes protervi,*
*Nec tibi somnos adimunt, amatque janua limen.*

16 *Nullum hujus simile factum?* These Words are to be supposed spoken with Vehemence, and an Air of Indignation against the other, who was so unlike this Example of Sobriety. The Reader too must be highly diverted to find *Demea* so lavish in his Praise of the Person who was chiefly in fault, and for whose sake alone the Assault was committed.

18 *Homine imperito.* By *homo imperitus*, *Micio* here means one who knows not the World, and the Practices of it. As the
Circle

DE. Fores effregit, atque in ædes irruit
Alienas: ipsum dominum atque omnem familiam
Multavit usque ad mortem: eripuit mulierem,       10
Quàm amabat. clamant omnes indignissimè
Factum esse? hoc advenienti quot mihi, Micio,
Dixere? in ore est omni populo. denique
Si conferendum exemplum est, non fratrem videt
Rei dare operam, ruri esse parcum ac sobrium?       15
Nullum hujus simile factum? hæc cùm illi, Micio,
Dico, tibi dico. tu illum corrumpi sinis.
MI. Homine imperito nunquam quidquam injustius,
Qui, nisi quod ipse fecit, nihil rectum putat.
DE. Quorsum istuc? MI. quia tu, Demea, hæc malè
    judicas.       20
Non est flagitium, mihi crede, adolescentulum
Scortari, neque potare; non est, neque fores
Effringere. hæc si neque ego, neque tu fecimus,
Non sivit egestas facere nos. tu nunc tibi
Id laudi ducis, quod tum fecisti inopiâ.       25
Injurium est. nam si esset unde id fieret,
Faceremus? & tu illum tuum, si esses homo,
Sineres nunc facere, dum per ætatem licet,
Potiùs quàm, ubi te exspectatum ejecisset foras,
Alieniore ætate post faceret tamen.       30
DE. Proh Jupiter! tu homo adigis me ad insaniam.
Non est flagitium facere hæc adolescentulum? MI. ah,
Ausculta, ne me obtundas de hac re sæpiùs.

*DE. Effregit fores,*
*atque irruit in æ-*
*des alienas: mul-*
*tavit ipsum domi-*
*num atque omnem*
*familiam usque ad*
*mortem: eripuit*
*mulierem, quam a-*
*mabat; omnes cla-*
*mant esse factum in-*
*dignissime. Quot*
*dixere hoc mihi ad-*
*venienti, Micio?*
*Est omni populo in*
*ore. Denique, si ex-*
*emplum est conferen-*
*dum, non vidit fra-*
*trem dare operam*
*rei, & esse parcum*
*ac sobrium ruri?*
*Nullum factum si-*
*mile hujus? Cum*
*dico hæc illi, Micio,*
*dico tibi; tu sinis*
*illum corrumpi. MI.*
*Nunquam quid-*
*quam est injustius*
*homine imperito, qui*
*putat nihil rectum,*
*nisi quod ipse fecit.*
*DE. Quorsum istuc?*
*MI. Quin tu, De-*
*mea, judicas hæc*
*male. Non est fla-*
*gitium, crede mihi,*
*adolescentulum scor-*

*tari, neque potare; non est: neque effringere fores. Si neque ego, neque tu fecimus hæc,*
*egestas non sivit nos facere. Tu nunc ducis id laudi tibi, quod fecisti tum inopia. Injurium est.*
*Nam si esset unde id fieret, faceremus: &, tu si esses homo, nunc sineres illum tuum facere*
*hæc, dum licet per ætatem: potius quam ubi ejecisset te expectatum foras, faceret tamen post,*
*alieniore ætate. DE. Proh Jupiter! tu homo adigis me ad insaniam. An non est flagitium*
*adolescentulum facere hæc? MI. Ah, ausculta, ne obtundas me sæpius de hac re.*

## ANNOTATIONS.

Circle of his Acquaintance is very narrow, and his Notions of things for the most part contracted; he is apt to blame every little Deviation from his own Manner, as a real Crime.

21 *Non est flagitium,* &c. *Micio* seems here to carry his Indulgence too far; but we are to reflect, that it is more to oppose *Demea*'s Surliness, than from any real Approbation of his Son's Follies, that he speaks in this manner: for towards the end of the Scene he owns that he was not a little concern'd for this late Behaviour of *Æschinus,* who rather carried his Extravagancies too far. It is evident, however, that both *Greeks* and *Romans* were very complaisant to their Children in this Article, and seldom check'd them, but when they gave themselves entirely up to Gallantry, or were expensive beyond Reason. They, moreover, seem to have distinguish'd between *peccatum* and *flagitium.* Thus Gallantry and Intriguing came under the Denomination *peccatum,* but they would not allow it to be what they call'd *flagitium.* The following Passage from *Cicero* will give the Reader a clearer Apprehension of the Notion of the Ancients in this particular, than any thing I can say. *Pro. Cæl.* 20. "Verum "si quis est, qui etiam meretriciis amoribus "interdictum juventuti putet, est ille qui- "dem valde severus: negare non possum: "sed abhorret non modo ab hujus seculi li- "centia, verum etiam à majorum consuetu- "dine atque concessis. Quando enim hoc "factum non est? Quando reprehensum? "Quando non permissum? Quando denique "fuit, ut, quod libet, non liceret?"

27 *Si esses homo.* That is, say some, *Si esses humanus, non tyrannus erroribus juve-num*

me with these stories.   You gave me this Son to adopt him : he is now become mine : if he is guilty of any Fault, *Demea*, it is to me : I bear the Burden of all.   Does he treat?   Does he drink?   Does he smell of Perfumes?   'Tis all at my charge.   Does he wench?   He shall have Money of me, while I can supply him ; when I have no more to give, he may perhaps then be discarded.   Has he broke open a Door?   they shall have another.   Has he torn any one's Clothes? they shall be mended.   I have, thank God, enough to do all these things, and as yet, they don't hurt me.   In fine, either cease complaining, or choose some one to judge between us : I'll make it appear that you're more to blame in this Affair than I.

*Dem.*  Dear me! learn to be a Father from those who know what it is to be really so.

*Mic.*  You are his Father by Nature, but I by my Care and Instructions.

*Dem.*  You a Father to him by your Instructions!

*Mic.*  Nay, if you go on at this rate, I'll leave you.

*Dem.*  Is this your way?

*Mic.*  Must I be so often tormented with the same Story?

*Dem.*  It touches me very near.

*Mic.*  And me too.   But, *Demea*, let each take care of what he ought : you of your Son, and I of mine.   For to pretend to the care of both, is, in a manner, to demand back him whom you have given me.

*Dem.*  Ah, *Micio!*

*Mic.*  So it seems to me.

*Dem.*  What's all this? if you like it, let him squander, spend and destroy ; 'tis nothing to me.   If henceforth I say one word—

*Mic.*  You again put yourself into a passion, *Demea*.

*Dem.*  Don't you believe me? Do I demand back him I gave you? 'tis very hard : I'm no Stranger, if I do oppose these Courses ... but I have done.   You desire me to take care of one ; I do : and thank Heaven, he is just such as I would have him.   That Spark of yours will be sensible of it in time ; I don't care to say any thing worse of him at present.

*Mic.*  There is something in what he says, tho' it be not all true ;

nor

*ANNOTATIONS.*

*num irascens, cum veniam te illis deceret dare.* But this does not so well agree with what follows, by which it is evident, that *Micio* means, if he would act wisely.   *Homo* singly taken often signifies Courage, Prudence, or any good Quality that renders one worthy of the name of a Man.   Thus, *Plaut. Epid.* III. 4. 57.

    *Pugnasti, Homo es,*

And *Cic. Fam.* 7. 29. *At illa nostra prædicatio quanti est, non quod simus, quod habeamus, quod homines existimemur, id omne abis habere.* Att. 4. 15. *Si vis Homo esse, re-*

*cipe te ad nos.*   *Si esses Homo*, if you acted like a Man of common Prudence.

'35 *Is meus est factus.*'  This was the Law of Adoption among the *Romans* : for the Person adopted was immediately considered as the Son of him who adopted him ; and to him was thenceforth transferred all the Power and Authority of the Father.

'39. *Fortasse excludetur foras.*  These Words are of ambiguous Signification : for they may either mean that his Mistresses will then discard him, or that *Micio* himself will

send

| | |
|---|---|
| Tuum filium dedisti adoptandum mihi : | *Dedisti tuum filium* |
| Is meus est factus: si quid peccat, Demea,   35 | *mibi adoptandum:* |
| Mihi peccat: ego illi maximam partem feram. | *is est factus meus:* |
| Opsonat? potat? olet unguenta? de meo. | *si peccat quid, De-* |
| Amat? dabitur a me argentum, dum erit commodum? | *mea, peccat mihi:* |
| Ubi non erit, fortasse excludetur foras. | *ego feram maxi-* |
| Fores effregit? restituentur. discidit   40 | *mam partem illi.* |
| Vestem? resarcietur. est, Dis gratia, | *Opsonat? Potat?* |
| Et unde hæc fiant, & adhuc non molesta sunt. | *Olet unguenta? fa-* |
| Postremo aut desine, aut cedo quemvis arbitrum : | *cit de meo. Amat?* |
| Te plura in hac re peccare ostendam. DE. hei mihi ! | *argentum dabitur* |
| Pater esse disce ab illis, qui vere sciunt.   45 | *à me, dum erit com-* |
| MI. Natura tu illi pater es, consiliis ego. | *modum: ubi non erit,* |
| DE. Tun' consulis quidquam? MI. ah! si pergis, abiero. | *fortasse excludetur* |
| DE. Siccine agis? ME. an ego toties de eadem re audiam? | *foras. Effregit fo-* |
| DE. Curæ est mihi. MI. & mihi curæ est: verum, | *-res? Restituentur.* |
|   Demea, | *Discidit vestem?* |
| Curemus æquam uterque partem: tu alterum,   50 | *Resarcietur. Gra-* |
| Ego item alterum. nam ambos curare, propemodum | *ia diis, est mihi* |
| Reposcere illum est, quem dedisti. DE. ah Micio! | *unde hæc fiant, &* |
| MI. Mihi sic videtur. DE. quid istic? tibi si istuc placet, | *adhuc non sunt* |
| Profundat, perdat, pereat, nihil ad me attinet. | *molesta. Postremo* |
| Jam si verbum unum posthac. MI. rursum, Demea,   55 | *ut desine, aut ce-* |
| Irascere? DE. an non credis? repeton' quem dedi? | *lo quemvis arbi-* |
| Ægre est. alienus non sum. si obsto ... hem, desino. | *trum: ostendam te* |
| Unum vis curem: curo: & est Dis gratia, | *peccare plura in* |
| Quam ita, ut volo, est. iste tuus ipse sentiet | *hac re. DE. Hei* |
| Posterius: nolo in illum gravius dicere.   60 | *mihi! Disce esse* |
| MI. Nec nihil, neque omnia hæc sunt, quæ dicit. tamen | *pater, ab illis qui* |
| | *vere sciunt. MI.* |
| | *Tu es pater illi na-* |
| | *tura, ego consiliis.* |
| | *DE. Tune consulis* |
| | *quidquam? MI.* |
| | *Ab! si pergis, abi-* |
| | *erò. DE. Siccine* |
| | *agis? MI. An ego* |
| | *audiam toties de ea-* |
| | *dem re? DE. Est* |

*mibi curæ. MI. Et est mihi curæ: verum, Demea, uterque curemus æquam partem: tu al-*
*terum, ego item alterum: nam curare ambos, est propemodum reposcere illum, quem dedisti,*
*DE. Ab Micio! MI. Sic videtur mibi. DE. Quid istic? Si istuc placet tibi, profundat,*
*perdat, pereat, attinet nihil ad me. Jam si addidero verbum unum posthac— MI. Demea,*
*rursum irascere? DE. An non credis? Repeton quem dedi? est ægre: non sum alienus, si*
*obsto, hem, desino. Vis curem unum: curo: & est gratia diis, quum est ita ut volo: iste tu-*
*ui, ipse sentiet posterius; nolo dicere quid gravius in illum. MI. Nec nihil, neque omnia*
*hæc quæ dicit, sunt vera; tamen hæc sunt non nihil molesta mihi:*

## ANNOTATIONS.

send him packing. I am rather inclin'd to follow the first, as it is more agreeable to *Micio's* Character of a fond easy Father. Nor ought we to pass over, without Remark, the Tenderness and Good-nature that appears in his manner of expressing himself. He does not say absolutely, *he will be discarded; excludetur foras:* but *perhaps he may; fortasse excludetur foras.* He loves his Son so well, and has so good an opinion of him, as to flatter himself he will be agreeable to them, even without the Recommendation of Presents. There is an inexpressible Beauty and Elegance in the word *fortasse.*

*Donatus* too was sensible of it, and expresses himself thus: *Et mire fortasse dicit, ut pater indulgens, & credens adolescentem posse etiam amari ab amica. Non enim affirmavit, ut diceret, excludetur foras.*

46 *Natura tu illi pater es, consiliis ego.* This is *Micio's* Answer to *Demea,* charging him with not knowing the Duty of a Father; intimating, that he thought Nature not of so great Importance in training up of Children, as Deliberation and Prudence. A real Father may be often blinded by his Affection, but in the case of one, whose liking was founded upon the Merit of the Person beloved,

nor am I wholly free from Concern on this account
willing that he should see my Uneasiness: for such
the Man, that when I want to pacify him, I oppose
Huff him; and yet he is scarce able to contain him
to humour him in his Passion, or blow the Coal, I fl
Madman than he. And yet after all, *Æschinus* has
well in this Affair. What Girl is there but he has
with, or made some Present to? Besides, lately (I
then sick of these Follies) he promised me to marry.
that the high Tide of his Youth was now over, and w
at it. But see, he has begun again: however I am
it whatever it is, and will find out my Gentleman
*Forum.*

*ANNOTATIONS.*

beloved, there was less reason to think that
he would be biased by Passion, and that,
therefore, he could judge of his Behaviour
without Prejudice, and give such Advice
as was most agreeable to his real Circum
stances.

6. *Non nibil molesta hæc sunt mibi.* *Terence* shews great Judgment in his way of
managing *Micio's* Character. It is evident
that the Poet inclines to the milder way of
educating children; and that *Micio* was a
favourite Character with him, which he
meant as a Pattern for Imitation. He ha
set him off with Affability, Good-nature,
and every amiable endearing Quality; nor i
his Indulgence to *Æschinus* founded on any
other Consideration, than that he sees him of
a Temper there was no danger of spoiling.
He therefore judged it better to give him hi
way a little for the present, that by being

acquainted with the F
the World, he might b
when reason came to be
cio had seem'd to car
far before *Demea*; T
Spectators, and to prev
Impressions to his Di
him here, after his Br
what uneasy and distur
had done. *Donatus's* R
cellent, and well worth
" Optime poeta Mici
' tum; ne si omnino
" indulgere adoptivo f
" non curare videretu
" servat placidum anin
" neat patris affectum.'
7. *Dixit velle uxore*
several Places gives us
may partly understand

---

# ACT II. SCENE

ARGUMENT.

*The Old Men being now dismissed, we have*
*quarrelling with the Cock-bawd, about the Gi*
*by force out of his House; a Scene that r*
*the Confidence and Boldness of a forward Yo*

SANNIO, ÆSCHINUS,

*Sannio* FOR Heaven's sake, good Neighbours, giv
to a miserable, innocent Man: help the

*ANNOTATIONS.*

We have seen in the preceding Scene, that
*Demea* had been informed of *Æschinus's*
coming into *Sannio's* House, and taking

thence by force a N
Scene therefore seems
sentation of that scuffle

Non nihil molesta hæc sunt mihi: sed ostendere,
Me ægre pati, illi nolui. nam ita est homo:
Cùm placo, adversor sedulo, & deterreo;
Tamen vix humanè patitur: verùm si augeam, 65
Aut etiam adjutor sim ejus iracundiæ,
Insaniam profecto cum illo. etsi Æschinus
Nonnullam in hac re nobis facit injuriam.
Quàm hic non amavit meretricem, aut cui non dedit
Aliquid? Postremò nuper (credo jam omnium 70
Tædebat) dixit velle uxorem ducere.
Sperabam jam deservisse adolescentiam:
Gaudebam ecce autem dé integro: nisi, quidquid est,
Volo scire, atque hominem convenire, si apud forum est.

*sed nolui ostendere illi, me ægre pati. Nam homo est ita; cùm placo, adversor sedulo, & deterreo; tamen vix patitur humanè: verùm si augeam, aut etiam sim adjutor ejus iracundiæ, profecto insaniam cum illo. Etsi Æschinus facit nonnullam injuriam nobis in hac re. Quàm meretricem hic non amavit? Aut cui non dedit*

*aliquid? Postremò nuper (credo jam tædebat omnium) dixit se velle ducere uxorem. Sperabam adolescentiam jam deservisse. Gaudebam. Ecce autem rapit de integro: nisi (sed) quidquid est, volo scire, atque convenire hominem, si est apud forum.*

## ANNOTATIONS.

Play, and that even from Persons who are themselves ignorant of it: for although *Micio* knew nothing of *Æschinus*'s Love for *Pamphila*; yet he says here, *Credo jam omnium tædebat, & dixit se velle uxorem ducere.* This was extremely well imagined in the Poet; that *Micio*, who was so indulgent to his Son, and encouraged him to hide nothing from him, might not appear wholly ignorant of so important a Transaction. For hence we are let to understand, that it was not want of Candour in *Æschinus*, or that he desired to deceive his Father; for we see he had intended to discover all, and had actually begun it, but, restrained by Modesty and Awe, had gone no farther than to tell him, that he was now weary of the Follies of Youth, and had some Thoughts of marrying. His real Intentions are clear'd up in the Progress of the Play.

7² *Sperabam jam deservisse adolescentiam.* The Heat and Fire of Youth is frequently expressed by the Word *fervor*, a Metaphor taken from the Rage and Impetuosity of a stormy Sea. Hence the abating and subsiding of this Heat, is signified by the Verb *deferveo. Cic. pro Cæl.* 18. "Multi & nostra, "& patrum majorumque memoria, judices, "summi homines, & clarissimi cives fue- "runt; quorum cum adolescentiæ cupidi- "tates *deservissent,* eximiæ virtutes, firma- "ta jam ætate, extiterunt." In like manner, in his Book *de Senectute, Cap.* 13. "Epulabar igitur cum sodalibus omnino mo- "dice; sed erat quidam fervor ætatis, qui "progrediente, omnia fient indies mitiora."

---

# ACTUS II. SCENA. I.
## ARGUMENTUM.

*Omissis senibus, describitur Æschini factum, jurgantis cum lenone, propter puellam ereptam. Protervi adolescentis fidentia & impetus hac scena exprimitur.*

### SANNIO, ÆSCHINUS.

OBsecro, populares, ferte misero atque innocenti auxilium:

*ORDO.*
Sa. OBsecro, populares, ferte auxilium misero atque innocenti

## ANNOTATIONS.

Reader preposterous, and contrary to the Order of Time. To obviate this Difficulty, we are to observe, that *Æschinus* had no less than two Quarrels with *Sannio*. The first, when

*Æfch.* (*To the Mufick-Girl.*) Stand juft there where you are, with-out fear. Why do you look back? there's no danger. I'll under-take, he does not offer to touch you while I am here.

*Sann.* But in fpite of the World, I will——

*Æfch.* Tho' he be a Villain, he'll fcarce do any thing to provoke me to give him a fecond Drubbing.

*Sann.* Hark ye, *Æfchinus*; that you may'nt afterwards pretend to have been ignorant of my Profeffion; I'm a Woman-Merchant.

*Æfch.* I know it.

*Sann.* And as honeft in my way as ever Man was. Your pretend-ing to clear yourfelf afterwards, by telling me, that you're forry for it, and could heartily wifh it had never happened, fhall have no weight with me: for, be affur'd, I'll purfue my Right; nor fhall all your fine words be able to atone for the real Injury you have done me. I know the common Excufes on thefe Occafions. *I'm heartily forry for it, I'll take my Oath you did not deferve it:* when, mean-time, I have been treated in the moft unworthy manner.

*Æfc.* (*To* Parmeno.) Run before quickly, and open the Door.

*Sann.* 'Tis all to no purpofe.

*Æfc.* (*To* Parmeno) In with her now.

*Sann.* (*Stepping between.*) But I'll take care to prevent it.

*Æfc.* Come hither, *Parmeno*: you're got too far on that fide; ftand here clofe by this Rafcal. There, juft fo: take care now to keep your Eyes always fix'd on mine; that when I tip the wink, you may inftantly give him a flap in the Face.

*Sann.* I'd have him try that.

*Æfc.* Hip! take care, *Parmeno*, (*he ftrikes*) (*to* Sannio.) Let go the Woman.

*Sann.* O fcandalous!

*Æfc.* He'll repeat it, unlefs you take care. [*Parmeno ftrikes again.*

*Sann.* O miferable!                                                    *Æfc.*

ANNOTATIONS.

when he broke into his Houfe, and carried off the Mufick-Girl. As this could not be done without a great deal of noife, and gathering a croud of People about the Door, the Ru-mour of it flew all over the Town in an in-ftant; and reaching *Demea*, he runs to his Brother *Micio*, to complain, and reproach him with it. This is what we have feen in the laft Scene. Mean time, *Æfchinus*, bring-ing home the Mufick-Girl, is followed by the Pimp, who perfecutes him all the way, till he comes to *Micio's* Door; and endea-vuurs to hinder him from conveying her into the Houfe, which gives rife to another Squab-ble. This is evident from the Circumftances of the Story itfelf: for *Sannio*, fpeaking of the former Affault, fays;

'*Domo me eripuit, verberavit: me invito adduxit meam:*'

*Homini mifero plus quingentos colaphos in-fregit mibi.*

Whereas in this latter Quarrel *Æfchinus* fays to his Servant: *abi præftrenue ac fo-res aperi: Fores fcilicet ædium Micionis patri Æfchini:* And afterwards, *I intro num jam.*'

2 *Otiofe: nunc jam illico bic confifte.* Thefe Words are addreffed to the Mufick-Girl who no doubt lik'd better to be in the Hand of *Æfchinus* than *Sannio*, and had followed with a Mixture of Joy and Fear. Hence *Æfchinus* ufes the Word *otiofe*, which, as *Donatus* explains it, is equivalent to *fecure Illico* is an Adverb of Place, not of Time Stand perfectly eafy and unconcerned, *illico bic*, in this very place.

7 *Leno ego fum.* He declares this to *Æf-chinus*, to intimidate him, becaufe the Mer-chant

Subvenite inopi. Æs. etiose: nunc jam illico hic consiste:
Quid respectas? nihil pericli est: nunquam, dum ego
   adero, hic te
Tanget. Sy. ego istam inviti' omnibus.
Æs. Quanquam est scelestus, non committet hodie un-
   quam iterum ut vapulet.        5
Sa. Æschine, audi: ne te ignarum fuisse dicas meorum
   morum;        [fide quisquam optima.
Leno ego sum. Æs. scio. Sa. at ita, ut usquam fuit
Tu quod te posterius purges, Hanc injuriam mihi nolle
Factam esse; hujus non faciam. crede hoc, ego meum
   jus persequar;        [feceris. 10
Neque tu verbis solves unquam, quod re mihi male-
Novi ego vestra hæc: Nollem factum: Jusjurandum
   dabitur, te esse        [ceptus modis.
Indignum injuria hac; indignis cùm egomet sim ac-
Æs. Abi præstrenuè, ac fores aperi. Sa. cæterùm hoc
   nihil facis.        [accede illuc, Parmeno;
Æs. I intro nunc jam. Sa. at enim non sinam. Æs.
Nimiùm istoc abisti: hic propter hunc assiste. hem,
   sic volo.        15
Cave nunc jam oculos à meis oculis quoquam demoveas
   tuos,        [malâ hæreat.
Ne mora sit, si innuerim, quin pugnus continuò in
Sa. Istuc volo ergo ipsum experiri. Æs. hem, serva.
   omitte mulierem.     [Sa. hei misero mihi!
Sa. O facinus indignum! Æs. geminabit, nisi caves

*Subvenite inopi. Æs. Jam, nunc consiste illico hic otiose: quid respectat? est nihil periculi: hic nunquam tanget te, dum ego adero. Sa. Ego tangam istam invitis omnibus. Æs. Quanquam est scelestus, non unquam committet quidquam, ut vapulet iterum. Sa. Audi, Æschine: ne dicas te fuisse ignarum morum meorum; ego sum leno. Æs. Scio. Sa. At ita optima fide, ut usquam quisquam fuit. Quod tu purges te posterius, dicens te nolle hanc injuriam esse factam mihi; non faciam hujus: crede hoc, ego persequar meum jus. Neque tu unquam solves verbis, quod malefeceris mihi re. Ego novi hæc vestra verba: Nollem factum: Jusjurandum dabitur te esse*

*indignum hac injuria; cum egomet sim acceptus indignis modis. Æs. Abi præstrenuè, ac aperi fores. Sa. Cæterum nihil facis hoc. Æs. Jam nunc i intro. Sa. At enim non sinam. Æs. Parmeno, accede illuc, abisti nimium istoc: assiste hic propter hunc: hem volo sic. Cave nunc jam ne demoveas tuos oculos quicquam à meis oculis, ne sit mora, si innuerim; quin pugnus continuo hæreat in malâ. Sa. Volo ergo ipsum experiri istuc. Æs. Hem, serva, omitte mulierem. Sa. O indignum facinus! Æs. Geminabit, nisi caves. Sa. Hei mihi misero!*

## ANNOTATIONS.

chants, who dealt in Slaves, had great Privileges at *Athens*, by reason of the Advantages the Commonwealth drew from them. And it was forbid to abuse them, under pain of Disinheritance. Hence, in *Lucian*, a young Man complaining that he had been injuriously disinherited by his Father, says, *Is there any Merchant of Slaves, who accuses me of having used him ill?*

9 *Hujus non faciam.* It is necessary, to compleat the Sense, that some Action or Gesticulation be supposed to accompany these Words; as either that be held something of little or no value in his hand, and pointed it to *Æschinus*, or snapp'd his Fingers, or did something else of the like nature.

11 *Nollem factum! jusjurandum dabitur, &c.* In this the Poet shews the usual Refuges of young Fellows, when they had abused any one who resented it so far, as to pursue them upon it. Nay, and it is evident, that the Injured were often appeased by Submissions of this kind. Thus in *Plautus, Amph.* 3. 2. 7. *Alcmena* charg'd with Baseness by her Husband *Amphitruo*, says,

   —— *Quin ego illum aut deseram,*
*Aut satisfaciat mihi: atque adjuret in-*
   *super,*
*Nolle esse dicta, quæ in me insontem præ-*
   *tulit.*

*Sannio* here threatens, that however prevalent he may have found these Excuses on some Occasions, yet they should have no weight with him.

19 *Hem, serua. Sannio,* after saying *istuc volo ergo ipsum experiri,* had laid hold of the Girl,

*Æsc.* (*To* Parmeno.) I didn't give the wink; however, err rather on that fide. Now go in.

*Sann.* What means this? Do you reign here, *Æschinus?*

*Æsc.* If I did, you fhould be handled as you deferve.

*Sann.* What Bufinefs have you with me?

*Æsc.* None.

*Sann.* What! Do you know who I am?

*Æsc.* I don't want to know.

*Sann.* Did I ever touch any thing of yours?

*Æsc.* If you had, you fhould have anfwer'd for it.

*Sann.* What greater Right have you to my Slave, whom I fairly paid for? anfwer me.

*Æsc.* You had better not make all this Difturbance before the Door; for if you continue to be troublefome, I'll have you dragg'd in immediately, and there lafh'd without mercy.

*Sann.* What! A Free-man, and lafh'd!

*Æsc.* It fhall be juft fo.

*Sann.* O fhamelefs Man! Is it here that they pretend all Men enjoy equal Liberty?

*Æsc.* If you have done with raving, Mr *Pimp*, pray hear me now a little.

*Sann.* Have I been raving at you, or you at me?

*Æsc.* Let that pafs, and come to the Point.

*Sann.* To what Point? Where fhall I come?

*Æsc.* Are you willing now, that I fhould fpeak to you about your own Affairs?

*Sann.* With all my heart; let it only be with juftice.

*Æsc.* Pretty, truly: a Cock-bawd cautions me againft Injuftice.

*Sann.* I am a Bawd, I own it, the common Bane of Youth, a perjured Wretch, a public Scourge; yet I never injured you.

*Æsc.* No: for that's to come.

*Sann.* Pray, *Æfchinus*, return to your firft Propofal.

*Æsc.* You bought her for threefcore Pounds, and may your Bargain never thrive. You fhall have the Money for her again.

*Sann.* What if I don't choofe to fell her? Will you force me?

*Æsc.* By no means.

*Sann.* I was afraid you would.

*Æsc.* Nor do I think fhe can be fold, who is a Free-woman; for I
here

ANNOTATIONS.

Girl, which occafions *Æfchinus's* turning fuddenly to *Parmeno*: *Hem, ferva*; and then, with a peremptory Air to the Pimp; *Omitte mulierem.* But as he ftill keeps his hold, *Parmeno* gives him a Blow on the Face, when he exclaims, *O facinus indignum!* And as *Æfchinus* tells him, *geminabit, nifi caves, Parmeno* haftily, without expecting the Signal from his Mafter, gives him another; which draws from him that Lamentation, *Hei mifero mibi!* Upon which *Æfchinus* fays to *Parmeno; Non innueram: verum in iftam partem potius peccato tamen.*

23 *Quid? noftin' qui fim?* Donatus has a Remark upon thefe Words, which deferves particular Explanation; *Proprie: fic enim dicit qui nibil quidquam debet,* NUM ME NOVIT? *non quod ignoretur, fed quod in jure non cernatur.* " Sannio here anfwers very " properly, for this was the common An-
" fwer

ÆS. Non innueram: verùm in istam partem potiùs
    peccato tamen,            20
I nunc jam. SA. quid hoc rei est? regnumne, Æschine,
    hîc tu possides?
ÆS. Si possiderem, ornatus esses ex tuis virtutibus.
SA. Quid tibi rei mecum est? ÆS. nihil. SA. quid?
    nostin' qui sim? ÆS. non desidero.
SA. Tetigin' tui quidquam? ÆS. si attigisses, ferres in-
    fortunium.            [gentum dedi? 25
SA. Qui tibi magis licet meam habere, pro quâ ego ar-
Responde. ÆS. ante ædes non fecisse erit melius hîc
    convicium:            [que ibi
Nam si molestus pergis esse, jam intro abripiere, at-
Usque ad necem operiere loris. SA. loris liber? ÆS.
    sic erit.            [esse æquam omnibus
SA. O hominem impurum! hiccine libertatem aiunt
ÆS. Si satis jam debacchatus es, leno, audi si vis nunc
    jam.            30
SA. Egon' debacchatus sum autem, an tu in me? ÆS.
    mitte ista, atque ad rem redi.
SA. Quam rem? quò redeam? ÆS. jamne me vis di-
    cere id, quod ad te attinet?
SA. Cupio, æqui modò aliquid. ÆS. vah, leno iniqua
    me non volt loqui!            [tium,
SA. Leno sum, fateor, pernicies communis adolescen-
Perjurus, pestis: tamen tibi à me nulla est orta injuria.
ÆS. Nam hercle etiam hoc restat. SA. illuc quæso re-
    di, quò cœpisti, Æschine.            36
ÆS. Minis viginti tu illam emisti, quæ res tibi vortat
    male:            [lo vendere?
Argenti tantum dabitur. SA. quid, si ego tibi illam no-
Coges me? ÆS. minimè. SA. namque id metui. ÆS.
    neque vendundam censeo,

*Æs. Non innuerim: verumtamen peccato potius. In istam partem. I nunc jam. SA. Quid rei est hoc? Æschine, tune possides, regnum hîc? Æs. Si possiderem, esses ornatus ex tuis virtutibus. SA. Quid rei est tibi mecum? Æs. Nihil. SA. Quid? Nostine qui sim? Æs. Non desidero. SA. Tetigine quidquam tui? Æs. Si attigisses, ferres infortunium. SA. Qui magis licet tibi habere meam puellam, pro quâ ego dedi argentum? responde. Æs. Erit melius non fecisse convicium hic ante ædes: nam si pergis esse molestus, jam abripiere intro, atque ibi operiere loris usque ad necem. SA. Egone liber operiar loris? Æs. Sic erit. SA. O hominem impurum! Hiccine aiunt libertatem esse æquam omnibus. Æs. Si es jam debacchatus satis, leno, audi nunc jam, si vis. SA. Egone autem sum debacchatus in te, an tu es debacchatus in me? Æs. Mitte ista, atque redi ad rem. SA. Ad quam rem? Æs. Visne me jam dicere id, quod attinet ad te? SA. Cupio, modo dic aliquid æqui. Æs. Vah, leno vult me loqui non iniqua! SA. Sum leno, fateor, communis pernicies adolescentium, perjurus, pestis; tamen nulla injuria est orta tibi à me. Æs. Nam hercle hoc etiam restat. SA. Quæso, Æschine, redi illuc, quo cepisti. Æs. Tu emisti illam viginti minis, quæ res vortat male tibi: tantum argenti dabitur. SA. Quid si ego nolo vendere illam tibi, coges me? Æs. Minime. SA. Namque metui id. Æs. Neque censeo illam esse vendundam,*

## ANNOTATIONS.

" swer of a Man who owed nothing, *Does
" he know me?* Not that the Person to
" whom he spoke did not know him, but
" because he had no Action against him
" in any Court of Justice." Thus, *nosti me?
nosti qui sim?* are Terms drawn from the
Practice and Formalities of the Bar. Instead of saying, *I owe you nothing,* the usual
Phrase was, *Do you know me?* For a Debtor
was generally well known to his Creditor;
and *Æschinus's* Answer, that he did not desire to know him, is much the same as if he
had said, *I don't want to have any Demands
upon you.* Thus all the Pleasantry of this
Passage consists in the equivocal Meaning of
the Terms, which must be lost in the
Translation, as our Language annexes no
double Sense to the Words. *Dacier.*

  26 *Convicium. Quasi convicium, seu multorum junctus clamor.* Hence it is used to
        signify

here claim her by an Action of Freedom. Now fee which you'll
choofe: to take the Money, or try your Caufe. Think of it, I fay,
Mr Bawd, till I return.

*Sann.* (*Alone.*) O almighty *Jove!* truly I don't much wonder
that Men run mad under Oppreffion. He dragg'd me out of my
own Houfe, beat me, took away my Girl from me by force, and has
given me above five hundred Blows; and in return for all this fine
ufage, wants that I fhould give her for what fhe coft me. True:
fince he deferves of me fo well, let him have her: he demands but
his right. Well: I could even be content to quit her after all, were
I fure of the Money. But this is what I fufpect, when I have confented to give her for fo much, he'll immediately take Witneffes of
her being fold. As to my having the Money, 'tis a mere Dream:
*Don't fear, you fhall have it; call again to-morrow.* Nay, I could
bear with that too, unjuft as it is, were I but fure of it at laft. But
the real truth of the Matter is this: when a Man has once begun fuch
a Trade; he muft refolve to bear in filence the Affronts of thefe
young Blades. But here is nobody to pay me; it is in vain for me
to be making up Accounts with myfelf.

A N N O T A T I O N S.

fignify any Noife, Scuffle or Difturbance.
*Cic. pro Arch.* 6. *Quia fuppeditat nobis, ubi
& animus ex hoc forenfi ftrepitu reficiatur,
& aures convicio defeffæ conquiefcant.*

*4°. Nam ego liberali illam affera caufa ma-
nu.* Thefe Words may be thus paraphrafed:
*Quia liberam mulierem, quæ vendi non poteft,
alienare vis, ego illam liberali caufa,* i. e.
*directa legis, qua liberos homines alienare pro-
bibitum eft, actione, affero manu.* This
*Æfchinus* fays to *Sannio,* to frighten him
into the Compofition which he had refufed. *Plaut. Curc.* V. 2. 66.

*Et tens hic debet nobis triginta minas.*
PH. *Quamobrem iftuc?* TH. *Quia ille ita
repromifit mihi,*

*Si quifquam hanc liberali afferuiffet manu,
Sine controverfia omne argentum reddere.
Afferere manu,* was therefore a Law Phrafe,
and implied the undertaking to defend any
one as free. Thefe Defenders of Liberty
were called *Affertores,* and the Action which
they commenced to evince this Liberty,
*Caufa liberalis,* an Action of Freedom.
"Locutio inde orta (fays *Wefterbovius*) quod
"qui hominem in fervitute conftitutum de-
"fendere vellet, & effe liberum dicere, eum
"juxta fe collocatum coram prætore & ma-
"nu apprehenfum quafi affereret feu planta-
"ret, dicens, *Hunc ego hominem, jure Qui-*
"*ritium liberum effe aio.* Eft enim *ferere*
"non tantum femen in-terram mittere, fed
"&

---

## ACT II. SCENE II.

### ARGUMENT.

Sannio *complains of the Injury done him by* Æfchinus; *and is
deceived by the Cunning of* Syrus, *who artfully brings him
to confent to take the Money for the Girl in queftion.*

SYRUS, SANNIO.

*Syrus.* (*TO* Æfchinus *within.*) Say no more; I'll go meet him myfelf, and foon make him glad to take the Money; nay, and
he

A N N O T A T I O N S.

Æfchinus, in the preceding Scene, had
left *Sannio* abruptly, having firft alarm'd
him with an apprehenfion, that he intended to ftand upon his Defence, and affert the
Freedom

Quæ libera est: nam ego liberali illam affero causâ
   manu.                                   40
Nunc vide utrum vis, argentum accipere, an caufam
   meditari tuam.                     [Jupiter!
Deibera hoc, dum ego redeo, leno. SA. proh supreme
Minimè miror, qui insanire occipiunt ex injuria.   43
Domo me eripuit, verberavit: me invito abduxit meam.
Ob malefacta hæc tantidem emtam postulat sibi tradier.
Homini misero plus quingentos colaphos infregit mihi.
Verùm enim, quando bene promeruit, fiat: suum jus
   postulat.                            [hariolor:
Age, jam cupio, modò si argentum reddat. sed ego hæc
Ubi me dixero dare tanti, testes faciet illico,
Vendidisse me: de argento somnium: mox, Cras redi.
Id quoque possum ferre, si modò reddat: quanquam in-
   jurium est.                            51
Verùm cogito id, quod res est: quando eum quæstum
   occeperis,
Accipiunda & mussitanda injuria adolescentium est.
Sed nemo dabit: frustra egomet mecum has rationes
   puto.

*ORDO.* — quæ est libera: nam ego, manu assero, illam causa liberali. Nunc vide utrum vis, accipere? argentum, an meditari tuam causam, Delibera hoc, leno, dum ego redeo. SA. Proh supreme Jupiter! minimè miror, qui occipiunt insanire ex injuria. Eripuit me domo, verberavit: abduxit meam puellam me invito: infregit plus quam quingentos colaphos mihi misero homini. Ob hæc malefacta postulat eam emptam, viginti minis tradi sibi tantidem. Verum etiam fiat, quando promeruit bene: postulat suum jus. Age jam cupio, si modo reddat argentum. Sed ego hariolor hæc. Ubi dixero me dare illam tanti, illico faciet testes me vendidisse eam: de argento erit somnium: dicet, Habebis mox, redi cras. Possum ferre id quoque, quanquam est injurium, si modo reddat. Verum cogito id quod res est: quando occeperis eum quæstum, injuria adolescentium est accipienda, & mussitanda. Sed nemo dabit argentum mihi; egomet frustrà puta bas rationes mecum.

### *ANNOTATIONS.*

" & plantam vel surculum figure. Unde
" asserere simpliciter pro defendere usurpa-
" tur. *Flor.* I. 11. *Latini quique Tarqui-*
" *nios asserebant.*"

41 *Caufam meditari tuam.* This carries in it something of the Air of a Proverb. *Cic. Att.* 8. 11. *Vidit, quam caufam mediter.* He also in another Place calls it, *commentari caufam.*

46 *Plus quingentos colaphos infregit mihi.* Donatus observes a poetical Beauty in the word *infregit;* which *Sannio,* he supposes, pronounced in such manner, as that it might carry some Resemblance of the rebounding of the Blows he had received. *Infregit,* i. e. *illisit, inflixit.*

## ACTUS II. SCENA II.

### ARGUMENTUM.

*Sannio queritur de injuria sibi facta ab Æschino, & Syri consiliis eluditur; qui eum callide impellit ut accipiat pretium pro erepta virgine.*

### SYRUS, SANNIO.

TACE, egomet conveniam ipsum: cupidè accipiat
   jam faxo, atque etiam

*jam faxo ut accipiat cupidè, atque etiam ut*

*ORDO.* SY. Tace, egomet conveniam psum; &

### *ANNOTATIONS.*

Freedom of the Musick-Girl. Accordingly we find *Sannio,* when left alone, reflecting with himself, what was best for him to do; and, as is usual in these Cases, resolves to put

up

he shall say he has been well used too. (*To Sannio.*) What's this, Sannio? I hear you have had I don't know what Quarrel with my Master.

*Sann.* Quarrel! I never saw a more unequal one in my Life. He with beating, and I with being beaten, were both of us tired sufficiently.

*Syr.* 'Twas your own fault.

*Sann.* What could I do?

*Syr.* You should have yielded to the young Gentleman.

*Sann.* What cou'd I do more? when I even gave my Face to his Blows?

*Syr.* Well, do you know what I am going to say? To seem to slight Money on some occasions, is often the surest gain. How! Was you afraid, greatest of all Fools, that if you had parted with a little of your Right now, and humoured the young Gentleman, it would not in the end have return'd to you with Interest?

*Sann.* I don't like to pay for my Hope.

*Syr.* You'll never be rich. Away, Fool, you don't know how to take in young Blades.

*Sann.* I believe it might have been the better Way: but I was never yet so cunning as not to prefer the ready Money, when I could get it.

*Syr.* Well, come, I know your Spirit: as if threescore Pounds were any thing to you, in comparison of obliging my Master. Besides, they say you are going to *Cyprus.*

*Sann.* Hah!

*Syr.* That you have bought up a whole Stock of Goods to carry thither; and hired a Vessel: I know you're in suspense; however, I hope you'll make it up, when you come back.

*Sann.*

*A N N O T A T I O N S.*

up the Affront, and rest satisfied, if he can but obtain his own. *Æschinus,* in the mean time was not easy, he knew the severe Penalties he was liable to, did *Sannio* prosecute the Suit, and therefore, was willing by all means to come to an Agreement with him. For this purpose he applies to *Syrus,* a Slave of great Cunning, and expert in these Affairs. *Syrus* undertakes it, and is here represented as coming out from his Master, and talking to him within, giving him Assurances that he will soon bring *Sannio* to Terms.

2 *Quid issue, Sannio est?* It is worth while to remark here, how *Terence* varies his Style, and always suits it to the Genius, Character, and Designs of the Person who speaks. In the former Scene, *Æschinus* carries it with a high Hand, disdains to make any Concessions to *Sannio;* and instead of calling him by his own Name, in contempt denominates him by his Profession: *Delibera hoc, dum ego redeo, leno.* This Behaviour is natural enough in a young Man of the Town, arrogant and fierce; and who, no doubt, thought the only way to humble his Adversary, was to shew that he undervalued and despised him. But *Syrus,* who wanted to make up matters, begins with a softer Tone, and addresses him by his own Name; which was doing great Honour to a Man who got his Living by so sordid an Employment; for we find that this Familiarity was a mark of Esteem and Affection, even among People of Condition. Both in Poets and Historians, nothing is more common than this plain simple Address. In the *Eunuch,* when *Thais* wants to ingratiate herself with the Soldier, it is, *Salve, mi Thraso;* and when afterwards she speaks in Anger and Resentment, *Miles, nunc adeo edico tibi.*

3 *Nunquam vidi iniquius certationem comparatam.*

Bene dicat fecum effe actum. Quid iftuc, Sannio, eft,
  quod te audio             [di iniquius·
Nefcio quid cum hero concertaffe? SA. nunquam vi-
Certationem comparatam, quàm hæc hodie internos fuit.
Ego vapulando, ille verberando, ufque ambo defeffi fu-
  mus.            [rem geftum oportuit.  6
SY. Tua culpa. SA. quid agerem? SY. adolefcenti mo-
SA. Quî potui meliùs, qui hodie ufque os præbui? SY.
  age, fcis quid loquar?       [lucrum. hui!
Pecuniam in loco negligere, maxumum interdum eft
Metuifti, fi nunc de tuo jure conceffiffes paululùm,
Atque adolefcenti effes morigeratus, hominum homo
  ftultiffime;                10
Ne non tibi iftuc fœneraret? SA. ego fpem precio non
  emo.                 [Sannio.
SY. Nunquam rem facies: abi, nefcis inefcare homines,
SA. Credo iftuc melius effe : verùm ego nunquam adeò
  aftutus fui,             [fentiâ.
Quin, quidquid poffem, mallem auferre potiùs in præ-
SY. Age, novi tuum animum: quafi jam ufquam tibi
  fint viginti minæ,          15
Dum huic obfequare. præterea autem, te aiunt pro-
  ficifci Cyprum.  SA. hem.
SY. Coëmiffe hinc, quæ illuc veheres, multa; navem
  conductam : hoc fcio,      [hoc ages,
Animus tibi pendet : ubi illinc, fpero, redieris, tamen

*dicat effe etiam bene fecum. Quid iftuc eft, Sannio, quòd audio te concertaviffe nefcio ob quid cum bero? SA. Nunquam vidi certationem comparatam iniquius, quam bæc fuit comparata inter nos bodie. Ego vapulando, ille verberando ambo ufque fumus defeffi. SY. Culpa eft tua. SA. Quid agerem? SY. Oportuit merem fuiffe geftum adolefcenti. SA. Quî potui melias, qui bodie præbui ufque os? SY. Age, fcis quid loquar? Negligere pecuniam in loco, interdum eft maximum lucrum. Hui! Homo ftultiffime bominum, metuifti, fi conceffiffes paululum nunc de tuo jure, atque effes morigeratus adolefcenti, ne iftuc non fœneraret tibi? SA. Ego non emo fpem*

*precio. SY. Nunquam facies rem. Abi, Sannio, nefcis inefcare bomines. SA. Credo iftuc effe melius : verùm ego nunquam fui adeo aftutus, quin mallem potius auferre quidquid poffem in præfentia. SY. Age, novi tuum animum : quafi viginti minæ fint jam ufquam tibi, dum obfequare buic : præterea autem aiunt te proficifci Cyprum. SA. Hem. SY. Aiunt te coëmiffe multa, quæ veberes binc illuc : navem effe conductam. Scio boc, animus pendet tibi : tamen ubi redieris illinc, fpero, ages boc.*

### ANNOTATIONS.

*paratam.* This Anfwer is founded upon what *Syrus* had juft faid, for by the word *concertaffe;* he feem'd to put Æfchinus and *Sannio* upon an Equality; hence, in the Anfwer we meet with *comparatam,* a Term drawn from the Combats of Gladiators, where it was the Cuftom to choofe out fuch as feem'd to be moft upon a level, and match them together.

8 *Hui.* Guido *Juvenal* afcribes this to *Sannio,* who here interrupts *Syrus.* Interjectio (fays he) *ridentis, quafi leno rideat dicta fervi, & contemnat.* But I think it reads much better, if we fuppofe it to come from *Syrus,* who here makes a fudden Paufe, as wondering that *Sannio* did not fee that by humouring Æfchinus for the prefent, he might be able to make him his Dupe afterwards.

9 *Si nunc de tuo jure conceffiffes paululum.* *Sannio* maintain'd it as his Right, that he could not be forced to fell the Mufic-Girl. This is what *Syrus* refers to here : You ought not to have infifted fo rigoroufly, but, as you found him fo earneft, your beft way was to have yielded, which would have been certain gain to you in the end. *Concedere de jure tuo,* i. e. *paululum de jure remittere.* Cic. Fam. XI. 3. *Illud vero quemadmodum ferendum fit, tute cogita : non licere prætoribus, concordiæ ac libertatis caufa, per edictum de fuo jure decedere, quin Cof. arma minetur.* And *Off.* 2. 18. *Eft enim non modo liberale, paulum nonnunquam de fuo jure decedere, fed interdum etiam fructuofum. Habenda autem eft ratio rei familiaris, quam quidem dilabi finere flagitiofum eft : fed ita, ut illiberalitatis avaritiæque abfit fufpicio. Poffe enim liberalitate uti, non fpoliantem fe patrimonio, nimirum is eft pecuniæ fructus maximus.*

12 *Abi, nefcis inefcare bomines, Sannio.*

*Sann.* I don't stir a Foot. Ruin'd, by *Jupiter!* it was upon this Hope they built their Project.

*Syr.* He's afraid, I see: I have aim'd right.

*Sann.* O Baseness! only see how he has nick'd me in the very critical Article. I have bought several Women Slaves, and other things to carry to *Cyprus.* Unless I get thither before the Fair is over, I shall be a very great Loser; and if I leave this Business unfinish'd now, 'twill come to nothing. When I return, it will be all over, the Affair will be quite forgotten. What, are you come at last? Why did you neglect it so long? Where have you been? Insomuch, that I had better lose it altogether, than either stay here so long till it is paid; or sue for it after my Return.

*Syr.* Well, have you done yet with computing the Gains of your Voyage?

*Sann.* Is this acting honourably? Is this becoming in *Æschinus?* to attempt to take my Girl from me by downright force?

*Syr.* [*Aside.*] He sinks, I perceive — I have this one Proposal to make, see whether it will please you. Rather than run the hazard of saving or losing all, *Sannio,* compound with him; take one half: he'll some way or other contrive to scrape thirty Pounds together.

*Sann.* Wretch that I am! What! am I in danger of losing part even of the Principal? Is he past shame? he has beat out all my Teeth; my whole Head is full of Bumps with the Blows he gave me; and would he moreover defraud me? I'm going no where.

*Syr.* As you will: Have you any thing more to say before I go?

*Sann.* Yes, my dear *Syrus,* I have this to request: however these things have been, yet rather than go to Law, let him give me back my own, at least what she cost me: *Syrus,* I know, you never yet had any occasion for me in a friendly way; but you'll say I'm neither unmindful nor ungrateful.

*Syr.* I'll do the best I can for you. But I see *Ctesipho* coming: he's all in Spirits, that he has got his Mistress.

*Sann.* Will you do as I ask?

*Syr.* Stay a little.

<hr>

ANNOTATIONS.

Compare this with *Plautus, Asin.* I. 3. 63.

*Non tu scis? hæc noster quæstus aucupii si-
millimu'st.*

*Auceps quando concinnavit aream, offundit
cibum,*

*Aves adsuescunt: necesse est facere sumptum,
qui quærit lucrum.*

*Sæpe edunt: semel si sunt captæ, rem
solvunt aucupi.*

*Itidem hic apud nos: ædis nobis area est,
auceps sum ego;*

*Esca est meretrix; lectus illex est; ama-
tores aves.*

21 *Emtæ mulieres, complures et item hinc
alia, quæ porto Cyprum.* Guyetus will not al-
low that *Sannio* had bought these Slaves at Athens, to carry them to *Cyprus*; but contrariwise, that they had been bought at *Cyprus,* to carry to *Athens*; and upon this Supposition, he changes and alters the Text at pleasure. But he seems to have forgot, that it was the Practice of the Merchants to range all over *Greece,* and buy up Women-Slaves, to sell them at a celebrated Fair, which was kept at *Cyprus*; and that the Profits which *Greece,* especially the *Athenians,* drew from this Commerce, was the Cause of their granting so many Privileges to the Merchants of Slaves.

28 *Jamne enumerasti,* &c. This Passage has been generally misunderstood, in being supposed to refer to the Music-Girl; where-

Sa. Nufquam pedem. perii hercle: hac illi fpe hoc in-
    ceperunt. Sy. timet:
Injeci fcrupulum homini. Sa. ô fcelera! illud vide, 20
Ut in ipfo articulo oppreffit. emptæ mulieres
Complures, & item hinc alia, quæ porto Cyprum.
Nifi eo ad mercatum venio, damnum maxumum eft.
Nunc fi hoc omitto, actum agam: ubi illinc rediero,
Nihil eft, refrixerit res : Nunc demum venis?    25
Cur paffus? ubi eras? ut fit fatius perdere,
Quàm aut hic manere tam diu, aut tum perfequi.
Sy. Jamne enumerafti id quod ad te rediturum putes?
Sa. Hoccine illo dignum eft? hoccine incipere Æf-
    chinum?
Per oppreffionem ut hanc mî eripere poftulet?    30
Sy. Labafcit. unum hoc habeo. vide fi fatis placet:
Potiùs quàm venias in periclum, Sannio,
Servefne an perdas totum, dividuum face.
Minas decem conradet alicunde. Sa. hei mihi!
Etiam de forte nunc venio in dubium mifer.    35
Pudet nihil: omnes dentes labefecit mihi.
Præterea colaphis tuber eft totum caput.
Etiam infuper defraudet? nufquam abeo. Sy. ut lubet.
Numquid vis, quin abeam? Sa. imo hercle hoc quæfo,
    Syre;
Ut ut hæc funt facta, potiùs, quàm lites fequar,    40
Meum mihi reddat, faltem quánti empta eft. Syre,
Scio te non ufum antehac amicitiâ meâ:
Memorem me dices effe, & gratum. Sy. fedulo
Faciam. fed Ctefiphonem video : lætus eft    44
De amicâ. Sa. quid, quod te oro? Sy. paulifper mane.

*Sa. Feto pedem nufquam. Perii her-*
*cle: illi incêpêrunt hoc hac fpei Sy.*
*Timet? injeci fcru-*
*pulum homini. Sa.*
*O fcelera! vide il-*
*lud, ut oppreffit me*
*in ipfo articulo:*
*Complures mulieres*
*funt emptæ, & item*
*alia, quæ porto hinc*
*Cyprum. Nifi venio*
*eo ad mercatum,*
*damnum eft maxi-*
*mum. Sed fi omit-*
*to hoc nunc, agam*
*actum: ubi rediero*
*illinc, eft nibil, res*
*refrixerit. Dicent:*
*Venis nunc demum &*
*Cur paffus es? Ubi*
*eras? ut fit fatius*
*perdere, quàm aut*
*minere hic tam diu,*
*aut perfequi tum.*
*Sy. Jamne enume-*
*ravifti id quod putes*
*rediturum ad te?*
*Sa. Hoccine eft dig-*
*num illo? Æfchi-*
*num incipere. hocci-*
*ne? Ut poftulet eri-*
*pere hanc mibi per*
*oppreffionem? Sy.*
*Labafcit. Habeo*
*hoc unum dicere tibi,*
*vide fi placet fatis:*
*potius, Sannio, quam*
*venias in periculum,*

*fervefne an perdas tetum, fac dividuum. Corradet decem minas alicunde. Sa. Hei mibi.*
*Mifer, venio etiam nunc in dubium de forte. Pudet nibil: labefecit omnes dentes mibi.*
*Præterea totum caput eft tuber colapbis. Infuper etiam defraudet? abeo nufquam. Sy.*
*Ut lubet. Numquid vis, quin abeam? Sa. Imo hercle quæfo hoc, Syre; ut ut hæc funt facta,*
*potius quam fequar lites, reddat meum mibi, faltem quanti eft empta. Scio, Syre, te antehac*
*non ufum fuiffe mea amicitia: dices me effe memorem & gratum. Sy. Faciam fedulo. Sed*
*video Ctefiphonem: eft lætus de amicâ. Sa. Quid facies, quod oro te? Sy. Mane paulifper.*

## ANNOTATIONS.

as it is really a Piece of Cunning in *Syrus*, to turn the Difcourfe to another Subject; and, by his feeming Unconcern, increafe the Fears and Anxiety of the Pimp. He demands, therefore, whether he had computed the Gains he expected to make by his Voyage, which as it made *Sannio* fenfible that they knew the Neceffity he was under, was like to bring him fooner to fubmit to Terms.

*35 Etiam de forte nunc venio in dubium mifer.* Sors is properly the principal Sum, lodg'd any where for the accumulating of Intereft, it is call'd alfo *caput*, the capital Stock, and the Intereft granted upon it *mercet*. Hor. Lib. I. Sat. 2.

*Quinas hic capiti mercedes exfecat.*

*Sannio* here ufes the word *fors*, in fpeaking of the original Price, which he gave for the Mufic-Girl, becaufe he confidered that as a kind of Capital, and the Profit he expected in felling her again, as the Intereft. To be deprived of this latter, was to him a heavy Misfortune; but to lofe part, even of the Principal, appear'd quite intolerable. He, therefore exclaims againft the Injuftice, and, repeating all the ill Ufage he had already received, afks of *Syrus*, whether he can carry his Bafenefs fo far, as moreover to defraud him?

## ACT II. SCENE III.

### ARGUMENT.

Ctesipho *commends and praises his Brother, and thanks him in his Absence, for the Service he had done him.*

### CTESIPHO, SYRUS.

*Ctesipho.* IT gives one pleasure to receive a Benefit from any Hand, where the Want is pressing: but it doubles the Joy, when it comes from one, from whom we have reason to expect it. O Brother, Brother! In what Words shall I now praise you? This I know well enough, that all I am able to say, must come far short of your Merit: for I reckon myself particularly happy in this, beyond all other Men; that no one can boast of having a Brother more distinguish'd for every good Quality, than mine.

*Syr.* O *Ctesipho!*

*Ctes.* O *Syrus!* Where's *Æschinus?*

*Syr.* He's at home there, waiting for you.

*Ctes.* Oh!

*Syr.* What's the Matter?

*Ctes.* The Matter? But for him, *Syrus,* I had not now been alive. Delightful Man! who disregarded every Consideration that might have restrained him, when my Happiness was at stake, and took all the Reproach, Infamy, Intrigue, and Fault upon himself.

*Syr.* He could, indeed, do no more.

*Ctes.* But what noise is that at the Door?

*Syr.* Stay, stay, he's coming out himself.

### ANNOTATIONS.

The Rape of this Music-Girl was not upon *Æschinus's* own account, but for his Brother. Endeavours had been used to obtain her fairly from *Sannio*; but he insisted upon Conditions, which it was impossible for them to comply with. This reduced *Ctesipho* to the greatest Despair, insomuch, that he was upon the point of leaving his Country. *Æschinus* seeing the Consequences were like to prove so terrible, resolves upon Violence, and, as we have seen, carries the Girl off by force. *Ctesipho* had, by this time, heard of it, and is here introduced full of Joy at his good Fortune, and of Gratitude to a Brother who had done so much for him.

*7 O Ctesipho!* CT. *O Syrus! Æschinus ubi est?* Nothing can be better conducted than this Meeting of *Ctesipho* and *Syrus.* O' is an Interjection of Joy or Surprise. *Syrus sees Ctesipho* happy and possess'd of all

## ACTUS II. SCENA II.

### ARGUMENTUM.

*Ctesipho fratrem laudat & commendat, agitque gratias absenti pro accepto beneficio.*

CTESIPHO, SYRUS.

| | ORDO. |
|---|---|
| ABS quivis homine, cùm est opus, beneficium acci-<br>　　pere gaudeas:　　　　　　[facere, is bene facit.<br>Verùm enimvero id demum juvat; si, quem æquom est<br>O frater, frater, quod ego nunc te laudem? satis certò<br>　　scio,　　　　　　　　　　　[superet tua.<br>Nunquam ita magnificè quidquam dicam, id virtus quin<br>Itáque unam hanc rem me habere præter alios præci-<br>　　puam arbitror,　　　　　　　　　　　　5<br>Fratrem homini nemini esse primarum artium magi'<br>　　principem.　[lum, te exspectat domi. CT. hem.<br>SY. O Ctesipho. CT. ô Syre, Æschinus ubi est? SY. el-<br>SY. Quid est? CT. quid sit? illius operâ, Syre, nunc vi-<br>　　vo. festivum caput!<br>Qui　omnia sibi post putârit esse præ meo commodo.<br>Maledicta, famam, meum amorem, & peccatum in se<br>　　transtulit.　　　　　　　　　　　　　　10<br>SY. Nihil pote supra. CT. quidnam fores crepuit?<br>　　SY. mane, mane, ipse exit foras. | CT. *Audeat accipere beneficium abs quovis homine, cum est opus: verum enim-vero id demum juvat, si is bene facit, quem est æquum facere ita. O fra-ter, frater, quid ego nunc laudem te? scio satis certo, ut nunquam dicam quidquam ita mag-nifice, quin tua vir-tus superet id. Ita-que arbitror me ha-bere hanc unam rem præcipuam præter alios, esse nemini homini fratrem ma-gis principem pri-marum artium.* SY. *O Ctesipho.* CT. |

*O Syre. Ubi est, Æschinus? SY. Ellum, expectat te domi. CT. Hem. SY. Quid est? CT. Quid sit? Nunc vivo, Syre, illius opera. Festivum caput! qui putaverit omnia esse sibi post, præ meo commodo. Transtulit in se maledicta, famam, meum amorem, & meum peccatum. SY. Nihil pote supra. CT. Quidnam fores crepuit? SY. Mane, mane, ipse exit foras.*

### ANNOTATIONS.

his Wishes. *Ctesipho* is address'd unexpected-ly by *Syrus*, and turns to him with an Emo-tion of Surprise, *ô Syre!* But as his Thoughts are full of *Æschinus*, the very first Question regards him; *Ubi est Æschinus?*

8 *Festivum caput! qui omnia sibi postputa-vit esse,* &c. There is nothing that affects us with equal Pleasure, as what we are satisfied comes from the Heart. The Ex-pressions here made use of by *Ctesipho*, as they are the manifest Overflowings of a grateful Mind, must sensibly touch every Reader who knows how to distinguish what is amiable and praise-worthy in a Character. For as Ingratitude is one of the blackest Vices, and, if well represented, must excite Horror; so the contrary Character is in pro-portion pleasing and lovely.

## ACT II. SCENE IV.

### ARGUMENT.

*The two Brothers talk together. It is agreed upon to dis-*
*charge the Bawd, and make ready a Supper.*

ÆSCHINUS, SANNIO, CTESIPHO, SYRUS.

*Æschinus.* WHERE's that Scoundrel?

*Sann.* He wants me: does he bring any thing with
him? I'm quite undone, I fee nothing.

*Æsc.* (*Seeing* Ctesipho.) Hah, you're come very fortunately, I
wanted you. How goes it, *Ctesipho*? All's safe: no more of your
grave Faces.

*Cte.* I have done with them, by *Hercules*, having such a Brother
as you. O my *Æschinus*! O my Brother! but I'm unwilling to
praise you any more before your Face, left you should suspect it rather
Flattery than Gratitude.

*Æsc.* Away Fool, as if we did not now perfectly know one another. This grieves me, that we knew it so late, and that the matter
was almost come to that pass, that, had all Mankind desired it, it
had not been in their power to serve you.

*Cte.* Modesty hindred me.

*Æsc.* Pshaw! that is Folly, not Modesty. To be upon the point
of leaving your Country for such a trifle. It ought never to be
mention'd: Heaven forbid it.

*Cte.* I own my fault.

*Æsc.* (*To* Syrus.) What says *Sannio* to us at last?

*Syr.* He's now very tame.

*Æsc.* I'll to the *Forum* directly, and discharge him; get you in to
your Girl, *Ctesipho*.

*Sann.* Syrus, urge it.

*Syr.* Let us dispatch him; for he wants to be at *Cyprus*.

*Sann.* Not in any such haste; tho' I have no need to loiter away
my time here.

*Syr.* You shall have your Money, don't be afraid.            *Sann.*

### ANNOTATIONS.

*Æschinus* again appears, and with the same
haughty Air towards *Sannio*, as knowing
that was the most likely way to humble him,
and bring him to Terms. In this Scene,
the several Characters are preserved with
wonderful Exactness; the Discourse runs
upon different Subjects, but each is mindful
of what it was natural to think should most
employ his Thoughts. *Sannio* is attentive
only to the Recovery of his Money. Every
thing he does or says tends to this. *Æschi-*
*nus* still speaks with his usual Haughtiness,
and a threatening Tone; but withal whif-
pers *Syrus*, to know how the Bawd stood inclin'd; and, when told that he was come to
Terms, resolves to go immediately and difcharge him. *Ctesipho*'s first Concern is, to
express his Gratitude to his Brother: which,
when done, he thinks how to provide against
his Father's hearing any thing of what had
happen'd; and for this purpose begs of *Sy-*
*rus*, that *Sannio* may be discharged as soon as
possible.

[1] *Me quærit.* So we ought to read, without an Interrogation; for *Sannio* no sooner
hears the words *ubi est ille sacrilegus*? than
he understands that they are meant of him,
and applies them accordingly. *Me quærit.*
We are to suppose too, that he says this with
an Air of Complacency, as expecting that
*Æschinus* had brought the Money with him;
but when he sees no Marks of that, he soon
changes

## ACTUS II. SCENA IV.

### ARGUMENTUM.

*Colloquüntur fratres; agitur de pecunia reddenda leuoni,*
*& de paranda cæna.*

ÆSCHINUS, SANNIO, CTESIPHO, SYRUS.

| | ORDO. |
|---|---|
| UBI ille eſt ſacrilegus? SA. me quærit. numquid-<br>    nam effert? occidi:    [quid ſit, Cteſipho?<br>Nil video. ÆS. ehem, opportunè: teipſum quærito.<br>In tuto eſt omnis res: omitte verò triſtitiam tuam.<br>CT. Ego illam hercle verò omitto, qui quidem te ha-<br>    beam fratrem, ô mi Æſchine!    [pliùs, 5<br>O mi germane! ah, vereor coràm in os te laudare am-<br>Ne id aſſentandi magis, quàm quò habeam gratum, fa-<br>    cere exiſtumes.    [nos, Cteſipho<br>ÆS. Age inepte, quaſi nunc non nôrimus nos inter<br>Hoc mihi dolet, nos penè ſerò ſciſſe, & penè in eum<br>    locum    [liarier.<br>Rediſſe, ut, ſi omnes cuperent, nihil tibi poſſent auxi-<br>CT. Pudebat. ÆS. ah, ſtultitia eſt iſtæc non pudor:<br>    tam ob parvolam    10<br>Rem pene è patria! turpe dictu. Deos quæſo, ut iſtæc<br>    prohibeant.    [jam mitis eſt.<br>CT. Peccavi. ÆS. quid ait tandem nobis Sannio? SY.<br>ÆS. Ego ad forum ibo, ut hunc abſolvam, tu intro ad<br>    illam, Cteſipho. [Cyprum. SA. ne tam quidem;<br>SA. Syre, inſta. SY. eamus; namque hic properat in<br>Quamvis etiam maneo otioſus hîc. SY. reddetur, ne<br>    time.    15 | Æs. UBI eſt<br>ille ſa-<br>crilegus? SA.<br>Quærit me: num-<br>quidnam effert?<br>occidi: video nil.<br>ÆS. Ehem, oppor-<br>tune: quærito te-<br>ipſum: quid ſit,<br>Cteſipho? Omnis<br>res eſt in tuto: o-<br>mitte vera tuam<br>triſtitiam. CT. E-<br>go hercle vere omit-<br>to illam, qui qui-<br>dem habeam te<br>fratrem, O mi<br>Æſchine! O mi<br>germane! ab, ve-<br>reor laudare te am-<br>plius coram in os,<br>ni exiſtumes me fa-<br>cere id magis aſ-<br>ſentandi cauſa,<br>quam quo habeam<br>me gratum. ÆS.<br>Age inepte, quaſi<br>nunc non noverimus<br>nos inter nos, Cteſi-<br>pho. Hoc dolet mi-<br>bi, nos penè ſero |

*ſciſſe, & rediſſe pene in eum locum, ut, ſi omnes cuperent, nibil poſſent auxiliari tibi. CT. Pu-*
*debat. ÆS. Ab, iſtæc eſt ſtultitia, non pudor: fugiſſe pene è patria ob tam parvulam rem!*
*turpe dictu. Quæſo Deos, ut probibeant iſtæc. CT. Peccavi. ÆS. Quid Sannio tandem ait*
*nobis? SY. Eſt mitis jam. ÆS. Ego ibo ad Forum, ut abſolvam bunc. Tu, Cteſipho, abi in-*
*tro ad illam. SA. Syre, inſta. SY. Eamus: namque bic properat in Cyprum. SA. Ne*
*tam propere quidem; quamvis etiam maneo otioſus bic. SY. Argentum reddetur, ne time.*

### ANNOTATIONS.

changes his Note. *Occidi! nil video.* No-thing can be juſter than this: *Sannio* is not at all concern'd at the hard Names given him, thoſe go for nothing, as no doubt he was uſed to them in that Profeſſion; but not to ſee Money, when he expected it, was a real Affliction.

5 *Coram in os te laudare amplius.* Coram, ſays *Donatus,* ad ipſum pertinet qui laudat, & ad eos qui audiunt: in os ad ipſum qui laudatur. Nam coram laudes, qui non tacet apud alios, & hoc agit non per epiſtolam, ſed ipſe præſens. In os, qui apud ipſum loquitur, quem collaudat. *Pene è patria.* We are told by *Donatus,* that in *Menander,* the young Man was

about to kill himſelf in deſpair. But as that appear'd too tragical; *Terence* has taken care to ſoften it a little, which is improving upon his Original.

14 *Eamus; namque hic properat in Cyprum.* *Syrus* takes a malicious Pleaſure in vexing *Sannio,* who was always ſtartled at hearing his Voyage to *Cyprus* named, as dreading that *Æſchinus* would take advantage of it; whence his Anſwer, *Ne tam quidem.*

15 *Quamvis etiam maneo otioſus hic.* Commentators ſeem to have miſtaken the Senſe of theſe Words, when they explain them, *I am at leiſure to ſtay here, as long as you will.* I take them rather to expreſs his De-

*Sann.* But shall I have it all?

*Syr.* I tell you, you shall have all; only be silent, and follow us.

*Sann.* I will.

*Ctes.* Hark ye, hark ye, *Syrus.*

*Syr.* What now?

*Ctes.* Pray discharge that mean Wretch as soon as possible, lest, if he should be further provok'd, the Story may reach my Father, and then I'm ruin'd for ever.

*Syr.* That shan't happen: Fear nothing; but enjoy yourself with her meanwhile within Doors; and order the Cloth to be laid for us, and every thing to be in readiness: for as soon as the Affair is ended, I'll come home with Store of Provisions.

*Ctes.* Do, pray; and since all has succeeded so well, let us e'en make a chearful Day of it.

### ANNOTATIONS.

*fire of being dispatch'd as soon as possible.* The whole runs thus, *I am in no such haste to be at Cyprus, although I am here idling away my Time.* As if he had said, I have no Business that calls me to *Cyprus,* yet is it not the less inconvenient to be hanging on here, when I have other important affairs to call me elsewhere? and therefore pray dispatch me as soon as possible.

*17. Observo bercle, hominem istum imperitissimum.* *Ctesipho* had gone in to his Mistress, but recollecting, that if *Sannio* was not discharged, he might make a noise, and the Story come to his Father's Ears, he calls after *Syrus,* to caution him upon that Head. His manner of expressing himself, as *Donatus* observes, is suitable to the Character of one who had all his Life time been bred in the Country, and therefore was too modest to use the word *lens.* This Remark may, perhaps, to some appear too refin'd; and, indeed, it was common, when speaking of any one who either by his Profession or sordid Character, was a proper Object of Contempt, to describe

---

# ACT III. SCENE I.

### ARGUMENT.

*The Poet introduces Sostrata full of Anxiety for her Daughter, who is big with Child by Æschinus.*

### SOSTRATA, CANTHARA.

*Sostrata.* FOR Heaven's sake, dear Nurse, how is she like to be?

*Cant.* Like to be, say you? very well, I hope.

*Sost.* Her Pains, Nurse, seem to be just beginning.

*Cant.* You're as much afraid now, as if you had never been present at a Labour, or cry'd out yourself.     *Sost.*

### ANNOTATIONS.

*Æschinus,* in one of his Night-Rambles, had happened to meet an Athenian Virgin, one *Pamphila,* the Daughter of *Sostrata,* who, tho' poor, was yet well descended, and had been virtuously educated. After a violent Struggle, he forced her; but chancing to drop his Ring, *Pamphila* secur'd it, as thinking it might be a means of discovering some time or other who this Author of her Misfortune was. *Æschinus,* when he came to reflect on what he had done, convinced of the Baseness of ruining a young Creature, who had probably nothing beside her Virtue to depend upon, resolves to make Reparation. He goes to them, excuses the late Insult, and promises to marry the Girl. Thus all is hush

SA. At ut omne reddat. SY. omne reddet, tace modò,
　　ac fequere hac. SA. fequor.
CT. Heus, heus, Syre. SY. hem, quid eft? CT. obfecro
　　hercle, hominem iftum impuriffimum
Quamprimùm abfolvitote, ne, fi magis irritatus fiet,
Aliqua ad patrem hoc permanet, atque ego tùm per-
　　petuò perierim. 　　　　　　　[oblecta interim, 20
SY. Non fiet: bono animo es. tu cum illâ te intus
Et lectulos jube fterni nobis, & parari cætera,
Ego jam transactà re convortam me domumcum opfonio.
CT. Ita quæfo: quando hoc bene succeffit, hilarem
　　hunc fumamus diem.

SA. *At fac ut red-
dat itaque. SY. Red-
det omne, modo fa-
ce, ac fequere me
hac. SA. Sequor.
CT. Heus, heus,
Syre. SY. Hem,
quid eft? CT. Ob-
fero hercle, abfol-
vitote quamprimum
iftum impuriffimum
hominem, ne fi fiet
magis irritatus, hoc
permanet aliqua ad
patrem, atque ego
tum perpetuo peri-*

*erim. SY. Non fiet: es bono animo: tu interim oblecta te cum illâ intus, & jube lectulos
fterni nobis, & cætera parari. Ego, re transactâ, jam convertam me domum cum opfonio.
CT. Fac ita quæfo: &, quando hoc succeffit bene, fumamus hunc diem hilarem.*

## ANNOTATIONS.

defcribe him in the very fame Terms that
Cæfipho ufed here. *Cic. pro Cluent.* 25. *Quæ
pecunia fimulatque ad eum delata eft, homo
impuriffimus ftatim cæpit in ejufmodi mente
& cogitatione verfari: nihil effe fuis rationi-
bus utilius.*

22. *Ego jam transactâ re convortam me domum cum opfonio.* Donatus has upon this
the following judicious Remark: *Convortam,
magnifice dictum: verbum eft enim r. magni
moliminis & agminis ingentis. Nam con-
vertere se, dicitur, quem pompa præcedit: ut
imperator proprie convertit exercitum. Et*
*fpectatur, ut moribus arrogantes ferui
fint; quàm lætantur.* "Convortam carries
"something magnificent in the very Ex-
"preffion, for it is a word peculiar to a
"great Train and Attendance. *Converfere
"fe* is properly faid of one who is preceded
"by fome folemn Pomp, as in a Triumph:
"in like manner, *converti:* is ufed of a Ge-
"neral, when he changes the March of his
"Army. In this, therefore, we fee the boaft-
"ing and vain-glorious Humour of Slaves,
"when things go on profperoufly with them."

# ACTUS III. SCENA I.

## ARGUMENTUM.

*Solicitam inducit Softratam, ob filiæ, quæ ex Æfchino gra-
vida eft, vicinum partum.*

### SOSTRATA; CANTHARA.　　　　ORDO.

OBfecro, mea nutrix, quid nunc fiet? CA. quid fiet,
　　rogas? 　　　　　　　　　　[cipiunt primulùm.
Rectè ædepol, fpero. So. modò dolores, mea tu, oc-
CA. Jam nunc times, quafi nunquam adfueris, nun-
　　quam tute pepereris.

So. *Obfecro me-
a nutrix,
quid fiet nunc?
CA. Rogas, quid
fiet? ædepol. fpero
rectè. So. Mea tu,
modo dolores primu-*

*lam occipiunt. CA. Jam nunc times, quafi nunquam adfueris in partu, quafi tute nunquam
pepereris.*

## ANNOTATIONS.

hufh and quiet; *Pamphila,* mean time, proves
with Child; and the Mother is here introduced full of Anxiety, becaufe her painful
Moments feem to be juft at hand.
*Modo dolores, mea tu.* Thefe Words,
which, in almoft all Editions, have been a-
fcribed to *Softrata,* Tanaquil Faber contends
muft belong to the Nurfe. The whole Paffage
he reads thus:
So. *Obfecro, mea nutrix, quid nunc fiet?*
CA. *Quid fiet, rogas?*
*Rectè, ædepol, fpero. Modo dolores, mea
tu, occipiunt primulùm.*

*Soft.* Alas! I have nobody with me, we're all alone: *Geta* too
is absent; nor is there a Soul to send for the Midwife, or call *Æschinus.*

*Cant.* He'll be here presently, I know: for he never suffers one
Day to pass without coming.

*Soft.* He's my only Consolation amidst all my Misfortunes.

*Cant.* It could not have happened better, as the thing is, Mistress,
than that, as your Daughter was forced, it should be by one so much
of a Gentleman, of so noble and generous a Spirit, and so well
descended.

*Soft.* 'Tis, indeed, as you say, Nurse: pray Heaven he may be
preserved to us.

ANNOTATIONS.

*Jam nunc times, quasi nunquam adfueris,
nunquam tute pepereris.*
But besides that this last Line does not come
in so well, as if we suppose, *Modo dolores,
mea tu,* to be said by *Sostrata;* the very
Expression, *mea tu,* is too familiar from a
Servant to her Mistress.

8 *E re nata;* &c.   In this manner, says
*Donatus,* we speak of things which happen

to us contrary to our Inclination, as in the
present Case, the Virgin's Misfortune. The
Words, therefore, may be thus paraphras'd:
*E re nata,* i. e. *postquam res ita nata erat,
ut nimirum filiæ tuæ offerretur vitium:
melius fieri haud potuit,* i. e. malum illud ad
majorem salutem converti non potuit, quam
quod ad Æschinum attinet, illum esse talem. This Congratulation from *Canthara,*
to.

---

## ACT III. SCENE II.

### ARGUMENT.

*In this Scene,* Geta, *a faithful Servant of* Sostrata, *relates,
with great Concern, how* Æschinus, *forgetting his first Love
and abandoning an Athenian* Virgin, *whom he had debauch'd,
had taken a Music-Girl by force from a Cock-bawd.*

GETA, SOSTRATA, CANTHARA.

*Geta.* **N**OW is our Misfortune such, that were all Mankind to
combine and unite their Counsels for a Remedy to this
Disaster which has happened to me, my Mistress, and her Daughter,
all would be ineffectual. How wretched a Situation is this! So many Calamities beset us at once, out of which it is impossible for us
to extricate ourselves. Violence, Poverty, Injustice, Solitude, Infamy: What a base Age! O the Wickedness of Men! O sacrile-
gious Race! O perfidious Man!

*Soft.*

ANNOTATIONS.

The Poet, by the short Conversation between *Canthara* and *Sostrata,* in the preceding Scene, prepares for what is to happen
here. While they are in discourse, talking
of *Æschinus,* as the only Support of the Family, and praying to Heaven for his Safety,
*Geta* appears. He chanced to be passing
along the Street where *Sannio* lived, when

the Scuffle happened, and saw *Æschinus* carry
off the Music-Girl by force. It was natural
enough for him to conclude, that all this was
done on his own account, and that the Music-Girl must be some new Mistress he had
fallen in love with. *Geta,* who was *Sostrata's*
Servant, one well affected to the Family, and
whose Labour and Industry was their chief
Support

So. Miseram me, neminem habeo, solæ sumus: Geta
  autem hic non adest:
Nec quem ad obstetricem mittam, nec qui accersat Æs-
  chinum. 5
CA. Pol is quidem jam hic aderit: nam nunquam u-
  num intermittit diem, [remedium.
Quin semper veniat. SA. solus mearum miseriarum est
CA. E re natâ melius fieri haud potuit, quàm factum est,
  hera; [potissimùm,
Oblatum quando vitium est, quod ad illum attinet
Talem, tali genere atque animo, natum ex tantâ fa-
  miliâ. 10
So. Ita pol est, ut dicis. salvus nobis, Deos quæso, ut siet.

*è re nata, quam est factum, hera; quando vitium est oblatum filiæ tuæ, quod attinet, potis-*
*simum ad illum talem, tali genere, atque animo, & natum ex tanta familia. So. Pol est ita,*
*ut dicis. Quæso Deos, ut sit salvus nobis.*

So. *Heu me mise-*
*ram, habeo nemi-*
*nem, sumus solæ:*
*Geta autem non ad-*
*est hic, nec ullus*
*alius, quem mittam*
*ad obstetricem, nec*
*qui accersat Æs-*
*chinum.* CA. *Pol*
*is quidem jam ad-*
*erit hic: nam nun-*
*quam intermittit*
*unum diem, quin*
*semper veniat.* So.
*Ille solus est reme-*
*dium mearum mise-*
*riarum.* CA. *Haud*
*potuit fieri melius*
*..., quod attinet, potis-*
*... So. Pol est ita,*

## A N N O T A T I O N S.

to *Sostrata*, is for this reason brought in here
by the Poet, that the shock which *Geta*'s
Relation gives in the following Scene, might
appear the greater. *Bentley* reads, *E re na-*
*tæ*, which he explains, *Ex commodo filiæ tuæ,*
*melius haud fieri potuit, quam factum est*. So
*Phormio* V. 7. 76.
  *Non hercle ex re istius me instigasti, Demipho.*

10 *Tali genere, ex tanta familia*. *Genus,*
according to some, refers to the Nobility and
Splendor of his Race; *familia,* with its E-
pithet, represents their Power and Wealth.
*Ex tanta familia*. i. e. *ex tam divite &*
*potenti domo*. *Bentley* reads; *Tali ingenio*
*atque animo*.

---

## ACTUS III. SCENA II.
### ARGUMENTUM.

*Hic Geta, Sostratæ servus fidelis, vehementer commotus, re-*
*fert quomodo Æschinus alio amore captus, puellam lenoni eri-*
*puerit, deserta ac spreta Attica virgine.*

### GETA, SOSTRATA, CANTHARA.

NUNC illud est, quod, si omnes omnia sua con-
  silia conferant, [ferant;
Atque huic malo salutem quærant, auxilii nihil af-
Quod mihique, heræque, filiæque herili est. væ misero
  mihi!
Tot res repente circumvallant, unde emergi non potest,
Vis, egestas, injustitia, solitudo, infamia. 5
Hoccine seclum? ô scelera! ô genera sacrilega! ô ho-
  minem impium!

Ge. NUNC il-
lud est
nostrum infortuni-
um, quod, si om-
nes homines con-
ferant omnia sua
consilia, atque quæ-
rant salutem huic
malo, quod est fa-
ctum mihique, he-
ræque, filiæque he-
rili, afferant nihil

*auxilii. Væ misero mihi! Tot res repente circumvallant nos, unde non potest emergi, vis,*
*egestas, injustitia, solitudo, infamia. Hoccine est seclum? O scelera! O genera sacrilega!*
*O hominem impium!*

## A N N O T A T I O N S.

Support, bewails, bitterly, this   alarming, was now quite alienated from them, Want
Misfortune. Æschinus, in all probability,  and Infamy threatened them; nor was the
  Calamity

*Sof.* Alas! What can be the meaning of *Geta's* haſtening to us in ſuch a Fright?

*Get.* Whom neither Honour, nor Oaths, nor common Humanity, have been able to reſtrain, or ſoften to Pity; nor that the poor young Creature, whom he ſo ſhamefully abuſed, was big with Child by him, and near her Time.

*Sof.* I don't well underſtand what he ſays.

*Can.* Let us, pray, *Soſtrata*, go a little nearer.

*Get.* Wretch that I am! I'm almoſt bereft of my Senſes, ſo far has my Anger tranſported me. There is nothing I ſo much wiſh for, as to meet the whole Family of them, that I may diſcharge all my Vengeance againſt them, while the Wound is freſh; for I would contentedly incur any Puniſhment to obtain but my full Revenge. Firſt of all, I'd tear out the Soul of the old Wretch, who produced that Monſter of Wickedneſs; and then as for *Syrus*, the Prompter to this Miſchief, ah, what Torments would I not invent for him? I'd firſt ſnatch him by the middle, then daſh his Head againſt the ground, and ſtrew the Way with his Brains. Tho ſweet Youth himſelf, I'd tear his Eyes out, and afterwards tumble him over ſome Precipice. The reſt I'd ruſh upon, drive them before me, drag them, trample on them, and cruſh them to pieces. But why do I linger to inform my Miſtreſs of her Misfortune?

*Sof.* Let us call him back: *Geta!*

*Get.* Piſh, let me alone, whoever you are.

*Sof.* 'Tis *Soſtrata*.

*Get.* Where is ſhe? 'Tis you I want, and am looking for. It is very fortunate that I have met you, Miſtreſs.

*Sof.* What's the matter? Why do you tremble?

*Get.* Alas!

*Sof.* Why do you hurry yourſelf ſo? Take Breath a little, *Geta*.

*Geta.*

*ANNOTATIONS.*

Calamity ſuch as admitted any Alleviation. Theſe his Complaints are overheard by *Soſtrata*; who goes up to him to know what is the matter.

15 *Satis mihi id habiam ſupplicii, dum ille ulhiſcar modo.* It is not eaſy to aſcertain the proper Senſe of theſe Words. The more general, and received way of explaining them is, thus, "That he would be ſatisfied and "think it Puniſhment enough, could he "but take what Revenge upon them he "pleas'd." But this is flat, and ſeems to eaſy with it, no conſiſtent Meaning. Madam *Dacier*, therefore, endeavours to give them another turn, "En verité (*ſays ſhe*) "ce ſeroit là un choſe bien ſurprenante que "*Geta* crût ces gens là aſſez punis, s'il avoit "arrache le cœur à l'un, & ecraſe le tête à "l'autre. Je m'etonne que l'on n'ait ſenti "que cela fait un tres mauvais ſens. Sati- "baberem id ſupplicii, ſignifie, je ſuffrirois "tel ſupplice que l'on voudroit." *Donatus* ſeems to have taken the Words in the ſame ſenſe, when he ſays: "Moraliter loquitur: "nam fere quando quiſquam iraſcitur, ſibi "videtur fortis, tanquam qui plus audet." It may not, perhaps, be amiſs, to ſuppoſe that *Geta*, in the heat of Anger, ſpeaks with too much Hurry and Inattention to be accurate; and, therefore, notwithſtanding ſome little Difficulty in the Conſtruction, we may very naturally ſuppoſe him ſpeaking thus: "Nor "is there any thing I wiſh more, than to "have the whole Family in my power, that "I may diſcharge my Vengeance upon "them without Reſerve; for I care not "what becomes of myſelf, if I can but "have my Revenge on them."

10 *Seni animam exſtinguerem ipſi.* This may be underſtood either of *Demea* or *Micio*, because

So. Me miseram, quidnam est, quòd sic video timidum
  & properantem Getam?
Ge. Quem neque fides, neque jusjurandum, neque il-
  lum misericordia    [bat prope,
Repressit, neque reflexit, neque quòd partus insta-
Cui miseræ indignè per vim vitium obtulerat. So. non
  intelligo    10
Satis quæ loquatur. Ca. propiùs, obsecro, accedamus,
  Sostrata. Ge. ah,    [cundiâ.
Me miserum, vix sum compos animi, ita ardeo ira-
Nihil est, quòd malim, quàm totam familiam dari mi-
  hi obviam,    [hæc est recens:
Ut iram hanc in eos evomam omnem, dum ægritudo
Satis mihi id habeam supplicii, dum illos ulciscar modo.
Seni animam primùm exstinguerem ipsi, qui illud pro-
  duxit scelus:    16
Tum autem Syrum impulsorem, vah, quibus illum la-
  cerarem modis!    [terram statuerem,
Sublimem medium primùm arriperem, & capite in
Ut cerebro dispergat viam.
Adolescenti ipsi eriperem oculos, post hæc præcipitem
  darem.    20
Cæteros ruerem, agerem, raperem, tunderem, & pro-
  sternerem.    [cemus. Geta. Ge. hem,
Sed cesso hoc malo heram impertiri propere? So. revo-
Quisquis es, sine me. So. ego sum Sostrata. Ge. ubi ea
  est? teipsam quærito:    [viàm,
Te exspecto. oppidò opportunè te obtulisti mi ob-
Hera. So. quid est? quid trepidas? Ge. hei mihi!
  So. quid festinas, mi Geta?    25

*So. O me miseram, quidnam est, propter quod illico Getam sic timidum & properantem? Ge. Quem neque fides, neque jusjurandum, neque misericordia, repressit illum; neque reflexit, neque quod partus prope instabat virgini, cui miseræ indigne obtulerat vitium per vim. So. Non satis intelligo quæ loquitur. Ca. Obsecro, Sostrata, accedamus propius. Ge. Ah, me miserum, vix sum compos animi, adeo ita iracundia. Et nihil est, quod malim, quam totam familiam dari obviam mihi, ut evomam hanc omnem iram in eos, dum ægritudo hæc est recens: habeam id satis supplicii mihi, dum modo ulciscar illos. Primùm extinguerem animam ipsi seni, qui produxit illud scelus. Tum autem, quod ad Syrum, impulsorem, vah, quibus modis lacerarem illum! primum arriperem medium sublimem, & statuerem eum capite in terram, ut dispergat viam cerebro. Eriperem oculos ipsi adolescenti, post hæc darem præcipitem: ruerem, agerem, raperem, tunderem, & prosternerem cæteros. Sed cesso propere impertiri heram hoc malo? So. Revocemus. Geta. Ge. Hem, quisquis es, sine me. So. Ego sum Sostrata. Ge. Ubi ea est? Quærito teipsam: exspecto te. Obtulisti te obviam mihi oppidò opportune, bene. So. Quid est? Quid trepidas? Ge. Hei mihi! So. Quid festinas, mi Geta?*

## ANNOTATIONS.

because *produxit*, will refer either to the be-
getting or educating of *Æschinus*. It will,
however, have a better Effect, if we apply it
to *Demea*. *Geta*, in the heat of his Passion,
talks at random, without regard to nice dis-
criminating Circumstances. How much so-
ever *Demea* might disapprove of his Son's
Behaviour; *Geta*, in his present Fury, thinks
it Crime enough that he begot him.

19 *Ut cerebro dispergat viam.* Tanaquil
*Faber* observes, that the original Reading
must have been *dispergeret*; for that the *Latins* never said, *Illum invaderem, ut interfici-
am*; but, *ut interficerem*, in like manner it
ought to be, *Arriperem, & statuerem capite
in terram, ut dispergeret.*

21 *Ruerem, agerem, raperem.* These are
all Terms borrowed from the Art of War,
and aptly chosen to suit *Geta's* present Temper, who, in the heat of his Rage, thinks
himself irresistibly strong.

23 *Quisquis es, sine me.* Madam *Dacier*
observes upon this Place, that in *Greece*
the People often took a pleasure to stop and
detain Servants in the Streets, that they
might be lash'd when they got home, for
staying out so long.

25 *Quid festinas, mi Geta?* Nothing can
exceed

*Get.* Quite——

*Soſt.* What, quite!

*Get.* Ruin'd! undone!

*Soſt.* Say, for Heaven's ſake, what's the matter?

*Get.* Now!——

*Soſt.* What, now, *Geta?*

*Get.* Æſchinus——

*Soſt.* What of him?

*Get.* Is no more attach'd to our Family.

*Soſt.* Ah! undone! Why ſo?

*Get.* He has got another Miſtreſs.

*Soſt.* Wretch that I am.

*Get.* Nor does he affect to conceal it: He himſelf openly forc'd her from the Bawd.

*Soſt.* Are you perfectly ſure of this?

*Get.* Perfectly ſure! I myſelf was an Eye-witneſs to it, *Soſtrata.*

*Soſt.* Unhappy Wretch that I am! What can one believe now, or whom? What, our *Æſchinus!* the very Life of us all; our only Hope and Support, who ſwore that it would be impoſſible for him ever to live a ſingle Day without her; who ſaid, he would place the Infant on his Father's Knees, and in that manner conjure him to give his Conſent to their Marriage!

*Get.* Miſtreſs, forbear your Tears, and let us rather conſult what is beſt to be done in the preſent Conjuncture; whether we ſhould ſubmit patiently, or diſcover it to ſome Friend.

*Can.* Ah, ah, Man, have you loſt your Seuſes quite? Is this a Buſineſs to make known to any one?

*Get.* I indeed think not. For, firſt, it is evident that he is now wholly alienated from us. If therefore we make the thing public, he'll deny it; I know very well. Your Reputation, and the Honour and Repoſe of your Daughter will ſuffer. Nay, ſhould he even confeſs all, as his Affections are now with another, it were not prudent

dent



exceed the Juſtneſs and Maſterly Strokes of this Deſcription. *Geta,* when he comes to acquaint his Miſtreſs with the Misfortune that had befallen her, as he knew how much pain it muſt give her, finds himſelf almoſt deprived of the Power of Speech. He was too much ſhock'd to be able to expreſs himſelf any otherwiſe than in ſingle Words, or broken and interrupted Sentences. *Hei mihi —— prorſus ——periimus! actum eſt——Jam ——Æſchinus,—— &c.* This, almoſt every one's Experience can inform him to be Nature itſelf. For in ſpeaking with another, eſpecially where awed by Friendſhip and Reſpect; whatever we ſay with Reluctance, or foreſee will be diſagreeable, and give pain, comes out with great difficulty. Our Speech,

in ſpite of ourſelves, will be broken and abrupt, and Breath ſeems to fail us in uttering our Words.

3° *A lenone ipſus eripuit palam.* Donatus's remark upon this Paſſage is well worth the tranſcribing, as it diſcovers a hidden Art in the Poet, that might otherwiſe eſcape our Notice. " Sic renuntiat, ut ultima pejora " ſint. Et his argumentis vult probare, quod " immodice amavit Æſchinus, qui plus quam " virginem, id ipſum quod pudor nec hortatur, nec conſulit, amat. Quis autem magis potuit impudens eſſe, quam qui poſt " honeſtum amorem, ab lenone ſinet? hoc " etenim ſignificat meretricem. Ergo non " honeſtum, ſed ab lenone r non per alium, " ſed ipſus; nec emit, aut abduxit, ſed ob " impatientiam

| | |
|---|---|
| Animam recipe. GE. prorſus. So. quid iſtuc prorſus ergo eſt ? GE. periimus. | *Recipe animam. GE. Prorſus. So. Quid ergo eſt iſtuc prorſus? GE. Periimus. actum eſt.* |
| Actum eſt. So. eloquere ergo, obſecro te, quid ſit. GE. jam. So. quid jam, Geta? | *So. Obſecro te ergo eloquere, quid ſit. GE. Jam. So. Quid jam, Geta?* |
| GE. Æſchinus, So. quid is ergo ? GE. alienus eſt ab noſtrâ familiâ. So. hem, | *GE. Æſchinus, So. Quid is ergo? GE. Eſt alienus ab noſtra familia. So.* |
| Perii, quare? GE. amare occepit aliam. So. væ miſeræ mihi! | *Hem, perii, quare? GE. Occepit amare aliam. So. Væ miſeræ mihi! GE.* |
| GE. Neque id occultè fert. à lenone ipſus eripuit palàm. | *Neque fert id occulte: ipſe palam eripuit puellam à lenone.* |
| So. Satin' hoc certum eſt ? GE. certum. hiſce oculis egomet vidi, Soſtrata. So. ah,    31 | *So. Eſtne hoc ſatis certum? GE. Eſt certum. Egomet vidi biſce oculis, Soſtrata.* |
| Me miſeram ? quid credas jam ? aut cui credas ? noſtrumne Æſchinum,       [omnes ſitæ | *So. Ah, me miſeram! Quid credas jam? Aut cui credas? Noſtrumne Æſchinum facere* |
| Noſtram vitam omnium, in quo noſtræ ſpes opeſque | *ita, noſtram vitam omnium, in quo omnes noſtræ ſpes o-* |
| Erant, qui ſine hac jurabat ſe unum nunquam victurum diem     34 | *peſque erant ſuæ, qui jurabat ſe nun-quam victurum u-num diem ſine hac,* |
| Qui ſe in ſui gremio poſiturum puerum dicebat patris, | *qui dicebat ſe poſi-turum puerum in* |
| Ita obſecraturum, ut liceret hanc ſibi uxorem ducere ! | |
| GE. Hera, lacrumas mitte, ac potiùs, quod ad hanc rem opus eſt, porro proſpice, | *GE. Hera, mitte la-* |
| Patiamurne, an narremùs cuipiam ? CA. au, au, mi homo, ſanuſne es ? an ſquidem non placet, | *an narremus cuiquam? CA. Au, au, mi homo, ſanuſne es? An hoc videtur tibi eſſe uſquam* |
| Hoc proferendum tibi videtur eſſe uſquam ? GE. mihi | *proferendum? GE. Non* |
| Jam primùm, illum alieno animo à nobis eſſe, res ipſa indicat.     40 | *alieno à nobis. Nunc ſi* |
| Nunc ſi hoc palàm proferimus, ille inficias ibit, ſat ſcio ; | |
| Tua fama, & gnatæ vita in dubium veniet. tum ſi maxuimè | |
| Fateatur, cum amet aliam, non eſt utile hanc illi dari. | |

*gremio ſui patris, obſecraturum ita, ut liceret ſibi ducere hanc uxorem! GE. Hera, mitte la-crymas, ac potius porro proſpice quod eſt opus ad hanc rem: patiamurne, an narremus cuiquam? CA. Au, au, mi homo, ſanuſne es? An hoc videtur tibi eſſe uſquam proferendum? GE. Non quidem placet mihi. Jam primum ipſa res indicat illam eſſe animo alieno à nobis. Nunc ſi proferimus hoc palam, ille, ſat ſcio, ibit inficias; tua fama, & vita gnatæ veniet in dubium: tum ſi maxime fateatur, cum amet aliam, non eſt utile hanc dari illi.*

## ANNOTATIONS.

" impatientiam valde amantis *eripuit*. Ne-
" que id *occulte*, ut qui celaret factum, tan-
" quàm ſatisfacturus uxori videretur ; ſed
" *palam*." The Reader, perhaps, will be ſurpriſed to find ſo much Art and Judgment in a Paſſage that appear'd to him quite eaſy and unaffected : nay, and expreſſed in the only manner in which it ſeem'd capable of being expreſs'd. This, indeed, is the Perfection of Art, to employ it with that Prudence and Reſerve, that it appears not to have any hand in the Compoſition ; and it is a ſure ſign the Poet has attain'd this, when things are told in the very Words, which every one thinks he would uſe himſelf in the like Circumſtances.

31 *Noſtrumne Æſchinum.* There is a particular Emphaſis and Beauty in the Addition of *noſtrum* to *Æſchinus*'s Name. This ſingle word aſſembles a Croud of tender Ideas. One is inſenſibly led to reflect upon all the endearing Inſtances of *Æſchinus*'s Love and Generoſity. Hence *Soſtrata*'s Diſtreſs appears in a ſtronger Light, and the Compaſſion of the Spectators begins to be warmly engaged for her.

35 *Qui ſe in ſui gremio poſiturum puerum dicebat patris.* Not to meddle with the Diſputes and Cavils of Commentators, with reſpect either to the Reading or Conſtruction of this Paſſage ; I think it enough to propoſe the following Explanation of it from *Weſterbovius,*

dent to give him your Daughter: For which reason, I think, we ought at any rate to keep all secret.

*Soſt.* Ah, by no means! I'll not do it.

*Get.* What do you resolve upon then?

*Soſt.* I'll make it public.

*Get.* Ha, *Soſtrata!* take care what you do.

*Soſt.* The thing can't be worſe than it is already. For firſt, ſhe has no Fortune: then beſides, ſhe has loſt that which might have ſerved inſtead of a Fortune: ſhe cannot now be made to paſs for a Maid: and ſhould he deny it, I have ſtill this Reſource; the Ring which he loſt in the Struggle will witneſs againſt him. In fine, as I am conſcious to myſelf that there is no Reproach on my ſide, and that neither Avarice, nor any diſhonourable View was the Cauſe of this Misfortune; I'll even venture to make it public, *Geta.*

*Get.* What can one ſay? As you ſeem to ſpeak with more Juſtneſs, I readily yield.

*Soſt.* Run, therefore, immediately to *Hegio,* her Kinſman, and tell him the whole Story exactly as it is: for he was our *Simulus's* beſt Friend, and has always behaved with great regard to us.

*Get.* For, truly, nobody elſe takes any notice of us.

*Soſt.* Do you, *Canthara,* make haſte to bring the Midwife, that ſhe mayn't be wanting when we have occaſion for her.

*A N N O T A T I O N S.*

*Weſterbovius,* as what ſets it in a clear and intelligible Light, " Qui dicebat, ſe " poſiturum puerum recens natum in gre- " mio patris ſui Micionis, atque ita obſecra- " turum, & patris miſericordiam implora- " turum, ut ex qua ſuſcepiſſet hunc pue- " rum, hanc ſibi liceret uxorem ducere."

47 *Quæ ſecunda ei dos erat, periit.* The Ancients ſet a great Value upon Chaſtity; that alone was often a ſufficient Recommen- dation, and made one reſpected where Fortune and the Splendor of a Name were wanting. Thus, in the *Phormio, Antipho* complaining of the continual Anxiety he was under for fear of his Father's Diſpleaſure, becauſe he had married a Girl of no Fortune, is thus anſwer'd by *Phædria,* his Companion and Equal:

*Ut ne addam quod ſine ſumptu, ingeniam,* *liberalem, nactus es:* *Quod habes, ita ut voluiſti, uxorem ſine ma-* *la fama.*

We are not, therefore, to wonder, that in ancient Comedy, we ſo often meet with young Gentlemen of Fortune, in love with Girls of lower Rank, and earneſt to have them in Marriage. The Poets have taken care to paint them with Chaſtity unſtain'd; and this ſingle Circumſtance, they thought, carried in it a ſufficient Vindication. Compare this with the two following Quotations from *Plautus, Amphit.* II. 2. 209. where *Alcmena* ſays:

*Non ego illam mihi dotem eſſe duco, quæ dos* *dicitur:* *Sed pudicitiam, & pudorem, & ſedatam* *cupidinem.*

*Aul.* II. 2. 61.

*En. At nihil eſt dotis, quod dem.* Me. *Ne duas:* *Dummodo morata recte vivat, dotata eſt* *ſatis.*

" En. But I have no Fortune to give with " her. Me. What then? give her none; " provided ſhe is chaſte, and of Morals un- " ſtain'd, that is Fortune ſufficient." *Horace* too, in that famous Ode of his, where he gives ſo fine a Deſcription of the Innocence and virtuous Manners of the *Scythians,* does not forget to mention it to their Honour.

Quapropter quoquo pacto tacito est opus. So. ah, mi-
   nimè gentium :
Non faciam. Ge. quid ages ? So. proferam. Ge. hem,
   mea Sostrata, vide quam rem agas.          45
So. Pejore res loco non potis est esse, quam in hoc,
   quo nunc sita est.                 [dos erat,
Primùm indotata est ! tùm præterea, quæ secunda ei
Periit : pro virgine dari nuptum non potest. hoc relli-
   quom est,                    [serat.
Si inficias ibit, testis mecum est annulus, quem ami-
Prostremò, quando ego conscia mihi sum, à me culpam
   esse hanc procul,                50
Nec precium, neque rem ullam intercessisse illâ aut me
   indignam ; Geta,
Experiar. Ge. quid istic ? accedo, ut melius dicas. So.
   tu, quantum potes,           [nem ordine :
Abi, atque Hegioni cognato hujus rem enarrato om-
Nam is nostro Simulo fuit summus, & nos coluit ma-
   xumè.           [tu, mea Canthara: 55
Ge. Nam hercle alius nemo respicit nos. So. propera
Curre, obstetricem arcesse, ut, cum opus sit, ne in mo-
   rà nobus siet.

Quapropter opus est tacito quoquo pacto. So. Ah, minimè gentium : non faciam. Ge. Quid ages ? So. Proferam. Ge. Hem, mea Sostrata, vide quam rem agas. So. Res non est potis esse in pejore loco, quam in hoc, quo est nunc sita. Primùm est indotata : tum præterea, quæ erat secunda dos ei; periit : non potest dari nuptum pro virgine. Hoc est reliquum, si ibit insidias, annulus, quem amiserat, est testio mecum. Postremo, quando ego sum conscia mihi, hanc culpam esse procul à me, & nec precium, neque ullam rem intercessisse indignam illâ aut

me ; experiar, Geta. Ge. Quid istic ? Accedo tibi, ut qui dicas melius. So. Tu abi, quantum potes, atque enarrato omnem rem ordine Hegioni, cognato hujus : nam is fuit summus amicus nostro Simulo, & coluit nos maxime. Ge. Nam hercle nemo alius respicit nos. So. Propera tu, mea Canthara, curre, arcesse obstetricem, ut ne sit in mora nobis, cum opus sit.

## ANNOTATIONS.

nour, that Virtue and Chastity are what they chiefly regard in the Choice of their Wives. L. 3. Ode 24. 17.

   *Illic matre carentibus*
     *Privignis mulier temperat innocens.*
   *Nec dotata regit virum*
     *Conjux, nec nitido fidit adultero.*
   *Dos est magna, parentium*
     *Virtus, & metuens alterius viri*
   *Certo fœdere castitas ;*
     *Et peccare nefas, aut pretium est mori.*

I have been the more large upon this, to shew that the ancient Comic Poets are liable to no Censure or Ridicule, for painting Manners so greatly different from ours.

52 *Quid istic ? accedo ut melius dicas.* These Words have greatly perplexed Commentators, chiefly because of the Difficulty of reconciling them with what follows. The Sense generally received, and which, indeed, seems most naturally to offer itself, is this ; *What are you about ? I beg you will resolve* on something better. But this would have undoubtedly drawn from *Sostrata*, if not a further Defence of her Design, at least an express Declaration that she would not change it : whereas she speaks to *Geta*, as one who was come into her Opinion ; and desires him to run and acquaint *Hegio* with the whole Affair. We are, therefore, under a Necessity of explaining *Geta*'s Answer, so as to make it imply an Assent ; and this is what I have endeavoured to do. *Quid istic ! accedo tbi, ut qui dicas melius.* " Say no more : " I submit to you, as one that seems to have " a juster Notion of what is best in the pre- " sent Exigence." *Westerbovius* supposes that *Sostrata* had shewn some Symptoms of Anger, and on that account explains, *Ut melius dicas ; ut bona verba loquaris : Rather than offend you, or incur your displeasure.* But this, besides that it is too strain'd, would be no satisfying Answer to *Sostrata*.

## ACT III. SCENE III.

### ARGUMENT.

Demea *is in great Distress, having heard that his Son* Ctesipho *was present, when* Æschinus *carried off the Music-girl.*

### DEMEA.

I'M perfectly distracted : I have heard that my Son *Ctesipho* was with *Æschinus*, at the carrying off of this Girl. It completes my Misfortune, if he should draw him too into Debauchery, who otherwise promises so fair. Where shall I inquire for him ? I doubt they have carried him into some bad House : that profligate Brother of his has persuaded him, I do believe. But I see *Syrus* coming this way ; he, probably, can inform me. But now I think on't, he's one of the Gang ; if he perceives that I want him, the Rogue will never tell. I'll not let him see my Design.

### ANNOTATIONS.

*Demea* is introduced here in great Concern, because he had been told that his other Son, *Ctesipho*, had also been present when *Æschinus* broke into the Cock-Bawd's House. He is afraid that this Youth, of whom he had conceived great Hopes, might be seduced by his Brother, and give into the same Debaucheries. He therefore appears here considering with himself where to seek for him, that he may carry him home, and remove him from so dangerous a Companion. Mean-time he spies *Syrus*, and as he can't guess where to meet with his Son, resolves artfully to draw the Secret from him.

4 *Qui alicuri rei est. Sub.* natus, aptus, idoneus. *Eugraphius* seems to have read *alicujus spei :* but the Alteration is unnecessary, as the other reading is agreeable enough to the common Forms of Speech ; for so *Plautus, Stich.* 5. 4. 38.

*Nolo*

## ACT III. SCENE IV.

### ARGUMENT.

Ctesipho *is praised*, Micio *and* Æschinus *are blamed ; both by* Syrus, *who here exerts all his Cunning.* Demea, *again, is highly delighted, with hearing a recital of* Ctesipho's *Virtues.*

### SYRUS, DEMEA.

*Syrus.* WE just now told the Old Gentleman the whole Exploit, as it had been conducted. I never saw any thing better pleased in my Life.

*Dem.* My God ! The Folly of the Man !

*Syr.* He commended his Son, and thank'd me, who put him upon the Project.

*Dem.*

### ANNOTATIONS.

This Scene is one of the most diverting in the whole Play, and represents how Men of a severe rigid Character, tenacious of Virtue and Honesty, are generally ridicul'd or hated, wherever they come. In the second Act *Æschinus* and *Syrus*, followed by *Sannio*, went to the Forum to look for *Micio*. They had told him by this time the whole Affair as it happened ; and the old Man, far from being angry, was rather delighted with the Humour of the Thing, and told down the Money immediately, to discharge *Sannio*. As he imagined the young Sparks, pleased that their Project had succeeded, would like to spend the Day in Mirth and Jollity ; he moreover gives *Syrus* half a *Mina* to lay out on Provisions, &c. These he had brought home, and is preparing to have them dressed, when he is accosted by *Demea*. The Conversation is full of Humour and Variety, and perhaps

# ACTUS III. SCENA III.

## ARGUMENTUM.

*Male est Demeæ, quod filium Ctesiphonem audiverit una adfuisse cum eriperet mulierem Æschinus.*

DEMEA

DIsperii. Ctesiphonem audivi filium
Unà fuisse in raptione cùm Æschino.
Id misero restat mihi mali, si illum potest,
Qui alicui rei est, etiam ad nequitiem eum abducere.
Ubi ego illum quæram? credo abductum in ganeum
Aliquo. persuasit ille impurus, sat scio.                6
Sed eccum Syrum ire video. hinc scibo jam, ubi siet.
Atque hercle hic de grege illo est: si me senserit
Eum quæritare, nunquam dicet carnufex.
Non ostendam id me velle.                               10

ORDO.

DIsperii. Audivi filium Ctesiphonem una fuisse cum Æschino in raptione. Id mali restat mihi misero, si potest abducere illum, qui est aptus alicui rei, abducere inquam etiam cum ad nequitiam. Ubi ego quæram illum? Credo eum esse abductum aliquo in ganeum.

*Ille impurus persuasit ei, sat scio. Sed eccum video Syrum ire. Jam scibo hinc, ubi sit: at hercle hic est de illo grege. Si carnifex senserit me quæritare eum, nunquam dicet. Non ostendam me velle id.*

## ANNOTATIONS.

*Nolo ego nos pro summo bibere: nulli rei crimus postea.*

Demea himself too, says above, in his first Conversation with *Micio: Non fratrem rei dare operam videt, ruri esse parcum ac sobrium?*

6 *Persuasit ille impurus.* Suademus faci-

lia persuademus *difficilia. Et suadere facientis est, persuadere perficientis.* Impurus *autem pro improbo ponitur apud Terentium. Et hic quoque excusata voluntas est Ctesiphonis, cui a majore fratre et improbi ingesta sit persuasione nequitia.* Donat.

---

# ACTUS III. SCENA IV.

## ARGUMENTUM.

*Commendatur Ctesipho, vituperanter Micio Æschinus: callide utrumque Syrus facit. Demea autem narratione virtutum Ctesiphonis plurimum gaudet.*

SYRUS, DEMEA.

OMnem rem modò seni,
Quo pacto haberet, enarramus ordine.
Nil quidquam vidi lætius. DE. proh Jupiter,
Hóminis stultitiam! SY. collaudavit filium:
Mihi, qui id dedissem consilium, egit gratias.            5

ORDO.

SY. ENarramus modò omnem rem ordine seni, quo pacto haberet se: vidi nil quidquam lætius. DE. Proh Jupiter, stultiam hominis! SY. Collaudavit filium: egit gratias mihi, qui dedissem id consilium.

## ANNOTATIONS.

perhaps one of the best conducted in all *Terence.* Here we see the Fondness of a Father towards his favourite Son; the Pleasure he takes to encourage a Discourse that flatters his Partiality; and the artful Management of a cunning Slave, who, taking advantage of the old Gentleman's Bias, exposes him all the while to the Ridicule of the Spectators.

2 *Enarramus.* By an Enallage of the Tense for *enarravimus.* This Figure, in its



original

*Dem.* I shall burst.

*Syr.* He told down the Money directly, and gave me, moreover, a Piece and Half to spend; that's laid out as I could wish.

*Dem.* So! if you would have any thing done to purpose, leave it to this Gentleman.

*Syr.* Ha, *Demea!* I did not see you: how goes it?

*Dem.* How should it go? I can't enough wonder at your manner of living.

*Syr.* Silly enough, truly, not to diffemble, and abfurd. *(To Dromo within.)* *Dromo*, gut and fcale the reft of the Fish: let the great Conger-Eel play a little in the Water; when I come back, he shall be honed; not before.

*Dem.* Are Enormities like thefe to be endur'd?

*Syr.* Indeed, I don't half like them; nay, I often exclaim against them. *Stephanio*, fee that the falt Fish are well foak'd.

*Dem.* Good God! Is this done on purpofe, or does he imagine it will be to his Credit to ruin his Son? Wretch that I am! methinks I fee the Day when this young Spark will be obliged to run away for want, and lift himfelf for a Soldier.

*Syr.* O *Demea!* that, indeed, is being wife, not only to take care of the prefent; but look forward, alfo, into what's to come.

*Dem.* What! Is this Mufick-girl now with you?

*Syr.* For certain: fhe's within.

*Dem.* Why, fure, he don't defign to keep her at home?

*Syr.* Nay, I believe he's mad enough.

*Dem.* Is is poffible?

*Syr.* The foolifh Lenity of his Father, and an Eafinefs greatly to be blamed.

*Dem.* Why, truly, I'm quite afhamed and forry for my Brother.

*Syr.* There's too great Difference; nor do I fay it, *Demea*, becaufe you are here prefent; there is by far too great a Difference between you. You, in every thing, are Wifdom itfelf: he's a mere Dreamer. Would you fuffer your Son to go on in this way?

*Dem.* I fuffer him? Or would I not have fmelt him out, think ye fix whole Months, before he attempted any fuch Project?

*Syr.*

DE. Disrumpor. SY. argentum adnumeravit illico:
Dedit praeterea in sumtum dimidium minae:
Id distributum, sanè est ex sententiâ. DE. hem,
Huic mandes, si quid rectè curatum velis.
SY. Ehem Demea, haud aspexeram te: quid agitur? 10
DE. Quid agatur? vostram nequeo mirari satis
Rationem, SY. est hercle inepta, ne dicam dolo,
Atque absurda. Pisces caeteros purga, Dromo:
Congrum istum maxumum in aquâ sinito ludere
Tantisper: ubi ego rediero, exossabitur; 15
Priùs nolo. DE. haeccine flagitia? SY. mihi quidem
    non placent:
Et clamo saepe. Salsamenta haec, Stephanio,
Fac macerentur pulchrè. DE. Di vostram fidem;
Utrum studione id sibi habet, an laudi putat
Fore, si perdiderit gnatum? vae misero mihi! 20
Videre videor jam diem illum, cùm hinc egens
Profugiet aliquò militatum. SY. ô Demea,
Istuc est sapere, non quod ante pedes modò est,
Videre, sed etiam illa, quae futura sunt,
Prospicere. DE. quid? istaec jam penes vos saltria est?
SY. Ellam intus. DE. eho, an domi est habiturus?
    SY. credo, ut est 26
Dementia. DE. haeccine? fieri? SY. inepta lenitas
Patris, & facilitas prava. DE. fratris me quidem
Pudet, pigetque. SY. nimium inter vos, Demea; ac
Non quia ades praesens, dico hoc, pernimium interest.
Tu, quantus quantus, nihil nisi sapientia es: 31
Ille somnium, sineres verò illum tu tuum
Facere haec? DE. sinerem illum? aut non sex totis
    mensibus
Priùs olfecissem, quàm ille quidquam coeperit?

*DE. Disrumpor. SY. Adnumeravit argentum illico? dedit praeterea dimidiam minae in sumptum: sanè id est distributum ex sententiâ. DE. Hem, si velis quid curatum rectè, mandes huic. SY. Ehem Demea, haud aspexeram te? quid agitur? DE. Quid agatur? Nequeo satis mirari vostram rationem. SY. Hercle est inepta, ne dicam dolo, atque absurda. Dromo, purga caeteros pisces: sinito istum maximum congrum ludere tantisper in aqua: ubi ego rediero, exossabitur; nolo prius. DE. Haeccine flagitia? SY. Quidem non placent mihi: & clamo saepe; Stephano, fac ut haec salsamenta macerentur pulchre. DE. Dii vestram fidem; utrumne habet id studio sibi? an putat fore laudi, si perdiderit gnatum? Vae misero mihi! videor jam videre illum diem, cum egens profugiet hinc aliquo militatum. SY. O Demea, istuc est sapere, non modo videre quod est ante pedes, sed etiam*

*prospicere illa, quae sunt futura. DE. Quid? An istaec psaltria est jam penes vos? SY. Ellam intus. DE. Eho, an est habiturus eam domi? SY. Credo, ut dementia est. DE. Haeccine fieri? SY. Inepta linitas patris & facilitas prava facit. DE. Quidem pudet pigetque me, fratris. SY. Nimium, Demea, inter vos, ac non dico hoc, quia ades praesens, pernimium interest. Tu quantus quantus, es nihil nisi sapientia: ille somnium: an vero tu sineres illum tuum facere haec? DE. Sinerem illum? Aut non olfecissem sex totis mensibus, priusquam ille coeperit quidquam?*

## ANNOTATIONS.

large over-grown Eel. It was in great esteem among Men of a delicate Taste. They came mostly from *Sicyon*, and were generally brought over alive.

21 *Videre videor, &c.* A Way of speaking somewhat singular, yet not without Example. *Cicero Fam.* 16. 21. *Quomodo ego mihi nunc ante oculos tuum jucundissimum conspectum propono? videor enim videre ementem te rusticatis res, cum villico loquentem, in lacinia servantem ex mela secunda semina.*

33 *An non sex totis mensibus, prius olfecissem?* The Poet has purposely contrived in this Scene to make *Demea* appear in the most ridiculous Light possible. *Syrus* extols his Wisdom, and pretends to admire him greatly, but manifestly sneers all the while. *Demea* seems to have no Suspicion, but that he is serious: for Men of his Character are apt to put a great Value upon themselves, and implicitly swallow every kind of Praise, because they think they deserve it. The Poet



gives

*Sy.* Need I to be told of your Foresight?

*Dem.* Pray Heaven he may be always such as he is at present.

*Syr.* As Fathers breed up their Sons, so they generally prove.

*Dem.* But about this Son of mine : Have you seen him to-day?

*Syr.* Who, your Son?—I'll dispatch him into the Country.—I fancy he's hard at work in the Fields, by this time.

*Dem.* Are you sure he's there?

*Syr.* Sure? when I went so far with him myself.

*Dem.* That's well : I was afraid he might be loitering here somewhere.

*Syr.* And in a mighty Paffion too.

*Dem.* For what?

*Syr.* He fell a scolding at his Brother in the Forum, about this Musick-girl.

*Dem.* Say you so, indeed?

*Syr.* He did; and in very free Language too. For as by chance we were telling down the Money, the Gentleman came unexpectedly upon us : So, Æschinus, cry'd he, *Are these your ways? Are you not ashamed to dishonour our Family by such Courses?*

*Dem.* Oh, I weep for Joy.

*Syr.* 'Tis not the Money only that you destroy, but your very Life, *your good Name.*

*Dem.* Heaven preserve him ; I hope he'll be like his Forefathers.

*Syr.* No doubt of it.

*Dem.* Syrus, he's full of these Maxims.

*Syr.* Well he may ; he had one at home to teach him.

*Dem.* I do it with all the Care I am able; I overlook nothing, but endeavour to make Virtue habitual. In a Word, I tell him to look into the Lives of Men, as into a Glass, and thence to take Example. Do this———

*Syr.* Perfectly well!

*Dem.* Shun that———

*Sy.* Excellent!

*Dem.* This is praise-worthy———

*Syr.* There you have it again.

*Dem.* That were blameable———

*Syr.*

## ANNOTATIONS.

gives an Inftance of this Weaknefs in the Paffage now referred to. *Demea* imagines himfelf a Man of too great Quicknefs and Penetration to be deceived. It were impoffible for his Son to make a falfe Step, but he would difcover it immediately; nay, could difcern the very firft Inclinations and Propenfities to go aftray. This muft be highly entertaining to the Reader, who knows the while that *Ctefipho* is chiefly in fault, and that this fo very wife Father is the Dupe of the whole Family.

44 *Abigam hunc rus.* This *Syrus* fays in a kind of Whifper, turning to the Spectators.

44 *Vah, nibil reticuit. Syrus,* as he knew it would give *Demea* Joy to find that his Son *Ctefipho* refembled him, takes care to omit no Circumftance that he thought would take with the old Man, *Ctefipho,* though the younger Brother, attacks *Æfchinus,* nor does the Difparity of Age keep him in awe, he makes no fcruple to fpeak his Mind freely : *nibil reticuit.* This was the more agreeable to *Demea,* as it refembled perfectly his own Carriage towards his Brother *Micio.*

43 *Intervenit homo de improvifo. Interrogire,*

SY. Vigilantiam tuam tu mihi narras? DE. fic fiet 35
Modo, ut nunc, eft, quæfo. SY. ut quifque fuum volt
esse, ita eft.
DE. Quid eum? vidiftin' hodie? SY. tuumne filium?
(Abigam hunc rus) jamdudum aliquid ruri agere ar-
bitror. [optumè eft.
DE. Satin' fcis ibi effe? SY. oh, quiegomet produxi. DE.
Metui, ne hæreret hic. SY. atque iratum admodum. 40
DE. Quid autem? SY. adortus jurgio fratrem apud forum
De pfaltriâ iftac. DE. ain' verò? SY. vâh, nil reticuit:
Nam, ut numerabatur forte argentum, intervenit
Homo de improvifo: cœpit clamare; Æfchîne,
Hæccine flagitia facere te? hæc te admittere 45
Indigna genere noftro? DE. oh, oh, lacrumo gaudio.
SY. Non tu hoc argentum perdis, fed vitam tuam.
DE. Salvus fit: fpero, eft fimilis majorum fuûm. SY. hui.
DE. Syre præceptorum plenus iftorum ille. SY. phy;
Domi habuit, unde difceret. DE. fit fedulo: 50
Nil prætermitto: consuefacio: denique
Infpicere, tanquam in fpeculum, in vitas omnium
Jubeo, atque ex aliis fumere exemplum fibi.
Hoc facito. SY. rectè fanè. DE. hoc fugito. SY. callide.
DE. Hoc laudi eft. SY. iftæc res eft. DE. hoc vitio datur.

*SY. An tu narrae mihi tuam vigilantiam? DE. Quæfo fic fit, ut eft nunc modo. SY. Ut quifque vult fuum effe, ita eft. DE. Quid eum? Vidifine hodie? SY. Tuumne filium? (abigam hunc rus) arbitror eum jamdudum agere aliquid ruri, DE. Satifne fcit eum effe ibi? SY. Ob, qui egomet produxi. DE. Eft extime? metui ne hæreret hic. SY. Atque produxi admodum iratum. DE. Ob quid autem? SY. Adortus, eft fratrem jurgio apud forum de iftac pfaltriâ. DE. Aifne verò? SY. Vah, reticuit nil: nam forte ut argentum numerabatur, homo intervenit de improvifo, cæpit clamare: Æfchine, oportuitne te facere hæc flagitia? Te admittere hæc indigna noftro genere? DE. Ob, ob, lacrumo gaudio. SY. Tu non modo perdis hoc argentum, fed perdis tuam vitam. DE. Sit falvus: fpero, eft fimilis majorum fuorum. SY. Hui. DE. Syre, ille eft plenus iftorum præceptorum. SY. Phy, habuit domi unde difceret. DE. Fit fedulo: prætermitto nibil: confuefacio: denique jubeo illum infpicere in vitas omnium tanquam in fpeculum, atque fumere exemplum fibi ex aliis. Facito hoc. SY. Rectè funè. DE. Fugito hoc. SY. Callide. DE. Hoc eft laudi. SY. Iftæc eft res. DE. Hoc datur vitio.*

## ANNOTATIONS.

aire, eft in medio negotio, quafi ex infidiis fupervenire, & opprimere in ipfo actu eos, qui rem celatam vellent. Et vide quam oratorie narret geftionem rei, quæ nunquam facta fit: his enim fides fit. *Donatus.*

46 *Lacrumo gaudio.* We fee that *Demea* is here prone to believe every thing to the advantage of his favourite Son, of whom he had before boafted fo highly.

*Non fratrem videt.*
*Rei dare operam, ruri effe parcum, ac fobrium?*

Unde (fays *Donatus*) mirâ poetæ arte, & initia, & media, & poftrema fibi congruunt atque refpondent.

52 *Infpicere, tanquam in fpeculum.* Dona-tus feems to doubt, whether *fpeculum* comes in properly here, where the Poet fpeaks of examining into the Lives of other Men, to af-certain the proper Standard for our own Con-duct. I think it enough to obferve, that as we make ufe of a Glafs to correct thofe Faults and Blemifhes, which Cuftom or Negligence may have given us, and to find out the Air, Drefs and Manner that beft becomes us: in like manner, we ought to look into the Lives of others, to learn what is infamous and re-proachful, and what on the contrary is laud-able and praife-worthy; for we are fooner apt to fee what is faulty in others, than in ourfelves; becaufe, in the one Cafe, we judge without Partiality, in the other, Self-love mifleads us. *Cicero, Off.* I. 41. *Non eft in-commodum, quale quodqoe eorum fit, ex aliis judicare: ut, fi quid dedecat alter, vitemus & ipfi. Fit enim refcio quomodo, ut magis in aliis cernamus, quam in nobifmet ipfis, fi quid delinquitur.* This, I fay, is what the Poet means by looking into the Lives of others, as into a Glafs, not that they reprefent our Lives to us, as a Mirrour reflects the Objects placed before it.

54 *Hoc facito, hoc fugito, hoc laudi eft, hoc vitio datur.* The Character of *Demea* is very natural, and very happily conducted. A Man of his Turn and Way of Life cannot be

*Syr.* Admirable!

*Dem.* Besides——

*Syr.* Why, truly, Sir, I am not at leisure to hear you out now; I have got some excellent Fish to dress, and must take care they ben't spoiled; for that were as great a Crime among us, *Demea*, as for you to neglect those Precepts you have been just inculcating. And, as far as I am able, I instruct my Fellow-Servants in the same Strain. This is too salt: that's quite burnt: this isn't wash'd enough: that's perfectly well: pray remember to do so another time. I am ever giving them the best Advice I can, according to my Capacity. In fine, *Demea*, I bid them look into their Dishes, as into a Glass, and tell them what they are to do. I confess that these, our Matters, are trifling enough; but what can one do? As the Man is, so we must study to humour him. Have you any thing else?

*Dem.* That you may learn more Wisdom.

*Syr.* You are going into the Country, I suppose?

*Dem.* Directly.

*Syr.* For what should you do here? where, give you ever such good Advice, nobody regards it. [*Exit.*

*Dem.* I, indeed, go hence, since he, for whose sake I came, is gone into

## ANNOTATIONS.

be supposed capable of instructing his Son in that part of Philosophy, which explain'd the Reasons of things; why some Actions were good, and some bad. His Lessons must be suited to his Figure in Life; that of a plain Country Gentleman, who advises his Son to make Example from others, and points out what is praise-worthy or blameable in the several Characters within his Observation. To enter into all the Elegance and Beauty of this Passage, the Reader may compare it with what *Horace* says upon the same Subject. Sat. 4. Lib. I. where he evidently copies what our Poet says here; for he makes his Father give him the very same Instructions, as those of *Demea* to *Ctesipho*. I shall transcribe the Passage at length. Verse 105.

*Insuevit pater optimus hoc me,*
*Ut fugerem exemplis vitiorum quæque notando.*
*Cum me hortaretur, parce, frugaliter, atque*
*Viverem uti contentus eo, quod mi ipse parasset:*
*Nonne vides, Albi ut male vivat filius? Utque*
*Barus inops? Magnum documentum, ne patriam rem*
*Perdere quis velit. A turpi meretricis amore*
*Cum deterreret: Sectani dissimilis sis.*
*Ne sequerer mæchas, concessa cum Venere uti*

*Possem: deprensi non bella est fama Treboni,*
*Aiebat. Sapiens vitatu quidque petitu*
*Sit melius, causas reddet tibi: mi satis*
*est, si*
*Traditum ab antiquis morem servare, tuamque*
*Dum custodis eges, vitam famamque tueri.*
*Incolumem possim; simul ac duraverit ætas*
*Membra, animumque tuum, nabis sine cortice. Sic me*
*Formabat puerum dictis:*

" 'Twas after this manner, that the best of
" Fathers taught me to shun Vice, pointing
" out its Enormity by living Examples.
" When he recommended Frugality, and
" good Oeconomy, and advised me to live
" contented with what he had provided for
" me: Don't you see, said he, the Misery
" to which the Son of *Albius*, and indigent
" *Barus* have reduced themselves? A re-
" markable Lesson to deter young Men from
" wasting their paternal Estates. When
" he counselled me against the Love of pro-
" fligate Women; Beware, said he, of the
" Example of *Sectanus*. When he would
" dissuade me from Gallantry with married
" Women, and press me to seek only after
" lawful Pleasures; You see how *Trebonius*
" has lost his Reputation, ever since his cri-
" minal Intrigues were discovered. The
" Philosophers, added the good Man, will
" explain the Reasons why some things are
" to be sought after, and others to be avoid-
" ed.

Sy. Probissumè. De. porro autem. Sy. non hercle
   otium est                                                56
Nunc mihi auscultandi. pisces ex sententiâ
Nactus sum: hi mihi ne corrumpantur, cautio est.
Nam id nobis tam flagitium est, quàm illa, Demea,
Non facere vobis, quæ modò dixti: &, quod queo, 60
Conservis ad eundem istunc præcipio modum.
Hoc salsum est, hoc adustum est, hoc lautum est parum;
Illud rectè, iterum sic memento: sedulo
Moneo, quæ possum pro meâ sapientiâ.                      64
Postremò, tanquam in speculum, in patinas, Demea,
Inspicere jubeo, & moneo quid facto usu' sit.
Inepta hæc esse, nos quæ facimus, sentio.
Verùm quid facias? ut homo est, ita morem geras.
Numquid vis? De. mentem vobis meliorem dari. 69
Sy. Tu rus hinc ibis? De. rectâ. Sy. nam quid tu hîc
Ubi, si quid bene præcipias, nemo obtemperet? [agas,
De. Ego verò hinc abeo, quando is, quamobrem huc
    veneram,

*Sy. Probissimè. De. Porro autem. Sy. Hercle non ... mihi nunc etiam auscultandi. Nactus sum pisces ex sententia: cautio est mihi, ne ti corrumpantur. Nam id, Demea, est tam flagitium nobis, quam est vobis non facere illa, quæ modò dixisti: &, quod queo, præcipio conservis ad istunc eundem modum. Hoc est salsum, hoc est adustum, hoc est parum lautum: illud rectè; memento sic facere iterum. ... moneo sedulo quæ ... possum pro mea sapientia. Postremo, Demea, jubeo inspicere in patinas tanquam in spe-*

*-culum, & moneo quid usus sit facto. Sentio hæc, quæ nos facimus, esse inepta. Verum quid facias? Ut homo est, ita geras morem. Numquid vis? De. Mentem meliorem dari vobis. Sy. An tu ibis hinc rus? De. Rectà. Sy. Nam quid tu agas hic, ubi, si præcipias quid boni, nemo obtemperet? De. Ego vero abeo hinc, quando is, quamobrem veneram huc.*

## ANNOTATIONS.

" ed. 'Tis enough, for a Man of my Con-
" dition, to observe the Train of *Culture*
" used by our Ancestors, and keep your Life
" and Character clear from Reproach, while
" you stand in need of a Director. When
" Age shall have ripened your Judgment, as
" well as bodily Strength, you will then be
" your own Master, and be able to walk
" without a Guide. 'Twas thus that, when
" a Child, he formed me to Virtue by his
" Precepts." The Remark which *Donatus*
makes here, is somewhat akin to that above:
" Non philosophicè, sed civiliter monet.
" Non enim dixit, hoc bonum; sed, hoc laudi
" est. Nec hoc malum; sed, vitio datur.
" Ergo ut idiota & comicus pater, non ut
" sapiens & præceptor."

56 *Non hercle etiam est.* *Syrus* now begins to lose Patience; especially when *Demea*, after so long and particular a Detail, comes out with *porro autem;* two Words that seem'd to threaten a long Discourse. He therefore interrupts him; and, to prevent his being any more teazed with these sage Lessons, turns all he had said into Ridicule, by gravely applying the very Expressions *Demea* had used, to the Directions, he, in quality of Head-cook, gave the Servants under him.

64 *Pro meâ sapientiâ.* *Syrus* had said before to *Demea*, *Tu quantus quantus nihil nisi sapi-*entia es; but here speaking of himself, he affects to talk diminutively. As if he had said, " Your Lessons are the Dictates of Wisdom " itself." I too, according to my small Capacity, observe the same Method, in instructing my Fellow-Servants. *Donatus* observes, that *sapientia* is to be understood here equivocally, not only in its common Acceptation, but as a Term of Cookery; for Cooks, in seasoning, are directed by Taste and Relish; *gustu, & sapore.* But this, perhaps, may be refining too much.

69 *Mentem vobis meliorem dari.* *Demea* maintains to the last, his Character of Surliness and Rusticity. He will not answer in the common Way, *rectè* or *valeas.* " Sed " hic (says *Donatus*) ne vel abiens blandus " esset, pro salutationibus ipsis amara sup-" ponit. Et memento etiam hunc eundem " insalutatum relinquere, qui adveniens nec " salutaverat, nec resalutaverat fratrem. " *Meliorem* autem pro bona ac tolerabili po-" suit. Non enim bonam credit, ut melio-" rem optet." Sic *Virgilius* Georg. 3. 513. *Dii meliora piis, erroremque hostibus illum.*

70 *Tu rus hinc ibis?* This ought to have after it a Mark of Interrogation; and it is further to be observed, that these Interrogations are not so much from a view of Information, as Admonition, when we want to
insinuate

into the Country. He is my whole Care; he belongs to me. Since my Brother will have it so, let him look after that other Spark himself. But who's that I see at some distance there? Isn't it *Hegio* of our Ward? If I see right, it is the very same. Ah, a Man I have lived in Friendship with from a Child. Good Gods! How few have we, now-a-days, such Citizens as he? A Man of ancient Probity and Strictness; one, that would not for the World be guilty of any thing to give Offence. How I rejoice to find that there are still some Remains of this Race! Ah, now I think there's some Pleasure in Life. I'll wait for him here, to salute and have some Discourse with him.

### ANNOTATIONS.

insinuate to any one, whose Absence we desire, what they ought to do. His Question, therefore, implies an Advice: and he pronounces it with such an Air, as shews that he made no doubt, what he hinted at, would be done; and approves of it too. For when *Demea* says, *recta*; he has his Answer immediately ready, *Nam quid tu hic agas?* which is inforcing his Advice, and insinuating-Dispatch.

73 *Illum curo unum.* The Poet conducts here with great Judgment: *Demea* means his favourite Son, whom he was more inclined to look after, and where there was nobody to controul him. But it was no easy matter for him to forget *Æschinus*: it would not have looked like a Father, much less such a Father as *Demea* is represented to be. He therefore still shews how anxious he was for him, and that if he did not any more concern himself about him, it was not so much owing to any Indifference in his Temper, as because his Brother would have it so. *Quando ita volt frater, de istoc ipse viderit.*

76 *Tribulis noster.* We are told that the ancient *Athenians* were divided into Tribes; but Writers are not agreed as to their Number. Some tell us they were twelve, in imitation of the *Jewish* tribes; a far-fetch'd Conjecture, for what Connexion was there between the *Athenians* and *Jews?* It is more probable that this Number was derived from the twelve Months, into which the Year was divided; for we also find that there were in every Tribe thirty Sub-divisions, in allusion to the Number of Days in a Month.

81 *Quam gaudeo, ubi etiam hujus generis reliquias restare video!* We have here another Instance, with what a masterly Judgment the Poet handles his Subject. *Hegio* is
to

---

## ACT III. SCENE V.

### ARGUMENT.

*Hegio* here acquaints Demea, *that Æschinus had debauch'd Sostrata's Daughter, and now added to his other ill Usage, that of abandoning her.*

HEGIO, GETA, DEMEA, PAMPHILA.

*Hegio.* IMmortal Gods, a base Action, *Geta!* Is it, indeed, as you tell me?

*Get.* It is indeed.

*Heg.* That any thing so dishonourable should come from so worthy

### ANNOTATIONS.

We have seen before, that *Geta* was dispatched by *Sostrata*, to acquaint *Hegio*, their Kinsman, of the Misfortune that had befallen her Daughter. This he had accordingly done. We see them here coming along together, and *Hegio* appears perfectly astonished at a Behaviour so base and dishonourable. *Demea*, who, in the former Scene, had spied him, and was resolved to wait his coming up, overhears part of their Conversation; and, as it regarded *Æschinus*, applies it to the Story of the Musick-girl, which he thought
*Hegio*

Rus abiit: illum curo unum: ille ad me attinet.
Quando ita volt frater, de istoc ipse viderit.
Sed quis illic est, quem video procul? estne Hegio   75
Tribulis noster? si satis cerno, is hercle est. vah,
Homo amicus nobis jam inde à puero. Di boni!
Næ illusmodi jam magna nobis civium
Penuria est. homo antiquâ virtute ac fide:
Haud citò mali quid ortum ex hoc sit publicè.   80
Quàm gaudeo, ubi etiam hujus generis reliquias
Restare video! vah, vivere etiam nunc lubet.
Opperiar hominem hîc, ut salutem & conloquar.

*abiit rus: curo illum unum; illud attinet ad me. Quando frater vult ita, ipse viderit de istoc. Sed quis est illic, quem video procul? Estn? Hegio noster tribulis? Si satis cerno, hercle est is. Vah, homo amicus nobis jam inde à puero. Dii boni! næ magna penuria est jam nobis civium illiusmodi. Homo antiqua virtute ac fide. Haud cito quid mali ortum sit publice ex hoc. Quàm gaudeo, ubi video reliquias etiam hujus generis restare! Vah, etiam nunc libet vivere. Opperiar hominem hîc, ut salutem & colloquar.*

## ANNOTATIONS.

to act a very important Part, he must deal with two Old-Men upon an Affair of the greatest Nicety; their Interest too is so very opposite to his Demands, that no other than a Character of the highest Moment, would have stood the least Chance to meet with any Regard or Notice from them. *Terence* has, therefore, taken care to represent him in such a Light, as gives the greatest Weight to every thing he says. He is a Man of the ancient rigid Virtue, and strictest Probity, consequently must be dear to *Demea*; nor would he be less rever'd by *Micio*, who was naturally inclined to Justness, and of invincible Good-nature. He was, besides, their Relation, and had lived in intimate Friendship with them, which gave him still more Authority. No wonder, therefore, if the Remonstrances of such a Man have great Weight: nor would they chuse much to be engaged in a suit, where, besides the Iniquity of the Cause itself, the very Character of the Man who managed it against them, must heighten the Odium. By all these Circumstances, has the Poet provided against our thinking the easy Consent of the Old Men improbable, or too hasty. *Demea* himself, when he sees him at a Distance, speaks of him with the utmost Respect, as a Man whom he, in a manner, rever'd. How could he therefore, deny a just Petition, represented so forcibly, and from such a Mouth?

# ACTUS III. SCENA V.

## ARGUMENTUM.

*Hegio docet Sostratæ filiam inique ab Æschino tractatam, tandem vitiatam esse: id factum nunc Demeæ narrat.*

### HEGIO, GETA, DEMEA, PAMPHILA.

PRoh Di immortales, facinus indignum, Geta! Quid narras? GE. sic est factum. HE ex illan' familia
GE. *Sic est factum.* HE. *Tamne illiberale facinus esse ortum ex illa familia?*

**ORDO.**

HE. PRoh Dii immortales, indignum facinus, Geta! Quid narras?

## ANNOTATIONS.

*Hegio* was much shock'd at, out of his Concern for their Family. But upon entering into Discourse with him, he is soon undeceived. Hence different Passions and Emotions on both sides. On *Demea*'s, Astonishment, Anger and Hesitation. He could not easily consent to his Son's marrying a Woman of no Fortune, and he was loth absolutely to reject a Demand that had so much Justice on its side, was urged with such force, and by a Person of so grave and weighty a Character. In *Hegio*, we see the manly Indignation of a free Spirit, that warmly resents every thing dishonourable; and tho' he addresses a Man considerably his Superior, yet he speaks with that Boldness and Confidence, which a
Consciousness

a Family? O *Æfchinus*, fure you never learnt this of your Father!

*Dem.* See now! he too has heard of this Mufick-wench, and, tho' a Stranger, is concern'd at it; yet this worthy Father of his thinks it nothing. Alas! were he but fomething nigh here, to overhear all this

*Heg.* If they refufe to do as they ought, they fhan't come off fo eafily.

*Get.* All our Hope, *Hegio*, is in you: you are our only Friend, our Patron, our Father. The Old Man on his Death-bed recommended us to you; if you abandon us, we are undone.

*Heg.* Take care what you fay: I'll never do it, nor, indeed, can I do it in honour.

*Dem.* I'll go up to him. *Hegio*, I falute you with the greateft Refpect and Friendfhip.

*Heg.* O *Demea*, your Servant: I wanted greatly to fee you.

*Dem.* For what, pray?

*Heg.* Your eldeft Son, *Æfchinus*, whom you gave to be adopted by your Brother, has acted neither like a Man of Worth, nor a Gentleman.

*Dem.* What has he done?

*Heg.* Did you know *Simulus*, a Friend and Companion of mine?

*Dem.* Perfectly well.

*Heg.* He has debauch'd his Daughter, a Virgin.

*Dem.* How!

*Heg.* Hold! you have not heard the worft yet, *Demea*.

*Dem.* What! Is there any thing worfe?

*Heg.* Worfe by much: for this will, in fome degree, admit of an Excufe: Night might prompt him, Love, Wine, or the Heat of Youth; there is nothing in this, but what may be attributed to human Frailty. When he was fenfible of what he had done, he came of himfelf to the Girl's Mother, weeping, praying, begging, protefting upon his Honour, and fwearing that he would take her home. It was pardon'd, hufh'd, and his Word taken: the Girl proved with Child; this is the tenth Month. He, fweet Youth, has got a Mufick-girl, forfooth, to live with, and hath caft off the other quite.

*Dem.* Is that certainly true which you fay?

*Heg.* Both the Girl and her Mother are here ready to fatisfy you; nay, the thing itfelf fpeaks but too plain. Befides, here's *Geta*, as Servants

---

A N N O T A T I O N S.

Confciousnefs of having Equity on our fide, always infpires.

³ *Tam illiberale facinus.* An Action fo difhonourable, fo unbecoming a Man born to Freedom, and thofe higher Notions, which Independency of Mind and Fortune ought to infpire.

⁴ *Haud fic auferent.* Vix. *Culpam, factum inultum.* They fhan't carry off Impunity

" of their Crime at this rate, on fuch eafy " Conditions." It is a Metaphor taken from Commerce, in which Merchants carry off their Goods, after the Conditions of Sale are once fettled. The Verb *auferre* too, has fometimes the fame Import with *impetrare;* according to which the Senfe may be, *Haud fic auferent veniam hujus facinoris illiberalis.* So *Cicero. ad Att.* 16. 16. *Adiimus ad Cæfarem.*

Tam illiberale facinus esse ortum ? ô Æschine,
Pol haud paternum istuc dedisti. DE. videlicet
De psaltria hac audivit; id illi nunc dolet    5
Alieno; pater is nihili pendit. hei mihi !
Utinam hic prope adesset alicubi, atque audiret hæc.
HE. Nisi facient quæ illos æquom est, haud sic auferent.
GE. In te spes omnis, Hegio, nobis sita est :
Te solum habemus: tu es patronus, tu pater :    10
Ille tibi moriens nos commendavit senex.
Si deseris tu, periimus. HE. cave dixeris :
Nec faciam, neque me satis piè posse arbitror.
DE. Adibo, salvere Hegionem plurimum
Jubeo. HE. oh, te quærebam ipsum; salve, Demea. 15
DE. Quid autem ? HE. major filius tuus Æschinus,
Quem fratri adoptandum dedisti, neque boni,
Neque liberalis functus officium est viri.    [lum,
DE. Quid istuc est ? HE. nostrum amicum nôras Simu-
Atque æqualem ? DE. quid ni ? HE. filiam ejus virgi-
    nem    20
Vitiavit. DE. hem ! HE. mane, nondum audisti, Demea,
Quod est gravissimum. DE. an quidquam est etiam
    amplius ?
HE. Verò amplius : nam hoc quidem ferundum aliquo
    modo est.
Persuasit nox, amor, vinum, adolescentia :
Humanum est. ubi scit factum, ad matrem virginis 25
Venit ipsus ultro, lacrumans, orans, obsecrans,
Fidem dans, jurans se illam ducturam domum.
Ignotum est, tacitum est, creditum est. virgo ex eo
Compressu gravida facta est. mensi, hic decimus est :
Ille bonus vir nobis psaltriam, si Dis placet,    30
Paravit, quicum vivat, illam deserat.
DE. Pro certon' tu istæc dicis ? HE. mater virginis
In medio est, ipsa virgo, res ipsa : hic Geta

*Ô Æschine, pol haud dedisti istud paternum. DE. Videlicet, audivit de hac psaltria; id nunc dolet illi alieno; is pater pendit nihili. Hei mihi ! utinam hic adesset alicubi prope, atque audiret hæc. HE. Nisi faciunt quæ æquum est illos facere, haud auferent sic. GE. Spes omnis, Hegio, est sita nobis in te : habemus te solum : tu es noster patronus, tu pater : ille ferus moriens commendavit nos tibi : si tu deseris, periimus. HE. Cave dixeris : nec faciam ; atque arbitror me posse satis pie. DE. Adibo. Jubeo Hegionem plurimum salvere. HE. Oh, quærebam teipsum; salvo, Demea. DE. Quid autem ? HE. Tuus major filius Æschinus, quem dedisti fratri adoptandum, functus est officium neque boni, neque liberalis viri. DE. Quid istuc est ? HE. Nôras Simulum nostrum amicum atque æqualem ? DE. Quid ni ? HE. Vitiavit filiam ejus virginem. DE. Hem. HE. Mane, nondum audivisti, Demea, quod est gravissimum. DE. An est etiam quidquam amplius ? HE. Amplius vero: nam hoc quidem est ferendum aliquo modo. Nox, amor, vinum, adolescentia, persuasit: humanum est; ubi scit factum, ipsus venit ultro ad matrem virginis, lacrymans, orans, obsecrans, dans fidem, jurans se ducturum illum domum. Ignotum est, tacitum est, creditum est. Virgo est facta gravida ex eo compressu. Hic est decimus mensis. Ille bonus vir, si Dis placet, paravit psaltriam nobis, quicum vivat, deserat illam. DE. Dicisne tu istæc pro certo ? HE. Mater virginis est in medio, ipsa virgo, ipsa res. Præterea hic Geta,*

## ANNOTATIONS.

sumus, verba facimus pro Eutrochiis, liberalissimum decretum abstulimus.

13. *Satis piè.*] Pietas in Latin, often stands for the Duty which results from the different Relations, which People bear to one another, especially that of a Father to a Son, or a Son to a Father. This Answer, therefore, depends upon what *Geta* had just said, *Tu patronus, tu pater.* But as the word *piety* in our Language, would not convey the same Idea; I have endeavoured in the Translation to conform to the present Manners, and Fashion of Speech.

2 30 *Si dis placet.* This was a common Form,

vants now are, no bad one, nor wanting in Diligence ; he maintains them, and by his Labour alone supports the whole Family. Take him, bind him, force the Truth from him.

*Get.* Nay, put me to the Torture, if you will, to be satisfied, *Demea :* besides, he won't deny it himself, bring us only together.

*Dem.* I'm quite ashamed, nor know not what to do, or how to answer him.

*Pam.* Wretch that I am, I am racked with Pains : *Juno Lucina* help, preserve me, I beseech you.

*Heg.* What ! Is she in Labour, pray ?

*Get.* For certain, *Hegio.*

*Heg.* Hah ! This young Creature, *Demea,* now implores your Honour and Compassion ; let her obtain, frankly, what the Law will otherwise oblige you to. Pray God you may do in this as you ought, and as becomes you ; but if you are resolved not, I'll defend her, and her deceas'd Father, to the utmost of my power. He was my Kinsman, we were bred up from Children together, and were constant Companions at home, and in the Wars : We have together too experienced the Hardships of Poverty. I am therefore resolved to do my utmost, pursue it vigorously, and try all means to obtain Justice : in fine, I'll rather abandon Life, than desert these poor Women. What do you say ?

*Dem.* I'll go meet my Brother, *Hegio :* whatever Advice he gives me in this Affair, I'll follow it.

*Heg.* But *Demea* ; see that you carry this in mind ; the more easy your Circumstances in Life ; the more powerful, rich, fortunate and noble you are ; so much the greater are your Obligations to act with Honour and Justice, if you value the Reputation of Probity.

*Dem.* Well, return : every thing shall be done as it ought to be.

*Heg.* This is as becomes you. *Geta,* shew me in to *Sostrata.*

*Dem.*

## ANNOTATIONS.

Form, where they wanted to aggravate an Action, or express a Detestation of it, and answers to our *Forsooth.*

34 *Ut captus est servorum.* Id est, ut se habet conditio servorum. Solet autem formula hæc, *ut captus est,* addi laudibus eorum, qui minus capaces sunt magnæ laudis. Ita *Cæs.* B. G. 4. 3. *Ad alteram partem succedunt Ubii, quorum fuit civitas ampla atque florens,* ut est captus *Germanorum.* We ought to observe here, that Slaves among the Ancients were but meanly thought of, nor was much Regard paid to their Testimony. This is the reason of *Hegio*'s being so particular in describing *Geta*'s good Qualities ; *Non malus neque iners :* where, by the by, we may take notice, that by *neque iners,* some understand one, that is *no Fool :* and all this to make *Demea* more apt to credit what he might say. *Non malus,* he is no Rogue, to say a thing without Foundation : *neque iners,* nor is he a Fool, one that can be easily imposed upon, or knows not what he says : *Iners, quasi sine arte.* But I rather take the whole to be a Commendation of his Faithfulness and Diligence ; especially, because of what immediately follows : *Alit illas : solus omnem familiam sustentat.*

40 *Differor doloribus.* Divellor, discrucior, dilaceror. Et proprie hoc genus querelæ convenit parturienti, & cui viscera distenduntur : & ei qui inexpertum dolorem nunc primum sentiat. *Donatus.*

41 *Juno Lucina, fer opem !* See the *Andrian,* Act III. Sce. I. 15.

53 *Paupertatem una pertulimus gravem.* There is nothing that more powerfully links Men together, than to be Companions in Adversity. The Heart is then at liberty to give full Scope to all its tenderest Feelings and Emotions ;

Præterea, ut captus est servorum, non malus,
Neque iners, alit illas; solus omnem familiam 35
Suftentat: hunc adduce, vinci: quære rem.
GE. Imò hercle extorque, nisi ita factum est, Demea:
Poftremò, non negabit, coram ipsum cedo.
DE. Pudet: nec, quid agam, neque quid huic re-
   spondeam,
Scio. PA. miseram me! differor doloribus. 40
Juno Lucina, fer opem, serva me obsecro. HE. hem!
Numnam illa, quæso, parturit? GE. certè, Hegio.
   HE. hem!
Illæc fidem nunc voftram implorat, Demea.
Quod vos vis cogit, id voluntate impetret.
Hæc primùm ut fiant, Deos quæso, ut vobis decet: 45
Sin aliter animus vofter est, ego, Demea,
Summâ vi defendam hanc, atque illum mortuum.
Cognatus mihi erat: unà à pueris parvolis
Sumus educti: unà semper militiæ domi
Fuimus: paupertatem unà pertulimus gravem. 50
Quapropter nitar, faciam, experiar, denique
Animam relinquam potiùs quàm illas deseram.
Quid mihi respondes? DE. fratrem conveniam, Hegio:
Is quod mihi de hac re dederit consilium, id sequar.
HE. Sed, Demea, hoc tu facito cum animo cogites, 55
Quàm vos facillime agitis, quàm estis maxumè
Potentes, dites, fortunati, nobiles,
Tam maxumè vos æquo animo æquè noscere
Oportet, si vos voltis perhiberi probos.
DE. Redito. fient, quæ fieri æquom est, omnia. 60
HE. Decet te facere. Geta, duc me intrò ad Softratam.

*ut eft captus servorum, non malus, neque iners, alit illas; solus suftentat omnem familiam: adduce hunc, vinci, quære rem: GE. Imo hercle extorque, Demea, nisi eft factum ita: poftremo non negabit, cedo coram ipsum. DE. Pudet: nec scio quid agam, neque quid respondeam huic. PA. O miseram me, differor doloribus! Juno Lucina, obsecro fer opem, serva me. HE. Hem! quæso numnam illa parturit? GE. Certè, Hegio. HE. Hem! illæc nunc implorat vestram fidem, Demea. Impetret voluntate id, quod vis cogit vos facere. Quæso, Deos primum, ut hæc fiant, ut decet vobis: sin vofter animus eft aliter, ego, Demea, defendam hanc, atque illum mortuum, summa vi. Erat cognatus mihi: sumus educti una, à parvulis pueris: fuimus semper una mi-* 

*paupertatem. Quapropter nitar, faciam, experiar, denique relinquam potius animam, quam deseram illas. Quid respondes mihi? DE. Conveniam fratrem, Hegio: sequar id confilium, quod is dederit mihi de hac re. HE. Sed, Demea, facito ut tu cogites hoc cum animo: quam vos agitis facillime, quam eftit maxime potentes, dites, fortunati, nobiles, tam maxime oportet vos noscere æqua æquo animo, si vultis vos perhiberi probos. DE. Redito: omnia fient, quæ æquum eft fieri. HE. Decet te facere. Geta, duc me intro ad Softratam.* 

## ANNOTATIONS.

Emotions; and as there are no Embarrass-
ments, no Avocations of Pleasure to en-
tangle it, it is glad to lay hold on those
Consolations which it possesses within itself.
For one of the greatest Philosophers of An-
tiquity has observed, that Friendship not only
doubles our Joys by a mutual Communica-
tion, but alleviates our Sorrows by the share
of them, our other Half seems to take upon
himself.

24. *Is quod mibi de bac re dederit consilium.* Commentators observe, that this Line
seems to be taken from the *Phormio* II. 3.

21. Where we read it Word for Word. It
does not, indeed, seem to come in here
with any Propriety: for *Micio* was the absolute Master of *Æschinus*; and, therefore,
all that *Demea* could do, was to offer his
Advice, and represent to *Micio*, what he
thought just and reasonable. Nor is it at
all likely, had he had the Disposal of
things, that he would have paid much
Regard to his Brother's Counsel. He does
not appear to be in such good Humour
with him, or so well satisfied with his
Conduct.

*Dem.* Thefe things don't happen without my foretelling them : I wifh from my Soul it may end here ; but I fear much that this immoderate Indulgence will turn at laft to fome heavy Misfortune. I'll go find out my Brother, and reproach him with thefe Extravagancies of his Son.

## ANNOTATIONS.

61 *Nen me incidente. Incidente*: i. e. *non dicente*, or *tacente.* This, as *Donatus* obferves, is an Expreffion harfh and unufual, but it comes very aptly from a Man in Anger.

Ibid. *Utinam hec fit modo defunctum.* Duo antiqui

---

# ACT III.  SCENE VI.

## ARGUMENT.

*Hegio comforts* Softrata, *and promifes to fupport her Daughter with his Friendfhip.*

### HEGIO.

BE quite eafy and chearful, *Softrata*, and comfort your Daughter. all in your power. I'll go meet *Micio*, if he's at the Forum, and inform him particularly of every Circumftance : if he is willing to do us Juftice, let him do it ; but if otherwife, let him declare it plainly, that I may know at once what I am to do.

## ANNOTATIONS.

*Donatus* obferves, that in fome Copies, this whole Scene is wanting ; and *Guyetus* thinks this Reafon enough to reject it altogether. He can't fee how *Hegio* comes to addrefs *Softrata*, who appears neither in this Scene, nor the preceding. But he feems not to have attended to what *Hegio* fays a little before to *Geta* : *Duc me intro ad Softratam.* While, therefore, *Demea* fpeaks the four next Verfes, and goes off the Stage ; *Hegio* is with *Softrata*, and here is feen coming out, and talking to her within ; juft as *Lefbia*, in the third Act of the *Andrian*, calls from without to *Archilles*, who was within with *Glycery* : and *Chremes*, in the Beginning of the fifth Act of the *Self-Tormentor*, fpeaks from the Scene to his Wife *Softrata* : Befides, in this Scene, *Hegio* fays, *Ego Micionem conveniam, fi apud forum eft.* Without this, the third Scene of the next Act, were we fee *Hegio* and *Micio* together, will not come in by far fo properly.

2. *Fac confolere. Pamphila* had many Caufes of Anxiety, and therefore ftood greatly in need of Confolation. She had Sicknefs to ftruggle with ; the Reflection upon her Misfortune muft alfo give her Uneafinefs, and as fhe was ftill unmarried, there would always be rifing fome little Apprehenfions that *Æfchinus* might abandon her ; for it is not likely, that in her prefent Situation, her Mother would acquaint her, what fhe be-
believed

De. *** me indicente hæc sciat. utinam hoc sit modo
Defunctum. Verùm nimia illæc licentia
Profecto evadet in aliquod magnum malum.
Ibo, requiram fratrem, ut in eum hæc evomam. 765

*magnum malum. Ibo, requiram fratrem, ut evomam hæc in eum.*

De. *** me indicente. Utinam modo hoc sit defunc- *** illæc nimia licentia evade: in aliqua

## ANNOTATIONS.

antiqui libri, Bembinus & Victorianus, uti- | id est, in hoc negotio: ne Æschinus pejora
nam hic habent. Ita *defunctum* impersonale | committat. *Factnus.*
erit; ut sit sensus: utinam sit defunctum hic,

---

# ACTUS III. SCENA VI.

### ARGUMENTUM.

*Hegio Sostratam consolatur, & profitetur amicitiam suam in filiam.*

### HEGIO.

BONO animo fac sis, Sostrata, & istam, quod potes,
  Fac consolere. ego Micionem, si apud forum est,
Conveniam, atque, ut res gesta est, narrabo ordine.
Si est, facturus ut sit officium suum,
Faciat: sin aliter de hac ré est ejus sententia;   5
Respondeat mi, ut, quid agam, quamprimùm sciam.

*est, ut sit facturus suum officium, faciat: sin sententia ejus de hac ré est aliter, respondeat mihi, ut sciam quamprimum quid agam.*

**ORDO.**

*Sostrata, fac ut sis bono animo, & fac consolere istam, quod potes: ego conveniam Micionem, si est apud forum, atque narrabo ordine, ut res est gesta. Si est, ut sit facturus suum officium, faciat. Si*

## ANNOTATIONS.

lived to be her real Misfortune. *Hegio's* Concern for the young Creature manifests great Good-nature and Humanity: this is perfectly agreeable to the Design of the Poet, who means to represent him as an amiable endearing Character.

6. *Ut, quid agam, quamprimum sciam.* Hegio expresses himself here with a becoming Modesty and Reserve. He is unwilling to say any thing harsh, or threaten, because it looks disrespectful, where there are any Hopes of obtaining an honourable Satisfaction; moreover he takes care to make *Sostrata* sensible, that he would not be remiss in her Affairs, if Justice were denied her, but take what further Measures might be necessary to redress her Wrongs; for that is evidently the Import of *ut, quid agam, quamprimum sciam.*

## ACT IV. SCENE I.

### ARGUMENT.

*This Scene shews that the Presence of Parents is sometimes irksome to Children, because it checks them in the gratifying their Inclinations, and keeps them under Restraint. It describes also the Behaviour and Character of a toward Youth. Syrus instructs Ctesipho in what manner he is to answer to his Father.*

### CTESIPHO, SYRUS.

*Ctesipho.* IS my Father gone into the Country, say you?
    *Syr.* Long ago.

*Ctes.* But tell me really.

*Syr.* I tell you he's at his Farm; and, I dare answer for it, labouring hard by this time in the Fields.

*Ctes.* I heartily wish, could it be without Prejudice to his Health, that he may so effectually tire himself, as not to be able to rise from Bed these three Days.

*Syr.* So be it: and something still better, if possible.

*Ctes.* True: for I greatly desire to spend this whole Day pleasantly, as I have begun it: nor is there any thing I so much hate that Country Seat of his for, as its being too near the Town. Was it farther off, Night would come on before he could return hither again. But now, when he finds I'm not there, I know very well he'll come back immediately. Where have you been, *Ctesipho*, will he say, that I have not seen you all this Day? What answer shall I make?

*Syr.* What! Can you think of nothing?

*Ctes.* Not one thing.

*Syr.* So much the worse. Have you no Client, Friend or Guest to plead?

*Ctes.* I have: What then?

*Syr.* That you was engaged to them.

*Ctes.* When I really was not engaged? what can never do.

*Syr.* It may.
                                       *Ctes.*

### ANNOTATIONS.

We have seen before, that *Syrus* dispatch'd *Demea* into the Country, making him believe that his Son was gone before him. *Ctesipho* himself was afraid, that upon his Father's missing him from home, he would come immediately, and inquire after him in Town. These his Fears he had probably been discovering to *Syrus*, who, in return, assures him, he had nothing to apprehend; for that he had himself contrived to send him into the Country. In this part of the Conversation they are introduced here, and is continued till they are interrupted by the Appearance of the old Gentleman himself. The whole Scene gives the Description of a modest Youth, unpractised in the Ways of Hypocrisy and Deceit; one who respects and stands in awe of his Father, and, therefore, anxious to conceal from him any thing that he knows will displease him.

³ *Quod cum salute ejus fiat.* Terence does not mean to represent *Ctesipho* an abandoned Character, but one carried away by Inclinations common to the Youth of that Age. He is, moreover, under the Eye of a severe and rigid Father who looked upon this Vice, as of the most heinous kind. Thus being under a Necessity of concealing his
                                    Fault,

# ACTUS IV. SCENA I.

### ARGUMENTUM.

*Ostendit, filios sæpe optare parentum absentiam; si quando solutius vivere & genio indulgere statuerunt. Probi adolescentis ingenium moresque hac scena exprimuntur. Syrus Ctesiphonem instituit, quem ad modum respondere debeat patri.*

CTESIPHO, SYRUS.

AIN' patrem hinc abisse rus? SY. jamdudum. CT.
    dic sodes. SY. apud villam est.
Nunc cum maxumè operis aliquid facere credo. CT.
    utinam quidem,
Quod cum salute ejus fiat, ita se defatigârit, velim,
Ut triduo hoc perpetuo prorsum è lecto nequeat surgere
SY. Ita fiat, & istoc si quid potis est rectius. CT. ita.
    nam nunc diem
Miserè nimis cupio, ut cœpi, perpetuum in lætitia
    degere.             [propè est:
Et illud rus nullâ aliâ causâ tam malè odi, nisi quia
Quod si abesset longius,
Priùs nox oppressisset illic, quàm huc revorti posset
    iterum.             [scio: 10
Nunc, ubi me illic non videbit, jam huc recurret; sat
Rogitabit me, ubi fuerim; quém ego hodie toto non
    vidi die:        [quidquam. SY. tanto nequior.
Quid dicam? SY. nihilne in mentem? CT. nunquam
Cliens, amicus, hospes, nemo est vobis? CT. sunt:
    quid postea?       [potest fieri. SY. potest:
SY. Hisce opera ut data sit. CT. quæ non data sit? non

*huc. Nunc, ubi non videbit me illic, sat scio, jam recurret huc; rogitabit me, ubi fuerim; quem ego non vidi hodie toto die: quid dicam? SY. Nibilne venit in mentem? OT. Nunquam quidquam. SY. Tanto nequior. Est nemo cliens, amicus, hospes vobis? CT. Sunt: quid postea? SY. Ut opera sit data hisce. CT. Quæ non sit data? Non potest fieri. SY. Potest.*

ORDO.

*CT. A isthc patrem abiisse hinc rus? SY. Jamdudum. CT. Dic sodes. SY. Est apud villam; nunc cum maxime credo eum facere aliquid operis. CT. Utinam quidem, quid velim, fiat cum salute ejus, ita se defatigaverit; ut nequeat surgere è lecto prorsum hoc perpetuo triduo. SY. Fiat ita, & rectius istoc, si quid est potis. CT. Ita. Nam nimis misere cupio degere hunc perpetuum diem in lætitia, ut cœpi: & nulla alia causa tam male odi illud rus, nisi quia est prope. Quod si abesset longius, nox oppressisset cum illic, prius quam posset iterum reverti*

## ANNOTATIONS.

Fault, and willing, at the same time, to indulge himself; he wishes it might so happen, that his Father were prevented from disturbing him; but, at the same time, with the Reserve becoming a dutiful Son, who is far from desiring any thing to his Father's real hurt.

5 *Ita fiat, & istoc si quid potis est rectius.* No one has succeeded better than our Poet, in distinctly marking his Characters. The young Gentleman himself speaks with Modesty, like one who had been bred up to Notions of Honour and Duty; but this Rogue of a Slave, whose Mind was of a very different make, observes no such Restraint, but roundly wishes the Old Man might effectually free them from all Apprehensions. However, he does not explain himself avowedly before the Son, whose virtuous Disposition he knew; but hides his meaning under equivocal Expressions, as if he meant no more than a longer Confinement. This shews the Poet's great Insight into Life and Manners. Servile low Minds seldom observe any Measure in their Wishes; especially in such Cases as this, where there was a Consciousness of Guilt, and a dread of Punishment, should it be discovered.

14 *Quæ non data sit? non potest fieri.* We must still admire Terence's Justness in the

*Ctef.* For the Day: but if I pafs the Night here, what Excufe can I pretend, *Syrus?*

*Syr.* Ah, how I fhould like it, were it the Cuftom to be engaged with Friends in the Night too; but make yourfelf quite eafy; I underftand his Humour perfectly, and, in his moft violent Tranfports of Rage, can make him as quiet as a Lamb.

*Ctef.* How?

*Syr.* He likes to hear you praifed: I make you a God to him, and reckon up all your Virtues.

*Ctef.* My Virtues!

*Syr.* Yours: immediately the Tears fall from him, as from a Child for Joy——Hah, take care.

*Ctef.* What's the matter?

*Syr.* The Wolf in the Fable.

*Ctef.* What, my Father?

*Syr.* The fame.

*Ctef.* Syrus, what fhall we do?

*Syr.* Get in quickly; I'll fee to that.

*Ctef.* If he afks any thing, you know nothing of me: you hear?

*Syr.* Can't you hold your tongue?

ANNOTATIONS.

Propriety of his Characters, and maintaining the Uniformity of them throughout. They are in every thing agreeable to the Precept of *Horace, De Arte Poet* Ver. 126.

 ——*Servetur ad imum*
 *Qualis ab inepto procefferit, & fibi conftet.*

*Ctefipho* had been brought up in the Country under a rigid Father, and is therefore a Stranger to Lying, Hypocrify and Deceit; Vices that fpring from Luxury, a Purfuit of Pleafure, and the Corruptions of a Town-Life. He cannot, therefore, be eafily prevailed on to have recourfe to Arts fo contrary to the Notions he had hitherto been train'd up in;

and if Neceffity obliges him at laft to confent, it is not till after he had fhewn a manifeft Reluctance.

 21 *Lupus in fabula.* This Proverb was equivalent to an enjoining of Silence. *Virgil* refers to it, in his ninth Eclogue, Ver. 54.

 ——*Vox quoque Mærin*
 *Jam fugit ipfa, lupi. Mærin videre priores.*

*Servius,* upon this Paffage, thus explains the Proverb. "Hoc etiam phyfici confirmant; "quod vox detrahitur ei, quem primum vi- "derit lupus; unde etiam proverbium hoc "natum eft, *lupus in fabula;* quotiens fu- "pervenit ille, de quo loquimur, & nobis fui "præfentia

---

## ACT IV. SCENE II.

### ARGUMENT.

Demea *complains that he can't find his Brother; and, inquiring of* Syrus, *is purpofely by him directed wrong.*

DEMEA, CTESIPHO, SYRUS.

*Demea.* I Verily think I'm one of the moft unfortunate Men alive: for firft, I can find my Brother nowhere: befides, while I

was

ANNOTATIONS.

In this Scene, we have a fecond Inftance of the Cunning of *Syrus,* and how artfully he deceives the good Old Man. We have feen

that, after parting from *Syrus,* with a defign to go into the Country; he was met by *Hegio,* and informed of all that had paffed between

CT. Interdiu : sed si hîc pernocto, causæ quid dicam, Syre?  15
SY. Vah, quàm vellem etiam noctu amicis operam
 mos esset dari.
Quin tu otiosus es : ego illius sensum pulchrè calleo.
Cùm servit maxumè, tam placidum quàm ovem red-
 do. CT. quomodo?  [deum :
SY. Laudarier te audit libenter. facio te apud illum
Virtutes narro. CT. meas? SY. tuas. homini illicò la-
 crumæ cadunt,  20
Quasi puero, gaudio. hem tibi autem. CT. quidnam
 est? SY. lupus in fabulâ.
CT. Pater adest? SY. ipsu'st. CT. Syre, quid agimus?
 SY. fuge modò intrò : ego videro.
CT. Si quid rogabit, nusquam tu me : audistin'? SY.
 potin' ut desinas?

*CT. Interdiu : sed si pernocto hic, Syre, quid causæ dicam? SY. Vah, quam vellem esset operam dari amicis etiam noctu. Quin tu es otiosus : ego pulchre calleo sensum illius : cum fervit maxime, reddo tam placidum quam ovem. CT. Quomodo? SY. Libenter audit te laudari : facio te deum apud illum : narro virtutes. CT. Meas? SY. Tuas. Illico lacrymæ cadunt homini quasi puero, gaudio. Hem autem tibi. CT.*

*Quidnam est? SY. Lupus in fabula. CT. Pater adest? SY. Ipsus est. CT. Syre, quid agimus? SY. Fuge modo intro; ego videro. CT. Si rogabit quid, tu vidisti me nusquam : audistine? SY. Potisne es ut desinas?*

### ANNOTATIONS.

" præsentia amputat facultatem loquendi." The same is observed by *Pliny*, L. 8. 22. and both are follow'd by *Isidorus*, Lib. I. Cap. 22. " Aiunt rustici, vocem hominem per-" dere, si eum lupus prior viderit. Unde & " subito tacenti dicitur illud proverbium : " *lupus in fabula*." But Mad..m *Dacier* is by no means satisfied with this Solution ; she will have it, that it was derived from the Stories about Wolves, which Women were frequently wont to tell their Children in the Fields. It often happened, that in the midst of their Relation, the very Animal they were speaking of, would suddenly appear. The Fear this occasioned, tied up their Tongues, and prevented them from going on with their Story. Hence the Proverb, *lupus in fabula*, to signify, that the Person, of whom one speaks, is at hand ; for this is evidently the Sense in which we are to take it here, as appears from *Ctesipho*'s Answer, who immediately asks, *pater adest?* It is thus too, that *Cicero* uses it in one of his Letters to *Atticus*, Lib. XIII. 33. " De Varrone loquebamur : " *lupus in fabula*. Venit enim ad me, & " quidem id temporis, ut retinendus esset. " Sed ego ita egi, ut non scinderem penu-" lam."

---

# ACTUS IV. SCENA II.

## ARGUMENTUM.

*Demea queritur, quod fratrem non repererit : idem à Syro deludi-
tur, locum in quo sit frater bifariam describente.*

DEMEA, CTESIPHO, SYRUS.   ORDO.

NÆ ego homo sum infelix! primùm fratrem nusquam invenio gentium.:

DE. NÆ ego sum homo infelix! primùm invenio fratrem nusquam gentium :

### ANNOTATIONS.

between *Æschinus* and *Pamphila*. Upon this, he changes his Resolution, and goes to look for his Brother ; but he can find him no-where. To add to his Misfortune, he meets a Workman from the Country, who tells him, that his Son *Ctesipho* was not there. He therefore appears here complaining of his bad Fortune ; and coming to his Brother's, to see whe-ther

was on the hunt for him, I met a Workman from my Country-Seat, who told me my Son was not there. I know not what to do.

*Ctef.* Syrus.

*Syr.* What?

*Ctef.* Does he afk for me?

*Syr.* Yes.

*Ctef.* I'm undone.

*Syr.* Have a good Heart.

*Dem.* What ill luck is this, in the name of Wonder? I can't conceive the Meaning of it; only, that it feems as if I were born to be miferable. I am always the firft to feel our Misfortunes, the firft to know every thing, the firft to carry the News of it *to my Brother*, and the only one that feels the Weight, if any thing happens.

*Syr.* I laugh to hear this: he fays, he is the firft to know every thing; when he's the only Man that knows nothing.

*Dem.* I now go back to fee if, perhaps, my Brother is return'd.

*Ctef.* Syrus, pray take care that he don't rufh in upon us fuddenly here.

*Syr.* Can't you hold your Tongue? I'll take care.

*Ctef.* But, by *Hercules*, I'll never truft that to your Management: for I'll go immediately and fhut myfelf up with her in fome fecure Retreat: that's fafeft.

*Syr.* Do; however, I'll take care to difpatch him.

*Dem.* But there's that Rogue *Syrus*——

*Syr.* By *Hercules*, there's no fuch thing as ftaying here, if this continues; I would gladly know how many Mafters I have; what a miferable Situation is this?

*Dem.* What's this Fellow whining and whimpering for? What would he have?—Hark ye, good Sir; is my Brother at home?

*Syr.* What the plague do you tell me of good Sir! I'm undone.

*Dem.* What's the matter?

*Syr.* The matter! *Ctefipho* has beat me and the Mufick-girl almoft to death.

*Dem.* Hah, what do you tell me?

*Syr.* See how he has tore my Lip!

*Dem.* Why?

*Syr.* He fays it was thro' me, that this Girl was bought.

*Dem.* Did you not juft now fay, that you had gone fo far with him into the Country?                                           *Syr.*

ANNOTATIONS.

ther he mayn't be return'd home; *Syrus* artfully contrives a Story, to make him eafy in refpect of *Ctefipho*; and then, to get rid of him effectually, fends him a wandering all over the Town In queft of his Brother. *A villa mercenarium vidi.* It was wife, fays *Donatus*, in the Poet, however near the old Gentleman's Country-Seat might be, to retain him in Town, as his Prefence was neceffary in other Parts of the Play, that were to come on fpeedily.

[8] *Primus, porro obnuncio.* Qui malam rem *nunciat,* obnunciat: *qui bonam,* annunciat, fays *Donatus; nam proprie* obnunciare *dicuntur Augures, qui aliquid mali ominis fævumque viderint.* The Explication here is undoubtedly good; but how far the making *obnunciare* the fame as *omen nunciare,* may

not

Præterea autem, dum illum quæro, à villâ mercenarium  
Vidi: is filium negat esse ruri; nec quid agam, scio.  
CT. Syre. SY. quid ais? CT. men' quærit? SY. verum.  
    CT. perii. SY. quin tu animo bono es.  
DE. Quid hoc, malu, infelicitatis? nequeo satis de-  
cernere:        5  
Nisi me credo huic esse natum rei, ferundis miseriis.  
Primus sentio mala nostra: primus rescisco omnia:  
Primus porrò obnuncio. ægrè solus, si quid sit, fero.  
SY. Rideo hunc: primùm ait se scire: is solus nescit  
omnia.  
DE. Nunc redeo: si fortè frater redierit viso. CT. Syre,  
Obsecro, vide ne ille huc prorsus se irruat. SY. etiam  
    taces?      11  
Ego cavebo. CT. nunquam hercle hodie ego istuc com-  
    mittam tibi.      [id tutissimum est.  
Nam me jam in cellam aliquam cum illâ concludam.  
SY. Age, tamen ego hunc amovebo. DE. sed eccum  
    sceleratum Syrum.      [potest. 15  
SY. Non hercle hic quidem durare quisquam, si sic fit,  
Scire equidem volo, quot mihi sint domini. quæ hæc  
    est miseria?      [hem, est frater domi?  
DE. Quid ille gannit? quid volt? Quid ais, bone vir?  
SY. Quid, malum, bone vir, mihi narras? equidem  
    perii. DE. quid tibi est?      [psaltriam  
SY. Rogitas? Ctesipho me pugnis miserum & istam  
Usque occidit. DE. hem, quid narras? SY. hem, vide  
    ut discidit labrum.      20  
DE. Quamobrem? SY. me impulsore hanc emtam esse  
    ait. DE. non tu eum rus hinc modo

*Præterea autem dum quæro, illum, vidi mercenarium à villâ: ... rure nec, scio, quid agam. CT. Syre. SY. Quid ais? CT. Quæritne me? SY. Verum. CT. Perii. SY. Quin tu is animo bono. DE. Quid hoc infelicitatis; malum? nequeo satis discernere: nisi credo me esse natum huic rei, ferendis miseriis. Primus sentio nostra mala: primus rescisco omnia: porro primus obnuncio: si quid sit, ego solus fero ægre. SY. Rideo hunc: ait se primùm scire: is solus nescit omnia. DE. Nunc redeo: viso, si fortè frater redierit. CT. Syre, obsecro vide, ne ille prorsus irruat se huc. SY. Etiam taces? ego cavebo. CT. Nunquam hercle ego committam, istuc tibi hodie; nam jam concludam me in aliquam cellam cum illâ; id est tutissimum. SY. Age, tamen ego amovebo hunc. DE. Sed eccum*

*sceleratum Syrum. SY. Hercle quidem nen quisquam potest durare hic, si sit hic. Equidem volo scire quot domini sint mihi: quæ miseria est hæc? DE. Quid ille gannit? Quid vult? Quid vis, bone vir? Hem, est frater domi? SY. Quid, malum, narras, bone vir, mihi? equidem perii. DE. Quid est tibi? SY. Rogitas? Ctesipho usque occidit me miserum & istam psaltriam pugnis. DE. Hem, quid narras? SY. Hem, vide ut discidit labrum. DE. Quamobrem? SY. Ait hanc esse emptam, me impulsore. DE. Non tu aiebas modo te produxisse eum hinc rus?*

## ANNOTATIONS.

not be an over-nice Refinement, I leave to the Reader to judge. I am rather apt to think, that it resembles the Compounds *obloquor, obrogo, obtrudor,* and such like; in all which the Particle *ob* has something importunate and disagreeable in its Signification. *Scilicet,* says *Westerhovius, magistratus magistratui dicebatur obnunciare, denuncians rem, de qua is acturus erat cum populo, differendam esse in aliud tempus; prætextu religionis vel auspiciorum, quibus collega ille simulabat se operam dare reipublicæ causâ. Quum igitur de cælo servaturus dixisset collegæ, alio die, nulla erant comitia, sed maxime quæ in urbe, ne ..., unde* ... *auspicia erant captanda, abigerentur.* Thus, *Cicero pro Sextio* 15. *Lata lex est, ne auspicia valerent, ne quis obnunciaret, ne quid legi intercederet.*

10 *Syre, observe, vide.* Ctesipho is not now standing with *Syrus;* but must be supposed to have retired behind the Door, or to speak from a Window.

17 *Quid ille gannit? Alii garrit,* sed melius *gannit: gannire* enim proprie catulorum est, & de catulis gementibus dicitur, unde *gannitus* sæpe ponitur pro plorato vapulantium.

18 *Quid, malum, bone vir, mihi narras? Malum* hic interjectio est, & illud ...

*Syr.* I did: but he return'd like a perfect Madman, sparing nobody: might he not have been ashamed to beat an old Man, who dandled him t'other day in my Arms, scarce thus high.

*Dem.* I commend you, *Ctesipho*, you're Father right: come, I see you're a Man.

*Syr.* Commend him, say you? Nay, he'll keep his Hands to himself another time, if he's wise.

*Dem.* Brave!

*Syr.* Mighty brave, sure, to beat a poor Woman, and me a Slave, that dar'd not to strike again! Oh yes, wonderfully brave!

*Dem.* He could not have done better.  He thought the same as I, that you was the Ring-leader of this Plot.  But is my Brother within?

*Syr.* No.

*Dem.* I'm thinking where to look for him.

*Syr.* I know where he is, but am determin'd not to tell.

*Dem.* Hah, what's that you say?

*Syr.* Even so.

*Dem.* I'll break your Head for you this instant, you Rascal,

*Syr.* I don't know the Man's Name at whose House he is, but I know the Place.

*Dem.* Tell me the Place then.

*Syr.* Do you know the *Portico* down this way, just by the Market?

*Dem.* How should I but know it?

*Syr.* Go directly up that Street; when you come to the end, there is a Descent backwards; go down that: afterwards, on this side, you'll see a Chapel; and near to that there is a narrow Lane.

*Dem.* Whereabouts?

*Syr.* Just where the great wild Fig-tree stands: do you know it?

*Dem.* I do.

*Syr.* Keep directly through that.

*Dem.* But that Lane is no Thorow-fare?

*Syr.* True, by *Jupiter:* what a Fool I am? I was out: return again to the *Portico*; this will be a much nearer way, and easier found. Do you know the House of this rich Fellow, *Cratinus?*

*Dem.* Yes.

*Syr.* When you have pass'd that, keep directly along the Street on your left Hand, till you come to *Diana*'s Temple, then turn to the Right: before you come to the Gate, just by the Pond, there is a Mill, and over against it a Joiner's Shop: he's there.

*Dem.* What does he there?                                        *Syr.*

*A N N O T A T I O N S.*

Syros repetit, *quasi diceret,* Quid, malum! mihi illud, *bene vir,* occinis, meque irrides, quasi parum sim miser, & parum afflictus, recentem injuriam & verbera Ctesiphonis filii tui passus.  The Conduct here is so extremely natural, and well imagined, that *Demea* could never take it for a Feint; and, *Syrus,* to give it the greater Air of Truth, tears his

Lip a little, and affects to shew it to the old Man.

[32] *Produxe.* Here, for *produxisse,* a Liberty frequent with the Poets.  Thus, in *Catullus,* we read *promisse* for *promisisse*; in *Virgil,* *explesse* for *explevisse*; and in *Horace* *surrexe* for *surrexisse.*

[34] *Tantillum: in manibus gestavi meis?*

This

Prodexe aiebas ? Sy. factum verùm venit pòst infaniens :
Nihil pepercit. non puduiffe verberare hominem fenem,
Quem ego modò puerum tantillum in manibus geftavi
    meis ?
De. Laudo, Ctefipho : patriffas. abi, virum tejudico.    25
Sy. Laudas ? næ ille continebit pofthac, fi fapiet, manus!
De. Fortiter. Sy. perquàm ; quia miferam mulierem
    & me fervolum,
Qui referire non audebam, vicit : hui, perfortiter !
De. Non potuit melius. idem, quod ego, fenfit, te effe
    huic rei caput.                             [ram, cogita.    30
Sed eftne frater intus ? Sy. non eft. De. ubi illum quæ-
Sy. Scio ubi fit, verùm hodie nunquam monftrabo. De.
    hem, quid ais ? Sy. ita.                        men nefcio
De. Diminuetur tibi quidem jam cerebrum. Sy. at no-
Illius hominis, fed locum novi ubi fit. De. dic ergo
    locum                                 [De. quidni noverim ?
Sy. Noftin' porticum apud macellum hanc deorfum i
Sy. Præterito hac rectà plateà furfum. ubi eò veneris,    35
Clivus deorfum vorfus eft, hac præcipitato : poftea
Eft ad hanc manum facellum : ibi angiportum proptèr
    eft.                                    [De. novi. Sy. hac pergito.
De. Quónam ? Sy. illîc, ubi etiam caprificus magna eft.
De. Id quidem angiportum non eft pervium. Sy. ve-
    rum hercle. vah,                              [fum redi.    40
Cenfen' hominem me effe ? erravi. in porticum rur-
Sanè hac multo propiùs ibis, & minor eft erratio.
Scin' Cratini hujus ditis ædes ? De. fcio. Sy. ubi eas
    præterieris,
Ad finiftram hac rectà plateà : ubi ad Dianæ veneris,
Ito ad dextram : priùs, quàm ad portam venias, apud
    ipfum lacum
Eft piftrilla, & exadvorfum fabrica : ibi eft. De. quid
    ibi facit ?                                          45

*Ubi veneris ea, eft clivus vorfus deorfum, præcipitato hac : poftea eft facellum ad hanc manum : ibi eft angiportum propter. De. Quónam ? Sy. Illic, ubi eft etiam magna caprificus. De. Novi. Sy. Pergito hac. De. Id angiportum quidem non eft pervium. Sy. Verùm hercle. Vah, cenfefne me effe hominem ? erravi. Redi rurfum in porticum. Sane ibis multo propiùs hac via, & erratio eft minor. Scifne ædes hujus ditis Cratini ? De. Scio. Sy. Ubi præterieris eas, ito ad finiftram hac rectà platea : ubi veneris ad templum Dianæ, ito ad dextram : priufquam venias ad portam, eft piftrilla apud ipfum lacum, & exadverfum fabrica : eft ibi. De. Quid facit ubi ?*

## ANNOTATIONS.

This, in the Action, was accompanied with
fome Gefture, to exprefs his full Meaning,
that he had dandled *Ctefipho* in his Arms,
when but a meer Infant.
    +? *Cenfen' hominem me effe ? erravi.* Cal-
liditas eft maxima, fays *Donatus*; deprehen-
fum mendacium non defendere, fed fateri; ut

opinionem fimplicitatis acquirat. Vides igitur, ut ipfe fibi fuccenfeat; tanquam imprudens erraverit, non dolofus impulerit inter-
rogantem. Et mire fe negat hominem;
tanquam homo corde fit, non corpore.
    ++ *Prius, quam ad portam venias.* By this
we are let to underftand, that *Syrus* had
                                        contrived

Sy. Eft facilè : ve-
rum venit poft infa-
niens : pepercit nihil;
An non oportuit pu-
duiffe eum verberare
hominem fenem, eum
inquam, quem ego
modo geftavi plurum
tantillum in meis ma-
nibus ? De. Laudo
te, Ctefipho : patrif-
fas, ubi, judico te
virum. Sy. Lau-
das ? næ ille contine-
bit manus pofthac,
fi fapiet. De. For-
titer. Sy. Perquam ;
quia vicit miferam
mulieram, & me fer-
vulum, qui non au-
debam referire : hui,
perfortiter ! De. Non
potuit feciffe melius ;
fenfit idem, quod ego
fentio, te effe caput
huic rei. Sed eftne
frater intus ? Sy.
Non eft. De. Cogi-
to, ubi quæram il-
lum. Sy. Scio ubi fit,
verum nunquam mon-
ftrabo hodie. De.
Hem, quid ais ? Sy.
Ita. De. Cerebrum
quidem jam diminue-
tur tibi. Sy. At
nefcio nomen illius
hominis, fed novi lo-
cum ubi fit. De.
Dic locum ergo. Sy.
Noftine hanc porti-
cum deorfum apud
macellum ? De.
Quidni noverim ?
Sy. Præterito hac
rectà platea furfum.

*Syr.* He has ordered some oaken-legged Tables to be made to set in the Sun.

*Dem.* For you to drink upon : mighty well, truly.  But why do I delay going to him ?

*Syr.* Go then : I'll exercise you to-day, as you deserve, old Dotard. *Æschinus* stays intolerably ; Dinner's quite spoil'd : *Ctesipho* thinks of nothing but his Mistress : I too will provide for myself : for I'll go directly, and pick out the choicest Bit I can find ; and sipping off my Cups leisurely, will prolong the Day all I can.

*ANNOTATIONS.*

contrived to send *Demea* a wandering as far as the very Walls and Extremity of the Town : *Apud ipsum lacum.* We learn from *Varro,* that near the Gates of their Cities, the Ancients commonly had large Basons of Water, where their Horses were led to drink, and whence they might be supplied on any sudden Emergence of Fire.

46 *Lectulos in sole ilignis pedibus.* It was frequent with the Ancients to sit, lie, or walk in the Sun, and considered by them as one of the great Preservatives of Health, as we learn from *Celsus,* L. I. Thus *Syrus* being ask'd a Question, that possibly he had not foreseen, has recourse to this, and is circumstantial enough in his Answer to prevent Suspicion ; for he is particular in the Design and Form of them : thus, first *lectulos,* then, *lectulos in sole collocandos ;* and lastly, *lectulos ilignis pedibus faciundos.* Where we are to observe, that the Legs to Couches, among the Ancients, were generally made of Oak ; so their Tables were, for the most part, of Maple Wood, often of Ivory, and sometimes Silver.

48 *Silicernium.* There is great Debate, among Grammarians, about the Signification and Etymology of this Word ; but I shall content myself with observing here, that it is most generally allowed to signify an old Man that stoops as he walks, *Quasi silicem cernens.*                49 *Præbium*

## ACT IV.  SCENE III.

### ARGUMENT.

Hegio *begs of* Micio, *that he will go himself to* Sostrata, *and satisfy her that the Suspicion of* Æschinus's *being alienated from* Pamphila, *was owing entirely to his having carried off the Musick-girl for his Brother* Ctesipho.

MICIO, HEGIO.

*Micio.* I Can see nothing in all this that deserves such mighty Praises, *Hegio* : I only do my Duty, and give satisfaction for the Faults of my own Family : unless you took me to be one of those Men, who think it an Injury to expostulate with them for Wrongs they

*ANNOTATIONS.*

*Hegio,* after parting from *Sostrata,* goes to the Forum, where he has the good Luck to find *Micio.* He acquaints him with the whole Business ; and instead of meeting with Denials, or evasive Answers, as he apprehended, is heard with great Candour and Compassion, and obtains a Promise of ample Redress. This naturally draws from *Hegio* many Praises and Commendations, which *Micio,* whose Character is that of Goodness itself, modestly declines. In this part of their Conversation they are introduced by the Poet, who has so framed and contrived their Discourse, that it is easy from it to understand all that had passed between them before. An artful Management, and justly to be admir'd,

as

SY. Lectulos in sole ilignis pedibus faciundos dedit.
DE. Ubi potetis vos? bene sanè. sed cesso ad eum per-
    gere? [diam.
SY. I sanè: ego te exercebo hodie, ut dignus es, siliter-
Æschinus odiosè cessat: prandium corrumpitur:
Ctesipho autem in amore est totus. ego jam prospiciam
    mihi.                                                      50
Nam jam adibo, atque unum quidquid, quod quidem
    erit bellissimum,
Carpam, & cyathos sorbillans paulatim hunc producam
    diem.

*SY. Dedit lectulos faciundos iligxis pedibus, ponendos in sole. DE. Ubi vos ponetis? bene sanè. Sed cesso pergere ad eum? SY. I sanè, ego exercebo te benè, siliternium, ut es dignus. Æschinus cessat odiosè: prandium corrumpitur: Ctesipho autem est totus in amore. Ego*

*jam prospiciam mihi. Nam jam adibo, atque carpam unum quidquid, quod erit quidem bel-
lissimum, & sorbillans cyathos paulatim producam hunc diem.*

## ANNOTATIONS.

49. *Prandium corrumpitur.* The *Greeks* and *Romans* generally made but one Meal in a Day, which was Supper; the Dinner here spoken of, is for two debauched young Sparks, who confin'd themselves to no Rules. Hence, in the last Scene of this Play, *Demea,* among other ironical Commendations of *Syrus,* mentions his preparing a Repast, while it was yet early in the Day. *Apparare de die convivium;* where we are to observe, that the Words *de die,* make the chief Beauty of the Irony.

52 *Hunc producam diem.* Both *Donatus* and *Madam Dacier* take *producere* as a metaphorical Term borrowed from the Language of Funerals, and think it of the same import as *condere diem, condere soles.* But this certainly can't be *Syrus*'s meaning here, as may be made evident from his own Words: For first he says, *Cyathos sorbillans,* which is a going on leisurely, to take in the whole Relish of the Pleasure, and lengthen it out as much as possible; besides the word *paulatim* is of itself sufficient to ascertain the proper Sense of *producam diem* in this place, which can signify no other than, *I will make this Day a long one.* Thus, *Mart.* II. 89. 1.

*Quod nimio gaudes noctem producere vino;
Ignosco.*

---

# ACTUS IV. SCENA III.

## ARGUMENTUM.

*Rogat Micionem Hegio, ut Sostratam adeat, narraturus illi suspicionem alienati à Pamphila Æschini, ortam esse propter ereptam Ctesiphoni psaltriam.*

### MICIO, HEGIO.

EGO in hac re nihil reperio, quamobrem lauder,
    tantopere, Hegio.                    [est, corrigo.
Meum officium facio: quod peccatum à nobis ortum
Nisi si me in illo credidisti esse hominum numero, qu[i
    ita putant

*est ortum à nobis; nisi si credidisti me esse in illo numero hominum, qui ita putant*

*ORDO.*
*MI. EGO[He]gio, reperio nihil in hac re, quamobrem lauder tantopere. Facio meum officium: corrigo peccatum quod ... putant*

## ANNOTATIONS.

as it throws great Light upon the Characters, and comes nearer to the Standard of Nature.

3 *Qui ita putant,* &c. Commentators have been greatly perplexed to unravel the Construction of this Passage, which is very obscure. *Stephens,* in his elegant Edition of
    1540,

they themselves have done, and who are always the first to accuse.
Do you now thank me because I have not acted in this manner?

*Heg.* Ah! not in the least; I never believed you to be other than
what I now find you; but I beg, *Micio,* that you will go with me
to the Virgin's Mother, and tell her yourself what you have now
told me; that this Suspicion is on his Brother's account, and that
the Musick-girl was for him.

*Mic.* If you think I ought, or that it is necessary to do it, let
us go.

*Heg.* 'Tis mighty good in you; for it will greatly relieve her
Mind, that now languishes in Misery and Distress, and you will
have acquitted yourself of your Duty: but if you had rather not,
I'll tell her myself, what you have said.

*Mic.* Nay. I'll go myself.

*Heg.* You do well: People in Circumstances of Distress are always, I know not how, more apt to be suspicious: They construe
every thing into an Affront, and fancy themselves flighted because
of their Poverty: 'Twill be therefore more satisfying, if you justify
him to them yourself.

*Mic.* You say right, and what is perfectly just.

*Heg.* Follow me therefore in.

*Mic.* I do.

### ANNOTATIONS.

1540, in the smallest Character, prints it
thus:

> *Qui itam putant,*
> *Sibi fieri injuriam, ultro si quam fecere ipsi,*
> *expostulant,*
> *Et ultro accusant.*

According to which, the Construction may
run thus: *Qui putant injuriam fieri sibi; si
aliqui expostulant eam injuriam, quam ipsi ultro
fecero, & ultro accusant.* Some Criticks contend earnestly for *expostules. Legendum est,*
says *Faërnus, ex libro Bembino* expostules, *et
sensus est,* de facta ab eis tibi injuria, etiam
insuper te accusant.

*Propter suam impotentiam se semper cre-
dunt negligi.* There are two Things remarkable in this Verse; first, that *impotentia* is
used instead of *paupertas,* or *inopia.* The Reason is evident, because in Poverty People are
generally of little Account and Consideration.
*Cicero* gives us an Example of it in this
sense, *pro Mur.* 28. *Valeant hæc omnia ad
salutem innocentium, ad opem impotentium, ad
auxilium calamitosorum.* Another Thing to
be observed here is, the strong Opposition
that *negligi* meets with from *Faërnus,* who is
for substituting in place of it *calvier,* the
Infinitive of the Verb *calvor,* a Word very
much in use in the Times of *Scipio* and *Lælius,*
and which he proves by a Variety of Quotations, to have been often used passively, and of
the same Import, with *decipi, frustrari.* The
reason

A C T

Sibi fieri injuriam, ultrò fi, quam facere ipfi, expoftulant;
Et ultro accufant. id quia non eft à me factum, agi'
   gratias?                           5
HE. Ah, minimè: nunquam te aliter, atque es, in
   animum induxi meum.              [Micio;
Sed quæfo, ut unà mecum ad matrem virginis eas,
Atque iftæc eadem, quæ mihi dixti, tute dicas mulieri;
Sufpicionem hanc propter fratrem ejus effe & illam
   pfaltriam.
MI. Si ita æquum cenfes, aut fi ita opus eft facto, ea-
   mus. HE. bene facis:                 10
Nam & illi animum jam rellevabis, quæ dolore ac
   miferià                           [putas,
Tabefcit; & tuo officio fueris functus. fed fi aliter
Egomet narrabo quæ mihi dixti. MI. imo ego ibo.
   HE. bene facis.             [nefcio quo modo
Omnes, quibu' res funt minu' fecundæ, magi' funt
Sufpiciofi: ad contumeliam omnia accipiunt magis: 15
Propter fuam impotentiam, fe femper credunt negligi.
Quapropter teipfum purgare ipfi coràm, placibilius eft.
MI. Et rectè, & verum dicis. HE. fequere me ergo
   hac intrò. MI. maxumè.

injuriam fieri fibi, fi aliqui expeftulant eam injuriam, quam ipfi ultro fecere; et ultro accufant. Agis gratias quia id non eft factum à me? HE. Ab! minimè; nunquam induxi in animum meum credere te effe aliter atque es; fed quæfo, Micio, ut eas una mecum ad matrem virginis, atque ut tute dicas muliere eadem iftæc dixifti mibi; viz. hanc fufpicionem effe propter fratrem ejus, et illam pfaltriam. MI. Si cenfes ita effe æquum, aut fi opus eft facto ita, eamus. HE. Facis bene: nam et jam relevabis animum illi, quæ tabefcit dolore ac miferia; et fueris functus tuo officio. Sed fi putas aliter, egomet narrabo quæ dixifti mibi. MI. Imo ego ibo. HE. Facis bene: Omnes, quibus res funt minus fecundæ, funt, nefcio quo modo magis fufpiciofi: magis accipiunt omnia ad contumeliam: femper credunt fe negligi, propter fuam impotentiam. Quapropter eft placibilius te purgare ipfum ipfi, coram. MI. Dicis et rectè, et verum. HE. Ergo fequere me intro hac via. MI. Maximè.

## ANNOTATIONS.

reafon of all this is, becaufe he thinks this
Word of greater Force, and more fuited to
the Poet's Defign than *negligi*. It likewife
better expreffes the Senfe of the original
Lines of *Menander*, whence thefe are taken.
But if we confider that *negligi* is the Reading
almoft univerfally found, and that it fignifies not only *bare Neglect*, but fometimes too
implies *Contempt and Scorn*, there will appear lefs Neceffity for receding from the
common reading.

[17] *Quapropter teipfum purgare ipfi, coram, placibilius eft.* Thefe Words, which appear at firft fomewhat intricate, may be thus construed: *Quapropter placibilius eft, te Micionem purgare ipfum Æfchinum, ipfis matri et virgini; coram,* id eft, te præfentem, & coram præfentibus, as *Donatus* explains it. *Placibilius,* h. e. ad placandum aptius.

## ACT IV. SCENE IV.

### ARGUMENT.

*Æschinus is greatly perplexed for the Suspicion he had fallen into with Sostrata and Pamphila, as if he was himself in love with this Music-girl, whom he had carried off, not on his own account, but to oblige his Brother.*

### ÆSCHINUS.

I Am perfectly on the Rack: This cruel Misfortune, to come so unexpectedly upon me, that I neither know what to do with myself, nor how to behave: Fear enfeebles my Limbs; my Mind is stupid through Surprize; my Breast is incapable of Counsel. Ah! How shall I free myself from this Perplexity? The Suspicion against me is so strong, and seemingly but too well grounded. Sostrata believes I have bought this Musick-girl for myself: So much I learned from old Nurse; for as she was going to call the Midwife, happening to see her, I immediately went up to her. How is Pamphila, said I? Is she in labour? Are you going for the Midwife? Away, away, Æschinus, cries she, you have deceived us long enough; you have enough amused us with your fine Promises. Hah! what's the meaning of this, said I? Farewel, says she, enjoy her that pleases you so much better. I was aware immediately of what they suspected; however, I check'd myself, nor would discover any thing relating to my Brother to that prating old Woman, lest it might by this means be divulg'd. But what shall I do now? Shall I tell them that this Girl was for my Brother? The Thing in the world that requires the greatest Secrecy. Well, let that pass; 'tis possible it might never go any farther. I doubt whether they will even believe
it,

### ANNOTATIONS.

We here find Æschinus represented in a very different Light from what he has appeared in, in former Scenes. There he is a Town-Rake, and engaged in some of the Exploits so usual to young Gentlemen of that Stamp; but here he is a Lover, full of Tenderness, and conscious of all the Anxieties, Fears and Emotions, that are so apt to thrust themselves in, where this Passion prevails. There is nothing more instructing than this Diversity of Character in the same Person, when justly represented, as it serves more immediately to guide us through all the Mazes and Windings of the human Heart, and shew the different Shapes Men are apt to appear in, according to the several Passions they are actuated by, and their different Degrees of Prevalence. For Æschinus, when he carries off the Musick-girl from *Sannio*, affects a haughty Disdain, as he knew the only way to bring him to Terms was by Brow-beating, and daunting him. But here his Heart is laid open, and he appears not in a counterfeit Light, as formerly, but in his native Colours. He had learn'd from the Nurse, whom he accidentally met as she was going for the Midwife, the Suspicion he lay under to *Sostrata*, and the Grounds of it. This perplexes him extremely. He is anxious to make them easy, and vindicate himself, but is at a loss how to do it. To inform them of the whole matter as it really was, would expose his Brother, whose Story he was unwilling to let be known to any: nay, and should he even do this, confiding in their Discretion and Prudence, yet there were so many probable Circumstances against him, that it was doubtful how far they would believe him. He therefore determines to rouze effectually, acquaint his Father with the Situation he was in, and beg *Pamphila* in Marriage; for by this so evident a Proof of his

## ACTUS IV. SCENA IV.

### ARGUMENTUM.

*Dolet vehementer Æschinus in suspicionem se venisse apud Sostratam et Pamphilam, quod amare psaltriam cœperit; quam non sibi, sed fratri ut gratum faceret, ab lenone eripuerat.*

### ÆSCHINUS.

<table>
<tr><td>

Discrucior animi. hoccine de improviso mali mihi objici<br>
           [certum fiet?<br>
Tantum, ut neque quid me faciam, nec quid agam,<br>
Membra metu debilia sunt: animus timore obstupuit:<br>
Pectore consistere nihil consilii quit. vah,<br>
Quomodo me ex hac expediam turbâ?      5<br>
Tanta nunc suspicio de me incidit. neque ea immeritò.<br>
Sostrata credit mihi me psaltriam hanc emisse: id anus<br>
Mihi indicium fecit.<br>
Nam ut hinc fortè ea ad obstetricem erat missa, ubi<br>
    vidi eam, illico<br>
Accedo, rogito, Pamphila quid agat, jam partus adsiet;<br>
Eóne obstetricem accersat, illa exclamat, Abi, abi jam,<br>
    Æschine:          10<br>
Satis diu dedisti verba, sat adhuc tua nos frustrata est<br>
    fides.      [beas illam quæ placet.<br>
Hem, quid istuc obsecro, inquam, est? Valeas, ha-<br>
Sensi illicè id illas suspicari: sed me reprehendi tamen,<br>
Ne quid de fratre garrulæ illi dicerem, ac fieret palàm.<br>
Nunc quid faciam? dicam fratris esse hanc? quod minimè est opus        15<br>
Usquam efferri. age, mitto: fieri potis est, ut nequà exeat.

</td><td>

**ORDO.**

Æs. Discrucior animi: hoccine tantum mali objici mihi de improviso, ut sit certum, neque quid faciam de me; nec quid agam? Membra sunt debilia metu: animus obstupuit timore: nihil consilii quit consistere in pectore. Vah, quomodo expediam me ex hac turba? tanta suspicio nunc incidit de me, neque ea est immeritò. Sostrata credit, me emisse hanc psaltriam mihi: anus fecit id indicium mihi: nam ut forte eà erat missa hinc ad obstetricem, ubi vidi eam, illico accedo, rogito, quid Pamphila agat, an partus jam adsit; accersatne

</td></tr>
</table>

*obstetricem eo. Illa exclamat, Abi, abi, Æschine; jam dedisti verba nobis satis diu: adhuc tua fides sat frustrata est nos. Hem, inquam, quid obsecro est istuc? Valeas, habeas illam quæ placet tibi. Sensi illico illas suspicari id: sed tamen reprehendi me, ne dicerem quid de fratre illa garrulæ, ac res fieret palam. Nunc quid faciam? Dicam hanc esse amicam fratris? Quod est minimè opus efferri usquam. Age, mitto: est potis fieri ut ne exeat que.*

### ANNOTATIONS.

Sincerity, he knew he should remove all their Scruples at once, and moreover, compleat his own Wishes.

*13 Sed me reprehendi tamen.* Æschinus here gives a very great Proof of his Discretion. When any thing alarms us suddenly, or we see ourselves injur'd in the Opinion of one we have a Value for, it is the hardest matter in the World to check the Impatience we feel of being justified: nor are we apt in such a Case to regard the Consequences. But Æschinus, however anxious he was to remove his *Pamphila*'s Suspicions, is yet too discreet, to do it at the hazard of his Brother's

Repose. He knew the Genius of old Women, fond of Tattle, and eager to communicate every little Story they heard, to their Gossips. This, which is but too much their Character, was still more to be apprehended in *Canthara*, who was a Nurse, a Creature of all others the most given to prating; hence his own Remark upon her: *Sed me reprehendi tamen, ne quid de fratre garrulæ illi dicerem, ac fieret palam.*

*16 Age, mitto: fieri potis est, &c.* These Words have occasioned some Disputes among Commentators, each wresting them his own way, without regarding their Connexion
with

it, so many probable Circumstances are against me. I myself carried her off : I told down the Money : She was brought home to me. I am very much in fault here : Ought I not to have acquainted my Father with what had happened ? I might have obtain'd his Consent to marry her. I have been too negligent hitherto ; now, Æschinus, it is time to rouze. The first Thing is to go and clear myself to them. I'll to the Door : Death ! I always fall a trembling, when I advance to knock at these Doors. Soho ! 'Tis Æschinus : Somebody open the Door quickly. Who can this be coming out ? I'll retire hither.

### ANNOTATIONS.

with the other Parts of Aeschinus's Speech, which might have easily led them into their genuine Sense. He would say nothing of his Brother's Affair to the Nurse, as knowing her prating Humour, and that it would be soon spread all over the Town. But now that she is gone, he is considering in his own Mind how he shall clear himself to Pamphila and her Mother. Shall I, says he, tell them that this Wench was for my Brother ? a

Story that I am very unwilling should take air. However (continues he) I dismiss that Fear ; 'tis possible, for their own sakes, they may be discreet enough to keep it secret. But I doubt whether they will believe me : there are so many Circumstances that make it likely the Girl was for myself, that my telling them she was for my Brother, may appear a meer temporary Shift. Had Westerhovius attended to this natural, and easy Connexion,

---

# ACT IV. SCENE V.

## ARGUMENT.

Micio, *by an ingenious Fiction, alarms Æschinus, pretending that* Pamphila *would be obliged to wed another. At last, easing his Fears, and growing serious with him, he fills him with Joy, by promising his Consent to the Marriage.*

MICIO, ÆSCHINUS.

*Micio.* DO as I told you, *Sostrata* ; I'll go meet *Æschinus*, that he may know from me how Matters are. But who was this knocked at the Door ?

*Æsc.* Death ! It is my Father. I'm undone.

*Mic.* Æschinus.

*Æsc.* What Business can he have here ?

*Mic.* Was it you that knock'd at this Door ? He's silent. Why shouldn't I play upon him a little ? 'Twill be better, because he never trusted me with this Secret. Do you answer me nothing ?

*Æsc.* I don't know that I knock'd.

*Micio.*

### ANNOTATIONS.

We have seen before, that *Micio* had gone along with *Hegio* to *Sostrata*, to remove her Suspicions with regard to *Æschinus*, and at the same time make her sensible that she had nothing to apprehend from him ; who would

be so far from opposing the Marriage, that he would further it all in his power. Meantime, *Æschinus*, informed of *Sostrata's* Suspicions, is hastening to justify himself, and knocks at the Door just as his Father is coming out.

It

Ipfum id metuo ut credant: tot concurrunt verifimilia : | *Metuo ut credant id*
Egomet rapui : ipfe egomet folvi argentum : ad me | *ipfum : tot verifimi-*
   abducta eft domum. | *lia concurrunt. Ego-*
Hæc adeo meâ culpâ fateor fieri, non me hanc rem | *met rapui : ipfe ego-*
   patri,                                                      19 | *met folvi argentum :*
Ut ut erat gefta, indicaffe ? exoraffem, ut eam ducerem. | *abducta eft domum ad*
Ceffatum ufque adhuc eft : nunc porro, Æfchine, ex- | *me : adeo fateor hæc*
   pergifcere.                      [accedam ad fores. | *fieri mea culpa. An*
Nunc hoc primum eft : ad illas ibo, ut purgem me. | *non oportuit me in-*
Perii, horrefco femper, ubi pultare hafce occipio fores | *dicaffe hanc rem pa-*
   mifer.                                [tum oftium. | *tri, ut ut eras gefta?*
Heus, heus: Æfchinus ego fum : aperite aliquis actu- | *Exoraffem, ut duce-*
Prodit nefcio quis. concedam huc.                      25 | *rem eam. Eft ceffatum*

*ut purgem me. Accedam ad fores. Perii mifer : femper horrefco, ubi occipio pultare hafce fores. Heus, heus: ego fum Æfchinus : aperite aliquis oftium actutum : nefcio quis prodit : concedam huc.*

## ANNOTATIONS.

he might have fpared his Conjecture of *mu-tio* for *mitto*; a Reading which, if received, would only ferve to involve the Text in ftill greater Obfcurity.

21 *Expergifcere.* He means, that he muft now rouze from a State of Indolence and Sloth, for fo the Word is often ufed, where an Exertion of Vigour and Induftry is intend-ed. *Saluft. Catil.* 20. Quin igitur *expergif-cimini*: And 52. *Expergifcimini* aliquando et capeffite rempublicam.

24 *Aperite aliquis oftium.* *Aliquis* is here a Partitive, that is, a Word fignifying ma-ny feverally, or one by one : Hence, though it is here in the fingular Number, it has all the force of the plural ; *aperite aliquis.*

---

# ACTUS IV. SCENA V.

### ARGUMENTUM.

*Mire faceto commento pater Æfchino novum incutit metum; oftendens alii viro nupturam Pamphilam. Tandem, amoto ludo, agere ferio incipiens, filii animum gaudeo explet, futurum promittens, ut illam ipfe ducat uxorem.*

### MICIO, ÆSCHINUS.

ITA, ut dixi, Softrata,      [do acta hæc funt, fciat. | ORDO.
  Facite: ego Æfchinum conveniam, ut, quo mo- | Mi. **F**Acite ita,
Sed quis oftium hoc pultavit? Æs. pater hercle eft : |    ut dixi,
   perii. Mi. Æfchine.                    [fores? tacet. | *Softrata : ego conve-*
Æs. Quid huic hîc negotî eft? Mi. tune has pepulifti | *niam Æfchinum, ut*
Cur non ludo hunc aliquantifper? melius eft :      5 | *fciat quomodo hæc*
Quandoquidem hoc nunquam mihi ipfe voluit credere. | *funt acta. Sed quis*
Nil mihi refpondes? Æs. non quidem iftas quod fciam. | *pultavit hoc oftium?*

*Tune pepulifti has fores? Tacet. Cur non ludo hunc aliquantifper? Eft melius : quandoquidem ipfe nunquam voluit credere hoc mihi. Refpondes nil mihi? Æs. Equidem non pepuli iftas quod fciam.*

## ANNOTATIONS.

It is eafy to conceive how much he would be furprifed to fee him there, and accordingly he, with fome Earneftnefs, afks the reafon of it : *Micio* finding every thing to be as he would have it ; and ftill retaining his ufual Good-Humour, refolves to divert himfelf a little at his Son's Expence, out of revenge, becaufe he all along had conceal'd this his Engagement with *Pamphila* from him. Ac-cordingly he ingenioufly feigns a Story to

*Mic.* So I thought: for I wonder'd what Bufinefs you could have here. He blufhes: All's well.

*Æfc.* But do, Father, tell me: What was it brought you here?

*Mic.* Nothing relating to myfelf. A Friend juft now brought me higher with him from the Forum, to affift him in an Affair.

*Æfc.* What!

*Mic.* I'll tell you. There are fome poor Women that live here. I fuppofe you know nothing of them; nay, and I'm perfectly fure of it, for they are but lately come.

*Æfc.* Well, and what elfe?

*Mic.* A young Woman with her Mother.

*Æfc.* Go on.

*Mic.* The young Woman has loft her Father; this Friend of mine it feems is her neareft Relation, and the Laws oblige her to marry him.

*Æfc.* Undone!

*Mic.* What's the matter?

*Æfc.* Nothing: very well; proceed.

*Mic.* He's come to take her with him, for he lives at *Miletus*.

*Æfc.* How! To take the young Woman with him?

*Mic.* Yes.

*Æfc.* What, to *Miletus*, pray?

*Mic.* Ay.

*Æfc.* It wounds me to the Soul. Well, but as to them: What do they fay?

*Mic.* What do you think they fhould? Juft nothing: The Mother indeed pretends that there is a Child by another Man; I can't tell who, nor does fhe name him. He is the firft, they fay, and therefore this other ought not to have her.

*Æfc.* Well, and did you not think thefe Reafons fufficient?

*Mic.* No.

*Æfc.* Blefs me! no. Shall he carry here hence, Father?

*Mic.* Why fhould he not?

*Æfc.* 'Tis very hard and cruel in you; and if I may fpeak my Mind plainly, Father, unhandfome.

*Mic.* Why fo?

*Æfc.* Why fo? What do you think muft be the Condition of the unhappy Youth her firft Lover, who perhaps is ftill as fond of her as ever, when he fhall fee her thus hurried away, and torn from his Sight for ever? 'Tis really an unworthy Action, Father.

*Mic.*

### ANNOTATIONS.

alarm him, and with the defired Effect. But unwilling to torment him too much, at laft undeceives him, and at the fame time fills him with Joy, by promifing his Confent to the Marriage.

9 *Erubuit: falva res eft.* In *Micio*'s Character we fee a ftrong Difpofition to Generofity and Juftice. He was inclin'd from the very firft to make Reparation to the unfor-

tunate young Girl for the Injury that had been done her; and appears here anxious to have his Son of the fame mind. He therefore watches his Looks, and finding them promifing, is highly pleafed. *Erubuit: falva res eft.* Reafons of Advantage or Convenience are not fufficient to blot out his Regard for Honour and Juftice. He is more delighted to fee his Son humane and gene-

MI. Ita? nam mirabar quid hîc negoti esset tibi.
Erubuit: salva res est. Æs. dic sodes, pater,
Tibi vero quid istic est rei? MI. nihil mihi quidem. 10
Amicus quidam me à foro abduxit modò
Huc advocatum sibi. Æs. quid? MI. ego dicam tibi.
Habitant hîc quædam mulieres pauperculæ:
Ut opinor. has non nosse te, & certò scio:
Neque enîm diu huc commigrarunt. Æs. quid tum
    postea? 15
MI. Virgo est cum matre. Æs. perge. MI. hæc vir-
    go orba est patre:
Hic meus amicus illi genere est proxumus:
Huic leges cogunt nubere hanc. Æs. perii. MI. quid est?
Æs. Nil: rectè: perge. MI. is venit, ut secum avehat:
Nam habitat Mileti. Æs. hem, virginem ut secum
    avehat? 20
MI. Sic est. Æs. Miletum usque, obsecro? MI. ita.
    Æs. animo male est. [enim.
Quid ipsæ? quid aiunt? MI. quid illas censes? nihil
Commenta mater est, esse ex alio viro
Nescio quo puerum natum, neque eum nominat:
Priorem esse illum, non oportere huic dari. 25
Æs. Eho, nonne hæc justa tibi videntur postea?
MI. Non. Æs. obsecro, non? an illam hinc abducet,
    pater?
MI. Quid illam ni abducat? Æs. factum à vobis duriter,
Immisericorditerque, atque etiam, si est, pater,
Dicendum magis apertè, inliberaliter. 30
MI. Quamobrem? Æs. rogas me? quid illi tandem
    creditis
Fore animi misero, qui illi consuevit prior,
Qui infelix, haud scio, an illam miserè nunc amat,
Cùm hanc sibi videbit præsens præsenti eripi,
Abduci ab oculis? facinus indignum, pater! 35

*MI. Ita? Nam mirabar quid negoti esset tibi hic. Erubuit: res est salva. Æs. Pater, die sodes, quid rei vero est tibi istic? MI. Quidem nihil mihi. Amicus quidam modo abduxit me advocatum sibi huc, à foro. Æs. Ob quid? MI. Ego dicam tibi. Quædam paupercula mulieres habitant hic. Ut opinor, et scio certo, te non nosse has: neque enim commigrarunt huc diu. Æs. Quid tum postea? MI. Est virgo cum matre. Aes. Perge. MI. Hæc virgo est orba patre: hic meus amicus est proximus genere illi: Leges cogunt hanc nubere huic, Aes. Perii. MI. Quid est? Aes. Nil: recte: perge. MI. Is venit ut avehat eam secum: nam, habitat Mileti. Aes. Hem, an venit ut avehat virginem secum? MI. Est sic. Aes. Obsecro ut avehat eam usque Miletum? MI. Ita. Aes. Est male animo meo. Quid ipsæ? Quid aiunt?*

*MI. Quid censes illas dicere? enim nihil. Mater commenta est, puerum esse natum ex nescio quo alio viro, neque nominat eum: illum esse priorem, non oportere eam dari huic. Aes. Eho, nonne hæc videntur justa tibi postea? MI. Non. Aes. Obsecro, non? An abducet illam hinc, pater? MI. Quid ni abducat illam? Aes. Factum est duriter à vobis, immisericorditerque, atque etiam, pater, si est dicendum magis aperte, illiberaliter. MI. Quamobrem! Aes. Rogas me? Quid animi tandem creditis fore illi misero, qui prior consuevit illi, qui infelix, haud scio, an nunc amat illam misere, cum præsens videbit hanc eripi sibi præsenti, et abduci ab oculis? Est indignum facinus, pater.*

## ANNOTATIONS.

rous, ready to make satisfaction for what he had done in the Heat of Passion, than hunting after a Match that might ennoble or enrich him.

18 *Huic leges cogunt nubere hanc.* There is frequent mention of this Law at *Athens*, in the Writings of the Ancients. *Orbam proximus ducat, lex Attica est.* It is remarkable that this same Law was established by *Moses* among the *Jews. Numb.* xxxvi. 6. *Omnis filia, quæ succedit in hæreditatem, in familia quacumque Israelitarum; alicui qui sit originis familiæ ejusdem paternæ uxor erit. Grotius,* upon the Place, conjectures that this Law was first borrowed from the *Hebrews* by the *Phœnicians*, and from them transmitted, to the *Athenians. Dacier.*

23 *Factum à vobis duriter, immisericorditerque,*

*Mic.* Why so ? Who contracted her ? Who gave her away ? When, and to whom was she married ? Who was the Manager of this Affair ? Why did he espouse another's Right ?

*Æsc.* Was it for a Girl of her Age to sit at home, waiting till her Kinsman should come from such a Distance ? You ought to have represented this, Father, and urg'd it.

*Mic.* Ridiculous ! Was I to plead against the Man whom I came to befriend ? But what's all this to us, *Æschinus* ? Or, what Business have we with them ? Let us go. What's the matter ? Why those Tears ?

*Æsc.* Father, I beg you'll hear me ?

*Mic. Æschinus,* I have heard, and know all already : for I love you ; for which Reason, every Thing you do concerns me nearly.

*Æsc.* Dear Father, so may you, as long as you live, find me deserving of your Love, as I am sincerely sorry for this Fault I have committed, and ashamed to see you.

*Mic.* I believe it sincerely ; for I know your generous Temper : But I doubt you are too negligent. In what City pray do you think you live ? You have debauc'd a Virgin, whom the Laws forbid you to touch. This is a great Fault, a very great one, tho' but too common : Others have often done it before you, and even Men of Worth too. But after this happened, tell me what Circumspection have you shewn ? Or did you consider with yourself what was to be done, and in what manner ? If you was ashamed to tell it me yourself, might you not have contrived some other means to let me know

of



*terque,* &c. Although *Æschinus* here keeps upon the Reserve, as not designing at present to acquaint his Father with his Passion, yet the Poet takes care not to lose sight of the Lover. *Æschinus* here affects to plead for another, yet it is easy to discern, that his own Interest is concern'd. He expresses himself with so much Warmth and Earnestness, and the Words are so particularly adapted to his inward Feelings, that, had *Micio* known nothing of it before, he might easily have guessed now how the Case stood.

36 *Quis despondit ? Quis dedit ? Cui ? quando nupsit ? Micio* repeats here, in a few Words, the Conditions requisite to render a Marriage valid, and with the more Assurance, as he knew *Æschinus* could give no consistent Answer. He had been guilty of a Rape, the Business had been all along kept private, none of the usual Ceremonies observed, no Relation on either side made acquainted with it. Instead of *Cui ? quando nupsit ?* Some read *qui, quando nupsit ?* But the usual reading rather answers better. *Quis despondit ? Quis dedit ? Cui data est ? Quando nupsit ?*

39 *An sedere oportuit domi virginem tam grandem ? Grandem* here respects her Age ; full grown, ripe for a Husband.

45 *Æschine, audivi omnia. Micio* still preserves the Character of an indulgent Father, he had tormented *Æschinus* enough, and was unwilling to overwhelm him still more with the Pain of a Confession. *Virg. Æneid.* I. 389.

- - - *Nec plura querentem,*

*Passa Venus, medio sic interfata dolore est.*

" Bene ergo (*says* Donatus) intelligunt, " qui sic accipiunt, perrecturum adhuc fuisse " Micionem, nisi victus affectu, fallaciam " projecisset."

47 *Ita velim me promerentem ames.* There is a great Beauty in this Answer. *Æschinus* is not contented with saying *ita velim ames me,* but he adds *promerentem,* signifying that he wish'd to be lov'd by him, and to deserve that Love. Perhaps his Father's Partiality was such, as might overlook very considerable Faults in him ; but *Æschinus* cannot be satisfied with a random Affection ; he would have his Father therefore to love him ; because he merited it.

MI. Quâ ratione istuc? quis despondit? quis dedit?
Cui, quando nupsit? auctor his rebus quis est?
Cur duxit alienam? Æs. An sedere oportuit
Domi virginem tam grandem, dum cognatus huc
Illinc veniret, exspectantem? hæc, mi pater,     40
Te dicere æquom fuit, & id defendere.
MI. Ridiculum! advorsumne illum causam dicerem,
Cui veneram advocatus? sed quid illa, Æschine,
Nostra? aut quid nobis cum illis? abeamus; quid est?
Quid lacrumas? Æs. pater, obsecro, ausculta.  MI.
   Æschine, audivi omnia,                         45
Et scio: nam te amo: quo magis, quæ agis, curæ
   sunt mihi.                                 [pater,
Æs. Ita velim me promerentem ames, dum vivas, mi
Ut me hoc delictum admisisse in me, id mihi vehe-
   menter dolet;                              [ovi tuum
Et me tui pudet. MI. credo hercle: nam ingenium
Liberale: sed vereor ne indiligens nimium sies.   50
In quâ civitate tandem te arbitrare vivere?
Virginem vitiasti, quam te jus non fuerat tangere.
Jam id peccatum primum magnum, magnum, at hu-
   manum tamen.                              [cedo,
Fecere alii sæpe, item boni, at postquam id evenit,
Numquid circumspexti? aut numquid tute prospexti
   tibi,                                          55
Quid fieret, quâ fieret? si teipsum mihi puduit dicere;

*me admisisse hoc delictum in me, et pudet me tui. MI. Hercle credo: nam novi tuum ingenium liberale: sed vereor ne sis nimium indiligens. Nam qua tandem civitate arbitrare te vivere? Vitiasti virginem, quam non fuerat jus te tangere. Jam primum id est magnum peccatum, magnum inquam, at tamen humanum. Alii, item boni, fecere sæpe. At postquam id evenit, cedo, numquid circumspexisti? aut numquid tute prospexisti tibi, quid fieret, qua fieret? si puduit teipsum dicere id mihi.*

Right-margin paraphrase:

*MI. Qua ratione dicis istuc? Quis despondit eam? Quis dedit? Cui, quando, nupsit? Quis est auctor his rebus? Cur duxit alienam? Æs. An oportuit virginem tam grandem sedere domi, expectantem dum cognatus veniret illinc huc? Mi pater, æquum fuit te dicere hæc, et defendere id. MI. Ridiculum! dicerem ne causam adversum illum, cui veneram advocatus? Sed quid ista nostra, Æschine? Aut quid nobis cum illis? Abeamus. Quid est? Quid lacrumas? Æs. Pater, obsecro, ausculta. MI. Æschine, audivi omnia, et scio: nam amo te, quo magis quæ agis sunt curæ mihi. Æs. Mi pater, velim ita ames me promerentem, dum vivas, ut id vehementer dolet mihi,*

## ANNOTATIONS.

50 *Ne indiligens nimium sies.* It is a wondrous Instance of Clemency In the Father to forgive so frankly the Offence, and even when he mentions it, to speak of it in Terms that are equivalent to an Apology. The whole Strain of his Reproof here is conceived in Terms of so much Mildness, that he rather seems to be excusing him to himself. In order to apprehend better the Force and Energy of this, we must suppose, that *Æschinus* discovers great Confusion in his Looks, as if, from a Consciousness of his Fault, ashamed to be seen by his Father. *Micio* sensible of this, and unwilling to put him to too much Pain, puts on a soft forgiving Air, to assure and encourage him. And the Poet has contrived to make this more powerful to correct the Youth, than all the Methods of Harshness and Severity could probably have been.

51 *In qua civitate.* *Micio* begins his Reproof in a very grave and solemn Tone. Have you forgot that you live at *Athens*, a City where such a strict Obedience is requir'd to the Laws? But he soon changes his Note, and instead of exaggerating his Son's Offence, endeavours to excuse and soften it. *Jam id peccatum magnum; magnum, at humanum tamen: fecere alii sæpe, item boni.*

54 *Ad postquam id evenit.* Criticks observe on this Reproof of *Micio,* that he makes choice of Terms peculiarly mild. Thus here he does not say, *postquam id commissum est,* but *postquam id evenit,* an Expression of abundant less Asperity. The first represents a Thing, criminal, and done in consequence of a Design laid and concerted before-hand; the other looks more like the Effect of Chance, Surprize, or some sudden Start of Passion.

of it? In this Uncertainty ten Months have been loft. You have gone near to undo yourfelf, the poor Girl, and your Son. What! Did you imagine the Gods would accomplifh thefe Things for you, without any Care of your own, and miraculoufly convey her into your Bed-chamber? I fhould be forry to find you equally negligent, in other Affairs. However, chear up, you fhall marry her.

*Æfc.* Hah!

*Mic.* Chear up, I fay.

*Æfc.* Pray, Father, do you banter me now?

*Mic.* I banter you! Why?

*Æfc.* I don't know: but that the more paffionate I am to have it fo, the greater is my Anxiety left it fhould not.

*Mic.* Go home, and pray to the Gods, that you may have your Wife: go.

*Æfc.* What, have her now?

*Mic.* Now.

*Æfc.* Now!

*Mic.* Now: as foon as poffible.

*Æfc.* May all the Gods hate me, Father, if I don't love you better than my very Eyes.

*Mic.* What! than her too?

*Æfc.* As well.

*Mic.* That's faying a great deal.

*Æfc.* But what's become of the *Milefian?*

*Mic.* He's gone, he's embark'd; he's quite vanifhed before now. But why do you linger?

*Æfc.* Nay, Father, do you rather go and pray to the Gods; for I know they will regard you more, as you're fo much the better Man.

*Mic.* I am going in, that every thing may be in readinefs; do you as I faid, if you're wife.

*Æfc.* What can one think here? Is this being a Father? Or this. being a Son? Had he been my Brother or Companion, how could he have been more indulgent or complaifant? Ought I not to love him? to carry him in my Bofom? Indeed I am now brought under the moft powerful Engagements to beware of doing any thing inconfider-
ately,

*ANNOTATIONS.*

63 *Ego te? Quamobrem? Donatus* has a Remark upon this Paffage, too beautiful to be omitted. *Micio* anfwers his Son here, as if he were furprized how he fhould fufpect him capable of bantering him in fo ferious an Affair. This may perhaps ftartle the Reader, who will be apt to call to mind the Story of the *Milefian* he has but juft done with. The Solution given of this Difficulty by the above mentioned Critick is extremely judicious, and may be admitted as an indifputable Maxim in Morals. *Eft enim amantis,* fays he, *in falfum metum conjicere imminente lætitia, quælibet fententia: inimici vero, in falfum gaudium quemquam impellere, fub alicujus mæroris adventum.* " It is allowable " to banter a Perfon we love, by raifing falfe " Alarms, when we have it in our power to " diffipate thefe Fears in a moment, and fill " them with real Joy. But it is a deceitful " and cruel Part to fill one with imaginary " Joys, when we forefee that Sadnefs and " Sorrow are like to enfue.".

69 *Abiit, periit, navem afcendit.* Facete, *abiit:* ne diceret, mentitus fum. Atque ita dixit, ut infantibus nutrices de terriculis dicere folent: quas, cum ipfæ confinxerint, abolitas volunt, poftquam illos vident nimium pavere.

Quâ resciscerem? hæc dum dubitas, menses abierunt
    decem.                [quidem in te fuit.
Prodidisti te, & illam miseram, & gnatum, quod
Quid? credebas dormienti hæc tibi confecturos Deos?
Et illam sine tuâ operâ in cubiculum iri deductum do-
    mum?                60
Nolim cæterarum rerum te socordem eodem modo.
Bono animos es, duces uxorem hanc. Æs. hem! Mi.
    bono animo es, inquam. Æs. pater,
Obsecro, num ludis tu nunc me? Mi. ego te? quàm-
    obrem? Æs. nescio:        [magis.
Quia tam miserè hoc esse cupio verum, ideo vereor
Mi. Abi domum, ac Deos comprecare, ut uxorem ac-
    cersas: abi.            65
Æs. Quid? jamne uxorem? Mi. jam. Æs. jam? Mi.
    jam. quantum potest. Æs. Di me, pater,
Omnes oderint, ni magi' te quàm oculos nunc ego
    amo meos.       [Æs. quid? ille ubi est Milesius?
Mi. Quid? quàm illam? Æs. æquè. Mi. perbenignè.
Mi. Abiit, periit, navem ascendit. sed cur cessas?
Æs. abi, pater:
Tu potiùs Deos comprecare: nam tibi eos certò scio 70
Quo vir melior multo es quàm ego, obtemperaturos
    magis.         [ut dixi, si sapis.
Mi. Ego eo intro, ut, quæ opu' sunt, parentur. tu fac.
Æs. Quid hoc negoti? hoc est patrem esse? aut hoc est
    filium esse?
Si frater aut sodalis esset, qui magi' morem gereret?
Hic non amandus? hiccine non gestandus in sinu est?
    hem!           75
Itaque adeo magnammi injecit suâ commoditate curam,

*ce quam mens oculos. Mi. Quid? quam amas illam? Æs. Æquè. Mi.
Quid: Ubi est ille Milesius? Mi. Abiit, periit, ascendit navem. Sed cur cessas? Æs. abi,
pater, comprecare. tu potius Deos: nam scio certo eos magis obtemperaturos tibi, quò es vir
multo melior quam ego. Mi. Ego eo intro, ut quæ opus sint, parentur; fac tu, ut dixi, si
sapis. Æs. Quid negotii est hoc? Hoc est esse patrem? Aut hoc est esse filium? Si esset
frater aut sodalis, qui magis generet morem? Hic non est amandus? Hiccine non est gestandus
in sinu? Hem! Itaque adeo injecit magnam curam mihi suâ commoditate,*

## ANNOTATIONS.

pavere. Et mihi videtur ridens hæc dixisse: ut intelligat Æschinus, Micionem joco fuisse mentitum. *Donatus.*

70 *Tu' potius deos comprecare.* It is a nice, and, for the most part, a disagreeable Task, for a Son to praise his Father to his face. *Terence* has found the Art of making *Æschinus* do it here without offending Delicacy. Religion furnishes him with the Opportunity of a Panegyrick, and in excusing himself from addressing the Gods in the present Case, he finds a natural Occasion of bestowing on his Father, in a few Words, the finest Commendation that could possibly be given him. Just in the same manner in the *Æneis*, *Æneas* says to *Anchises*, II. 717.

> *Tu, genitor, cape sacra manu, patriosque*
>     *penates.*

"Do you, Father, carry in your Hand these "sacred Symbols; and the Images of our "native Gods." He himself would carry his Father, but his Father must carry the Gods. *Donatus, Dacier.*

76 *Itaque adeo magnam mi injecit curam.* *Terence* is particularly careful to make his Readers sensible of the good Effects which

the

ly, that may give him uneasiness. But why don't I go in, that I may not myself be a hindrance to my Marriage?

### ANNOTATIONS.

the Complaisance of Fathers may produce. But we are to take notice, that he all along means a Complaisance founded in good Sense, and an exact Knowledge of the Genius and Temper of the Person to whom it is shewn: For if blind and without distinction, it may produce very mischievous Effects. This latter is far from being the Case with *Micio*, as is evident from what he says above, ver. 59. *Credo hercle, nam ingenium novi tuum liberale.* And still more apparently from what afterwards passes between him and *Demea, Act* 5. *Scene* 1.

---

## ACT IV. SCENE VI.

### ARGUMENT.

*Demea, fatigu'd with walking, complains of Syrus, that he had not distinctly enough describ'd the Place where he might find his Brother.*

### DEMEA.

I'M quite tired with walking: Almighty *Jove* confound thee *Syrus*, with that Direction of thine. I've trotted all over the Town, been at the Gate, the Pond, every where. There was no Joiner's Shop there, nor had any Soul I met seen my Brother. But now I'm resolv'd to wait for him at his own House, till he comes home.

### ANNOTATIONS.

*Demea*, after wandering over the whole Town in consequence of the wrong Direction given him by *Syrus*, returns complaining of the Fatigue he had undergone, and all to no purpose; for that neither could he find his Brother, nor meet with any one who had seen him. He therefore resolves to give over a vain Pursuit, and wait for him at his own House, till he comes home.

5 *Domi obsidere. Donatus* takes the Word *ob-*

---

## ACT IV. SCENE VII.

### ARGUMENT.

*Demea complains to Micio of the Injury done to the young Virgin by Æschinus: At first he is in a violent Passion, but by degrees is brought to a little better Temper.*

### MICIO, DEMEA.

*Micio.* I'LL go and tell them, that there is now no hindrance on our side.

*Dem.* But here he comes.——I've been looking for you this long while, *Micio. Mic.*

### ANNOTATIONS.

*Micio*, having got every thing in readiness for the intended Marriage of his Son, is going to acquaint the Bride and her Mother, when he is met by *Demea*, who had been seeking him so long. Hence a Conversation begins; at first warm and passionate on the side

Ne forte imprudens faciam, quod nolit, sciens cavebo.
Sed cesso ire intro, ne moræ meis nuptiis egomet siem?
*cesso ire, intro, ne eg omet sim moræ meis nuptiis?*

| |
|---|
| *et sciens cavebo, ne*<br>*forte imprudens fa-*<br>*ciam, quod nolit. Sed* |

### ANNOTATIONS.

1. 41. *Video sapere, intelligere, in loco ve-*
*reri, inter se amare: scire est liberum ingeni-*
*um, atque animum: quovis illos tu die reducas.*
Thus far was necessary to observe, that it
might not be thought, that the Poet encourages a Complaisance without Restriction in
Fathers. He means only to recommend it,
where it will evidently have a better Effect,
than the contrary Method of Harshness and
Severity.

# ACTUS IV. SCENA VI.

## ARGUMENTUM.

*Demea, ambulando fatigatus, de Syro queritur, quod non aperte
satis commonstravit locum, ubi frater esset Micio.*

### DEMEA.   ORDO.

DEfessus sum ambulando. ut, Syre, te cum tuâ
  Monstratione magnus perdat Jupiter. [cum,
Perreptavi usque omne oppidum, ad portam, ad la-
Quò non? nec fabrica illic ulla erat, nec fratrem homô
Vidisse se aiebat quisquam. nunc verò domi   5
Certum obsidere est usque donec redierit.

*De. SUM defess. s
ambulando,
utinam Syre, ut
magnus Jupiter per-
dat te cum tua mon-
stratione: Perrepta-
vi usque omne oppi-
dum, ad portam, ad*

*lacum, quo non? Nec ulla fabrica erat illic, nec quisquam homo aiebat se vidisse fratrem. Nunc
vero est certum me obsidere domi, usque donec redierit.*

### ANNOTATIONS.

*obsidere* here in its most general Sense, as when
it is used to signify the investing or laying
Siege to a Town. *Proprie obsidere dixit; convenit enim et irato, et repente aggressuro.* But
had the Poet intended this, he would undoubtedly have said *obsidere domum,* and not *domi. Obsidere* is no more here than *diu sedere,* just
as *Plautus, Pseud.* III. 2. 18. speaking of one
who had attended all Day at the Forum, in
hopes of being hir'd, calls him *obsessor Fori.*

# ACTUS IV. SCENA VII.

## ARGUMENTUM.

*Demea de vitio virgini oblato, et nuptiis rescicit: is fingitur jam
tumultuari, sed postea placatur.*

### MICIO, DEMEA.   ORDO.

IBO, illis dicam nullam esse in nobis moram.
  DE. Sed eccum ipsum. Te jamdudum quæro.
  Micio,

*Mi. IBO, et di-
cam illis esse
nullam moram in no-
bis. De. Sed eccum*

*ipsum. Micio, quæro te jamdudum.*

### ANNOTATIONS.

side of *Demea,* who fancying his Brother
knew nothing of the Rape *Aeschinus* had
committed, makes no doubt, but upon hearing it, he will be thoroughly provok'd, and
no less forward than he, in condemning this
licentious Youth. But *Micio,* who was appriz'd

*Mic.* What's the matter now?

*Dem.* I bring other Enormities to you, shocking ones, of that hopeful Youth.

*Mic.* Look ye there, now!

*Dem.* New, capital Offences.

*Mic.* What, at it again?

*Dem.* Ah! you little know what sort of a Man he is.

*Mic.* I do.

*Dem.* O Simpleton! thou fanciest, I warrant, that I mean the Musick-wench: no, this is a Crime against an *Athenian* Virgin.

*Mic.* I know it.

*Dem.* How! Know it, and bear with it?

*Mic.* Why shou'dn't I bear with it?

*Dem.* Tell me; don't you exclaim? Don't you rave?

*Mic.* No: I'd rather, indeed, *it had not happened,*

*Dem.* There's a Son born too.

*Mic.* Heaven bless it.

*Dem.* The Girl has nothing.

*Mic.* So I have heard.

*Dem.* And he must marry her without a Fortune.

*Mic.* No doubt of it.

*Dem.* What's to be done in this Case?

*Mic.* What the thing itself points out to us; the young Woman must be brought hither.

*Dem.* O *Jupiter!* Is that the way then?

*Mic.* What can I do else?

*Dem.* What can you do? If you are not really concern'd at this, it were decent however to seem so to be.

*Mic.* But I have already contracted them, the Business is concluded; the Marriage goes forward; I have remov'd all their Fears: this I think is more decent and becoming.

*Dem.* But are you pleas'd with this Adventure, *Micio?*

*Mic.* No, If I could help it: But now, that I can't, I bear it patiently. The Life of Man is, as when we play at Dice; if the
Throw

*ANNOTATIONS.*

prized of it before, hears him with great Calmness, which perfectly astonishes *Demea,* who therefore tries whether by Raillery he can gain any thing: but the other still continuing unmoved, and answering with his wonted Good-humour; he laments with himself the Destruction which he foresees coming upon his Brother's Family.

4 *Ecce autem.* *Ecce* dicitur, quum repente triste aliquid rebus intervenit lætis, aut certe, quum aliud agitur, aliud emergit novum: ut *Virg. Æn.* 2. 203.

*Ecce autem gemini à Tenedo tranquilla per alta.*

*Horresco referens, immensis orbibus angues.*
Et *Ibid.* 403.

*Ecce trahebatur passis Priameïa virgo Crinibus.*

Sic Cicero etiam, Verr. 5. 34.

*Ecce autem repente, ebrio Cleomene, esurientibus cæteris, nunciatur piratarum naves esse in portu Edissæ.* Donatus.

9 *Non, malim quidem.* These Words are variously descanted upon by Commentators. Some divide them, referring *malim quidem* to *Demea;* thus, *Demea,* after informing him of the Crime *Æschinus* had been guilty of, asks, *Non clemas? Non insanis?* *Micio* replies, *non.* Upon which the other immediately says, *malim quidem;* and to make it so, if possible, subjoins another Aggravation and Inconvenience, attending the present Charge; *Puer natus*

MI. Quidnam? DE. fero alia flagitia ad te ingentia
Boni, illius adolescentis. MI. ecce autem. DE. nova,
Capitalia. MI. ohe, jam. DE. ah, nescis qui vir sit.
    MI. scio.	5
DE. O stulte, tu de psaltriâ me somnias
Agere. hoc peccatum in virginem est civem. MI. scio.
DE. Eho, scis, & patere? MI. quidni patiar? DE.
    dic mihi,
Non clamas? non insanis? MI. non; malim quidem.
DE. Puer natu' est. MI. Dî bene vortant. DE. virgo
    nihil habet.	10
MI. Audivi. DE. & ducenda indotata est? MI. scilicet.
DE. Quid nunc futurum est? MI. id enim quod res
    ipsa fert:
Illinc huc transferetur virgo. DE. ô Jupiter!
Istoccine pacto oportet? MI. quid faciam amplius?
DE. quid facias? si non ipsâ re tibi istuc dolet,	15
Simulare certè est hominis. MI. quin jam virginem
Despondi: res composita est: fiunt nuptiæ:
Demsi metum omnem. hæc magis sunt hominis. DE.
    cæterùm,
Placet tibi factum, Micio? MI. non, si queam
Mutare: nunc, cùm non queo, æquo animo fero.	20
Ita vita est hominum, quasi, cùm ludas tesseris;

*MI. Quidnam? DE. Fero ad te alia ingentia flagitia, illius boni adolescentis. MI. Ecce autem. DE. Nova, capitalia. MI. Ohe, jam. DE. Ah, nescis qui vir sit. MI. Scio. DE. O stulte, tu somnia: me agere de psaltria; hoc peccatum est in virginem civem. MI. Scio. DE. Eho, scis, & patere? MI. Quidni patiar? DE. Dic mihi, non clamas? non insanis? MI. Non: malim quidem non evenisse. DE. Puer est natus. MI. Dii vortant bene. DE. Virgo habet nihil. MI. Audivi. DE. Et est ducenda indotata? MI. Scilicet. DE. Quid est futurum nunc? MI. Id enim quod ipsa res fert: virgo transferetur illinc huc. DE. O Ju-*
*piter, Oportetne fieri istoc pacto? MI. Quid faciam amplius? DE. Quid facias? Si istuc non dolet tibi ipsa re, certe est hominis simulare. MI. Quin jam despondi virginem: res est composita: nuptiæ fiunt: dempsi omnem metum: hæc magis sunt officia hominis. DE. Cæterùm, an factum placet tibi Micio? MI. Non, si queam mutare: nunc, cum non queo, fero æquo animo. Vita hominum est ita, quasi, cum ludas tesseris;*

## ANNOTATIONS.

*natus est.* To which *Micio* still the same, and not to be moved by these Representations of his Brother, answers, *Dii bene vortant.* Others give them to *Micio*, who was probably to have compleated the Sentence, by adding *non evenisse*, or some such Expression; but is interrupted by *Demea*, who impatient to see his Brother so mild, endeavours to aggravate the Crime, by adding *puer natus est.* This has the greater Air of Probability, because of what soon after follows in the same Scene, Ver. 19. DE. *Placet tibi factum, Micio?* He answers in just the same manner as here; *Non, si queam mutare: nunc, quum non queo; æquo animo fero.*

12 *Quid nunc futurum est?* More irascentium, quum ipse sciverit quid futurum sit, Micionem interrogat. Et hujusmodi interrogatio, secundum figuram suam non habet responsionem; sed Micio sic respondit, quasi simpliciter inquirenti. *Donatus.*

18 *Hæc magis sunt hominis.* Micio could not have fram'd a better Answer to *Demea*, than this which is now referr'd to. We are not always in every thing to proceed with the utmost Severity and Rigour. It becomes us, as Men, to make Allowances, to enter into one anothers's Foibles, and, as far as is consistent with Reason and Prudence, to indulge one another's Wants and Desires. The Poet has contriv'd to give *Micio*, along with his Mildness and Affability, a strong Biass to Justice. This appears in all his Behaviour. No sooner does *Hegio* represent *Pamphila's* Case to him, than he is willing to make her full Reparation, and is even anxious to find *Aeschinus* the same way inclin'd. And here when *Demea* exclaims against this unequal Match, he checks him, by telling him that it was the more just and humane part, as an Injury had been offered, to give the Satisfaction that the Law required, and not suffer the Motives of a sordid Avarice to stifle all Regard for Equity. This is an uncommon Stroke of Delicacy, to represent the affable, easy, indulgent *Micio*, as of a more upright and unbiass'd Virtue, than *Demea* with all his Rigour and Severity.

21 *Ita vita est hominum, quasi, cum ludas tesseris.* The Poet had probably in his Eye here

Throw that was most wanted comes not up, we must correct that
by Skill which Chance has sent us.

*Dem.* A Corrector! You have already, forsooth, with this mighty
Skill of yours, thrown away sixty Guineas upon a Musick-wench,
whom we must now strive to get rid of at any Price; if not for
Money, for nothing at all.

*Mic.* Not in the least; nor indeed have I any Design to sell her.

*Dem.* What will you do then?

*Mic.* I'll keep her at home.

*Dem.* Great *Jupiter!* A Whore and a Wife in the same House!

*Mic.* Why not?

*Dem.* Do you imagine you are in your Senses?

*Mic.* Indeed I think so.

*Dem.* As I hope for Mercy your Folly appears such to me, that
I believe you keep her to be entertain'd with her Musick.

*Mic.* Why not?

*Dem.* And the young Wife, I suppose, is to be her Scholar.

*Mic.* No doubt on't.

*Dem.* You too will trip it along, and lead the Dance.

*Mic.* Like enough.

*Dem.* Like enough!

*Mic.* You shall make one of the Party too, if there's occasion.

*Dem.* My God! Are you not asham'd of these Follies?

*Mic.* Come, *Demea,* lay aside for the present, this Sullenness of
yours, and be free and merry as you ought at your Son's Wedding:
I'll just step to the Bride and her Mother, and return immediately.

*Dem.* O *Jupiter!* Here's a Life for you! Here are Manners!
Here's Madness! A Wife without a Fortune; a Musick-Wench in
keeping; an expensive House; a Youth sunk in Luxury; a doating
old Father. Providence itself, however desirous, will never be able
to save this Family.                                                A C T

*ANNOTATIONS.*

here a Passage of the Tenth Book of *Plato's*
Commonwealth, where that Philosopher
says, " That we should make it our endea-
" vour to reap the Fruits of Wisdom from
" the Operations of Chance, and, as in a
" Game at Dice, employ all our Skill in
" turning that to our Profit, which Fortune
" has thrown up to us; that by thus using
" the Lights which Reason gives us, we
" may turn even seeming Misfortunes into
" Benefits." These moral Maxims come in
very aptly in Comedy, which is a Picture of
human Life. The *Tesseræ* among the Ancients seem to have been the same with our
Dice, for so they are describ'd by *Stephanus,*
upon the Word *Tesseræ,* Κυβὸς, *Cubus* sive
solidum quadratum. *Tesseræ* quibus in ta-
bula lusoria luditur: sunt enim quadratæ, et
quibusdam punctis notatæ. *Tesseræ* a Cube
or solid Square; *Tesseræ,* those which are
play'd with in a Gaming-Table: They are
square, and mark'd with certain Spots.

34 *Tu inter eas restim ductans saltabis.*
*Restis,* a Cord or Rope. *Ducere restim,* to lead
or draw the Cord, is therefore a Phrase that
requires to be particularly explained. One
should be apt to think, that in those times,
when any Number of Persons danc'd in
Company, they all held a Cord, and he who
was first of the Train, was said *ducere restim.*
But many Reasons may be offered against
this. To what purpose a Cord? Could they
not dance Hand in Hand? This is much
more likely, that a Company dancing in
train, and link'd together by the Hands,
gave rise to the Expression. This Notion derives Credit from a Passage of *Livy,*
*Lib.* 27. where describing the Solemnity of twenty seven young Virgins, who
went dancing in procession to the Temple of
*Juno,* he has these Words; *Cap.* 37. *In fo-*
*ro pompa constitit, et per manus reste ducta,*
*virgines sonum vocis pulsu pedum modulantes,*
                                                                        *in-*

Si illud, quod maxumè opus est jactu, non cadit,
Illud, quid cecidit fortè, id arte ut corrigas.
De. Corrector! nempe tuá arte viginti minæ
Pro psaltriá periere : quæ, quantum potest,                    25
Aliquò abjicienda est ; si non precio, gratiis.
Mi. Neque est, neque illam sanè studio vendere.
De. Quid igitur facies ? Mi. domi erit. De. proh
    divûm fidem !
Meretrix & mater familias uná in domo ! [dem arbitror.
Mi. Cur non ? De. sanum te credis esse ? Mi. equi-
De. Ita me Dii ament, ut video ego tuam ineptiam,
Facturum credo, ut habeas quicum cantites. [scilicet.
Mi. Cur non ? De. & nova nupta eadem hæc discet ? Mi.
De. Tu inter eas restim ductans saltabis. Mi. probè.
De. Probè ? Mi. & tu nobiscum uná, si opus sit. De.
    hei mihi !                                                 35
Non te hæc pudent ? Mi. jam verò omitte, Demea,
Tuam istanc iracundiam, atque ita, uti decet,
Hilarum ac lubentem fac te gnati in nuptiis.
Ego hos conveniam, post redeo.   De. ô Jupiter !
Hanccine vitam ! hoscine mores ! hanc dementiam !   40
Uxor sine dote veniet : intus psaltria est :
Domus sumtuosa : adolescens luxu perditus :
Senex delirans : ipsa si cupiat Salus,
Servare prorsus non potest hanc familiam.

*Scilicet. De. Tu saltabis inter eas ductans restim. Mi. Probè. De. Probè ? Mi. Et tu uná nobiscum, si sit opus. De. Hei mihi, an non hæc pudent te ? Mi. Jam vero, Demea, omitte istanc tuam iracundiam, atque fac te ita hilarum ac lubentem, uti decet, in nuptiis gnati. Ego conveniam hos, post redeo. De. O Jupiter ! Hanccine vitam ! hoscine mores ! hanc dementiam ! uxor veniet sine dote : psaltria est intus : domus sumptuosa : adolescens perditus luxu : senex delirans : Salus ipsa, si cupiat, prorsus non potest servare hanc familiam.*

## ANNOTATIONS.

incesserunt. *Where we are to observe, that per manus reste ducta does not signify holding with their Hands a Cord,* but *making a Cord of their Hands,* i. e. having them link'd together, and lengthening out the Procession ; for that it was the custom to dance Hand in Hand, appears from *Horace,* Book 2. Ode 12.

> *Nec vertare joco, nec dare brachia*
> *Ludentem nitidis virginibus.*

This, which is the main of what Madam *Dacier* offers in support of the above Notion, tho' it may not perhaps amount to a full Proof, yet renders it extremely probable. The Quotation from *Lucretius,* as it depends upon a conjectural Variation, which she proposes in the Text, I omit here, and shall only add, that I am the more Inclin'd to follow this Explication, because it is that which *Donatus* had given before her. His Words are : " *Lusus est natus ab eo fune, quo in-* " *troductus equus Durius in Trojam est, cum* " *nexis manibus fune, chorum ducunt sal-*
" *tantes. Hoc à quibusdam dicitur, sed ego* " *puto, manu consertos choros puellorum* " *puellarumque cantantes,* restim ducere ex- " *istimari, et id maxime convenire ad exa-* " *gitandam importunitatem senis, veluti pu-* " *eros imitantis. Simul etiam, quia est* " *connexus manuum lascivus ac petulans* " *adimit discretionem conditionis, dignita-* " *tis, ætatis, inter meretricem, novam nup-* " *tam & senem.*"

43 *Ipsa si cupiat Salus.* Preservation, Safety, Providence itself, can't save this Family from Ruin. An hyperbolical Way of speaking, to signify that the Current of Destruction was so strong, nothing could stop it. So *Plaut. Capt.* III. 3. 14.

> *Neque jam Salus servare, si vole, me potest.*

*Mostell.* II. 1. 4.

> *Nec Salus nobis saluti jam esse, si cupiat,*
>      *potest.*

In like manner, *Cicero pro Font.* Salus ipsa virorum fortium innocentiam tueri non potest.

An

## ACT IV. SCENE VIII.

### ARGUMENT.

*Syrus comes out drunk upon the Stage, exulting that he had regaled himself so plentifully. Demea observing it, reprimands him severely for his Drunkenness.*

### SYRUS, DEMEA.

*Syrus.* WHY truly, my *Syrus*, thou haſt cared for thyſelf delicately, and acted thy Part to excellent purpoſe. Thou Wag! But after filling myſelf with all that's choice within, I thought proper to take an Airing here.

*Dem.* See, for Heaven's ſake, this rare Model of their Diſcipline.

*Syr.* But here comes our old Man!———What's the matter? Why so demure?

*Dem.* O Villain!

*Syr.* O Mr. *Wiſdom*; are you come to throw away your fine Maxims here?

*Dem.* Were you my Servant?

*Syr.* You'd be rich, *Demea*; and improve your Eſtate to a wonder.

*Dem.* I'd take care you ſhould be an Example to all others.

*Syr.* Why ſo? What have I done?

*Dem.* Why! In the heat of a Diſturbance: and during a moſt heinous Crime, which is not yet fully pacify'd, you've got drunk, you Raſcal, as if all was quiet and well.

*Syr.* I wiſh I had kept within doors.

### ANNOTATIONS.

As *Demea*, at the end of the laſt Scene, is reflecting upon the threatning Situation, as he ſuppoſes, of his Brother's Family, a freſh Reaſon occurs to increaſe theſe Apprehenſions. *Syrus* comes out drunk, with great Aſſurance and Confidence, and commending himſelf for having acted his Part ſo well. A more provoking Circumſtance could not have happened to *Demea*, already almoſt diſtracted at the repeated Debaucheries of his Son, and the overſtrained Indulgence of his Brother; than to ſee this flagrant Inſtance of Licentiouſneſs, and that the Infection ran thro' the whole Family. But it is the Poet's Aim all along, to multiply *Demea's* Vexations, as will appear in the following Scenes.

3 *Abi.* Verbum vel ſibi, vel alteri cum laudatione blandientis. Nam ſic dicunt, qui jam compotes ſunt vitorum omnium, perfectique in rebus univerſis. *Donatus.*

5 *Exemplum Diſciplinæ!* Dacier renders this; *There goes a fine Model, for the training up of Children:* for, ſays ſhe, *Demea* regards *Syrus* as the Maſter and Governour of his

# ACTUS IV. SCENA VIII.

## ARGUMENTUM.

*Redit in proscenium Syrus temulentus, exultans se laute opipareque cænatum esse: hunc Demea ob temulentiam objurgat.*

SYRUS, DEMEA.

| | ORDO. |
|---|---|
| EDepol, Syrisce, te curasti molliter, | EDepol, Syrisce, curasti te molliter, adminiftra- |
| Lautéque munus adminiftrasti tuum. | stique tuum munus |
| Abi. sed poftquam intus sum omnium rerum satur, | laute. Abi. Sed |
| Prodeambulare huc libitum eft. DE. illud sis vide | poftquam sum satur |
| Exemplum difciplinæ! SY. ecce autem hic adeft  5 | omnium rerum in- |
| Senex nofter.   Quid fit? quid tu es triftis? DE. oh, | tus, libitum eft pro- |
| fcelus! | deambulare huc. |
| SY. Ohe, jam tu verba fundis hic; fapientia? | DE. Vide sis illud |
| DE. Tun'? fi meus effes. SY. dis quidem effes, Demea, | exemplum difcipli- |
| Ac tuam rem conftabiliffes. DE. exemplum omnibus | næ! SY. Ecce au- |
| Curarem ut effes. SY. quamobrem? quid feci? DE. | tem hic nofter senex |
| rogas?                                         10 | adeft. Quid fit? |
| In ipsâ turbâ, atque in peccato maxumo, | quid tu es triftis? |
| Quod vix fedatum fatis eft, potafti, fcelus, | DE. Ob fcelus! SY. |
| Quafive bene geftâ. SY. fane nollem huc exitum. | Obe, fapientia tu |
| | jam fundis hic ver- |
| | ba? DE. Tune? |
| | Si effes meus. SY. |

*Effes dis quidem, Demea, ac conftabiliffes tuam rem. DE. Curarem ut effes exemplum omnibus. SY. quamobrem? Quid feci? DE. Rogas? in ipfa turba, atque in maximo peccato, quod vix eft fatis fedatum, potafti, fcelus, quafi in re bene gefta. SY. Sane nollem exitum huc.*

## ANNOTATIONS.

his Son, whom *Micio* had adopted. But to me the Words feem to imply no more, than that *Syrus* was an Example of the ruinous Difcipline that prevailed in his Brother's Family.

6 *Quid fit? Quid tu es triftis?* The Poet very happily in this Place expreffes the Careleffnefs and Security of one in drink. *Syrus* difcovers no Fear at the Approach of the old Man, as in former Scenes. He has no Forethought, no Apprehenfion of Danger, but is quite lulled in Eafe and Indolence.

7 *Sapientia.* This is the Title under which he addreffes *Demea* in allufion to what he had faid in a former Scene. *Tu quantus quantus es, nihil nifi fapientia es.* To conftrue *fapientia verba*, would deftroy the whole Beauty and Energy of the Paffage; for nothing can be more fuited to the forward Petulance of one in drink, than to addrefs the Perfon he fpeaks to by the Title of Mr. *Wifdom*, as he knew that to be the Character he valued himfelf upon.

ACTUS

## ACT IV. SCENE IX.

### ARGUMENT.

*By the unseasonable Appearance of* Dromo, Ctesipho *is betrayed to his Father.* Syrus *endeavours to hinder the old Man from going in, but in vain.*

DROMO, SYRUS, DEMEA.

*Dromo.* D'Ye hear, *Syrus,* Ctesipho *desires you to come back.*

 *Syr.* Hush.

*Dem.* What's this he says of *Ctesipho?*

*Syr.* Nothing.

*Dem.* How, you Hangdog: is *Ctesipho* within?

*Syr.* He is not.

*Dem.* How comes he to name him then?

*Syr.* 'Tis another of the same Name, a little Parasite: don't you know him?

*Dem.* I will know presently.

*Syr.* What now? Where are you going?

*Dem.* Let me alone.

*Syr.* I tell you I won't.

*Dem.* Hands off, Villain, or I'll beat out your Brains this Instant.

*Syr.* He's gone. I foresee, by *Jove,* that he'll prove but an unwelcome Guest, especially to *Ctesipho.* What shall I do now? why, even creep into some quiet Corner, till this Storm is laid, and there sleep off the present Load. That will be best.

### ANNOTATIONS.

The Poet still contrives to heap fresh Troubles upon *Demea.* His Brother, notwithstanding all his Remonstrances, is irreclaimable; he is reflecting upon the Ruin that threatened his Brother's Family, when, as an additional Proof of it, *Syrus* comes out drunk; and now to compleat his Misfortunes, he learns, by the unseasonable Appearance of *Dromo,* that his favourite Son *Ctesipho* makes one of the revelling Company within. Thus has the Poet contrived to raise his Passion by several Gradations to the highest Pitch, till

 finding

# ACTUS IV. SCENA IX.

## ARGUMENTUM.

*Exitu Dromonis. Ctesipho Demeæ proditu: Syrus senem ab ingressu avertere conatur, sed frustra.*

DROMO, SYRUS, DEMEA.

| | ORDO. |
|---|---|
| HEUS Syre, rogat te Ctesipho, ut redeas. Sy. abi.<br>DE. Quid Ctesiphonem hic narrat? Sy. nihil.<br>DE. eho, carnufex,<br>Est Ctesipho intus? Sy. non est. DE. cur hic nominat?<br>Sy. Est alius quidam, parafitafter parvolus;<br>Noftin'? DE. jam scibo. Sy. quid agis? quò abis? DE.<br>    mitte me.                  5<br>Sy. Noli, inquam. DE. non manum abftines, maftigia?<br>An tibi jam mavis cerebrum difpergam hîc? Sy. abît.<br>Edepol comiffatorem haud fanè commodum,<br>Præfertim Ctefidoni. quid ego nunc agam?<br>Nifi, dum hæ filefcunt turbæ, interea in angulum  10<br>Aliquò abeam, atque edormifcam hoc villi. fic agam. DE. | HEus Syre, Ctefipho rogat te, ut redeas. Sy. Abi. DE. Quid hic narrat Ctefiphonem? Sy. Nibil. DE. Ebo, carnifex, eft Ctefipho intus? Sy. Non eft. DE. Cur hic nominat? Sy. Eft alius quidam, parvulus parafitafter; noftine? DE. Jam fcibo. Sy. Quid agis? Quò abis? DE. Mitte me. Sy. Noli, inquam. DE. Non abftines |

manum, maftigia? An mavis jam ut difpergam cerebrum tibi hic? Sy. Abiit. Edepol conjicio eum effe comiffatorem haud fane commodum, præfertim Ctefiphoni. Quid ego agam nunc? Nifi interea, dum hæ turbæ filefcunt, abeam aliquo in angulum, atque edormifcam hoc villi. Sic agam.

## ANNOTATIONS.

finding it uneafy to himfelf, and of no manner of Purpofe; he, at laft, of Choice, embraces the mild and eafy Temper.

8 *Edepol comiffatorem haud fane commodum.* The whole Beauty here lies in the Word *comiffatorem.* *Comiffator* is properly a Man, who after having been already engaged in a Debauch, goes mafk'd to another, and enters fuddenly, making a great Noife. The Word is, therefore, very happily applied to *Demea,* who rufhes fuddenly into *Micio's* Houfe; where they are revelling in Mirth, and raifes a hideous Uproar and Difturbance. Thefe Ironies are very proper in Comedy, and greatly divert the Spectators.

11 *Hoc villi,* i. e. *Hoc vini.* As *unus ullus, afinus afellus, vinum villum.*

## ACT V. SCENE I.

### ARGUMENT.

*Demea, who is now appris'd of his Son* Ctesipho's *Amours, exclaims, and falls bitterly upon* Micio, *as the common Corrupter of their Children, but is at length appeas'd, and brought into temper with both* Ctesipho *and* Æschinus.

### MICIO, DEMEA.

*Micio.* EVERY thing's ready with us, when you will, *Sostrata,* as I said before: but who's this that makes our Door fly open with such Fury?

*Dem.* Alas! What shall I do? How shall I behave? Where direct my Complaints, or to whom exclaim? O Heaven! O Earth! O *Neptune!* Ruler of the Seas.

*Mic.* See now: he has discover'd all; that makes him exclaim so; I foresee a Storm: but I must help the young Man.

*Dem.* Here comes the common Corrupter of our Children.

*Mic.* Moderate, at length, your Passion, and return to yourself.

*Dem.* I have moderated it; I am myself; I forbear all Reproaches; let us come to the Point: it was agreed upon between us, and the Proposal too was your own; that you should take no Concern in my Son, nor I in yours. Answer me.

*Mic.* It was so; I don't deny it.

*Dem.* Why is he now revelling at your House? Why do you receive him? Why purchase a Mistress for him, *Micio?* Ought I not to have the same Justice from you, as you have from me? As I don't meddle with your Son, don't you with mine.

*Mic.* You don't reason fairly? you don't indeed: for it is an old Saying, *Among Friends, all Things are common.*

*Dem.* Very pretty, truly: you have at length then found this Salvo.

*Mic.* Hear me a little, *Demea,* if you can but muster up so much Patience.

### ANNOTATIONS.

In this Scene *Micio* is seen coming out from *Sostrata,* after having given her what Instructions he thought proper relating to the Marriage. At the same Time *Demea,* who had rush'd into his Brother's, and there found *Ctesipho* wantoning and enjoying himself with his Musick-wench, driven almost to Distraction, comes out in great Fury. This naturally begets a Conversation full of Anger and Passion on one Side, full of Meekness and Good-nature on the other. *Micio* finding that his Brother was too greatly provoked by what he had lately discovered, to think of calming him in the usual Way, by either huffing him, or appearing unconcerned; resolves to dissemble no longer, but to lay before him the Principles upon which he acted, and the Motives that led him to prefer Lenity to Rigour. All this he does with so much Temper and good Sense, that *Demea* is at last pacified, and yields to his Brother.

[1] *Parata à nobis sunt.* It is evident, that the fifth Act ought to begin here, which some have injudiciously carried back two Scenes farther. At the end of the last Scene, *Demea* goes in to his Brother's; *Syrus,* retires to sleep off his Dose, and *Micio* is with *Sostrata.* Thus all have left the Stage, and the Time that *Micio* spends with *Sostrata,* makes a sufficiently long Interval.

[2] *Hei mihi, quid faciam? Quid agam?* We ought not to pass over here without Notice the Poet's Art and Judgment, who labours to raise *Demea's* Resentment and Passion

# ACTUS V. SCENA I.

## ARGUMENTUM.

*Cognito Ctesiphonis amore, Demea exclamat, et Micionem jurgio adoritur, ut liberorum corruptelam : per quem placatur tandem et Æschino et Ctesiphoni.*

|  |  |
| --- | --- |
| MICIO, DEMEA. | ORDO. |

PARATA à nobis sunt, ita ut dixi, Sostrata,
  Ubi vis. quisnam à me pepulit tam graviter fores?
DE. Hei mihi, quid faciam? quid agam? quid cla-
  mem, aut querar?
O cœlum, ô terra, ô maria Neptuni! MI. hem tibi,
Rescivit omnem rem : id nunc clamat. ilicet,                5
Paratæ lites : succurrendum est. DE. eccum adest
Communis corruptela nostrûm liberûm.
MI. tandem reprime iracundiam, atque ad te redi.
DE. Repressi, redii, mitto maledicta omnia :
Rem ipsam putemus. dictum hoc inter nos fuit,           10
Ex te adeo est ortum, ne tu curares meum,
Neve ego tuum. responde. MI. factum est, non nego.
DE. Cur nunc apud te potat? cur recipis meum?
Cur emis amicam, Micio? numquid minus
Mihi idem jus æquom est esse, quod mecum est tibi? 15
Quando ego tuum non curo, ne cura meum.
MI. Non æquom dicis; non : nam vetus verbum hoc
  quidem est,
Communia esse amicorum inter se omnia.
DE. Facete! nunc demum istæc nata oratio est.
MI. Ausculta paucis, nisi molestum est, Demea.       20

ORDO.

MI. Omnia sunt parata à nobis, ubi vis, ita ut dixi, Sostrata : quisnam pepulit fore tam graviter à me? DE. Hei mihi, quid faciam? quid agam? quid clamem, aut querar? O cœlum, o terra, o maria Neptuni! MI. Hem tibi, rescivit rem omnem : clamat nunc ob id : ilicet, lites sunt paratæ : succurrendum est juveni. DE. Eccum, (communis) corruptela nostrorum liberorum adest. MI. Reprime tandem iracundiam, atque redi ad te. DE. Repressi, redii, mitto omnia maledicta : putemus ipsam rem. Hoc fuit dictum inter nos, est ortum adeo ex te, ne tu curares meum, neve ego curarem tuum filium. Responde. MI. Est factum : non nego. DE. Cur nunc Ctesipho potat apud te? Cur recipis meum? Cur emis amicam ei, Micio? Numquid est minus æquum, ideo jus esse mihi tecum, quod est tibi mecum? Quando ego non curo tuum, ne cura tu meum. MI. Non dicis æquum, non : nam hoc quidem est verbum vetus; Omnia amicorum esse communia inter se. DE. Facete! istæc oratio est nata nunc demum. MI. Ausculta paucis, Demea, nisi est molestum.

## ANNOTATIONS.

Passion upon discovering his Son *Ctesipho's* Excesses, as much above what he felt for *Æschinus*, as his Tenderness towards the one is greater than towards the other. When he talks with his Brother of the Debauches of *Æschinus*, he says, *Rogas me quid tristis sim?* But upon the least Suspicion, that *Ctesipho* was concern'd with *Æschinus* in these Projects, he changes his Style quite: *Disperii! Ctesiphonem audivi filium una defuisse in raptione cum Æschino.* And a little after: *Næ ego sum homo infelix.* But here, when he finds that it is really so, he gives way to Rage too big for Expression: *Quid faciam? quid agam?* He is unable to express himself; he invokes Heaven, Earth, and Sea, all the Elements, and all the Gods. This is agreeable to Nature, and the Conduct of the most approved Poets, who, when they want to describe any tempestuous Emotion of Soul, too great for Utterance, always use Interrogations and Exclamations. Thus *Virgil*, when he represents *Orpheus* again deprived of his dear *Eurydice, Georg.* 4. 504.

*Quid faceret? Quo se rapta bis conjuge*
  *ferret?*
*Quo fletu Manes, qua Numina voce moveret?*
" What should he do? Whither should he
" turn him, his Love being twice snatched
" away? With what Tears assuage the *Manes?*
" With what Accents the infernal Powers?"

17 *Non æquum dicis, non,* *Micio* is here sorely pressed, and at a loss to find an Excuse; hence he affects the greater Air of Confidence,

Patience. First, if you are grieved at the Expence your Sons make; pray, consider with yourself, that formerly you maintained both, suitably to your Fortune, which you thought would be sufficient for them; for at that time you made no doubt but I would marry. Observe now this your wonted Rule: hoard, scrape together, save, do all you can to leave them handsome Fortunes, and take the whole Credit to yourself: but let them make free with mine, as it comes to them beyond Expectation. Your Stock will not be diminished; and all they have from me you ought to regard as clear Gain. If you will but weigh these things impartially in your own Mind, you'll save me, them, and yourself a world of trouble, *Demea.*

*Dem.* I don't talk of the Expence; 'tis the ill Habits they contract.

*Mic.* Have patience: I understand you: I was coming to that. There are many signs in Men, Brother, from which it is easy to conjecture, that when two Persons do the same thing, it may prove very hurtful to the one, but not so to the other, from no Difference in the thing itself, but in the Persons who do it. I see in your Sons, what makes me confident, they will answer our Wishes. They have good Sense, Discretion, Modesty enough upon occasion, and love one another entirely; whence 'tis easy to discern in them a dutiful Nature, and noble Soul; nor will you find it a hard Task at any time to reclaim them. But, perhaps, you're afraid lest they should be indiscreet and negligent as to their Fortunes. O Brother *Demea,* in every thing else we are made wiser by Age, but this one Vice is inseparable from it, that we are all apt to be more worldly than is needful: believe it then, that Age will make them sufficiently careful.

*Dem.* Have a care, *Micio,* that these fine Reasonings, and this impartial Mind of yours, don't in the End undo us all.

*Mic.* Peace! there is no danger: think no more of these things, but for this Day be directed by me; smooth up your Countenance.

*Dem.* Nay, at present things are so, that I must do it: but to-morrow I'll into the Country with my Son by Break of Day.

*Mic.* At Midnight, if you please; only be chearful to-day.

*Dem.* And carry that Musick-girl along with me too. *Mic.*

## ANNOTATIONS.

dence, and finding no other Pretence, has recourse to a Proverb, which rather makes against him, than for him.

35 *Multa in homine, Demea.* Micio is here hard put to it, his Discourse is obscure, and discovers something of Incoherence and Confusion. He undertakes to defend a thing that will but ill-bear being defended; for, however it may be prudent sometimes, to overlook and wink at the Extravagance of Youth, yet to justify or patronize them is carrying it too far. Let us however, interpret *Micio's* Discourse candidly. He is offering an Apology for his own Lenity and Indulgence; and does it from this Consideration, that although it might in some Cases be dangerous, yet he had Reason from the Disposition and Temper of the Two Youths to judge it would be otherwise with them. Were they wholly restrained, it would be only adding a Spur to their Desires; but if a little indulged, Experience would soon convince them of the Vanity and Folly of these youthful Sallies, and then it would be an easy Matter to reclaim them. And this so far influences *Demea,* that we find him immediately coming into *Micio's* Sentiments.

48 *Attentiores sumus,* &c. Old Age brings Care and Anxiety, and, from an overstrained Foresight, is apt to fall into the Vice here mentioned. *Cicero* exposes the Folly of it in his Treatise *de Senectute* 18. *Avaritia vero senilis*

Principio, si id te mordet, sumtum filii
Quem faciunt; quæso, hoc facito tecum cogites:
Tu illos duo olim pro re tollebas tuâ,
Quòd sati' putabas tua bona ambobus fore:
Et me tum uxorem credidisti scilicet    25
Ducturum. eandam illam rationem antiquam obtine:
Conserva, quære, parce, fac quamplurimum
Illis relinquas. gloriam tu istam obtine:
Mea, quæ præter spem evenere, utantur sine:
De summâ nihil decedet: quod hinc accesserit,    30
Id de lucro putato esse omne. hæc si voles
In animo vere cogitare, Demea,
Et mihi, & tibi, & illis demseris molestiam.
DE. Mitto rem: consuetudinem ipsorum. MI. mane:
Scio: istuc ibam. multa in homine, Demea,    35
Signa insunt, ex quibu' conjectura facilè fit,
Duo cùm idem faciunt, sæpe ut possis dicere,
Hoc licet impunè facere huic, illi non licet:
Non quo dissimilis res sit, sed quò is qui facit:
Quæ ego in illis esse video: ut confidam fore    40
Ità, ut volumus. video sapere, intellegere, in loco
Vereri, inter se amare. scire est liberum
Ingenium, atque animum: quovis illos tu die
Reducas. At enim metuas, ne ab re sint tamen
Omissiores paulo. O noster Demea,    45
Ad omnia alia ætate sapimus rectiùs:
Solum unum hoc vitium adfert senectus hominibus;
Attentiores sumus ad rem omnes, quàm sat est:
Quod illos sat ætas acuet. DE. ne nimiùm modò
Bonæ tuæ istæ nos rationes, Micio,    50
Et tuus istæ animus æquus subvortat. MI. tace,
Non fiet: mitte jam istæc: da te hodie mihi:
Exporge frontem. DE. scilicet, ita tempus fert,
Faciundum est: cæterùm rus cras cum filio
Cum primo lucu ibo hinc. MI. de nocte, censeo:
Hodie modo hilarum te fac. DE. & istam psaltriam

*Principio, si id mordet te, sumtum quem filii faciunt; quæso, facito ut cogites hoc tecum: tu olim tollebas illos duo pro re tua, quod putabas tua bona fore satis pro ambobus. Et scilicet credidisti tum me esse ducturam uxorem: obtine eandam illam antiquam rationem: conserva, quære, parce, fac ut relinquas quamplurimum illis: obtine tu istam gloriam, sine utantur mea, quæ evenere præter spem: nihil decedet de summa: quod accesserit illis hinc, putato omne id esse de lucro. Si, Demea, voles cogitare hæc vere in animo, demseris molestiam, & mihi, & tibi, & illis. DE. mitto rem: vide consuetudinem ipsorum. MI. Mane: scio: ibam istuc. Multa signa insunt in homine, Demea, ex quibus conjectura fit facile, ut, cùm duo faciunt idem; sæpe possis dicere, licet huic facere hoc impune, non licet illi: non quo res sit dissimilis, sed quo is qui facit: quæ ego video esse in illis: ut confidam fore ita, ut volumus. Video eos sapere, intelligere, vereri in loco, amare inter se. Est facile scire esse illis liberum ingenium atque animum: tu reducas illos quovis die. At enim metuas, ne sint tamen paulo emissiores ab re. O noster Demea, sapimus rectius ad omnia alia ætate: senectus adfert solum hoc unum vitium hominibus; sumus omnes attentiores ad rem, quam est satis: ad quod ætas satis acuet illos. DE. Cave modo, Micio, ne istæ tuæ bonæ rationes, & iste tuus animus æquus, nimium subvertat vos. MI. Tace, non fiet: mitte istæc jam: da te mihi hodie: exporrige frontem. DE. Scilicet, tempus fert ita, est faciendum; cæterum cras ibo hinc rus cum filio cum primo luce. MI. Censeo, de nocte: modo fac te hilarum hodie. DE. Et abstraham istam psaltriam*

## ANNOTATIONS.

*senilis quid sibi velit, non intelligo; potest enim quidquam esse absurdius, quam, quo minus viæ restat, eo plus viatici quærere?*

50 *Et istam psaltriam,* Demea had con-sented to assume an Air of Good-humour, finding it vain to do otherwise, and partly moved by the Reasoning of his Brother. But as Characters change slowly, and with



great

*Mic.* There you have it ; for by that means you'll keep your Son
at home ; only take care to secure her.

*Dem.* I'll see to that ; and by setting her a baking or grinding,
keep her constantly bedaub'd with Ashes, Meal, and Smoke. Besides, in the Heat of the Day, I'll send her to gather Stubble ; till
she be sun-burnt, and as black as a Coal.

*Mic.* Excellent ! now you seem to be wise : nay, and I would
then have you even force your Son to lie with her.

*Dem.* Do you banter me ? you're a happy Man, I think, to be
of so easy and indifferent a Temper.

*Mic.* Ah ! Are you at it again ?

*Dem.* I have done, I have done.

*Mic.* Go in then ; and since this is a Day destined to Mirth, let
us think of nothing else.

*ANNOTATIONS.*

great Difficulty ; *Terence* represents this Humour as retaining still a Tincture of savage
Rusticity. If he consents to stay in Town to-
day to celebrate his son's Wedding, he resolves to depart with his other Son early next
Morning ; and if he takes the Musick-girl
with

---

# ACT V.   SCENE II.

### ARGUMENT.

*Demea,* now sensible that Severity and Rigour towards Children
is generally disliked, resolves upon a different Behaviour ; and,
rejecting his stern rustick Manner, aims at Complaisance and
Affability.

DEMEA.

THERE is no Man has so well computed the Measures of Life,
but Experience, Years, and Custom will be still bringing something new, still furnishing some Lesson ; insomuch, that you must
own your Ignorance of many Things you fancied you knew, and
often reject upon Trial, what before you believed unexceptionable ;
as is the Case with me at present : for tho' my Race is almost run, I
yet resolve to renounce the rigid and painful Life I have hitherto led.
Why so ? because I have found by Experience, that nothing is more
advantageous to a Man, than Mildness and Complaisance. This will
be

*ANNOTATIONS.*

This Scene sets before us a very uncommon Example ; that of an old Man rejecting
his former rigid Course of Life, and embracing
one more complaisant, polite, and fashionable.
The Poet has taken great care to prepare
for this Change, that it mayn't appear capricious or ridiculous, which would have but ill
suited the Character of the Person on whom
it is wrought. *Demea* has, thro' the Course
of the Play, met with many Mortifications.
His Passion, Complaints, Advice, are all
slighted ; his Brother is loved and followed,
himself shunned ; add to that, the Conversation he had lately held with *Micio,* was conceived in a Strain that must affect him. No
wonder, therefore, if, when left by himself,
he begins to ruminate and reflect on all this,
and resolves to abandon his Severity thro'
meer Impatience, because he finds it avails
nothing. It is not then so much thro' Consent
and Approbation, that he assumes a different
Behaviour, as because he is under a necessity
of doing it. He still thinks Fathers ought to
be severe in checking the Miscarriage of their
Children, but that it is a Temper odious to
Youth, and apt to lessen filial Affection.

*Ecce*

Unà illac mecum hinc abstrahant. MI. pugnaveris.
Eo pacto prorsum illi alligaris filium;
Modò facito, ut illam serves. DE. ego istuc videro.
Atque ibi favillæ plena, fumi ac pollinis!                      60
Coquendo sic faxo, & molendo : præter hæc,
Meridie ipso faciam ut stipulam colligat.  [MI. placet.
Tam excoctam reddam atque atram, quam carbo est.
Nunc mihi videre sapere, atque equidem filium,
Tum etiam si nolit, cogam ut cum illà unà cubet.
DE. Derides ? fortunatus, qui isto animo sies,              66
Ego sentio. MI. ah, pergisne ? DE. jam, jam desino,
MI. I ergo intro, & cui rei est, ei rei hunc sumamus diem.

Consilium placet; nunc videre mihi sapere, atque equidem etiam tum cogam filium, si nolit, ut cubet una cum illa. DE. Derides ? fortunatus es, ego sentio, qui sis isto animo. MI. Ah, pergisne ? DE. Jam ut, jam desino. MI. I intro ergo, et sumamus hunc diem ei rei dicatus.

ORDO.
MI. Pugnaveris. Eo pacto prorsum alligaris filium illi. Facito modo, ut serves illam. DE. Ego istuc videro. Atque faxo coquendo & molendo ibi, ut sit plena favillà, fumi, ac pollinis : præter hæc faciam ut colligat stipulam ipsa meridie. Reddam eam tam excoctam atque atram, quam est carbo. MI.

#### A N N O T A T I O N S.

with him, it is not so much out of Complaisance to his Son, as to render her in a little time an object of his Disgust.

57. *Pugnaveris.* Magnam rem feceris. nam sic Lucilius;

*Vicimus, ô socii, & magnam pugnavimus pugnam.*

---

## ACTUS V. SCENA II.

### ARGUMENTUM.

*Demea, cum videat non probari vulgo severitatem in liberos, diversam institutionis viam meditatur : atque ex duro atque agresti studet fieri benignus.*

DEMEA.

NUnquam ita quisquam bene subductâ ratione ad
     vitam fuit,
Quin res, ætas, usus semper aliquid apportet novi,
Aliquid moneat : ut illa, quæ te scire credas, nescias ;
Et quæ tibi putaris prima, in experiundo ut repudies.
Quod nunc mi evenit. nam ego vitam duram, quam
     vixi usque adhuc,                             [ipsâ repperi, 6
Prope jam excurso spatio, mitto : id quamobrem ? re-
Facilitate nihil esse homini melius, neque clementiâ.
Id esse verum, ex me, atque ex fratre, cuivis facile
     est noscere.
Ille suam semper egit vitam in otio, in conviviis :

quam vixi adhuc : quamobrem facio id ? repperi ipsa re, nihil esse melius homini facilitate, neque clementiâ. Facile est mihi noscere ex me, atque ex fratre; id esse verum. Ille semper egit suam vitam in otio, in conviviis.

ORDO.
DE. Nunquam quisquam sciit ratione ita bene subducta ad vitam, quin res, ætas, usus, semper apportet aliquid novi, moneat aliquid : ut nescias illa, quæ credas te scire, et ut repudies in experiundo prima, quæ putaveris. Quod nunc evenit mihi. Nam ego, spatio prope jam excurso, mitto vitam duram.

#### A N N O T A T I O N S.

1. *Bene subductâ ratione.* Id est (says Donatus) bene disposita, bene computata : ducere enim est digitis computare. Sed ducere, est apud alium & palam : subducere, apud seipsum & secreto. *Demea*, therefore, means, that no man has so well regulated and computed with himself the Measures of Life; but that in a course of Time he will often find Reason to change his Mind ; to approve what he had rejected, and reject what he had approved. *Cicero* used the same Phrase with great Elegance, *Fam.* 1. 9. *Ille*

H 4

be manifest to any one who but considers me and my Brother. He
has spent his whole Life in Gaiety and Ease, mild, agreeable, inoffensive, and always chearful; in a word, he has lived for himself,
spent for himself: all Men speak well of him, all Men love him. I
again, that rustic, rigid, morose, saving, stern, covetous Wretch,
must needs marry: What a Source of Misery has this proved? Two
Sons were born to me, a new Care. Besides, in studying to acquire
a Fortune for them, I have worn out my Life and best Days; and
now my Course almost finished, the Return I have for all my Labour, is their Hate. My Brother, again, without any Trouble on
his part, enjoys all the Advantages of a Father. They love him,
and shun me; they trust him with all their Secrets, are fond of him,
like both to be with him: I am forsaken: They wish that he may
live long, but expect my Death with Impatience. Thus, at a small
Expence, he has made them his own, for whom I took so much pains
in bringing them up. I have all the Trouble, he the Pleasure. Come,
come, let us see whether I too can't be complaisant and liberal, since
he forces me to it. I want too to be loved and respected by my
Children. If that is to be obtained by Indulgence and Bounty, I
shan't be behind with him. Money will fail; but that least concerns
me, who am the oldest.

### ANNOTATIONS.

cum humano consilio efficere potui, circumspectis
rebus meis omnibus, rationibusque subductis,
summam feci cogitationum mearum omnium; quam
tibi, si potero, breviter exponam.'

10 Nulli lædere os. The Expression here
is remarkable, and imports the saying any
thing to a Person that will shock him, or
make him change Countenance in testimony
of Surprize or Indignation. Augustine had,
very properly, this Passage in view, in his
first Book de Civitate Dei, where speaking of
those who are afraid to tell others of their
Faults; he says, Vel cum laboris piget, vel os
eorum verecundamur offendere.

13 Quam ibi miseriam vidi? The Latins
often use videre for pati, experiri; in imitation of the Greeks, who borrowed that Way
of speaking from the Eastern Nations.

22 Meam autem mortem exspectant. Exspectant is here to be taken in the most invidious
Sense, as if he had said, optant ut moriar.
'Tis thus used by Cicero. Parad. 6. 1. Si
testamenta amicorum exspectas, aut ne exspectas
quidem, at ipse supponis: hæc utrum abundan-
tis, an egentis signa sint?

24 Provocat. Locutio à singulari certa-
mine translata. Cic. fin. 2. 22. Cum Galla
apud Anienem depugnavit provocatus.

26 Non posteriores feram. Sub. Partes.
Sensus est, Non ero secundo loco aut pretio.
Translatio desumpta à personis comicis, in
quibus aliæ primarum, aliæ secundarum, aliæ
denique

Clemens, placidus, nulli lædere os, arridere omnibus: 10
Sibi vixit: sibi sumtum fecit: omnes benedicunt, amant.
Ego ille agrestis, sævus, tristis, parcus, truculentus, tenax,
Duxi uxorem: quam ibi miseriam vidi? nati filii,
Alia cura: heia autem, dum studio illis ut quamplu-
ox Trimum [meam: 15
Facerem, contrivi in quærundo vitam, atque ætatem
Nunc exactâ ætate hoc fructi pro labore ab iis fero,
Odium ille alter sine labore patria potitur commoda:
Illum amant, me fugitant: illi credunt consilia omnia:
Illum diligunt: apud illum sunt ambo, ego desertu' sum.
Illam, ut vivat, optant; meam autem mortem ex-
spectant scilicet. 20
Ita eos meo labore eductos maxumo, hic fecit suos [dia.
Paulo sumtu. miseriam omnem ego capio; hic potitur gau-
Age, age, nunc jam experiamur porro contra, ecquid
ego possiem [vocat.
Blande dicere, aut benigne facere, quando huc pro-
Ego quoque à meis me amari & magni pendi postulo. 25
Si id fit dando atque obsequendo, non posteriores feram.
Deerit: id meà minime refert, qui sum natu maxumus.

*clemens, placidus, lædere os nulli, arridere omnibus: vixit sibi, fecit sumtum sibi: omnes benedicunt & amant eum. Ego ille agrestis, sævus, tristis, parcus, truculentus, tenax, duxi uxorem: quam miseriam vidi ibi? filii sunt nati, Alia cura: heia autem, dum studui ut facerem quamplurimum illis, contrivi meam vitam atque ætatem in quærendo: nunc ætate exacta, fero hoc fructi ab iis pro labore, nempe odium. Ille alter sine labore potitur patria commoda: amant illum, fugitant me: credunt omnia sua consilia illi: diligunt illum: sunt ambo apud illum: ego sum desertus. Optant illum ut vivat; Autem expectant meam mortem scilicet. Ita hic fecit eos, eductos meo maximo labore, suos, paulo sumptu. Ego capio omnem miseriam, hic potitur gaudia. Age, age, nunc jam porro experiamur contra, ecquid ego possiem dicere blande, aut facere benigne, quando frater provocat me huc. Ego quoque postulo me amari & magni pendi à meis. Si id fit dando atque obsequendo, non feram posteriores. Res deerit: id minime refert mea, qui sum natu maximus.*

## ANNOTATIONS.

denique posteriorum erant partium. *Westerhovius.*

27 *Deerit: id mea minime refert.* The Poet still shews *Demea* in his proper Character, that of one who has a strong Attachment to his Wealth, and can't be easily reconciled to Expence. Without this, the Change must have appeared overstrained and unnatural. *Demea,* tho' now fully convinced that Liberality was the only Way to gain the Affection of his Children, yet can't help reflecting upon the great Havock it will make of his Estate; however, he comforts himself with the Thought, that there is enough for the short Remainder of his Days; and when he is gone, they may provide for themselves. *Plautus* has much the same Thought, *Trin.* II. 2. 38.

*Mibi quidem ætas acta est ferme: tua istuc
refert maxume.*

## ACT V. SCENE III.

### ARGUMENT.

*Demea addresses Syrus in a Style of Flattery, and, contrary to his natural Temper, endeavours to be affable.*

#### SYRUS, DEMEA.

*Syrus.* D'Ye hear, *Demea*, your Brother begs you won't go any where out of the Way.

*Dem.* Who's that? O, our *Syrus*, your Servant; how is it? How goes it?

*Syr.* Very well.

*Dem.* (*Aside.*) Excellent! I have now first brought out these three Expressions contrary to my Nature. *Our* Syrus, *How is it? How goes it?* (to *Syrus*) You shew yourself to be a very worthy Servant, and I'll gladly embrace an Opportunity of doing you a good Office.

*Syr.* I thank you.

*Dem.* I promise you indeed, *Syrus*, and you shall find it too, very soon.

#### ANNOTATIONS.

Demea here gives a Specimen of his new Conduct, and the Poet has contrived on purpose to give every Thing he says an Air of Impertinence and Ridicule, to shew that it is the hardest Thing in the World to change one's natural Disposition, or avoid running from one Extreme into another. *Demea*, instead of complaisant, is a mean servile Flatterer; instead of generous, is extravagantly profuse. The Poet's Judgment in this cannot be enough admired.

3 *Jam nunc hæc tria primum addidi.*

These

---

## ACT V. SCENE IV.

### ARGUMENT.

*Demea continues to affect Affability and Complaisance.*

#### GETA, DEMEA.

*Geta.* (TO Sostrata *within.*) I'm going to see for them, Mistress; that they may send for the Bride as soon as possible.——But here's *Demea*, your Servant.

*Dem.* O, what's your Name, pray?

*Get.* *Geta.*

*Dem.* *Geta*, I have concluded you this Day to be a Man of great Worth; for I look upon him as an undoubtedly good Servant, who has a real Concern for his Master, as I have found you to have, *Geta*; for which Reason, I'll gladly do something for thee, when Opportunity shall offer.——I'm endeavouring to be affable, and it succeeds pretty well.

*Get.*

#### ANNOTATIONS.

Demea soon after accosts *Hegio* in the same Strain of Complaisance, and with the same ridiculous Affectation. Nothing can be more impertinent than the Compliment he makes him, when he was a Stranger even to his very Name.

3 *Lubens*

# ACTUS V. SCENA III.

## ARGUMENTUM.

*Demea Syro præter naturam adulatur, & contra ingenium suum*
*blandus esse conatur.*

### SYRUS, DEMEA.

HEUS Demea, rogat frater, ne abeas longiùs.
  DE. Quis homo? ô Syre noster, salve: quid sit?
  quid agitur?               [mùm addidi
SY. Rectè. DE. optumè est. jam nunc hæc tria pri-
Præter naturam, O noster, Quid sit? Quid agitur?
Servóm haud illiberalem præbes te, & tibi       5
Lubens bene faxim. SY. gratiam habeo. DE. atqui, Syre,
Hoc verum est, & ipsâ re experiere propediem.

*fit? Quid agitur? præbes te servum haud illiberalem, & libens bene faxim tibi. SY. Habeo*
*gratiam. DE. Atqui, Syre, hoc est verum, & experiere ipsâ re propediem.*

**ORDO.**

SY. *HEus De-*
*mea, fra-*
*ter rogat, ut ne abeas*
*longius.* DE. *Quis*
*homo? O noster Syre,*
*salve: quid sit? quid*
*agitur?* SY. *Rectè.*
DE. *Optimè est. Nunc*
*jam primum addidi*
*hæc tria præter na-*
*turam, O noster, Quid*

### ANNOTATIONS.

These Words make the chief Beauty of this Scene, as they represent *Demea* reflecting with himself, and applauding his own Performance and Proficiency. Every one's Experience will teach him, that this is Nature itself, because we are apt to feel the very same Motions in our own Minds, when we attempt to display any new Accomplishments, we never aimed at before.

---

# ACTUS V. SCENA IV.

## ARGUMENTUM.

*Pergit Demea adulando comis videri.*

### GETA, DEMEA.

HERA, ego huc ad hos proviso, quàm mox virginem
  Accersant. sed eccum Demeam. Salvus sies.
DE. Oh, qui vocare? GE. Geta. DE. Geta, hominem
Precii esse te hodie judicavi animo meo.     [maximi
Nam is mihi profectò est servus spectatus satis,   5
Cui dominus curæ est, ita uti tibi sensi, Geta:
Et tibi ob eam rem, si quid usus venerit,
Lubens bene faxim. meditor esse affabilis,

*Nam profectò is est servus satis spectatus mihi, cui dominus est curæ, ita uti sensi esse tibi, Geta*
*&, si quid usus venerit, libens bene faxim tibi ob eam rem. Meditor esse affabilis,*

**ORDO.**

GE. *HEra, e-*
*go pro-*
*viso huc ad hos, ut*
*quàm mox accersant*
*virginem. Sed eccum*
*Demeam, Sis salvus.*
DE. *Ob, qui vocare?*
GE. *Geta.* DE. *Ge-*
*ta, judicavi te ho-*
*die animo meo esse ho-*
*minem maximi pretii,*

### ANNOTATIONS.

8. *Lubens bene faxim.* It is artful in the Poet to represent *Demea* as a meer Rustick, and of a sudden affecting the fine Gentleman, at a loss how to express himself, and obliged to use the same Words over and over again. By this too he prepares us for the Part he is to act in the ensuing Scenes.

10 *Paulatim*

*Get.* You're extremely good, Sir, to think so.

*Dem.* I begin with the loweſt, and ſtrive to gain them by degrees.

### ANNOTATIONS.

10 *Paulatim plebem.* The Poet here had in his eye the Practice of ambitious Candidates, when they were ſuing for any Office or Preſerment in the State. They began with the

---

## ACT V. SCENE V.

### ARGUMENT.

*Æſchinus is provoked to ſee his Marriage retarded by the great Formality of Preparations. Demea addreſſes him in very ſmooth Language, and adviſes to pull down an old Wall, for the more conveniently transferring the Bride.*

### ÆSCHINUS, DEMEA, SYRUS, GETA.

*Æſchinus.* I Proteſt they quite kill me with their Delays: In this Formality of Preparation they waſte the whole Day.)

*Dem.* Æſchinus, how goes it?

*Æſc.* Hah! Was you here, Father?

*Dem.* Your Father indeed, both by Nature and Affection; who love you more than my very Eyes. But why don't you ſend for your Wife?

*Æſc.* I deſire it: but wait for the Flutes, and the Chorus to ſing the nuptial Song.

*Dem.* Pſhaw! Will you take an old Man's Advice?

*Æſc.* What?

*Dem.* Let theſe things alone; the nuptial Song; the Crouds of Company; the Lights and Muſick; and order this old Stone-wall in the Garden to be thrown down with all diſpatch; convey the Bride this way; join the two Houſes in one; and bring over the Mother too, and the whole Family.

*Æſc.* Excellent Advice, moſt charming Father!

*Dem. To himſelf.)* So, I'm now called charming. My Brother's Houſe will be a Thoroughfare; whole Crouds will flock to it; Expence will increaſe, and largely too: what is it to me? I'm accounted a charming Man, and get into Favour.————Order *Babylo* to tell down

### ANNOTATIONS.

. In this Scene, *Æſchirus* comes out, impatient at their tedious Delays in preparing for the Wedding. His Father addreſſes him ſmoothly, and, the more effectually to gain upon him, complies with all his Humours. This takes; *Æſchines* is pleaſed, admires the Expedient he propoſes for the more conveniently transferring the Bride, and commends him as the beſt of Fathers. Hence we have a Leſſon, how ungrateful Cenſure is to Youth; how agreeable Flattery and Indulgence; for by means of this laſt we may inſenſibly poſſeſs ourſelves of their Paſſions, and wind them which way we will.

7 *Hymenæum. Sub: Carmen:* the nuptial Song; from *Hymen,* the Son of *Bacchus* and *Venus,* who firſt inſtituted Marriage; and hence came to be accounted the God of that Solemnity.

10 *Hanc in örtte maceriam. Maceria,* properly

Et bene procedit. GE. bonus es, cum hæc exiſtumas.
DE. Paulatim plebem primulùm facio meam. 10

*Primulùm facio plebem paulatim meam.*

## ANNOTATIONS.

the People, addreſſing them by their Names, and endeavouring to ſteal into their Favour by Flattery and Complaiſance. *Liv. Lib.*

III. 14. *Paulatim, permulcendo, tractandoque manſueſcerent plebem.*

---

# ACTUS V. SCENA V.

## ARGUMENTUM.

*Indignatur Æſchinus nimio apparatu differri nuptias: hunc De-
mea blande alloquitur; & maceriam dirui jubet, quæ puerperam
traducat.*

ÆSCHINUS, DEMEA, SYRUS, GETA.

OCcidunt me, equidem ...dem nimi' ſanctas nuptias
   Student facere, in apparando conſumunt diem.
DE. Quid agitur. Æſchine? Æs. ehem, pater mi, tu hîc
DE. Tuus hercle verò & animo, & naturâ pater, [eras?
Qui te amat plus quàm hoſce oculos. ſed cur non do-
   mum            [eſt, 5
Uxorem accerſis? Æs. cupio: verum hoc mihi mora
Tibicina, & hymenæum qui cantent. DE. eho.
Vin' tu huic ſeni auſcultare? Æs. quid? DE. miſſa hæc
   face,
Hymenæum, turbas, lampadas, tibicinas:
Atque hanc in horto maceriam jube dirui,    10
Quantum poteſt; hac transfer, unàm fac domum:
Tranſduce & matrem & familiam omnem ad nos. Æs.
   placet,
Pater lepidiſſime. DE. euge, jam lepidus vocor.
Fratri ædes fient perviæ: turbam domum
Adducet, ſumtam admittet: multa: quid meâ?    15
Ego lepidus ineo gratiam. jube nunc jam
Dinumeret illi Babylo viginti minas.

*...riam in horto dirui, quamtum poteſt: transfer uxorem hac: fac domum unam: tranſduce & matrem & omnem familiam ad nos. Æs. Pater lepidiſſime, conſilium placet. DE. Euge, jam vocor lepidus: ædes fient perviæ fratri: adducet turpam domum, admittet ſumptum, multa, quid refert mea? ego lepidus ineo gratiam, Jube nunc jam ut Babylo dinumeret illi viginti minas.*

**ORDO.**

*Æs. Equidem occidunt me, dum ſtudent facere nuptias nimis ſanctas, conſumunt diem in apparatu. DE. Æſchine, quid agitur? Æs. Ehem, mi pater, an in eras hîc? DE. Hercle tuus pater, vero, & anima, & natura, qui amat te pluſquam hoſce [meos] oculos. Sed cur non accerſis uxorem domum? Æs. Cupio: verum hoc eſt mihi mora, v.z. tibicina, & qui cantent hymenæum. DE. Eho, viſne tu auſcultare huic ſeni? Æs. Quid? DE. Fac hac miſſa, hymenæum, turbas, lampades, tibicinas? atque jube hanc mace-*

## ANNOTATIONS.

properly a Wall about any Piece of Ground.

12. *Dinumeret illi Babylo viginti minas.* Theſe Words have greatly perplexed Commentators, nor in truth can they be any otherwiſe explained, than by Conjecture; for it is neither eaſy to find to whom they are addreſſed, nor who Demea here means by Ba-bylo. Some think *Babylo* here, refers to *Micio*, whom he ſtyles a *Babylonian* on account of his Riches and Luxury; but as this carries in it the Appearance of a Reproach, and would be repugnant to *Demea's* Deſign, who wants rather to ingratiate himſelf, we muſt reject it. Others explain *illi Babylo,*

down sixty Pounds immediately.——*Syrus*, why don't you go and do as I ordered you?

*Syr.* What?

*Dem.* Down with the Wall. You, *Geta*, go and bring them hither.

*Get.* May the Gods bless you, *Demea*, for acting in so friendly a manner towards our Family.

*Dem.* I think they deserve it. (*To Æschinus.*) What say you to this Project?

*Æsc.* I like it prodigiously.

*Dem.* 'Tis much better than to bring the sick lying-in Woman along the Street.

*Æsc.* I never saw any thing better contrived, Father.

*Dem.* 'Tis my Way: but here comes *Micio!*

## ANNOTATIONS.

*illi impuro, profano*, and refer it to *Sanio*. But *Demea* knew, by what he overheard from *Syrus*, in a former Scene, that that Money was already paid. Let us see then, whether we can't light upon some probable Conjecture. *Demea* had been before reflecting upon the Expence that the present Courses must occasion. *Sumptum admittet ; multa :* and then concludes, *quid mea ?* He resolves then, instead of checking this Expence, to forward it, and turning to *Æschinus*, says, *Jube jam nunc dinumeret;* &c. Where we are to observe,

---

## ACT V. SCENE VI.

### ARGUMENT.

*Micio is prevailed upon, after much Intreaty, to marry Sostrata, not without the Diversion of the Spectators. Demea, contrary to his Nature, studies to be complaisant.*

MICIO, DEMEA, ÆSCHINUS.

*Micio.* DOES my Brother order it, say you? Where is he? *Demea*, is this your Order?

*Dem.* I did, indeed, order it, and in this and every thing else should be glad to unite, serve, oblige, and in a Word, to make this Family one with our own.

*Æsc.* Pray, Father, let it be so.

*Mic.* Nay, I'm not against it.

*Dem.* 'Tis, indeed, what we ought to do. First, here's your Son's Wife's Mother.

*Mic.* What then?

*Dem.*

## ANNOTATIONS.

*Syrus*, according to *Demea's* Order, was busy in throwing down the Garden-Wall, *Micio* observes it, and enquires the Reason; and, understanding that it was by his Brother's Order, wonders at the sudden Change, and comes out, to be satisfied whether it was so really. The meeting of the two Brothers occasions quite a new Scene; for *Demea* carrying every thing to Excess, is not satisfied with bringing over the whole Family, and joining the two Houses in one; but will have *Micio* to marry the Bride's Mother. *Æschinus*

Syre, ceffas ire, ac facere? SY. quid ergo? DE. dixdixi.
Tu, illas, abi, & traduce. GE. Dii tibi, Demea,
Benefaciant, cùm te video noftræ familiæ    20
Tam ex animo factum velle. DE. dignos abitror
Quid tu ais? Æs. fic opinor. DE. multo rectiu' eft,
Quàm illam puerperam hunc duci huc per viam
Ægrotam. Æs. nihil enim vidi melius, mi pater.
DE. Sic foleo. fed eccum; Micio egreditur foras.    25

*Æs. Opinor fic. DE. Eft multo rectius, quam illam puerperam ægrotam nunc duci huc per viam.*
*Æs. Equidem, mi pater, vidi nihil melius. DE. Soleo fic. Sed eccum, Micio egreditur foras.*

*ORDO.*
*Syre, ceffas ire, ac facere? SY. Quid ergo? DE. Dixe. Tu abi, & traduce illas. GE. Dii faciant bene tibi, Demea, cum video te velle factum tam ex animo, noftra familiæ. DE. Arbitror dignos. Quid tu ais?*

## ANNOTATIONS.

ferve, that the greater Part of Manufcripts read *ille Babylo* *Babylo*, I take to be the proper Name of the Banker, in whofe Hands *Micio's* Money was lodged; and that the Words themfelves are addreffed to *Æfchinus*. *Jube nunc jam, ut ille Babylo dinumeret tibi viginti Minas.* " Order that Banker of " my Brother's *Babylo*, to let you have " threefcore Pounds." This *Demea* thought would be grateful to *Æfchinus* at this time, as it would enable him to have every thing at the Wedding to his own liking. He then turns to *Syrus* to quicken him to his Part,

---

# ACTUS V. SCENA VI.

## ARGUMENTUM.

*Micio fuadetur, ut uxorem ducat Softratam, ac vix tandem per-*
*fuadetur, & non fine rifu fpectantium. Demea præter naturam*
*facilis effe ftudet.*

### MICIO, DEMEA, ÆSCHINUS.

JUBET frater? ubi is eft? tune jubes hoc, Demea?
  DE. Ego vero jubeo, & hac re & aliis omnibus
Quàm maxumè unam facere nos hanc familiam;
Colere, adjuvare, adjungere. Æs. ita quæfo, pater.
MI. Haud aliter, cenfeo. DE. imo hercle, ita nobis
    decet.    5
Primùm hujus uxoris eft mater. MI. quid poftea?

*Æs. Pater, fit ita quæfo. MI. Haud cenfeo aliter. DE. Imo hercle ita decet, nobis; primum eft mater uxoris hujus. MI. Quid poftea?*

*ORDO.*
*ANi jubet hoc? Ubi is eft? Demea, tune jubes hoc? DE. Ego vero jubeo; & volo nos hac re, & omnibus aliis facere hanc familiam quam maxime unam, colere, adjuvare, adjungere.*

## ANNOTATIONS.

too, joins in the Requeft, and with much difficulty, he is at laft perfuaded to confent. I don't know whether the Poet is not here liable to fome Cenfure, as he expofes to ridicule a Character that has all along appeared extremely amiable. For *Micio's* Complaifance hitherto, when we confider the Reafons, which he himfelf alledges for it, and the Temper of the Youth, to whom it is fhewn, will admit of fome Excufe; but his Compliance at prefent carries a manifeft Appearance of Simplicity and Folly. here begins his Propofal; but at a Diftance, infomuch that *Micio* might underftand his Meaning, before he came to explain himfelf directly. This is the conftant Practice of Orators, where what they have to Propofe, is of fuch a Nature, that the firft Mention of it might fhock. An Inftance of this we have in *Virgil*, where *Iris* perfuades the *Trojan* Matrons to fet fire to their Ships; the Advice itfelf is the very laft thing fhe mentions, after having premifed a great number of Arguments.

*Dem.* A modest, good kind of Woman.

*Mic.* So they say.

*Dem.* Well in Years too.

*Mic.* I know it.

*Dem.* Long past Child-bearing, quite solitary, and has nobody to regard her.

*Mic.* What does he mean?

*Dem.* You ought to marry her;—and you, *Æschinus*, should endeavour to persuade him to it.

*Mic.* I marry her?

*Dem.* You.

*Mic.* I?

*Dem.* You, I say.

*Mic.* Ridiculous!

*Dem. To Æschinus.)* If you have any Spirit in you, he'll do it.

*Æsc.* Father!

*Mic.* What, Fool, do you mind what he says?

*Dem.* 'Tis in vain to refuse; it can't be otherwise.

*Mic.* You're mad, sure.

*Æsc.* Do, Father, let me prevail with you.

*Mic.* 'Tis all Folly and Extravagance; away.

*Dem.* Come, pray oblige your Son.

*Mic.* Are you in your Senses? Shall I at threescore and five now first marry? And a decrepit old Woman too? Is that your Counsel?

*Æsc.* Do: I have promised it.

*Mic.* Promised too! Pray, Boy, promise for yourself.

*Dem.* Come, what if he should ask a still greater Favour?

*Mic.* As if this was not the greatest.

*Dem.* Comply.

*Æsc.* Father, pray don't refuse.

*Dem.* Do, promise.

*Mic.* Will you not have done?

*Æsc.* Not till I have prevailed.

*Mic.* This is downright Force.

*Dem.* Come, *Micio*, oblige us for once.

*Mic.* Tho' this appears to me foolish, absurd, ridiculous, and repugnant to my Way of Life; yet, if you are so much set upon it, let it be.

*Æsc.* 'Tis mighty good in you: with Reason, I love you, Father.

*Dem.* Well, what shall I say now? this succeeds to my Wish. What more remains to be done?——*(Aloud.) Hegio* is their nearest Relation, our Kinsman too, and poor; we ought, by all means, to do something for him.                                    *Mic.*

DE. Proba & modesta. MI. ...niunt. DE. ...gra-
dior.
MI. Scio. DE. parere jam diu hæc per an... non po...
Nec, qui eam respiciat, quisquam est: sola est. M...
... ...agit?
DE. Hanc te æquum est ducere, & te operam, ut
fiat, dare.                                              10
MI. Me ducere autem? DE. te. MI. me? DE. te,
inquam. MI. ineptis. DE. si tu sis homo,
Hic faciat. Æs. mi pater. MI. quid? tu autem huic,
asine, auscultas? DE. nihil agis.
Fieri aliter non potest. MI. deliras. Æs. sine te exo-
rem, mi pater.
MI. Insanis? aufer. DE. age, da veniam filio. MI.
sati' sanus es?
Ego novus maritus anno demum quinto & sexagesimo
Fiam, atque anum decrepitam ducam? idne estis
auctores mihi?                                          16
Æs. Fac: promisi ego illis. MI. promisti autem? de
te largior, puer.
DE. Age, quid, si quid te majus oret? MI. quasi non
hoc sit maxumum.
DE. Da veniam. Æs. ne gravere. DE. fac, promitte.
MI. non omittitis?
Æs. Non, nisi te exorem. MI. vis est hæc quidem.
DE. age prolixe, Micio.                                 20
MI. Etsi hoc mihi pravum, ineptum, absurdum, atque
alienum à vitâ meâ
Videtur; si vos tantopere istuc voltis, fiat. Æs. bene
facis:
Merito te amo. DE. verùm quid ego dicam? hoc con-
fit quod volo.
Quid nunc quod restat? Hegio his est cognatus prox-
umus,
Affinis nobis, pauper: bene nos aliquid facere illi
; decet.                                                25

Non omittitis? Æs. Non, nisi exorem te. MI. Hæc quidem est vis. Micio. MI. Etsi hoc videtur mihi pravum, ineptum, absurdum, atque alienum à vitâ vitâ; si vos vultis istuc tantopere, fiat. Æs. Facis bene: merito amo te. DE. Verùm quid ego dicam? hoc quod volo confit. Quid est quod restat nunc? Hegio est proximus cognatus his affinis nobis, pauper; decet nos facere aliquid bene illi.

DE. Proba & modesta. MI. ...unt ita. DE. Gradior natu. MI. Scio. DE. Jam diu hæc non potest parere per annos: nec est quisquam, qui respiciat eam: est sola. MI. Quam rem hæc agit? DE. Est æquum te ducere hanc, & te dare operam ut fiat. MI. Me autem ducere? DE. Te. MI. Me? DE. Te, inquam. MI. Ineptis. DE. si sis homo, hic faciat. Æs. Mi pater. MI. Quid? tu autem asine, auscultas hæc? DE. Agis nihil; non potest fieri aliter. MI. Deliras. Æs. Sine ut exorem te, mi pater. MI. Insanis? aufer. DE. Age, da veniam filio. MI. An es satis sanus? ego demum fiam novus maritus anno sexagesimo & quinto, atque ducam anum decrepitam? Estisne auctores mihi ad id? Æs. Fac: ego promisi illis. MI. Promisisti autem? largitor de te, puer. DE. Age, quid si oret te quid majus? MI. Quasi hoc non sit maximum. DE. Da veniam. Æs. Ne gravere. DE. Fac, promitte. MI. ... DE. Age, prolixe, ...

## ANNOTATIONS.

20 *Age prolixe.* H. e. *Benigne, liberaliter.* Cic. Fam. 7. 5. *Neque mehercule minus ei prolixe de tua voluntate promisi, quam eram solitus-d: mea pollicari.*

22 *Si vos tantopere istuc vultis, fiat.* I have already observed, that the Poet's Con- duct here is justly liable to Censure: the only Consideration that can be urged in his Defence is, that he meant to shew the Inconveniencies arising from a Good-nature too extensive; as that it is apt sometimes to betray us into very ridiculous Actions, and such as

*Mic.* Do! What?

*Dem.* There's a little Farm near the Town, which you lett out, let us give it to him to live upon.

*Mic.* A little one, do you say?

*Dem.* Were it a great one, he ought to have it. He is instead of a Father to the young Bride, he is a worthy Man, and our Relation, nor can you bestow it better: besides, Brother, I now adopt the Saying, which you not long ago so happily applied, *'Tis the common Vice of us all, to grow covetous as we grow old.* We ought to avoid this Reproach; 'tis a true Saying, and worthy to be observed.

*Mic.* What's all this? He shall have it, if my Son desires it.

*Æsc.* Dear Father.

*Dem.* Now are you my Brother in Soul as well as Body.

*Mic.* I'm glad on't.

*Dem.* I foil him at his own Weapons.

A N N O T A T I O N S.

we may have occasion to repent of afterwards. But I think *Micio* has all along been | represented so agreeable, and possessed of so much Judgment, good Sense, and Knowledge of

## A C T  V.  S C E N E  VII.

### A R G U M E N T.

*At* Demea's *Request,* Syrus *and his Wife are both made free, and the two young Gentlemen have all their Desires granted:* Demea *too acquaints* Micio *with the Reason of the sudden Change in his Temper.*

SYRUS, DEMEA, MICIO, ÆSCHINUS.

*Syrus.* 'TIS done as you ordered, *Demea.*

*Dem.* A brave Man!——Why, truly, in my Opinion, *Syrus* ought to have his Freedom to-day.

*Mic.* He, his Freedom? for what?

*Dem.* For many things.

*Syr.* O our *Demea,* you're a good Man: I have taken care of these your two Sons from their Cradles; taught them, instructed them, and given them all the good Advice in my power.        *Dem.*

A N N O T A T I O N S.

This Scene gives us the Conclusion of the Play, and sends the Spectators away happy and contented, because all the several Persons concerned in it, obtain the full Completion of their Wishes. We have already seen *Æschinus* and *Pamphila* made happy; *Sostrata* and *Hegio* provided for; so that our only remaining Anxiety is for *Ctesipho,* that he obtain his Wishes; and that the faithful honest *Syrus* be rewarded. The profuse lavish Turn | that had seized *Demea,* happily accomplishes this for us. *Syrus* had obey'd his Orders, and levelled the Wall. He returns to tell him so, and hence he takes the Hint to propose making him free. It is done, and to compleat his Happiness, his Wife *Phrygia* too has her Freedom given her. *Micio* wondering at this strange Change of Temper in his Brother, enquires the Reason of it; *Demea* satisfies him in a grave Speech, and at the

MI. Quid facere ? DE. agelli est hîc sub urbe paulu-
lum, quod locitas foras :
Huic demus, quî fruatur. MI. paululum id autem ?
DE. si multum est, tamen
Faciundum est : pro patre huic est, bonus est, noster
est ; recte datur.
Postremò, non meum illud verbum facio, quod tu,
Micio,                              [omnium est,        30
Bene & sapienter dixti dudum : vitium commune
Quòd nimium ad rem in senectâ attenti sumus. hanc
maculam nos decet
Effugere. dictum est verè, & ipsâ re fieri oportet.
MI. Quid istic ? dabitur quidem, quando hic volt.
ÆS. mi pater.
DE. Nunc tu mihi es germanus pariter corpore &
animo. MI. gaudeo.
DE. Suo sibi gladio hunc jugulo.                       35

portet fieri ipsa re. MI. Quid istic ? quidem dabitur, quando hic vult. ÆS. Mi pater. DE.
Nunc tu es germanus mibi pariter corpore & animo. MI. Gaudeo. DE. Jugulo hunc suo gladio
sibi.

MI. Facere quid ?
DE. Est paululum
agelli hic sub urbe,
quod locitas foras :
demus huic, qui fru-
atur. MI. Vocas id
autem paululum ?
DE. Si est multum,
tamen est faciun-
dum : est huic novæ
nuptæ pro patre :
est bonus : est noster :
datur rectè. Postre-
mo, Micio, nunc fa-
cio illud verbum me-
um, quod tu dixti
bene & sapienter du-
dum : est vitium com-
mune omnium, quod
sumus nimium attenti
ad rem in senecta :
decet nos effugere
hanc maculam : dic-
tum est vere, & o-
portet fieri ipsa re. ÆS. Mi pater. DE.
DE. Jugulo hunc suo gladio
sibi.

## ANNOTATIONS.

of the World, that this last Piece of Extravagance must shock Probability, and offend the
Delicacy of the Spectator.

---

# ACTUS V. SCENA VII.

## ARGUMENTUM.

*Hortatu Demeæ Syrus cum uxore libertate donatur, & filiis am-
bobus optata conceduntur : Causam etiam Micioni refert Demea, cur tam repentè mores mutaverit.*

SYRUS, DEMEA, MICIO, ÆSCHINUS.

FActum est, quod jûsti, Demea.
   DE. Frugi homo es. ego edepol hòdie, meâ qui-
      dem sententiâ,
Judico, Syrum fieri, esse æquom, liberum. MI. istunc
      liberum ?
Quodnam ob factum ? DE. multa. SY. ô noster De-
      mea, edepol vir bonu' es :
Ego istos vobis usque à pueris curavi ambos sedulò ;    5
Docui, monui, bene præcepi semper, quæ potui, omnia.

depol es vir bonus : ego sedulo curavi istos ambos vobis usque à pueris : docui, monui, semper bene
præcepi omnia, quæ potui.

ORDO.

SY. Quod jussisti est factum, Demea. DE. Es homo frugi : equidem ego mea quidem sententia judico esse æ-
quum, Syrum fieri hodie liberum. MI. Istunc esse, liberum ? ob quodnam factum ? DE. Ob multa. SY. O noster Demea, e-
monui, semper bene

## ANNOTATIONS.

the same time informs him of the Part he
intended to act for the time to come. But
Æschinus, tho' he submits, yet still anxious
for his Brother, takes occasion to mention
him. The Answer is favourable, and promises Indulgence. Thus all ends happily.

I 2

8  Apparare

*Dem.* The thing's apparent: besides, to cater, to provide a Girl with secrecy, and prepare a Repast in the Morning for them, are no ordinary Accomplishments.

*Syr.* O the delightful Man!

*Dem.* Nay, he too assisted in buying this Musick-Wench; 'twas he that managed the whole Affair; we ought to reward him, it will be an encouragement to others: besides *Æschinus* too desires it.

*Mic.* Do you desire it?

*Æsc.* I do.

*Mic.* Nay, if you desire it; *Syrus* come hither, be free.

*Syr.* 'Tis generously done: I return my Thanks to you all, and to you in particular, *Demea*.

*Dem.* I rejoice at it.

*Æsc.* And I too.

*Syr.* I believe it. I wish this my Joy were compleat, and that I might see my Wife *Phrygia* free too.

*Dem.* An excellent Woman, truly!

*Syr.* And the first that suckled my young Master's Son, your Grand-Son to-day.

*Dem.* Seriously, and indeed? Nay then, if she verily was the first that suckled him, without all Dispute she ought to be made free.

*Mic.* What, for that?

*Dem.* For that: in fine, you shall have the Price of her Freedom from me.

*Syr.* May the Gods ever grant you all your Desires, *Demea!*

*Mic.* *Syrus*, this has been a happy Day to you.

*Dem.* If moreover, Brother, you'll do your Duty, and let him have some small matter before-hand to begin with; he'll soon repay it.

*Mic.* Not this.

*Æsc.* He's an industrious honest Fellow.

*Syr.* I'll return it, indeed; let me have it but.

*Æsc.* Do, Father.

*Mic.* I'll consider of it.

*Dem.* He'll do it.

*Syr.* O excellent Man!

*Æsc.* O delightful Father!

*Mic.* What means all this, Brother? Whence this sudden Change
in

## *A N N O T A T I O N S.*

[8] *Apparare de die convivium.* The main Emphasis here lies upon *de die*, which signifies in the Morning, before Noon or Mid-day. This, as I have before observed, was accounted Debauchery among the Ancients. The whole Strain of *Demea*'s Speech here is ironical, tho' it passes very well among those to whom it is addressed.

[24] *Istoc vilius.* This, in the Representation, was accompanied with some particular Gesture, expressive of *Micio*'s Intention, as that he held in his Hand, or pointed at something of small Value.

[27] *Quod prolubium?* This Passage is taken from a Comedy of *Cæcilius*:

 ——— *Mea rastraria,*

Quod proluvium, *quæ voluptas, quæ te-*
  *listat. largitas?*

Only that, in the one, we have *prolubium,* which signifies Whim, Caprice, Extravagance;
and

DE. Res apparet. & quidem porro hæc; opsonare,
  cum fide
Scortum adducere, apparare de die convivium.
Non mediocris hominis hæc sunt officia. SY. ô lepi-
  dum caput!
DE. Postremò, hodie in psaltriâ istac emundâ hic ad-
  jutor fuit, 10
Hic curavit: prodesse æquom est: alii meliores erunt.
Denique hic volt fieri. MI. vin' tu hoc fieri? Æs. cu-
  pio. MI. siquidem
Tu vis; Syre eho, accede huc ad me, liber esto. SY.
  bene facis.
Omnibu'gratiam habeo,& seorsum tibi præterea, Demea.
DE. Gaudeo. Æs. & ego. SY. credo. utinam hoc per-
  petuum fiat gaudium, 15
Phrygiam ut uxorem meam unâ mecum videam liberam.
DE. Optumam quidem mulierem. SY. & quidem tuo
  nepoti, hujus filio
Hodie primam mammam dedit hæc. DE. hercle verò
  serio, [quom siet.
Siquidem primam dedit, haud dubium quin emitti æ-
MI. Ob eam rem? DE. ob eam. postremo, à me ar-
  gentum, quanti est, sumito. 20
SY. Dii tibi, Demea, omnes semper omnia optata
  offerant. [Micio,
MI. Syre, processisti hodie pulchrè. DE. siquidem porro,
Tu tuum officium facies, atque huic aliquid paululum
  præ manu
Dederis, unde utatur: reddet tibi citò. MI. istoc vilius.
Æs. Frugi homo est. SY. reddam hercle: da modò.
Æs. age, pater. MI. pòst consulam. 25
DE. Faciet. SY. ô vir optime. Æs. ô pater mi festi-
  vissime. [tuos?
MI. Quid istuc? quæ res tam repentè mores mutavit

*DE. Ob eam: postremo sumito argentum, quanti est, à me. SY. Dii omnes, Demea, semper of-
ferant omnia optata tibi. MI. Syre, processisti pulchre hodie. DE. Siquidem, Micio, tu porro
facies tuum officium, atque dederis paululum aliquid huic, unde utatur, reddet tibi cito. MI. Vilius istoc. Æs. Est frugi homo. SY. Hercle reddam: da modo. Æs. Age, pater. MI.
Consulam post. DE. Faciet. SY. O vir optime. Æs. O mi pater festivissime. MI. Quid istuc?
Quæ res tam repente mutavit tuos mores?*

The right-hand paraphrase column reads:

*DE. Res apparet: & quidem porrò; opsonare, adducere scortum cum fide, apparare convivium de die: hæc, inquam, sunt officia hominis non mediocris. SY. O lepidum caput! DE. Postremò hic fuit adjutor in emendâ istac psaltriâ hodie, hic curavit: est æquum prodesse: alii erunt meliores. Denique hic vult id fieri. MI. Visne tu hoc fieri? Æs. Cupio. MI. Si tu quidem vis; Syre, eho, accede huc ad me, esto liber. SY. Facis bene: habeo gratiam omnibus, & præterea seorsum tibi, Demea. DE. Gaudeo. Æs. Et ego. SY. Credo: utinam hoc gaudium fiat perpetuum, ut videam Phrygiam uxorem meam liberam unâ mecum. DE. Optimam mulierem quidem. SY. Et quidem hæc dedit primam mammam hodie tuo nepoti, filio hujus. DE. Hercle verò serio, si quidem hæc dedit primam mammam ei, haud dubium est, quin fiet æquum eam emitti. MI. Ob eam rem?*

# ANNOTATIONS.

and in the other, *preluvium*, *Profusion*. This,
it is not unlikely, may have also been the
original Reading in *Terence*, as by that the
Sense will be better, and more agreeable to
the Poet's Design. Besides, *prolubium* is seldom used, but when the Discourse regards
Women. Thus *Accius*, in his *Andromeda*:
*Muliebre ingenium, prolubium, occasio.*

And *Laberius*: *Prolubium meretricis.* Dacier.

Ibid. *Quæ istæc subita est largitas.* Criticks
distinguish betwixt *largitas* and *largitio*.
*Largitio*, they tell you, is used in speaking of
particular Acts of Profusion or Liberality.
*Largitas* denotes a Byass, Inclination, or Pro-
pensity. This Distinction answers very well
here.

in your Temper? What Profusion? What an hasty Fit of Prodigality?

*Dem.* I'll tell you. In order to make you senfible, that your paffing for an eafy agreeable Man, is not from your real Life, or founded on Equity and good Senfe: but from your overlooking Things, from your Indulgence, and giving them whatever they want. Now, Æfchinus, if I am, therefore, odious to you, becaufe I don't wholly humour you in every thing, right or wrong; I'll concern myfelf with you no farther; fquander, buy, do whatever you have a mind to. But if you had rather that I check and reftrain you in Purfuits, which, by reafon of your Youth, you are not aware of the Confequences of, where Paffion mifleads you, or prompts you too far; and as Occafion offers direct you: behold me ready to do you that Piece of Service.

*Æfc.* Father, we fubmit to you entirely: you beft know what is fit and proper. But how will you do with my Brother?

*Dem.* I confent that he may have his Girl, provided his Follies end there.

*Æfc.* That's well.——(*To the Spectators.*) Your Applaufe.

## ANNOTATIONS.

here. *Micio* is aftonifhed at fo many Acts of Profufion in *Demea*, and therefore regards them not as Inftances of Good-nature, but as proceeding from a fuddenly contracted Bent or Byafs to Liberality.

32 *Nunc adeo, fi ab eam rem.* Here *Demea* returns to his proper Character, and unriddles to his Brother the Myftery of his fudden Change of Manners; that he only meant to fatisfy him, that his blind Complaifance and Indulgence for his Children, was the fole Caufe of the Affection they had for him, and that it was an eafy Matter to gain it, where one could reconcile himfelf to the Means. The oppofite Characters of thefe two Brothers, and the Inconveniencies they bring upon themfelves, clearly point out to Parents the middle Courfe they ought to hold in the training up of their Children, between exceffive Rigour on the one Side, and an overftrained Indulgence on the other. This is the Part which *Demea* at laft affumes, indulging *Ctefipho* in his Mufick Wench, provided he keeps within Bounds, and don't launch into new Extravagancies. Thofe purer Notions of Morality which Chriftianity infpires, will not allow of this Complaifance; but among the ancient *Greeks* and *Romans*, it was not accounted criminal.

4°. *Iftuc recte.* Thefe Words are generally given to *Æfchinus*, tho' *Donatus*, in his Remarks, afcribes them to *Micio*. The Manner too, in which he explains them, is very ingenious, as if he meant this in a way of Reproach to *Demea*, for adopting an Indulgence he had fo often condemned. " Et
" Micio

Quod prolubium? quæ istæc subita est largitas? De.
   dicam tibi.
Ut id oftenderem, quòd te isti facilem & festivum putant,
Id non fieri ex verâ vitâ, neque adeo ex æquo & bono,
Sed ex assentando, indulgendo, & largiendo, Micio. 31
Nunc adeo, si ob eam rem vobis mea vita invisa est,
   Æschine;
Quia non justa, injusta, prorsus omnia omnino obsequor;
Missa facio, effundite, emite, facite quod vobis lubet.
Sed si id voltis potiùs, quæ vos propter adolescentiam 35
Minu' videtis, magis impensè cupitis, consulitis parùm,
Hæc reprehendere & corrigere me, & obsecundare in
   loco;
Ecce me, qui id faciam vobis. Æs. tibi, pater, per
   mittimus:
Plus scis, quid facto opus est. sed de fratre quid fiet?
   De. sino, 39
Habeat: in istac finem faciat. Æs. istuc rectè. Plaudite.
     CALLIOPIUS RECENSUI.

*scentiam minus videtis, cupitis magis impensè, & consultis parùm, & obsecundare in loco; ecce me qui faciam id vobis. Æs. Pater, permittimus nos tibi: scis plus quid opus est facto: sed quid fiet de fratre? De. Sino ut habeat istam psaltriam: faciat finem in istac. Æs. Istuc est rectè: Plaudite.*

*Quod prolubium? Quæ est istæc subita largitas? De. Dicam tibi. Ut oftenderem id, Micio: quod isti putant te facilem & festivum, id non fieri ex vera vita, neque adeo ex æquo & bono, sed ex assentando, indulgendo, & largiendo. Nunc adeo, Æschine, si mea vita est invisa vobis ob eam rem, quia non obsequor omnino omnia, injusta prorsus ac justa: facio missa; effundite, emite, facite quod libet vobis. Sed si potius velis id: me reprehendere & corrigere hæc, quæ vos propter adole-*

## ANNOTATIONS.

" Micio non discessit de proposito suo, qui ut
" peccasse alias oftenderet fratrem ob nimi-
" am asperitatem, cum exceptione quadam
" laudans verba ejus *istuc rectè* dixit. Qua-
" si diceret, *non & cætera.* Et simul repo-
" suit ei, qui supra dixerat, *ut id oftenderem,*
" *quod te isti facilem, & festivum putant, id*
" *non fieri ex vera vita; neque adeo ex æquo*
" *& bono.*" But it is more natural to think that as *Æschinus* put the Question to his Father, and received a favourable Answer, he makes this Reply, expressing that he was fully satisfied at the Indulgence granted his Brother. Besides, it is not likely, that the Poet, at the Conclusion of the Play, would admit Ironies or Reproaches; it is more for his Purpose to shew them all happy, contented, and in Good-humour.

 PUBLII

# PUBLII TERENTII PHORMIO.

---

# TERENCE's PHORMIO.

# *TERENCE's*

# PHORMIO.

## *The* TITLE.

THIS PLAY WAS EXHIBITED AT THE RO-
MAN GAMES, WHEN L. POSTUMIUS ALBI-
NUS, AND L. CORNELIUS MERULA WERE
CURULE ÆDILES. IT WAS ACTED BY THE
COMPANIES OF L. AMBIVIUS TURPIO, AND
L. ATTILIUS PRÆNESTINUS. FLACCUS THE
FREEDMAN OF CLAUDIUS COMPOSED THE
MUSICK, WHICH WAS PERFORMED ON UN-
EQUAL FLUTES. IT IS TAKEN WHOLLY
FROM A GREEK COMEDY OF APOLLODORUS,
CALLED EPIDICAZOMENOS. IT WAS FOUR
TIMES ACTED UNDER THE CONSULSHIP
OF C. FANNIUS, AND M. VALERIUS.

## ANNOTATIONS.

[1] *Ludis Romanis.* We are told by *Dona-tus,* in his Preface to this Play, that it was acted at the *Megalesian* Games. But *Dona-tus* must certainly be mistaken, for this Play was not brought upon the Stage till after the *Eunuch,* and in the same Year. It could not, therefore, be acted at the Feast of *Cy-bele,* because, on that occasion, the *Eunuch* was represented. We must, therefore, refer it to some other Feast that came after this, and that of the *Romans* all went extremely well, for it was held in the Month of *September,* whereas that of *Cybele* was in *April.* These *Ludi Romani* were very ancient Games, instituted at the first building of the *Circus* by *Tarquinius Priscus.* Hence, in a strict Sense, *Ludi Circenses* are often used to signify the same Solemnity. They were de-signed to the Honour of the three great Dei-ties, *Jupiter, Juno,* and *Minerva.* The old *Fasti* make them to be kept nine Days together, from the Day before the Nones, to
the

# P. TERENTII

# PHORMIO.

## TITULUS seu DIDASCALIA.

ACTA LUDIS ROMANIS, L. POSTU-MIO ALBINO, L. CORNELIO MERU-LA ÆDIL. CUR. EGERE L. AMBIVI-US TURPIO, L. ATTILIUS PRÆNE-STINUS. MODOS FECIT FLACCUS CLAUDII, TIBIIS IMPARIBUS. TOTA GRÆCA APOLLODORU EPIDICA-ZOMENOS. FACTA IV, C. FANNIO, M. VALERIO COSS.

**ORDO.**

Hæc Comœdia fuit acta [1] Ludis Romanis, L. Postumio Albino, L. Cornelio Merula Ædilibus Curulibus. L. Ambivius Turpio, L. Attilius Prænestinus egere. Flaccus Libertus Claudii fecit modos, tibiis imparibus. Est tota Comœdia Græca Apollodoru, dicta [2] Epidicazomenos. [3] Facta erat IV, C. Fannio, & M. Valerio Consulibus.

## ANNOTATIONS.

the Day before the Ides of *September*.

[2] *Epidicazomenos*. For the right understanding of this, see the Notes upon the Prologue. The Word is *Greek*, and respects the Subject of the Play.

[3] *Facta IV.* *Donatus* explains this *edita quarto loco*, that it was acted the Fourth of *Terence*'s Pieces. But there is great Reason to doubt whether this be a just Account of the Matter: for supposing it to be true, that the *Andrian* was the first of *Terence*'s Plays that was brought upon the Stage, yet it would be an Error to maintain that the *Phormio* was his fourth Piece. The Title says expressly, that it was acted at the *Roman* Games. It is, therefore, his fifth Play, in as much as the *Eunuch* was exhibited the same Year during the Feast of *Cybele*, which was before that of the *Romans*. *Facta quarto,* therefore signifies here, that this Comedy was acted four Times the first Year, and this doubtless to mark the Merit of the Piece, which was the chief Intent of those who composed these Titles. It was acted, we are told, when *C. Fannius Strabo*, and *M. Valerius Messala* were Consuls, the same Year in which the *Eunuch* was exhibited.

# *The* ARGUMENT *to the* PHORMIO *from* MURETUS.

CHREMES, and Demipho, were Brothers, both Athenians. Chremes had married at Athens, one Nausistrata, a *Woman with* a large Fortune, and by her had a Son named Phædria. Nausistrata, besides her other *Wealth*, had rich Possessions in Lemnos. *Thither* Chremes went yearly, to let them out, and gather in the Rents. *While* he stays there, chancing to fall in love with a poor *Woman*, he takes her also to *Wife*, and has a Daughter by her, whom he calls Phany; and, to prevent the Story from taking air, he changes his Name, and at Lemnos passes under that of Stilpho. The Revenues of his Athenian *Wife's* Possessions in Lemnos, furnish'd enough to support his other *Wife* there, and her Daughter; and at his Return home, he excused himself under different Pretences; ill Health, the Lowness of Markets, or such like. Demipho too had a Son named Antipho. *When therefore* Phany had now arrived at her fifteenth Year, the Brothers agree between themselves; Chremes, to bring his Lemnian *Wife* and Phany privately to Athens; and Demipho to marry his Son Antipho to Phany. For this purpose, Chremes goes to Lemnos; and it happened at the same time, that De- mipho was under a Necessity of undertaking a Journey to Cilicia. At their Departure, they leave the Care of their Sons to Geta, one of De- mipho's Servants. No sooner are the old Men gone, than Phædria falls in love with a Musick-girl: but there was this unlucky Circumstance in it, that he had nothing wherewith to purchase her from the Cock-bawd to whom she belonged. Meantime, the Lemnian *Wife* urged by Poverty, and no longer able to wait for the Arrival of her Husband, who pro- bably had been away from her beyond his ordinary time, embarks in a Ship, and sails for Athens, together with her Daughter, and the Nurse. There they enquire after Stilpho, but in vain; no one of that Name was to be found at Athens. This Misfortune affected the Mother so deeply, that she died soon after; and Antipho chancing to see Phany, who with the Nurse was paying the last Offices to the deceas'd, falls desperately in love with her. He comes next Day to the Nurse, begging that she will resign her to him, but is rejected, unless he will consent to marry her. He would gladly do any thing, but dreads his absent Father; till at last, Phormio, a Parasite, gives him the following Counsel. There was a Law, among the Athenians, in favour of Orphans, obliging those who were next akin to them, either to marry them, or give them a Portion: I, says the Parasite, will pretend to have been this young *Woman's* Father's Friend, that therefore I undertake her Cause, bring an Action against you as her nearest Relation, and insist that you marry her according to the Terms of the Law. You, on the contrary, must manage so as to give me an easy Victory, and have yourself cast. By this means, you will obtain what you so much desire; and, when your Father returns, have a good Excuse ready. Every thing is conducted as the Parasite had advised. The Marriage is concluded, and soon after the old Men arrive, both on

the

# M. Ant. Mureti ARGUMENTUM.

CHREMES, & Demipho, fratres Athenienses erant. Chremes Athenis uxorem divitem, ac bene donatam duxerat Nausistratam: & ex ea susceperat filium Phædriam. Habebat Nausistrata, præter cæteras opes, opima prædia in Lemno. Eo igitur Chremes quotannis, ad ea locanda, capiendosque fructus, commeabat. Dum illic residet, paupercula cujusdam mulieris amore correptus, eam quoque ducit uxorem, & ex ea suscipit filiam Phanium; ac ne res emanaret, commutato nomine, Stilphonem se Lemni vocari jubet. Detrahebat autem è fructibus prædiorum uxoris Atheniensis, quantium satis esset ad illam alteram unum cum filia nutriendam. Deinde Athenas reversus, ut calamitatem, aut vilitatem, aut tale aliquid causabatur. Erat Demiphoni filius Antipho. Quum igitur Phanium quindecim jam haberet annes, conveniunt inter se Chremes & Demipho, ut Chremes quidem & Lemniam uxorem, & Phanium Athenas clanculum adduceret; Demipho vero Phanium filio suo uxorem daret. Ejus rei causa proficiscitur in Lemnum Chremes. Eodem tempore accidit, ut Demiphoni quoque iter esset in Ciliciam. Abeuntes ambo, Geta (is Demiphonis servus erat) filios committunt suos: profectis senibus, Phædria se statim citharistriæ cujusdam amore implicat. Sed hoc erat incommodi, quod, qui à lenone emeret, quod daret, nihil habebat. Interea uxor è Lemno, quæ propter paupertatem, viri diutius forte, quam solebat morantis, adventum expectare non posset, conscensa navi, Athenas una cum filia, & nutrice ipsius venit: quærunt Stilphonem frustra. Athenis, qui quenquam eo nomine nosset, reperiebatur nemo. Ibi mater (tanta eam ægritudo ceperat) moritur. Ei funus una cum nutrice procurantem Phanium quum adspexisset Antipho, subito amore illius exarsit. Venit ad nutricem postridie, ut ejus sibi copiam faceret, obsecrans: illa se, nisi puellam uxorem duceret, facturam negat. Illi, quum & quidvis facere cuperet, & patrem absentem vereretur, Parasitus Phormio hoc consilium dedit. Lex erat Athenis, ut orbas puellas, qui eis genere proximi essent, ducere, aut, si id nollent, dotem eis dare cogerentur. Ego, inquit parasitus, simulabo, me patri virginis amicum fuisse, ideoque causam illius suscipere: vocabo te in judicium, tanquam illius cognatum, tecumque lege agam, ut eam ducas. Tu ita te defendes, ut mihi facilem victoriam præbeas: ita condemnabere. Sic fiet, ut & tu potiaris tua, &, patre reverso, paratam excusationem habeas. Ita fiunt omnia, ut parasitus suaserat. Confectis jam nuptiis, eodem die ambo redeunt senes: turbati uterque:

ille,

the *fame Day* ; *and are extreamly difconcerted by the News, the one, that his Son had married a Wife without a Fortune, the other, left by lofing this Opportunity of marrying his Daughter, the whole Story of his Amour might come to be divulged. At the fame Time, the Cock-bawd, who had the Difpofal of the Mufick Girl, whom* Phædria *was in love with, threatens that he will fell her to another, unlefs they immediately pay him ninety Pounds for her. To obtain this,* Geta *frames the following Device : He pretends to the old Men, that he had conferred with* Phormio, *and brought him to confent to take* Antipho's *Wife home to himfelf, provided he has with her a Portion of ninety Pounds.* Demipho *immediately gets the Money of* Chremes, *and tells it down to* Phormio, *who gives it to* Phædria, *and* Phædria *to the Cock-bawd for his Miftrefs. Thefe Things are no fooner over, but* Phany *comes to be known. This proves matter of great Joy to the old Men, that a Marriage, which they had before concerted between themfelves, fhould by chance be concluded in their Abfence, and without their knowing any thing of it. But ftill they were difturbed, that they had parted with the ninety Pounds. At firft, they endeavour to recover it by gentle Methods ; but, finding thefe ineffectual, proceed to Threats and Violence. Mean-time,* Phormio, *who had now learnt the whole Story of* Chremes's *two Wives, goes and difcovers all to* Naufiftrata. *She, upon this, complains heavily of her Hufband, but at length is pacified, and agrees to be determined by her Son's Judgment.*

ille, quod filius indotatam uxorem, se absente, duxisset. Hic, quod vereretur, ne, erepta sibi hac collocandæ filiæ occasione, tota res fierat palam. Eo ipso die, leno, citharistriæ, quam Phædria amabat, dominus, nisi sibi pro ea triginta minæ darentur, venditurum se eam, minitabatur. Ad eas conficiendas hanc fallaciam Geta confingit: ait Anidus, se cum Phormione collocutum: Phormionem vero, si sibi dotis triginta minæ darentur, paratum eam uxorem accipere, quam duxisset Antipho. Eam pecuniam Demipho à Chremete sumptam numerat Phormioni: is eam Phædriæ. Phædria lenoni pro amica tradit. Quum hæc jam confecta essent, agnoscitur Phanium. Ibi vero senes gaudere, quod, quas nuptias ipsi facere molebantur, eæ ipsis absentibus, atque inscientibus, factæ essent. Sed dolebant, sibi periisse triginta minas. Eas dum à Phormione, primo blanditiis, postea etiam per vim eripere conantur; Phormio, qui jam de duabus Chremetis uxoribus, deque tota re intellexerat, inclamat Nausistratam, atque aperit omnia. Illa, quum aliquamdiu de viro conquesta esset, tandem placatur; filiique ipsius judicio omnia se permissuram pollicetur.

PER-

# PERSONS *of the* PLAY.

The Speaker of the PROLOGUE.
ANTIPHO, a young Gentleman, the Son of *Demipho.*
CHREMES, an old Man, *Demipho*'s Brother.
CRATINUS,
CRITO, } Counsellors.
HEGIO,
DAVUS, Servant to some unknown Master.
DEMIPHO, an old Man, Brother to *Chremes.*
DORIO, a Cock-bawd.
GETA, *Demipho*'s Servant.
NAUSISTRATA, an *Athenian* Matron, and Wife to *Chremes.*
PHÆDRIA, a young Gentleman, the Son of *Chremes.*
PHORMIO, a Parasite.
SOPHRONA, Nurse to *Phany.*


# MUTES.

DORCY, a Waiting-Maid.
PHANY, a young Lady, the Daughter of *Chremes.*


## SCENE, *ATHENS.*

# DRAMATIS PERSONÆ.

P R O L O G U S.
A N T I P H O, *adolescens, filius Demiphonis.*
C H R E M E S, *senex, frater Demiphonis.*
C R A T I N U S, ⎫
C R I T O, ⎬ *Advocati.*
H E G I O, ⎭
D A V U S, *servus incerti heri.*
D E M I P H O, *senex, frater Chremetis.*
D O R I O, *leno.*
G E T A, *servus Demiphonis.*
N A U S I S T R A T A *matrona, uxor Chremetis.*
P H Æ D R I A, *adolescens, filius Chremetis.*
P H O R M I O, *Parasitus.*
S O P H R O N A, *nutrix Phanii.*

## PERSONÆ MUTÆ.

D O R C I U M, *ancilla.*
P H A N I U M, *adolescentula, filia Chremetis.*

### S C E N A est *ATHENIS.*

## The PROLOGUE.

THE old Bard finding it impossible to make our Poet abandon his Studies, and embrace a Life of Idleness, endeavours by Invectives to deter him from Writing. For he pretends that in all his former Plays, the Characters are too simple, and the Style not sufficiently raised; because, forsooth, he never described a frantick Youth, who fancied he saw a Hind closely pursued by the Hounds, bemoaning her Fate, and imploring his Aid. But were he sensible that his Play, when it was first represented, owed its Success more to the Address of the Actor, than any Merit in the Piece itself; he would not, perhaps, be so rash in giving Offence. Now, if any one among you should say or think, that had not the old Bard first attacked our Poet, he would not have known how to write a Prologue, having no one to abuse, let this serve for an Answer: That the Prize of Honour is proposed in common to all who apply to the Poetick Art. He aimed at driving our Poet from his Studies into Indigence and Want, who again means this only as an Answer, not an Invective. Had he opposed him in gentle Terms, he had met with a gentle Reply. He has only repaid in kind the Injury, which he first offered. But henceforth I shall take no farther Notice of him, since he ceases not daily to expose himself. Attend now what it is I request of you. I present you to-day a new Play, which the *Greeks* call *Epidicazomenos*,

but

### ANNOTATIONS.

[1] *Vetus Poeta.* *Luscius Lanuvinus*, the same mentioned in former Prologues. We see from this, that all his Attempts were the Effect of Jealousy. He was afraid that *Terence* would eclipse him, and obscure the Fame he had enjoyed so long, and, therefore, endeavoured to crush him in his first Essays; but not succeeding, he takes all possible ways to detract from his Merit, and decry his Writings.

[5] *Tenui esse oratione, & scriptura levi.* The Distinction between *oratio* and *scriptura* ought not to pass unregarded. *Eugraphius* interprets the Passage: *Soliditatem in verbis nullam, nullam in rebus*; which Explication seems also to be adopted by Madam *Dacier*, who refers *oratio* to the Characters, and *scriptura* to the Style. To this last he objects, that it was low and creeping, *levis*; in like manner as *Horace* says of some of the Verses of *Ennius*, that they were *gravitate minores*, void of Weight, Force, and Solidity. In this we may observe how injudicious the old Critick was in his Censures, thus to exclaim against what was the chief Ornament and Beauty of Comedy, a Style simple, unaffected, and void of Pomp.

[4] *Quia nusquam insanum scripsit adolescen-* *tulum.* This Verse serves to illustrate the foregoing, and confirms the Explication we have given of it; for here the Poet gives us a Specimen of his Rival's Genius and Taste. He was fond of bringing upon the Stage frantick Youths, acting up to all the Excesses of Folly and Distraction, Characters extravagant, unnatural, and overstrained: hence the Language and Stile must be of a piece, impetuous, turbulent, full of Rant, full of Affectation. No wonder, therefore, if he could not relish the Compositions of our Poet, whose Characters are drawn from Nature, and Still Life, and the Language suitably artless and simple.

[10] *Actoris opera stetisse.* This *Terence* adds in Complaisance to his Audience, that he might not seem to charge them with want of Judgment in approving a Piece so wretched as that he had been just censuring. He ascribes its Success neither to the Merit of the Piece, nor want of Judgment in the Spectators, but to the Address of the Actors. Just Action is of irresistible force, and helps out many a lame Performance. Our own Times are a Proof of it. How many Plays are well received upon the Stage, and afterwards, when published, scarce ever read?

*Minus*

# PROLOGUS.

POSTQUAM poeta vetus poetam non poteſt
  Retrahere à ſtudio, & tranſdere hominem in otium ;
Maledictis deterrere, ne ſcribat, parat :
Qui ita dictitat, quas antehac fecit fabulas,
Tenui eſſe oratione, & ſcripturâ levi,      5
Quia nuſquam inſanum ſcripſit adoleſcentulum
Cervam videre fugere, & ſectari canes,
Et eam plorare, orare ut ſubveniat ſibi.
Quòd ſi intellegeret, cùm ſtetit olim nova,
Actoris operâ magis ſtetiſſe, quàm ſuâ :    10
Minu' multo audacter, quàm nunc lædit, læderet.
Nunc ſi quis eſt, qui hoc dicat, aut ſic cogitet,
Vetu' ſi poeta non laceſſiſſet prior,
Nullum invenire prologum potuiſſet novus
Quem diceret, niſi haberet, cui malediceret :   15
Is ſibi reſponſum hoc habeat ; in medio omnibus
Palmam eſſe poſitam, qui artem tractant muſicam.
Ille ad famam hunc ab ſtudio ſtuduit reicere :
Hic reſpondere voluit, non laceſſere.
Benedictis ſi certaſſet, audiſſet bene    20
Quod ab illo allatum eſt, ſibi id eſſe relarum putet.
De illo jam finem faciam dicundi mihi,
Peccandi cùm ipſe de ſe finem non facit.
Nunc quid velim, animum attendite. apporto novam
Epidicazomenòn quam vocant comœdiam   25

ORDO.

POſtquam vetus poeta non poteſt retrahere noſtrum poetam à ſtudio, & tranſdere hominem in otium ; parat deterrere cum maledictis, ne ſcribat : qui dictitat ita, fabulas, quas noſter poeta fecit antehac eſſe tenui oratione, & levi ſcriptura, quia nuſquam ſcripſit inſanum adoleſcentulum videre ſervam fugere, & canes ſectari, & eam plorare, & orare ut ipſe ſubveniat ſibi. Quod ſi intelligeret, cum nova ejus comedia olim ſtetit, eam ſtetiſſe magis opera acteris, quam ſua ; læderet multo minus audacter, quam lædit nunc. Nunc ſi eſt quis, qui dicat hoc, aut cogitet ſic, ſi vetus poeta non prior laceſſiſſet, novus potuiſſet invenire nullum prologum, quem diceret, niſi haberet, cui malediceret : is habeat hoc reſponſum ſibi ; palmam eſſe poſitam in medio omnibus, qui tractant artem muſicam. Ille ſtuduit reicere hunc ab ſtudio ad famam : et

gum, quem diceret, niſi haberet, cui malediceret : is habeat hoc reſponſum ſibi ; palmam eſſe poſitam in medio omnibus, qui tractant artem muſicam. Ille ſtuduit reicere hunc ab ſtudio ad famam : et hic voluit reſpondere, non laceſſere. Si certaſſet benedictis, audiſſet bene : putet id eſſe relatum ſibi, quod eſt allatum ab illo. Jam faciam finem mihi dicendi de illo, cum ipſe non facit finem peccandi de ſe. Nunc animum attendite, quid velim. Apporto novam comœdiam, quam Græci vocant Epidicazomenon.

## *ANNOTATIONS.*

11 *Minu' multo audacter*, &c. In moſt Editions of *Terence*, the following Verſe comes after this :

  *Et magis placerent quas feciſſet fabulas.*
The *Cambridge* Edition, however, has rejected it, and indeed I am aſtoniſhed that it was ſuffered in this Prologue ſo long ; for beſides that it is manifeſtly taken from the Prologue to the *Andrian*, it makes here no Senſe as all, or a very ridiculous one.

16 *In medio omnibus palmam eſſe poſitam.* This does not ſeem a direct Anſwer to what *Terence* is reproached with, yet is ſufficient to ſtop the Mouths of his Adverſaries, as it ſignifies that his attacking his Rival was Compulſion and Self-defence. He has, in a former Prologue, ſhewn in what manner he would have acquitted himſelf, had he not been reduced to the Neceſſity of anſwering the malicious Inſinuations of the old Bard. Prol. *Andr.* 5.

  *Nam in prologis ſcribundis operam abuſi-*
    *tur,*
  *Non qui argumentum narret, ſed qui male-*
    *voli*
  *Veteris poetæ maledictis reſpondeat.*

23 *Peccandi cum ipſe de ſe finem non facit.* De ſe is here either for *ultro*, or *de ſua parte, quod ad ſe attinet.* *Wielingius* explains it ; *Non faciam finem, cum ipſe finem non facit.*

25 *Epidicazomenon.* This Word is originally *Greek*, and implies one who demands Juſtice of another. This was *Phormio* the

but the *Latins*, *Phormio*; becaufe he who acts the chief Part is *Phor-mio*, a Parafite, by whom the Plot is moftly conducted. If you are difpofed to encourage the Poet, attend with Silence, and an impartial Ear, that we mayn't meet with the like Difafter as once before, when our Company was by a Tumult driven from their Places, which the Merit of the Actors, feconded by your Candour and Goodnefs, has fince reftored to us.

## ANNOTATIONS.

*Parafite.* Hence, in the Original, the Play was call'd *Epidicazomenes*, from *Phormio's* fuing *Antipho* to marry *Phany*, and in the *Latin* intitled *Phormio*, after his own proper Name.

32 *Nofter Grex motus loco eft.* It is generally

Græci, Latini Phormionem nominant;
Quia primas partes qui aget, is erit Phormio
Parasitus, per quem res geretur maxumè.
Voluntas vostra, si ad poetam accesserit,
Date operam, adeste æquo animo per silentium:  30
Ne simili utamur fortunâ, atque usi sumus,
Cùm per tumultum noster grex motus loco est:
Quem actoris virtus nobis restituit locum,
Bonitasque vostra adjutans, atque æquanimitas.

*Latini nominant Phormionem; quia is, qui aget primas partes, erit Phormio parasitus, per quem res maxime geretur. Si vestra voluntas accesserit ad poetam, date operam, adeste æquo animo per silentium; ne utamur simili fortuna, atque*

*usi sumus, cum noster grex est motus loco per tumultum: quam locum virtus actoris, bonitasque vostra, atque æquanimitas adjutans, restituit nobis.*

## A N N O T A T I O N S.

rally supposed that *Terence* means here, the *Hecyra*, which was not acted quite through till after several Attempts and Repulses, as | will be taken notice of on the Prologue to that Play.

K 3                    PHOR-

# *TERENCE's*
# PHORMIO.

## ACT I. SCENE I.

### ARGUMENT.

*Davus, coming out, tells us that he brings with him an old Debt
due to* Geta. *He is introduced on purpose to give* Geta *an Opportunity in Conversation with him to explain the Subject of
the Play.*

### DAVUS.

MY very good Friend and Countryman *Geta* came to me yesterday. There was a trifle of Money of his in my hands, the
Balance of an old Account, which he wanted me to make
up; I have done so, and now bring it with me: for I hear that his
Master's Son is married, and suppose this is scraped together as a Present for the Bride. How unjust is Custom; that they who have but
little, are always adding to the Abundance of the Rich! All that this
poor Wretch has been able to save by little and little out of his small
Allowance, denying himself almost every Indulgence, must go at once
to her, who never thinks of the Pains with which it was got. Besides,
*Geta* must provide another Gift, when his Mistress shall be brought

to

### ANNOTATIONS.

*Terence* proceeds here, in the same manner
as in his former Plays: introduces *Davus*,
and soon after *Geta*, to let us into the Plot,
and prepare us for what is to follow. *Geta*
had requested of *Davus*, to let him have a
trifle of Money he owed him, which *Davus*
here brings; and as he had heard that *Geta's*
young Master was lately married, he naturally enough conjectures, that it was intended
as a present for the Bride. This leads him
into several beautiful Reflections upon the
Inequality of the Lot of Man, till by the
Appearance of *Geta* he is interrupted.

*Popularis.* This Word does not always
signify one born in the same Country or City:
often it imports no more than that he lived
in the same District, and had his Name writ-
ten in the same Roll or List. Hence it
sometimes stands for an intimate Friend, or
familiar Acquaintance, because those of the
same Division or Tribe were generally well
known to one another.

[2] *Erat ci de ratiuncula.* *Terence* here
speaks of a small Sum, and therefore purposely uses Diminutives, *pauxillulum* and *ratiuncula*; this conveys the Idea the more
strongly, and makes way for the Reflection
that follows, of the great Hardship that Servants should be deprived of the little they have
with so much pains saved. The Sense is,
*Debebam ei nonnihil ex ratione antiqua.*

[9] *Quod ille unciatim vix de demenso suo.*
This Passage is beautiful beyond Expression,
and requires to be particularly explained.
Servants, says *Donatus*, received four Measures of Bread-Corn every Month, and this
monthly Allowance was call'd *Demensum*,
perhaps from *mensis* the Term of Payment,
or rather from *demetiri*, because it was mea-
sured out to them four *Medii* or Bushels.
Hence the Word came to be used for Servants Wages of every kind. *Unciatim per
uncias*, by Ounces. It was impossible to choose
a happier Term, as it refers to Wages paid

in

# P. TERENTII
# PHORMIO.

## ACTUS I. SCENA I.

### ARGUMENTUM.

*Davus exiens dicit adferre se, quam debet Getæ, pecuniam, & hæc persona extra argumentum inducitur, cui rem gestam narraturus est Geta.*

### DAVUS.

<table>
<tr><td>

AMICUS summus meus, & popularis Geta
Heri ad me venit : erat ei de ratiuncula
Jampridem apud me reliquum pauxillulum
Nummorum : id ut conficerem. confeci : affero.
Nam herilem filium ejus duxisse audio          5
Uxorem ei, credo, munus hoc conraditur.
Quam inique comparatum est, ii, qui minus habent,
Ut semper aliquid addant divitioribus.
Quod ille unciatim vix de demenso suo,
Suum defrudans genium, comparsit miser,        10
Id illa universum abripiet, haud existumans
Quanto labore partum. porro autem Geta
Ferietur alio munere, ubi hera pepererit:

</td><td>

ORDO.

GETA amicus summus amicus & popularis venit heri ad me : et jampridem pauxillulum nummorum, quum reliquum ei apud me de ratiuncula : l operi ut conficerem, id q; confeci : affero. Nam audio herilem filium ejus duxisse uxorem : credo, hoc munus conraditur ei. Quam inique est comparatum, ut ii, qui habent minus, semper addant aliquid divi-

</td></tr>
</table>

*tioribus. Quod ille miser vix comparsit unciatim de suo demenso, defraudans suum genium, illa abripiet id universum, haud existimans quanto labore sit partum. Porro autem Geta ferietur alio munere, ubi hera pepererit:*

### ANNOTATIONS.

in Corn." Observe, therefore, the Force of the whole Sentence. 'He saves it, *de demenso suo*, from his monthly Pittance of Corn *unciatim* by Ounces, and even that with great difficulty, *vix.* The following Verse still heightens the Description, as it denotes the Pains and Anxiety it cost him to scrape it together: *Vix comparsit, defraudans suum genium.* Not a Word, but what is strong, significant, and expressive, and tends to heighten still the Description as you go on, making the whole a regular *Climax.* This Image of Poverty and Distress, that saves a trifle with so much Labour, is finely contrasted in the next Line, where it is quite swallowed up, and disappears at once, without making any sensible Addition to the Person who receives it, or leaving any Impression of the Pains it cost to acquire it. *Id illa universum abripiet, haud existumans quanto labore sit partum.* Observe

the Opposition. *Quod ille* conradit: *illa* abripiet: *Quod ille miser vix comparsit.* unciatim de suo demenso : *illa abripiet* Id universum ; *haud existumans quanto labore sit partum.*

13 *Ferietur alio munere."* It will be struck for another Present ; a Phrase peculiar to common Conversation, and very expressive: *Ex consuetudine ferietur* (says *Donatus*) *non & plagam, damnum & sumptum,* sanguinem nostrum dicimus. In truth, *ferire* is often used, where any thing is like to happen to us, that it is supposed will be uneasy and vexatious. As in *Horace*, Book II. Sat. I. where *Trebatius* threatens him with Coldness and Indifference from his powerful Friends

——— O puer, ut sit
*Titanis, metus, & majorum ne quis amicus*
*Frigore te feriat.*

to Bed, and, moreover, another upon the Anniversary of the Boy's
Nativity, when he shall be initiated. All this the Mother carries
off, tho' the Child serves for the Pretence. But isn't that *Geta* there?

### ANNOTATIONS.

15 *Ubi initiabunt.* This refers to the
Custom of Initiation among the Ancients,
of which there were several kinds, nor is it
easy to fix upon any one particular here with

Certainty. We read in *Varro*, that Children
were initiated *edulia*, *& poticæ*, *& cubæ*, i.
e. *divis edendi, & potandi, & cubandi, ubi
primum à lacte; & curis, ad solidiores cibos*

---

# ACT I. SCENE II.

## ARGUMENT.

Geta *tells* Davus *of both the old Mens going from home, soon
after which* Antipho, Demipho's *Son, falls in love with a
young Girl, whom, by the Persuasion and Artifice of a Parasite,
he is induced to marry.*

### GETA, DAVUS.

*Geta.* **T**O them within.) If a red-haired Man should enquire for me—
     *Dav.* Here he is, say no more.

*Get.* O, *Davus!* I was just coming out to meet you.

*Dav.* Take it here, 'tis good Coin, and the exact Sum I owe you.

*Get.* I love you, and thank you for not forgetting me.

*Dav.* Especially as Times now are: the World is come to that
pass, that a Man must be extremely thankful, if he receives but his
own. But why so grave?

*Get.* Who I? You little know the Terror and Danger I am in.

*Dav.* What is it, pray?

*Get.* You shall know, if you'll promise to be secret.

*Dav.* Away, Simpleton: are you afraid to trust him with Words,
whom you have found faithful in your Money? What Advantage
can I propose by betraying you?

*Get.* Be attentive then.

*Dav.* I promise you I will.

*Get.* Do you know *Chremes*, our old Master's elder Brother?

*Dav.* Know him! perfectly well.

*Get.* What! And his Son *Phædria* too?

*Dav.* As well as I know you.

*Get.* It happened that both the old Men were obliged to take a Journey at the same time, *Chremes* to *Lemnos*, and our good Man to *Cilicia,*

### ANNOTATIONS.

*Davus* is interrupted by the Appearance
of *Geta*, who is here seen coming out to
look for him, and leaving Instructions at
home, if perhaps he should enquire for him
after he was gone. When they meet, they
fall into Conversation, in which the whole
Mystery of the Play is laid open: the Dan-

ger that threatened *Geta*, by the precipitate
Behaviour of his Master's Son; the Anxiety the young Gentleman himself lay under, lest, at his Father's Return, his *Phany*
might be ravished from him, and the Distress
*Phædria* was in, that he could not come at
the Possession of his Musick-Girl. All these
are

Porro autem alios, ubi erit puero natalis dies,
Ubi initiabunt; omine hoc mater auferet :          15
Puer causa erit mittundi. Sed videon' Getam?

*hoc omne: puer erit causa mittundi. Sed videsne Getam?*

*porro autem alios, ubi natalis dies erit pue-ro, uti initiabunt cum? mater auferet*



*& lectulos transibant.* But Madam *Dacier* rejects this, because it was a Custom purely *Roman*, whereas the present Piece is translated from the *Greek*. She supposes it is to be understood of their being initiated in the grand Mysteries of *Ceres*, which was commonly done while they were yet very young.

## ACTUS I. SCENA II.

### ARGUMENTUM.

*Geta narrat, quo sunt profecti senes Demipho & Chremes; qua occasione cœperit amare Demiphonis filius Antipho: & quomodo captus amore virginis, eam opera parasiti uxorem duxerit.*

### GETA, DAVUS.

SI quis me quæret rufus—DA. præsto est, desine. GE. oh,
At ego obviam conabar tibi, Dave. DA. accipe, hem :
Lectum est, conveniet munerus, quantum debui.
GE. Amo te, & non neglixisse habeo gratiam.
DA. Præsertim ut nunc sunt mores ; adeo res redit :   5
Si quis quid reddit, magna habenda est gratia.
Sed quid tu es tristis? GE. egone? nescis quo in metu &
Quanto in periclo simus. DA. quid istuc est? GE. scies,
Modo ut tacere possis. DA. abi sis, insciens :
Cujus tu fidem in pecuniâ perspexeris,        10
Verere ei verba credere? ubi quid mihi lucri est
Te fallere? GE. ergo ausculta. DA. hanc operam tibi
   dico.
GE. Senis nostri, Dave, fratrem majorem Chremem
Nostin'? DA. quidni? GE. quid? ejus gnatum Phæ-
   driain?
DA. Tanquam te. GE. evenit, senibus ambobus simul,
Iter illi in Lemnum ut esset, nostro in Ciliciam   16

GE. SI quis homo rusus quæret me.---- DA. Præsto est, desine. GE. Obi, ego conabor ire obviam tibi, Dave. DA. Hem, accipe; argentum est lectum, munerus, conveniet, habes quantum debui. GE. Amo te, & habeo gratiam; non neglexisse ... DA. Præsertim ut mores sunt nunc, res redit; adeo, si quis reddit, quid, magis gratia est habenda ei. Sed ob quid tu es tristis? GE. Egone? nescis in quo metu, & in quanto periculo simus. DA. Quid est istuc? GE. Scies, modo ut possis ...

taceas. DA. Abi sis, insciens: verere credere verba ei, cujus fidem tu perspexeris in pecuniâ? Ubi est quid lucri mihi fallere te? GE. Ausculta ergo. DA. Dico hanc operam tibi. GE. Nostine, Dave, Chremem, majorem fratrem nostri senis? DA. Quidni? GE. Quid? Nostine Phædriam gnatam ejus? DA. Tanquam novi te. GE. Evenit, ut esset iter ambobus senibus simul, illi in Lemnum, nostro in Ciliciam.



are strongly represented; the Passions of the Audience gradually moved, and the Way prepared for the Appearance of the other Characters, and the Parts they are to act.

3. *Lectum est*; i. e. *Argentum est integrum, non adulterium, sed justi ponderis & pretii.*

7 *Sed quid tu es tristis?* By this we are led to understand, that *Geta* had from the Beginning appeared thoughtful and perplexed, as if his Attention was taken up with something
   thing

*cia*, to an old Acquaintance there, who wheedled him over by Letters, promising him Mountains of Gold, and what not.

*Dav.* To him, who had so much, and more than he could use?

*Get.* Hold your tongue: 'tis his way.

*Dav.* O! I ought certainly to have been a King.

*Get.* When the old Gentlemen set out, they left me as Tutor to their Sons.

*Dav.* O *Geta!* you had a hard Task to enter upon.

*Get.* That I know well from Experience. I'm satisfied my good Genius abandoned me that day in anger. At first, I began to oppose them: what need of Words? while I study to be faithful to the old Men, my Shoulders smarted.

*Dav.* I thought as much, for 'tis Madness to kick against the Pricks.

*Get.* I then began to do as they would have me, and humour them in every thing.

*Dav.* You knew how to make your Market.

*Get.* Our Youth run into no Mischief at first: but *Phædria* immediately found out a Musick-girl, whom he became desperately fond of. She was in the hands of a sordid covetous Wretch of a Cock-bawd, nor had they any thing to give, their Fathers had taken care of that. All he could do, therefore, was to feed his Eyes with her, dangle after her, lead her to School, and back again. We, who had nothing to employ us, were commonly with *Phædria.* Right over-against the Musick-School, where this Girl learnt, was a Barber's Shop: here we generally waited her coming out, to attend her home. One day, as we sat there, a young Man came in with Tears in his Eyes: we wondered what could be the matter, and asked him the reason. Never, said he, did Poverty seem to me so grievous and heavy a Burden, as it doth now. I have just seen an unfortunate young Creature of this Neighbourhood lamenting her dead Mother. She sat over-against the Body, nor was any Friend, Acquaintance, or Relation

lation

## ANNOTATIONS.

thing of moment. *Donatus* goes so far as to observe, that this may be even gathered from his Conversation: for that *si quis me quærit :  at ego, obviam conabar tibi, Dave :* and, *amo te, & non neglexisse habeo gratiam :* are Expressions that evidently carry in them an Indication of Anxiety and Concern in the Mind of him who speaks. Whatever may be in this, I am apt to think that *Geta*'s Concern appeared more from the Air and Cast of his Countenance, than any thing in the Expressions he uses.

18. *Modo non montes auri pollicens.* Modo non, here for *tantum non; ferme, propemodum.* As if he had said; promising almost Mountains of Gold.

20. *Ob, regem me esse oportuit. Rex* is often used for a rich Man, or a Man of Power, as if *Davus* had said; *I ought by all means to have been rich :* agreeable to the usual Vanity of People in low Life, who think that Wealth is for the most part thrown away upon those that possess it, and that did it belong to them, they would know better how to use it. We are therefore to compleat the Sentence ourselves: I ought certainly to have been a King, or a great Man: I should have known how to use Riches, how to be liberal, and how to bound my Desires when I had enough, nor undertaken a long and hazardous Voyage to increase a Stock that was already overgrown.

24. *Reliqui me Deo irato meo.* The Ancients had a Persuasion, that each Man had

Ad hospitem antiquom, is senem per epistolas
Pellexit, modò non montes auri pollicens.
DA. Cui tanta erat res, & supererat? GE. desinas:
Sic est ingenium. DA. oh, regem me esse oportuit. 20
GE. Abeuntes ambo hîc tum senes me filiis
Relinquunt quasi magistrum. DA. ô Geta, provinciam
Cepisti duram. GE. mihi usus venit, hoc scio.
Memini relinqui me Deo irato meo.
Cœpi advorsari primò: quid verbis opu' st? 25
Seni fidelis, dum sum, scapulas perdidi:
DA. Venere in mentem mihi istæc: namque inscitia est,
Advorsum stimulum calces. GE. cœpi his omnia
Facere, obsequi quæ vellent. DA. scisti uti foro.
GE. Noster mali nil quidquam primò: hic Phædria 30
Continuò quandam nactus est puellulam
Citharistriam: hanc amare cœpit perditè.
Ea serviebat lenoni impurissimo:
Neque, quod daretur, quidquam: id curarant patres.
Restabat aliud nihil, nisi oculos pascere, 35
Sectari, in ludum ducere, & reducere:
Nos otiosi operam dabamus Phædriæ.
In quo hæc discebat ludo, exadvorsùm illico
Tonstrina erat quædam. hic solebamus fere
Plerumque eam opperiri, dum inde iret domum. 40
Interea dum sedemus illic, intervenit
Adolescens quidam lacrumans: nos mirarier:
Rogamus, quid sit, nunquam æquè, inquit, ac modò
Paupertas mihi onus visum est & miserum, & grave.
Modò quandam vidi virginem hîc viciniæ 45
Miseram, suam matrem lamentari mortuam.
Ea sita erat exadvorsùm: neque illi benevolens,

*ad antiquum hospitem is pellexit senem per epistolas, pollicens modo non montes auri. DA. Cui tanta res erat, & supererat? GE. Oro ut desinas: ingenium est sic. DA. Oh, oportuit me esse regem. GE. Ambo senes tum abeuntes relinquunt me hic quasi magistrum filiis. DA. O Geta, cepisti duram provinciam. GE. Scio hoc, usus venit mihi. Memini me relinqui Deo meo irato. Primo cœpi adversari iis: quid opus est verbis? dum sum fidelis seni, perdidi scapulas. DA. Istac venere in mentem mihi: namque est inscitia jactare calces adversum stimulum. GE. Cœpi facere omnia his, obsequi quæ vellent. DA. Scisti uti foro. GE. Noster primo egit nihil quidquam mali, hic Phædria continuo nactus est quandam puellulam citharistriam capit amare hanc perdite. Ea serviebat impurissimo lenoni: neque erat quidquam iis quod daretur, patres*

*curaverant id. Nihil aliud restabat, nisi pascere oculos, sectari eam, ducere in ludum, & reducere. Nos otiosi dabamus operam Phædriæ. Illico exadversum ludo, in quo hæc discebat, erat quædam tonstrina. Hic plerumque fere solebamus opperiri eam, dum iret inde domum. Interea dum sedemus illic, quidam adolescens intervenit, lacrumans: nos cœpimus mirari: rogamus quid sit. Inquit, Paupertas nunquam est visum mihi onus & miserum & grave, æque ac modo. Modo vidi quandam virginem viciniæ hic, lamentari suam matrem mortuam. Ea erat sita exadvorsum: neque benevolens quisquam*

## ANNOTATIONS.

a. Genius or guardian Deity, who constantly attended him: and that when he fell into any Misfortune, or was guilty of any Crime, it was because his good Genius had abandoned him.

29 *Scisti uti foro.* A Metaphor taken from Traffick, in which, Merchants suit themselves to the Times, and fix a Price upon their Commodities according to the Course of the Market.

36 *In ludum ducere.* To lead her to School.

In *Greece* were Schools appropriated to Singing, Musick, and Dancing. There is something satirical in this Representation; *Phædria*, a Youth qualified to attend the Lessons of Philosophers, is here seen dangling after a young Girl to School.

39 *Tonstrina erat quædam.* Barbers Shops in *Athens* and *Rome* were Places of publick Resort for Conversation, much of the Nature of our Coffee-houses.

tition prefent, to affift at the Funeral, excepting one poor old Woman.    I pitied her from my Soul.    The Girl herfelf too a compleat Beauty.    To be fhort, we were all moved at the Story.    Then fays *Antipho*, What d'ye think ? Shall we go and fee her ? Go by all means, fays another: pray lead us to her.    We go, come to the Place, and fee the Girl.    She was beautiful beyond Expreffion; and, as an incontestible Proof of it, appeared fo, though deftitute of every Advantage to recommend her.    Her Hair loofe; her Feet bare; her Drefs mean; her Countenance disfigured with Grief; and her Eyes drowned in Tears: fo that had fhe not poffeffed a native Stock of Charms, thefe Circumftances muft have quite extinguifhed her Beauty.    The other Spark, that was enamoured of the Mufick-girl, only faid; She's well enough : but our Youth——

*Dav.* I guefs it already : was fmitten.

*Get.* But can you imagine how deeply ? obferve the Confequence. Next Day he goes to the old Woman, and begs that he may have the Girl. She refufes; nor was it juft in him, fhe told him, to require it : that fhe was a Citizen of *Athens*, virtuous, and well defcended : if he meant to marry her, that he might lawfully do ; but otherwife it was in vain to hope. My young Mafter was quite at a lofs what to do: he had a ftrong Inclination to marry her, but dreaded his abfent Father.

*Dav.* Would not his Father, if he was returned, give his Confent ?

*Get.* He confent to his marrying a Girl of obfcure Birth, and no Fortune ! he'd never do it.

*Dav.* What's come of it then ?

*Get.* What's come of it ? There is one *Phormio*, a Parafite, a ftrange confident Fellow, who, Perdition blaft him——

*Dav.* What has he done ?

*Get.* Gave this Counfel I am now about to tell you. There is a Law which ordains, that Orphan Girls fhall marry thofe who are neareft to them in Blood, and contrarywife the fame Law obliges their neareft Relations to marry them. I'll fay you are related to her, and pretending to be her Father's Friend, commence a Suit againft you. We'll bring it before the Judges : as to who was her Father, who her Mother, or how fhe is related to you ; all that I'll feign, fo as may beft ferve our Purpofe. When you difprove none of thefe Articles, I fhall gain the Caufe. Your Father will come home; he'll have a pull with me : what care I ? the Girl will be ours.

*Dav.* A droll Piece of Affurance !                              *Get.*

<hr>

### ANNOTATIONS.

77. *Tibi fcribam dicam. Dica: actio, lis, qu. In jus te vocabo. Plaut. Aul.* 4. 10. 30.

*Jam quidem hercle te ad prætorem rapiam, & tibi fcribam dicam.*

81. *Quod erit mihi bonum atque commodum.* Commentators are not agreed how thefe Words ought to be explained. Some take them in connexion with the former Part of the Sentence, *confingam, quid erit mihi bonum atque commodum.* I'll frame the whole Story fo as may beft anfwer my Purpofe. Others detach them altogether, as if *Phormio* were reprefenting the Iffue of their Project, *viz.* The Advantage arifing from this Propofal is, that when you difprove none of the Articles, I fhall gain my Suit.

Neque notus, neque cognatus, extra unam aniculam,
Quisquam aderat, qui adjutaret funus. miseritum est.
Virgo ipsa facie egregiâ. quid verbis opu'st?        50
Commôrat omnes nos. ibi continuò Antipho,
Voltisne eamus visere? alius, Censeo,
Eamus, duc nos sodes. imus, venimus,
Videmus, virgo pulchra: & quo magi' diceres,
Nihil aderat adjumentî ad pulchritudinem.        55
Capillus passus, nudus pes, ipsa horrida:
Lacrumæ, vestitus turpis, ut, ni vis boni
In ipsâ inesset formâ, hæc formam exstinguerent.
Ille, qui illam amabat fidicinam, tantummodo,
Satis scita, inquit: noster verò—DA. jam scio;        60
Amare cœpit. GE. scin' quam? quò evadat, vide.
Postridie ad anum rectà pergit: obsecrat,
Ut sibi ejus faciat copiam: illa enim se negat:
Neque eum æquom ait facere: illam civem esse At-
   ticam,
Bonam, bonis prognatam: si uxorem velit,        65
Lege id licere facere: sin aliter, negat.
Noster, quid ageret, nescire. & illam ducere
Cupiebat, & metuebat absentem patrem.
DA. Non, si redisset, ei pater veniam daret?
GE. Ille indotatam virginem atque ignobilem        70
Daret illi? nunquam faceret. DA. quid fit denique?
GE. Quid fiat? est parasitus quidam Phormio,
Homo confidens: qui, illum Dii omnes perduint—
DA. Quid is fecit? GE. hoc consilium, quod dicam,
   dedit.
Lex est, ut orbæ, qui sint genere proxumi,        75
Iis nubant: & illos ducere eadem hæc lex jubet.
Ego te cognatum dicam, & tibi scribam dicam:
Paternum amicum me adsimulabo virginis:
Ad judices veniemus. qui fuerit pater,
Quæ mater, qui cognata tibi sit, omnia hæc        80
Confingam: quod erit mihi bonum atque commodum.
Cùm tu horum nihil refelles, vincam scilicet.
Pater aderit: mihi paratæ lites: quid meâ?
Illa quidem nostra erit. DA. jocularem audaciam!

*neque notus, neque cognatus, qui adjutaret funus, aderat illi, extra unam aniculam. Miseritum est. Virgo ipsa egregia facie: quid opus est verbis? commoverat nos omnes. Ibi Antipho continuo ait, Vultisne ut eamus visere eam? athue respondit: Censes, eamus, duc nos sodes. imus, venimus, videmus, Virgo verò pulchra, & quo diceres magis, nihil adjumenti aderat ad pulchritudinem. Capillus passus, pes nudus, ipsa horrida: Lacrymæ cadebant, vestitus turpis erat, ni vis boni inesset in ipsa forma, hæc extinguerent formam. Ille, qui amabat illam fidicinam, (tantummodo inquit, Est satis scita: verò noster—DA. Scio jam: cœpit amare. GE. Scisne quam? vide, quo evadat. Postridie pergit recta ad anum: obsecrat, ut faciat copiam ejus sibi, illa enim negat se facturam, nequit ait esse æquum eum facere id: ait illam esse civem Atticam, bonam prognatam bonis: si velit eam uxorem, licere facere id lege: sin aliter, negat. Noster, nescire quid ageret: & cupiebat ducere illam, & metuebat absentem patrem. DA. An non pater daret veniam*

ei, si redisset? GE. Ille daret illi virginem indotatam atque ignobilem? nunquam faceret. DA.
Quid fit denique? GE. Quid fiat? Est quidam Phormio parasitus, homo confidens, quem Dii
omnes perdant illum. DA. Quid is fecit? GE. Dedit hoc consilium, quod dicam. Est lex, ut
orbæ nubant iis, qui sunt proximi genere, & hæc eadem lex jubet illos ducere eas. Ego, inquit
Phormio, dicam te esse cognatum ejus, & scribam dicam tibi; adsimulabo me esse paternum a-
micum virginis: veniemus ad judices. Qui fuerit pater, quæ mater, qui si cognata tibi, confingam omnia hæc: quod erit bonum atque commodum mihi. Cum tu refelles nihil horum, scilicet
vincam. Pater aderit: lites erunt parata mihi: quid refert mea? Illa quidem erit nostra.
DA. Jocularem audaciam!

*Get.* He perſuaded my Gentleman: immediately they ſet about it: the Trial came on: we were caſt: he married.

*Dav.* What do you tell me?

*Get.* 'Tis juſt as you have heard.

*Dav.* O *Geta!* what will become of you?

*Get.* I can't tell, indeed; but this one thing I know, that whatever Fortune lays upon me, I'll bear it with Courage and Firmneſs.

*Dav.* I like to hear this. Hah, ſpoken like a Philoſopher.

*Get.* All my Hope is in myſelf.

*Dav.* I commend you.

*Get.* Suppoſe I apply to ſome one to intercede for me, who, forſooth, may make ſome ſuch Speech as this: Pray forgive him this once, if he ever does ſo again, I have done with him. 'Tis well, if he don't add, When I'm gone, e'en hang him.

*Dav.* But what of the Muſick-girl's Hero? What Project has he in hand?

*Get.* Juſt none at all.

*Dav.* He has but little perhaps to give.

*Get.* Nay, nothing at all but *fine Promiſes* and Hope.

*Dav.* Is his Father come home, or not?

*Get.* Not yet.

*Dav.* Well: but when do you expect your old Man?

*Get.* I don't know for certain, but I heard juſt now, that there is a Letter come from him, and left with the Inſpectors of the Port; I'll go ſee for it.

*Dav.* Is there any thing elſe you want with me, *Geta?*

*Get.* Nothing, but that I wiſh you well.——Here, Boy. What will nobody anſwer? take this, and carry it to *Dorcium.*

A N N O T A T I O N S.

94 *Quid pædagogus ille, qui citharistri-* | *pædagogus* vocatur. Hi enim antiquo ævo à
*am?* Subaudi *ſectabatur, in ludum ducebat,* | præceptoribus diſtincti in ludum comitabantur
*& reducebat.* Qui adoleſcens amans lepide | liberos ingenuos, iiſque quaſi cuſtodes additi
                                                 erant,

---

# ACT I. SCENE III.

ARGUMENT.

*Antipho complains, that by his Raſhneſs he was expoſed to his Father's Reſentment. They contend which is the more miſerable. Phædria ſhews, that we are apt to be ſatiated with our own Enjoyments, and to admire the Fortune of others, though often more croſs than our own.*

ANTIPHO, PHÆDRIA.

*Antipho.* IS it come to this, *Phædria*, that I ſhould be afraid of him who wiſhes me ſo well, that I ſhould dread my own Father,

A N N O T A T I O N S.

This Scene furniſhes a very uſeful Leſſon, | out regard to Conſequences, yet when the
that tho' we are apt to covet Pleaſures with- | bent of Enjoyment is over, and Reaſon begins

GE. Persuasum est homini: factum est: ventum est:
    vincimur: 85
Duxit. DA. quid narras? GE. hoc, quod audis. DA.
    ô Geta,
Quid te futurum est? GE. nescio hercle. unum hoc scio:
Quod fors feret, feremus æquo animo. DA. placet:
Hem, istuc viri est officium. GE. in me omnis spes
    mihi est.
DA. Laudo. GE. ad precatorem adeam, credo, qui mihi
Sic oret: nunc amitte quæso hunc: cæterùm 91
Posthac si quidquam, nihil precor. tantummodò
Non addit, Ubi ego hinc abiero, vel occidito.
DA. Quid pædagogus ille, qui citharistriam?
Quid rei gerit? GE. sic, tenuiter. DA. non multum
    habet 95
Quòd det fortasse. GE. imo nihil, nisi spem meram.
DA. Pater ejus rediit, an non? GE. nondum. DA. quid?
    senem
Quoad exspectatis vostrum? GE. non certum scio:
Sed epistolam eb eo allatam esse audivi modò, &
Ad portitores esse dalatam: hanc petam. 100
DA. Numquid, Geta, aliud me vis? GE. ut bene sit tibi.
Puer, heus. nemon' huc prodit? cape, da hoc Dorcio.

*GE. Persuasum est homini: factum est: ventum est: vincimur: duxit. DA. Quid narras? GE. Hoc, quod audis. DA. O Geta, quid futurum est de te? GE. Hercle nescio: scio hoc unum; feremus æquo animo, quod fors feret. DA. Dictum placet; bem, istuc est officium viri. GE. Omnis istec est mihi in me. DA. Laudo. GE. Adeam ad precatorem, qui, credo, sic oret mihi: Quæso amitte hunc nunc: cæterùm. si admittet quidquam posthac, precor nihil: tantum modo non addit Ubi ego abiero hinc, vel occidito. DA. Quid ille pædagogus gerit, qui amabat citharistriam? Quid rei gerit? GE. Sic, tenuiter. DA. for-*

*tasse non habet multum, quod det. GE. Imo habet nihil, nisi meram spem. DA. Pater ejus rediit, an non? GE. Nondum. DA. Quid? Quoad exspectatis vestrum senem? GE. Non scio certum: sed audivi modo epistolam esse allatam ab eo, & esse delatam ad portiores: petam hanc. DA. Num vis me quid aliud, Geta? GE. Ut sit bene tibi. Puer, heus, nemone prodit huc? cape, da hoc Dorcio.*

### ANNOTATIONS.

erant, præceptoribus artes & scientias docen-
tibus. *Plaut. Merc. Prol.* 89.
*Servam una mittit; qui olim à puero par-
vulo*

*Mibi pædagogus fuerat.*
100 *Portitores.* Officers who attended at
the Port, and collected the Duties laid upon
Goods exported or imported.

## ACTUS V. SCENA III.

### ARGUMENTUM.

*Querela Antiphonis, metuentis patrem, & Phædriæ correptio: contendunt autem inter se, uter magis miser sit: Phædria probat, nostra nobis sordere, & improbas aliorum fortunas admirari.*

ANTIPHO, PHÆDRIA.     ORDO.

ADEON' rem redisse, ut, qui mihi consultum op-
    tumè velit esse, [adventi venit?
Phædria, patrem ut extimescam, ubi in mentem ejus

*AN. Edtne rediisse adeo, Phædria, ut ut extimescam meum patrem, qui velis esse optime consultum mihi, uti cogitatio adventi ejus venit in mentem mihi?*

### ANNOTATIONS.

gins to resume her Province, we are then
sensible of our Rashness, and regret that our

Choice is not equally free at first. Hence
an essential Maxim to our Happiness, that
before

ther, as oft as I think of his Return. Had I not been a thoughtless Fool, I might have waited for him, as was fit I should.

*Phæd.* What's the Matter now?

*Ant.* Do you ask that Question, who have been my Confident in so bold a Feat? I wish it had never come into *Phormio*'s Mind to persuade me to it; or urge me in the Heat of my Passion to a Thing which is the Source of all my Misfortunes. I should not have obtained her. What then? I might have been uneasy, perhaps, for a few Days; but should not have suffered under this hourly and perpetual Anxiety.

*Phæd.* I hear you,

*Ant.* While I am every Moment in expectation of his Return, who will tear from me what I hold so dear.

*Phæd.* Others grieve, because they cannot have what they love; you, on the contrary, complain, because you have too much. You abound in Happiness, *Antipho*; for I know no Situation in Life more to be desired and coveted than yours. As I wish for Heaven, to be so long in possession of what I love, I would contentedly die the next Moment. Do but consider, what pain I must suffer in being excluded from every Indulgence, and what Pleasure you may enjoy, in the full Possession of your Desires. Not to mention your good Fortune in obtaining without Expence a Virgin well born, and virtuously educated; that you have according to your own Desire a Wife of unblemished Reputation. How evidently happy, were not one Thing wanting; a Mind capable to bear your Lot with becoming Prudence. Had you to do with the Cock-bawd that I must treat with, you'd soon be

*ANNOTATIONS.*

before we yield to the Impetuosity of Passion, we weigh impartially every Circumstance, and cast up the Balance fairly, taking this for our Rule, *nocet empta dolore voluptas.* *Antipho*, before his Marriage with *Phany*, 'tis plain, would have sacrificed every thing to obtain her; but how, when his first Heat is allay'd, can envy *Phædria*, who, if he was still disappointed of his Wishes, had it yet in his Power to make a free Choice, and proceed or retreat, as he found it most expedient. *Tu contra mihi nunc videre fortunatus, Phædria; cui de integro est potestas etiam consulendi, quid velis: retinere, amare, amittere.* To pursue Pleasure with that Caution, that we can renounce it, if it threatens us with any Misfortune, is undoubtedly the great Art of living.

9 *Qui adimat hanc mihi consuetudinem.* The Poet here makes *Antipho*, amidst all his Perplexity, behave with great Propriety. What he says here is extremely well judged, and was necessary, to prevent the Audience from suspecting that all these fine Reflections, and this Concern he seemed to be under, proceeded from some Disgust at her, he had so fond-ly wished for. This must have made him appear in a very disadvantageous Light, as capricious, fickle, and unsteady. But here, on the contrary, we see, that it was partly from Respect to his Father, whom he could not bear to offend, partly from an Apprehension of losing what of all Things he held most dear. And as both these are Indications of a good Disposition, they of Course beget Impressions and Wishes in his Favour; a Thing of great Consequence, and never to be neglected by a Poet in his favourite Characters. The Remark of *Donatus*, on this Place, is judicious and well worth transcribing. " Quam amatorie loquatur Antipho! " errant qui putant eum pœnitere sui deside- " rii. Nam si hoc est, nec maritus firmus vi- " debitur fore. Sed hoc dicit : facilius fuisse " abstinere virgine intacta, quam ea cum " qua jam consueverit.",

10 *Ut ne addam quod sine sum'u.* Nothing can be more naturally framed, than the Conversation of these two. Each speaks in a Strain adapted to his Character and Circumstances. *Antipho*, who had compassed his

Desires,

Quod in fuissem incogitans, ita cum exspectarem, ut
  par fuit.
PH. Quid istuc est? AN. rogitas, qui tam audacis
  facinoris mî conscius sis?
Quod utinam ne Phormioni id suadere in mentem in-
  cidisset,                                                    5
Neu me cupidum eò impulisset, quod mihi principium
  est mali.                                               [dies
Non potius essem: fuisset tum illos mihi ægrè aliquot
At non quotidiana cura hæc angeret animum. PH. audio.
AN. Dum exspecto quàm mox veniat, qui hanc mihi
  adimat consuetudinem.
PH. Aliis, quia desit quod amant, ægrè est: tibi, quia
  superest, dolet.                                            10
Amore abundas, Antipho.
Nam tua quidem hercle certe vita hæc expetenda op-
  tandaque est.
Ita me Di bene ament; ut mihi liceat tam diu, quod
  amo, frui,
Jam depecisci morte cupio. tu conjicito cætera,
Quid ego ex hac inopiâ nunc capiam, & quid tu ex
  istac copiâ:                                               15
Ut ne addam, quòd sine sumtu, ingenuam, liberalem,
  nactus es:
Quòd habes, ita ut voluisti, uxorem sine malâ famâ:
  palàm
Beatus, ni unum desit, animus qui modestè istæc ferat.
Quòd si tibi res sit cum eo lenone, quocum mihi est,
  tum sentias.

pia, et quid voluptatis tu ex istac copia; ut ne addam, quod nactus es sine sumptu virginem ingenuam & liberalem, quod, ita ut voluisti, habes uxorem sine mala fama: palàm beatus, ni unum
desit, viz. animus qui ferat istæc modeste. Quod si res sit tibi cum eo lenone, quocum est mihi, tum
sentias.

## ANNOTATIONS.

Desires, but sees Misfortunes threatening him, laments his Fate, and envies *Phædria*, who, though he had been crossed in his Wishes, had yet no Fears to alarm him. *Phædria* again, impatient that his Happiness was deferred, magnifies *Antipho*'s good Fortune, and opposes it to his own, every way perverse and untoward. This Opposition is finely set off by *Donatus*: " Contra ea quæ patitur, " ista posuit omnia. Hujus in amore co- " piam; suam inopiam. Hujus desiderium " nullo constitisse sumptu: sibi à lenone in- " isse emendam puellam. Hujus ingenuam; " suam servam. Hujus liberalem; suam " citharistriam. Hunc nactum esse; se " sectari tantum. Hujus uxorem; amicam " suam. Hujus amorem maritalem esse; " suum velut prodigi, velut scortatoris."

17 *Quòd habes, ita ut voluisti, uxorem sine mala fama.* These Words admit of a two-fold Construction. *Quod habes sine mala fama,* that you have got a Wife without any hurt or prejudice to your Character. But this can scarce be *Phædria*'s Meaning; seeing in appearance the thing was otherwise. *Antipho* had married a Girl of obscure Birth, and of no Fortune. We ought, therefore to make it *uxorem sine mala fama.* A Wife of unspotted Reputation, without Blemish or Reproach.

be sensible of the Difference. But such we are almost all by Nature, never to be contented with our own Condition.

*Ant.* But you now, *Phædria*, seem to me on the contrary to be the fortunate Man, as you have it still in your power to resolve on what pleases you best; either to keep her, love her, or leave her. I have fallen into that unhappy Situation, that I cannot think of parting with her, and yet have it not in my power to retain her. But what can this be? Isn't that *Geta* I see running hither in such haste? 'Tis he himself. Alas! how do I dread that he brings some bad News.

---

# ACT I. SCENE IV.

### ARGUMENT.

Geta *acquaints* Antipho *that his Father was returned from* Cilicia; *at which the Youth, conscious of his Fault, is so much terrified, that to avoid being seen by him, he forthwith retires.*

GETA, ANTIPHO, PHÆDRIA.

*Get.* (*To himself.*) *Geta*, thou art undone, unless thou can't quickly find some Expedient; so many sudden Misfortunes threaten thee wholly unprepared: nor do I know either how to shun them, or in what manner to extricate myself from them; for the bold Step we have taken cannot now be long a Secret, and, if Care is not taken to prevent it, my Master or I must be unavoidably ruined.

*Ant.* (*To* Phædria.) What comes he in such a Panick for?

*Get.* (*To himself.*) Then I have but a minute left to bethink myself; my Master's at hand.

*Ant.* What Mischief is this?

*Get.* (*To himself.*) When he comes to hear of it, what Method can I think of to pacify him? Shall I speak? 'twill inflame him the more. Shall I be silent? even that will provoke him. Shall I attempt to clear myself? 'twill be labour in vain. Wretch that I am? while I tremble for myself, I am also in pain for *Antipho*; 'tis him that I pity; my greatest Fears are for him; he keeps me here: for had not he been concerned, I should have well provided for my own Security, and

Ita plerique ingenio sumus omnes: nostri nosmet pœ-
  nitet.   20
An. At tu mihi contà nunc videre fortunatur, Phædria.
Cui de integro est potestas etiam consulendi, quid velis;
Retinere, amare, amittere: ego in eum invidi infelix
  locum,
Ut neque mihi ejus sit amittendi, nec retinendi copia.
Sed quid hoc est? videon' ego Getam currentem huc
  advenire?   25
Is est ipsus. hei, timeo miser, quàm hic nunc mihi
  nunciet rem.

*Videone ego Getam currentem advenire huc? Est is ipsus: hei, ego miser timeo, quam rem hic nunc nunciet mihi.*

---

## ACTUS I. SCENA IV.
### ARGUMENTUM.

*Geta Antiphoni narrat, è Cilicia rediisse patrem, quo nuntio tan-
tus injicitur metus male sibi conscio adolescenti, ut subducat illico sese.*

### GETA, ANTIPHO, PHÆDRIA.

NUllus es, Geta, nisi jam aliquod tibi consilium
  celere repperis,
Ita subito nunc imparatum tanta te impendent mala:
Quæ neque uti devitem scio, neque quomodo me inde
  extraham:
Nam non potest celari nostra diutius jam audacia:
Quæ, si non astu providentur, me aut herum pessum
  dabunt.   5
An. Quidnam ille commotus venit?
Ge. Tum, temporis punctum mihi ad hanc rem est,
  herus adest. An. quid istuc mali est?
Ge. Quod cùm audierit, quod ejus remedium invenim
  iracundiæ?   [laterem lavem.
Loquarne? incendam: taceam? instigem. purgem me?
Eheu me miserum! cùm mihi paveo, tum Antipho me
  excruciat animi:   10
Ejus me miseret: ei nunc timeo: is nunc me retinet.
  nam absque eo esset,

*um inveniam ejus iracundiæ? Loquarne? incendam. Taceam? instigem. Purgem me? lavem laterem. Eheu me miserum! cum paveo mihi, tum Antipho excruciat me solicitudine animi: miseret me ejus: timeo nunc ei: is nunc retinet me: nam absque eo esset,*

**ORDO** (sidebar paraphrase)

Ita plerique omnes sumus ingenio, pænitet nosmet nostri. AN. At ia contra, Phædria, vane cuidere fortunatus, tibi tui potestas consuledi etiam de integro, quid velis; retinere, amare, amittere: ego infelix incidi in eum locum, ut neque sit mihi copia amittendi ejus, nec retinendi. Sed quid est hoc?

ORDO. GE. ES nullus, Getà, nisi jam reperis aliquod celere consilium, tibi, tanta mala ita subito nunc imperdent te imparatum: quæ neque scio uti devitem, neque quomodo extrabam me inde: jam nostra audacia non potest jam diutius celari: quæ mala si non providetur est, pessum dabunt me aut herum. AN. Ob quidnam ille venit commotus? GE. Tum est punctum temporis mihi ad hanc rem: herus adest. AN. Quid mali est istuc? GE. Quod cum audierit, quid remedi-

---

and been revenged on the old Man for his Perverseness: I had scraped what I could together, and taken to my Heels with all speed.

*Ant.* What scraping up and Flight is this he's contriving?

*Get.* But where shall I find *Antipho*, or which Way go to look for him?

*Phæd.* He names you.

*Ant.* I expect to hear I don't know what terrible Misfortune by this Messenger.

*Phæd.* Ah, are you in your Senses?

*Get.* I'll go see at home, he's most commonly there.

*Phæd.* Let's call him back.

*Ant.* You Sir, stop immediately.

*Get.* Hy, hy! a pretty imperious Air, whoever you are.

*Ant. Geta!*

*Get.* The very Person I wanted to meet.

*Ant.* Tell me, pray, what News you bring, and if possible dispatch it in a Word.

*Get.* I will.

*Ant.* Out with it then.

*Get. I saw* just now at the Port——

*Ant.* My Father?

*Get.* You've hit it.

*Ant.* I'm ruin'd.

*Phæd.* Hah!

*Ant.* What shall I do?

*Phæd.* What's that you say?

*Get.* That I saw his Father, your Uncle.

*Ant.* What Remedy can be found for this sudden Calamity? for if it is my Fortune to be torn from my dearest *Phany*, Life will be no longer desireable.

*Get.* Therefore, *Antipho*, since Things are so, you have the more need to rouze and look about you. Fortune helps the Brave.

*Ant.* I'm not myself.

*Get.* But now it is more than ever necessary that you should be, *Antipho*; for if your Father perceives any thing of Fear about you, he'll conclude you're in fault.

*Phæd.* That's true.

*Ant.* I cannot change my Nature.

*Get.* What would you do, were you involved in some more perplexing Business?

*Ant.*

# ANNOTATIONS.

<sup>18</sup> *Conrasissem.* Videtur à mulitibus castra moventibus, præsertim in fuga translata; id enim *vasa conclamare* dixerunt. MSS. quidem *corrasissem* habent, quod ferme idem.

<sup>19</sup> *Satis pro imperio.* H. e. *satis imperiose.* So *Livy*, Lib. 2. 56. *Nec illum ipsum pro imperio submovere posse more majestatis.* Donatus supposes that he says so in contempt of

Recte ego mihi vidissem, & senis essem ultus iracun-  
   diam:                     [nam in pedes.  
Aliquid convasissem, atque hinc me conjicerem proti-  
AN. Quam hic fugam aut furtum parat?  
GE. Sed ubi Antiphonem reperiam? aut quâ quærere  
   insistam viâ?                 15  
PH. Te nominat. AN. nescio quod magnum hoc nun-  
   cio exspecto malum.  
PH. Ah, sanu' ne es? GE. domum ire pergam: ibi  
   plurimum est. PH. revocemus  
Hominem. AN. sta illico. GE. hem!  
Satis pro imperio, quisquis es. AN. Geta. GE. ipse est,  
   quem volui obviam.  
AN. Cedo, quid portas, obsecro? atque id, si potes,  
   verbo expedi.              20  
GE. Faciam. AN. eloquere. GE. modò apud portum——  
AN. meumne? GE. intellexti. AN. occidi. GE.  
   hem!  
AN. Quid agam? PH. Quid ais? GE. huju' patrem  
   vidisse me, patruum tuum.     [inveniam miser?  
AN. Nam quod ego huic nunc subito exitio remedium  
Quòd si eò meæ fortunæ radeunt, Phanium, abs te ut  
   distrahar,  
Nulla est mihi vita expetenda. GE. ergo istæc cùm  
   ita sint, Antipho,            25  
Tanto magis te advigilare æquom est. fortes fortuna  
   adjuvat.  
AN. Non sum apud me. GE. atqui opus est. nunc cum  
   maxumè ut sis, Antipho:  
Nam si senserit te timidum pater esse, arbitrabitur  
Commeruisse culpam. PH. hoc verum est. AN. non  
   possum immutarier.  
GE. Quid faceres, si aliud quid gravius tibi nunc faci-  
   undum foret?            30

*ego recte vidissem mihi, & ultus essem iracundiam senis: convacissem aliquid, atque protinam conjicerem me hinc in pedes. AN. Quam fugam aut furtum hic parat? GE. Sed ubi reperiam Antiphonem? aut qua via insistam quærere? PH. Nominat te. AN. Expecto nescio quod magnum malum hoc nuncio. PH. Ah, esne sanus? GE. Pergam ire domum, est ibi plurimum. PH. Revocemus hominem. AN. Sta illico. GE. Hem, quisquis es, jobes satis pro imperio. AN. Geta. GE. Est ipse, quem volui obviam. AN. Obsecro, cedo quid portas? atque, si potes, expedi id uno verbo. GE. Faciam. AN. Eloquere. GE. Modo apud portum —— AN. Vidistine meum patrem? GE. Intellexti. AN. Occidi. GE. Hem! AN. Quid agam? PH. Quid ais? GE. Me vidisse patrem hujus, tuum patruum. AN. Nam quod remedium ego miser nunc inveniam huic subito exitio? Quod si meæ*

*fortunæ redeunt eo, ut distrahar abs te, Phanium, nulla vita est expetendi mihi. GE. Ergo, Antipho, cum istæc ita sint; tanto magis æquum est te advigilare. Fortuna adjuvat fortes. AN. Non sum apud me. GE. Atqui nunc cum maxime opes est ut sis, Antipho. Nam si pater senserit te esse timidum, arbitrabitur te commeruisse culpam. PH. Hoc est verum. AN. Non possum immutari. GE. Quid faceres, si quid aliud gravius foret nunc faciendum tibi?*

## ANNOTATIONS.

of his Master; but it is evident he did not know who it was that addressed him in so imperious a Strain, both from what he subjoins immediately, *quisquis es*, and because afterwards, when he finds it to be *Antipho*, he speaks with an Air of Surprize: *Ipse est, quem volui obviam.*

22. *Hujus patrem vidisse me, patruum tuum.*

'Tis artful in the Poet to make *Geta* only just hint the Matter to *Antipho*, but expreſs himself rather over-copiously to *Phædria*. The one's Imagination is quickened by his own Fears and Apprehensions, the other is easy and secure, and therefore less ready to anticipate.



31. *Hoc*

*Ant.* If I am unequal to this, I should be still more so to the other.

*Get.* Pshaw, this is doing nothing, *Phædria*; leave him to himself: why do we waste our Time here to no Purpose? I'll be gone.

*Phæd.* And I too.

*Ant.* Pray now suppose I put on a confident Air, thus; will it do?

*Get.* You do but trifle.

*Ant.* Observe my Countenance: Hah, will not this do?

*Get.* No.

*Ant.* What if I look thus?

*Get.* Almost.

*Ant.* What if thus?

*Get.* 'Twill do: bah, keep to that, and answer him Word for Word: be sure that you return like for like, nor suffer him by Rant and Blustering to disconcert you.

*Ant.* I understand.

*Get.* Say you was obliged to it against your Will, by Law and the Sentence of the Judges: you take me? But what old Man is that I see at the farther end of the Street?

*Ant.* 'Tis he himself: I cannot stand it.

*Get.* Ah, what are you about? Where now, *Antipho?* Stay, I say.

*Ant.* I know myself and my Fault too well: I trust my *Phany* and my Life to your Management.

*Phæd.* What shall we do now, *Geta?*

*Get.* You'll be scolded at perhaps, but I shall be trussed up directly, or I am very much deceived. But what were we just now advising *Antipho* to, that we *must* put in practice ourselves, *Phædria.*

*Phæd.* Hang your *musts:* command me at once what I am to do.

*Get.* Do you remember, when we first entered upon this Project, what was agreed upon as the most proper Defence? that their Cause was just, clear, unanswerable, and the fairest in the World.

*Phæd.* I remember it.

*Get.* Well, this is the Plea we must make use of now, or something still better, and more subtil, if you can think of it.

*Phæd.* I'll do it manfully.

*Get.* Do you advance first. I'll lie here in Ambush as a Reserve to sustain you, if you shall happen to give ground.

*Phæd.* Come on then.

## *ANNOTATIONS.*

31 *Hoc nibil est.* *Geta* is supposed to express himself thus in contempt, and speak of *Antipho* as an Animal good for nothing. *Hoc*, i. e. *hic Antipho.* Others make *hoc* a Relative, and point the Sentence thus, *Hoc? nibil est*, q. d. *Hoc non potes, quod niLil est?*

36 *Protelet.* Protelare, *longe propellere, percutere, perturbare.* Locutio translata à telis militum.

42, *Justam illam causam, facilem, vincibilem.* *Geta* here repeats what had been agreed upon among them, at the first concerting of this Enterprize. As they foresaw that *Antipho*'s Father would be offended, they had taken care to provide an Excuse, *viz.* that the Virgin's Cause was made clear and evident, so as to leave no room for Opposition. This same Plea, *Geta* says, is now to be made, as being the most specious one they could think of in the present Exigence. *Vincibilem* is to be understood here actively, *quæ facile vincat*, in the same manner as *orator impetra-*

AN. Cùm hoc non possem, illud minu' possem. GE.
  mi hoc nihil est, Phædria: illicet:
Quid conterimus operam frustra? quin habeo. PH. &
  quidem ego. AN. obsecro,
Quid si adsimulo? satin' est? GE. garris. AN. voltum
  contemplamini, hem,
Satine sic est? GE. non! AN. quid si sic? GE. prope-
  modum. AN. quid sic? GE. sat est.
Hem istuc serva, & verbum verbo, par pari ut respon-
  deas,    35
Ne te iratus suis sævidicis dictis protelet. AN. scio.
GE. Vi coactum te esse invitum, lege, judicio: tenes?
Sed quis hic est senex, quem video in ultima platea?
  AN. ipsus est.    [tipho? 40
Non possum adesse. GE. ah, quid agis? quo abis, An-
Mane, inquam. AN. egomet me novi, & peccatum me-
Vobis commendo Phanium, & vitam meam.  [um
PH. Geta, quid nunc fiet? GE. tu jam lites audies:
Ego plectar pendens, nisi quid me fefellerit.
Sed quòd modò hic nos Antiphonem monuimus,
Id nosmetipsos facere oportet, Phædria.    45
PH. Aufer mihi oportet: quin tu, quid faciam, impera.
GE. Meministi olim ut fuerit vostra oratio
In re incipiundâ ad defendam noxiam?
Justam illam causam, facilem, vincibilem, optumam.
PH. Memini. GE. hem, nunc ipsa eâ est opus, aut, si
  quid potest,    50
Meliore, & callidiore. PH. fiet sedulo.
GE. Nunc prior adito tu: ego in insidiis hîc ero
Succenturiatus, si quid deficies. PH. age.

AN. Cùm non pos-
sum facere hoc, mi-
nus possem facere il-
lud. GE. Hoc est
nihil, Phædria: ili-
cet: quod conterimus
operam frustrà? quin
abeo. PH. Et qui-
dem ego. AN. Ob-
secro, quid si adsi-
mulo? Estne satis?
GE. Garris. AN.
Contemplamini vol-
tum, hem, estne satis
sit? GE. Non. AN.
Quid si sic? GE.
Propemodum. AN.
Quid sic? GE. Sat
est; hem, serva ist-
uc, & ut respondeas
verbum verbo, par
pari, ne ille iratus
protelet te suis sæ-
vidicis dictis. AN.
Scio. GE. Dic te
invitum esse coactum
vi, lege, judicio: te-
nes? Sed quis senex
est hic, quem video
in ultima platea?
AN. Est ipsus: non
possum adesse. GE.
ah, quid agis? Quo
abis, Antipho? ma-
ne, inquam. AN. E-
gomet novi me, &
meum peccatum: com-
mendo Phanium, &
meam vitam vobis.
PH. Geta, quid fiet?
Sed oportet nosmet-
PH. Aufer oportet mibi:
in incipiendâ re, ad
noxiam. PH. Memini,
tale potest venire in
insidiis succenturiatus, si

nunc? GE. Tu jam audies lites, ego plectar pendens, nisi quid fefellerit me
ipsos, Phædria, facere id, quod nos modo monuimus Antipphonem hic. PH. Aufer oportet mihi:
quin tu impera, quid faciam. GE. Meministi ut vestra oratio fuerit olim in incipiendâ re, ad
defendam noxiam? viz. illam causam esse justam, facilem, vincibilem, optimam. PH. Memini.
GE. Nem, nunc opus est ea ipsa oratione, aut meliore & callidiore, si quid tale potest venire in
mentem. PH. Fiet sedulo. GE. Nunc tu prior adito: ego ero hic in insidiis succenturiatus, si
deficies quid. PH. Age.

## ANNOTATIONS.

imperabilis signifies often *qui facile impetrat quod vult.*

52 *Ego in insidiis hic ero succenturiatus.* — In several Manuscripts we read *in subsidiis*; which makes no material Alteration in the Sense. These last *subsidia*, were properly Bodies of Reserve, to support an Army, and restore the Battle, if in any Place the Tropps were like to give ground. *Succenturiati* were Men enlisted to fill up the Vacancies in the Centuries or Companies, when they were impaired by a Battle, or a Discharge of those deemed unfit for the Service. 'Tis therefore as if he had said; *Tum partes suscipiam, tibique opem feram, quasi post primas militum centurias collocatus, seu post primam aciem.*

L 4       ACTUS

## ACT II. SCENE IV.

### ARGUMENT.

Demipho *is greatly troubled to find that his Son* Antipho *had married in his Absence.* Phædria *and* Geta *endeavour to defend him. At laſt* Demipho *determines to meet with* Phormio, *whom he ſuppoſed to have promoted the Marriage, and expoſtulate the Injury with him.*

DEMIPHO, GETA, PHÆDRIA.

*Demipho.* IS it poſſible that *Antipho* has married without my Conſent ? To ſhew no regard to my Authority—but I wave Authority ; not even to be awed by the Dread of my Diſpleaſure ? To diveſt himſelf thus of all Shame ? O audacious Crime ! O *Geta,* thou hopeful Tutor !

*Get.* I am brought in then at laſt.

*Dem.* What will they ſay, I wonder, or what Excuſe will they find ?

*Get.* (*To* Phædria,) I have got one already, think you of another.

*Dem.* Will he pretend that he did it againſt his Will ? That the Law obliged him to it ? I hear him, and allow it.

*Get.* Well ſaid.

*Dem.* But knowingly, and without offering at a Defence to give up the Cauſe to his Adverſaries, did the Law oblige him to that too ?

*Phæd.* That ſtrikes home.

*Get.* I'll clear up that, leave it to me.

*Dem.* I don't know what to do, for this is an Accident I could not have expected or foreſeen, and I am ſo enraged too, that I can't compoſe my Mind to think. We ought all therefore, when Fortune ſmiles moſt upon us, to conſider with ourſelves, in what manner to bear Adverſity. Returning from abroad, let us think of Dangers, Loſſes, Exile, an untoward Son, the Death of a Wife, or a Daughter ſick : that theſe are common Accidents of Life, and may poſſibly happen : thus nothing will be new or unexpected to us ; and if things fall

### ANNOTATIONS.

In this Scene we have *Demipho* expreſſing his Diſpleaſure at his Son's Behaviour ; and *Phædria* and *Geta* defending him to the utmoſt of their power. *Geta* wiſely for ſome time keeps out of the way, and watches to overhear what Reception *Phædria* meets with, reſolving to take his Meaſures accordingly ; for we have ſeen what a Panick he was in, and no doubt, had *Phædria's* Apologies been ſternly received, he would have made off immediately, nor expoſed his Back to inſtant Peril. But finding things go on ſmoothly, and that *Phædria* acted his Part to Admiration, he ventures to advance. By their joint Pleading, *Demipho* is a little pacified ; and, conſidering *Phormio* as the Author of all the Miſchief, deſires to meet, and expoſtulate the matter with him. There is one thing more, that ought not be paſſed over without Notice here. In ſeveral Editions of *Terence,* this is made the firſt Scene of the ſecond Act, a Miſtake ſo palpable, that it's a wonder any one ſhould have fallen into it, for the leaſt Attention to the Concluſion of the laſt Scene would have prevented it. There *Geta* ſays to *Phædria ;* *Do you advance firſt, I'll lie in ambuſh to ſupport you.* He accordingly does it, and *Demipho*

## ACTUS I. SCENA V.

### ARGUMENTUM.

*Filium Antiphonem se absente uxorem duxisse, admodùm ægrè fert*
*Demipho: à Phædria ille & Geta servo defenditur. Ad postre-*
*mum Demipho convenire Phormionem constituit, ut injuriam*
*cum eo expostulet, qui ducendæ puellæ auctor fuerat.*

### DEMIPHO, GETA, PHÆDRIA.

ITANE tandem uxorem duxit Antipho injussu meo?
Nec meum imperium, ac mitto imperium, non
          [Geta
    sic multatem meam
Revereri saltem? non pudere? ô facinus audex! ô
Monitor! GE. vix tandem! DE. quid mihi dicent?
    aut quam causam reperient?
Demiror. GE. atqui reperi jam: aliud cura. DE. an   5
    hôc dicet mihi?
Invitus feci: lex coegit. audio: fateor. GE. placet.
DE. Verùm scientem, tacitum causam tradere adver-
    sariis.           [pediam: sine.
Etiamne id lex coegit? PH. illud durum. GE. ego ex-
DE. Incertum est, quid agam, quia præter spem, at-
    que incredibile hoc mihi obtigit.
Ita sum irritatus, animum ut nequeam ad cogitandum
    instituere.           10
Quamobrem omnes, cùm secundæ res sunt maxumè,
    tùm maxumè.         [nam serant.
Meditari secum oportet, quo pacto advorsam ærum-
Pericla, damna, exsilia peregrè rediens semper cogitet,
Aut fili peccatum, aut uxoris mortum, aut morbum filiæ:
Communia esse hæc; fieri posse: ut ne quid animo sit
    novum:           15

### ORDO.

DE. Itane tandem Antipho duxit uxorem injussu meo? nec revereri meum imperium, ut mitto imperium, non revereri saltem meam simultatem? Non pudere? O facinus audax! O Geta monitor! GE. Vix tandem. DE. Quid dicent mihi? Aut quam causam reperient? demiror. GE. Atqui reperi jam; cura aliud. DE. An dicet hoc mihi? Feci invitus: lex coegit. Audio: fateor. GE. Placet. DE. Verum illum scientem, tacitum, tradere causam adversariis, legne coegit id etiam? PH. Illud durum. GE. Ego expediam: sine. DE. Incertum est, quid agam quia hoc obtigit mihi praeter spem, atque incredi-bile. Sum ita irritatus, ut nequeam instituere animum ad cogitandum. Quamobrem, cum res sunt maxime secunda, tum maximè oportet omnes meditari secum, quo pacto ferant adversam ærumnam. Rediens peregre semper cogitet pericla, damna, exilia, aut peccatum filii, aut mortem uxoris, aut morbum filiæ: hæc esse communia; posse fieri: ut ne quid sit novum animo:

### ANNOTATIONS.

...mipho and he enter into Conversation imme-diately, without any Pause or Interruption: It is, therefore, without all Dispute, the fifth Scene of the first Act.

*Si Atqui reperi jam*, &c. It may be translated: *That's provided already; think of something else:* [...] *Illud durum.* Several Commentators ascribe these Words to *Geta*, and the following; *ego expediam: sine,* to *Phædria*; because, say they, 'tis he only that reasons the matter with *Demipho*, and breaks the first Sallies of his Indignation. It is not very material which way we determine it, but were one to argue from Propriety, as *Geta* had before said *placet; illud durum,* comes best from *Phædria*, as a kind of Antithesis to the former; and then *ego expediam* serves. *Geta* by way of Reply, and at the same time very happily describes the Vanity of those Slaves, who are apt to fancy every thing within the reach of their Cunning.

*Quamobrem omnes, cùm,* &c. *Cicero,* in the third Book of his *Tusculan Questions,* translates this Sentence from *Euripides,* whence *Terence* had taken it. 'Tis *Theseus* that speaks:

" Nam,

fall out different from what we apprehended, we may account it fo much clear Gain.

*Get.* O *Phædria*, 'tis incredible how much I furpafs my Mafter in Wifdom! I have already, confidered with myfelf all the Evils that threaten me. If my Mafter return, I muft expect to be fent to the Mill-houfe, to be whipped, or put in Irons, or doomed to labour in the Fields. None of thefe things will be new ; and whatever happens beyond Expectation, I fhall look upon as real Gain. But why don't you go up to the old Gentleman, and foften him with fair Words?

*Dem.* I fee *Phædria*, my Brother's Son, coming to meet me.

*Phæd.* Uncle, your Servant.

*Dem.* Your Servant : but where's *Antipho* ?

*Phæd.* I'm glad to fee you fafe returned.

*Dem.* I believe you : but pray anfwer my Queftion.

*Phæd.* He's very well, and juft by here ; but are all things according to your Defire ?

*Dem.* I wifh they were.

*Phæd.* What's amifs, pray ?

*Dem.* Is that a Queftion, *Phædria* ? You have made a fine Marriage among you here in my Abfence.

*Phæd.* What, are you angry with him for that ?

*Get.* Excellent !

*Dem.* Have I not reafon to be angry with him ? I wifh he would but come into my fight ; he fhould foon be fenfible that of a gentle Father his Folly has made me a very fevere and terrible one.

*Phæd.* But really, Uncle, he has done nothing to deferve your anger.

*Dem.* Look ye there, they are all of a piece, all hang together ; know one, and you know all.

*Phæd.* It is not fo indeed.

*Dem.* If this one's in fault, the other's ready to defend him : is he again to blame ? this is fure to ftand up for him : they help one another by turns.

*Get.* The old Man has given a truer Picture of them, than he thinks for.

*Dem.* For were it not as I fay, you would not offer to vindicate him, *Phædria*.

*Phæd.* Indeed, Uncle, had *Antipho* committed any Fault, injurious either to his Intereft or Reputation, I would not once interpofe, but

leave

<hr>

*ANNOTATIONS.*

" Nam, qui hæc audita à docto memi-
" niffem viro,
" Futuram pacem commentabar miferias :
" Aut mortem acerbam, aut exilii me-
" tum fugam,
" Aut femper aliquam molem meditabar
" mali [...]
" Ut, fi quæ invecta divitas cafu foret,

" Ne me imparatum cum laceraret re-
" pens."
This was one of the favourite Maxims of the *Stoicks*, who maintained, againft the *Epicureans*, that it was not induftrioufly feeking matter of Grief and Anxiety, but taking the wifeft Precautions againft them ; for fo the fame great Philofopher, *Philip.* xi. 3.
" Eft

Quidquid præter spem eveniat, omne id deputare esse
    in lucro.                                    [sapientiâ.
GE. O Phædria, incredibile est, quanto herum anteeo
Meditata mihi sunt omnia mea incommoda: herus si
    redierit,                                    [compedes:
Molendum usque in pistrino: vapulandum: habendæ
Opus ruri faciundum. horum nil quidquam accidet
    animo novum:                                 20
Quidquid præter spem eveniet, omne id deputabo esse
    in lucro.                                    [alloqui?
Sed quid cessas hominem adire, & blandè in principio
DE. Phædriam mei fratris video filium mihi ire obviam.
PH. Mi patrue, salve. DE. salve. sed ubi est Antipho?
PH. Salvum advenire—DE. credo: hoc responde mihi.
PH. Valet: hîc est. sed satin' omnia ex sententiâ? 26
DE. Vellem quidem. PH. quid istuc est? DE. rogitas,
    Phædria?
Bonas me absente hîc confecistis nuptias.      [bum!
PH. Eho, an id succenses nunc illi? GE. artificem pro-
DE. Egon' illi non succenseam? ipsum gestio    30
Dari mî in conspectum, nunc suâ culpâ ut sciat
Lenem patrem illum factum me esse acerrimum.
PH. A qui nil fecit, patrue, quod succenseas.
DE. Ecce autem similia omnia: omnes congruunt:
Unum cognoris, omnes noris. PH. haud ita est.  35
DE. Hic in noxa est, ille ad defendendam causam adest.
Cùm ille est, hic præsto est: tradunt operas mutuas.
GE. Probè horum facta imprudens depinxit senex.
DE. Nam ni hæc ita essent, cum illo haud stares,
    Phædria.
PH. Si est, patrue, culpam ut Antipho in se admiserit, 40
Ex quâ re minus rei foret aut famæ temperans;

*Quidquid eveniat præter spem, deputare omne id esse in lucro. GE. O Phædria, incredibile est, quanto anteeo herum sapientia. Omnia mea incommoda sunt meditata mihi: si herus redierit, molendum usque in pistrino: vapulandum: compedes habendæ: opus faciendum ruri: nil quidquam horum accidet novum animo: quidquid eveniat præter spem deputabo id omne esse in lucro. Sed quid cessas adire hominem, & alloqui eum blande in principio? DE. Video Phædriam filium mei fratris ire obviam mihi. PH. Mi patrue, salve. DE. Salve. Sed ubi est Antipho? PH. Gaudeo te advenire salvum. DE. Credo: responde hoc mihi. PH. Valet: est hic: Sed omniane sunt satis ex sententia? DE. Vellem quidem. PH. Quid istuc est? DE. Rogitas, Phædria? confecistis bonas nuptias hic, me absente. PH. Eho, an nunc succenses illi ob id? GE. Probum arti-*

*ficem! DE. Egone non succenseam illi? gestio ipsum dari in conspectum mihi, ut nunc sciat me illum lenem patrem esse factum acerrimum sua culpa. PH. Atqui fecit nil, patrue, quod succenseas. DE. Ecce autem omnia similia: omnes congruunt: cognoveris unum, noveris omnes. PH. Haud est ita. DE. Hic est in noxa, ille ad est ad defendendam causam. Cum ille est, hic est præsto: tradunt operas mutuas. GE. Senex imprudens probe depinxit facta horum. DE. Nam ni hæc essent ita, haud stares cum illo, Phædria. PH. Si est, patrue, ut Antipho admiserit culpam in se, ex qua re foret minus temperans rei aut famæ;*

## ANNOTATIONS.

" Est enim sapientis, quidquid homini acci-
" dere possit, id præmeditari ferendum mo-
" dice esse, si evenerit. Majoris omnino est
" consilii, providere, ne quid tale accidat:
" sed animi non minoris, fortiter ferre, si
" evenerit." What *Seneca* says upon the
same Subject, is highly deserving of our Notice. (*Ep.* 18.) " In ipsa securitate animus
" ad difficilia se præparet, & contra injurias
" fortunæ, inter beneficia firmetur. Miles
" in media pace decurrit sine ullo hoste, val-
" lum jacit, & supervacuo labore lassatur, ut
" sufficere necessario possit. Quem in ipsa
" re trepidare nolueris, ante rem exerce."
25 *Salvum advenire.* Sub. *te, gaudeo.*
But *Demipho's* Impatience interrupts him before he had concluded the Sentence. *Credo.
Hoc responde mihi.* The Emphasis lies in *hoc.*

leave him to suffer what he deserved. But if any one maliciously lays
a Snare for our Youth, and by artful Management succeeds; does the
Blame belong to us, or the Judges, who oft through Envy take from
the Rich, and through Compassion add to the Poor?

*Get.* Were I not privy to the Affair, I should fancy he spoke truth.

*Dem.* Can any Judge know your Right, when like him you offer
not a word in defence of it.

*Phæd.* He behaved like a modest young Gentleman; when he
came before the Judges, he could not say what he had prepared,
Shame and his natural Fearfulness had so confounded him.

*Get.* I commend you, *Phædria*: but why don't I go up directly to
him myself? Master, your Servant; I'm glad to see you safe return'd.

*Dem.* Oh, good Mr. *Tutor*, your Servant, thou Prop and Pillar of
my Family, to whose Care I committed my Son at my departure!

*Get.* I hear you have been accusing us very undeservedly, and me
most undeservedly of all. For what would you have me to have done,
for you in this Business? The Laws don't allow a Servant to plead in
Court, nor is his Evidence taken.

*Dem.* I grant it all: add too, that the Youth unused to Courts,
and those publick Appearances, was fearful; allow all this, I say, and
that you're only a Slave: yet was she ever so nearly related to him,
there was no necessity for his marrying her; you might, as the Law
requires, have given her so much for a Portion, and left her to seek
out another Husband: what could move him rather to take home a
Wench that had nothing?

*Get.* 'Twas no particular Reason that moved him, but Want of
Money.

*Dem.* He might have borrowed it somewhere.

*Get.* Somewhere! nothing easier said.

*Dem.* In fine, if he could not get it otherwise, he should have taken it upon Interest.

*Get.* Hy, well said; as if any one would have given him Credit,
while you are alive!

*Dem.* No, it must not continue so, it cannot be: shall I suffer her
to remain with him so much as a single Day? I can see no manner of
　　　　　　　　　　　　　　　　　　　　　　　　Temptation

*ANNOTATIONS.*

I want to know of *Antipho*; answer me that
and defer your Congratulations. One can't but
wonder how *Guyetus* should so far mistake,
as to be for discarding this *hoc*, which makes
the whole Beauty, and Spirit of the Reply.
*Qui sæpe propter invidiam adimunt di-
tiit.* Judges, often, through meer Compassion, are byassed to the Poor, and sometimes,
through Envy, unjustly decide against the
Rich. This latter Principle, in the Mind of
one whose Decisions ought to be governed by
the most inviolable Equity, is always vicious,
nay, and even the former may be overstrained,
For although Compassion and Pity have
something noble and generous in them, and
deserve to be cherished; yet they ought never
to influence our Judgment, so far as to make
us swerve from a steady Adherence to Justice.
Hence, in that divine System of Laws, given
to the *Israelites* by *Moses*, this is particularly
cautioned against. *Neither shalt thou pity the
Condition of the Poor. Thou shalt not regard
the Person of the Poor in Judgment.* This is
an Injunction often repeated, and clearly de-
monstrates the Wisdom of that Institution,
in so particularly guarding us against this
　　　　　　　　　　　　　　　　　　　　　　　　Vice,

Non causam dico, quin, quod meritus sit, serat.
Sed si quis forte malitia fretus sua
Insidias nostræ fecit adolescentiæ,
Ac vicit; nostran' culpa ea est, an judicum;   45
Qui sæpe propter invidiam adimunt diviti,
Aut propter misericordiam addunt pauperi.
GE. Ni nollem causam, crederem vera hunc loqui.
DE. An quisquam judex est, qui possit noscere
Tua justa, ubi tute verbum non respondeas,   50
Ita ut ille fecit? PH. functus adolescentuli est
Officium liberalis: postquam ad judices
Ventum est, non potuit cogitata proloqui:
Ita eum tum timidum ibi obstupefecit pudor.   54
GE. Laudo hunc: sed cesso adire quamprimùm senem?
Here, salve: salvum te advenisse gaudeo. DE. oh,
Bone custos, salve, columen vero familiæ,
Cui commendavi filium hinc abiens meum.
GE. Jamdudum te omnes nos accusare audio
Immeritò, & me horunc' omnium immeritissimò   60
Nam quid me in hac re facere voluisti tibi?
Servum hominem causam orare leges non sinunt:
Neque Testimonii dictio est. DE. mitto omnia.
Addo istuc: imprudens timuit adolescens: sino:
Tu servus. verùm si cognata est maxumè,   65
Non fuit necesse habere; sed, id quod lex jubet,
Dotem daretis; quæreret alium virum.
Quâ ratione inopem potiùs ducebat domum?
GE. Non ratio, verùm argentum deerat. DE. sumeret
Alicunde. GE. alicunde? nihil est dicto facilius.   70
DE. Postremò, si nullo alio pacto, fenore.
GE. Hui, dixti pulchrè, siquidem quisquam crederet,
Te vivo. DE. non, non sic futurum est; non potest.
Egone illam cum illo ut patiar nuptam unam diem?

*non dico causam, quin ferat, quod sit meritus; sed si forte quis fraus sua malitia fecit insidias nostra adolescentiæ, ac vicit; estne ea nostra culpa, an judicum; qui sæpe adimunt diviti propter invidiam, aut addunt pauperi propter misericordiam. GE. Ni nossem causam, crederem hunc loqui vera. DE. An est quisquam judex, qui possit noscere tua justa; ubi tute non respondeas verbum, ita ut ille fecit? PH. Functus est officium adolescentuli liberalis: postquam est ventum ad judices, non potuit proloqui cogitata: ibi pudor, ita obstupefecit. tum timidum. GE. Laudo hunc: sed cesso quamprimum adire senem? here, salve: gaudeo te advenisse salvum. DE. O bone custos salve, columen familiæ vero, cui abiens hinc commendavi meum filium. GE. Jamdudum audio te accusare omnes nos immerito, & me immeritissimo, horunc omnium. Nam quid voluisti me facere tibi in hac re? leges non*

*sinunt hominem servum orare causam; neque est dictio testimonii. DE. Mitto omnia; addo istuc: adolescens imprudens timuit: sino: tu servus. Verum si est maxime cognata, non fuit necesse eum habere hanc, sed, id quod lex jubet, daretis dotem; quæreret alium virum. Quâ ratione ducebat potius inopem domum? GE. Non ratio, verum argentum deerat. DE. Sumeret alicunde. GE. Alicunde? nihil est facilius dicto. DE. Postremo, si nullo alio pacto, sumeret fænore. GE. Hui, dixti pulchre, siquidem quisquam crederet, te vivo. DE. Non, non est futuram sic; non potest. Egone ut patiar illam nuptam cum illo unum diem?*

## ANNOTATIONS.

Vice, because it is apt to impose upon the Mind with the shew of Virtue.

v. 66. *Sed, id quod lex jubet.* For the Law runs thus: *Orbæ qui sint genere proximi, eis nubunto; aut iis orbis dotem danto.* "Let "Orphans be married to those who are their "nearest Relations, or let those nearest Re-"lations allow them a Portion."

72 *Siquidem quisquam crederet, te vivo. Alexander ab Alexandro Genial. Dier. L. I.* takes notice of an ancient Decree of Senate, derived to the Romans from a Law of *Solon.* In this was a Proviso against lending Money to young Men, during the Life of their Fathers, lest the Sons of great Families being intangled in Debt, and impatient to extricate themselves

Temptation for it. I could wish to meet with this Fellow, or be
directed where he lives.

*Get.* *Phormio* do you mean?

*Dem.* The Wench's Patron.

*Get.* I'll bring him here immediately.

*Dem.* But where can *Antipho* be?

*Phæd.* Gone out a little.

*Dem.* Do, *Phædria*, find him out, and bring him hither.

*Phæ.* I'll go directly.

*Get.* (*Aside.*) Yes, to *Pamphila.*

*Dem.* (*Alone.*) I'll first step home, and thank the Gods for my
safe Return; thence I'll to the Forum, and get some of my Friends
to be present in this Affair, that I may not be unprovided, if *Phormio* come.

### ANNOTATIONS.

themselves, might be prompted to use dishonourable Means, or even to hasten a Parent's
Death. The Words of the Decree are thus:
" Placere, ne cui qui filio familias mutuam
" pecuniam dedisset, etiam post mortem pa-
" rentis, cujus in potestate fuisset, actio pe-
" titioque daretur; ut scirent, qui pessimo
" exemplo fœnerarent, nullius posse filiifa-

" milias bonum nomen, inde expectata pa-
" tris sui morte, fieri." Hence we may understand the Reason of *Geta's* Defence.

75 *Nil suave meritum est.* These Words
have greatly perplexed Commentators: As it
would be tedious to recount their various O-
pinions, I shall content myself with observing, that *Gronovius* seems to me to have
hit

---

# ACT II. SCENE I.

### ARGUMENT.

*Phormio is introduced to defend what he had done, who there-
fore here prepares for an Encounter with the old Man.*

PHORMIO, GETA.

*Phormio.* HOW do you say? *Antipho* gone, afraid to be seen by his
Father?

*Get.* Very much afraid.

*Phor.* That *Phany* is left by herself?

*Get.* The same.

*Phor.* And the old Man in a Rage?

*Get.* A great one.

*Phor.* The whole Business then, *Phormio*, rests upon you alone.
You

### ANNOTATIONS.

*Phædria*, we have seen in the end of the
last Act, had been dispatched away to find
out *Phormio*, and here they present themselves together. *Geta* had been informing the
Parasite by the way, of what had passed,
particularly of *Antipho's* Terror and Flight
upon seeing his Father. This rouzes *Phormio*, who plainly perceives he must take all
the Burden upon himself; *Geta* urges him to

it, and, finding him resolute and determined,
commends him, but seems to fear that his
Boldness may some time or other bring him to
trouble. This gives rise to a very pleasant
Conversation, which is at last interrupted by
the Appearance of *Demipho*, with his Train
of Advocates. Some have made this the
second Scene of the second Act; but the Error is evident upon the least Consideration?
For

Nil suave meritum est, hominem commonstrarier      75
Mihi istum volo, aut, ubi habitet, demonstrarier.
GE. Nempe Phormionem? DE. istum patronum mu-
   lieris.                                         [PH. foris.
GE. Jam faxo hîc aderit. DE. Antipho ubi nunc est?
DE. Abi, Phædria; eum require atque adduce huc.
   PH. eo                                        [DE. at
Rectâ viâ quidem illuc. GE. nempe ad Pamphilam.
Ego Deos penates hinc salutatum domum            8i
Devortar. inde ibo ad forum, atque aliquot mihi
Amicos advocabo, ad hanc rem qui adsient,
Ut, ne imparatus sim, si adveniat Phormio.

*Nempe ad Pamphilam. DE. At ego devortar hinc domum salutatum Deos penates; inde ibo ad forum, atque advocabo aliquot amicos mihi, qui adsient ad hanc rem, ut ne sim imparatus, si Phormio adveniat.*

ORDO.

*Est nihil adeo suave meritum. Volo istum hominem commonstrari mihi, aut demonstrari, ubi habitet. GE. Nempe Phormionem? DE. Istum patronum mulieris. GE. Faxo aderit hic jam. DE. Ubi est Antipho nunc? PH. Foris. DE. Abi, Phædria; require eum, atque adduc huc. PH. Eo quidem rectâ viâ illuc. GE. ... penates; inde ibo ad ... ne imparatus, si Phormio ...*

## ANNOTATIONS.

hit upon their true Meaning: his Words are, *Nil suave meritum est: hoc est, nihil est tanti: nihil est pretii aut lucri tam magni, quod libeat capiam, si habendum sit ea conditione, ut hoc feram.*

  *At ego Deos penates.* Every Citizen and Father of a Family had in his House some peculiar Gods, whom he privately worshipped, and considered in an especial manner, as the Guardian Deities of him and his Houshold. These were call'd, *Dii Penates, Domestici, or Lares familiares.* Cic. pro Domo. 41. *Quid est sanctius? Quid omni religione munitius, quàm domus uniuscujusque civium? hìc aræ sunt, hìc foci, hic Dii penates, hic sacra, religiones, cæremoniæ, continentur.*

---

# ACTUS II. SCENA I.

## ARGUMENTUM.

*Adducitur Phormio ut factum defendat, qui hic se instruit cum sene litigaturus.*

### PHORMIO, GETA.

ITANE patris ais conspectum veritum hinc abiisse?
  GE. admodum.
PH. Phanium relictam solam? GE. sic. PH. & iratum
  senem?                                         [redit?
GE. Oppidò. PH. ad te summa solum, Phormio, rerum

*Sic. PH. Et senem esse iratum? GE. Oppidò. PH. Summa rerum redit ad te solum, Phormio.*

ORDO.

*Isne ita, Antiphonem abiisse hinc veritum conspectum patris? GE. Admodum. PH. Phanium esse relictam solam? GE. ...*

## ANNOTATIONS.

For at the End of the last Scene, all the several Persons disappear. *Geta* goes to find out *Phormio*, and *Demipho* to return Thanks to the Gods for his safe Arrival, and thence to the Forum to call some Friends; all which require a pretty long Interval.

  *Itane patris ais conspectum?* Donatus has preserved a Tradition concerning *Terence* and *Ambivius Turpio*, which he says was current even in his Time. The Poet causing this Piece one day to be rehearsed before a few select Friends; *Ambivius,* who was to play the Part of *Phormio,* entered drunk, which highly exasperated *Terence.* But *Ambivius,* with an unconcerned Air, and scratching his Head with his Finger, repeated some Verses, which the Poet no sooner heard, than he immediately resumed his wonted Good-humour; protesting, that when he composed these Lines, he had in his Mind the Idea of such a Parasite as *Ambivius* then appeared to be. This Tradition deserves Notice, as it gives us some Notion of the Manner of the Actors of those Times.

4   T. etc.

You have made up this Pill, and must yourself swallow it down. To work then.

*Get.* Prithee, *Phormio.*

*Phor.* Suppose he should ask.

*Get.* All our Hope's in you.

*Phor.* 'Twill do. But if he should reply?

*Get.* You put us upon it.

*Phor.* Ay, now I think I have it.

*Get.* Do, help us then.

*Phor.* Let the old Gentleman come; all my Measures are settled.

*Get.* What do you propose to do?

*Phor.* What do you think? but that *Phany* continue with him still, to clear *Antipho* of all Blame, and turn the old Man's Anger wholly upon myself.

*Get.* O brave Man, and best of Friends! But I'm very much afraid, *Phormio*, lest this Courage of yours prove your Ruin at last.

*Phor.* Ah, there's no manner of Danger; I have already made trial, and ponder'd the Paths of my Feet. How many Men, think you, both Foreigners and Citizens, have I battered almost to death. The more I know, the bolder I am. Tell me, did you ever hear of an Action of Damages brought against me.

*Get.* How comes it that you escape so well?

*Phor.* Because the Net is never spread for the Hawk or the Kite, that do mischief, but for such Birds as are quite harmless; because in these last there is some Profit, the others were lost Labour. Just so, they only are in danger from others, who have any thing to lose. They know I have nothing. But, say you, They'll obtain Judgment against me, take me home, and confine me. Far from it; they'll never choose to maintain a devouring Fellow like me; and faith, in my Opinion, they're wise, not to do me the greatest Kindness, in return for the many Tricks I have play'd them.                *Get.*

## ANNOTATIONS.

4 *Tute hoc intristi. Intritum,* call'd also sometimes *moretum,* we are told was a mixed Composition, consisting of Garlick, Onions, Cheese, Eggs, and other Ingredients.

5 *Obsecro te.* What *Geta* says in these two Verses, makes a continued Speech of itself, and no way refers to what comes from the Parasite. *Obsecro te, in te spes est. Tu impulisti. Subberi.* The same is to be said of *Phormio,* he is all the while taken up with his own Thoughts, and contriving how to deal with the old Man. Two Things offer themselves to *Phormio's* Mind. *Si rogabit.* Should he question me upon this Affair, and desire that I would make it appear how *Phany* is related to him; for so it seems requisite to supply this abrupt Sentence. The proper Answer occurs to him immediately. *Eccere,* i. e. *ecce habeo: hem tibi; habeo quod respondeam:* for *Plautus* uses both *ecce* and *eccere* in the same Sense. *Mill.* II. 2. 48. *Phormio* goes on; *Quid si reddet?* to which he opposes *sic opinor. Sub. me responsurum, & confutaturum senem verbis.* Here his Deliberations end, and he thinks himself abundantly prepared. That this is the real way of understanding these two Lines, appears from what follows in the next Verse. *Cedo senem: jam instructa sunt mihi in corde consilia omnia.*

" *In nervum erumpat denoque.* There are several Conjectures offered to explain these Words. Some consider them figuratively, as taken from an Archer's drawing the Bow till the String breaks. Others will have them to allude to the Custom of binding those who for any Misdeeds were sentenced to Confinement; for the Expression commonly used in these Cases, was *in nervum conjicere. Est enim nervus,* says a learned Commentator,
*Varch.?*

Tute hoc intriſti, tibi omne ex exedendum : accingere.
GE. Obſecro te. PH. ſi rogabit. GE. in te ſpes eſt. PH.
   eccere, 5
Quid ſi reddet? GE. tu impuliſti. PH. ſic opinor. GE.
   ſubveni. [ſilia omnia.
PH. Cedo ſenem : jam inſtructa ſunt mihi in corde con-
GE. Quid ages? PH. quid vis? niſi uti maneat Phani-
   um, atque ex crimine hoc [rivem ſenis?
Antiphonem eripiam, atque in me omnem irem de-
GE. O vir fortis, atque amicus. verùm hoc ſæpe,
   Phormio, 10
Vereor, ne iſtæc fortitudo in nervum erumpat denique.
   PH. ah, [via.
Non ita eſt : factum eſt periclum ; jam pedum viſa eſt
Quot me cenſes homines jam deverberaſſe uſque ad
   necem,
Hoſpites? tùm cives? quò magi' novi, tanto ſæpius.
Cedo dum, en unquam injuriarum audiſti mihi ſcri-
   ptam dicam 15
GE. Qui iſtuc? PH. quia non rete accipitri tenditur,
   neque miluo,
Qui malè faciunt nobis : illis, qui nil faciunt, tenditur :
Quia enim in illis fructus eſt, in illis opera luditur.
Aliis aliunde eſt periclum, unde aliquid abradi poteſt :
Mihi ſciunt nihil eſſe. Dices, Ducent damnatum do-
   mum. 20
Alere nolunt hominem edacem : & ſapiunt meâ ſen-
   tentiâ,
Pro-maleficio ſi beneficium ſummum nolunt reddere.

*tute intriſti tibi, jam-
ne eſt exedendum ti-
bi : accingere. GE.
Obſecro te. PH. Si
rogabit. GE. Spes
eſt in te.. PH. Ec-
cere, quid ſi reddet?
GE. Tu impuliſti.
PH. Sic opinor. GE.
Subveni. PH. Cedo
ſenem : jam omnia
conſilia ſunt inſtructa
intel in corde. GE.
Quid ages? PH.
Quid vis? niſi uti
Phanium maneat, at-
que eripiam Anti-
phonem ex hoc cri-
mine, atque dirivem
omnem iram ſenis in
me? GE. O vir fortis,
atque amicus.
Verum ſæpe vereor
hæc, Phormio, ne i-
ſtæc fortitudo erum-
pat denique in ner-
vum. PH. Ah, non
eſt iſta : periculum eſt
factum, via pedum
eſt jam viſa. Quot
homines, hoſpites, tum
cives, cenſes me jam
deverberaſſe uſque ad
necem? quo magis
novi, tanto ſæpius.
Cedo dum, en unquam
audiſti dicam inju-
riarum ſcriptam mi-
hi? GE. Qui iſtuc?*

*PH. Quia rete non tenditur accipitri, neque milvio, qui faciunt male nobis : tenditur illis qui faciunt nil : quia enim eſt fructus in illis : opera luditur in illis. Periculum aliunde eſt aliis, unde aliquid poteſt abradi : ſciunt eſſe nihil mihi. Dices, Ducent me damnatum domum. Nolunt alere hominem edacem : & meâ ſententiâ ſapiunt, ſi nolunt reddere ſummum beneficium pro ma-leficio.*

## ANNOTATIONS.

*Vinculi lignei genus, in quod pedes conjecti arc-tantur.* This laſt is the Interpretation more generally followed ; and is, moreover, con-firmed by the Sequel, where *Phormio* ſays, Ver. 20. *Dices, Ducent damnatum demum;* which appears to allude to this Paſſage.

12. *Jam pedum viſa eſt via.* Marutius fancies this a Metaphor taken from Dogs in hunting ; but it more probably refers to Tra-vellers, who having travelled any Road often, are perfectly acquainted with it, and know where to tread ſure ; unleſs we make it re-late to the preceding Verſe, wherein *Geta* ſpeaks of the Danger he was in of having his Feet faſtened. *Phormio* anſwers, that this is no new Trade to him, and that he has by long Experience learned to ſecure his Feet against all Danger.

13 *Deverberaſſe.* This Word is here me-taphorical, inſtead of *evertiſſe, bonis ſpol aſſe per fraudem & calumniam.*

14. *Quo magi' novi, tanto ſæpius.* The more I know, the more bold and adventu-rous I am ; either becauſe his Experience directed him in a ſure and ſafe Road ; or becauſe the more he knew of the World, the more he was ſatisfied, that Villainy with addreſs was ſecure of Impunity, and hence he boldly ventured. Some think that the Words here are deſignedly inverted, and that *Phormio* ſays *quo magis novi, tanto ſævius,* in-ſtead of *quo ſævius, tanto magis novi.*

*Dicens damnatum domum.* By the Ro-man Laws, Debtors were adjudged the Slaves

*Get.* *Antipho* will never be able to requite you sufficiently, for this Favour.

*Phor.* Nay, 'tis we, on the contrary, that can never sufficiently requite our Patrons for their Favours. For you to sit at free cost, anointed, bath'd, easy in your Mind; while he has all the Trouble and Expence of providing what he thinks you'll like best. He frets, you laugh; are honour'd with the first Cup, placed at the upper End of the Table: a dubious Supper is serv'd up.

*Get.* Dubious! What's that?

*Phor.* Where the Variety is such, that you are in doubt what to eat of most. When you consider within yourself how delicious and costly all these are, don't you account him a very God who provides them for you?

*Get.* The old Man's coming; mind what you're about: The first Onset's the fiercest; if you can but stand that, all the rest will be mere Play and Pastime.

A N N O T A T I O N S.

of their Creditors, till the Debt was discharged. Thus *Phormio*, if cast in an Action of Damages, as he was insufficient to pay the Sum awarded, would have been in the Situation of an insolvent Debtor.

24 *Nemo sati' pro merito gratiam regi refert.* In the *Eunuch,* *Terence* has given the Character of a higher Order of Parasites; Men, who had arrived at great Skill and Eminence in the Art of Flattery; here a lower Rank of them is described, those who offered themselves to others as proper Tools to accomplish their Designs, and hence from their Cunning and Address were often in high Favour, invited to Supper, and admitted to sit at the same Table with the Master of the Feast. *Rex* is often used for a great or a rich Man, and was a common Apellation too for the Master of the Feast, he who invited and entertained the Company.

25 *Tene asymbolum.* We learn from *Donatus,* that this Passage was not taken from *Apollodorus,* but imitated from some Lines of the sixth Satire of *Ennius,* where a Parasite says:

*Quippe*

# ACT II. SCENE II.

### ARGUMENT.

*This Scene contains the Encounter of* Demipho *with* Phormio *the Parasite:* Antipho *had married unknown to his Father, who upon his Return insists that he part with his Wife.* Phormio *opposes it.*

DEMIPHO, GETA, PHORMIO.

*Dem.* TO the *Advocates.*) Did you ever hear of a more outrageous Insult offered to any one than this to me? Pray come and stand by me.

*Get.*

A N N O T A T I O N S.

This Scene is artfully conducted by the Poet. *Geta* and *Phormio* see *Demipho* at a Distance, advancing with his Train of Advocates behind him, but continue the Conversation, as if they saw him not. Thus *Geta* is overheard by his Master defending his cause with great Warmth, and proceeding even to Reproaches against *Phormio.* All this with design to ward off the Blow from himself, and make it appear as if he was not any way to blame in what had been done. In the Conversation that ensues upon *Demipho*'s coming up; *Phormio,* in spite of all his Cunning and artful Evasions, appears more than once disconcerted, and in danger of betraying himself. There is, perhaps, more Merit in this, than most Readers are aware of; the Poet would not represent

Knavery

Ge. Non poteſt ſati' pro merito ab illo tibi referri gratia.
Ph. Imo enim nemo ſati' pro merito gratiam regi refert.
Tene aſymbolum venire, unctum, atque lautum è bal-
   neis,                              25
Otioſum ab animo; cùm ille & curâ, & ſumtu abſu-
   mitur,
Dum tibi fit, quod placeat; ille ringitur, tu rideas?
Prior bibas, prior decumbas; cœna dubia apponitur?
Ge. Quid iſtuc verbi eſt? Ph. ubi tu dubites, quid
   ſumas potiſſimum.
Hæc, cùm rationem ineas, quàm ſint ſuavia, & quàm
   cara ſint;                            30
Ea qui præbet, non tu hunc habeas planè præſentem
   Deum?                          [rima:
Ge. Senex adeſt, vide quid agas, prima coitio et acer-
Si eam ſuſtinueris, poſtilla jam, ut lubet, ludas licet.

*Ge. Gratia non poteſt ſatis referri tibi. ab illo, pro merito. Ph. Imo enim, nemo ſatis refere gratiam. regi pro merito. Tene venire aſymbolum, unctum, atque lautum. è balneis, otioſum ab animo; cum ille abſumitur & cura, & ſumptu, dum quod placeat ſit tibi; ille ringitur, tu rideas? prior bibas, prior decumbas; cœna dubia apponitur? Ge. Quid verbi eſt iſtuc? Ph. Ubi tu dubites quid potiſſimum ſumas. Cum*

*ineas rationem, quam ſuavia hæc ſint, & quam cara ſint; non tu habeas hunc plane præſentem Deum, qui præbet ea? Ge. Senex adeſt; vide quid agas: prima coitio eſt acèrrima: ſi ſuſtinue-ris eam, jam poſt illa, licet ludas ut lubet.*

## ANNOTATIONS.

*Quippe ſine cura, lætus, lautus, quum ad-*
   *venis,*
*Inſertis malis, & expedito brachic,*
*Alacer, celſus, lupino exſpectans impetu.*
*Max dum alterius abligurias bona: quid*
*Cenſes dominis eſſe animi? Pro Divom fi-*
   *dem!*
*Ille triſtis cibum dum ſervat, tu ridens vo-*
   *ras.*

" For when you ſit down at Table devoid
" of Care, chearful, bathed and perfumed,
" with Jaws ready for Havock, and an
" active right Hand, keen, wrathful, and
" eager like a Wolf after his Prey: When
" afterwards you be,... :he delicious Repaſt,
" and gorge at another's Expence: what do
" you imagine is the Condition of your En-
" tertainer? Good Heavens! While he
" with a Heart full of Anguiſh ſerves you
" all round, you chearfully diſpatch his
" Bounty."

28 *Cœna dubia apponitur?* Phormio himſelf explains the meaning of this in the next Line. Horace uſes the ſame Phraſe in the ſecond Satire of the ſecond Book, where recommending Temperance, and deſcribing the miſchievous Effects, which a Variety of Meats jumbled together in the Stomach muſt produce, he ſays:

----- *Vides, ut pallidus omnis*
*Cœna deſurgat dubia?*

# ACTUS II. SCENA II.

### ARGUMENTUM.

*Hæc ſcena concertationem habet Demiphonis & paraſiti. Clam patre uxorem duxerat Antipho: domum reverſus pater illum vult ejicere: contra dicit Phormio.*

DEMIPHO, GETA, PHORMIO.

E N unquam cuiquam contumelioſiùs
   Audiſtis factam injuriam, quàm hæc eſt mihi?

*tumelioſius cuiquam, quàm hæc eſt facta mihi?*

ORDO.

De. E N unquam audiſtis injuriam factam con-

## ANNOTATIONS.

Knavery in too triumphant Circumſtances. Phormio, tho' old in the Practice of Roguery, and hardened to Deceit, yet cannot ſo far conquer the Conviction of his own Mind, but it will in ſpight of all his Endeavours diſcover itſelf, by a certain Incoherence and Heſitation in his Anſwers.

1 *En unquam cuiquam.* He is ſpeaking

      here

*Get.* He's in a Passion.

*Phor.* (*softly*) Pray hold your tongue, ſt. I'll ſoon rouze him ef-fectually; (*aloud*) Immortal Gods! Does *Demipho* deny that *Phany* is related to him? What, *Demipho* deny that ſhe is related to him?

*Get.* He does.

*Phor.* Or that he knows any thing who her Father was?

*Get.* He denies it.

*Dem.* This I believe is the very Man I was ſpeaking of. Follow me.

*Phor.* Or that he knows who even *Stilpho* was?

*Get.* He denies it.

*Phor.* Becauſe, poor Creature, ſhe was left deſtitute, her Father's diſown'd, herſelf neglected: See the Effects of Avarice!

*Get.* If you accuſe my Maſter of Avarice, you ſhan't eaſily eſcape.

*Dem.* Unparallel'd Impudence! Is he even come to accuſe firſt?

*Phor.* As to the young Man, I can't reaſonably be angry with him, if he did not know him; becauſe, as *Stilpho* was much in years, poor, and ſupported himſelf only by his Labour, he kept almoſt always in the Country:-there he farm'd a ſmall Piece of Ground of my Fa-ther. The old Man was wont often to complain to me, how he was neglected by this his Kinſman. But what a Man did he thus neglect? The very beſt I ever ſaw in my Life.

*Get.* See that you ſay no more either of him or yourſelf than you can make good.

*Phor.* You go and be hang'd; for had I not known him to be ſo, I would never have raiſed ſuch powerful Enemies to myſelf in your Fa-mily, for her ſake whom your Maſter now ſo ungenerouſly ſlights.

*Get.* What, do you perſiſt ſtill, you Wretch, to abuſe my Maſter in his abſence?

*Phor.* He deſerves it.

*Get.* Say you ſo, you Jail-Bird?

*Dem.* Geta.

*Get.* Thou common Defrauder, thou Perverter of the Laws.

*Dem.* Geta.

*Phor.* Anſwer him.

*Get.* Who's that? Oh!

*Dem.* Hold your tongue.

*Get.* This Fellow, Sir, has been charging you to-day in your ab-ſence,

ANNOTATIONS.

here to the three Lawyers, whom he has brought from the Forum, to conſult with in the preſent Cauſe; for we are to ſuppoſe that he had by the way been informing them of the particular Circumſtances of it, after which he puts this Queſtion to them.

.3 *Quin tu hic age*, &c. In moſt Editions we read *quin tu hic ages* without the Addi-tion of *ii*. T...nus was the firſt who re-ſtored the true reading from the Remark of *Donatus*, who obſerves that this *quin tu hic age* amounts to an Injunction of Silence. This from the common and natural Signi-fication of theſe Words could never have been conjectured, without ſome ſuch Addi-tion as *ii*, which is an evident Note of Si-lence. This Emendation he moreover con-firms by ſeveral other Reaſons, all very ſtrong and convincing.

4 *Proh Deum immortalium!* What a Per-

Adeste quæso. GE. iratus est. PH. quin tu hoc age. st.
Jam ego hunc agitabo. proh Deum immortalium!
Negat Panium esse hanc sibi cognatam? Demipho? 5
Hanc Demipho negat esse cognatam? GE. negat.
PH. Neque ejus patrem se scire, qui fuerit? GE. negat.
DE. Ipsum esse opinor, de quo agebam. sequimini.
PH. Nec Stilphonem ipsum scire, qui fuerit? GE. negat.
PH. Quia egens relicta est misera, ignoratur parens, 10
Neglegitur ipsa. vide. avaritia quid facit.
GE. Si herum insimulabis malitiæ, male audies.
DE. O audaciam! etiamne ultro accusatum advenit?
PH. Nam jam adolescenti nihil est quod succenseam,
Si illum minus norat: quippe homo jam grandior, 15
Pauper, cui opera vita erat, ruri fere
Se continebat: ibi agrum de nostro patre
Colendum habebat. sæpe interea mihi senex
Narrabat, se hunc neglegere cognatum suum.
At quem virum? quem ego viderim in vita optumum.
GE. Videas te, atque illum, ut narras. PH. abi in
    malam crucem: 21
Nam ni ita eum existumassem, nunquam tam graves
Ob hanc inimicitias caperem in vostram familiam,
Quam is aspernatur nunc tam inliberaliter.
GE. Pergin' hero absenti male loqui, impurissime? 25
PH. Dignum autem hoc illo est. GE. ain' tandem,
    carcer? DE. Geta.
GE. Bonorum extortor, legum contortor. DE. Geta.
PH. Responde. GE. quis homo est? hem. DE. tace.
GE. absenti tibi,

*quæso adisse. GE. Est iratus. PH. Quin tu hoc age, st. Jam ego agitabo hunc. Proh Deum immortalium! An Demipho negat hanc Phanium esse cognatam sibi? Demipho negat hanc esse cognatam? GE. Negat. PH. Neque se scire patrem ejus, qui fuerit? GE. Negat. DE. Opinor hunc esse ipsum, de quo agebam. Sequimini. PH. Nec scire ipsum Stilphonem, qui fuerit? GE. Negat. PH. Quia misera est relicta egens, parens ignoratur, ipsa neglegitur, vide quid avaritia facit. GE. Si insimulabis herum malitiæ, audies male. DE. O audaciam! Etiamne ultro advenit accusatum? PH. Nam jam est nihil propter quod succenseam adolescenti, si minus noverat illum: quippe homo jam grandior, pauper, cui opera erat vita, continebat se fere ruri: ibi habebat agrum co-lendum de nostro patre. Sæpe interea senex narrabat mihi, hunc suum cognatum neglegere se. At quem virum? optimum quem ego viderim in vita. GE. Videas ut narras te atque illum. PH. Abi in malam crucem: nam ni existimassem eum ita, nunquam caperem tam graves inimicitias in vostram familiam ob hanc, quam is nunc aspernatur tam inliberaliter. GE. Pergisne, impurissime, loqui male hero absenti? PH. Hoc autem est dignum illo. GE. Aisne tandem, carcer? DE. Geta. GE. Extortor bonorum, contortor legum. DE. Geta. PH. Responde. GE. Quis homo est? hem. DE. Tace. GE. Nunquam cessavit hodie dicere contumelias tibi absenti,*

## ANNOTATIONS.

...nio had said before to Geta, was in a low whispering Voice, but here he raises his Tone, on purpose to be heard by Demipho, and thus is the first to accuse the Person he had injured. To compleat the Sentence, we must supply *fidem*; as in the *Andrian* we read *proh Deum atque hominum fidem*.

[21] *Videas te, atque illum, ut narras.* These Words have been wrested into six or seven different Meanings by Commentators. The most natural and obvious Construction is thus: *Videas ut narras te atque illum.* See what you say, what account you give of yourself and him. Phormio had been extolling Stil-pho, the pretended Father, as a Man of great Worth, which included a heavy Reflection upon *Demipho* for his neglect of him. Hence *Geta*, with an affected Zeal for his Master, interrupts him: *Take care you say no more than you can prove, for you'll be called upon to make it good.* I don't say but this Explication may be liable to Objections, yet it seems less so than any of the others that have been offered.

[23] *In vostram familiam.* In some Editions we read *nostram familiam*; the Difference is not material.

[27] *Bonorum extortor, legum contortor.*


This

fence, with such Things as are unworthy of you, and worthy only of himself.

*Dem.* Well, have done. Young Man, with your good leave, I'd first afk this Question, if you'll be pleafed to give me an Anfwer. Who, do you fay, this Friend of yours was? Explain that Point, and how he claim'd Relation to me.

*Phor.* You queftion me, forfooth, as if you knew nothing of the Matter.

*Dem.* I know?

*Phor.* Yes, you.

*Dem.* I deny it: You, who affert it, rub up my Memory.

*Phor.* I warrant you did not know your own Coufin!

*Dem.* You diftract me : Tell me his Name.

*Phor.* His Name! I will,

*Dem.* Why don't you then?

*Phor.* I'm undone by *Hercules*, I've forgot the Name.

*Dem.* Ha! what's that you fay?

*Phor.* (*Afide to* Geta.) *Geta*, if you remember the Name I mentioned juft now, whifper it to me. (*To* Demipho.) I'll not tell you ; as if you did not know it already ; you come to pump me.

*Dem.* I come to pump you!

*Get.* (*fofily to* Phormio.) *Stilpho.*

*Phor.* And after all, what is it to me? 'Tis *Stilpho.*

*Dem.* Whom do you fay?

*Phor.* I fay, *Stilpho* ; you knew him.

*Dem.* I neither knew him, nor was ever related to any one of that Name.

*Phor.* Say you fo? Are you not afhamed of fuch Doings? But had he left behind him an Eftate of ten Talents——

*Dem.* The Gods confound thee!

*Phor.* You'd have been the firft to trace minutely the Detail of your Pedigree, from Grandfather, and Great-Grandfather.

*Dem.* Perhaps fo : I fhould then, had I undertaken it, have made it appear how fhe was related to me : Now do you the fame. Tell me which way we are related.

*Get.* (*To* Demipho.) Faith, Mafter, well urg'd. (*To* Phormio.) You, Sir, take care of yourfelf.

*Phor.* I made the Thing plain where I ought, before the Judges : If it was falfe, why did not your Son then difprove it?

*Dem.* Speak not to me of my Son, whofe Folly was beyond expreffion.

*Phor.* But you who are fo wondrous wife, apply to the Magiftrates,

A N N O T A T I O N S.

This feems to have been a common Reproach to Sycophants and Sharpers, and as it has an immediate Reference to what *Phormio* had lately done, muft in the Eye of *De-* *mipho* ftrike more deep. *Cicero* endeavours by a like Figure to augment the Odium of a bafe Behaviour ; *in Pifonem* Cap. 17. "Age, "fenatus odit te, quod eum tu facere jure "concedis,

Te indignas, seque dignas contumelias
Nunquam cessavit dicere hodie. DE. ohe, desine. 30
Adolescens, primùm abs te hoc bonâ veniâ peto,
Si tibi placere potis est, mihi ut respondeas:
Quem amicum tuum ais fuisse istum? explana mihi:
Et qui cognatum me sibi esse diceret.
PH. Proinde expiscare, quasi non nosses. DE. nossem?
    PH. ita. 35
DE. Ego me nego: tu, qui ais, redige in memoriam.
PH. Eho, tu sobrinum tuum non noras? DE. enecas:
Dic nomen. PH. nomen? maxumè. DE. quid nunc
    taces? [PH. Geta,
PH. Perii hercle, nomen perdidi. DE. hem, quid ais?
Si meministri id quod olim dictum est, subjice. hem,
Non dico: quasi non noris, tentatum advenis. 41
DE. Egon' autem tento? GE. Stilpho. PH. atque adeo,
    quid meâ? [noveras?
Stilpho est. DE quem dixti? PH. Stilphonem, inquam
DE. Neque ego illum noram, neque mihi cognatus fuit
Quisquam isto nomine. PH. itane? non te horum pudet?
At si talentûm rem reliquisset decem— 46
DE. Di tibi male faciant. PH. primus esses memoriter
Progeniem vostram usque ab avo atque atavo proferens.
DE. Ita ut dicis, ego tum cùm advenissem, quî mihi
Cognata ea esset, dicerem: itidem tu face. 50
Cedo, quî est cognata? GE. eu noster, rectè. heus tu
    cave.
PH. Dilucidè expedivi, quibus me oportuit
Judicibus. tum, id si falsum fuerat, filius
Cur non refellit? DE. filium narras mihi?
Cujus de stultitiâ dici, ut dignum est, non potest. 55
PH. At tu, qui sapiens es, magistratus adi,

*indignas te dignas-
que se. DE. Ohe,
desine. Adolescens,
primùm peto hoc abs
te bona venia, si est
potis placere tibi, ut
respondeas mihi:
quem ais istum tuum
amicum fuisse? ex-
plana mihi: & qui
diceret me esse cogna-
tum sibi. PH. Ex-
piscare proinde, quasi
non nosses. DE.
Nossem? PH. Ita.
DE. Ego nego me
nosse: tu qui ais,
redige in memoriam.
PH. Eho, tu non no-
ras tuum sobrinum?
DE. Enecas: dic
nomen. PH. Nomen?
maxime. DE. Quid
taces nunc? PH.
Perii hercle, perdidi
nomen, DE. Hem,
quid ais? PH. Geta,
si meministri id no-
men quod dictum est
olim, subjice. Hem,
non dico: quasi non
noris, advenis tenta-
tum. DE. Egone au-
tem tento? GE. Stil-
pho. PH. Atque a-
deo, quid refert mea?
est Stilpho. DE.
Quem dixti? PH.
Inquam Stilphonem,
noveras? DE. Ne-
que ego noveram il-
lum, neque quisquam
isto nomine fuit cog-*

*natus mihi. PH. Itane? Non pudet te horum? at si reliquisset rem decem talentum. DE. Dii
male faciant tibi. PH. Esses primus memoriter proferens progeniem vestram usque ab avo, atque
atavo. DE. Ita ut dicis, ego tum, cum advenissem, dicerem qui ea esset cognata mihi: tu face
itidem: cedo qui est cognata? GE. Eu noster, rectè: heus tu, cave. PH. Expedivi dilucidè
judicibus, quibus oportuit me: si id fuerat falsum, cur filius non tum refellit? DE. Narras filium mihi? de cujus stultitia non potest dici, ut est dignum. PH. At tu qui es sapiens, adi magistratus,*

## ANNOTATIONS.

" concedis, afflictorem, & perditorem, non
" modo dignitatis & auctoritatis, sed omnino
" ordinis ac nominis sui."

51 *Eu noster, rectè.* These Words are addressed to *Dmipho*, applauding him for push-
ing the Question so close. *Heus tu! cave,*
these again are pronounced, turning to *Phormio*; but 'tis uncertain whether they are to
be understood as spoken aloud, or in a soft
whispering Tone. If the first, they are a
pretended Check or Mènace, to deter him
from Evasions, and compel him to come directly to the Point: if a Whisper, they are
a Caution to *Phormio* to be upon his Guard.
Hitherto he had pretty well sustained the old
Man's Attack, but at present he is very
hard pressed. It was almost impossible to
avoid giving a direct Answer, which yet could
not be done without hazarding a Discovery
of the whole Plot. This alarms *Geta*; but



*Phormio*

ſtrates, and procure a ſecond Deciſion in the ſame Cauſe; as you ſeem to be Sovereign here, and the only Man that can claim a Prerogative of having the ſame Cauſe try'd over again.

*Dem.* Altho' I am manifeſtly injur'd, yet rather than engage in a Law-Suit, or be plagu'd with your Tongue: Free me of her, and as if ſhe was really any Relation, take fifteen Guineas, the Portion which the Law allows.

*Phor.* Ha! ha! ha! A pleaſant kind of Man!

*Dem.* What's the Matter? Do I aſk any Thing unreaſonable? Can't I obtain even this, which is common Juſtice?

*Phor.* Say you ſo, truly? Does the Law allow, that after you have abuſed a Citizen, you ſhould diſmiſs her with a Reward, as if ſhe were a Whore? Or is it not rather to prevent a Citizen's bringing any Scandal upon herſelf thro' Poverty, that the Law enjoins a Marriage with her next Relation, that ſhe may paſs her Life with one Man? A Thing which you here mean to hinder.

*Dem.* Ay, ay, with her next Relation: But whence are we related to her? Or why muſt we be concern'd with her?

*Phor.* Well well, the Thing's now done, and you can't undo it.

*Dem.* Not undo it? Nay, I ſhan't deſiſt till I have gone through with it.

*Phor.* 'Tis all a Joke.

*Dem.* See the End of it then.

*Phor.* In fine, *Demipho,* you are no way concern'd in the Affair: 'Tis your Son, and not you, that's caſt: For your Marriage-Days are over long ago.

*Dem.* Suppoſe 'tis he ſays all this to you that I now ſay; or I'll turn both him and this Wife of his out of Doors.

*Get.* (*Aſide.*) He's angry.

*Phor.* You'll be better adviſ'd, I hope.

*Dem.* Are you thus determined, you unlucky Raſcal, to do me all the Miſchief you can?

*Phor.* (*Aſide to Geta.*) He's afraid of us, for all he ſtrives to hide it.

*Get.* (*Aſide to Phormio.*) You've begun well.

*Phor.* Even bear with Patience what can't be avoided: 'Twill be acting like yourſelf to keep up a Friendſhip between us.

*Dem.* Do I value your Friendſhip, or deſire to have, ſee, or be acquainted with you?

*Phor.* If you can but agree with her, you'll have one to be the Joy and Delight of your old Age: Pray conſider your Time of Life.

*Dem.*

*ANNOTATIONS.*

*Phormio* eſcapes the Danger, by ſaying that he had already made it appear before the proper Judges, and had no Intention to give a ſecond Detail.

58 *Quandoquidem ſolus regnas.* This is an invidious Jeer; for in *Athens,* a City tenacibus of its Freedom, the Name of King, or the affecting of regal Power was extremely odious; and to claim a ſecond Judgment in a Cauſe that had been already determined, looked ſomewhat tyrannical, as if a Man meant to ſet himſelf above the Laws, and controul them at his Pleaſure.

79 *Tute idem melius feceris.* Commentators

Judicium de eadem causâ iterùm ut reddant tibi:
Quandoquidem solus regnas, & soli licet.
Hic de eadem causâ bis judicium adipiscier.
De. Etsi nihil facta injuria est, verumtamen    160
Potius quàm lites secter, aut quàm te audiam,
Itidem ut cognata si sit, id quod lex jubet
Dotem dare, abduce hanc, minas quinque accipe.
Ph. Ha, ha, hæ, homo suavis! De. quid est? num
    iniquom postulo?    164
An ne hoc quidem ego adipiscar, quod jus publicum est?
Ph. Itane tandem, quæso, item ut meretricem, ubi
    abusu' sis,
Mercedem dare lex jubet ei, atque amittere? an,
Ut ne quid turpe civis in se admitteret
Propter egestatem, proxumo jussa est dari,
Ut cum uno ætatem degeret? quod tu vetas.    70
De. Ita, proxumo quidem: at nos unde? aut quam-
    obrem? Ph. ohe.
Actum, aiunt, ne agas. De. non agam? imo haud
    desinam,
Donec perfecero hoc. Ph. ineptis. De. sine modò.
Ph. Postremò tecum nihil rei nobis, Demipho, est:
Tuus est damnatus gnatus, non tu: nam tua    75
Præterierat jam ad ducendum ætas. De. omnia hæc
Illum putato, quæ ego nunc dico, dicere:
Aut quidem cum uxore hac ipsum prohibebo domo.
Ge. Iratus est. Ph. tute idem melius feceris.
De. Itane es paratus facere me advorsum omnia    80
Infelix? Ph. metuit hic nos, tametsi sedulo
Dissimulat. Ge. bene habent tibi principia. Ph. quin,
    n ob quod est
Ferundum fers? tuis dignum factis feceris,
Ut amici inter nos simus. De. egon' tuam expetam
Amicitiam? aut te visum, aut auditum velim?    85
Ph. Si concordabis cum illà, habebis, quæ tuam
Senectutem oblectet: respice ætatem tuam.

*ut iterum reddant judicium tibi de eadem causa: quandoquidem solus regnas hic, & licet tibi soli adipisci hic judicium bis de eadem causa. De. Etsi injuria est facta nihil, verumtamen potius quàm secter lites, aut quàm audiam te; itidem ut si sit cognata, abduce hanc, & accipe quinque minus, id quod lex jubet dare dotem. Ph. Ha, ba, bæ, homo suavis! De. Quid est? Num postulo iniquum? An ego ne adipiscar hoc quidem, quod est publicum jus? Ph. Itane quæso tandem lex jubet, ubi sis abusus civem item ut meretricem, dare mercedem ei, atque amittere? An at civis ne admitteret quid turpe in se propter egestatem, jussa est dari proximo, ut degeret ætatem cum uno? quod tu vetas. De. Ita quidem, proximo. At unde nos sumus proximi? aut quamobrem? Ph. Ohe, aiunt, ne agas actum. De. Non agam? imo haud desiram, donec perfecero hoc. Ph. Ineptis. De. Sine modo. Ph. Postremo, Demipho, est nihil rei nobis tecum: tuus gnatus est damnatus, non tu: nam tua ætas ad ducendum jam præterierat. De. Putato illum dicere omnia hæc, quæ ego nunc dico: aut quidem prohibebo ipsum cum hac uxore domo. Ph. Tute feceris idem melius. Ge. Est iratus. De. Itane es paratus infelix facere omnia adversum me? Ph. Hic metuit nos, tametsi sedulo dissimulat. Ge. Principia habent bene tibi. Ph. Quin fers quod est ferendum? feceris dignum tuis factis, ut nos simus amici inter nos. De. Egone expetam tuam amicitiam, aut velim te visum & auditum? Ph. Si concordabis cum illà, habebis nutum, quæ oblectet tuam senectutem: respice tuam ætatem.*

## ANNOTATIONS.

...differ greatly as to the Meaning of these Words; some explain them; *You'll scarce venture to put your Threats in execution:* Others; *You'll think them of it.* It may, perhaps, have been a common Form of Speech, where Threats were despised as impotent: Such is that of *Davus* in the *Andria: Pena verbis, quasi.*

Geta,

*Dem.* Let her be your Delight; take her to yourſelf.

*Phor.* Moderate your Paſſion.

*Dem.* Mark what I ſay, for we have had too many Words already: If you don't quickly take away this Wench, I'll turn her out; I have ſaid it, *Phormio.*

*Phor.* If you offer to uſe her in any Manner unworthy a Gentlewoman, I'll bring a heavy Action againſt you; I have ſaid it, *Demipho*—(*aſide to* Geta.) If you ſhould happen to want me, I'll be at home.

*Get.* I underſtand you

---

## ACT II. SCENE III.
### ARGUMENT.

Demipho *conſults the Advocates in regard to his Son's Marriage. One adviſes a Proceſs, the other diſſuades from it, and the third, inſtead of joining with either of the others, requires time to deliberate.*

### DEMIPHO, GETA, HEGIO, CRATINUS, CRITO.

*Dem.* WHAT Care and Anxiety does my Son bring upon me, by entangling himſelf and me in this unhappy Marriage? Nor does he offer to come near me, that I may know what he can ſay, or what his Sentiments may be. Do you go and ſee whether he is come home, or no.

*Get.* I will.

*Dem.* You ſee now, Gentlemen, how the Caſe ſtands. What muſt I do? Say, *Hegio.*

*Heg.* Who, I? I think *Cratinus* ſhould give his Opinion firſt, if you pleaſe.

*Dem.* Say *Cratinus.*

*Crat.* Muſt I ſpeak?

*Dem.* You.

*Crat.* I'd have you do what's moſt for your Advantage. 'Tis my Opinion, that what your Son did in your Abſence, ought in Reaſon and Juſtice to be made void, and the Law will grant it. I have told you *my* Sentiments.

*Dem.* Say now, *Hegio.*

*Heg.* I believe *Cratinus* has ſpoke his real Thoughts; but as the Saying is, *So many Men, So many Minds:* every one has his Way.

I

### ANNOTATIONS.

Geta, in the Beginning of this Scene, is ſent to enquire after *Antipho*; and *Phormio* had retired. *Demipho* is therefore left with his three Counſellors, to whom he addreſſes himſelf, and enquires their Opinion of the Cauſe, now that they had heard more particularly about it. They give their Judgment with great Form and Ceremony, contradict one another, and leave *Demipho* in greater Uncertainty than ever; who finding that he was like to receive but little Benefit from the Advice of his learned Council, reſolves to wait his Brother's Return, and be guided by him.

7 *Dic,*

DE. Te oblectet: tibi habe. PH. minue verò iram.
 DE. hoc age:
Satis jam verborum eft. nifi tu properas mulierem
Abducere, ego illam ejiciam: dixi, Phormio.        90
PH. Si tu illam attigeris fecus, quà dignum eft liberam.
Dicam tibi impingam grandem: dixi, Demipho.
Si quid opus fuerit, heus, domo me. GE. intellego.

*DE. Oblectet te, habe eam tibi. PH. Vero minue iram. DE. Age hoc: jam eft fatis verborum; nifi tu properas abducere mulierem, ego ejiciam illam: dixi, Phormio. PH. Si tu attigeris illam fecus,*

*quam eft dignum attingere liberam, ego impingam grandem dicam tibi: dixi, Demipho. Si quid fuerit opus, heus, continebo me domo. GE. Intelligo.*

---

# ACTUS II. SCENA III.

### ARGUMENTUM.

*Confulit Demipho advocatos fuper filii conjugio: unus fuadet, diffuadet alter; tertius, qui fe alterutri addere debuiffet, ejufmodi fententiam dicit, ut rurfus deliberatione opus effe videatur.*

DEMIPHO, GETA, HEGIO, CRATINUS, CRITO.    ORDO.

QUANTA me curâ, & folicitudine afficit
   Gnatus, qui me & fe hifce impedivit nuptiis?
Neque mî in confpectum prodit, ut faltem fciam,
Quid de hac re dicat, quidve fit fententiæ.
Abi tu, vife redieritne jam, an nondum, domum.      5
GE. Eo. DE. videtis quo in loco res hæc fiet.
Quid ago? dic, Hegio. HE. ego? Cratinum cenfeo,
Si tibi videtur. DE. dic, Cratine. CRA. mene vis?
DE. Te. CRA. ego, quæ in rem tuam fint, ea velim
   facias. mihi
Si hoc videtur: quod te abfente hîc filius             10
Egit, reftitui in integrum, æquom eft & bonum:
Et id impetrabis. dixi. DE. dic nunc, Hegio.
HE. Ego fedulo hunc dixiffe credo. verùm ita eft,
Quot homines, tot fententiæ: fuus cuique mos.

*DE. Quanta cura & folicitudine gnatus afficit me, qui impedivit me & fe hifce nuptiis? neque prodit mibi in confpectum, ut faltem fciam, quid dicat de hac re, quidve fententiæ fit illi. Abi tu, vife redieritne domum jam, an nondum. GE. Eo. DE. Videtis in quo loco hæc res fit. Quid ago? dic Hegio. HE. Ego? cenfeo Cratinum prius confulendum fi videtur tibi. DE. Dic, Cratine.*

*CRA. Vifne me dicere? DE. Volo te. CRA. Ego velim facias ea quæ fint in tuam rem. Hoc fic videtur mihi: quod filius egit hic, te abfente, eft æquum & bonum id reftitui in integrum, & impetrabis id. Dixi. DE. Dic nunc, Hegio. HE. Ego credo hunc dixiffe fedulo: verum eft ita, quot homines funt, tot fententiæ funt: fuus mos eft cuique.*

### ANNOTATIONS.

7 *Dic, Hegio.* This was the Form of Addrefs ufed in defiring a Counfellor to fpeak his Sentiments of any Caufe. The fame was ufed too by the Confuls, when they afked a Senator's Opinion in the Houfe.

12 *Et id impetrabis.* The Reader may, perhaps, wonder how *Cratinus* could give this as his Opinion, when it is feveral times hinted above, that it was meer Folly and Extravagance once to attempt the getting Judgment reverfed. To obviate this Difficulty, I fhall here quote the Sentiments of a learned Senator of *Holland*, who being confulted by *Wefterbovius* upon this very Paffage of our Poet, returned for Anfwer: " Res quidem " judicata inter eafdem perfonas pro veritate " habetur. Sed hic damnatus erat filius, " non pater. Quid ergo prohibebat, quo- " minus pater, jure poteftatis patriæ, ean- " dem litem ageret; apud eofdem judices, &
                                                " fua

I don't think that what the Law has once done, can be annulled: and it is wrong to attempt it.

*Dem.* Say, *Crito.*

*Crit.* I think we ought to deliberate farther upon it: 'tis an Affair of great Consequence.

*Heg.* Do you want any thing more of us?

*Dem.* You've done very well.———I'm now more to seek than ever.

*Get.* They say he's not come home yet.

*Dem.* I must wait the return of my Brother. Whatever Advice he shall give me in this Affair, I'll follow it. I'll go to the Port, and enquire when the Ship is expected.

*Get.* And I'll go find out *Antipho*, that he may know what has passed here. " But O, I see he comes just in the nick of time."

A N N O T A T I O N S.

" sua interesse probaret, filium, se invito,
" non elocari ? Absente, nec audito patre,
" judicium actum erat. Poterat igitur ipse
" judices adire, & causam, non tam filii,
" quam suam agere. Si ita hæc intelligas,
" de appellationibus ex jure Attico inanis
" est omnis disputatio,"

24 *Sed eccum ipsum.* There must certainly be some Mistake here. This is made the Conclusion of the second *Act*, and yet there is apparently no Pause or Interval, in as much as *Antipho* comes on immediately, and enters into Conversation with *Geta.* This has moved some to continue this Act a great deal

---

# A C T  III.  S C E N E  I.

A R G U M E N T.

*Antipho blames himself for shunning his Father so precipitately, and by that inconsiderate Flight leaving his Cause to be defended by others : at length he learns from* Geta *the whole of what had passed.*

Antipho, Geta.

*Antipho.* INDEED, *Antipho*, you are greatly to be blamed for this Timorousness of Spirit. Was it excusable in you to run away thus, and trust your whole Happiness to the Management of others ? Did you imagine that they would take more real Concern in your Affairs than yourself ? for however other things were, you ought at least to have thought of her, whom you have now at home ; that she be not deceived, or suffer any Misfortune from the Confidence she has reposed in you, who are now her only Hope and Resource.

*Get.* Why truly, Master, we have been accusing you heavily in your Absence, for leaving us.                    *Ant.*

A N N O T A T I O N S.

*Antipho,* who was naturally of a timorous Disposition, and in danger of betraying himself, by the Confusion he was apt to discover, when questioned about any thing, had, as we have seen, from a Consciousness of this, retired upon his Father's Approach. But afterwards reflecting with himself, of what ill Consequence this might be to his Affairs, as he was obliged to leave them to the Management of others, whom it could not be supposed

Mihi non videtur, quod sit factum legibus,  15
Rescindi posse : & turpe inceptum est. DE. dic, Crito.
CRI. Ego amplius deliberandum censeo :
Res magna est; HE. numquid noscris ? DE. secistis
  probe :
Incertior sum multo, quàm dudum. GE. negant
Rediisse. DE. frater est exspectandus mihi :  20
Is quod mihi dederit de hac re consilium, id sequar.
Percontatum ibo ad portum, quoad se recipiat.
GE. At ego Antiphonem quæram, ut, quæ acta hîc
  sint, sciat.
Sed eccum ipsum video in tempore huc se recipere.

*Videtur mihi, id quod sit factum legibus, non posse rescindi : & inceptum est turpe. DE. Dic, Crito. CRI. Ego censeo deliberandum amplius ; res est magna. HE. Nam vis nos facere quid aliud ? DE. Fecistis probe : sum multo incertior, quam dudum. GE. Negant filium rediisse. DE. Frater ex expectandus mihi :*

*sequar id consilium, quod consilium is dederit mihi de hac re. Ibo ad portum percontatum, quoad recipiat se. GE. At ego quæram Antiphonem, ut sciat quæ sint acta hîc. Sed eccum video ipsum recipere se huc in tempore.*

## ANNOTATIONS.

deal further, and to begin the third Act with, Quid ? Qua profectus causa hinc est Lemnum, Civem ? Indeed there seems to be great Confusion in the Division of the Acts of this Play. We have, however, in this, as in every thing else, conformed to the *Cambridge* Edition, though perhaps the other Division is the truer. Madam *Dacier*, who here also concludes the second Act, retrenches this last Line, to prevent the apparent Absurdity of continuing the Play without Intermission, where the Interval between the two Acts is supposed.

---

# ACTUS III. SCENA I.

### ARGUMENTUM.

*Antipho reversus seipsum incusat, quod patris conspectum veritus fugerit, quodque ita inconsulto discedens, causam suam aliis defendendam reliquerit : rem totam denique ex Geta cognoscit.*

### ANTIPHO, GETA.

ENimvero, Antipho, multimodis cum istoc animo
  es vituperandus.
Itane te hinc abiisse, & vitam tuam tutandam aliis de-
  disse ?  [versuros ?
Alios tuam rem credidisti, magis quàm tete, animad-
Nam, ut ut erant alia, illi certe, quæ nunc tibi domi
  est, consuleres :
Ne quid propter tuam fidem decepta pateretur mali :  5
Cujus nunc miseræ spes opesque sunt in te uno omnes
  sitæ.  [incusamus, qui abieris.
GE. Et quidem, here, nos jamdudum hîc te absentem

*mali propter tuam fidem : cujus miseræ omnes spesque sunt nunc sitæ in te uno. GE. Et quidem, here, nos hîc jamdudum incusamus te absentem, qui abieris.*

**ORDO.**

*AN. ENimvero, Antipho, es multimodis vituperandus cum istoc animo. Tene abiisse hinc ita, & dedisse tuam vitam tutandam aliis ? Credidisti, alios animadversuros tuam rem magis, quam tete ? nam, ut ut alia erant, certe consuleres illi, quæ est nunc domi tibi : ne decepta pateretur quid*

## ANNOTATIONS.

supposed they touched so nearly, he resolves to make off this Weakness, if possible, and maintain his own Cause. He accordingly appears full of these Thoughts, and is overheard

*Ant.* I was looking for you.

*Get.* But we were never the lefs diligent for that.

*Ant.* Speak, pray: in what pofture are my Affairs? How is my Deftiny like to be? Does my Father fufpect any thing?

*Get.* Nothing at all.

*Ant.* But is there any Hope for me?

*Get.* I can't tell.

*Ant.* Ah!

*Get.* Unlefs *Phædria* had left nothing undone in your Favour—

*Ant.* 'Tis nothing new in him.

*Get.* Then *Phormio* in this, as in all other Affairs, has behaved like a true Hero.

*Ant.* What has he done?

*Get.* He out-hectored the old Gentleman, angry as he was.

*Ant.* Well done, *Phormio!*

*Get.* I too did what I could.

*Ant.* Honeft *Geta,* I love you all.

*Get.* The firft fetting out was as I fay; hitherto, matters go fmoothly; and your Father intends to wait your Uncle's Arrival.

*Ant.* Why wait for him?

*Get.* He faid that he would be determined by his Advice in what relates to this Bufinefs.

*Ant.* How I dread my Uncle's coming home now, *Geta!* for by his Sentence alone I underftand, I muft live or die.

*Get.* Here comes *Phædria.*

*Ant.* Where?

*Get.* See there, he's coming out from his School of Exercife.

## ANNOTATIONS.

overheard by *Geta,* who immediately lets him know, that they no lefs blamed his Abfence, than he did himfelf; but, however, had not been negligent of his Intereft.

[10] *Numquid patri fubolet?* This relates to his acting in concert with *Phormio:* he is anxious to know whether his Father had any Sufpicion of that. Much depended on this; for if his Father imagined him innocent, and that all was owing to the Tricks and Devices of *Phormio,* he would not find it fo hard a matter to pacify him, and perhaps in time might reconcile him to the Match.

[13] *Confutavit. Confutare,* in its proper and original Signification means, to allay the Heat and Rage of boiling Water, by pouring cold Water into it. This was done from a Veffel, call'd by the Ancients *futum. Confutare,* i. e. *futo aquam ferventem compefcere.* Hence the Word, by an elegant Tranfition, was ufed to exprefs, calming the Tranfports of Paffion.

[20] *Ab fua palæftra. Palæftra* was properly the Place where the *Grecian* Youth practifed their Exercifes; as running, vaulting, riding, &c. In allufion to this, *Geta* pleafantly

An. Teipſum quærebam. Ge. ſed eâ causâ nihilo
   magis defecimus.         [tùnæ meæ ?
An. Loquere, obſcero ; quónam in loco ſunt res & for-
Numquid patri ſubolet ? Ge. nil etiam. An. ecquid
   ſpei porro eſt ? Ge. neſcio. An. ah.     10
Ge. Niſi Phædria haud ceſſavit pro te eniti. An. nihil
   fecit novi.       [nuum hominem præbuit.
Ge. Tum Phormio itidem hac re, ut in aliis, ſtre-
An. Quid is fecit ? Ge. confutavit verbis admodum
   iratum ſenem.       [Geta, omnes vos amo.
An. Eu Phormio. Ge. ego, quod potui porro. An mi
Ge. Sic habent principia ſeſe, ut dico : adhuc tran-
   quilla res eſt :              15
Manſuruſque patruum pater eſt, dum huc adveniat.
   An. quid eum ? Ge. ut aiebat,    [attinet.
De ejus conſilio ſeſe velle facere, quod ad hanc rem
An. Quantus metus eſt mihi, venire huc ſalvum nunc
   patruum, Geta :        [ſententiam :
Nam per ejus unam, ut audio, aut vivam aut moriar
Ge. Phædria tibi adeſt. An. ubinam ? Ge. eccum ab
   ſuâ palæſtrâ exit foras.         20

An. *Quærebam te-ipſum.* Ge. *Sed nibilo magis defecimus ea cauſa.* An. *Obſcero, loquere, quonam in loco ſunt meæ res & fortunæ ? Numquid ſubolet patri ?* Ge. *Etiamdum nil.* An. *Eſt ecquid ſpei porro ?* Ge. *Neſcio.* An. *Ab,* Ge. *Niſi Phædria baud ceſſavit eniti pro te——*An. *Fecit nibil novi.* Ge. *Tum Phormio præbuit ſe ſtrenuum bominem in bac re, itidem ut in aliis.* An. *Quid is fecit ?* Ge. *Confutavit verbis ſenem admodum iratum.* An. *Eu Phormio.* Ge. *Ego porro, feci quod potui.* An. *Mi Geta, amo vos omnes.*

Ge. *Principia babent ſeſe ſic, ut dico : rés adbuc eſt tranquilla : pater eſt manſurus patruum, dum adveniat buc.* An. *Quid manſurus eum ?* Ge. *Ut aiebat, ſeſe velle facere quod attinet ad banc rem, de conſilio ejus.* An. *Quantus metus eſt mibi, Geta, patruum nunc venire buc ſalvum : nam per unam ſententiam ejus, ut audio, aut vivam aut moriar.* Ge. *Phædria adeſt tibi,* An. *Ubinam ?* Ge. *Eccum exit foras ab ſua palæſtra.*

## ANNOTATIONS.

pleaſantly calls the Cock-bawd's Houſe, *Phædria*'s School of Exerciſe. For *Pamphila*, with whom this Youth was in love, belonged to the Bawd ; hence *Phædria*'s Viſits there were very frequent. *Dorio* too threatened him with ſelling her to another ; and to counterplot the Artifices and Cunning of the Bawd, to ſtruggle with his own Wants and ill Fortune, was exerciſe enough in all conſcience. In like manner, *Plautus* ſpeaking of the Houſe of a Courtezan, ſays : *Baccb.* A. 1. S. 1. Ver. 32.

—————— *Quid ego metuam, rogitas ? bome*
   *adoleſcentulus .*
*Pedetrare bujuſmodi in palæſtram, ubi damnis deſudaſcitur,*
*Ubi pro diſco damnum capiam, pro curſura dedecus ?*

" Do you aſk me what it is I fear ſo much ?
" for a young Man to enter into this School
" of Exerciſe, where Ruin muſt enſue ;
" where inſtead of contending for the Prize
" of the Quoit, or of the Courſe, he muſt
" ſtruggle with Loſſes and Diſgrace ?"

## ACT III.  SCENE II.

### ARGUMENT.

*Phædria begs of the Cock-bawd not to be too hasty in giving up
the Girl to the Soldier, to whom he threatened to sell her; for
that in three Days he would tell down the Money he had promised for her Redemption.*

PHÆDRIA, DORIO, ANTIPHO, GETA.

*Phædria.* DORIO, pray hear me.

*Dor.* I will not.

*Phæd.* But a moment.

*Dor.* Let me alone.

*Phæd.* Hear what I have to say.

*Dor.* I'm tired with hearing the same thing a thousand times over.

*Phæd.* But now I have something to say that will please you.

*Dor.* Well, speak; I hear.

*Phæd.* Can't I prevail with you to stay but for these three Days?
Where are you going now?

*Dor.* I should wonder much, if you had any thing new to offer.

*Ant. (To* Geta.) I fear the Bawd will work himself no good.

*Get.* I fear too.

*Phæd.* Don't you believe me?

*Dor.* You have guess'd it.

*Phæd.* But I give my Promise.

*Dor.* All stuff.

*Phæd.* You shall have reason to say, that the kindness was well
repaid.

*Dor.* Meer Words.

*Phæd.* Believe me, you shall never repent it; 'tis true indeed.

*Dor.* A very Dream!

*Phæd.* Do but try; the time is not long.

*Dor.* The same Story over again.

*Phæd.* You shall be my Kinsman, my Father, my Friend, my——

*Dor.* Talk on.

*Phæd.* To be of a Temper so hardened and inexorable, as can
neither be softened by Pity nor Entreaties——

*Dor.* And for you, *Phædria*, to be so silly and simple, as to imagine you can make me the Dupe of your fine Speeches, and get my
Girl for nothing.                                           *Ant.*

### ANNOTATIONS.

This Scene furnishes a Proof, how justly *Geta* had called the Cock-bawd's House, *Phædria*'s School of Exercise, for here we have a lively Example of it. The Youth accosts him with the most earnest Importunities, the time he demands too is but short; three Days; but nothing avails. *Antipho* and *Geta* also join in the Request, with the very same Success. He is inexorable to every thing they say; and, like a true Bawd, lets them know that Interest alone governs him. He had an Offer of ready Money for his Slave, and would not, by all the whining and whimpering they could use, be brought to relinquish present Certainty for Prospects distant and future. He therefore tells them, that as the Money was to be paid the next Morning: if they miss'd this
Offer

## ACTUS III. SCENA II.

### ARGUMENTUM:

*Phædria lenonem orat, ut venditam militi Pamphilam non tam
cito abducendam tradat: se intra triduum nummos adnume-
raturum, quos pro illius redemptione sit pollicitus.*

PHÆDRIA, DORIO, ANTIPHO, GETA.

DORIO, audi absecro. Do: non audio: Ph. pa-
   rumper. Do. quin omitte me:
PH. Audi quod dicam. Do. at enim tædet jam audire
   eadem millies.            [re, audio:
PH. At nunc dicam, quod lubenter audias. Do. loque-
PH. Nequeo te exorare, ut maneas triduum hoc ? quo
   nunc abis ?
Do. Mirabar, si tu mihi quidquam afferres novi.   5
AN. Hei, metuo lenonem, ne quid suo suat capiti. GE.
   idem ego metuo.       [do. Do. fabulæ.
PH. Non mihi credis ? Do. hariolare. PH. sin fidem
PH. Feneratum istuc beneficium pulchrè tibi dices.
  Do. logi.          [Do. somnia.
Ph. Crede mihi, gaudebis facto : verum hercle hoc est.
PH. Experire, non est longum. Do. cantilenam: ean-
   dem canis.           10
PH. Tu mihi cognatus, tu parens, tu amicus, tu—Do.
   garri modò.
PH. Adeon' ingenio esse duro te atque inexorabili,
Ut neque misericordiâ neque precibus molliri queas ?
Do. Adeon' te esse incogitantem atque impudentem,
  ·Phædria,
Ut phaleratis dictis ducas me, & meam ductes gratiis ?

*verum. Do. Somnia. PH. Experire, non est longum. Do. Canis eandem cantilenam. PH. Tu eris
mibi cognatus, tu amicus, tu parens, tu----Do. Garri modo. PH. Tene esse ingenio adeo duro
atque inexorabili, ut aqueas molliri neque precibus ? Do. Tene, Phædria, esse adeo incogitantem
atque impudentem, ut dicat me phaleratis dictis, & ductes meam gratiis ?*

ORDO:

PH. DOrio, ob-
secro au-
di. Do. Non audio.
PH. Parumper. Do.
Quin omitte me. PH.
Audi quod dicam.
Do. At enim jam
tædet audire eadem
millies. PH. At nunc
dicam id; quod au-
dias libenter. Do.
Loquere, audio. PH.
Nequeo exorare te,
ut maneas hoc tri-
duum ? Quo abis
nunc. Do. Mirabar,
si tu adferres quid-
quam novi mihi. AN.
Hei, metuo lenonem,
ne suat quid suo ca-
piti. GE. Ego me-
tuo idem. PH. Non
credis mihi ? Do.
Hariolare. PH. Sin
do fidem. Do. Fa-
bulæ. PH. Dices
istuc beneficium pul-
chre fœneratum tibi.
Do. Logi. PH. Cre-
de mihi. gaudebis
facto : hercle hoc est

### ANNOTATIONS.

Offer of it before that time, he would receive
the first Comer as usual, but otherwise they
had nothing to expect.

10 *Metuo lenonem, ne quid suo suat capiti.*
It were endless to repeat the several Conjectures of Commentators upon this Passage.
One of the most specious is that of *Muretus*,
who tells us, that in a Manuscript of his,
the Text runs thus : *Metuo lenonem, ne quid
suo capiti.* Which he thus explains : After
*Antipho* had said *metuo lenonem, ne quid suat,*
i. e. *machinetur, struat ;* and the Spectators
naturally supposed he was to add, *Phædria*
*capiti,* he suddenly changes the Form of

the Expression; and turns it into an Imprecation against the Pimp himself ; by saying,
*Suo capiti, q. d. Quæ res ipsi lenoni male
veriat.* But in my Opinion, a much easier
and more simple Explication may be given of
the Words, what even naturally offers itself
upon the first Reading : *Antipho* had overheard *Phædria* earnest and importunate ; and
the Bawd obstinate and inflexible. He therefore dreads that this Brutality may provoke
*Phædria* to some Act of Violence ; *Ne suat
quid suo capiti ;* bring Vengeance upon his
own Head. *Suo,* to sew, join, or fasten together.

*Ant.* (*To* Geta.) I pity him.

*Phæd.* (*Aside.*) Alas, I know it to be too true.

*Get.* (*To* Antipho.) How well they keep up to their Characters!

*Phæd.* For this Misfortune to happen to me at a time too, when *Antipho* is taken up with the same Cares?

*Ant.* Ah, *Phædria*, what's the matter?

*Phæd.* O happy, happy, *Antipho*.

*Ant.* Who, I?

*Phæd.* Who have what you love in your own possession, nor was ever reduced to the Necessity of encountering such a Plague as this.

*Ant.* I, in my possession, say ye? Yes indeed, as the Saying is, *I have a Wolf by the Ears*. For I neither know how to part with her, nor is it in my power to keep her.

*Dor.* 'Tis my very Case with this Spark.

*Ant.* (*To* Dorio) Well said: don't be a Bawd by halves. (*To* Phædria.) Has he done any thing yet?

*Phæd.* Who, he? the Part of an inhuman Wretch: he has sold my *Pamphila*.

*Get.* What! sold her?

*Ant.* Say you so? Sold her!

*Phæd.* He has sold her.

*Dor.* A horrid Crime, sure, to sell a Wench bought with my own Money.

*Phæd.* I can't prevail with him to stay, and break off the Bargain with the other, only for three Days, till I get the Money of my Friends, which they have promised to lend me; if I give it you not then, don't be put off an Hour longer.

*Dor.* You perfectly stun me.

*Ant.* It is not a long time, that he asks, *Dorio*; let him prevail, he'll requite you double, and you'll deserve it.       *Dor.*

## ANNOTATIONS.

16 *Hei, veris vincor.* These Words are uttered by *Phædria* in a low Voice, so as not to be overheard by *Dorio.* *Veris vincor*, i. e. *vera prædicat leno, neque enim more fit, ut quis gratiis ductet amicam ab avaro lenone; mibi vero, quod dem, nibil est.*

Ibid. *Quam uterque est similis sui?* Madam *Dacier* observes here, that this Reflection of *Geta* is occasioned by what *Phædria* had just said; *bei, veris vincor.* For in this, says she, *Phædria* preserves the Character of a Man of Sense and Judgment, who readily submits to Reason, and the Cock-bawd likewise keeps up to his Character in continuing obstinate and inflexible.

17 *Neque, Antipho alia cum occupatus esset solicitudine.* This Passage has been hitherto misunderstood; I flatter myself I have hit upon the true Sense of the Original. *Westerbovius*, who seems to have come nearest the Author's Meaning, gives this Order of the Words: *Neque malum hoc objectum* *mibi esse tum, cum Antipho alia solicitudine esset occupatus.* Something is evidently wanting here to Clearness and Perspicuity. I have therefore ranged them thus: *Hoc malum esse objectum mibi tum, cum Antipho esset occupatus utque alia solicitudine.* "For this "Misfortune happened to me at a time "too, when *Antipho* is taken up with the "same Cares." *Neque alia solicitudine;* *With Cares no way different, of the same kind.* For *Phædria* was in danger of losing his Mistress, as *Dorio* threatened to sell her to another; and *Antipho* too was in the same unhappy Situation, now that his Father was returned, and fully purposed, if he could, to annul the Marriage. This was an unhappy Circumstance to *Phædria*; because *Antipho*, intent upon his own Affairs, was not at leisure to assist him. Hence the Ground of the present Complaint. The Translator of *Terence*, in three Volumes, renders it *When Antipho is in full Possession of his Love, that I* *should*

AN. Miſeritum eſt. PH. hei, veris vincor. GE.
  quàm uterque eſt ſimilis ſui ?          16

PH. Neque, Antipho alià cùm occupatus eſſet ſolici-
  tudine,

Tum hoc eſſe mihi objeĉtum malum ? AN. ah, quid
  iſtuc autem eſt, Phædria ?

PH. O fortunatiſſime Antipho, AN. egone ? PH. cui
  quod amas, domi eſt ;

Nec cum hujuſmodi unquam uſus venit ut confliĉtares
  malo.          20

AN. Mihin' domi' ſt ? immo id quod aiunt, auribus
  teneo lupum :         [neam, ſcio.

Nam neque, quomodo à me amittam, neque utì reti-

Do. Ipſum iſtuc mihi in hoc eſt. AN. heia, ne parum
  leno ſies.         [humaniſſimus :

Numquid hic confecit ? PH. hiccine ? quod homo in-

Pamphilam meam vendidit. GE. quid ? vendidit ? AN.
  ain' vendidit ?         25

PH. Vendidit. Do. quàm indignum facinus, ancillam
  ære emtam ſuo !         [mutet fidem,

PH. Nequeo exorare, ut me maneat, & cum illo ut
'Triduum hoc, dum id, quod eſt promiſſum, ab amicis
  argentum aufero.         [tus ſies.

Si non tum dedero, unam præterea horam ne opper-

Do. Obtunde. AN. haud longum eſt id quod orat,
  Dorio : exoret, ſine :         30

Idem hic tibi, quod bene promeritus fueris, conduplicaverit.

hominem vendere *ancillam emptam ſuo ære !* PH. *Nequeo exorare, ut maneat me hoc triduum, et ut mutet fidem cum illo, dum aufero id argentum ab amicis, quod eſt promiſſum, ſi non dedero tum, ne ſis oppertus unam horam præterea.* Do. *Obtunde.* AN. *Id quod orat haud eſt longum, Dorio : ſine, exoret : hic conduplicaverit idem tibi, quod fueris bene promeritus.*

AN. *Miſeritum eſt.*
PH. *Hei, vincor ve-*
*ris.* GE. *Quam u-*
*terque eſt ſimilis ſui ?*
PH. *Hoc malum eſſe*
*objeĉtum mihi tùm,*
*cum Antipho eſſet oc-*
*cupatus neque alia ſo-*
*licitudine ?* AN. *Ab,*
*Phædria, quid au-*
*tem eſt iſtuc ?* PH.
*O fortunatiſſime An-*
*tipho.* AN. *Egone ?*
PH. *Cui quod amas*
*eſt domi ; nec uſus*
*venit, ut unquam*
*confliĉtares cum ma-*
*lo hujuſmodi.* AN.
*Mihine domi eſt ?*
*imo id quod aiunt,*
*teneo lupum auribus ;*
*nam neque ſcio, quo-*
*modo amittam a me,*
*neque utì retineam.*
Do. *Iſtuc ipſum eſt*
*mihi in hoc.* AN.
*Heia, ne ſis parum*
*leno. Numquid hic*
*confecit ?* PH. *Hic-*
*cine ? Quod homo in-*
*humaniſſimus poſſet*
*conficere : vendidit*
*meam Pamphilam.*
GE. *Quid ! Vendi-*
*dit ?* AN. *Aſne ?*
*Vendidit ?* PH. *Ven-*
*didit.* Do. *Quam*
*indignum facinus,*

## A N N O T A T I O N S.

ſhould have this *Plague.* Than which nothing can be more remote either from Faĉt,
or the Poet's Intention.

  21 *Auribus teneo lupum.* This was a common Proverb, when one foreſaw Difficulties
to be encounter'd which ever way he took.
We learn from *Suetonius,* that it was frequently in the Mouth of *Tiberius,* when he
heſitated in what manner to oppoſe the Dangers he ſaw approaching.

  23 *Ipſum iſtuc mihi in hoc eſt.* De *Phædria hæc dicit leno, q. d. Hic mihi lupus eſt,
quem neque ferre diutius, quia nihil numerat,
neque abſolvere poſſum, quia improbe blandus eſt,
& multa pollicendo me obtundit.*

  Ibid. *Ne parum leno ſies. Laudat hæc
verba Aſconius Pedianus, ad Cic Verr. I. 38.
Habent autem correĉtionem ironicam verborum
lenonis, q. d. Dicis, tibi ita rem eſſe cum*

*Phædria, ut videaris lupum tenere auribus,
quia metuis, ne param ſis leno, l. e. ne minus ſis flagitioſus, quam vulgus lenonum ſolet,
non ſatis magno pretio vendens puellam. Su-
mitur autem perſona ipſa pro moribus.* Plaut.
Perſ. 4. 6. 4.

  *Ne non ſat eſſes leno, id metuebas miſer.*
*Weſterovius.*

  26 *Quam indignum facinus, ancillam ære
emtam ſuo.* Theſe Words are by the Bawd
addreſs'd to the Speĉtators with a ſarcaſtical
Air. It is worth while too to obſerve the
different Manners of the Speakers. *Phædria* expreſſes himſelf with Tenderneſs and
Love : he calls her *meam Pamphilam. Dorio* again uſes the undervaluing Epithet *Ancilla.*

  27 *Cum illo ut mutet fidem.* The Expreſſion is ſomewhat rare and uncommon ;



*mutare*

*Dor.* All mere Words.

*Ant.* (*To* Phædria.) Will you suffer your Mistress to be ravished from this Place? (*to Dorio.*) Or can you be so cruel as to tear these Lovers from one another?

*Dor.* 'Tis neither I nor you, that do it.

*Get.* May the Gods grant you every thing you deserve.

*Dor.* I have, contrary to my natural Temper, borne with you for several Months, promising, whimpering, but bringing me nothing. Now, on the contrary, I have found one who will give *freely*, without sniveling : *therefore I say*, give place to your Betters.

*Ant.* Why certainly, if I remember right, there was once a Day fix'd upon, when you was to give him the Money.

*Phæd.* There was.

*Dor.* Do I deny it?

*Ant.* Is that Day past then?

*Dor.* No; but this is come before it.

*Ant.* Are not you asham'd of your Treachery?

*Dor.* Not at all, when it's for my Interest.

*Get.* Sordid Wretch!

*Phæd.* *Dorio*, is this right now, do you think?

*Dor.* 'Tis my Way, if you like me, use me.

*Ant.* Do you offer to deceive him in this manner?

*Dor.* Nay, *Antipho*, 'tis rather he that deceives me, for he knew me to be the Person I was, but I fancied him to be a quite different Man. 'Tis he that has disappointed me, for I am the same to him as ever. But however these things are, I'll yet do this, the Captain has promised to bring me the Money to-morrow Morning ; if you bring it before then, *Phædria*, I'll keep to my old Rule of preferring him who brings the Money first. Your Servant.

ANNOTATIONS.

*mutare fidem cum aliquo*, instead of *fidem alteri datam fallare.* Vide Fabri Thesaur, Latin. Voce *cum.*

49 *Ut potior sit, qui prior ad daudum est.*

We see the Character of the Cock-bawd preserved with admirable Uniformity throughout this whole Scene. All Methods are try'd with him, but to no purpose, nor would it have

---

# ACT III. SCENE III.

## ARGUMENT.

*The two Youths, with great difficulty, prevail on* Geta *to set about some Artifice for obtaining Money to be given to the Cockbawd for the Musick-Wench.*

PHÆDRIA, ANTIPHO, GETA.

*Phædria.* WHAT shall I do? Wretch that I am, where shall I now, that am worse than nothing, raise Money so speedily

for

ANNOTATIONS.

We see the perplexing Situation in which *Phædria* is left; he must procure the Money immediately, or submit to lose his Mistress.

The Time allow'd is so short, as leaves him not the least glimmering Hope; so that he is giving way to Despondency, when *An-*

*tipho*

Do. Verba istæc sunt. An. Pamphilamne hac urbe
   privari sines ?
Tum præterea horunc' amorem distrahi poterin' pati ?
Do. Neque ego, neque tu. Ge. Di tibi omnes, id,
   quod es dignus, duint.
Do. Ego te complures, advorsum ingenium meum,
   menses tuli   35
Pollicitantem, & nil ferentem, flentem. nunc contra,
   omnia hæc ;
Repperi, qui det, neque lacrumet. da locum melioribus.
An. Certe hercle, ego si satis commemini, tibi, qui-
   dem est olim dies,        [ego istuc nego ?
Quam ad dares huic, præstituta. Ph. factum. Do. num
An. Jam ea præteriit ? Do. non, verum hæc ei ante-
   cessit. An. non pudet   40
Vanitatis ? Do. minimè, dum ob rem. Ge. sterquili-
   nium. Ph. Dorio,       [utere.
Itane tandem facere oportet ? Do. sic sum : si placeo,
An. Siccine hunc decipis ? Do. imo enimvero, Anti-
   pho, hic me decipit :     [credidi.
Nam hic me hujusmodi esse sciebat : ego hunc esse aliter
Iste me fefellit : ego isti nihilo sum aliter, ac fui.  45
Sed ut ut hæc sunt, tamen hoc faciam : cras manè ar-
   gentum mihi
Miles dare se dixit : si mihi prior tu attuleris, Phædria,
Meâ lege utar, ut potior sit, qui prior ad dandum est.
   vale.

rio, itane tandem oportet facere ? Do. Sic sum : si placeo, utere. An. Siccine decipis hunc ? Do. Imo enimvero, Antipho, hic decipit me : nam hic sciebat me esse hujusmodi : ego credidi hunc esse aliter. Iste fefellit me : ego sum nihilo aliter isti, ac fui. Sed ut ut hæc sunt, tamen faciam hoc : Miles dixit se dare argentum mihi cras manè, si tu prior attuleris id mihi, Phædria, utar mea lege, ut qui est prior ad dandum sit potior. Vale.

Do. Istæc sunt verba. An. Sinesne Pamphilam privari hac urbe ? tum præterea, tunc poteris pati amorem horunce distrahi ? Do. Neque ego, neque tu fuimus in causa. Ge. Dii omnes duint id tibi, quod es dignus. Do. Ego advorsum ingenium meum tuli te complures menses, pollicitantem et ferentem nil, flentem. Nunc, contra omnia hæc, repperi qui det, neque lacrumet : da locum melioribus. An. Certe hercle, si ego commemini satis, dies quidem est olim præstituta tibi, ad quam dares pecuniam huic. Ph. Est factam. Do. Num ego nego istuc ? An. An ea jam præteriit ? Do. Non, verum hæc antecessit ei. An. Non pudet te vanitatis ? Do. Minime, dum ob rem. Ge. Sterquilinium. Ph. Dorio,

*ANNOTATIONS.*

have been proper to make him relent. Even the small Concession which he makes is so contrived, as to throw still more Light upon his Character, and shew Avarice and Selfishness in perfection. Nothing could have been more happily imagin'd, nor can we too much admire the consummate Art and Judgment of the Poet.

---

## ACTUS III. SCENA III.

### ARGUMENTUM.

*Adolescentes persuadent Getæ, licet difficulter, ut per fallaciam argentum extorqueat, pro citharistria redimenda lenoni dandum.*

PHÆDRIA, ANTIPHO, GETA.    ORDO.

QUID faciam ? unde ego nunc tam subito huic
   argentum inveniam miser,

Ph. Quid faciam ? Unde ego miser, cui est

minus nihilo nunc tam subito inveniam argentum huic.

*ANNOTATIONS.*

...pho, concern'd for the Sufferings of his Friend, urges Geta to think of some Pro-ject, for getting the Money. Thus a new Plot comes on, in which Geta is one of the principal

for this Fellow ? Could he have been put off only for three Days, I had the Promife of it.

*Ant.* Geta, fhall we fuffer him to continue thus wretched, who fo lately affifted me in the friendly Manner you told me ? Shall we not now, that he ftands fo much in need of it, endeavour rather to return the Favour ?

*Get.* I know indeed 'tis but juft that we do it.

*Ant.* Set about it then, you are the only Man can ferve him.

*Get.* What can I do?

*Ant.* Procure the Money for him.

*Get.* I would with all my Soul: but tell; where can I have it ?

*Ant.* My Father's come home.

*Get.* I know it; but what then ?

*Ant.* Ah, a Word to the Wife is fufficient.

*Get.* Is that it then ?

*Ant.* It is.

*Get.* A moft excellent Advice truly ! Have done, have done, *Antipho* : Don't I triumph, think you, if I can efcape what I am threatened with from your Marriage; unlefs I hazard my Neck alfo on his account ?

*Ant.* 'Tis true that he fays.

*Phæd.* What ! Am I a Stranger amongft you then, *Geta?*

*Get.* Far from it : But does it feem nothing to you, that the old Gentleman is already provok'd againft us all ; unlefs we irritate him ftill farther, beyond all Hopes of Reconcilement ?

*Phæd.* Shall another bear her from my Sight into an unknown Land ? Ah, fpeak to me now, *Antipho,* look at me, while you may, while I am ftill with you.

*Ant.* Why fo ? What are you thinking of now ? Tell me.

*Phæd.* To whatever Part of the World fhe is carried ; I'm determin'd to follow, or perifh.

*Get.* Heaven profper the Defign : But don't be too hafty, however.

*Ant.* See, pray, *Geta,* if you can help him any Thing.

*Get.* Help him ! How ?

*Ant.* Do try, left peradventure he may do what we fhall be more or lefs forry for hereafter.

*Get.*

## ANNOTATIONS.

principal Actors, and *Phormio* has an Opportunity given him of exerting his Talents alfo in *Phædria*'s Caufe: The Project itfelf, and the Manner of its being conducted, will appear afterwards, in the Courfe of the Play.

8 *Dictum fapienti fat eft.* A Proverb frequently ufed among the *Romans,* and which anfwers exactly to that of ours. *A Word to the Wife.* Implying, that to one of *Geta*'s Sagacity and Penetration, a fingle Word was fufficient to make him underftand the Bufinefs. *Antipho* had faid *pater adeft* ; that

was enough. *Geta* himfelf would divine the reft ; that the old Man was, if poffible, to be cozen'd out of the Money. *Antipho* was not miftaken ; *Geta* knows his Meaning ; and in fact, as we fhall fee afterwards, procures the Money of the old Man, according to the Hint given him.

12 *Ego vobis, Geta, alienus fum ?* This Queftion arifes from *Geta*'s Manner of expreffing himfelf above ; *hujus caufa,* which feems to imply, as if *Phædria* was an Alien, a Stranger, one in whom *Geta* was not fo

nearly

Cui minu' nihilo eſt ? quod, ſi pote fuiſſet exorarier
Triduum hoc, promiſſum fuerat. AN. itane hunc pa-
  tiemur, Geta,                                [ter ?
Fieri miſerum ; qui me dudum, ut dixti, adjûerit comi-
Quin, cùm opus eſt, beneficium rurſum ei experimur
  reddere ?                                      5
GE. Scio equidem hoc eſſe æquom. AN. age ergo, ſo-
  lus ſervare hunc potes.
GE. Quid faciam ? AN. invenias argentum. GE. cu-
  pio : ſed, id unde, edoce.
AN. Pater adeſt hîc. GE. ſcio : ſed quid tum ? AN.
  ah, dictum ſapienti ſat eſt.
GE. Itane ? AN. ita. GE. ſane hercle pulchrè ſuades :
  etiam tu hinc abis ?
Non triumpho, ex nuptiis tuis ſi nil nanciſcor mali,  10
Ni etiam nunc me hujus causâ quærere in malo jubeas
  crucem ?               [nus ſum ? GE. haud puto :
AN. Verum hic dicit. PH. quid ? ego vobis, Geta, alie-
Sed parumne eſt, quòd omnibus nunc nobis ſuccenſet
  ſenex,
Ni inſtigemus etiam, ut nullus locu' relinquatur preci ?
PH. Alius ab oculis meis illam in ignotum abducet lo-
  cum, hem ;                               15
Tum igitur, dum licet, dumque adſum, loquimini
  mecum, Antipho :                 [facturus ? cedo.
Contemplamini me. AN. quamobrem ? aut quidnam
PH. Quoquò hinc aſportabitur terrarum, certum eſt
  perſequi,                            [tentim tamen.
Aut perire. GE. dii bene vortant, quod agas : pede-
AN. Vide, ſi quid opis potes adferre huic. GE. ſi quid ?
  quid ? AN. quære, obſecro,                 20
Ne quid plus minuſve faxit, quod nos pòſt pigeat, Geta.

*Quod ſi hic pote fuiſſet exorari hoc triduum, fuerat promiſſum. AN. Geta, itane patiemur hunc fieri miſerum ; qui dudum adjuverit me comiter, ut dixti ? Quin cum opus eſt, experimur reddere rurſum beneficium ei ? GE. Equidem ſcio hoc eſſe æquum. AN. Age ergo, ſolus potes ſervare hunc. GE. Quid faciam ? AN. Invenias argentum. GE. Cupio : ſed edoce, unde inveniam id. AN. Pater adeſt hic. GE. Scio : ſed quid tum ? AN. Ah, dictum eſt ſapienti. GE. Itane ? AN. Ita. GE. Sane hercle ſuades pulchrè : etiam tu abis hinc ? An non triumpho, ſi nanciſcor nil mali ex tuis nuptiis, ni etiam nunc jubeas me quærere crucem in mala causâ hujus ? AN. Hic dicit verum. PH. Quid ? An ego, Geta ſum alienus vobis ? GE. Haud puto : ſed hinc parum, quod ſenex nunc ſuccenſet nobis omnibus, ni etiam inſtigemus, ut nullus locus relinquatur preci ?*

PH. *Alius abducet illam ab meis oculis in ignotum locum ? hem ; tum igitur Antipho, dum licet, dumque adſum, loquimini mecum; contemplamini me.* AN. *Quamobrem ? Aut Quidnam es factu-rus ? Cedo.* PH. *Quoquo terrarum aſportabitur hinc, eſt certum perſequi, perire.* GE. *Dii vortant bene quod agas, tamen pedetentim.* AN. *Vide, ſi potes adferre quid opis huic.* GE. *Si quid ? Quid ?* AN. *Obſecro quære, Geta, ne faxit quid plus minuſve, quòd pigeat nos poſt.*

## ANNOTATIONS.

nearly concern'd, that he ſhould run any hazard for his ſake.

  [19] *Dii bene vortant, quod agas.* Some aſcribe theſe Words to *Antipho*, but it is evident they cannot with any propriety belong to him, who appears all along too much concern'd at his Friend's Suffering, to ſpeak of them in this mirthful Strain. They come much better from *Geta*, who alone had it in his Power to relieve him, and was by this time reſolv'd upon it. The Pleaſantry of the Paſſage conſiſts in *Geta*'s anſwering him in ſuch Manner as if he approved of this violent Reſolution he had taken of following his Miſtreſs. For 'tis as if he had ſaid, *Go, Sir, and Heaven proſper you.* This he utters with a grave and ſolemn Tone ; but immediately after, to prevent the Confuſion ſuch an Anſwer would be apt to occaſion, and inſpire him with Hope, he adds : *Pedetentim tamen* ; which implies, that Things are not yet quite deſperate, and ſomething may poſſibly be done for him. *Pedetentim,* i. e. *cautè a pedibus et tentando.*

  [21] *Ne quid plus minuſve faxit.* Caſaubon explains this, *ne quid omnino faciat ;* which

*Get.* I'm thinking about it—He's secure, as far as I can guess; but I fear I shall bring Vengeance upon myself.

*Ant.* Fear nothing: we'll share your Fortune, good or bad.

*Get.* How much Money do you want? Say.

*Phæd.* Only ninety Pounds.

*Get.* Ninety! Faith, she's very dear, *Phædria.*

*Phæd.* Nay, she's vastly cheap at that Price.

*Get.* Well, well, I'll get them for you.

*Phæd.* O the dear Man!

*Get.* Get away, get away.

*Phæd.* But I want them now.

*Get.* You shall have them now.   But I must have *Phormio* for an Assistant in this Business.

*Ant.* He's ready, I'll promise for him: Lay on boldly what Load you will, he'll bear it.   He's one of a thousand to serve his Friend.

*Get.* Let us go to him therefore directly.

*Ant.* Shall you have any Occasion for me?

*Get.* None; but go home, and comfort that poor Creature, whom I know to be almost dead with Fear.   Do you linger?

*Ant.* There's nothing I can do with so good a Will.

*Phæd.* How do you propose to accomplish this?

*Get.* I'll tell you by the Way; only let us hasten hence.

### ANNOTATIONS.

which is not exactly the Poet's Idea, for we are to compleat the Sentence by supplying *Quam æquum fit,* as in *Plautus; Cap.* v. 3. 18.

*Eheu! Cur ego plus minusve feci, quem æquom fuit!* 30 *Solus est homo amico amicus.* A manner

---

# ACT IV. SCENE I.

### ARGUMENT.

Demipho *and* Chremes, *both in Years, and Brothers, here converse together.   This latter acquaints the other with the Reason of his long Stay at* Lemnos; *they also touch upon* Antipho's *Marriage.*

### DEMIPHO, CHREMES.

*Dem.* WELL, *Chremes,* have you brought home your Daughter with you, as you proposed in going hence to *Lemnos?*

*Chr.* No.

*Dem.* Why have you not?                                           *Chr.*

### ANNOTATIONS.

The Poet conducts the Plot with great Judgment, it grows more and more interesting as it proceeds, and raises our Impatience to know the Issue.   A new Scene is going to present itself to us, this *Phany* so dear to *Antipho,* and whom he is so afraid of losing, is to turn out *Chremes*'s Daughter, and the very Person whom *Demipho* had before destin'd

GE. Quæro: falvus eft, ut opinor. verùm enim metuo malam.

AN. Noli metuere: unà tecum bona, mala tolerabimus.

GE. Quantum opus eft tibi argenti? loquere. PH. folæ triginta minæ.

GE. Triginta? hui, percara eft, Phædria. PH. iftæc verò vilis eft. 25

GE. Age, age, inventas reddam. PH. ô lepidum! GE. aufer te hinc. PH. jam opus eft. GE. jam feres. Sed opus eft mihi Phormionem ad hanc rem adjutorem dari. [feret:

AN. Præftò eft: audaciffimè quidvis oneris impone, & Solus eft homo amico amicus. GE. eamus ergo ad eum ociùs.

PH. Abi verò: dic, præftò ut fit domi. 30

AN. Numquid eft, quod opera mea vobis opu' fit? GE. nil: verum abi domum, & [tam metu, Illam miferam, quam ego nunc intus fcio effe exanima- Confolare. ceffas? AN. nihil eft, æquè quod faciam lubens, [te hinc amove.

PH. Quâ viâ iftuc facies? GE. dicam in itinere: modò

PH. *Abi vere; dic ut fit præfto domi. AN. Numquid eft, quod opus fit opera mea vobis? GE. Nil: verum abi domum, et confolare illam miferam, quam ego fcio effe nunc intus exanimatam metu. Ceffas? AN. Eft nibil, quod faciam æque lubens. PH. Qua via facies iftuc? GE. Dicam in itinere: modo amove te binc.*

ORDO.

*GE. Quæro: eft falvus, ut opinor. verum enim metuò malum. AN. Noli metuere; tolerabimus bona, mala, una tecum. GE. Quantum argenti eft opus tibi? Loquere. PH. Solæ triginta minæ. GE. Triginta? hui, percara eft, Phædria. PH. Vero iftæc eft vilis. GE. Age, age, reddam inventas. PH. O lepidum? GE. Aufer te binc. PH. Eft opus jam. GE. Feres jam. Sed opus eft Phormionem dari adjutorem mibi ad hanc rem. AN. Eft præfto: audaciffime impone quidvis oneris, et feret: eft bomo folus amicus amico. GE. Eamus ergo ad eum ocius.*

## ANNOTATIONS.

ner of fpeaking frequent among the *Latin* comic Poets. So *Plaut. Baccbid.* iii. 2. 2.

 *Homini amico, qui eft amicus, ita uti nomen*
  *poffidet,*
*Nifi Deos, ei nibil præftare.*

And *Mil.* iii. 1. 65.

 ----*Non invenies alterum*
 *Lepidiorem ad omnes res, nec qui amicus*
  *amico fit magis.*

---

# ACTUS IV. SCENA I.

### ARGUMENTUM.

*Demipho et Chremes fenes et fratres conloquuntur; narrat hic illi cur in Lemno diutius hæferit: fit et mentio nuptiarum Antiphonis.*

### DEMIPHO, CHREMES.

QUID? quâ profectus causâ hinc es Lemnum, Chremes,
Adduxtin' tecum filiam? CH. non. DE. quid ita non?
*num? adduxiftine filiam tecum? CH. Non. DE. Quid non ita?*

ORDO.

*DE. QUID? Chremes, qua caufa es profectus binc Lem-*

## ANNOTATIONS.

ftin'd for his Son. All this we are let into, not indeed by a minute Narration, which would have been tedious, but the Poet has fo contriv'd the Converfation of the Perfons concern'd, that by Hints from them, and a little Reflection we learn the whole. This pleafes the Reader, as it leaves fome Employment for him, to trace the Particulars of the Story, and gives Scope to his Fancy and Imagination. *Chremes* had fome Lands belonging

*Chr.* When her Mother found that I tarried here longer than ufual, and that the Girl's Age did not fuit with my Delays, they tell me fhe left *Lemnos* with all her Family, and came hither in fearch of me.

*Dem.* Pray what detain'd you there fo long then, when you heard of this?

*Chr.* Why truly an Illnefs.

*Dem.* How came you by this Illnefs? Or what was it?

*Chr.* Would you know? Why, Age itfelf is an Illnefs: But the Mafter of the Ship who brought them over, told me that they arrived fafe.

*Dem.* Have you heard, *Chremes*, what has happened to my Son in my abfence?

*Chr.* That's what reduces me to the greateft Perplexity; for fhould I offer my Daughter in marriage to a Stranger, I muft tell the whole Story of her being mine, and by whom I had her. I knew you to be faithful to me, as much as I can be to myfelf: but a Stranger that may be willing to become my Son-in-Law, will hold his tongue indeed fo long as we continue good Friends; but if he fhould happen to grow regardlefs of me, he'll know more a great deal than I care he fhould. And I fear that my Wife may fome way or other come to hear the Story, which were it to happen, I have no Courfe left but to march off, and leave the Houfe; for I am myfelf the only Friend I have at home.

*Dem.* I know it; and that's what makes me too uneafy; nor will I ceafe trying every Method I can think of, until I make good my Promife to you.

A C T

*A N N O T A T I O N S.*

longing to his Wife at *Lemnos*, whether he went yearly to gather in his Rents. There he cohabited with another Woman, and had by her a Daughter, who, when fhe was grown up, not knowing how to difpofe of her and keep the Bufinefs a Secret from his Wife, he communicates the whole Affair to his Brother *Demipho*; and it is agreed upon, that he fhall bring her from *Lemnos*, and marry her to *Antipho*, *Demipho*'s Son. When he went to *Lemnos*, he found that her Mother, impatient at his Delays, had fail'd for *Athens*; upon which he returns. Meantime his *Lemnian* Wife enquiring for *Stilpho*, for by that Name he had made himfelf pafs at *Lemnos* to prevent Difcovery, and finding no fuch Perfon, dies of Grief. *Phany*, as we have feen above, is married to *Antipho*. *Chremes* at his return hearing of this Marriage, and never once fufpecting it to be with his own Daughter, is grieved that all his Meafures are thus broke. This will explain to the Reader the Converfation of the two old Men in the prefent Scene; for *Demipho* had gone to the Port to enquire after his Brother, and there found that he himfelf was arriv'd. He naturally therefore afks, whether, as had been agreed upon, he had brought his Daughter with him from *Lemnos?*

[13] *Hanc conditionem fi cui tulero:* That is, *fi cui filiæ meæ matrimonium obtulero;* for *conditio* fignifies properly an Agreement or Contract of Marriage. Thus *Corn. Nepos,* in his Life of *Cimon:* " Egit cum Cimone, " ut eam fibi uxorem daret. Id fi impe- " traffet, fe pro illo pecuniam foluturum.

" Is

CH. Postquam vidit me ejus mater esse hîc diutiùs,
Simul autem non manebat ætas virginis
Meam neglegentiam; ipsam cum omni familiâ          5
Ad me profectam esse aiebant. DE. quid illìc tam diu
Quæso, igitur commorabare, ubi id audiveras?
CH. Pol me detinuit morbus. DE. unde? aut qui?
    CH. rogas?
Senectus ipsa est morbus. sed venisse eas
Salvas audivi ex nautâ qui illas vexerat.          10
DE. Quid gnato obtigerit, me absente, audistin', Chre-
    me?
CH. Quod quidem me factum consilii incertum facit:
Nam hanc conditionem si cui tulero extrario,
Quo pacto, aut unde mihi sit, dicendum ordine est.
Te mihi fidelem esse, æquè atque egomet sum mihi, 15
Sciebam. ille si me alienus affinem volet,
Tacebit, dum intercedet familiaritas:
Sin spreverit me; plus, quàm opus est scito, sciet:
Vereorque, ne uxor aliquâ hoc resciscat mea.
Quod si fit, ut me excutiam, atque egrediar domo,   20
Id restat. nam ego meorum solus sum meus.
DE. Scio ita esse, & istæc mihi res solicitudini est:
Neque defetiscar usque adeo experirier,
Donec tibi id, quod pollicitus sum, effecero.

CH. Mater ejus, post-
quam vidit me esse
diutius hic, simul
autem ætas virginis
non manebat meam
negligentiam; aie-
bant ipsam cum omni
familia esse profectam
ad me. DE. Quæ-
so, igitur, quid com-
morabare illic tam
diu, ubi audiveras
id? CH. Pol mor-
bus detinuit me. DE.
Unde? aut qui? CH.
Rogas? Ipsa senectus
est morbus. Sed au-
divi ex nauta qui
vexerat illas, eas
venisse salvas. DE.
Audistine, Chreme,
quid obtigerit gnato,
me absente? CH.
Quod factum quidem
facit me incertum
consilii; nam si tu-
lero hanc conditionem
cui extrario, dicen-
dum est ordine quo
pacto aut unde illa
filia sit mihi. Scie-
bam te esse fidelem

*mibi, æque atque egomet sum mibi. Si ille altenus volet me affinem, tacebit, dum familiaritas in-
tercedet: sin spreverit me; sciet plus, quam opus est cito. Vereorque ne mea uxor resciscat hoc aliqua via. Quod si sit, id restat, ut excutiam me, atque egrediar domo. Nam ego solus meorum sum
meus amicus. DE. Scio esse ita, et istæc res est solicitudini mibi: neque defetiscar experiri, usque adeo, donec effecero id tibi, quod sum pollicitus.*

## ANNOTATIONS.

" Is quum talem *conditionem aspernaretur.*"
*Suetan. Aug.* 69. " *Conditiones.* quæsitas per
" amicos, qui matres familias et adultas æta-
" te virgines denudarent, atque perspicerent,
" tanquam Thoranio Mangone vendente."
In like manner *Justin.* II. 7. *Tam pulcbra
conditio, prima regna felicitas videbatur.*

  Ibid. *Extrario. Extrarius,* according to
*Festus,* is one, *qui extra fecum, jufque noftrum
ac facramentum est. Muretus* will not allow it to be *Latin,* and therefore reads *ex-
traneo.* But we find it used by *Sueton. Vefp.*
5. " Præsente eo quondam, canis *extra-
" rius* è trivio manum humanam intulit,
" mensæque subjecit. Apuleii Apolog Præ-
" tore minabatur, si *extrario* nupsiset, nihil
" se filiis ejus ex paternis eorum bonis testa-
" mento relicturum." From which it is
plain, that *extrarius* is properly one *non*
*domesticus, non ex eadem familia.* For we
say *extraneus* and *extrarius* in the same manner as *præsentaneus* and *præsentarius : Pro-
letancus* and *Proletarius.*

  [20] *Ut me excutiam.* Madam *Dacier* observes, that it was the Custom of the *Greeks,*
and several oriental Nations, to shake their
Garments at the Door of the House, when
going out. Hence *excutere se* came to signify
going out of a House, leaving it, abandoning it.

  [21] *Ego meorum solus sum meus. Meus sum,*
i. e. *mibi faveo: nam nolter est, qui nobis
favet.* Thus in the *Andrian,* Act 5. Scene
6. 12. *Tuus est nunc Chremes.* What *Chremes* therefore means is, that nobody at home
will take his part, or endeavour to calm his
Wife, for they will all immediately side with
her. *Suus* again is said of one *qui sui arbitrii est.*

ACTUS

## ACT IV.  SCENE II.

### ARGUMENT.

*This Scene reprefents Geta exulting, that both the old Men were offered to him to practife his Artifices upon.*

### GETA.

*Geta.* **I** Never in my Life faw a more cunning Fellow than this *Phormio.* I came to him to tell him that we had need of Money, and how it might be procur'd. Scarce had I faid one half before he underftood me perfectly: the Project pleas'd him extremely: He commended me; begg'd to fee the old Man, and thank'd the Gods that an Opportunity was given him of fhewing himfelf no lefs a Friend to *Phædria*, than he had before done to *Antipho.* I defir'd him to wait at the Forum, whether I would bring the old Man to him. But here I fee he comes: Who's that other behind him? Oh! 'tis *Phædria*'s Father, I perceive. Fool that I am, what was I afraid of? Was it becaufe inftead of one, I have now two to make Dupes of? I think it beft to have two Strings to my Bow. I'll try him I firft defign'd to get it from; if I fucceed, 'tis well; but if I can make nothing of him, then have at the new Comer.

### ANNOTATIONS.

We are now to be let into the other Part of the Play, which regards *Phædria*, and the manner in which the Money is procur'd to redeem his Miftrefs. We have feen that *Geta* had undertaken it, and we fee here the Method by which he propofes to compafs it. In concert with *Phormio*, a Project is form'd which the next Scene will fully open. The prefent Scene contains the Praifes of the Parafite. *Geta* had communicated his Defign to him, and found him very quick at underftanding it, and very ready to enter into it. This may

---

## ACT IV.  SCENE III.

### ARGUMENT.

*Geta attacks the two old Men; artfully introduces the Money-Bufinefs, and carries off the thirty Minæ he wanted.*

### ANTIPHO, GETA, CHREMES, DEMIPHO.

*Ant.* **I** Every moment expect, that *Geta* will be here—But yonder I fee my Father and my Uncle ftanding together. 'Death! How I tremble to think what Influence his Return may have upon my Father!                                                           *Get.*

### ANNOTATIONS.

Here we are let into the Project which had been concerted between *Phormio* and *Geta*, for obtaining the Money they wanted. *Demipho* had before made the Parafite an Offer of five *Minæ* to rid him of any further Trouble in regard to this hated Marriage, but they were aware he would eafily confent to give more: Upon this Suppofition they proceed. *Phormio* feems willing to marry *Phany* himfelf, if they will give him a Portion of thirty *Minæ* with her. *Geta* is left to manage the Affair, and propofe it to his Mafter. Their Defign was, that having got the Money, which was prefently wanted, *Phormio* would artfully protract the Time, till *Phædria* receiv'd that which had

been

# ACTUS IV. SCENA II.

## ARGUMENTUM.

*Tota hæc scena est Getæ exultantis, duos sibi senes offerri, quos fallere possit.*

### GETA.

EGO hominem callidiorem vidi neminem,
Quàm Phormionem. venio ad hominem, ut dice-
rem
Argentum opus esse, & id quo pacto fieret :
Vixdum dimidium dixeram, intellexerat :
Gaudebat : me laudabat : quærebat senem :　5
Dîs gratias agebat, tempus sibi dari,
Ubi Phædriæ se ostenderet nihilo minùs
Amicum esse, quàm Antiphoni. hominem ad forum
Jussi opperiri : eò me esse adducturum senem.
Sed eccum ipsum. quis est ulterior ? at at Phædriæ　10
Pater venit. sed quid pertimui autem bellua ?
An quia, quos fallam, pro uno duo sunt mihi dati ?
Commodius esse opinor duplici spe utier.
Petam hinc, unde à primo instituit. si is dat, sat est.
Si ab eo nil fiet, tum hunc adoriar hospitem　15

### ORDO.

GE. *EGO vidi neminem heminem callidiorem, quam Phormionem : venio ad heminem, ut dicerem argentum esse opus nobis, et quo pacto id fieret. Vixdum dixeram dimidium, cum ille intellexerat : gaudebat : laudabat me : quærebat senem : agebat gratias Dis, tempus dari sibi, ubi ostenderet se esse nihilo minus amicum Phædriæ, quam Antiphoni. Jussi hominem opperiri ad forum : dixi me esse adducturum senem &c.*

*Sed eccum ipsum : Quis est ulterior ? At, at, pater Phædriæ venit. Sed quid autem ego bellua pertimui ? An quia, pro uno, duo sunt dati mihi, quos fallam ? Opinor esse commodius uti duplici spe. Petam argentum hinc, unde institui petere a primo : si is dat, est sat. Si nil fiet ab eo, tunc adoriar hunc hospitem.*

### ANNOTATIONS.

may be naturally supposed, pleases him. At last he observes both the old Men advancing, and expresses his Joy, that he had now two, instead of one, to practise upon.

5 *Gaudebat.* Terence is very happy in representing the real Characters of Men, ac-cording to Truth and Nature. *Phormio* is one of those Men who pride themselves in their Dexterity and Address, and accordingly is here fond of an Opportunity of exerting these Talents.

---

# ACTUS IV. SCENA III.

## ARGUMENTUM.

*Geta adoritur senes, et mira fallacia argentum cudit, et minas triginta ab ipsis aufert.*

### ANTIPHO, GETA, CHREMES, DEMIPHO.

EXSPECTO, quàm mox recipiat sese Geta ;
Sed patruum video cum patre adstantem. hei mihi,
Quàm timeo, adventus hujus quò impellat patrem !

### ORDO.

AN. *Exspecto quàm mox Geta recipiat sese huc : sed video patruum adstantem cum patre : hei mihi, quàm timeo quo adventus hujus impellat patrem !*

### ANNOTATIONS.

been promis'd him by his Friends, and then some Excuse could be fram'd for declining the Match, and the Portion be return'd. This is the Purpose of the Scene, but the

Poet

*Get.* I'll up to them : O, our *Chremes* ;

*Chr.* Your Servant, *Geta.*

*Get.* I'm glad to fee you fafe return'd.

*Chr.* I believe it.

*Get.* How goes all ?

*Chr.* Pretty much hurried, as is ufual at one's firft coming home : but I have heard a great deal of News fince my Arrival.

*Get.* No doubt : Have you been told what has happen'd to *Antipho ?*

*Chr.* All.

*Get.* What, did you tell him of it ? *(to* Demipho.) 'Tis a monftrous thing, *Chremes,* to be circumvented in this manner.

*Chr.* I was talking with him about it juft now.

*Get.* Nay, and I too, revolving it anxioufly in my own Mind, flatter myfelf I have found out a Remedy for this Evil.

*Dem.* How, *Geta* ; What Remedy ?

*Get.* As I went from you, by chance *Phormio* met me.

*Chr.* What *Phormio ?*

*Get.* He that patronizes the young Woman.

*Chr.* I underftand.

*Get.* It came into my Head to found him a little : I took him afide : *Phormio,* faid I, why don't you endeavour to make an End of this Affair, rather by fair means than foul ? My Mafter is generous, and hates Law-Suits : for I affure you all the reft of his Friends, with one Voice, counfell'd him to turn her out of Doors directly.

*Ant. (to himfelf)* What is he about, or where will this end at laft ?

*Get.* You'll fay, *perhaps,* that the Law will punifh him, if he turns her out. That Affair has been already canvafs'd. Let me tell you, you'll have enough to do, if once you engage with him, he can fpeak well. But fuppofe you caft him, 'tis not a Matter of Life and Death ; but a mere Money Bufinefs. When I found that thefe Words had funk a little the Gentleman's Courage, We are now here by ourfelves, faid I : come, tell me what would you demand now to drop this Suit with my Mafter, to rid us of this Girl, and trouble us no more ?                                              *Ant.*

*A N N O T A T I O N S.*

Poet has contriv'd to heighten it, and make it ftill more interefting, by introducing *Antipho,* who, in fome fecret Corner unobferv'd, overhears all that paffes. He not perfectly underftanding the Defign, is thrown into the greateft Perplexities, more efpecially when he finds that *Geta*'s Artifice had fucceeded.

6 *Multa advenienti, ut fit, nova hic compluria.* Thefe Words feem hitherto not to have been rightly underftood : they are fo explain'd as to make but one Sentence, and be clogg'd with a very difagreeable Redundancy of Words. *Multa compluria nova, ut fit adveni- ent.* This might eafily have been avoided, had proper Care been taken to point the Verfe diftinctly : Thus :

*Multa advenienti, ut fit : nova hic compluria.*

*Geta* afks, *Quid agitur ?* To which he returns : *multa, ut fit advenienti* ; and then, as his Thoughts were full of what had happened to *Antipho,* and his own Difappointment, he immediately fubjoins : *compluria nova narrantur, mihi hic.* This *Geta* eafily underftood, and anfwers accordingly : *Ita. De Antiphone audifti quæ facta ?*

9 *Id cum hoc agebam, commodum.* Commodum is of the fame Import with *opportune, admodum, jamiam, eo ipfo tempore.* As before

GE. Adibo hosce. ô noster Chremes! CH. salve, Geta.
GE. Venire salvum volupe est. CH. credo. GE. quid
  agitur?
CH. Multa advenienti, ut fit, nova hîc compluria. 6
GE. Ita. de Antiphone audistin' quæ facta? CH. omnia.
GE. Tun' dixeras huic? facinus indignum, Chreme,
Sic circumiri. DE. id cum hoc agebam commodùm. 9
GE. Nam hercle ego quoque id agitans mecum sedulo,
Inveni, opinor, remedium huic rei. DE. quid, Geta?
Quod remedium? GE. ut abii abs te, fit fortè obviam
Mihi Phormio. CH. qui Phormio? GE. is, qui istam.
  CH. scio.
GE. Visum est mihi, ut ejus tentarem sententiam.
Prêndo hominem solum: cur non, inquam, Phormio
Vides, inter vos sic hæc potiùs cum bonâ 16
Ut componantur gratiâ, quàm cum malâ
Herus liberalis est, & fugitans litium :
Nam cæteri quidem hercle amici omnes modò
Uno ore auctores fuere, ut præcipitem hanc daret. 20
AN. Quid hic cœptat? aut quò evadet hodie? GE. an
  legibus
Daturum pœnas dices, si illam ejecerit?
Jam id exploratum est. eia, sudabis satis,
Si cum illo inceptas homine: eâ eloquentiâ est.
Verùm pone esse victum eum : at tandem tamen 25
Non capitis ejus res agitur, sed pecuniæ.
Postquam hominem his verbis sentio mollirier,
Soli sumus nunc hîc, inquam : eho, quid vis dari
Tibi in manum, ut herus his desistat litibus,
Hæc hinc facessat, tu molestus ne sies? 30

*GE. Adibo hosce. O noster Chremes! CH. Salve, Geta. GE. Est volupe te venire salvum. CH. Credo. GE. Quid agitur? CH. Multa, ut fit advenienti, cempluria nova occurrunt mihi hic. GE. Ita: audivistine quæ sunt facta de Antiphone? CH. Omnia. GE. Tune dixeras huic? Est indignum facinus, Chreme, circumiri sic. DE. Agebam id cum hoc commodùm. GE. Nam hercle ego quoque agitans id sedulo mecum, opinor, inveni remedium huic rei. DE. Quid, Geta? quod remedium? GE. Ut abii abs te, forte Phormio fit obviam mihi. CH. Qui Phormio? GE. Is, qui defendit istam virginem. CH. Scio. GE. Visum est mihi, ut tentarem sententiam ejus. Prehendo hominem solum: inquam, Phormio, cur non vide, ut hæc sic componantur inter vos, potius cum bona gratia, quam*

*cum mala? Herus est liberalis, et fugitans litium: nam hercle quidem cæteri omnes amici fuere modo auctores uno ore, ut daret hanc præcipitem. AN. Quid hic cœptat? aut quo hodie evadet? GE. An dices eum daturum pœnas legibus, si ejecerit illam? Id est jam exploratum. Eia, sudabis satis, si inceptas cum illo homine: est eâ eloquentiâ. Verum pone eum esse victum: attamen tandem, res non ejus capitis, sed pecuniæ agitur. Postquam sentio hominem molliri his verbis, inquam, nunc sumus soli hic: eho, quid vis dari tibi in manum, ut herus desistat his litibus, ut hæc uxor facessat hinc, et ut tu ne sies molestus amplius?*

## ANNOTATIONS.

fore in the Eunuch, Act 2. Scene 3. 51. *Illa interea sese commodum huc adverterat in hanc nostram plateam.*

11 *Quid, Geta? quod remedium?* The Poet has very artfully contriv'd *Geta's* Part in this Scene: It is worth while to look back a little, and see with what Judgment he has prepared for it. *Demipho*, at his first coming home is greatly enrag'd at *Geta*, and considers him as one principally in fault. But all these Impressions are entirely remov'd; nay more in the second Scene of the second Act, *Geta* is introduc'd assailing *Phor-* *mio* with Reproaches, pretending not to see his Master, who was just by, and overheard all. Thus *Geta* is believ'd a great Enemy to the Parasite, and his Master begins to have Confidence in him. No one therefore was so proper to manage this Treaty, as he was himself; a Slave of great Address and Cunning, in concert with *Phormio*, and believ'd to be trusty and faithful by *Demipho*.

23 *Sudabis satis*, i. e. *satis laborabis.* Cic. Fam. III. 12. *Vides sudare me, jamdudum laborantem, quomodo ea tuear, quæ mibi tuenda sunt, et te non offendam.* And

Sensu

*Ant.* Have the Gods abandon'd the Wretch?

*Get.* For I know very well, that if you propose any thing reasonable, my Master is so good a Man, there will not be three Words to the Bargain.

*Dem.* Whose Orders had you to say so?

*Chr.* Nay he could not have contriv'd better to bring about what we want.

*Ant.* I'm undone.

*Chr.* Go on with your Story.

*Get.* At first the Fellow rav'd.

*Dem.* Tell me, what did he ask?

*Get.* What! Too much. Whatever his Fancy prompted him to.

*Dem.* But say what it was.

*Get.* Suppose he were to give me a great Talent.

*Dem.* Give him, the deuce: what, has he no Shame?

*Get.* I told him as much: Pray, said I, what could he do more, were he to portion out an only Daughter? He gains little by not having one of his own, when another is thus found, for whom he must provide a Fortune. But to be short, and pass over his many Impertinencies, he gave me at last this as his final Answer: I would, says he, from the very first have gladly married my Friend's Daughter, as was fit I should: For I was aware of her Misfortune, that being poor, and married into a rich Family, she would be rather a Slave than a Wife. But to be free with you, I wanted a Wife that could bring me somewhat to pay off my Debts; and even yet, if *Demipho* will give as much with her as is offered me with the Girl I am already engag'd to, there is no one I'd so much like to have for a Wife.

*Ant.* I can't tell what to say of this, whether I am to call it Folly or Malice, Stupidity, or Design.

*Dem.* What is it to us, if he owes his Soul?

*Get.* I have a Piece of Land, says he, mortgaged for thirty Pounds.

*Dem.* Well, well, let him marry her, I'll give him the Money.

*Get.*

*A N N O T A T I O N S.*

*Seneca Epist.* 4. *Parabile est quod natura desiderat, et appositum: ad supervacanea sudatur.* Hence any Work of great Labour and Difficulty, is by the Poets call'd *Opus sudatum.* Thus *Horace, Lib.* I. *Sat.* 10. 28.

 *Cum Pedius causas exsudet----*
 h. e. *Magno labore et cura agat.*

31 *Satin' illi Di sunt propitii?* These Words *Antipho* utters full of Perturbation and Perplexity, ignorant as he was of *Geta's* real Design, and dreading that he meant to tear *Phany* from him altogether. *Satin' illi Dii sunt propitii,* is a Phrase equivalent in sense to, *An Dii irati mentem ei ademerunt?* For thus *Plautus, Mil.* III. 1. 107. has *Dii tibi propitii sunt* for *sapis,* as the whole Run of the Passage leads us to explain it. Hence it was common, in wishing any Persons Judgment, Discretion, or a sound Mind, to wish the Gods might be propitious to them. Thus *Seneca,* Epist. 110. *Init. Ex Nomentano meo te saluto, et jubeo te habere mentem bonam, hoc est, propitios Deos omnes: quos habet placatos et faventes, quisquis sibi se propitiavit.*

33 *Tria non commutabitis verba. Commutare verba* is generally taken in an unfavourable Sense, being a Phrase that exactly answers to ours, of *having Words with any one,* which implies a quarrelling or falling out with them. " *Proprie,* says *Donatus,* " com-

AN. Satin' illi Di sunt propitii? GE. nam sat scio,
Si tu aliquam partem æqui bonique dixeris,
Ut est ille bonus vir, tria non commutabitis
Verba hodie inter vos. DE. quis te istæc jussit loqui.
CH. Imò non potuit melius pervenirier          35
Eò, quò nos volumus. AN. occidi. DE. perge eloqui.
GE. A primo homo insanibat. DE. cedo, quid postulat?
GE. Quid? nimium: quantum libuit. DE. dic. GE. siquis daret
Talentum magnum. DE. imo malum hercle: ut nil pudet!
GE. Quod dixi adeo ei: quæso, quid si filiam          40
Suam unicam locaret? parvi retulit
Non suscepisse. inventa est, quæ dotem petat.
Ut ad pauca redeam, ac mittam illius ineptias;
Hæc denique ejus fuit postrema oratio:
Ego, inquit, jam à principio amici filiam,          45
Ita ut æquom fuerat, volui uxorem ducere:
Nam mihi veniebat in mentem ejus incommodum,
In servitutem pauperem ad ditem dari:
Sed mihi opus erat, ut aperte tibi nunc fabuler,
Aliquantulum quæ afferret, qui dissolverem          50
Quæ debeo: & etiam nunc, si volt Demipho
Dare; quantum ab hac accipio, quæ sponsa est mihi,
Nullam mihi malim, quàm istanc, uxorem dari.
AN. Utrum stultitiâ facere ego hunc an malitiâ.
Dicam, scientem, an imprudentem, incertu' sum.  55
DE. Quid, si animam debet? GE. ager oppositu' est
pignori ob
Decem minas, inquit. DE. age, age, jam ducat: dabo.

*ita ut fuerat æquum: nam incommodum ejus veniebat in mentem mibi, hanc pauperem dari ad ditem in servitutem: Sed ut nunc fabuler tibi aperte, opus erat mihi uxore, quæ adferret aliquantulum, qui dissolverem quæ debeo; et etiam nunc, si Demipho vult dare, quantam accipio ab hac, quæ est sponsa, malim nullam uxorem dari mihi, quam istac. AN. Sum incertus utrum ego dicam hunc facere hoc stultitia, an malitia, scientem, an imprudentem. DE. Quid est mihi, si debet animam? GE. Ager, inquit, est oppositus pignori ob decem minas. DE. Age, age, jam ducat, dabo eas.*

*AN. Dii suntne latis prepitii illi? GE. Nam sat scio, si tu dixeris aliquam partem æqui bonique, ut ille est bonus vir, non commutabitis tria verba inter vos hodie. DE. Quis jussit te loqui istæc? CH. Imo non potuit melius pervenire eo, quo nos volumus. AN. Cecidi. DE. Perge eloqui. GE. A primo homo insaniebat. DE. Cedo, quid postulat? GE. Quid? nimium quantum libuit. DE. Dic. GE. Si quis daret magnum talentum. DE. Imo hercle malum daret: ut pudet nil! GE. Quod dixi adeo ei: quæso, quid si locaret suam unicam filiam? An daret plus? Parvi retulit eum non suscepisse filiam: alia est inventa, quæ petat dotem. Ut redeam ad pauca, ac mittam illius ineptias; hæc denique fuit ejus postrema oratio. Ego, inquit, jam à principio, volui ducere filiam amici uxorem,*

## ANNOTATIONS

" *commutare verba*" *est, quod altercari dicivius: sic enim dicebant jurgium significantes.* Thus in the *Adrian*, Act 2. Scene 4. 7. where *Davus* tells *Pamphilus*, that by pretending to consent to the Marriage, propos'd to him by his Father, he would leave no room for Chiding or Rebuke. We meet with the very same Phrase; *Crede, inquam, hoc mihi, Pamphile, nunquam hodie tecum commutaturum patrem unum esse verbum, si te dicis ducere.*

38 *Si quis daret talentum magnum.* The Attic great Talent consisted of sixty *Minæ*, and every *Minæ* was a hundred Drachms. We have already, in a former Note, explained the Value of these several Pieces of Coin. I shall only observe, that among ancient Writers we meet sometimes with the Word *Talent* simply; sometimes it is called a *great Talent*, and sometimes an *Attic Talent*, which all import the same, when to be understood of *Grecian* Money.

47 *Incommodum, in servitutem pauperem ad ditem dari. Terence* seems here to have had in his Eye a Passage of *Plautus*, *Aulularia* II. 2. 49.

*Get.* And a House for thirty more.

*Dem.* Hy, hy, that's too much.

*Chr.* Don't exclaim: you shall have these thirty from me.

*Get.* I must have a Maid for my Wife; I shall need some Furniture too, and a little Money to defray the Expence of the Wedding. For these, says he, you may at least allow thirty more.

*Dem.* Let him, if he will, bring six hundred Actions against me, I'll give nothing: to let the impure Wretch have such a Handle of triumphing over me.

*Chr.* Pray be easy, I'll give it: do you only bring your Son to marry the Woman we'd have him.

*Ant.* Wretch that I am! Ah, *Geta!* thou hast undone me by thy Treacheries.

*Chr.* 'Tis on my account she is turn'd off, and therefore in reason I ought to bear the Loss.

*Get.* Let me know, says he, as soon as possible, whether they give me this Girl, that I may dispatch the other, and not remain in Uncertainty; for her Friends have agreed to lay down the Portion directly.

*Chr.* He shall have the Money directly, let him break off with that other Girl, and marry this.

*Dem.* And may he have little Joy of his Purchase.

*Chr.* Very fortunately I have now Money by me; the Rents of my Wife's Farms at *Lemnos:* I'll take of that, and pretend to her that you had occasion for it.

*ANNOTATIONS.*

*Venit hoc mihi, Megadore, in mentem, te esse hominem divitem,*

*Factiosum; me autem hominum pauperum pauperrimum.*

*Nunc si filiam locassem meam tibi, venit in mentem,*

*Te bovem esse, et me esse asellum; ubi tecum conjunctus siem.*

*Ubi onus nequeo ferre pariter, jaceam ego asinus in luto:*

*Tu me bos magis haud respicias, gnatus quasi nunquam siem.*

16 *Sexcentas proinde scribito jam mihi dicas. Let him raise six hundred Actions against me.* Madam *Dacier* observes, that this Explication, tho' it is the more general and common, and gives more Life and Spirit to the Sentence, is yet liable to exception, because it was not at all *Phormio's* Part to begin an Action against *Demipho*, who on the contrary was more likely to attack him. She therefore offers another Interpretation: *Let him raise six hundred Articles, if he will, I'll give nothing.* Observing that *Dica* is frequently used to signify what we call *an Article of Account.* But this would almost wholly destroy the Energy and Beauty of Expression: nor is the Objection that she mentions of any force; for *Demipho* is here concerting whether he can rid himself

A C T

GE. Ædiculæ item sunt ob decem alias. DE. hoi, hui,
Nimium est. CH. ne clama : petito hasce à me decem.
GE. Uxori emunda ancillula est : tum pluscula          60
Supellectile opu' est, opus est sumptu ad nuptias.
His rebus pone sanè, inquit, decem minas.
DE. Sexcentas proinde scribito jam mihi dicas :
Nii do, impuratus me ille ut etiam irrideat ?
GE. Quæso, ego dabo, quiesce : tu modò filius          65
Fac ut illam ducat, nos quam volumus. AN. hei mihi!
Geta, occidisti me tuis fallaciis.
CH. Meâ causâ ejicitur : me hoc est æquom amittere.
GE. Quantum potest, me certiorem, inquit, face,
Si illam dant, hanc ut mittam, ne incertus siem :       70
Nam illi mihi dotem jam constituerunt dare.
CH. Jam accipiat : illis repudium renunciet :
Hanc ducat. DE. quæ quidem illi res vortat male.
CH. Opportunè adeo nunc mecum argentum attuli,
Fructum, quem Lemni uxoris reddunt prædia :            75
Id sumam : uxori, tibi opus esse, dixero.

GE. Item ædiculæ sunt oppignoratæ ob alias decem. DE. Hoi, hui, nimium est CH. Ne clama ; petito hasce decem a me. GE. Ancillula est emenda uxori : tum est opus plusculâ supellectile, est opus sumtu ad nuptias. Sane, inquit, pone decem minas his rebus. DE. Proinde jam scribito sexcentas dicas mibi : do nil. Ut ille impuratus etiam irrideat me ? CH. Quiesce, quæso, ego dabo. Modo tu fac, ut filius ducat illam, quam nos volumus. AN. hei mibi ! O Geta, occidisti me tuis fallaciis. CH. Ejicitur mea causa : æquum est me amittere hoc. GE. Face me certiorem, inquit, quantum potest, si dant illam, ut mitiam hanc, ne siem incertus : nam illi jam constituerunt dare dotem mibi. CH. Accipiat jam : renunciet repudium illis : ducat hanc. DE. Quæ res quidem vortat male illis. CH. Adeo opportunè nunc attuli argentum mecum, fructum quem prædia uxoris Lemni reddunt : sumam id : dixero uxori esse opus tibi eo.

## ANNOTATIONS.

himself of *Phany* upon easy Terms, by making some Concessions to *Phormio*, or if he must turn her off, and run the hazard of a Law-Suit. When therefore he finds *Phormio's* Demands so unreasonable, he resolves upon the latter Course, and to run the hazard of whatever Actions the Parasite might bring against him.

67. *Occidisti me tuis fallaciis.* The Word *occido* is frequently used by our Poet, and occurs twice in this very Scene ; here, where it is an active Verb, and before Verse 37, where it is *neuter*, they are both spelt the same way, and distinguish'd only by their Quantity. *Occido* here is active, and signifies to kill : *occidisti me tuis fallaciis.* It comes from *ob* and *cædo.* *Occido* again, Verse 37, is neuter, and signifies *to die, to perish,* or *be undone.* Its Derivation is from *ob* and *cado.*

75 *Fructum, quem Lemni uxoris reddunt prædia.* *Fructus* signifies properly and originally the Fruit and Produce of the Earth, thence it was transferred to signify Revenues of whatever kind, as here Money-Rents. *Cic. Parad. 6. 1. Multi ex te audierunt, cum diceres, neminem esse divitem, nisi qui exercitum alere posset suis fructus : quod populus Romanus tantis vectigalibus jampridem vix potest.*

## ACT IV. SCENE IV.

### ARGUMENT.

Antipho *fall heavily upon* Geta, *by whose Treachery he fancied himself in danger of losing his Wife: but* Geta *at length satisfies and appeases him.*

ANTIPHO, GETA.

*Ant.* GEta!

*Get.* Hah.

*Ant.* What have you done?

*Get.* Nabb'd the old Men of their Money.

*Ant.* Is that enough, think ye?

*Get.* Truly I don't know: 'twas what you desir'd, however.

*Ant.* Rascal, do you answer me in a manner from the Purpose?

*Get.* What would you be at then?

*Ant.* What would I be at? By your pretty Devices, Matters are brought to that pass, I may go hang myself. May all the Gods and Goddesses in Heaven and Hell confound thee for an Example to such Rascals. Hah, if there is any thing you are anxious to have succeed, be sure you commit it to this Fellow. Where was the necessity of touching upon this Sore, or naming my Wife? You have given my Father room to hope, that she may be turn'd off. Pray now tell me, if *Phormio* accepts the Portion, he must marry her without doubt. What will become of me?

*Get.* But he will not marry her.

*Ant.* I know that: but when they come to demand the Money back, I warrant he'll rather go to Jail than betray us.

*Get.* There is nothing, *Antipho*, but by ill telling may be made to appear the worse: you leave out what is good here, and mention only the bad. Hear now the other Side. If he takes the Money, he must take the Wife too, as you say: I grant it. But a little time will be allow'd him for making Preparation, for inviting his Friends, and discharging the usual Solemnities. Mean time *Phædria*'s Friends will procure him the Money they have promised, and he can return it out of that.

*Ant.* With what Face can he return it; or how excuse himself?

*Get.* Would you know? What Prodigies, *will he say*, have happen'd

since

### ANNOTATIONS.

We have seen that *Antipho* overheard all that was said in the last Scene, and what Perplexity he is thrown into by *Geta*'s ambiguous Behaviour. Now therefore that both the old Men are withdrawn, he comes up to him, and questions him upon it with great Heat and Impatience. *Geta* endeavours to satisfy him, that there is no Danger, and at last with some difficulty brings him to temper.

² *Satin' id est?* An usual Form of chiding, as in the *Eunuch*, Act V. Scene II. 12. where *Thais* pretends to rebuke *Chærea* her supposed Eunuch for running off. *Satin' id tibi placet?*

⁵ *Ad restim mihi res redit.* A manner of speaking usual, when one thought his Case desperate. Thus *Cæcilius*, *Synephebis:*

 *Ad restim res redit: immo Collus,*

  *Non res; nam ille argentum habet.*

⁸ *Huic mandes, quod quidem recte curatam velis.* In some Editions and Manuscripts we read, instead of this Verse,

*Huic*

## ACTUS IV. SCENA IV.

### ARGUMENTUM.

*Objurgat Antpho Getam, cujus opera se in periculum venisse putat, ne uxore excidat. Idem ab eodem placatur.*

ANTIPHO, GETA.

|  | ORDO. |
|---|---|
| GETA. Ge. hem. An. quid egisti? Ge. emunxi<br>    argento senes. | An. *Geta. Ge.<br>Hem. An.<br>Quid egisti? Ge.<br>Emunxi senes argen-* |
| An. Satin' est id? Ge. nescio hercle; tantum jussu' sum. | *to. An. Estne id sa-* |
| An. Eho, verbero, aliud mihi respondes, ac rogo? | *tis? Ge. Hercle nesa* |
| Ge. Quid ergo narras? An. quid ego narrem? operâ tuâ ad | *scio, jussus sum effi-* |
| Restim mihi quidem res rediit planissume.    5 | *cere tantum. An.* |
| Ut te quidem omnes Di, Deæque, superi, inferi | *Eho, verbero, res-* |
| Malis exemplis perdant. hem, si quid velis. | *pondes mihi aliud,* |
| Huic mandes, quod quidem rectè curatum velis, | *ac rogo? Ge. Quid* |
| Quid minùs utibile fuit, quàm hoc ulcus tangere, | *narras ergo? An.* |
| Aut nominare uxorem? injecta est spes patri,    10 | *Quid ego narrem?* |
| Posse illam extrudi. cedo nunc porro, Phormio | *res quidem tuâ operâ* |
| Dotem si accipiet, uxor ducenda est domum : | *planissumè rediit ad* |
| Quid fiet? Ge. non enim ducet. An. novi, cæterùm | *restim mihi. Ut qui-* |
| Cum argentum repetent, nostrâ causâ scilicet | *dem omnes Dii Deæ-* |
| In novum potiùs ibit. Ge. nihil est, Antipho,    15 | *que, superi, inferi* |
| Quin male narrando possit depravarier. | *perdant te malis ex-* |
| Tu id, quod boni est, excerpis : dicis, quod mali est. | *emplis. Hem, si v-* |
| Audi nunc contra jam. si argentum acceperit, | *esquid, quod quidem* |
| Ducenda est uxor, ut ais : concedo tibi : | *velis curatum rectè,* |
| Spatium quidem tandem apparandis nuptiis,    20 | *mandes huic. Quid* |
| Vocandi, sacrificandi dabitur paululum : | *fuit minùs utilule,* |
| Interea amici, quod polliciti sunt, dabunt : | *quàm tangere hoc ul-* |
| Inde iste reddet. An. quamobrem? aut quid dicet? | *cus, aut nominare* |
|     Ge. rogas? | *uxorem? Spes est in-<br>jecta patri, illam<br>posse extrudi. Cedo<br>nunc porro, si Phor-<br>mio accipiet dotem,<br>uxor est ducenda do-<br>mum : Quid fiet de* |

*me? Ge. Enim non ducet. An. Novi: cæterum cum repetent argentum, scilicet ibit potiùs in nervum nostra causa. Ge. Est nibil Antipho, quin possit depravari narrando male. Tu excerpis id quod est boni, dicis id quod est mali. Audi nunc jam contra. Si acceperit argentum, uxor est ducenda, ut ais : concedo tibi. Paululum quidem spatium dabitur tandem apparandis nuptiis, causa vocandi amicos, sacrificandi. Interea amici dabunt Phædriæ argentum, quod sunt polliciti, iste reddet inde. An. Quamobrem reddet? aut quid dicet? Ge. Rogas? dicet :*

### ANNOTATIONS.

*Huic mandes, qui te ad scopulum e tranquillo inferat.*
But the most judicious Criticks have rejected it as spurious.

9 *Quam hoc ulcus tangere.* Thus *Cic. Nat. Deor.* I. 37. *Quidquid enim horum attigeris, ulcus est.* " Est autem *tangere ulcus,* " says *Westerhovius,* mentionem facere rei, " quæ alteri, qui audit, ingrata sit ; tran- " slatione ab homine vomica, et ulceribus " obsito, quibus propter dolorem tangendis, " abstinendum est. *Plaut. Pers.* 2. 5. 11.    *To. Quid hoc hic in collo tibi tumet?*

*Sa. Vomica st, pressare parce.*
*Nam ubi qui mala tetigit manu, dolores cooriuntur.*

15 *In nervum potius ibit.* See the Note on Act II. Scene I. 11. of this Play.

16 *Nihil est, Antipho, quin male narrando possit depravarier.* Agreeable to what *Cicero* says, *Parad.* I. " Sed nihil tam incre- " dibile est, quod non dicendo fiat probabile ; " nihil tam horridum, tam incultum, quod " non splendescat oratione, et tanquam ex- " colatur."



24 *Quæ*

fince I confented to that Marriage ? A ftrange black Dog came *running* into the Houfe : a Snake fell off the Tiles, thro' my Spout into the Yard : my Hen crow'd : the Soothfayer forbad it, and the Soothfayer charg'd me not to meddle with any new Bufinefs till Winter. The beft Excufe in the World.   Thus will things be manag'd.

*Ant.* I heartily wifh they may.

*Get.* They will, truft me for that : but here comes your Father ! Go tell *Phædria* that the Money's procur'd.

*ANNOTATIONS.*

24 *Quot res poft illa monftra evenerunt mibi ?* So we read in the *Cambridge Terence,* and accordingly I have given it that Turn, both in the Verfion and *Ordo,* which it feems alone capable of admitting ; for as I have hitherto followed that Edition in the Text, I was unwilling to deviate from it here, tho' I think the Reading we meet with in fome other Editions far preferable :

    ----*Rogas ?*
*Quot res ? Poftilla, monftra evenerunt mibi !*
" Do you afk ? How many things may he " fay ? Since that Agreement, what Prodigies have happen'd to me ?" So that a Point of Interrogation is to come after *Quot res ?* and *poft illa* is equivalent to *ex eu tempore,* viz. *quo, dote data, Phanium mibi defponfata eft ;* as in the *Andrian,* Act V. Scene IV. 33. Where *Chremes* fpeaking of his Brother who had fail'd for *Afia,* and never been heard of afterwards, fays : *Poft ipfo nunc primum audio, quid illo fit factum.*

26 *Intreiit in ades,* &c. Many of thefe Superftitions prevail even at this Day ; whence

# ACT IV.   SCENE V.

### ARGUMENT.

*The old Men are converfing together about giving* Phormio *the Money.* Chremes *urges* Demipho *to difpatch that Affair with all hafte.*

DEMIPHO, GETA, CHREMES.

*Dem.* **B**E eafy, I fay ; I'll take care it fhall not be in his power to fhew his Knavery ; I'll never part with your Money rafhly, but have Witneffes prefent when I give it, and I'll mention too the Defign of its being given.

*Get.* How wary he is, where there is fo little Occafion !

*Chr.* You had need : and hafte, difpatch it while the Fit is upon him ; for fhould that other urge him warmly, he may perhaps throw us off.

*Get.* The very thing to be dreaded.

*Dem.* Lead me to him then.

*Get.*

*ANNOTATIONS.*

The two old Men again appear with the Money, upon which *Antipho* retires. As they both fufpected *Phormio* to be a mere Sharper, *Chremes* had been requefting *Demipho* not to be rafh in parting with the Money, till he had made fure of the Point in hand ; and *Demipho,* as they are coming along, is requefting *Chremes* to be eafy on that head, for he would take fuch wary Meafures, as fhould put it out of his power to impofe upon them.

3 *Ut caufus eft, ubi nil opus eft !* This

*Get*

Quot res poſt illa monſtra evenerunt mihi
Introiit in ædes ater alienus canis :
Anguis per impluvium decidit de tegulis :
Gallina cecinit ? interdixit hariolus :
Aruſpex vetuit ante brumam aliquid novi
Negotî incipere : quæ cauſa eſt juſtiſſima.
Hæc fient. AN. ut modo fiant. GE. fient : me vide.
Pater exit. abi, dic, eſſe argentum, Phædriæ.

*quot illa monſtra eve-*
25 *nerunt mibi poſt res*
*conventas de nup-*
*tiis ? Alienus ater*
*canis introiit in æ-*
*des : Anguis decidit*
*de tegulis per implu-*
*vium : Gallina ce-*
*cinit : Hariolus in-*
30 *terdixit : Aruſpex*
*vetuit me incipere a-*

*liquid novi negotii ante brumam ; quæ eſt juſtiſſima cauſa. Hæc fient. AN. Ut modo fiant. GE.*
*Fient, vide me. Pater exit. Abi, dic Phædriæ, argentum eſſe paratum.*

## ANNOTATIONS.

whence it is evident, that Mankind is much the ſame in all Ages. The Poet, as *Donatus* obſerves, ſeems here to ſneer at theſe Follies ſo prevalent in his Time.

29 *Aruſpex vetuit.* I ſhall here ſubjoin what *Perizonius* ſays upon the Origin and Derivation of this Word *ad Acliani Var. Hiſt.* III. 31. where, after refuting the Account given of it by *Dionyſius Halicarnaſſus*, he adds : " Nam revera *Haruſpices* ab " Hetruſco *Haruga*, eaque *ſpecienda*, ſunt " dicti, ut monet Donatus ad Terentii " *Phormionem. Haruga* autem eſt hoſtia, " vocabulum non *ab Hara formatum*, ut " idem Donatus putabat, ſed ex oriente et " lingua. orientali, cujus multa reperiuntur " apud Etruſcos ex Aſia ortos veſtigia tranſ- " latum. Ibi enim *Haruga*, ſignificat ca- " ſum, ſcil. Victimam, genere fœminino, " quia antiquiſſimis temporibus ſemella ad " ſacrificia maxime adhibebantur.

---

# ACTUS IV. SCENA V.

## ARGUMENTUM.

*Colloquuntur ſenes de tradendo Phormioni argento. Chremes Demiphonem inſtigat, ut argentum ſolvere feſtinet.*

### DEMIPHO, GETA, CHREMES.

QUietus eſto, inquam : ego curabo, ne quid verbo-
   rum duit.
Hoc temere nunquam amittam ego à me, quin mihi
   teſtes adhibeam,
Cùm dem : &, quam ob rem dem, commemorabo.
   GE. ut cautus eſt, ubi nil opu' ſt !
CH. Atque ita opus eſt facto : at matura, dum libido
   eadem hæc manet :
Nam ſi altera illa magis inſtabit, forſitan nos rejiciat. 5
GE. Rem ipſam putaſti. DE. duc me ad eum ergo.

ORDO.

DE. *E ſto quietus, inquam : ego curabo ne duit quid verborum no- bis. Ego nunquam amittam hoc temere a me, quin adhibe- am teſtes mihi, cum dem : et commemora- bo ob quam rem dem. GE. Ut cautus eſt, ubi eſt nihil opus ! CH. Atque ita opus eſt facto : at matura,*

*dum hæc eadem libido manet : nam ſi illa altera inſtabit magis, forſitan rejiciat nos. GE. Pu-*
*taſti ipſam rem. DE. Ergo duc me ad eum.*

## ANNOTATIONS.

Geta ſays in a low Voice to himſelf, ſmil- ing at the Concern the old Men appear to be in, which he knew to be groundleſs, as (the Money was indeed for *Phædria*) and according to their Scheme, would be re- turn'd again under various Pretences, as ſoon as *Phædria* could procure it of his Friends, as we learn from a former Scene.



35 *Ubi*

*Get.* When you will.

*Chr.* When you have done with him, step over to my Wife, that she may talk with the Girl before she goes: Let her tell her, that to prevent any Resentment on her Side, we have agreed to marry her to *Phormio,* who is much the fitter Match, as being her intimate Acquaintance, that we have in every thing acquitted ourselves of our Duty, and given *Phormio* what Portion he desir'd.

*Dem.* What the deuce, does that concern you?

*Chr.* A great deal, *Demipho.*

*Dem.* Are you not satisfied with having done your Duty, unless you have also the Applause of the Publick?

*Chr.* I'd have this done with her Consent, that she mayn't pretend she was forc'd away.

*Dem.* I can do all that myself?

*Chr.* But it will come better from one Woman to another.

*Dem.* Well, I'll ask her.

*Chr.* I'm now thinking with myself where I shall be most likely to find these Women.

### ANNOTATIONS.

**18.** *Ubi illas reperire poſſum.* This is to be underſtood of his *Lemnian* Wife and Daughter; he knew they were in *Athens,* but was quite a Stranger to their Adventures. Having therefore now settled every thing for annulling the former Marriage, and making way

---

# ACT IV.  SCENE VI.

### ARGUMENT.

*This Scene exhibits the meeting of* Sophrona *and* Chremes, *who at* Lemnos *had aſſumed the Name of* Stilpho. *From her he underſtands that his Daughter* Phany *was married to Antipho, which ſo unexpected good Fortune gives him great Joy: He takes proper Care however, that his Wife may hear nothing of it.*

### SOPHRONA, CHREMES.

*Soph.* WHAT shall I do? Where, in my present wretched State, shall I find a Friend? To whom shall I diſcloſe my Story? or whence look for Relief? For I tremble, lest the Advice I have given my Miſtreſs should be the Cauſe of her suffering any Indignity; as I hear the young Gentleman's Father is greatly offended at the Marriage.                                      *Chr.*

### ANNOTATIONS.

This Scene is very intereſting, as in it a Diſcovery is made that quite removes our Fears for *Antipho,* and his so much lov'd Bride. The Reader is already so much preposseſſed in their Favour, that every Check to their Happineſs gives him Pain; and of consequence this Diſcovery, which opens so fair a Prospect of compleating their Wishes, muſt give him proportionable Pleaſure. The several Incidents that lead to it, will easily

GE. non moror. CH. ubi hoc egeris,
Transito ad uxorem meam, ut conveniat hanc priùs.
  quàm hinc abit:
Dicat eamdare nos Phormioni nuptum, ne succenseat;
Et magis esse illum idoneum, qui ipsi sit familiarior;
Nos hostro officio nihil egressos esse; quantum is vo-
  lucrit,                                                      10
Datum esse dotis. DE. quid tuâ, malùm, id refert?
  CH. magni, Demipho.                              [probat?
DE. Non sat, tuum officium fecisse, si non id rama ap-
CH. Volo ipsius quoque voluntate hòc fieri, ne se
  ejectam prædicet                             [magi' congruet.
DE. Idem ego istuc facere possum. CH. mulier mulieri
DE. Rogabo. CH. ubi illas nunc ego reperire possim,
  cogito.

*te fecisse tuum officium, si fama non approbat id? CH. Volo hoc fieri ipsius voluntate quoque; ne prædicet se fuisse ejectam. DE. Ego possum facere istuc idem. CH. Mulier magis congruit mulieri. DE. Rogabo. CH. Cogito nunc, ubi ego possim reperire illas.*

ORDO.
*GE. Non moror. CH. Ubi egeris hoc, transito ad meam uxorem, ut conveniat hanc, priusquam abit hinc: dicat nos dare eam nuptum Phormioni, ne succenseat; et illum, qui sit familiarior ipsi esse magis idoneum maritum; nos esse nibil egressos nostro officio; tantum dotis esse datum, quantum is voluerit. DE. Quid, malum, id refert tua? CH. Magni, Demipho. DE. An non est sat,*

## ANNOTATIONS.

way for that of his Daughter, he naturally begins to think how he shall find her out, which was only wanting to compleat his Designs. This too, by an easy Transition, brings on the next Scene.

---

# ACTUS IV. SCENA VI.

## ARGUMENTUM.

*Hac scena Sophronæ nutricis, et Chremetis, qui Stilphonem se nominarat, mutua continetur agnitio. Deinde ex eâdem intelligit, filiam suam Phanium Antiphoni nuptam esse, ob cujus eventum inexpectatum, ingenti gaudio afficitur: cavet tamen, ne uxor hoc resciscat.*

### SOPHRONA, CHREMES.

QUID agam? quem mihi amicum misera inveni-
  am? aut cui
Consilia hæc referam? aut unde mihi auxilium petam?
Nam vereor, hera ne ob meum suasum indigna injuriâ
  afficiator:                                              [ter.
Ita patrem adolescentis facta hæc tolerare audio violen-

*ciatur indigna injuria ob meum suasum: audio patrem adolesentis tolerare hæc facta ita violenter.*

ORDO.
*So. MISERA, quid agam? quem amicum inveniam mihi? aut cui referam hæc consili? aut unde petam auxilium mihi? Nam vereor, ne hera affi-*

## ANNOTATIONS.

easily appear from what has been already remark'd on former Scenes, and therefore require not to be enlarg'd on here. I shall only observe, that in the Beginning of this Scene, the Poet has designed by introduc'd Sophrona complaining of her Misfortunes, and representing every thing in the most unfavourable Light, that the Reader may be the more sensible of the sudden Change occasion'd by her meeting with *Chremes,* from Sorrow and Despair, to Joy and Hope.

                                                         7 *Vita*

*Chr.* What old Woman can this be, that comes out from my Brother's with Looks so full of Concern?

*Soph.* The Diſtreſs we were in compell'd me to it, tho' I knew the Match was not good in Law: but I could think of no other way to prevent the Want that threaten'd her.

*Chr.* Why ſure, if I am not mightily miſtaken, if my Eyes don't inform me wrong, I ſee my Daughter's Nurſe.

*Soph.* Nor have we been able as yet————

*Chr.* What muſt I do?

*Soph.* To find her Father.

*Chr.* Had I beſt go up to her, or wait, and hear what more ſhe has to ſay?

*Soph.* For could he be found, I have nothing to fear.

*Chr.* 'Tis ſhe herſelf, I'll go ſpeak to her.

*Soph.* Who can this be ſpeaks here?

*Chr.* *Sophrona.*

*Soph.* And calls my Name too?

*Chr.* Look about to me.

*Soph.* God bleſs my Soul, is this *Stilpho?*

*Chr.* No.

*Soph.* Do you deny it?

*Chr.* Pray come a little this way from the Door there, *Sophrona,* and take care of ever calling me any more by that Name.

*Soph.* What! Are you not the ſame, pray, you always ſaid you were?

*Chr.* Huſh.

*Soph.* Why ſo greatly afraid of theſe Doors?

*Chr.* I have a Shrew of a Wife ſhut up here. Formerly I gave my-ſelf that falſe Name, out of fear, leſt ſome of you might indiſcreetly blab it about, and by that means the Story come to my Wife's Ears.

*Soph.* That's the very Reaſon why we have been ſo unhappy, as never to find you out here.

*Chr.* Well, but tell me what Buſineſs you had at that Houſe you came out of? Or where my Wife and Daughter are?

*Soph.* Alas!

*Chr.* Hah, what's the Matter? Are they alive?

*Soph.* Your Daughter is, but the poor Mother, after much Suffer-ing and Anxiety, died of Grief.

*Chr.* An unhappy Thing.

*Soph.* As for me, finding myſelf old, deſolate, needy, and un-known, I contriv'd, as well as I could, to marry your Daughter to the young Gentleman who is Maſter of this Houſe.

*Chr.* What, to *Antipho?*

*Soph.* The very ſame.

*Chr.* Has he, pray, two Wives?                              *Soph.*



7 *Vita ut in tuto foret.* That is, that ſhe might not be reduc'd to abſolute Want. *Vita* is frequently uſed by Poets for the ne-ceſſary Supports of Life. Thus in the ſecond Act of this ſame Play, Scene. 2. 16. *Quippe homo jam grandior, pauper, cui opera vita erat:*

CH. Nam quæ hæc anus est exanimata, à fratre quæ
    egressa est meo ?                                          5
So. Quod ut facerem, egestas me impulit ; cùm scirem
    infirmas nuptias                                    [foret.
Hasce esse ; ut id consulerem, interea vita ut in tuto
CH. Certe edepol, nisi me animus fallit, aut parum
    prospiciunt oculi,                        [CH. quid ago ?
Meæ nutricem gnatæ video. So. neque ille investigatur.
So. Qui est pater ejus. CH. adeon', an maneo, dum
    ea, quæ loquitur, magis cognosco ?                  10
So. Quòd si eum nunc reperire possim, nihil est, quod
    verear.   CH. ea ipsa est.
Conloquar. So. quis hîc loquitur ?  CH. Sophrona.
    So. & meum nomen nominat ?
CH. Respice ad me. So. Dî, obsecro vos : estne hic
    Stilpho ? CH. non. So. negas ?          [Sophrona.
CH. Concede hinc à foribus paululùm istorsum sodes,
Ne me istoc posthac nomine appellassis. So. quid ? non,
    obsecro, es                                         15
Quem semper te esse dictitasti ? CH. st. So. quid has
    metuis fores ?                               [de nomine.
CH. Conclusam hic habeo uxorem sævam. verùm istoc
Eò perperam olim dixi, ne vos fortè imprudentes foris
Effutiretis, atque id porro aliquâ uxor mea resciceret.
So. Istoc pol nos te hîc invenire miseræ nunquam po-
    tuimus.                                             20
CH. Eho, dic mihi, quid rei tibi est cum familiâ hac,
    unde exis ? aut           [vivuntne ? So. vivit gnata
Ubi illæ sunt ? So. miseram me ! CH. hem ! quid est ?
Matrem ipsam ex ægritudine miseram mors consecuta
    est.                          [deserta, egens, ignota,
CH. Male factum. So. ego autem, quæ essem anus
Ut potui, nuptum virginem locavi huic adolescenti, 25
Harum qui est dominus ædium. CH. Antiphonine ?
    So. hem, isti ipsi.   CH. quid ?

*CH. Nam quæ est hæc anus, quæ est egressa exanimata a meo fratre ? Sò. quod egestas impulit me, ut facerem, cum scirem hasce nuptias esse infirmas : ut consulerem id, ut vita ejus foret interea in tuto. CH. Certe adepol, nisi animus fallit me, aut oculi parum prospiciunt, video nutricem meæ gnatæ. So. Neque ille investigatur. CH. Quid ago ? So. Qui est pater ejus. CH. Adeone, an maneo, dum magis cognosco ea, quæ loquitur ? So. Quid si possim, nunc reperire eum, est nibil, quod verear. CH. Est ea ipsa, conloquar. So. Quis loquitur hic ? CH. Sophrona. So. Et nominat meum nomen ? CH. Respice ad me. So. Dii, obsecro vos ; estne hic Stilpho ? CH. Non. So. Negas ? CH. Concede hinc a foribus paululum istor- sodes, Sophrona, ne appellaveris me isto nomine postbæc. So. Quid ? obsecro, an non es, quem semper dictitavisti te esse ? CH. st. So. Quid metuis has fores ? CH. Habeo savam uxorem conclusam hic.*

*Verùm olim dixi me perperam istoc nomine eo, ne forte vos imprudentes effutiretis foris, atque porro mea uxor resciceret id aliquâ. So. Pol istoc nos miseræ nunquam potuimus invenire te hic. CH. Eho, dic mihi, quid rei est tibi cum hac familia, unde exis ? aut ubi illæ sunt ? So. Me miseram ! CH. Hem, quid est ? vivuntne ? So. Grata vivit. Mors est consecuta matrem ipsam miseram ex ægritudine. CH. Male factum. So. Ego autem que essem anus deserta, egens, ignota, ut potui, locavi virginem nuptam huic adolescenti, qui est dominus harum ædium. CH. Antiphonine ? So. Hem, isti ipsi. CH. Quid ?*

## ANNOTATIONS.

erat : i. e. whose Labours supplied him with the Necessaries of Life. And again, in the first Scene of the next Act, 5. *Etiam argentum est ultro objectum, ut sit, qui vivat, dum aliud aliquid flagitii conficiat.*

19 *Effutiretis.* Eloqueremini, evacuaretis, exinaniretis. *Effutire,* ab eo quod est effundere. Translatio est a vase, futili nomine : quod patulo ore, fundo acuto instabile, nihil prorsus continet ; unde *futilis* dicitur ejusmodi, ut nihil intra se contineat, et semper inanis sit.

23 *Ex ægritudine miseram mors consecuta est.* The Remark which Donatus has put upon
this

*Soph.* Nay, sure not he, he has none but her.

*Chr.* What's become of that other then, whom they pretend to be a-kin to him?

*Soph.* 'Tis your Daughter.

*Chr.* How do you say?

*Soph.* It was done by concert, that being in love with her he might marry her, portionless as she was.

*Chr.* Good Gods! how sometimes Chance directs things to favour us, more than we dare even wish for! Coming home, I find my Daughter match'd to the very Person, and in the very manner I would have her. What we were both so anxious, and at so much Pains to accomplish, this old Woman alone has by her own Care effected, without any Help from us.

*Soph.* Think now what's to be done, the young Man's Father is return'd, and they say is greatly offended at the Marriage.

*Chr.* There's no Danger there, but for God's sake take care that nobody know she is my Daughter.

*Soph.* Nobody shall know it of me.

*Chr.* Follow me then: you shall hear the rest, when we are got in.

*A N N O T A T I O N S.*

this is extremely judicious. The Poet (says he) has here observ'd a just Mean, in neither making *Chremes* appear wholly uncon-cern'd, nor too deeply affected. The particular Circumstances and Conjuncture too made such a Representation necessary; for two

---

# A C T  V.   S C E N E  I.

### A R G U M E N T.

*Demipho accuses himself, that by too anxiously studying to avoid the Stain of Avarice, he may be justly charged with Simplicity: for he mightily repines at the Money given away to* Phormio.

D E M I P H O, G E T A.

*Dem.* 'TIS our own fault that *some* Men find their Account in being Knaves; while we too much affect to be thought good, and generous. Run so as not to pass your own Gate, as the Saying is.

*A N N O T A T I O N S.*

We have seen, at the end of the last Scene, that *Chremes* goes in with *Sophrona* to *Demipho's,* to see his Daughter. Meanwhile *Demipho* and *Geta* are employed in settling Matters with *Phormio,* for which we are to allow a reasonable Time, especially if we reflect upon the Precautions the old Man was resolved to take, to prevent Deceit: Hence it appears that here we are to place the Interval between the Fourth and Fifth Acts; for we cannot suppose, that, when *Chremes* went with *Sophrona,* *Demipho* had already dispatch'd *Phormio,* and was returning from him; 'tis necessary to allow a little more Time. This first Scene therefore opens with *Demipho* and *Geta* returning from *Phormio.* The old Man, who parted with his Money with great Regret, shews his Discontent in every thing he says, while *Geta* artfully prepares the way for the

Duaſne is uxores habet? So. au, obſecro, unam ille
    quidem hanc ſolam.
Ch. Quid illam alteram, quæ dicitur cognata? So.
    hæc ergo eſt. Ch. quid ais?    [bere poſſet.
So. Compoſito eſt factum, quo modo hanc amans ha-
Sine dote. Ch. Dii voſtram fidem! quàm ſæpe forte
    temere                                        30
Eveniunt, quæ non audeas optare! offendi adveniens,
Quicum volebam, atque ut volebam, conlocatam filiam,
Quod nos ambo opere maxumo dabamus operam, ut
    ſieret,
Sine noſtrâ curâ maxumâ. ſuâ curâ hæc ſola fecit.
So. Nunc quid opus facto ſit, vide. pater adoleſcentis
    venit;                                        35
Eumque animo iniquo hoc oppidò ferre aiunt. Ch. ni-
    hil pericli eſt.
Sed per Deos atque homines, meam eſſe hanc, cave re-
    ſciſcat quiſquam.                        [audies.
So. Nemo ex me ſcibit. Ch. ſequere me: intus cætera.

*ſola fecit id, ſua cura, ſine noſtra maxima cura. So. Nunc vide, quid opus ſit facto; pater
adoleſcentis venit, aiuntque eum ferre hoc oppidò iniquo animo. Ch. Eſt nihil pericli. Sed per
Deos atque homines, cave quiſquam reſciſcat hunc eſſe meam. So. Nemo ſcibit ex me. Ch. Sequere me: audies cætera intus.*

*ORDO.* — *iſſe habet duas uxores? So. Ain obſecro, ille quidem habet hanc unam ſolam. Ch. Quid? habetne illam alteram, quæ dicitur cognata? So. Hæc ergo, eſt. Ch. Quid ais? So. Eſt factum compoſito, quomodo ille amans poſſet habere hanc ſine dote. Ch. Dii voſtràm fidem! quàm ſæpe forte ea venit temere, quæ non audeas optare! Advehilæ? offenti filiam cellocata mei, quicum volebam, atque ut volebam. Quod nos ambo dabamus operam maximo opere, ut ſieret, hæc anus*

## ANNOTATIONS.

two Wives in the ſame City muſt fill *Chremes* with ſo much Anxiety, as would have prov'd a greater Misfortune than the Sorrow ariſing from the Loſs of one of them. Nor in Comedy ought Deaths to appear in too affecting a Light, leſt thereby you change its very Nature, and give us rather a Tragedy.

# ACTUS V. SCENA I.

## ARGUMENTUM.

*Demipho ſeipſum incuſat, quod dum avaritiæ maculam ſtudet effugere, in ſtultitiæ reprehenſionem inciderit: dolet enim Phormioni datum eſſe urgentum.*

### DEMIPHO, GETA.

NOſtrapte culpâ facimus, ut malis expediat eſſe,
    Dum nimium dici nos bonos ſtudemus & be-
nignos.                                    [erat,
Ita fugias, ne præter caſam, quod aiunt. nonne id ſat

*ORDO.* — *De. Facimus noſtrapte culpa, ut expediat quiſdum hominibus eſſe malis, dum nimitum ſtudemus nos dici bonos et benignos. Ita fugias, ne fugias præter caſam, quod aiunt. Nonne id ſat erat.*

## ANNOTATIONS.

the Reſtitution, which in a few days he apprehended would be made.

  3 *Ita fugias, ne præter caſam.* There is no Paſſage in *Terence* has more perplex'd Commentators than this; and yet the Senſe g'ven it in the Tranſlation ſeems very obvious, and perfectly conſonant to *Demipho's* Diſcourſe. *Ita fugias, ne prætereas caſam tuam*

*Is.* Was it not enough to receive an Injury from him ? but we muſt go and voluntarily offer him Money too, that he may have where-with to ſupport himſelf, till he can contrive ſome new Piece of Roguery ?

*Get.* Moſt evidently.

*Dem.* You ſee there is a Reward for confounding right and wrong.

*Get.* But too true.

*Dem.* How ſimply we have behav'd in this Affair !

*Get.* 'Tis well enough, if he but keeps to his word, and marries her.

*Dem.* Is that to be doubted ?

*Get.* Why truly, Sir, he's ſuch a ſort of Man, that one can't be ſure he will not change his Mind.

*Dem.* Hah, change it too !

*Get.* I can't tell, but if perhaps he ſhould, I ſay.

*Dem.* I'll do as my Brother advis'd : I'll bring his Wife hither to talk with the Girl. Do you, *Geta*, go and give her notice that *Nauſiſtrata* will be with her.

*Get.* (*alone.*) Money is procur'd for *Phædria* ; Matters are all huſh and quiet ; Care is taken that *Phany* ſhall not be oblig'd to depart immediately. What more then ? What now remains to be done ? You're as deep in the Mire as ever : you muſt pay all with Intereſt, *Geta* : the Miſchief that threatned you, 'tis true, is put off to another Day ; but Vengeance will redouble, if you take not proper care. I'll now go home and teach *Phany* her Leſſon, that ſhe may fear nothing on the ſide of *Phormio*, nor be ſurpriz'd at the Converſation *Nauſiſtrata* is going to have with her.

*ANNOTATIONS.*

*tuam, quæ ſit tibi tutiſſimum receptaculum,* as *Donatus* has it : that is, fly ſo as not to go beyond the proper Bounds, and loſe ſight of Relief. I cannot however here omit the Explanation offered by *Gronovius*, who makes it, *So avoid one Danger, as not to run into a greater :* which anſwers extremely well to *Demipho*'s Speech ; and, but for its ſeeming a little too far fetch'd, muſt undoubtedly have the Preference. However, take it in his own Words : *Obſerv.* 3. g. " Proverbium eſt ruſticum, inter ergaſtu- " la natum : quod duo vocabula indicant, " *fugere*, et *caſa* : hanc enim ruris, illud " ſervorum fugitivorum intelligimus. Qui " fugiebant, ut id caute ac tutius facerent, " ex remotis plerumque et ultimis agri par- " tibus primulum ſe in pedes conjiciebant, " ubi a nemine obſervarentur. At caſam, " ſeu villam præterire velle : qui fugam pa- " raret, erat hominis de corio et capite ſuo " ludentis. Quid enim poterat expectare, " niſi ut aut domini, aut villici, aut ali- " cujus obſervantium familiarium, veniret " in manus, et manifeſta in noxa teneré- " tur ? Proprie igitur hoc conſilium fugiti- " vo datur, ſi fugam meditetur, ita eam " inſtituunt, ut *caſa domini non ſit prætere-* " *unda,* ne vitans ſervitutem, ærumnam, " compedes, incidat in ſupplicium, ſtigmata " crurifragium. Et pertinet ad omnes, " qui monendi ſunt, ne levius incommoduſſ " et onus gravati, in triſtiora et duriora " præcipitent. Itaque ſenex comicus, ut " Phryx, ſero ſapiens, increpat rem ab " ſeſe actam, qui metu columniæ et falſa- " rum litium illum, a quo injuria affectus " erat, pecunia donarat. Qui *præter caſam* " *fugit,*

A C T

Accipere ab illo injuriam? etiam argentum est ultro
    objectum,
Ut sit qui vivat, dum aliud aliquid flagitii conficiat. 5
GE. Planissimè. DE. his nunc præmium est, qui recta
    prava faciunt. [gesserimus
GE. Verissimè. DE. ut stultissimè quidem illi ren-
GE. Modò ut hoc consilio possiet discedi, ut istam du-
    cat.
DE. Etiamne id dubium est? GE. haud scio hercle, ut
    homo est, an mutet animum.
DE. Hem mutet autem? GE. nescio: verùm, si for-
    te, dico. 10
DE. Ita faciam, ut frater censuit; ut uxorem ejus huc
    adducam, [venturam.
Cum istâ ut loquatur. tu Geta ibi: prænuncia hanc
GE. Argentum inventum estPhædriæ: de jurgio siletur:
Provisum est, ne in præsentiâ hæc hinc abeat: quid
    nunc porro?
Quid fiet? in eodem luto hæsitas: vorsuram solves, 15
Geta: præsens quod fuerat malum, in diem abiit.
    plagæ crescunt, [edocebo.
Nisi prospicis. nunc hinc domum ibo, ac Phanium
Nequid vereatur Phormionem, aut ejus orationem.

*accipere injuriam ab illo? etiam argentum est ultro objectum, ut sit illi qui vivat; dum conficiat aliquid aliud flagitii. GE. Planissime. DE. Est nunc præmium his, qui faciunt recta prava. GE. Verissime. DE. Ut stultissime quidem gesserimus rem illi. GE. Modo ut possit discedi hoc consilio, ut ducat istam. DE. Etiamne id dubium est? GE. Hercle haud scio, ut est homo, an mutet animum. DE. Hem, mutet autem? GE. Nescio: verum dico, si forte: DE. Faciam ita, ut frater censuit: ut adducam, uxorem ejus huc, ut loquatur cum ista. Tu, Geta, abi: prænuncia illi, hanc esse venturam. GE. Argentum est inventum*

*Phædriæ: siletur de jurgio: provisum est ne hæc Phænium abeat hinc in præsentiâ: quid nunc porro? Quid fiet? hæsitas in eodem luto: solves versuram Geta: malum quod fuerat, præsens abiit in diem: plagæ crescunt nisi prospicis. Nunc ibo hinc domum, ac edocebo Phanium, ne quid vereatur Phormionem, aut orationem ejus, Nausistrata.*

***ANNOTATIONS.***

" fugit, videtur se prodere, ac velle capi:
" qui injuria accepta forum vitat nummos
" numerando, et presentem jacturam facit,
" et alteram injuriam invitat. Ita nuptias,
" et lites, et Phormionem fugere debeba-
" mus, ne nos ultro majori malo mulctare-
" mus."

8. *Modo ut hoc consilio possiet discedi.* That
is, *modo ut Phormio hac pecunia abduci possit, ut eam ducat.* Cic. ad Atticum, Lib.
II. *Si possum discedere ne causa optima in
senatu pereat.* That is, says *Aldus* upon the
Place, *si possum consequi,* and quotes this of
*Terence* as a similar Expression.

15 *Vosuram solves.* In some Copies we
meet with *vorsura,* and this Reading is generally approved by the Criticks. Est autem ( says *Westerhovius* ) *vorsura solvere,
debitori dissolvere pecunia aliunde fœnori accepta, ita ut creditor quidem mutetur, sed
debitum maneat,* Cic. Att. V. 15. *Ut verear, ne illud, quod tecum permutavi, versura
mihi solvendum sit.* Hic translate dicitur de
eo, qui cum expedire se conatur, in eodem
tamen hæret luto. Sed *versuram facere est
pecuniam fœnori accipere, mutuum accipere
sub usuris,* ut ex pluribus Ciceronis locis
evidentur apparet.

18 *Ne quid vereatur Phormionem, aut ejus
orationem. Ejus* here is not to be understood
of *Phormio,* but of *Nausistrata:* She was
to be sent to *Phany,* to reconcile her to
the Proposal of the Match with *Phormio.
Geta* justly apprehends, that such a Discourse might alarm her, and therefore runs
before to warn her that she has nothing to
fear from it. This makes way for his overhearing all that passes between her and *Chremes,* and makes all the remaining Parts of
the Play hang well together.

ACTUS

## ACT V.  SCENE II.

### ARGUMENT.

Nausistrata *complains of her Husband's Negligence in the*
*Management of his private Affairs:*

DEMIPHO, NAUSISTRATA, CHREMES.

*Dem.* COME, *Nausistrata*; shew here a little of your wonted Art;
keep the Girl in good Humour with us, and prevail upon
her to do voluntarily what we would have her.

*Nauf.* I will.

*Dem.* Help me with your Eloquence on this Occasion, as but just
now you have done with your Purse.

*Nauf.* I do it with Pleasure; but truly, Brother, 'tis less in my
Power than it ought to be, thro' my Husband's ill Management.

*Dem.* How so?

*Nauf.* Because he takes no proper care of the Estate so industriously acquir'd by my Father: He made two Talents a Year, with
ease, of these Farms.   Bless me, what difference there often is betwixt Man and Man!

*Dem.* Two Talents, pray!

*Nauf.* Yes indeed, two Talents, and in much worse Seasons too.

*Dem.* Hy!

*Nauf.* What! do you wonder at it?

*Dem.* Greatly.

*Nauf.* Would I had been born a Man, I'd have shewn——

*Dem.* I know it well.

*Nauf.* In what manner——

*Dem.* Spare yourself, pray, that you may be able to encounter the
young Woman, who else may perhaps be an Overmatch for you.

*Nauf.* I'll do as you say; but I see my Husband coming out from
your House.

*Chr.* O, *Demipho,* is the Money paid away yet?

*Dem.* It was done directly.

*Chr.* I'm sorry for it.   Ha, there's my Wife, I had almost said
too much.

*Dem.* Why sorry, *Chremes?*

*Chr.* Nothing; 'tis very well.

*Dem.* What have you done? Have you told her yet why we bring
your Wife to her?

*Chr.* I have

*Dem.* What says she then?

*Chr.* She can't be persuaded to it.

*Dem.* Why can't she?                                                    *Chr.*

### ANNOTATIONS.

We have seen before, that *Demipho* had | that she would go and reconcile *Phæ-*
gone in to *Nausistrata,* with the Request | the Match with *Phormio.*   In consequence
                                                                                          of

# ACTUS V. SCENA II.

### ARGUMENTUM.

*Nausistrata conqueritur de mariti negligentia in augenda re
familiari.*

DEMIPHO, NAUSISTRATA, CHREMES.

<table>
<tr><td>

A Gedum, ut soles, Nausistrata, fac illa ut placetur
    nobis;
Ut suâ voluntate id, quod est faciundum, faciat. NA.
    faciam.                     [tulata es.
DE. Parite nunc operâ me adjuves, ac re dudum opi-
NA. Factum volo: ac pol minu' queo viri culpâ, quam
    me dignum est            [ta indiligenter
DE. Quid autem? NA. quia pol mei patris bene par-
Tutatur: nam ex his prædiis talenta argenti bina  6
Statim capiebat. vir viro quid præstat! DE. bina quæso?
NA. Ac rebus vilioribu' multo, tamen duo talenta.
    DE. hui!                [me natam vellem:
NA. Quid hæc videntur? DE. Scilicet. NA. virum
Ego ostenderem. DE. certò scio. NA. quo pacto——
DE. parce sodes,                      10
Ut possis cum illâ; ne te adolescens mulier defetiget.
NA. Faciam, ut jubes: sed meum virum abs te exire
    video. CH. hem, Demipho,     [nollem datum.
Jam illi datum est argentum? DE. curavi illico. CH.
Hei, video uxorem: penè plus, quam sat erat. DE.
    cur nolles, Chremes?
CH. Jam rectè. DE. quid tu? ecquid locutus cum istâ
    es, quamobrem hanc ducimus?     15
CH. Transegi. DE. quid ait tandem? CH. abduci non
    potest. DE. quî non potest?

</td><td>

ORDO.

DE. A Gedum; Nausi-
strata, ut soles, fac
ut illa placetur no-
bis: ut faciat id
quod est faciundum
sua voluntate. NA.
Faciam. DE. Nunc
pariter adjuves me
opera, ac dudum opi-
tulata es re. NA.
Veib factum: ac pol
minus queo, quam est
dignum me, culpâ
viri. DE. Quid au-
tem? NA. Quia pol
indiligenter . tutatur
bene parta mei pa-
tris: nam statim ca-
piebat bina talenta
argenti ex his præ-
diis. Quid vir præ-
stat viro! DE.
Quæso bina? NA.
Ac rebus multo vili-
oribus, tamen capie-
bat duo talenta. DE.
Hui. NA. Quid, on
hæc videntur mi-
randa? DE. Scili-
cet. NA. Vellem me
natam viram: ego
ostenderem. DE. Scio

</td></tr>
</table>

certo. NA. Quo pacto---DE. Parce sodes, ut possis loqui cum illa, ne adolescens mulier defetiget te;
NA. Faciam, ut jubes; sed video meum virum exire abs te. CH. Hem, Demipho, an argentum est
jam datum illi? DE. Curavi illico. CH. Nollem datum. Hei, video uxorem: pene dixi plus, quàm
erat sat. DE. Cur nolles. Chreme? CH. Jam recte est. DE. Quid tu? Ecquid locutus es cum
istâ, quamobrem ducimus hanc? CH. Transegi. DE. Quid ait tandem?, CH. Non potest abduci.
DE. Qui non potest?

## ANNOTATIONS.

of this they are seen here coming out together, and *Demipho* is urging *Nausistrata*
to exert all her Art and Eloquence. Mean-
time *Chremes* joins them, who, now appriz'd
that *Phany* was his own Daughter, is hastening to prevent the Money's being given
away; but finding that done already, urges
*Demipho* to think no more of separating
*Antipho* and his new Bride. Hence a very
pleasant Conversation arises, while *Chremes*
on the one hand is endeavouring to make his
Brother understand him, and *Demipho* on
the other wonders at his sudden Change of
Mind. At last, after dismissing *Nausistrata*,
the whole Affair is clear'd up.

  3 *Ac redudum opitulata es.* This, no doubt,
respects the thirty *Minæ* which *Demipho* pretended to have borrowed of his Brother, to
discharge *Phormio*; for *dudum* does not always imply a remote Time, but often refers
to what is done but lately.

  7 *Statim*, h. e. *ita singulis annis ut
nunquam minus*, says *Westerhovius*. *Donatus*
explains it *perpetuo, æqualiter, et quasi uno
flatu.* It seems to import the same, as when
we say, with ease, without difficulty.

*Chr.* Becaufe they love one another.

*Dem.* What's that to us?

*Chr.* A great deal. Befides, I have found that fhe's our Relation.

*Dem.* How! Are you mad?

*Chr.* You'll find it fo, I don't fpeak at random; I have recollected her.

*Dem.* Are you in your Senfes?

*Nauf.* Nay, pray beware of injuring your Kinfwoman.

*Dem.* She is not.

*Chr.* Don't fay fo: her Father went by another Name, that was the occafion of your Miftake.

*Dem.* Did fhe not know her Father then?

*Chr.* She did.

*Dem.* Why did fhe call him by another Name?

*Chr.* Will you never yield to what I fay, nor underftand me?

*Dem.* If you fay nothing———

*Chr.* You ruin all.

*Nauf.* I wonder what this can be.

*Dem.* Upon my Life I don't know.

*Chr.* Would you know? As I hope for the Protection of Heaven, fhe has not a nearer-Relation in the World than are you and I.

*Dem.* Good Gods! Let us all go to her together. I want, one way or other, to be refolved in this.

*Chr.* Ah!

*Dem.* What's the Matter?

*Chr.* Have I fo little Credit with you then?

*Dem.* Would you have me believe you? Would you have me fubmit to this without farther Examination? Well, let it be fo. But fay, what's to be done with our Friend's Daughter?

*Chr.* She'll do well enough.

*Dem.* Muft we drop her then?

*Chr.* Why not?

*Dem.* And keep this Girl?

*Chr.* Yes.

*Dem.* Then, *Naufiftrata*, you may go home when you will.

*Nauf.* I think indeed 'tis much the better Refolution, that you keep her, than what you firft propofed; for fhe feem'd to me, when I faw her, to be very much of a Gentlewoman.

*Dem.* What can be the Meaning of this?

*Chr.* Has fhe fhut the Door yet?

*Dem.* Yes.

*Chr.* O *Jupiter!* The Gods certainly befriend us: I find 'tis my Daughter that is married to your Son.

*Dem.* Ha! How can that be?

*Chr.* This is not a proper Place to tell you.          *Dem.*



[19] *Redi mecum in memoriam.* I have recollected myfelf. This is the Senfe that most obviously occurs, tho' fome explain it as an Admonition to *Demipho* to recollect himfelf.

CH. Quia uterque utrique est cordi. DE. quid istuc no-
  stra? CH. magni. præter hæc,
Cognatam comperi esse nobis. DE. quid? deliras? CH.
  sic erit:                              [sati' ne sanus es?
Non temere dico: redi mecum in memoriam. DE.
NA. Au, obsecro, cave, ne in cognatam pecces. DE.
  non est. CH. ne naga:                                  20
Patris nomen aliud dictum est: hoc tu errasti. DE.
  non norat patrem?                      [concedes mihi?
CH. Norat: DE. cur aliud dixit? CH. nunquamne hodie
Neque intellegis? DE. si tu nil narras? CH. perdis:
  NA. miror quid hoc fiet.              [servet Jupiter,
DE. Equidem hercle nescio. CH. vin' scire? at ita me
Ut propior illi, quàm ego sum, ac tu, homo nemo est.
  DE. Dii vostram fidem!                                 25
Eamus ad ipsam unà omnes nos: aut scire, aut nescire
  hoc volo. CH. ah.
DE. Quid est? CH. itane parum mihi fidem esse apud
  te? DE. vin' me hoc credere?                [illà filia.
Vin' satis quæsitum mihi istuc esse? age, fiat. quid?
Amici nostri quid futurum est? CH. recte. DE. hanc
  igitur mittimus?
CH. Quidni? DE. illa maneat? CH. sic. DE. ire
  igitur tibi licet, Nausistrata                         30
NA. Sic pol commodius esse in omnes arbitror, quam
  ut cœperas,                                        [mihi.
Manere hanc: nam perliberalis visa est, cùm vidi,
DE. Quid istuc negoti est? CH. jamne operuit ostium?
DE. jam. CH. ô Jupiter,                     [filio. DE. hem,
Di nos respiciunt: gnatum inveni nuptam cum tuo
Quo pacto id potuit? CH. non satis tutus est ad nar-
  randum hic locus.                                      35

CH. Quia uterque est cordi utrique. DE. Quid istuc refert nostra? CH. Magni: præter hæc, comperi eum esse cognatam nobis. DE. Quid? Deliras? CH. Sic erit: non dica tibi: redi in memoriam mecum. DE. Ejne satis sanus? NA. Au, obsecro, cave ne pecces in cognatam. DE. Non est cognata. CH. Ne nega: nomen patris est dictum aliud: tu erravisti hoc. DE. An illa non noverat patrem? CH. Noverat. DE. Cur dixit aliud? CH. Nunquamne concedes mihi hodie? neque intellegis? DE. Si tu narras nil? CH. Perdis. NA. Miror quid hoc sit. DE. Hercle equidem nescio. CH. Visne scire? At ita Jupiter servet me, ut nemo homo est propior illi, quam ego sum, ac tu. DE. Dii vostram fidem! omnes nos eamus una ad ipsam: volo aut scire, aut nescire hoc. CH. Ah. DE. Quid est? CH. Itane fidem esse parum mihi apud te? DE. Vis-

ne me credere hoc? Visne istuc esse satis quæsitum mihi? age, fiat. Quid? quid est futurum de illa filia nostri amici? CH. Recte. DE. Igitur mittimus hanc? CH. Quidni? DE. Illa maneat? CH. Sic. DE. Igitur Nausistrata licet tibi ire. NA. Pol, sic arbitror esse commodius in omnes, hanc manere, quam ut cœperas: nam visa est mihi perliberalis, cum vidi, eam. DE. Quid negotii istuc? CH. Jamne operuit ostium? DE. Jam. CH. O Jupiter! DE. Dii respiciunt nos: inveni gnatam nuptam cum tuo filio. DE. Hem, quo pacto id potuit fieri? CH. Hic locus non est satis tutus ad narrandum.

## ANNOTATIONS.

himself. In this Case we must suppose, that *Chremes* means to signify how the Affair stood to his Brother, but by such obscure Hints as his Wife might not understand. Hence he says: Reflect a little with me; *i. e.* call to mind what has pass'd between us. Imagining that perhaps *Demipho* might by this be led to suspect what had happened. But the Thing was too remote from his Apprehension for him ever to take any such Hint, and therefore he is but the more aston.shed at *Chremes*'s Behaviour.

30 *Ire igitur tibi licet, Nausistrata.* As they had concluded to let things continue as they were without any Alteration, they had no farther occasion for *Nausistrata,* whose Service to prepare *Phany* for the Match with *Phormio,* must of course drop. The Poet contrives therefore to dismiss her, that *Chremes* might be at full liberty to let his Brother into the real Secret;

*Dem.* Go in then.

*Chr.* Hark-ye, I would not have even our Sons to know of this.

### ANNOTATIONS.

**36** *Ne filii quidem nostri hoc resciscant, volo.* *Chremes* appears thus anxious to keep this matter from his Wife, to prepare for the two last Scenes of the Play, in which *Phormio* threatens a Discovery to her, and at last actually makes it.

---

# ACT V. SCENE III.

### ARGUMENT.

*Antipho expresses his Joy at* Phædria's *having set his Mistress at liberty; but laments his own Fate, to be involved in Misfortunes, whence he could not extricate himself.*

### ANTIPHO.

HOwever my own Affairs go, I'm glad my Brother's have succeeded to his Wish. How wise it is, to give way only to Passions that can be gratified at a small Expence, even when things run cross! *Phædria,* as soon as he got the Money, was releas'd from all Care. I can contrive no method to rid myself of my present Fears. While this remains a secret, I am in perpetual Anxiety; if it be discover'd, I shall be disgraced; nor could I bear to go home, but for the small Hope I have of still retaining her. But where can I find *Geta,* that I may know of him, what will be the most proper time to meet my Father?

### ANNOTATIONS.

Here *Antipho* again makes his Appearance, reflecting on the different Situation of his own Affairs, from those of his Frend *Phædria.* He rejoices at his Friend's Success, but can't avoid repining at his own Fate in having thus subjected him to Misfortunes, that he found it so difficult to extricate himself from. However, he comforts himself in the best manner he can with the small Hopes that still remain of his being able to get the better of all these threatning Disasters.

¹ *Fratri obtigisse.* They were not really Brothers, but Brothers Sons. Cousin *Germans* are, however, by *Latin* Authors often called *fratres patrueles,* and sometimes simply *fratres.*

⁶ *Quin, si hoc celetur, in metu.* He means his

---

# ACT V. SCENE IV.

### ARGUMENT.

*Phormio tells how the Money had been paid down to the Cockbawd, and that, as now every thing had succeeded to his Wish, he intended to indulge himself a little.*

### PHORMIO, ANTIPHO.

*Phormio.* I Have received the Money, paid it to the Bawd, brought away the Wench; and put *Phædria* in possession of her

as

### ANNOTATIONS.

While *Antipho* is in this musing way, *Phormio* comes up to him; but very differently affected, and exulting in the Success of his Schemes. They enter into Conversation about

Dε. At tu intro abi. Cн. heus, ne filii quideni noſtri hoc reſciſcant, volo!

Dε. At tu abi intro.
Cн. Heus, volo ut ne noſtri quidem filii reſciſcant hoc.

---

# ACTUS V. SCENA III.

## ARGUMENTUM.

*Antipho redemptam Phædriæ amicam gratulatur; ſeque involu-*
*tam his malis queritur, unde expediri nequeat.*

### ANTIPHO.

LÆtu' ſum, ut ut meæ res ſeſe habent, fratri obti-
giſſe quod volt.
Quàm ſcitum eſt, ejuſmodi parare in animo cupiditates,
Quas, cùm res adverſæ ſient, paulo mederi poſſis!
Hic ſimul argentum repperit, curâ ſeſe expedivit:
Ego nullo poſſum remedio me evolvere ex his turbis, 5
Quin, ſi hoc celetur, in metu; ſin pateſit, in probro ſim.
Neque me domum nunc reciperem, ni mihi eſſet ſpes
oſtenta    [ut
Hujuſce habendæ. ſed ubinam Getam invenire poſſum,
Rogem, quod tempus conveniundi patris me capere ju-
beat?

ORDO.

UT ut meæ res habent ſeſe, ſum latus id obtigiſſe fratri, quod vult. Quam ſcitum eſt parare ejuſmodi cupiditates in animo, quas poſſis mederi paulo, cum res ſint adverſæ! Hic ſimul repperit argentum, expedivit ſeſe curâ: ego poſſum evolvere me ex his turbis nullo remedio; quin ſim in metu, ſi hoc celetur; ſin pateſit, ſim in probro: neque nunc reciperem me domum, ni ſpei habendæ hujuſce eſſet oſtenta mihi. Sed ubinam poſſum invenire Getam, ut rogem, quod tempus conveniundi patris jubeat me capere?

## ANNOTATIONS.

his being in league with *Phormio* to bring about his own Marriage. So long as this was conceived to be mere Force and Conſtraint, his Father, it was likely, would not acqu-eſce. So that he muſt remain in perpetual Fear, and ſhould he openly avow the Part he had in it, and that he could not bear to be ſepa-rated from his Wife, this would expoſe him to Reproach and Shame.

7 *Ni mihi eſſet ſpes oſtenta.* This refers to the Hopes that *Geta* had given him of *Phormio's* being able to break off his En-gagement with the old Men, and to keep things on the preſent footing. However faint theſe Hopes might be, *Antipho* is willing to encourage them; for we are glad of every flattering Circumſtance that ſaves us from abſolute Deſpair.

---

# ACTUS V. SCENA IV.

## ARGUMENTUM.

*Adnumeratam eſſe lenoni pecuniam narrat Phormio: &, quaſi*
*re beni geſta, nunc ſe curaturum cuticulam.*

### PHORMIO, ANTIPHO.

ARgentum accepi, tradidi lenoni: abduxi mulierem:

ORDO.

Pн. ACcepi argentum, tradidi lenoni: ab-duxi mulierem:

## ANNOTATIONS.

about *Phædria*, but are ſoon interrupted by *Geta*, who appears with an Air of Joy and

Triumph, at the good Fortune which had befallen his Maſter, whom he is therefore running

us his own, for she's now no longer a Slave.   One thing yet remains, which I must bring about ; and that is, to get leave of the old Men, to go and tope it a little, for I am resolved to spend these few Days merrily.

*Ant.* But here is *Phormio!* What say'st ?

*Phorm.* What !

*Ant.* What's *Phædria* upon now ? How does he propose to exhaust his Stock of Love ?

*Phorm.* He's going in his turn to act your Part.

*Ant.* What Part ?

*Phorm.* To shun his Father ; and begs, in the mean time, you'd act his, and plead his Cause for him, for he's to take a Glass at my House.   I'll pretend to the old Men, that I'm going to *Sunium* to the Fair, to buy the Girl that *Geta* spoke to them of lately, lest, if they see me not here, they may fancy, perhaps, that I'm spending their Money ; but the Door opens after you.

*Ant.* See who it is that's coming out.

*Phorm.* 'Tis *Geta.*



running to find, that he may communicate it to him,

* *Propria.* That is, as his own Right and Property ; for the Bawd had received his Money,

---

# ACT V.  SCENE V.

### ARGUMENT.

Geta *acquaints* Antipho, *that* Phany *had been discovered to be the Daughter of his Uncle* Chremes.

#### GETA, ANTIPHO, PHORMIO.

*Geta.* O Fortune ! O happy Fortune ! with what Favours, how suddenly too, have you made this Day overflow to my Master *Antipho !*

*Ant.* What can this be he is talking of ?

*Geta.* And delivered us, his Friends, from all our Fears ? But why do I linger ? Why don't I throw my Cloak over my Shoulder, and hasten to find him, that he may know what has happen'd ?

*Ant.* Do you comprehend what he says ?

*Phorm.* Do you ?
                                                              *Ant.*



While *Antipho* and *Phormio* are in difcourfe together ; *Geta* comes out with an Air of Joy and Triumph.  He had been fent by *Demipho,* to let *Phany* know that *Nausistrata* was coming to fee her.  But before that, *Chremes* had feen the Nurfe, and been led by her to his Daughter's Apartment. When *Geta,* therefore, comes to deliver his Meffage, he finds there is no Admittance. This raifes his Curiofity, he fteals foftly to the Door, and overhears a great Part of

what paffes between *Chremes* and *Phany.* Overjoy'd at the Difcovery, he runs out in hafte, to find his Mafter, and acquaint him with the good News ; and fo full he is of it, that 'tis fome time before he attends to *Antipho,* who calls feveral times.  The Youth, as is natural to think, is tranfported at the Difcovery, and hurries away with *Geta* to meet the old Men, and have all confirm'd to him.

' *O fortuna, O fors Fortuna.* Fors Fortung, feems

Curavi, propriâ eâ Phædria ut poteretur: nam emissa
    est manu.
Nunc una mihi res etiam restat, quæ est conficiunda,
    otium                              [sumam dies.
A senibus ad potandum ut habeam: nam aliquot hos
AN. Sed Phormio est. quid ais? PH. quid? AN. quid-
    nam nunc facturus Phædria?              5
Quo pacto satietatem amoris ait se velle absumere?
PH. Vicissim partes tuas acturus est. AN. quas? PH.
    ut fugitet patrem:                        [ceres:
Te suas rogavit rursum ut ageres; causam ut pro se di-
Nam potaturus est apud me: ego me ire senibus Sunium
Dicam ad mercatum, ancillulam emtum, dudum quam
    dixit Geta;                              10
Ne, cùm hîc non videant me, conficere credant ar-
    gentum suum.
Sed ostium concrepuit abs te. AN. vide, qui egre-
    diatur. PH. Geta est.

*potaturus apud me. Ego dicam senibus me ire Sunium ad mercatum, emtum ancillulam, quam Geta dudum dixit; ne, cum non videant me hic, credant me conficere suum argentum. Sed ostium concrepuit abs te. AN Vide, qui egrediatur. PH. Est Geta.*

ORDO.

*curavi, ut Phædria potiretur ea propria, nam est emissa manu. Nunc una res etiam restat mihi, quæ est conficiunda, ut habeam otium a senibus ad potandum? nam sumam bis aliquot dies hilariter. AN. sed hic est Phormio. Quid ais? PH. Quid AN. Quidnam est Phædria facturus nunc? Quo pacto ait se velle absumere satietatem amoris? PH. Est acturus tuas partes vicissim. AN. Quas? PH. Ut fugitet patrem. Rogavit te rursum ut suas, ut diceres causam pro se, nam est*

## ANNOTATIONS.

Money, and of consequence had no farther claim to her: his Right was transferred to *Phædria*, who had made her free; as is immediately added, *Nam emissa è manu est.*

---

# ACTUS V. SCENA V.

## ARGUMENTUM.

*Geta Antiphoni nunciat, Phanium inventam esse Chremetis filiam.*

### GETA, ANTIPHO, PHORMIO.

O Fortuna, ô Fors Fortuna, quantis commoditatibus,
    Quàm subito meo hero Antiphoni ope vestrâ hunc
    onerastis diem?                      [exonerastis metu?
AN. Quidnam hic sibi volt? GE. nosque amicos ejus
Sed ego nunc mihi cesso, qui non humerum hunc one-
    ro pallio;
Atque hominem propero invenire, ut hæc, quæ con-
    gerint, sciat?                            5
AN. Num tu intellegis, hic quid narret? PH. num tu?

*qui non onero hunc humerum pallio; atque propero invenire hominem, ut sciat hæc quæ contigerint? AN. Num tu intelligis, quid hic narret? PH. Num tu?*

ORDO.

*GE. O Fortuna, O Fors Fortuna, quantis commoditatibus, quam subito onerastis hunc diem meo hero Antiphoni vestra ope? AN. Quidnam hic vult sibi? GE. Exonerastisque nos amicos ejus metu? Sed ego nunc cesso mihi, ... sciat hæc quæ contigerint?*

## ANNOTATIONS.

seems to have been an Expression of the same import among the *Latins*, as when we say, *O happy Fortune*, and refers to some favourable Turn of Fortune, great and unexpected. | We meet with the same Expression in *Tacitus*, Annal. Lib. 2. where speaking of the publick Honours decreed at *Rome* to *Germanicus*, for his surprising Successes against the *Germans*,

*Ant.* Not a Word.

*Phorm.* Nor I.

*Get.* I'll directly to the Bawd's, they are likely to be there now.

*Ant.* Soho, *Geta!*

*Get.* Lookye there now : is it any thing strange or new to be call'd back, when one's in haste ?

*Ant. Geta.*

*Get.* Say on ; you shan't, with all your Importunity, be able to bring me back.

*Ant.* Will you not stay ?

*Get.* Go, be whipp'd.

*Ant.* That shall be your Portion, you Rascal, if you don't stop immediately.

*Get.* This must be one pretty familiar, it would seem by his Threats. But is it the Man I am looking for, or no ? It is the same.

*Phorm.* (*To* Antipho.) Up to him presently.

*Ant.* What's all this ?

*Get.* O happiest of all Men living ? for, without doubt, *Antipho,* you're the only Favourite of Heaven.

*Ant.* So I would have myself, but pray tell me how I shall believe that it is so ?

*Get.* Will it satisfy you, if I plunge you into a Sea of Joy ?

*Ant.* You kill me *with your Impertinence.*

*Phorm.* Have done with these Promises, and tell us what *good News* you bring.

*Get.* Oh, was you here too, *Phormio !*

*Phorm.* I was : but do you still keep us in Suspense ?

*Get.* Well, hear then : after giving you the Money at the Forum, we went directly home.—My Master, in the mean time, orders me to go to your Wife.

*Ant.* For what ?

*Get.* I omit that, *Antipho,* because 'tis nothing to the present Business. Just as I was going into her Apartment, her Boy *Mida* runs up to me, catches hold of me behind by the Cloak, and pulls me back.

I

## *ANNOTATIONS.*

Germans, he says ; *Fine anni arcus propter ædem Saturni, ob recepta signa cum Varo amissa, ductu Germanici, auspiciis Tiberii ; & ædes Fortis Fortunæ Tiberim juxta, in hortis quos Cæsar dictator populo Romano legaverat ; sacrarium genti Juliæ, effigiesque divo Augusto apud Bovillas, dicantur.* " At the end of " the Year, a triumphal Arch was raised " near the Temple of *Saturn,* as a Monu- " ment for the Recovery of the *Varian* " Eagles, under the Conduct of *Germanicus,* " and the *Auspices* of *Tiberius.*' A Temple " was dedicated to happy Fortune near the " *Tiber,* in the Gardens bequeathed to the " *Roman* People by *Cæsar,* the Dictator. A " Chapel was consecrated to the *Julian* Fa- " mily, and Statues to the deified *Augustus,* " in the Suburbs call'd *Bovillæ.*" To illustrate this still more, I shall subjoin the following Description of Fortune, which may serve as a Comment on the present Expression. *Cic. ad Herenn.* II. 23. *ex Paccvio.*

*Fortunam insanam esse, & cæcam, & brutam, perhibent philosophi.*

*Saxoque illam instare globoso prædicant volubilem :*

*Ideo, quo saxum impulerit sors, cadere eo fortunam autumant.*

*Cæcam*

AN. nil. PH. tantumdem ego.
GE. Ad lenonem hinc ire pergam: ibi nunc sunt. AN.
  heus, Geta. GE. hem tibi...
Num mirum, aut novum est, revocari, cursum cùm in-
  stitueris? AN. Geta. [AN. Non manes? 9
GE. Pergis hercle: nunquam tu odio tuo mé vinces.
GE. Vapula. AN. id quidem tibi jam fiet, nisi resistis,
  verbero. [lum.
GE. Familiariorem oportet esse hunc: minitatur ma-
Sed isne est, quem quæro, an non? ipse est. PH. con-
  gredere actutùm. AN. quid est?
GE. O omnium, quantum est, qui vivunt, homo
  hominum ornatissime:
Nam sine controversiâ ab Diis solus diligere, Antipho.
AN. Ita velim: sed quî istuc credam ita esse, mihi
  dici velim. 15
GE. Satin' est, si te delibutum gaudio reddo? AN.
  enecas. [cedo. GE. oh;
PH. Quin tu hinc pollicitationes aufer, &, quod fers,
Tu quoque hîc aderas, Phormio? PH. aderam: sed
  cessas? GE. accipe, hem. [domum
Ut modò argentum tibi dedimus apud forum, rectà
Sumus profecti: interea mittit herus me ad uxorem
  tuam. 20
AN. Quamobrem? GE. omitto proloqui: nam nihil
  ad hanc rem est, Antipho. [Mida
Ubi in gynæceum ire occipio, puer ad me accurrit
Pone apprehendit pallio, resupinat: respicio: rogo,

*AN. Nil. PH. Tantundem ego. GE. Pergam ire hinc ad lenonem: sunt ibi nunc. AN. Heus, Geta. GE. Hem tibi; num est mirum, aut novum, revocari, cum institueris cursum? AN. Geta. GE. Pergis hercle: tu nunquam vinces me tuo odio. AN. Non manes? GE. Vapula. AN. Id quidem jam fiet tibi, verbero, nisi resistis. GE. Oportet hunc esse familiariorem: minitatur malum. Sed esne is, quem quæro, an non? est ipse. PH. Congredere actutum. AN. Quid est? GE. O homo, ornatissime omnium hominum, quantum est, qui vivunt: nam sine controversia, solus Antipho diligere ab Diis. AN. Velim ita: sed velim dici mihi, qui credam istuc esse ita. GE. Estne satis, si reddo te delibutum gaudio? AN. Enecas. PH. Quin tu aufer pollicitationes*

*hinc, & cedo, quod fers. GE. Oh, tu quoque aderas hic, Phormio? PH. Aderam: sed cessas? GE. Hem, accipe. Ut modo dedimus argentum tibi apud forum, sumus profecti domum rectà: interea herus mittit me ad tuam uxorem. AN. Quamobrem? GE. Omitto proloqui, nam est nihil ad hanc rem, Antipho. Ubi occipio ire in gynæceum, puer Mida accurrit ad me: apprehendit pone pallio, resupinat: respicio: rogo,*

## ANNOTATIONS.

*Cæcam ob eam rem esse iterant, quia nihil cernat, quo sese applicet.*
*Insanum autem aiunt, quia atrox, incerta, instabilisque sit.*
*Brutam, quia dignum, atque indignum nequeat internoscere.*

8 *Num mirum, aut novum est, &c.* It was a common thing both at *Athens* and *Rome*, when a Servant was seen running in haste, to call out to him, on purpose to amuse and detain him. This, it would seem, was a Piece of fashionable Mirth and Waggery among the Vulgar. They diverted themselves with the Fancy, that when they went home, they should find their Master provoked against them for their Slowness and Delays.

9 *Nunquam tu odio tuo me vinces.* Odium is sometimes used to express Importunity, Teazing, or a Perseverance in disagreeable Talk. Thus, *Plaut. Asin.* II. 4. 40.
  *Jam hic me abegerit suo odio.*
And *Horace*, Sat. Lib. I. 7. 6.
  *Durus homo, atque odio quiposset vincere regem.*
In like manner, *Cicero, Attic.* 4. 2. *Sed tamen, cum horas tres fere dixisset, odio & strepitu senatus coactus est aliquando perorare.*
18 *Tu quoque hic aderas, Phormio?* The Poet artfully makes *Geta* trifle and procrastinate. This begets Eagerness and Impatience; besides the thing itself is extremely natural.
22 *Gynæceum.* Γυναικεῖον, *Sub.* οἴκημα.

I turn about, and afk why he ftops me.  He tells me, he had Orders
to let no one go into his Miftrefs.  *Sophrona*, fays he, juft now brought
in *Chremes*, your Mafter's Brother, and he is, at prefent, with them
in her Chamber.  When I heard this, I ftole foftly to the Door on
tiptoe; came clofe to it; ftood *hufh*: held my Breath: laid my Ear
*to the Key-hole*: and ftood in the moft attentive Pofture thus, catch-
ing every Word.

*Ant.* Excellent, *Geta!*

*Get.* There I heard a moft delightful Tale, that, by *Hercules*, made
me almoft cry out for Joy.

*Ant.* What Tale?

*Get.* What do you think?

*Ant.* I don't know.

*Get.* Indeed, the moft furprizing in the World: your Uncle is
found to be your Wife *Phany*'s Father.

*Ant.* Hah, what do you tell me?

*Get.* He had formerly fome private Converfation with her Mother
at *Lemnos*.

*Phorm.* A meer Dream! how could fhe be ignorant of her own
Father!

*Get.* Be fatisfied, *Phormio*, there's fome Reafon for it; but do you
imagine that I, who ftood without the Door, could underftand every
thing that paffed among them within?

*Ant.* Nay, I remember, indeed, to have heard the fame Story
myfelf.

*Get.* Befides, I will give you a ftill more convincing Proof.  While
I yet ftood there, your Uncle came out, and foon after return'd, and
went in again with your Father: both faid they left you at full Liberty to keep your Wife.  In fhort, I am fent to find you out, and
bring you to them.

*Ant.* Carry me then immediately; why do you linger?

*Get.* It fhall be done.

*Ant.* O my dear *Phormio*, farewel.

*Phorm.* Farewel, *Antipho*.  Let me die, if this be not a lucky Accident! and I heartily rejoice that Fortune has been fo favourable to
them, and, in a manner too, unexpected.  I have now a fine Opportunity offer'd me of bubbling the old Men, and eafing *Phædria* of
his Care about Money, that he mayn't be under the Neceffity of applying to any of his Companions for it.  For this fame Money, tho',
perhaps, it may be given, will yet be given with no good will; but I
have found a way that will do it effectually.  I muft now, therefore,

affume

*A N N O T A T I O N S.*

It fignifies an inner or remote Apartment,
and was call'd alfo *Gynæconitis*.  The following Quotation will ferve to throw fome light
upon this.  " Qvèm Romanorum pudet ux-
" orem ducere in convivium? aut cujus ma-
" terfamilias non primum locum tenet æ-
" dium, atque in celebritate verfatur?
" Quod multo fit aliter in Græcia, nam ne-
" que in convivium adhibetur, nifi propin-
" quorum: neque fedet nifi in interiore par-
" te ædium, quæ Gynæconitis appellatur:
" quo nemo accedit, nifi propinqua cogna-
" tione

Quamobrem retineat me : ait effe vetitum intrò ad he-
   ram accedere :
Sophrona modò fratrem huc, inquit, fenis introduxit
   Chremem.                                    25
Eumque nunc effe intus cum illis. hoc ubi ego audivi,
   ad fores
Sufpenfo gradu placidè ire perrexi : acceffi : aftiti :
Animam compreffi : aurem admovi : ita animum cœ-
   pi attendere,                          [pulcherrimum
Hoc modo fermonem captans. AN. eu, Geta. GE. hîc
Facinus audivi : itaque penè hercle exclamavi gaudio. 30
PH. Quod ? GE. quodnam arbitrare ? AN. nefcio. GE.
   atqui mirificiffimum :                          [hem,
Patruus tuus eft pater inventus Phanio uxori tuæ. AN.
Quid ais ? GE. cum ejus olim confuevit matre in Lem-
   no clanculùm.                          [aliquid credito,
PH. Somnium ! utin' hæc ignoraret fuum patrem ? GE.
Phormio, effe caufæ. fed me cenfen' potuiffe omnia 35
Intellegere extra oftium, intus quæ inter fefe ipfi ege-
   rint ?                                 [imo etiam dabo,
PH. Atque hercle ego quoque illam audivi fabulam. GE.
Quo magi' credas. patruus interea inde huc egreditur
   foras :
Haud multo pòft cum patre idem recipit fe intrò denuo :
Ait uterque tibi poteftatem ejus habendæ fe dare : 40
Denique ego miffus fum, te ut requirerem, atque ad-
   ducerem.                             [ô mi Phormio,
AN. Hem, quin ergo rape me : ceffas ? GE. fecero. AN.
Vale. PH. vale, Antipho. Bène, ita me Dii ament,
   factum : gaudeo,
Tantam fortunam de improvifo effe his datam :
Summa eludendi occafio eft mihi nunc fenes,      45
Et Phædriæ curam adimere argentariam,
Ne cuiquam fuorum æqualium fupplex fiet.
Nam idem hoc argentum, ita ut datum eft ingratiis,
Ei datum erit : hoc quî cogam, re ipsâ repperi.

*baud multo poft, idem denuo recipit fefe intro cum patre : uterque ait fe dare tibi poteftatem haben-
dæ ejus : denique ego fum miffus, ut requirerem te, atque adducerem. AN. Hem, quin ergo rape
me : ceffas ? GE. Fecero. AN. O mi Phormio, vale. PH. Vale, Antipho. Ita Dii ament me,
bene factum : gaudeo, tantam fortunam effe datam bis de improvifo. Nunc fumma occafio eft data
mihi eludendi fenes, & adimere Phædriæ curam argentariam, ne fit fupplex cuiquam fuorum æqualium. Nam idem hoc argentum, ita ut datum eft, erit-datum ei ingratiis : repperi re ipfa, qui
cogam hoc.*

*quamobrem retineat me : ait effe vetitum accedere intro ad heram. Sophrona, inquit modò introduxit Chremem fratrem fenis huc, eumque effe nunc intus cum illis : ubi ego audivi hoc, perrexi ire placide ad fores fufpenfo gradu acceffi : aftiti : compreffi animam : admovi aurem : ita cœpi attendere animum, captans fermonem hoc modo. AN. Eu, Geta. GE. Hic audivi pulcherrimum facinus : itaque hercle penè exclamavi gaudio. PH. Quod? GE. Quodnam arbitrare? AN. Nefcio. GE. Atqui eft mirificiffimum : patruus tuus eft inventus pater tuæ uxori Phanio. AN. Hem, quid ais? GE. Confuevit olim clanculum cum ejus matre in Lemno. PH. Somnium ! utine hæc ignoraret fuum patrem ? GE. Credito, Phormio, effe aliquid caufæ : fed cenfefne me potuiffe intelligere extra oftium, omnia quæ ipfi egerint intus inter fefe ? PH. Atque hercle ego quoque audivi illam fabulam. GE. Imo etiam dubo fignum, quo magis credas. Interea patruus egriditur inde huc foras :*

## ANNOTATIONS.

" tione conjunctus." *Corn. Nepos in Præ-
fatione.*

  29 *Pulcherrimum facinus.* The word *facinus*, tho', for the moft part, it carries the
Idea of fomething bad or difagreeable, yet it
is fometimes ufed in a favourable Senfe. As
in the *Heauton.* Act. 2. Sc. 2. 73. *Non fit
fine periclo facinus magnum & memorabile;* and
*Salluft. Jug. 2. Ingenii egregia facinora, fi-
cuti animæ, immortalia funt.*

  43 *Ingratiis ei datum erit.* Some Copies
read *bis*, viz. as Commentators explain it
                          *fenibus.*

affume a new Face, and a new Behaviour.　But it will be convenient for me to retire hence into this next Alley, and thence fhew myfelf to them, when they come out.　As to the Pretence of going to the Fair, I drop that.



*fenibus.*　But the Senfe is fo obvious and juft according to the other Reading, that it needs . . . ).

not many Reafons to confirm it.　*Phormio* wants to eafe *Phædria* of the Pain of applying

## ACT V.　SCENE VI.

### ARGUMENT.

*The old Men after difcovering who* Phany *was, want to get back their Money of* Phormio, *who refufes to make Reftitution: hence a Quarrel enfues.*

### DEMIPHO, PHORMIO, CHREMES.

*Demipho.* I Return Thanks to the Gods, and deservedly, Brother, that thefe things have turn'd out fo fortunately.　We muft now make what hafte we can to meet with *Phormio*, before he fquanders away the ninety Pounds, that we may recover it of him.

*Phorm.* I'll go and fee if *Demipho*'s at home, that I——

*Dem.* We were coming to you, *Phormio*.

*Phorm.* Upon this fame Affair perhaps.

*Dem.* Yes, indeed.

*Phorm.* I thought fo; but why that? A good Joke truly! Were ye afraid I fhould go back from what I had once promifed? Hark ye: how great foever my Poverty is, I have yet taken care of one thing, never to forfeit my Word.

*Chr.* Is'nt fhe, as I told you, a fine Girl?

*Dem.* She is really.

*Phorm.* And this it what I come to tell you of *Demipho*, that I'm ready: when you pleafe, give me my Wife.　For I poftpon'd every thing elfe, as was fit I fhould, when I underftood that you were fo defirous to have it fo.

*Dem.* But my Brother here diffuades me from giving her; for what, fays



As *Phormio*'s firft Scheme was now compleated, and *Antipho* made perfectly happy, nothing remains, but to make *Phædria* fo too.　He is fo in fome Degree already; his Miftrefs is in his Poffeffion, and the Bawd difcharged: but ftill he has a Money-Affair upon his hands; he knows it muft be reftor'd to the old Men in a few Days, and how to procure it is the Queftion.　This we may fuppofe would give fome Interruption to his Joy.　*Phormio* thinks he has it now in his power to make all fafe on this fide.　From

the late Difcovery he was fatisfied that the old Men would never confent to give him *Phany* according to their firft Propofal.　This was enough for him; he might fafely infift upon their making good the Agreement, and if they refufed to do it, as he knew they would, there was then a Colour for his detaining the Portion.　If that fail'd, his being acquainted with a Secret of fuch Importance to *Chremes*, would, he doubted not, compleat his Wifhes; and then *Phædria* had nothing to difturb him, or interrupt his

Nunc geſtus mihi, voltuſque eſt capiundus novus. 50
Sed hinc concedam in angiporum hunc proxumum :
Inde hiſce oſtendam me, ubi erunt egreſſi foras.
Quò me adſimularam ire ad mercatum, non eo.

*Nunc novus geſtus, novuſque vultus eſt capiendus mihi. Sed concedam hinc in hunc proximum, angiportum: inde oſtendam*

*me hiſce, ubi erunt egreſſi foras. Non eo, quo aſſimulaveram me ire ad mercatum.*

## ANNOTATIONS.

ing to his Friends for Money, and adds the Reaſon for his doing ſo. Becauſe, ſays he, tho' perhaps they may conſent to give it him, yet it will be with Reluctance; whereas I have found a way to ſecure it, without laying him under Obligations to any one.

## ACTUS V. SCENA VI.

### ARGUMENTUM.

*Cognita Phanio, ſenes à Phormione pecuniam repetunt: Phormio negat ſe redditurum: hinc contentio inter eos oritur.*

### DEMIPHO, PHORMIO, CHREMES.

DIIS magnas meritò gratias habeo, atque ago,
Quando evenere hæc nobis, frater, proſpere.
Quantum poteſt, nunc conveniendus Phormio eſt;
Priuſquam dilapidet noſtras triginta minas,
Ut auferamus: PH. Demiphonem, ſi domi eſt, 5
Viſam: ut quod—DE. at nos ad te ibamus, Phormio.
PH. De eadem hac fortaſſe causâ. DE. ita hercle. PH.
credidi.
Quid ad me ibatis? ridiculum: an veremini,
Ne non id facerem, quod recepiſſem ſemel? 9
Heus, quanta quanta hæc mea paupertas eſt, tamen
Adhuc curavi unum hoc quidem, ut mî eſſet fides.
CH. Eſtne ea ita, ut dixi, liberalis? DE. oppidò
PH. Itaque ad vos venio nunciatum, Demipho,
Paratum me eſſe: ubi voltis, uxorem date.
Nam omnes poſthabui mihi res, ita utì par fuit, 15
Poſtquam tantopere id vos velle animum advorteram.
DE. At hic dehortatus eſt me, ne illam tibi darem :

ORDO.

DE. MERITO habeo atque ago magnas gratias Diis, quando hæc evenere proſpere nobis, frater. Phormio eſt nunc conveniendus, quantum poteſt, priuſquam dilapidet noſtras triginta minas, ut auferamus eas. PH. Viſam Demiphonem, ſi eſt domi: ut quod---. DE. At nos ibamus ad te, Phormio. PH. Fortaſſe de hac eadem causâ. DE. Ita hercle. PH. Credidi. Quid ibatis ad me? ridiculum: an veremini, ne non facerem id, quod ſemel in me recepiſſem in me?

*heus, quanta quanta hæc mea paupertas eſt, tamen adhuc curavi hoc unum quidem, ut eſſet mihi fides. CH. Eſtre ea liberalis; ita ut dixi? DE. Oppido. PH. Itaque, Demipho, venio ad vos nunciatum, me eſſe paratum; ubi vultis, date uxorem; nam poſthabui omnes res mihi, ita utì fuit par, poſtquam unimum advorteram vos velle id tantopere. DE. At hic eſt dehortatus me, ne darem illam tibi :*

## ANNOTATIONS.

his Joys. But the Event anſwers not his Expectation. Demipho, who could not think of parting with ſo much Money, encourages his Brother, and violently ſeizes Phormio, to carry him before a Judge. The other, equally reſolute, calls aloud upon Nauſiſtrata, determined to diſcover all to her, and hoping that might occaſion ſome favourable Turn. 12 Eſtne ita ea ut dixi, liberalis? One cannot conceive any thing more happy or juſt, than theſe Words of Chremes. Demipho's Thoughts are wholly taken up how to recover

fays he, will be the Talk among the People, if you fhould do fo? Formerly, when fhe might have been difpofed of with Honour, no attempt was made: and now after a Marriage to force her away, were bafe and ungenerous. In fine, he repeated all the Reafons which you fo lately urg'd againft me.

*Phorm.* You treat me in a very infulting Manner.

*Dem.* How?

*Phorm.* How! Becaufe now I have no hope of marrying the other; for with what Face can I return to her I have fo much flighted?

*Chr.* Say; *Befides I fee that* Antipho *is unwilling to part with her.*

*Dem.* Befides I fee that my Son will not confent to part from her: therefore go *with us* to the Forum, *Phormio,* and order the Money to be paid me back again.

*Phorm.* When I have already paid it all away where it was owing?

*Dem.* What can be done then?

*Phorm.* If you are willing to let me have my Wife according to Agreement, I am ready to take her; but if you had rather fhe fhould remain with you, then 'tis but juft that her Portion remain with me, *Demipho.* For there is no Reafon that I fhould fuffer on your account, when, out of regard to your Honour I broke off another Match, where the Fortune offer'd me was equal.

*Dem.* Go be hang'd, you Rafcal, with your vain Rodomontades. Do you ftill imagine that I'm a Stranger to you and your ways?

*Phorm.* This is infupportable.

*Dem.* Would you marry this Girl, might you have her?

*Phorm.* Try me.

*Dem.* That my Son may cohabit with her at your Houfe; that was your Plot, *I prefume.*

*Phorm.* Pray, what's that you fay?

*Dem.* But do you give me my Money.

*Phorm.* Nay truely, do you give me my Wife.

*Dem.* Come before a Judge.

*Phorm.* Before a Judge! If you continue thus troublefome—

*Dem.* What will you do?

*Phorm.* Do? You think, perhaps, that I have only portionlefs Girls for my Clients; but I'd have you to know that I have thofe with Portions too.

*Chr.*

*ANNOTATIONS.*

cover the Money, and *Phormio* is no lefs intent upon his Scheme of retaining it; but *Chremes,* who was juft come from his Daughter, and had now firft feen her after a long Abfence, is reprefented with all the Fondnefs of a Father. He is regardlefs of their Difcourfe, nor can attend to any other Impreffions, than thofe fhe had left, and, impatient to know whether his Brother entertains Sentiments of her equally favourable with himfelf, puts the Queftion to him.

There is another Piece of Art in *Terence's* Management, which every Reader, perhaps, will not attend to; and that is, the Care he takes to fatisfy us of *Phany's* Beauty, for without this to recompenfe the Want of Birth and Fortune, *Antipho's* Behaviour muft appear very abfurd and inexcufable. It is not, therefore, enough, that we have the Teftimony of the young Men in the former Part of the Play; their Judgment might be influenced by Paffion, the Fire of Youth, and

*Pity*

Nam qui erit rumor populi, inquit, si id feceris?
Olim cùm honestè potuit, tum non est data:
Nunc viduam extrudi, turpe est: ferme eadem omnia,
Quæ tute dudum coràm me incusaveras:    21
PH. Satis superbe inluditis me. DE. quî? PH. rogas?
Quia ne alteram quidem illam potero ducere.
Nam quo redibo ore ad eam, quam contemserim?
CH. Tum autem Antiphonem video ut sese amittere 25
Invitum eam, inque. DE. tum autem video filium
Invitum sane mulierem ab se amittere.
Sed transi sodes ad forum, atque illud mihi
Argentum rursum jube rescribi, Phormio.
PH. Quodne ego descripsi porro illis, quibu' debui?    30
DE. Quid igitur fiet? PH. si vis mihi uxorem dare,
Quam despondisti, ducam: sin est, ut velis
Manere illam apud te, dos hîc maneat, Demipho:
Nam non est æquom me propter vos decipi;
Cùm ego vestri honoris causâ repudium alteræ    35
Remiserim, quæ dotis tantumdem dabat.
DE. I in malam rem hinc cum istac magnificentiâ,
Fugitive: etiam nunc credis te ignorarier,    [res,
Aut tua facta adeo? PH. irritor. DE. tunc hanc ducce-
Si tibi daretur? PH. fac periclum. DE. ut filius    40
Cum illâ habitet apud te, hoc vestrum consilium fuit.
PH. Quæso, quid narras? DE. quin tu mihi argen-
tum cedo.
PH. Imo verò uxorem tu cedo. DE. in jus ambula.
PH. In jus? enimvero, si porro esse odiosi pergitis;
DE. Quid facies? PH. egone? vos me indotatis modò
Patrocinari fortasse arbitramini:    46

*æquum est me decipi propter vos: cum ego causa vestri honoris remiserim repudium alteræ, quæ dabat tantundem dotis. DE. I hinc in malam rem, fugitive, cum istac magnificentia: etiam nunc credis te, aut tua adeo facto ignorari? PH. Irritor. DE. Tune duceres hanc, si daretur tibi? PH. Fac periculum. DE. Hoc suit vestrum consilium, ut filius habitet cum illa, apud te. PH. Quæso, quid narras? DE. Quin tu cedo argentum mihi. PH. Imo vero, cedo tu uxorem. DE. Ambula in jus. PH. In jus? enimvero, si porro pergitis esse odiosi; DE. Quid facies? PH. Egone? vos fortasse arbitramini me patrocinari modo indotatis:*

# ANNOTATIONS.

Pity for a young Girl they saw in Distress. But here it is confirm'd from the Mouth of a sedate cool old Man. And if we look back into the second Scene of this Act, we shall meet with another Confirmation of it from *Nausistrata,* Ver. 31.

*Sic, pol commodius esse in omnes arbitror,*
    *quam ut cæperas,*
*Manere hanc. Nam perliberalis visa est,*
    *quum vidi, mihi.*

It is not without Design, the Poet makes every one who sees her give this Testimony to her Charms. It disposes the Spectator to favour *Antipho,* whose Character *Terence* meant should be that of a fond, tender, and passionate Lover.

29 *Argentum rursum jube rescribi. Scribere, rescribere, perscribere,* were Terms used chiefly in Dealings that regarded Money. *Scribere,* was to take up or borrow any Sum of Money; *rescribere,* to pay it back again; and *perscribere,* to employ it promiscuously in the common Uses of Life, Business, or Traffic. For all these things were generally managed

*Chr.* What's that to us?

*Phorm.* Nothing. But I know a certain Lady of this Town, whofe Husband——

*Chr.* Hah!

*Dem.* What's the matter?

*Phorm.* Had another *Wife* at *Lemnos.*

*Chr.* I'm ruin'd.

*Phorm.* And had a Daughter by her, whom he brings up privately.

*Chr.* I'm bury'd.

*Phorm.* This I'll go tell her of immediately.

*Chr.* For Heaven's fake don't.

*Phorm.* Oh, ho! What are you the Man?

*Dem.* What a Jeft he makes of us!

*Chr.* We difcharge you.

*Phorm.* A mere Story!

*Chr.* What would you have? we forgive you the Money you've got of ours.

*Phorm.* I hear: but why then do you trifle fo fcandaloufly with me, by thefe childifh filly Speeches! I won't, I will: I will, I won't again: keep it, give it me back: what you fay one Moment, you contradict the next: what now you refolve to do, you are for undoing again.

*Chr.* How in the World could he know this?

*Dem.* I can't imagine: but I'm certain I told nobody of it.

*Chr.* 'Tis quite aftonifhing, as I hope to live.

*Phorm.* I have nettled them.

*Dem.* The Deuce! Shall the Rafcal carry off fuch a Sum of Money, and laugh at us to our very Face? I'd fooner die, by *Hercules,* than fuffer it! Summon all your Refolution and Prefence of Mind. You fee that this Slip of yours has got abroad, nor will it now be poffible to conceal it long from your Wife: 'tis therefore better to tell her ourfelves, what fhe is likely foon to hear from others; and then we may revenge ourfelves on this Rogue, as we pleafe.

*Phorm.* By *Jupiter,* if I don't look out fharp, I'm undone, they make to me with an Air fo ftern and threatning.

*Chr.* (*To* Demipho.) But I doubt fhe'll never be brought to forgive me.

*Dem.* Fear nothing; I'll make all up between you, depend on it,

*Chremes;*

ANNOTATIONS.

managed by Writing, much in the manner of our Orders upon Bankers, or Bills of Exchange. It is obferved by Criticks, that the three laft Scenes of this Act, are the moft finifhed and beautiful of the whole Play, and yet *Guyetus* is fo far diffatisfied with them, that he is for retrenching them altogether. But his Criticifm is approved by very few.

41 *Etiam detetis folco.* Some think that

*Phormio* has here in his Eye *Naufiftrata,* the Wife of *Chremes,* whofe Part he was refolved to take againft her Hufband, who had injured her. But there is no Neceffity for fuch Refinement: *Phormio* talks the natural Language of a Man, who, thinking himfelf undervalued, wants to appear confiderable, without confining his Thoughts to any particular Inftance.

65 *Vides*

Etiam dotatis soleo. CH. quid id nostra? PH. nihil.
Hic quandam noram, cujus vir uxorem—CH. hem.
　　DE. quid est?
PH. Lemni habuit aliam. CH. nullus sum. PH. ex
　　quâ filiam
Suscepit: & eam clàm educit. CH. sepultu' sum.　50
PH. Hæc adeo ego illi jam denarrabo. CH. obsecro,
Ne facias. PH. oh, tun' is eras? DE. ut ludos facit!
CH. Missum te facimus. PH. fabulæ. CH. quid vis
　　tibi?
Argentum quod habes, condonamus te. PH. audio:
Quid vos, malùm, ergo me sic ludificamini,　55
Inepti vostrâ puerili sententiâ?
Nolo, volo: volo, nolo rursum: cape, cedo:
Quod dictum, indictum est: quod modò erat ratum,
　　irritum est.
CH. Quo pacto, aut unde hæc hic rescivit? DE. nescio;
Nisi, me dixisse nemini, certò scio.　60
CH. Monstri; ita me Dii ament, simile. PH. injeci
　　scrupulum. DE, hem,
Hiccine ut à nobis hoc tantum argenti auferat,
Tam apertè irridens? emori hercle satius est.
Animo virili præsentique ut sis, para.
Vides peccatum tuum esse elatum foras,　65
Neque jam id celare posse te uxorem tuam:
Nunc quod ipsa ex aliis auditura sit, Chreme,
Id nosmet indicare placabilis est.
Tum hunc impuratum poterimus nostro modo
Ulcisci. PH. at at, nisi mihi prospicio, hæreo:　70
Hi gladiatorio animo ad me affectant viam.
CH. At vereor, ut placari possit. DE. bono animo es:
Ego redigam vos in gratiam? hôc fretus, Chreme,

*soleo etiam patrocinari dotatis. CH. Quid id refert nostra? PH. Nil. Noveram quandam uxorem hic, cujus vir--- CH. Item. DE. Quid sit? PH. Habuit aliam uxorem Lemni: CH. Sum nul'us. PH. Ex qua suscepit filiam, & educit illam clam. CH. Sum sepultus. PH. Ego adeo jam denarrabo haec illi. CH. Obsecro, ne facias. PH. Ob, tune eras is? DE. Ut facit ludos! CH. Facimus te missum. PH. Fabulae. CH. Quid vis tibi? condonamus te argentum, quod habes. PH. Audio; quid ergo, malum, vos inepti sic ludificamini me vestra puerili sententia? Nolo, volo; volo, nolo rursum: cape, cedo: quod erat dictum est, indictum; quod modo erat ratum, est irritum. CH. Quo pacto, aut unde hic rescivit haec? DE. Nescio, nisi certo scio me dixisse nemihi. CH. Ita Dii ament me, est monstri simile. PH. Injeci scrupulum. DE. Hem, ut hiccine auferat hoc tantum argenti nobis, irridens tam aperte? Hercle est satius emori. Para, ut sis animo virili praesentique. Vides tuum peccatum esse elatum foras, neque te posse jam celare id tuam uxorem. Nunc, Chreme, est placabilius nosmet indicare id, quod ipsa sit auditura ex aliis. Tum poterimus ulcisci hunc impuratum nostra modo. PH. At, at, nisi prospicio mihi, haereo. Hi affectant viam ad me gladiatorio animo. CH. At vereor, ut possit placari. DE. Es bono animo, ego redigam vos in gratiam, si fretus hoc, Chreme,*

## ANNOTATIONS.

65 *Vides peccatum tuum esse elatam foras.* The different Characters of the two Brothers are admirably preserved throughout this Scene. *Chremes* is of a peaceable Temper, and loves Quiet. He stands greatly in awe of his Wife, and will submit to any thing, rather than the present Story should come to her Ear. Accordingly, when *Phormio* threatens him, he readily offers to forgive him the Money, and make up Matters with him. But *Demipho* is of a quite different Turn. The losing so much Money appears to him insupportable, nor will he so much as bear of it: he encourages his Brother to behave with Spirit and Resolution, and promises that he himself will make up Matters between him and his Wife.

71 *Gladiatorio animo.* That is, with a bold, resolute, intrep'd Air; a Metaphor taken from Gladiators, who entered the Lists with a Resolution either to kill or be killed.

*Chremes*; especially as the Woman, by whom you had this Daughter
is *dead and* out of the way.

*Phorm.* Is this the way you deal with me? indeed, methinks you
attack me very cunningly; but you won't, I believe, Mr. *Demipho*, find
it much for his advantage, that you have provoked me. Say you
then? When you have been following your Pleasures abroad, without any regard to this worthy Gentlewoman, but injur'd her in the
most unheard of manner; come you now to wash away your Offence
with *feign'd* Submissions? I'll so rouze her by a Recital of these
your Ways, that you shan't find it possible to appease her, were you
even to melt into Tears.

*Dem.* May all the Gods and Goddesses wreck their Vengeance on
him! That any Man should be possessed of such amazing Confidence! Does not a Wretch like this deserve to be publickly banish'd
into some solitary Desert?

*Chr.* I'm reduced to that Dilemma, I know not what in the world
to do with him.

*Dem.* I know: let us drag him to Justice.

*Phorm.* To Justice! Here rather if you please.

*Dem.* Follow him, and hold him back, till I call out the Servants.

*Chr.* I'm not able by myself; run *and help me.*

*Phorm.* (*To* Demipho.) I have an Action against you.

*Chr.* Bring it then *when you will.*

*Phorm.* And another against you, *Chremes.*

*Dem.* (*To the Servants.*) Away with him.

*Phorm.* Are you at that then? I must exert my Voice, I perceive;
*Nausistrata*, come out hither.

*Chr.* Stop his Mouth.

*Dem.* See how strong the Villain is!

*Phorm. Nausistrata*, I say.

*Chr.* Will you not hold your tongue?

*Phorm.* Hold my tongue?

*Dem.* If he will not follow, punch him in the Belly, or dash his
Eyes out.

*Phorm:* I know how to be soundly revenged.

*ANNOTATIONS.*

83 *Malum, quod isti di deæque omnes
duint. Malum,* in magna ira, aut indigna-
tione, usitatissima interjectio, ut supra, 4, 5.
*Quid tua, malum, id refert?* Hanc igitur vocem (quæ vox alioquin infausta est) cum justa
Demiphoni his expressisset indignatio: omnem diritatem (ita enim illi de talibus verbis
judicabant) statim a se deprecatur, & Phormioni imprecatur, dum addit, *quod isti,* &c.
*Mer: Casaubonus.*

88 *In jus eamus.* *Ph. In jus? huc, si
quid lubet.* The old Men were for carrying
*Phormio*

Cùm è medio excessit, unde hæc suscepta est tibi.
PH. Itane agitis mecum? satis astutè aggredimini.        75
Non hercle ex re istu' me instigasti, Demipho.
Ain' tu? ubi quæ libitum fuerit peregrè feceris,
Neque hujus sis veritus feminæ primariæ,
Quin novo modo ei faceres contumeliam;
Venias nunc precibus lautum peccatum tuum?        80
Hisce ego illam dictis ita tibi incensam dabo,
Ut ne restinguas, lacrumis si exstillaveris.
DE. Malum, quod isti Di, Deæque omnes duint.
Tantâne affectum quenquam esse hominem audacia?
Non hoc publicitùs scelus hinc deportarier        85
In solas terras? CH. in id redactus sum loci,
Ut quid agam cum illo, nesciam prorsum. DE. ego scio.
In jus eamus. PH. in jus? huc, si quid lubet.
DE. Assequere, retine, dum huc ego servos evoco.
CH. Enim solus nequeo: accurre. PH. una injuria est        90
Tecum. CH. lege agito ergo. PH. altera est tecum,
    Chreme.                                        [pus.
DE. Rape hunc. PH. sic agitis? enimvero voce est o-
Nausistrata, exi. CH. os opprime. DE. impurum vide.
Quantum valet: PH. Nausistrata, inquam. CH. non
    taces?                                        [ingere.
PH. Taceam? DE. Nisi sequitur, pugnos in ventrem
Veloculum exclude. PH. est ubi vos ulciscar probè.        96

*cum illo. DE. Ego scio. Eamus in jus. PH. In jus? imo eamus huc,*
*Assequere, retine, dum ego evoco servos huc. CH. Enim solus nequeo, accurre.*
*injuria tecum, Demipho. CH. Ergo agito lege. PH. Est altera tecum, C*
*hunc. PH. Sic agitas? enimvero est opus voce. Nausistrata, exi. CH. Op*
*impurum, quantum valet. PH. Nausistrata, inquam. CH. Non taces? PH.*
*sequitur, ingere pugnos in ventrem, vel exclude oculum. PH. Est ubi ulciscar*

### *A N N O T A T I O N S.*

*Phormio* to the Forum, or some public Court of Justice. He, on the other hand, points to *Chremes*'s House, *huc, si quid lubet*, and makes the best of his way towards it; which *Demipho* perceiving, calls out to *Chremes*, *assequere, retine, dum huc ego servos evoco.*

90 *Una injuria est tecum.* These Words are address'd to *Demipho*, who had come back to aid *Chremes* in keeping him from forcing in to *Nausistrata*; and what follows, *Lege agito ergo*, ought not in my opinion to be ascrib'd to *Chremes*, as it almost always is, but to *Demipho*, who despises his Threats.

95 *Nisi sequitur, pugnos in ventrem ingere.* These Words are spoken to the Servants, who had by this Time come out, and were dragging him away.

## ACT V. SCENE VII.

### ARGUMENT.

Chremes, *who had been false to his Wife* Nausistrata, *being charged with the Crime in her Presence by* Phormio, *is severely reproached to* Phormio's *great Satisfaction.* Demipho *intercedes for his Brother, and begs of his Wife to forgive him. At last,* Phædria *is chosen to settle this Contest between his Parents.*

NAUSISTRATA, CHREMES, PHORMIO, DEMIPHO.

*Nauf.* WHO's that calls me?

*Chr.* Ah!

*Nauf.* What Disturbance, pray, Husband, is this?

*Phor.* Hah, what are you now mute?

*Nauf.* What Man is this? Don't you answer me?

*Phor.* How should he answer you, who hardly knows where he is?

*Chr.* Beware how you believe any thing he says.

*Phor.* Go touch him, Madam, my Life on't he's all in a cold Sweat.

*Chr.* 'Tis nothing.

*Nauf.* What is it then that he means?

*Phor.* You shall know it presently; hear me only.

*Chr.* Are you then resolv'd to believe him?

*Nauf.* What should I believe, when he has told me nothing?

*Phor.* Poor Soul, he's bereft of his Senses through Fear.

*Nauf.* It must be no Trifle this, that you are in such a Fright.

*Chr.* I in a Fright!

*Phor.* Nay then, since you're in no Fright, and what I'm going to say is just nothing at all; tell it yourself.

*Dem.* Is he to tell it at your desire, Villain?

*Phor.* O yes; 'tis quite right to stand up warmly for your Brother.

*Nauf.* Will you not tell me then, Husband?

*Chr.* Why——

*Nauf.* Why?

*Chr.* There is no need for telling it.

*Phor.* Not to you, I believe, but 'tis highly needful that she know it.——In *Lemnos*——

*Chr.* Hah, what are you doing?

*Dem.* Will you not be silent?

*Phor.* Unknown to you——

*Chr.* Ruin'd.                                                    *Phor.*

### ANNOTATIONS.

This Scene is properly a Continuation of the foregoing. *Phormio*, when he found that they would not suffer him to get at *Nausistrata*, but dragg'd him away by force, has recourse to his Voice, and calls as loud as he can upon *Nausistrata*. She hear-ing herself named, comes running out to see what is the Matter. This makes way for the Discovery of all, whence ensues much Resentment on the side of *Nausistrata*, much Anguish and Vexation on that of *Chremes*, *Demipho*, acts the Part of a Mediator, and at last,

## ACTUS V. SCENA VII.

### ARGUMENTUM.

*Chremes adulterii reus, Nausistratæ uxori à Phormione proditus, ab ea possimè audit, eumque graviter objurgat; unde Phormio magnopere exultat. Tum Demipho pro Chremete intercedit, uxor ut ipsi crimen condonet. Et Phædria contentionis parentum suorum sedandæ, arbiter constituitur.*

NAUSISTRATA, CHREMES, PHORMIO, DEMIPHO.

QUI nominat me? DE. hem. NA. quid istuc tur-
   bæ est, obsecro,        [homo est?
Mi vir? PH. hem, quid nunc obstupuisti? NA. quis hic
Non mihi respondes? PH. hiccine ut tibi respondeat?
Qui hercle, ubi sit, nescit. CH. cave isti quidquam
   creduas
PH. Abi: tange: si non totus friget, me eneca.   5.
CH. Nihil est. NA. quid ergo? quid istic narrat? PH.
   jam scies:        [ero,
Ausculta. CH. pergin' credere? NA. quid ego, obse-
Huic credam, qui nil dixit? PH. delirat miser
Timore. NA. non pol temere est, quòd tu tam times.
CH. Ego timeo? PH. rectè sane: quando nihil times, 10
Et hoc nihil est, quod dico ego, tu narra. DE. scelus,
Tibi narrat? PH. eho tu: factum est abs te sedulò
Pro fratre. NA. mi vir, non mihi narras? CH. at.
   NA. quid at?        [huic opus
CH. Non opus est dicto. PH. tibi quidem: at scito
In Lemno—CH. hem, quid ais? DE. non taces? PH.
   clam te—DE. hei mihi!        15

ORDO.

NA. QUI nominat me? DE. Hem? NA. Obsecro, mi vir, quid turbæ est istuc? PH. Hem, q ud obstupuisti nunc? NA. Quis homo est hic? non respondet mihi? PH. Hiccine te spondeat tibi? qui hercle nescit ubi sit. CH. Cave credas quidquam isti. PH. Abi, tange, si non totus friget, eneca me. CH. Est nihil. NA. Quid ergo? quid istic narrat? PH. jam scies: ausculta. NA. Pergisne credere? NA. Obsecro, quid ego credam huic, qui dixit nil? PH. Miser delirat timore. NA. Pol non est temere, quod tu tam dico, est nihil, tu pro fratre. NA. PH. Quidem tibi:

*times. CH. Ego timeo? PH. Rectè sane: quando times nibil, et boc, quod ego dico, est nibil, tu narra. DE. Scelus, narret tibi? PH. Eho tu: factum est sedulo abs te pro fratre. NA. Mi vir, non narras mibi? CH. At. NA. Quid at? CH. Non opus est dicto. PH. Quidem tibi: at opus est scito huic. In Lemno----CH. Hem, quid ais? DE. Non taces? PH. Clam te----CH. Hei mibi!*

### ANNOTATIONS.

last, with some difficulty, brings *Nausistrata* to temper. *Phormio*, in the meantime, who was anxious for himself and *Phædria*, interposes, and owns his having receiv'd Money of the old Man, and how he had employ'd it. *Nausistrata*, who seems to have been partial towards her Son, leaves all to his Determination, and invites *Phormio* to supper. Here the Poet concludes, leaving the Spectators to supply the rest. And indeed it is easy to suppose, that as *Chremes* would gladly yield to his Son, to have peace at home, *Phædria*, having his Desires comply'd with, would be no less

ready to gratify his Father. *Demipho* too, finding the Money not engross'd by the Parasite, but given to one of the Family, would rest contented; and *Phormio*, who had been so useful and zealous in the young Gentleman's Cause, would not pass unrewarded.

4 *Ubi sit, nescit.* It is an usual Effect of Terror and Consternation, to throw the Mind into such Disorder and Confusion, that it is render'd incapable of Reflection. Thus *Plautus*, in a like case, makes one say, *Equidem quo eam, aut ubi sim, aut quo sim, nequeo cum animo certum investigare.*

7 *Pergin' credere?* He had before said,

*Phor.* He married another.

*Nauf.* Hah ! Heaven forbid.

*Phor.* 'Tis certainly true.

*Nauf.* Wretch that I am, I'm undone !

*Phor.* And has a Daughter by her too, whom you never dreamt of.

*Chr.* (to Dem.) What shall we do ?

*Nauf.* Immortal Gods ! What Treachery and Basefness is this !

*Phor.* 'Tis as I tell you.

*Nauf.* Can any thing be imagin'd more ungenerous ? And yet these Husbands, when with their Wives, are then forsooth old and good for nothing. *Demipho*, I address myself to you, for I have not patience to speak with him : were thefe his frequent Journeys, and long Stays at *Lemnos* ? Was this the Cheapnefs *of Grain*, that so much lower'd our Rents ?

*Dem.* I don't deny, *Naufiftrata*, that he is highly to blame in this Bufinefs ; but yet the Crime is not wholly unpardonable.——

*Phor.* He preaches to the Wind.

*Dem.* For 'twas neither thro' any Averfion nor Contempt of you that he did it ; but being once about fifteen Years ago over-heated with Wine, he got this Woman with child, and had a Daughter by her, nor ever touch'd her afterwards. She is now dead ; the only Scruple that remain'd in this Affair is remov'd : Therefore I beg that you will exert the fame Prudence here you are wont to do on other Occafions, and bear it with Patience and Calmnefs.

*Nauf.* What should I bear with Patience ? I heartily wish indeed that it might end here : but what Reafon have I to hope ? Can I flatter myfelf that Age will reclaim him ? He was then old enough, were Years a Security for his Behaviour. Are my Age and Beauty more attractive now than formerly, *Demipho* ? What can you offer to make me think or hope that it will not any more be fo ?

*Phor.* Whoever has a mind to attend at *Chremes*'s Funeral, now is the tune. 'Tis thus I retaliate. Come then and provoke *Phormio*, who dares : he shall be ferved the fame Sauce. Why even let him re-



*advc. ifei quidquam credat*, and here expoftu-lates as if fhe was already giving ear to him, when in reality nothing had been faid. Thefe n'ce and delicate Strokes difcover the moft exact Knowledge of the human Frame. A Man confcious of Guilt, how much foever it may be his Intereft to conceal it, will yet often betray himfelf by his own Fears, and an overftrained Anxiety. This particular Caft of Mind, fo infeperable from a Heart cor-rupted and bafe, is admirably exprefs'd by *Phæ-drus* in the following Lines ; *Lib.* 3. *Prol.* 45.

  *Sufpicione fi quis errabit fua,*
    *Et rapiet ad fe quod erit commune omnium,*
    *Stulte notabit animi confcientiam.*

  ó *Mi bome. Dii melius duint.* Some fup-pofe thefe Words directed to her Hufband, not imagining that fhe would ufe an Expref-fion fo familiar as *mi bomo* to *Phormio.* But this Criticifm is trifling. *Mi bomo* was a common Form of Addrefs at that time, and ufed promifcuoufly, even to People of low Rank. In the Tranflation however I have exprefs'd it fo as to fuit the Manners of the prefent Age.

  30 *Ea mortem abiit : e medio abiit.* De-mipho dwells upon this Circumftance, repeat-ing it twice, as upon this chiefly his Hopes depended of being able to bring about a Re-conciliation. And here we ought to obferve, how judicioufly the Poet has conducted his Plot, in contriving to remove the *Lemnian* Wife out of the way. For had fhe been ftill alive, it muft have prov'd an infur-
         mountable

PH. Uxorem duxit. NA. mihi homo, Dii melius duint.
PH. Sic factum est. NA. perii misera. PH. & inde filiam
Suscepit jam unam, dum tu dormis. CH. quid agimus?
NA. Proh Di immortales, facinus indignum & malum!
PH. Hoc actum est. NA. an quidquam hodie est fac-
    tum indignius?                                        20
Qui mi, ubi ad uxores ventum est, tum fiunt senes.
Demipho, te apello: nam me cum hoc ipso distædet
    loqui.
Hæcine erant itiones cræbræ, & mansiones diutinæ
Lemni? hæccine erat ea, quæ nostros fructus minue-
    bat, vilitas?
DE. Ego, Nausistrata, esse in hac re culpam meritum
    non nego,                                            25
Sed ea quin sit ignoscenda. PH. verba fiunt mortuo.
DE. Nam neque neglegentiâ tuâ, neque odio id fecit tuo
Vinolentus fere abhinc annos quindecim mulierculam
Eam compressit, undæ hæc nata est, neque postilla un-
    quam attigit.
Ea mortem obiit: è medio abiit: qui fuit in re hac
    scrupulus.                                           30
Quamobrem te oro, ut alia facta tu sunt, æquo animo
    hoc feras,                                    [defungier,
NA. Quid ego æquo animo? cupio misera in hac re jam
Sed quid sperem? ætate porro minu' peccaturum putem?
Jam tum erat senex, senectus si verecundos facit.
An mea forma atque ætas nunc magis expetenda est,
    Demipho?                                             35
Quid mihi hîc affers, quamobrem exspectem, aut spe-
    rem porro non fore?                         [hem tempus est.
PH. Exsequias Chremeti, quibus est commodum ire,
Sic dabo: age nunc, Phormionem, qui volet, lacessito:
Faxo tali eum mactatum, atque hic est, infortunio.

*PH. Duxit uxorem. NA. Mihi homo, Dii duint melius. PH. Sic est factum. NA. Misera perii. PH. Et jam suspecit unam filiam inde, dum tu dormis. CH. Quid agimus? NA. Proh Dii immortales, facinus indignum et malum! PH. Hoc est actum. NA. An quidquam hodie est factum indignius? Qui, ubi est ventum ad uxores, fiunt tum senes mihi. Demipho, appello te: nam distædet me loqui cum hoc ipso. Hæccine erant crebræ initiones, et diutinæ mansiones Lemni? hæccine erat ea vilitas, qui minuebat nostros fructus? DE. Ego, Nausistrata, non ego sum esse meritum culpam in hac re; sed quin ea sit ignoscenda. PH. Verba fiunt mortuo. DE. Nam fecit id neque tua negligentia, neque tuo odio. Fere quindecim annos ab hinc, vinolentus compressit eam mulierculam, unde hæc est nata, neque unquam attigit illam postilla. Ea obiit mortem: abiit e medio: qui fuit scrupulus in hac re. Quamobrem oro te, ut alia tua facta sunt, feros hoc æquo animo. NA. Quid ego feram æquo animo? Misera, cupio jam defungi in hac re, sed quid sperem? Putem porro, eum minus peccaturum ætate? Si senectus facit verecundos, jam tum erat senex. An mea forma atque ætas est magis expetenda nunc, Demipho? Quid affers mihi hic; quamobrem expectem, aut sperem tale quid non porro fore? PH. Hem, est tempus celebrare exsequias Chremeti, iis quibus est commodum ire. Sic dabo: age nunc, lacessito Phormionem qui volet: faxo eum mactatam tali infortunio, atque hic est:*

## ANNOTATIONS.

mountable Obstacle to the reconciling of the several Parties.

37 *Exsequias Chremeti.* The Pleasantry of this Passage consists chiefly in *Phormio's* employing the very Terms that were used in proclaiming Funerals. *L. Titio exsequias ire quoi commodum est, jam tempus est, ollus defertur.*

38 *Sic dabo.* That is, *In this manner will I treat him;* or, *Thus will I revenge the Injury.* *Phormio* triumphs in the Success of his Scheme; *age, age, nunc, Phormionem, qui volet, lacessito.* He imagines himself invincible, and talks in the genuine Style of a vain Parasite, conceited of his own Wit, and who imagines himself an Overmatch for every body.

39 *Tali mactatam infortunio.* This manner of speaking is very familiar to *Plautus. Mactare,* in its proper and orginal Signification,

return again to Favour, I've had Revenge enough; she has something to ring in his Ear as long as he lives.

*Nauf.* Possibly. I deserved this: Ah *Demipho*, what need is there now to repeat how faithful I have been to him in every thing?

*Dem.* I know it all, as well as yourself.

*Nauf.* Do you think then that I deserved such Usage?

*Dem.* Far from it: but since Reproaches can't annul what is already past, forgive him. He begs pardon, owns his Fault, and makes an Apology for it; what would you have more?

*Phor.* But truly before she pronounces the Pardon, I must secure myself and *Phædria.* Hark ye, *Nausistrata*, before you answer rashly in the present Case, hear me a little.

*Nauf.* What's the matter?

*Phor.* I drew from your Husband by Stratagem ninety Guineas: These I gave to your Son, and he has given them to *Dorio* the Bawd for a Mistress.

*Chr.* Hah, what is that you say?

*Nauf.* What? Does it appear a Crime so heinous to you, that your Son a young Man keeps one Mistress, when you yourself have got two Wives? Are you not asham'd? With what Face can you reprove him? Answer me.

*Dem.* He'll do as you'd have him.

*Nauf.* Nay, that you may know my mind, I neither forgive, nor promise aught, nor give any Answer at all, till I see my Son: I refer all to his Determination, and will agree to whatever he proposes.

*Phor.* You're a wise *prudent* Woman, *Nausistrata.*

*Nauf.* Does that satisfy you then?

*Phor.* Nay, I come off delightfully, and beyond my Hopes.

*Nauf.* But pray tell me your Name.

*Phor.* My Name? Phormio; a *real* Friend to your Family, and particularly to *Phædria.*

*Nauf.* Well, *Phormio*, and you may depend upon it that henceforward I will serve you as far as I am able in Word and Deed.

*Phor.* You're very obliging.

*Nauf.* Nay, indeed you deserve it.

*Phor.* Will you then do a thing that will mightily please me, *Nausistrata*, and make your Husband's Eyes ake?

*Nauf.* With all my Soul.

*Phor.* Invite me to Supper.                                     *Nauf.*

ANNOTATIONS.

tion, is an Expression equivalent to *magis augere.* 'Tis thus that *Horace* uses it; *Lib.* I. *Sat.* 2. *Macte virtute esto, inquit sententia dia Catonis.* That is, *magis aucte esto.* Hence we sometimes meet with this Phrase of *mactare Deos bestia;* both in *Plautus* and *Cicero.*

42 *At meo merito, credo.* It will be necessary to observe here, that these Words *at vero*, or as some read, *an*, and *credo*, do not so often denote an Interrogation, as mark an Irony or Sneer. Thus *Sulpicius ad Cic. Fam.* 4, 5. *An.* illius vicem, *credo*, doles? And *Lucretius, Lib.* 5. V. 175.

An, credo, in tenebris vita, ac mærore jacebat?

Redeat fane in gratiam : jam fupplicii fatis eft mihi. 40
Habet hæc, ei quod, dum vivat, ufque ad aurem ob-
　ganniat.　　　　　　　　　　　[morem, Demipho,
NA. At meo merito, credo. quid ego nunc ea comme-
Singillatim, qualis ego in hunc fuerim? DE. novi æque
　omnia　　　　　　　　　　　　[minimè gentium:
Tecum. NA. merito hoc meo videtur factum? DE.
Verùm, quando jam accufando fieri infectum non po-
　teft,　　　　　　　　　　　　　　　　　45
Ignofce: orat, confitetur, purgat: quid vis amplius?
PH. Enimvero, priufquam hæc dat veniam, mihi pro-
　fpiciam & Phædriæ.
Heus, Naufiftrata; priufquam huic refpondes temerè,
　audi.　NA. quid eft?
PH. Ego minas triginta ab ifto per fallaciam abftuli:
Eas dedi tuo gnato: is pro fuâ amicâ lenoni dedit. 50
CH. Hem, quid ais? NA. adeon' indignum tibi vide-
　tur, filius　　　　　　　　　　　　[duas?
Homo adolefcens unam fi habet amicam, tu uxores
Nil pudere? quo ore illum objurgabis? refponde mihi.
DE. Faciet, ut voles. NA. imo, ut meam jam fcias
　fententiam,
Neque ego ignofco, neque promitto quidquam, neque
　refpondeo,　　　　　　　　　　　　　55
Priufquam gnatum videro. ejus judicio permitto om-
　nia:　　　　　　　　　　　　　　[fiftrata.
Quod is jubebit, faciam. PH. mulier fapiens es, Nau-
NA. Satin' tibi eft? PH. imo vero pulchrè difcedo,
　& probè,　　　　　　　　　　　[mîn' Phormio,
Et præter fpem. NA. tu tuum nomen dic quod eft. PH.
Veftræ familiæ hercle amicus, & tuo fummus Phæ-
　driæ.　　　　　　　　　　　　　　　60
NA. Phormio, at ego ecaftor pofthac tibi, quod pote-
　ro, & quæ voles,　　　　　　　　[tum eft tuum.
Faciamque & dicam. PH. benignè dicis. NA. pol meri-
PH. Vin' primùm hodie facere, quod ego gaudeam,
　Naufiftrata,　　　　　　　　　　[cœnam voca.
Et quod tuo viro oculi doleant? NA. cupio. PH. me ad

*Sane redeat in gra-*
*tiam: eft jam fatis*
*fupplicii mihi, Hæc*
*habet, quod obganni-*
*at ei ad aurem, ufque*
*dum vivat. NA.*
*At credo, meo meri-*
*to. Quid ego nunc,*
*Demipho, commemo-*
*rem ea fingillatim,*
*qualis uxor fuerim*
*in hunc? DE. Novi*
*omnia, æque tecum.*
*NA. Hoc videtur*
*factum meo merito?*
*DE. Minime genti-*
*um: verum, quando*
*jam non poteft fieri*
*infectum accufando,*
*ignofce: orat confite-*
*tur, purgat: quid*
*vis amplius? PH.*
*Enimvero, priufquam*
*hæc dat veniam ei,*
*profpiciam mihi et*
*Phædriæ. Heus,*
*Naufiftrata; priuf-*
*quam refpondes te-*
*mere huic, audi.*
*NA. Quid eft? PH.*
*Ego abftuli triginta*
*minas ab ifto per fal-*
*laciam: dedi eas tuo*
*gnato: is dedit eas*
*lenoni pro fua amica.*
*CH. Hem, quid ais?*
*AN. Videturne tibi*
*adeo indignum, fi fi-*
*lus homo adolefcens*
*habet unum amicam,*
*tu duas uxores?*
*Pudere nil? Quo ore*
*objurgabis illum?*
*Refponde mihi. DE.*
*Faciet, ut voles. NA.*
*Imo, ut jam fcias me-*
*am fententiam, neque*
*ego ignofco, neque*
*promitto, neque re-*
*fpondeo quidquam,*
*priufquam videro*

*gnatum. Permitto omnia ejus judicio: faciam quod is jubebit. PH. Es mulier fapiens, Naufiftrata.*
*NA. Efîne fatis tibi? PH. Imo vero difcedo pulchre, et probe, et præter fpem. NA. Tu dic*
*quod eft tuum nomen. PH. Mihine? Phormio, amicus hercle veftræ familiæ, et fummus amicus*
*tuo Phædriæ. NA. Phormio, at ego ecaftor pofthac faciamque, et dicam tibi, quæ potero, et*
*quæ voles. PH. Dicis benigne. NA. Pol, eft tuum meritum. PH. Vifne primum facere bodie,*
*Naufiftrata, quod ego gaudeam, et quod oculi doleant tuo viro? NA. Cupio. PH. Voca me ad*
*cœnam.*

## ANNOTATIONS.

53 *Quo ore illum objurgabis? Terence* takes
care from time to time to inftruct as well as
divert his Readers, and convey to their
Minds the jufteft Sentiments of Morality.
Here we have an important Leffon to Parents, that they ought to have a guard upon
　　　　　　　　　　　　　　　　their

*Nauf.* I do invite you heartily.
*Dem.* Let us now go in.
*Nauf.* Agreed. But where's *Phædria* our Judge?
*Phor.* I'll bring him presently. [*To the Spectators.*] Farewel,
and give us your Applause.

## ANNOTATIONS.

their Actions, if it were but for the sake of their Children; for with what Face can they reproach others for a Crime they are conscious of being guilty of themselves?

65 *Sed ubi est Phædria judex noster?* This we are to conceive pronounc'd with a facetious, pleasant Air, and refers to what she had said a little before: *Ejus judicio permitto omnis.*

NA. Pol verò voco. DE. eamus intrò hinc. NA. fiat.
    fed ubi eſt Phædria
Judex noſter ? PH. jam hîc favo aderit.   Vos valete,
    & plaudite.
        CALLIOPIUS RECENSUI.

NA. *Pol verò voco.*
DE. *Eamus intro*
NA. *Fiat. Sed ubi*
*eſt Phædria noſter*
*judex ?* PH. *Faxo*
*aderit bic jam. Vos*
*valete & plaudite.*

## ANNOTATIONS.

*pia.* He only was now wanting to compleat the Peace. The Poet leaves it to the Reader to conceive the reſt, it being ſo obvious, that all will end to their mutual Satisfaction. For there was no great Likelyhood that *Phædria,* who was at that very time indulging himſelf with a Miſtreſs, would paſs any ſevere and rigorous Sentence againſt his Father, for a Fault of the ſame kind.

P. TE-

ВОЛКЪ

ВОЛКЪ

# P. TERENTII

# HECYRA.

---

## THE

# HECYRA

OF

# *TERENCE.*

# THE
# HECYRA
## OF
## *TERENCE.*

### *The* TITLE.

THIS PLAY WAS EXHIBITED AT THE ROMAN GAMES, WHEN SEXTUS JULIUS CÆSAR, AND CNEUS CORNELIUS DOLABELLA WERE CURULE ÆDILES. IT WAS NOT ACTED QUITE THROUGH. FLACCUS THE FREEDMAN OF CLAUDIUS COMPOSED THE MUSICK, WHICH WAS PERFORMED ON EQUAL FLUTES, UNDER THE CONSULSHIP OF CNEUS OCTAVIUS, AND T. MANLIUS. IT WAS ATTEMPTED AGAIN AT SOME FUNERAL GAMES. IT WAS BROUGHT ON A THIRD TIME, WHEN Q. FULVIUS, AND L. MARCIUS WERE CURULE ÆDILES.

### *ANNOTATIONS.*

The Title to this Play is very perplexed, and varies exceedingly in different Editions. Some make it to be acted at the *Roman* Games, others at the Feast of *Cybele,* some tell us it is taken from the *Greek* of *Menander,* others from *Apollodorus.* That given here, as in all the rest, is from the *Cambridge* Edition. But as the Title prefix'd to this Play by *Westerhovius* in his accurate Edition of our Poet, seems to be the fullest and most exact of any yet published, I shall here, for the Sake of the Reader, give it entire.

*P. Terentii Hecyra, acta Ludis Mega-*

*lensibus, Sexto Julio Cæsare, et Cneo Cornelio Dolabella Ædilibus Curulibus. Non est peracta. Modos fecit Flaccus Claudi, tibiis paribus. Tota Græca Apollodoru facta est. Acta primo sine prologo. Data secundo, Cneo Octavio, et T. Manlio Consulibus. Relata est L. Æmilio Paulo ludis funebribus. Non est placita. Tertio relata est, Q. Fulvio, L. Marcio Ædilibus Curulibus. Egit L. Ambivius Turpio. Placuit.*

The Reader will the better understand this Title, and the Reason of the Play's being so often attempted

before

# P. TERENTII

# HECYRA.

## TITULUS *seu* DIASCALIA.

ACTA LUDIS ROMANIS, SEX. JU-
LIO CÆS. CN. CORNELIO DOLA-
BELLA, ÆDIL. CUR. NON EST PER-
ACTA TOTA. MODOS FECIT
FLACCUS CLAUDII. TIBIIS PARIB.
CN. OCTAVIO, T. MANLIO COSS.
RELATA EST ITERUM LUDIS FU-
NEBRIBUS. RELATA EST TERTIO,
Q. FULVIO, L. MARCIO ÆDILI-
BUS CURULIBUS.
*lata est Tertio, Q. Fulvio, & L. Marcio Ædilibus Curulibus.*

ORDO.

*Hæc Comœdia fuit acta Ludis Romanis Sexto Julio Cæfare, et Cneo Cornelio Dolabella Ædilibus Curulibus. Non est tota peracta. Flaccus, Libertus Claudii, fecit modos tibiis paribus ; Cneo Octavio, et T. Manlio Confulibus Relata est iterum Ludis funebribus. Re-*

## ANNOTATIONS.

before it could be acted quite thro', after having read the two Prologues with the Remarks upon them.

1 *Tibiis paribus.* That is, with two equal Flutes, either right-handed or left-handed, according to the different Occasions on which it was acted.

2 *Cn. Octavio, T. Manlio Coss.* That is, in the Year of the City 588, and 165 Years before the Birth of Christ, the Year after the Representation of the *Andrian.*

3 *Relata est iterum ludis funebribus.* *Donatus,* in his Remarks upon the Prologue, tells us, that it was acted upon Occasion of the Funeral Games of L. *Æmilius Paulus.* But this is scarce to be credited, because Æmi-lius *Paulus* died not till five Years after the first Attempt of bringing it upon the Stage, and it is not likely, that the Poet, who knew that the Opposition it met with was not owing to want of Merit in the Performance, but the extravagant Fondness for Rope-Dancers, which prevail'd at that time, would have neglected the reviving it so long, if he had any Thoughts of bringing it on again at all, as it appears by the Prologue he had from the very Beginning. I am therefore to apt think that the Funeral Games here mentioned, were celebrated towards the latter End of the same Year in which this first Attempt was made.

# *The* ARGUMET *to the* HECYRA, *from* MURETUS.

**P**AMPHILUS, *the Son of* Laches *by his Wife* Sostrata, *was desperately in love with one* Bacchis *a Courtezan. One Night as he was coming drunk to her House, he chanced to meet with* Philumena *the Daughter of* Phidyppus *and* Myrrhina, *and by Force enjoyed her; and as it was in the dark, neither of them knew the other. In the Struggle, however, he took a Ring from her, and made a Present of it to* Bacchis. *Some time after, his Father, both to wean him from this unlawful Love, and to have some Support in his old Age, prevailed on him to marry. It fortun'd that this very Girl was given him to Wife, whom a little before he had ravish'd, her Mother greatly rejoicing; who, as she was alone conscious to her Misfortune, was glad to have her given away in Marriage as soon as possible; hoping by this means to hide the Disaster. But it fell out far otherwise than she expected. For* Pamphilus, *who had with great Reluctance consented to marry, because he found it impossible so all of a sudden to shake off his Passion for* Bacchis, *abstain'd from all nuptial Commerce with his Wife.* Bacchis, *again, to whom* Pamphilus *had promised, that during her Life he never would marry, greatly resenting the Injury which she imagined was done her, did not behave to him now with her usual Complaisance and Good-humour. This provok'd* Pamphilus, *and gradually weakened his Affection, insomuch that his Passion soon took a new Turn, and he became fond of the Wife he had before despis'd. Mean time an Affair happens, that calls* Pamphilus *from home. During his Absence,* Philumena *sensible that she was every day advancing in her Pregnancy, began to avoid all Company, and especially that of her Stepmother. In fine, when she found there was no Probability of concealing it longer, she forms a Pretence of going to assist her Mother at a Sacrifice, and continues with her, who alone was let into the Secret of what had befallen her. Some few Days after* Sostrata *sends for her, but is answered, that she is sick. She goes to see her, and is refus'd Admittance.* Laches *hearing this, accuses his Wife, and lays all the blame upon her. She clears herself, and endeavours to make it appear, that the Charge is without Foundation, as being conscious of nothing that should make her Company disagreeable to her Daughter-in-law. Mean time* Pamphilus *returns, and so it fortun'd, that the very day of his Arrival at* Athens, Philumena *was brought to bed. When therefore, impatient to see her, (for he understood she was ill, and lov'd her to Distraction) he had suddenly rush'd in, he finds that she is delivered of a Child.* Myrrhina *as he is retiring, follows him, and with Tears requests him (as it could no way injure him to keep this Affair secret, nor was he required to take back his Wife unless it was his own Choice)*

*that*

# *M. Ant. Mureti* ARGUMENTUM.

*PAMPHILUS*, Lachetis e Sostrata uxore filius, Bacchidem
meretricem deperibat. Is quum aliquando noctu ad eam temulentus iret, in Philumenam, Phidippi et Myrrhinæ filiam, incidit, eamque in via per vim compressit: atque ita effugit, ut neque ipse eam,
neque puella ipsam cognoscere potuerit. In illa autem lucta etiam annulum ei detraxit, eamque Bacchidi dono dedit. Paulo post patrem eum,
tum ut a meretricio amore averteret, tum ut præsidium suæ senectuti
pararet, ad uxorem ducendam perpulit. Contigit, ut ea ipsa uxor ei
daretur, quam ipse constupraverat: gaudente admodum puellæ matre, quæ
quia sola conscia erat filiam e stupro; gravidam esse, quamprimum eam
collocare properabat, ut, si forte post aliquot menses pareret, nuptiis,
quemadmodum sæpe fit, obtegeretur stuprum; cecidit res longe aliter ac
putabatur. Etenim Pamphilus, qui invitissimus adjecisset animum ad rem
uxoriam, quia avellere se derepente a Bacchidis amore non posset, ita dor-
mit cum uxore, ut eam ne attigerit quidem. Bacchis, quod, ea viva, nunquam se uxorem ducturum, sæpe ei promiserat Pamphilus, nonnullam
sibi ab eo factam injuriam putans, multo ei minùs, quam solebat, pla-
cida et obsequens esse cœpit. Eo factum est, ut Pamphilus ei se paul-
latim subduxerit, quamque prius spernebat uxorem, ejus mirificum
quendam amorem animo conceperit. Interea quiddam accidit, ut iter
Pamphilo in Imbrum esset. Profecto eo, Philumena, quæ intumescere
sibi uterum sentiret, quum aliorum, tum socrus imprimis suæ conspectum refugiebat. Tandem quum in eo esset, ut cæleri vix posse amplius videretur, sumpta occasione, per sacrificandi speciem, ad matrem
se, unam omnium rerum consciam, confert. Post dies complusculos mittit Sostrata, qui eam arcesserent. Respondetur, ægrotam esse. It, ut
eam saltem viseret: non admittitur. Laches accusare uxorem, et dicere, hæc omnia illius culpa contingere. Illa contra excusare se; et
culpam deprecari: nullius se rei consciam esse, cur sua consuetudo nurui
odiosa esse debeat. Interea rediit Pamphilus, atque ita sors tulit, ut
quo die ipse Athenas appulit, eo ipso Philumena partu levaretur. Quum
igitur, videndi cupidus (ægrotare enim acceperat, et ita amabat, ut
qui vehementissime) subito ad eam ingressus esset, peperisse deprehendit.
Ibi eum Myrrhina exeuntem prosecuta, lacrumans, obtestari cœpit, quando ea res nihil ipsi nocitura esset; ne reciperet quidem uxorem, si ita
videretur: sed tamen ne famam illius proderet. Ita se facturum
recipit. Quum igitur neque vellet uxorem recipere, neque rursum

*that he would not betray her Daughter's Misfortune, and thereby ruin her Reputation. He gives his Promise. After this, when he would neither take back his Wife, nor assign the true Reason of his Refusal, the old Men begin to suspect that he is still enslav'd to Bacchis, and for that Reason so averse to live with his Wife. Laches therefore, sending for Bacchis, expostulates with her, but she wholly clears herself, and the old Man further requests of her, that she will go in to the Women, and try to remove also their Suspicions. Accordingly she goes in with the Ring upon her Finger, which Pamphilus in the struggle had taken from Philumena, and presented to her. By means of this Ring it is known that Pamphilus himself had ravish'd Philumena; upon which Pamphilus, full of Joy, takes home his Wife and Son.*

PER-

*vtram adferret caufam, fuspicati funt fenes, eum Bacchidis adhuc amore impeditum, ea de caufa ab uxore abhorrere. Arceffitam itaque Bacchidem objurgat Laches. Ea, quum fe illi purgaffet, jubetur ad mulieres ingredi, et eis quoque illam fuspicionem adimere. Ingreditur, annulum habens in digito, quem olim Philumenæ ereptum fibi dederat Pamphilus. Is annulus effecit, ut vitiatam effe ab ipfo Pamphilo Philumenam cognofceretur. Lætus Pamphilus, et uxorem et filium recipit.*

R 2 DRA-

## PERSONS *of the* PLAY.

The Speaker of the PROLOGUE.
BACCHIS, a Courtezan, Miſtreſs to *Pamphilus*.
MYRRHINA, Mother to *Philumena*.
LACHES, an old Man, Father to *Pamphilus*.
PAMPHILUS, the Son of *Laches* and *Soſtrata*.
PARMENO, Servant to *Soſtrata*.
PHIDIPPUS, an old Man, Father to *Philumena*.
PHILOTIS, a Courtezan.
SOSIA, Servant to *Pamphilus*.
SOSTRATA, Mother to *Pamphilus*.
SYRA, an old Bawd.

## MUTES.

PHILUMENA, the Daughter of *Phidippus*, married to *Pamphilus*.
SCIRTUS, a Servant.
A NURSE.
TWO MAIDS belonging to *Bacchis*.

# DRAMATIS PERSONÆ.

PROLOGUS.
BACCHIS, *meretrix, amica Pamphili.*
MYRRHINA, *mater Philumenæ.*
LACHES, *senex, pater Pamphili.*
PAMPHILUS, *filius Lachetis et Sostratæ.*
PARMENO, *servus Sostratæ.*
PHIDIPPUS, *senex, pater Philumenæ.*
PHILOTIS, *meretrix.*
SOSIA, *servus Pamphili.*
SOSTRATA, *mater Pamphili.*
SYRA, *anus, lena.*


# PERSONÆ MUTÆ.

PHILUMENA, *filia Phidippi, nupta Pamphilo.*
SCIRTUS, *servulus.*
NUTRIX.
ANCILLÆ DUÆ *Bacchidis.*

# *The* PROLOGUE.

THIS Comedy is called the Step-Mother. When it was firſt exhibited, a Folly and Diſaſter altogether new intervened, that neither could the Repreſentation be carried on, nor any Judgment form'd of it; the People were become ſo extravagantly fond of Rope-Dancing. It is therefore now offered as a new Play, for the Poet did not attempt then to bring it on a ſecond Time, that he might ſell it again to the Stage. You have ſeen and approv'd other Plays of his; be intreated to give this too a candid Hearing.

The

*A N N O T A T I O N S.*

[1] *Hecyra eſt huic nomen fabulæ.* The Name of this Play is deriv'd from a *Greek* Word ἐκυρα, which ſignifies a Mother-in Law, or Huſband's Mother. The Reaſon of this Title is, that ſome of the moſt intereſting Circumſtances of the whole Piece take their Riſe from Suſpicions form'd of *Soſtrata*, the Mother of *Pamphilus*.

Ibid. *Hæc cum data eſt nova, novum--- vitium.* It appears hence, that this was the ſecond time of an Attempt's being made to exhibit this Play, ſince the Words here plainly imply that they had eſſayed it before, but were repuls'd. *Vitium* Criticks obſerve to be a Word tranſlated from *Augury*, where it implied an unlucky Omen, and thence is put for any Misfortune or Diſaſter. The Poet juſtly calls the Fondneſs for Rope-Dancing, ſo prevalent at that Time, by this Name, as it was the Cauſe of the ill Reception his Play met with. Perhaps, too, it was intended to hint, that this fooliſh Preference was owing to a Corruption and Depravity of Taſte.

[4] *Ita populus ſtudio ſtupidus.* Here we diſcover the Poet's Anxiety to preſerve his Reputation. He tells us, the ill Reception his Play met with at its firſt Repreſentation, was not owing to any Defect or want of Merit on its ſide, but becauſe the Attention

tion

# PROLOGUS.

HEcyra eſt huic nomen fabulæ. hæc cùm data<br>
  Eſt nova, novum intervenit vitium & calamitas,<br>
Ut neque ſpectari, neque cognoſci potuerit :<br>
Ita populus ſtudio ſtupidus in funambulo<br>
Animum occuparat. nunc hæc planè eſt pro novâ : 5<br>
Et is, qui ſcripſit hanc, ob eam rem noluit<br>
Iterum referre, ut iterum poſſit vendere.<br>
Alias cognoſtis ejus : quæſo, hanc noſcite.

ORDO.

HEcyra eſt no-
men huic fa-
bulæ. Cum hæc eſt
data nova, novum
vitium, et nova cala-
mitas intervenit, ut
neque potuerit ſpec-
tari, neque cognoſci :
Populus ſtupidus ſtu-
dio ita occupaverat
animum in funam-

*bulo. Nunc hæc eſt plane pro nova: et is, qui ſcripſit hanc, noluit iterum referre ob eam rem, ut poſſit vendere iterum. Cognoviſtis alias comœdias ejus: quæſo, noſcite hunc.*

## ANNOTATIONS.

tion of the Audience was otherwiſe employ-ed. The Word *ſtupidus* does not ſignify the ſame here as *ſtupid*, in our Language, but denotes an earneſt Attention mixed with Aſtoniſhment and Wonder, a Keenneſs proceeding from Admiration and Surpriſe. *Turpilius* had before him uſed it in the ſame ſenſe. *Herus ſtupidus aſtat ; ita ejus aſpectus repens cor torporavit homini amore.*

7 *Ut iterum poſſit vendere.* It appears from this that *Terence* was very confident of the Merit of his Play ; and it is worthy our notice too, that he would rather be eſteem'd avaricious, than diffident of himſelf: for had he attempted to bring it on again, after the Rope-dancing Scene was over, he could not have ſold it a ſecond time as a new Play. But this Confeſſion of Avarice, if one may call it ſo, was a ſtrong Recommendation of the Play, becauſe the *Ædiles* or Actors would never have made another Purchaſe of it, unleſs they had conceived highly of its Merit.

8 *Alias cognoſtis ejus.* *Terence* wrote ſeveral Plays before the *Andrian*, tho' that is the only one left us of thoſe exibited by him before the *Hecyra*. *Voſſius*, and ſome others after him, tell us, that this ſecond Repreſentation was not till after the *Adelphi*. If ſo, the *Romans* had ſeen five Plays of his, for the *Adelphi* was the laſt Piece he wrote.



ALTER

## The SECOND PROLOGUE.

I COME in the Prologue-Speaker's Dress, an Envoy from the Poet; let me be a succesful one, nor lose, in my old Age, the Talent I poſſeſs'd in Youth, of reviving by repeated Trials exploded Plays, and hindering the Poet and his Works from ſinking into Oblivion. In thoſe new Plays of *Cecilius*, which I firſt ſtudy'd, ſome were hiſs'd off the Stage, others hardly ſtood their Ground. But becauſe I knew the Fortune of the Theatre to be fluctuating and variable, I ſubmitted to certain Toil, where the Hopes were very uncertain. I again attempted to bring them on, that from the ſame Poet I might with Care and Study learn other new Plays, nor diſcourage him from his Labours *for the Stage*. This Perſeverance obtain'd for them a fair Repreſentation, and, when ſeen, they fail'd not to pleaſe. Thus I reſtor'd the Bard to the Place he merited in your Eſteem, *and reſcued him*, whom now his Adverſaries had almoſt compell'd to abandon Study, Application, and the Poetick Art. But had I then deſpis'd his Plays, or aim'd at driving him from Study, to Indolence and Sloth, I could have eaſily deterr'd him from any new Attempts. Now therefore for my ſake hear with candid and impartial Minds what I am to ſay. I offer you again the Step-Mother, which I have never yet been able to act in Silence, ſo much did a *late* Misfortune prevail againſt it. This Misfortune your Judgment will now remove, if it joins in aid of our Labour and Addreſs. When I firſt began the Repreſentation, the Combats of the Prize-Fighters (an Expectation too was rais'd of a Scene of Rope-Dancing) the increaſing Crouds, Tumult, and Clamour of Women, compell'd me to withdraw before my time. Here then I attempt to revive an old Cuſtom, and perſevere in courting your Approbation. I bring it on again. In the

firſt

### ANNOTATIONS.

This Prologue is pen'd with wonderful Art, and an uncommon Power of Perſuaſion; for as it had been already twice at leaſt rejected, there was need of great Addreſs to bring it again upon the Stage. *Ambivius* himſelf is generally ſuppoſed to be the Speaker of the Prologue, one old in his Profeſſion, and in the higheſt Eſteem. His Authority therefore, approving both the Poet and the Poem, would carry in it a great deal of Weight. *Terence* is beſides compared with another of his Profeſſion, one of great Authority, and long ſtanding, I mean *Cacilius*. *Ambivius* argues from his Example, that this Play's being ſo often refuſed, ought to be no Objection to it at preſent, for the ſame had happened often to the other, and but once to our Poet.

1 *Orator ad vos venio.* Orator here is commonly underſtood to ſignfy an Envoy or Embaſſador, as in *Ennius*.

*Orator ſine pace redit, regique refert rem.* For altho' the proper Buſineſs of the Prologue was to relate the Subject of the Play, yet here *Ambivius* is an Embaſſador or Orator from the Poet to the Audience, to plead his Cauſe. See more of this in the Notes upon the Prologue to the *Self-Tormentor.*

4 *Novas qui exactus feci ut inveteraſcerent.* There is ſomething very ingenious in this. When I was but a young Actor, I made you in time reliſh Pieces that at firſt you had rejected; why ſhould I not now attempt the ſame in favour of this Play of *Terence*? I am old, have had long Experience, and therefore ought to be a better Judge of what will entertain and divert you. If I ſucceeded

then,

# ALTER, PROLOGUS.

ORator ad vos venio ornatu prologi;
Sinite exorator sim, eodem ut jure uti senem
Liceat, quo jure sum usus adolescentior,
Novas qui exactas feci ut inveterascerent,
Ne cum poetâ scripturâ evanesceret.
In his; quas primùm Cæcili didici novas,
Partim sum earum exactus, partim vix steti.
Quia scibam dubiam fortunam esse scenicam
Spe incertâ, certum mihi laborem sustuli.
Easdem agere cœpi; ut ab eodem alias discerem
Novas studiosè, ne illum ab studio abducerem.
Perfeci ut spectarentur: ubi sunt cognitæ,
Placitæ sunt, ita poetam restitui in locum,
Prope jam remotum, injuriâ advorsariûm,
Ab studio, atque ab labore, atque arte musicâ.
Quòd si scripturam sprevissem in præsentiâ, &
In derrendo voluissem operam sumere,
Ut in otio esset, potiùs quàm in negotio;
Deterruissem facilè, ne alias scriberet.
Nunc quid petam, meâ causâ, æquo animo attendite.
Hecyram ad vos refero, quam mihi per silentium
Nunquam agere licitum est; ita eam oppressit calamitas.
Eam calamitatem vostrâ intellegentia
Sedabit, si erit adjutrix hostræ industriæ.
Cùm primùm eam agere cœpi, pugilum gloria,
Funambuli eodem accessit exspectatio;
Comitum conventus, strepitus, clamor mulierum
Fecere, ut ante tempus exirem foras.
Vetere in novâ cœpi uti consuetudine.
In experiundo ut essem. refero denuo;

*terruissem, ne scriberet alias. Nunc meâ causâ attendite æquo animo, qui petam. Refero Hecyram, ad vos, quam, nunquam est licitum: mihi agere per silentium, calamitas ita oppressit eam. Vostra intelligentia, si erit adjutrix vostræ industriæ, sedabit eam calamitatem. Cum primùm cœpi agere eam, gloria pugilum, expectatio funambuli accessit eodem, conventus comitum, strepitus; clamor mulierum fecere, ut exirem foras ante tempus. Cœpi uti vetere consuetudine in nova fabula, ut essem in experiundo. Refero denuo;*

*ORDO.*

VEnio orator ad vos ornatu prologi; sine sim exorator, ut liceat senem uti eodem jure, quo jure sum usus adolescentior, qui feci novas exactas ut inveterascerent, ne scriptura evanesceret cum poeta. In his fabulis Cæcilii, quas novas primum didici, partim earum sum exactus, partim vix steti. Quia scibam fortunam scenicam esse dubiam, sustuli certum laborem mihi, incerta spe. Cœpi agere easdem, ut discerem alias novas studiose ab eodem, ne abducerem illum ab studio. Perfeci ut spectarentur: ubi sunt cognitæ, sunt placitæ. Ita restitui poetam in lætum, jam prope remotum injuria adire furiorem ab studio, atque ab labore, atque arte musica. Quod si sprevissem scripturam in præsentia, et voluissem sumere operam in deterrenda, ut esset in otio potius quam in negotio, facile deterruissem, ne scriberet alias. Nunc meâ causâ attendite æquo animo, qui petam. Refero Hecyram ad vos, quam, nunquam est licitum mihi agere per silentium, calamitas ita oppressit eam. ... Cum primùm ... conventus comitum, strepitus; ... Cœpi uti vetere consuetudine in nova fabula,

## ANNOTATIONS.

then, 'tis much more likely that I should succeed now; nor can you accuse me of Temerity or Forwardness for resuming an old Practice I have so great Reason to think well of.

*12 Perfeci ut spectarentur.* Cæcilius was one of the greatest Names among the Roman comic Poets. His Works were in great Esteem in After-Ages, and even at this very Time; and yet we plainly see from hence, with what difficulty they were at first receiv'd. The Bulk of the Audience are seldom capable of forming any true Judgment of the real Merit of a Performance. But we have here a very commendable Example in a celebrated Actor. He knew the Value of the Play, and therefore was not daunted by Opposition. His Steddiness and Perseverance procured the Poet a fair Hearing; and that the Audience might not think he claimed all the Merit to himself, he adds, *ubi sunt cognitæ, placitæ sunt.* Worth, if once set in a proper Light, will always recommend itself.

*25 Pugilum gloria.* To render the Sense compleat,

firſt Act I pleaſe, when mean time a Rumour ſpreads, that a Combat of Gladiators was to be exhibited. The People flock together, in tumultuous Crouds; Clamours, and a Contention for Places enſue, nor was it in the mean time poſſible for me to ſtand my Ground. Now there is no Diſturbance; but all Attention and Silence. I have now again an Opportunity granted of exhibiting this Play; 'tis yours properly *by a candid Judgment* to encourage and adorn theſe Dramatic Shews. Suffer not, by your Neglect, the Muſes and their Art to ſink into the Hands of a few; but make your Authority the Aid and Support of mine. If I never was governed by Avarice, in fixing the Price of my Art; but always accounted it my higheſt Gain to contribute as much as poſſible to your Pleaſure and Entertainment; allow me to obtain this of you, that a Poet, who commits his Works to my Defence, and throws himſelf upon your Protection, may not be injuriouſly expoſed to the Inſults of malicious Foes. For my Sake admit of this Plea, and attend with Silence, that other Poets too may be encouraged to write *for the Stage*, nor I be deterr'd from ſtudying new Plays, bought at my Hazard and Expence.

ACT

## ANNOTATIONS.

compleat, we muſt ſupply *acceſſit*. The Expreſſion is beautiful; *Pugilum gloria*, inſtead of *glorioſi pugiles*.

37 *Poteſtas condecorandi ludos, &c.* Madam *Dacier* obſerves upon this, that it is not his own Intereſt, that of the Poet, or even of the Audience, that be lays the chief Streſs upon. He affects a Concern for the ſacred Feſtivals of the Gods, which were in danger of being depriv'd of one of their chief Ornaments, if by a too great Severity they diſcouraged the Poets, who furniſhed the Theatrical Entertainments commonly exhibited on theſe Occaſions. There is great Force and Elegance in this.

39 *Facite, ut veſtra auctoritas, &c.* He means, that although at his Age, and with the Experience he may be ſuppoſed to have acquir'd, his Authority ought to be of the greateſt Weight, yet he ſtill wants to have the farther Support of their Aſſent and Concurrence, without which his Endeavours would be of little Service, and Poetry thus diſcouraged would ſink into the Hands of a few, and thoſe too probably Men of the loweſt Genius.

49 *Precio emtas meo.* Theſe Words I have rendered according to the literal Meaning, though there is great Diſpute among Commentators as to their real Import. *Donatus*, and after him, Madam *Dacier*, explain *pretio* by *æſtimatione*; that *Ambivius* aſcertained the Value of the Play, how much the *Ædiles* might give for it. This they think appears manifeſtly from the Concluſion of the firſt Prologue, where we are told, that the Action of the Play being interrupted, *Terence* would not attempt the Repreſentation of it a ſecond Time, that he might

ſell

Primo actu placeo ; cùm interea rumor venit,
Datum iri gladiatores ; populus convolat :
Tulmultuantur, clamant, pugnant de loco.
Ego interea meum non potui tutari locum.
Nunc turba nulla eft : otium, & filentium eft,  35
Agendi tempus mihi datum eft : vobis datur
Poteftas condecorandi ludos fenicos.
Notile finere per vos artem muficam
Recidere ad paucos. facite, ut veftra auctoritas
Meæ auctoritati fautrix adjutrixque fit.  40
Si nunquam avarè precium ftatui arti meæ,
Et eum efle quæftum, in animum induxi maxumum,
Quam maxumè fervire voftris commodis ;
Sinite impetrare me, qui in tutelam meam
Studium fuum, & fe in voftram commifit fidem,  45
Ne eum circumventum iniquè iniqui irrideant.
Meâ causâ caufam accipite, & filentium date,
Ut lubeat fcribere aliis, mihique ut difcere
Noyas expediat, pofthac precio emtas meo.

*placeo primo actu ; cum interea rumor venit gladiatores datum iri : populus convolat : tulmultuantur, clamant, pugnant de loco ; ego interea non potui tutari meum locum. Nunc eft nulla turba, eft otium et filentium. Tempus agendi eft datum mihi ; poteftas datur vobis condecorandi ludos fcenicos. Nolite finere per vos artem muficam recidere ad paucos. Facite, ut veftra auctoritas fit fautrix adjutrixque meæ auctoritati. Si nunquam ftatui precium meæ arti, et induxi in animum eum : efsè quæftum maximum ; fervire quam maxime veftris commodis, finite me impetrare, ne iniqui irrideant eum inique circumventum, qui commifit fuum ftudium in meam tutelam, et fe in veftram fidem. Accipite hanc caufam mea caufa, et date filentium, ut lubeat aliis fcribere, utque expediat mihi difcere novas, emtas pofthac meo precio.*

## ANNOTATIONS.

fell it as a new one upon fome other Occafion. Now had the Comedians bought it, it no longer belong'd to the Poet, but muft be entirely at their Difpofal. Madam *Dacier* therefore fuppofes the Cafe to be thus: When the *Ædiles* had a Mind to buy any Comedy for the Stage, they gave it to the Mafter of the Company, who was to perufe it, and fet a Price upon it. If it did not fucceed, the Mafter was bound to return the Money to the Magiftrates, which made it their proper Intereft to fupport the Piece with all their Credit, as the Lofs, if it was rejected, redounded to themfelves. This it muft be owned is ingenious, but has nothing to fupport it but Conjecture. We are entirely unacquainted with the Manner of thefe Tranfactions between the *Ædiles*, Players, and Poet, and therefore can pronounce nothing with Certainty about them. Befides, I believe it will be hard to find an Inftance where *Pretium* is put for *Æftimatio Pretii.* I am therefore more inclined to think, that on fome Occafions the *Ædiles*, on others the Mafter of the Company bought the Play, of which laft was the *Hecyra.* But how in either Cafe, if it was not received, the Poet could claim to fell it again ; is a Matter not eafy to be determined at this Diftance of Time.

o

P. TE-

# *TERENCE's*
# STEP-MOTHER.

## ACT I. SCENE I.

### ARGUMENT.

Philotis *and* Syra *are angry with* Pamphilus *for marrying, and abandoning* Bacchis, *to whom he had pretended Love.*

### PHILOTIS, SYRA.

*Phil.* VERILY, *Syra,* 'tis but seldom that we meet with a Lover who continues faithful to a Miſtreſs. Even this *Pamphilus,* how often has he ſworn to *Bacchis* (how ſolemnly too, that any one might have been induc'd to believe him) that he would never marry while ſhe liv'd! Well, he has married you ſee notwithſtanding.

*Sy.* I therefore earneſtly counſel and adviſe you to pity none; but to fleece, maul, and rend every one that comes in your way.

*Phil.* What to except none?

*Sy.* None. For know, that not one of theſe Sparks comes to you but with Deſign by his Flatteries to enjoy you at the cheapeſt Rate he can. And prithee ought not you in your turn, if poſſible, to countermine them?

*Phil.* But to ſerve all alike, is I think, *barbarous and unjuſt.*

*Sy.* Is there any Barbarity or Injuſtice in being revenged of our Enemies? Or drawing them into thoſe very Snares they had contriv'd againſt others? Alas! Why have not I that blooming Age and Beauty of yours, or you theſe Sentiments of mine!

ACT

### ANNOTATIONS.

The Poet here, as in all his other Plays, begins with letting us into as much of the Plot, as is neceſſary for underſtanding the ſeveral Incidents and Characters, according to the Order in which they are to appear. *Pamphilus* was ſo greatly attached to a Courtezan named *Bacchis,* that he had made a Promiſe never to marry while ſhe liv'd. *Philotis,* another Courtezan, who uſed to make one at their Merry-Meetings, was no Stranger to this. Being under a Neceſſity ſome time after of going to *Corinth,* ſhe is ſurprized at her Return to hear that *Pamphilus,* notwithſtanding his Promiſe, is actually married. This Breach of Faith makes the Subject of her Converſation with *Syra* in the preſent Scene. The latter, who was an old Bawd, takes hence Occaſion to give her ſome Inſtructions, with regard to her Management of the Men, that ſince

they

# P. TERENTII
# HECYRA.

## ACTUS I. SCENA I.

### ARGUMENTUM.

*Philotis et Syra indigne ferunt, Pamphilum uxorem duxisse, relicta quam amare videbatur Bacchide.*

#### PHILOTIS, SYRA.

PER pol quàm paucos reperias meretricibus
  Fideles evenire amatores, Syra.
Vel hic Pamphilus jurabat quoties Bacchidi,
Quàm sanctè, ut quivis facilè posset credere,
Nunquàm illâ vivâ ducturum uxorem domum :  5
En, duxit. SY. ergo propterea te sedulò
Et moneo, & hortor, ne cujusquam misereat,
Quin spolies, mutiles, laceres, quemque nacta sis.
PH. Utin' eximium neminem habeam? SY. neminem :
Nam nemo illorum quisquam, scito, ad te venit,  10
Quin ita paret sese, abs te ut blanditiis suis
Quam minimo precio suam voluptatem expleat.
Hiscine tu, amabo, non contra insidiabere?
PH. Tamen pol eandem injurium est esse omnibus.
SY. Injurium autem est ulcisci adversarios?  15
Aut quâ viâ te captent illi, eâdem ipsos capi?
Eheu me miseram! cur non aut istæc mihi
Ætas & forma est, aut tibi hæc sententia?

*quin ita paret sese, ut suis blanditiis expleat suam voluptatem abs te quam minima precio. Amabo, non tu contra insidiabere hiscine? PH. Tamen pol, injurium est esse eandem omnibus. SY. Injurium autem est ulcisci adversarios? Aut ipsos capi eadem via, qua illi captent te? Eheu me miseram! Cur non aut istæ ætas et forma est mihi, aut hæc sententia tibi?*

ORDO.

PH. POL, reperias perquam paucos fideles amatores evenire meretricibus, Syra. Vel hic Pamphilus quoties quam sanctè jurabat Bacchidi, ut quivis facilè posset credere. ei, se nunquam ducturum uxorem domum, illâ vivâ: en duxit, SY. Ergo propterea sedulo. et moneo. et hortor te, ne misereat te cujusquam, quin spolies, mutiles, laceres, quemque sis nacta. PH. Utine habeam neminem eximium? SY. Neminem: nam scito, nemo quisquam illorum venit ad te.

### ANNOTATIONS.

they were for the most part selfish and mercenary, and had no other Views than present Gratification, she ought to shew no Mercy, but make the most of them she can.

9 *Utin' eximium neminem habeam?* To exempt none, to give none the Preference, *Eximia pecora*, as *Donatus* observes, were those chosen from among the rest of the Flock, and fed with Care, either for the Master's own Use, or the Purposes of Sacrifice.

17 *Eheu me miseram*, &c. These two Lines are extremely happy in the Sentiment, and strongly mark the Character of this old Bawd. *Horace* seems to have had them in his Eye, B. 4. Ode 10. 7.

*Quæ mens est hodie, cur eadem non puero*
  *fuit?*
*Vel cur his animis incolumes non redeunt*
  *genæ.*

ACTUS

## ACT I. SCENE II.

### ARGUMENT.

Parmeno *tells* Philotis, *who was juft return'd from abroad, the whole Story of his Mafter, which ferves as an Argument to the Play.*

### PARMENO, PHILOTIS, SYRA.

*Par.* IF the old Man fhould afk for me, fay I'm juft gone to the Key to enquire about the Arrival of *Pamphilus.* Do you take me, *Scirtus?* If he afks for me, I fay, then you are to give this anfwer; if not, fay nothing at all; that I may have this Excufe to plead another time. But is not that *Philotis* there? Whence comes fhe, I wonder? *Philotis,* your very humble Servant.

*Phi.* O your Servant, *Parmeno.*

*Sy. Parmeno* I heartily wifh you well!.

*Par.* And I you by *Pollux, Syra.* Tell me, *Philotis,* where have you been a pleafuring this long while?

*Phi.* Very little Pleafure, Heaven knows I have had, who went to *Corinth* with a Soldier, the moft brutifh Fellow on Earth. There for two whole Years together I was forc'd to bear all his Impertinence and Rudenefs.

*Par.* I doubt not, *Philotis,* you have often repented of this foolifh Jaunt, and wifh'd to be in *Athens* again.

*Phi.* It is not to be exprefs'd how impatient I was to come home again, and leave this Soldier, that I might fee my old Friends, and enjoy the fame free Merry-Meetings with them as formerly. For there I durft not fpeak, but when, and what he pleas'd.

*Par.* It was not well methinks in the Captain, thus to lay a reftraint on your Tongue.

*Phi.* But what's this, *Parmeno?* What a ftrange Story has *Bacchis* been telling me juft now within? I could never have thought that he would confent to marry while fhe was living.

*Par.* Marry! I fay marry too.

*Phi.* Au! Is he not married?

*Par.* He is, but I doubt whether it will be a lafting Marriage.

*Phi.* So grant Heaven, if it is for *Bacchis*'s Advantage. But tell me, *Parmeno,* how fhall I believe it?                    *Par.*

### ANNOTATIONS.

While *Syra* and *Philotis* are difcourfing together, *Parmeno, Pamphilus*'s Servant comes out from his Mafter's. As from him they expect to learn the Particulars of the Story, and the Reafons of his Mafter's acting fo contrary to his Promife, *Philotis* enquires, and with fome difficulty prevails upon him to let her into all he knew. By his Account we are informed, that *Pamphilus,* much againft his Inclination, was by his Father's Importunity compell'd to marry. That after his Marriage, he ftill reforted to *Bacchis,* his Averfion to his Wife rather growing upon him. But as fhe was become peevifh and infupportable, and *Philumena* behaved with great Temper and Prudence, he by degrees contracts a Liking to her, and forgets the other. By the Death of a Friend, which happens about this time, he is call'd from home. *Philumena* is left with her Mother-in-Law. At firft they live together in great Harmony, but after fome time, *Philumena* pretending a Vifit to her Mother, refufes to return; which creates a Sufpicion that fome Mifunderftanding had happened. Matters therefore were at prefent in fuch

# ACTUS I. SCENA II.

## ARGUMENTUM.

*Redeunti peregere Philoti, Parmeno totius narrat argumentum*
*fabulæ.*

PARMENO, PHILOTIS, SYRA.     O R D O.

SENEX ſi quæret me, modò iſſe dicito
  Ad portum percontatum adventum Pamphili.
Audin', quiſ dicam, Scirte? ſi quæret me, utì
Tum dicas : ſi non quæret, nullus dixeris;
Aliàs ut uti poſſim caúsâ hac integrâ.    5
Sed videon' ego Philotium? unde hæc advenit?
Philotis, ſalve multùm. PH. ô ſalve, Parmeno.
SY. Salve mecaſtor, Parmeno. PA. & tu edepol, Syra.
Dic mihi, Philoti, ubi te oblectaſti tam diu?
PH. Minime equidem me oblectavi, quæ cum milite 10
Corinthum hinc ſum profecta inhumaniſſimo.
Biennium ibi perpetuum miſera illum tuli.
PA. Edepol te deſiderium Athenarum arbitror,
Philotium, cepiſſe ſæpe, & te tuum
Conſilium contemſiſſe. PH. non dici poteſt,    15
Quam cupida eram huc redeundi, abeundi à milite,
Voſque hic videndi, antiquâ ut conſuetudine
Agitarem inter vos liberè convivium.
Nam illî haud licebat niſi præfinitò loqui
Quæ illi placerent. PA. haud opinor commodè    20
Finem ſtatuiſſe orationi militem
PH. Sed quid hoc negoti eſt? modò quæ narravit mihi
Hîc intus Bacchis? quod ego nunquam credidi
Fore, ut ille hac vivâ poſſet animum inducere
Uxorem habere. PA. habere autem? PH. eho tu, an
     non habet?    25
PA. Habet : ſed firmæ hæ vereor ut ſint nuptiæ.
PH. Ita Dî Deæque faxint, ſi in rem eſt Bacchidis.
Sed qui iſtuc credam ita eſſe? dic mihi, Parmeno.

PAR. SI ſenex quæret me dicito me eſſe modo ad portum, percontatum adventum Pamphili. Audin', quid dicam, Scirte? uti tum dicas, ſi quæret me; ſi non quæret, nullus dixeris; ut alias poſſim uti hac cauſa integra. Sed videone ego Philotium? Unde hæc advenit? Philotis, ſalve multum. PH. O ſalve, Parmeno. SY. Salve mecaſtor, Parmeno. PA. Et edepol, Syra. Dic mihi, Philoti, ubi oblectaſti te tam diu? PH. Minime oblectavi me equidem, quæ ſum profecta hinc Corinthum cum milite inhumaniſſimo. Miſera tuli illum ibi perpetuum biennium. PA. Edepol, Philotium, arbitror deſiderium Athenarum ſæpe cepiſſe te, et te contemſiſſe tuum conſilium. PH. Non poteſt dici, quam cupida eram redeundi huc, abeundi a milite, videndique vos hic, ut

*antiqua conſuetudine agitarem convivium libere inter vos. Nam illic haud licebat loqui niſi præ-*
*finito quæ placerent illi. PH. Opinor militem haud commode ſtatuiſſe finem orationi. PH. Sed quid*
*negotii eſt hoc? Quæ Bacchis modo narravit mihi hic intus? Quod ego nunquam credidi fore, ut*
*ille poſſet inducere animum habere uxorem hâc viva. PH. Habere autem? PH. Eho tu, an non*
*habet? PA. Habet : ſed vereor ut hæ nuptiæ ſint firmæ. PH. Ita dii deæque faxint, ſi eſt in rem*
*Bacchidis. Sed qui credam iſtuc eſſe ita? Dic mihi, Parmeno.*

## ANNOTATIONS.

a Situation, that it was uncertain, whether at *Pamphilus*'s Return the Marriage would continue, or be broken off.

  8 *Salve mecaſtor, Parmeno.* The Ancients, as *Donatus* obſerves, were wont to add ſometimes to their Salutations the Form of an Oath, to give them the greater Air of Sincerity. *Mecaſtor* ſignifies the ſame as *by Caſtor :* in like manner *ædepol* quaſi *æde Pollucis,* by the Temple of *Pollux.*

  20 *Haud opinor commode.* It was not well methinks in the Captain, &c. This I take

                           to

*Par.* It is a thing not to be told, aſk me no more about it.

*Phi.* For fear, perhaps, left I ſhould divulge it. But by all that's Sacred I aſk not with a Deſign to ſpeak of it to any Body, but for my own private Satisfaction.

*Par.* All theſe fair Words ſhall never perſuade me to truſt my Back to your Diſcretion.

*Phi.* Nay don't, *Parmeno*; as if you now were not rather more impatient to tell me, than I am to know.

*Par.* What ſhe ſays is true; and that's my greateſt Failing. Promiſe to be ſecret, and I'll tell you.

*Phi.* That's like yourſelf. Come then, I promiſe.

*Par.* *Pamphilus* was then in the very Height of his Paſſion for *Bacchis*, when his Father began to importune him to marry, and urge all thoſe Reaſons that are commonly uſed by Parents in ſuch Caſes; as that himſelf was in Years, that he was his only Child, and that he wanted a Support in his old Age. At firſt *Pamphilus* refuſed; but his Father preſſing him ſtrongly, he began to waver, uncertain whether be ſhould yield to Duty, or Love. At length, by importunity and teazing, the old Man prevailed: he contracted him to his Neighbour's Daughter here. This did not ſo much af-fect *Pamphilus*, till he found himſelf on the very Point of Marriage: but when he ſaw all ready, and that there was now no Delay, but marry he muſt; then indeed, he laid it ſo much to Heart, that I perſuade myſelf, had even *Bacchis* been preſent, ſhe muſt have pi-tied him. As often as he had an Opportunity of being with me alone; *Parmeno*, would he ſay, I'm ruined, what have I done? Into what Calamities have I plunged myſelf! I cannot bear it, *Parmeno*, I'm miſerable and ruin'd for ever!

*Phi.* All the Gods and Goddeſſes confound thee, *Laches*, ſor teaz-ing him ſo. *Par.*

*A N N O T A T I O N S.*

to be the moſt eaſy and natural Meaning of the Words. Madam *Dacier* indeed gives them a different Turn. *Je croi en effet que tu capitaine te tailloit tes diſcours bien court, et que tu n'en etois pas trop contente.* She obſerves, that this very naturally paints their different Characters, that of a Woman, who loves to talk a great deal, and that of a Soldier, who, full of himſelf, and fond of engroſſing all the Diſcourſe, can't bear to hear another ſpeak. *Caſaubon* on the contrary finds Humour and Pleaſantry intend-ed in this Anſwer of *Parmeno*, and thinks there is in it an Alluſion to the Manners of *Rhetoricians* and their Scholars. *Jocan-di materiam arripit vernula more ſuo, ex verbis mulieris non alias ſane valde ambiguis, quaſi illa conqueſta fuiſſet, ſibi quaſi diſcipulæ Rhetoris cujuſdam non licuiſſe, niſi ad legem et regulam, ſeu ad amuſſim præceptorum Rhetoricorum loqui,* quam regulam non commode præſcripſerit rudis miles, et ipſi præceptorum artis oratoriæ non ſa-tis gnarus. I have mentioned theſe ſeveral Explications of this Paſſage, that the Reader may have an Opportunity of comparing them together, and chooſing what he thinks moſt natural and eaſy.

34 *Ah! noli Parmeno.* I doubt whether the Remark of *Donatus* here is not rather too refin'd. *Philotis* here, ſays he, pretends, that ſhe has no Fondneſs, no Deſire to know what ſhe had aſk'd. She thinks to per-ſuade him by this, that as ſhe had little Curioſity, ſhe was of Conſequence one that might be ſafely truſted with a Secret: for Curioſity is almoſt always a ſure Mark of an inceſſant Talker, that can keep nothing. Hence *Horace* juſtly ſays, Epiſt. 1. 18. 69.

*Percontatorem fugito, nam garrulus idem eſt.*
But to me, this ſeems to be no more than

PA. Non eſt opus prolato : hoc percontarier.
Deſiſte. PH. nempe eâ causâ, ut ne id fiat palàm.　30
Ita me Dii amabunt; haud propterea te rogo, ut
Hoc proferam, ſed ut tacita mecum gaudeam.
PA. Nunquam tam dices commodè, ut tergum meum
Tuam in fidem committam. PH. ah, noli, Parmeno :
Quaſi non tu multo malis narrare hoc mihi,　　35
Quàm ego, quæ percontor, ſcire. PA. vera hæc præ-
　　dicat :
Et illud mi vitium eſt maxumum. Si mihi fidem
Das te tacituram, dicam. PH. ad ingenium redis.
Fidem do, loquere. PA. auſculta. PH. iſtîc ſum. PA.
　　hanc Bacchidem
Amabat, ut cum maxumè, tum Pamphilus,　　40
Cùm pater, uxorem ut dicat, orare occipit :
Et hæc, communia omnium quæ ſunt patrum,
Seſe ſenem eſſe dicere, illum autem eſſe unicum :
Præſidium velle ſe ſenectuti ſuæ.
Ille ſe primò negare : ſed poſtquam acriùs　　45
Pater inſtat, fecit animi ut incertus foret,
Pudorin' ahne amori obſequeretur magis.
Tundendo atque odio denique effecit ſenex :
Deſpondit ei gnatam hujus vicini proxumi.
Uſque illud viſum eſt Pamphilo neutiquam grave,　50
Donec jam in ipſis nuptiis, poſtquam videt
Paratas, nec moram ullam, quin ducat, dari ;
Ibi demùm ita ægrè tulit, ut ipſam Bacchidem
Si adeſſet, credo, ibi ejus commiſereſceret.
Ubicunque datum erat ſpatium ſolitudinis,　　55
Ut conloqui mecum unà poſſet : Parmeno,
Perii : quid ego egi ? in quod me conjeci malum ?
Non potero hoc ferre, Parmeno : perii miſer.
PH. At te Dî Deæque perduint cum iſto odio, Laches.

PA. Non eſt opus prolato : deſiſte percontari hoc. PH. Nempè ea cáuſa, ne id fiat palam. Ita Dii amabunt me, haud propterea rogo te, ut proferam hæc, ſed ut tacita gaudeam mecum. PA. Nunquam dices tam commode, ut committam meum tergum in tuam fidem. PH. Ah, noli, Parmeno : quaſi tu non multa malis narrare hoc mihi, quam ego ſcire quæ percontor. PH. Hæi prædicat vera ; et illud eſt maximum vitum mihi. Si das fidem mihi te tacituram, dicam. PH. Redis ad ingenium : do fidem, loquere. PA. Auſculta. PH. Sum iſtîc. PA. Pamphilus tum amabat hanc Bacchidem, ut cum amabat eam maxime, cum pater occipit orare, ut ducat uxorem ; et dicere hæc, quæ ſunt communia argumenta omnium patrum, ſeſe eſſe ſenem, illum autem eſſe unicum filium. Se velle præſidium ſuæ ſenectuti. Ille primo negare ſe poſſe, ſed poſtquam pater inſtat acrius,

fecit ut foret incertus animi, obſequereturne magis pudori, anne amori. Denique ſenex tundendo atque odio effecit : deſpondit ei gnatam hujus proximi virini. Illud neutiquam eſt viſum grave Pamphilo, uſque donec jam in ipſis nuptiis : poſtquam videt eas paratas, nec ullam moram dari, quin ducat ; ibi demum tulit ita ægræ, ut credo commiſereſceret ipſam Bacchidem ejus, ibi ſi adeſſet. Ubicunque ſpatium ſolitudinis erat datum, ut poſſet colloqui una mecum : diceret : Parmeno, perii, quid ego egi ? In quod malum conjeci me ? Parmeno, non potero ferre hoc : perii miſer. PH. At Dii Deæque perduint te, Laches, cum iſto odio.

## ANNOTATIONS.

an ironical Reply, intimating that ſhe knew Parmeno too well not to be ſatisfied that he was as impatient to impart the Secret to her, as ſhe was to know it.

40 _Bacchidem amabat._ The Senſe and proper Diſpoſition of the Sentence is thus : Hanc Bacchidem tum amabat Pamphilus, at cum maxime amabat, quum pater uxorem, ut ducat, orare occipit. The whole is contriv'd to contain a Vindication of Pamphilus, that it was by Compulſion, and not Choice, he married, and forſook his Miſtreſs.

48 _Tundendo atque odio._ The Poet manages this Part of his Subject with great Dexterity and Art. Pamphilus is a favourite Character in the Play, and as his Breach of Promiſe to Bacchis ſeemed to carry ſome Appearance of Levity, Terence is ſolicitous



to

*Par.* To be short, he takes home his Wife : the first Night he offered not to touch her, the second it was the same.

*Phi.* How d'ye say ? A young Spark after a hearty Glass be in Bed with a Girl, and not offer to touch her ? It does not seem likely, nor do I believe it.

*Par.* I suppose it must appear incredible to you, because your Visitors generally come with good Appetites ; but he married her against his Will.

*Phi.* Well, what followed ?

*Par.* A few Days after *Pamphilus* took me aside, and told me that even then she remain'd a Virgin for him : that before he took his Wife home, he had hoped *Time* might reconcile him to the Marriage.   But as I cannot resolve to live with her any longer ; to abuse her, or not return her to her Parents untouch'd, as I received her, were dishonourable in me, and prejudicial to the Girl herself.

*Phi.* What you tell me of *Pamphilus*, argues him a Youth of good Principles and Modesty.

*Par.* For me, (continues he) to make known this my Design, would not do so well, and to return her to her Father without any Pretence of Blame, were insolent.   But I am in hopes, that when she finds it impossible to live with me, she'll go of herself.

*Phi.* But what did he all this while ? Did he continue his Visits to *Bacchis ?*

*Par.* Every Day : but as you may suppose, when she saw him given to another, she strait became ill-natur'd, and inaccessible.

*Phi.* Truly I don't wonder at it.

*Par.* And indeed this was what chiefly contributed to alienate him from her, after he had returned a little to himself, and began to know his Mistress and his Wife at home, estimating their Manners by Comparison.   His Wife, as might be expected from her Education and Birth, chaste, modest, patient under the Injuries and Ill-Treatment of her Husband, and anxious to hide his Faults.   Thus partly touch'd with Compassion for his Wife, partly

tir'd

*ANNOTATIONS.*

to vindicate him from this Charge. He shews how difficult it was to bring him to a Compliance, and that only the Sense of his Duty to a Parent could have conquered his Resolution.   Nor even after Marriage does he find it an easy Matter to withdraw his Affections from the Person on whom he had once placed them.   Time, Consideration, the peevish Behaviour of *Bacchis*, the Temper, Prudence, and good Sense of his Wife, all conspire to bring him to Reason and sound Reflection.

64 *Sese illa abstinere.* Although *abstinere* is here used in a Sense that regards the Passions, yet its common Acceptation for the most part is different. For *abstinentia* and *continentia* are used to express Virtues very distinct in their Natures.   The first denotes Moderation in Opportunities of enriching ourselves from the Publick, or from the private Fortunes of others entrusted to our Care. Hence it is generally used in speaking of Men in Power, Trust, and Authority. *Continentia* again imports a due Regulation of our Passions in Matters of Love and Desire.

73 *Sed quam decrêim.* We have in this Speech a manifest Proof of the natural good Disposition of *Pamphilus.* He could not reconcile himself to the Marriage, and, as he had determined to part from his Wife, he thought it would be doing her an Injury not to return her untouched, as he received

her.

PA. Ut ad pauca redeam, uxorem deducit domum: 60
Nocte illâ primâ virginem non attigit:
Quæ consecuta est nox, eam nihilo magis.
PH. Quid ais ? cum virgine unà adolescens cubuerit
Plus potus, sese illâ abstinere ut potuerit ?
Non verisimile dicis: nec verum arbitror. 65
PA. Credo ita videri tibi: nam nemo ad te venit,
Nisi cupiens tui: ille invitus illam duxerat.
PH. Quid deinde fit ? PA. diebus sane pauculis
Pòst, Pamphilus me solum seducit foras,
Narratque, ut virgo ab se integra etiam tum siet: 70
Seque ante, quàm eam uxorem duxisset domum,
Sperasse eas tolerare posse nuptias.
Sed quam decrêrim me non posse diutiùs
Habere, eam ludibrio haberi, Parmeno,
Quin integram itidem reddam, ut accepi à suis, 75
Neque honestum mihi, neque utile ipsi virgini est.
PA. Pium ac pudicum ingenium narras Pamphili.
PA. Hoc ego proferre, incommodum mihi esse arbitror.
Reddi patri autem, cui tu nihil dicas vitî,
Superbum est: sed illam spero, ubi hoc cognoverit, 80
Non posse se mecum esse, abituram denique.
PH. Quid interea? ibatne ad Bacchidem? PA. quotidie.
Sed, ut fit, postquam hunc alienum ab sese videt,
Maligna multo & magis procax facta illico est.
PH. Non edepol mirum. PA. atque ea res multo ma-
    xumè 85
Disjunxit illum ab illâ, postquam & ipse se,
Et illam, & hanc, quæ domi erat, cognovit satis,
Ad exemplum ambarum mores earum existumans.
Hæc, ita utì liberali esse ingenio decet,
Pudens, modesta; incommoda atque injurias 90
Viri omnes ferre, & tegere contumelias.
Hîc animus, partim uxoris misericordiâ

PA. Ut redeam ad pauca, deducit uxorem domum: Illa prima nocte non attigit virginem: quæ nox est consecuta, nibilo magis attigit eam. PH. Quid ais ? Adolescens plus potus cubuerit una cum virgine, ut potuerit sese abstinere illa ? Dicis non verisimile, nec arbitror esse verum. PA. Credo videri ita tibi; nam nemo venit ad te, nisi cupiens tui: ille invitus duxerat illam. PH. Quid deinde fit ? PA. Sane diebus pauculis post, Pamphilus seducit me solum foras, narratque, ut virgo etiam tum siet integra ab se: seque, antequam duxisset eam uxorem domum sperasse posse tolerare eas nuptias. Sed, Parmeno, eam, quam decreverim me non posse habere diutius, haberi ludibrio, quin itidem reddam integram, ut accepi a suis, neque est honestum mihi, neque utile ipsi virgini. PH. Narras pium ac pudicum ingeniam Pamphili. PA. Ego arbitror esse incommodum mihi proferre hoc, superbum autem

est, eam reddi patri, cui tu dicas nil vitii: sed spero illam, ubi cognoverit hoc, se non posse esse mecum, abituram denique. PH. Quid interea ? Ibatne ad Bacchidem ? PA. Quotidie, sed ut fit, postquam videt hunc alienum ab sese, illico est facta multo magis maligna et procax. PH. Edepol non mirum. PA. Atque ea res multo maxime disjunxit illum ab illa, postquam et ipse satis cognovit se, et illam, et hanc, quæ erat domi, existimans mores earum ad exemplum ambarum: hæc pudens, modesta, ita uti decet mulierem liberali ingenio esse; ferre incommoda atque omnes injurias viri, et tegere contumelias. Ille animus, partim devinctus misericordia uxoris, partim.

## ANNOTATIONS.

her. But still he is anxious how to compass this. To own the real Reason, would be highly improper; and to restore one to whom there could not be so much as pretended any tolerable Reason of Dislike, was insolent and assuming. He resolves therefore upon a middle Way, by continuing his Reserve, to make her sensible that there was no likelihood of their ever living with any Satisfaction together. By this means he persuaded himself she would at length resolve of herself to withdraw, and save him the Confusion that would be unavoidable by taking it upon himself.

88 *Ad exemplum ambarum mores earum existumans.* Some read *astumans,* and the



Measure

tir'd with the Infolence of his Miftrefs, he by Degrees withdrew his Love from *Bacchis*, and fettled it here, when he found her of a Temper that fo well accorded with his own. Mean while an old Relation of their's dies at *Imbrus*, whofe Eftate by Law fell to them. Thither love-fick *Pamphilus* was compelled to go by his Father; much againft his Will. He left his Wife here with his Mother: for the old Man is retir'd into the Country, and but feldom comes to Town.

*Phi.* What is there yet in this Marriage to hinder it from being lafting?

*Par.* Now you fhall hear. At firft for feveral Days they agreed mighty well; but all of a fudden fhe took a ftrange Averfion to *Soflrata*, nor was there ever any Quarrel or Words between them.

*Phi.* What then?

*Par.* If at any time her Mother-in-Law came to talk with her, fhe withdrew immediately, and feem'd to decline her Company. But when fhe could no longer endure the Houfe, fhe pretended her Mother had fent for her to affift at a Sacrifice, and accordingly went. When fhe had been abfent fome Days, her Mother-in-Law fent for her: They made fome, I know not what, Excufe. Again fhe fends, but in vain; no body returns. In fine, after feveral Meffages, they pretend fhe is fick: my Miftrefs went immediately to fee her, but was not admitted. When the old Man heard of this, he came Yefterday from the Country on purpofe, and waited immediately on *Philumena*'s Father. What paffed between them, I don't yet know, but muft own I'm in a good deal of Concern about the Iffue of it. You have here the whole Bufinefs, now I'll on my way.

*Phil.* And I too, for there is a Stranger I have appointed to meet with about this time. *Par.*

*A N N O T A T I O N S.*

Meafure of the Verfe feems to require it. The Manner of fpeaking here ufed, is elegant and expreffive, and may be thus paraphrafed. *Mores utriufque ex comparatione mutua æftimans, et de utrifque ex hac comparatione judicans.* There is a good deal of Addrefs in the Poet's manner here. *Philumena* is commended for her Modefty, good Breeding, and Patience. *Bacchis* is paffed over in filence, which as it is a tacit Cenfure, fo it avoids openly blaming one Courtezan in prefence of another. It were pity not to remark here the fine moral Inftruction conveyed in thefe few Lines. A virtuous Wife is always fufficient to reclaim a Hufband not quite deftitute of Reflection. If fometimes he fuffers himfelf to be led by wandering Paffions, yet his good Senfe will at length get the better of thefe irregular Sallies; and when he comes to compare Virtue and Merit, with thefe tinfel Allurements, and deceitful Attractions, that are often but too apt to infatuate weak Minds, he will foon gain the Maftery of himfelf, and recall his Affections to their proper Object.

[100] *Nam fenex rus obdidit fe.* This is a Circumftance particularly to be obferved, becaufe upon it the Conduct of the Plot in a great Meafure depends. *Nam fac præfentem fenem* (fays *Donatus*) *et nullus error in fabula eft.* "Suppofe the old Man not "to refide in the Country, and the whole "Intrigue finks to the Ground at once." Upon his Abfence depends the fuppofed Mifunderftanding between *Philumena* and her Mother-in-Law, which furnifhes Matter to the feveral Converfations of the old Men, and contributes much to conceal the real Caufe of her Departure. *Pamphilus* too hence draws a plaufible Pretext for declining to take her back, till fuch time as he comes to difcover the Truth, and all his Scruples are removed.

104

Devinctus, partim victus hujus injuriis,
Paulatim elapsu'st Bacchidi, atque huc transtulit
Amorem, postquam par ingenium nactus est.      95
Interea in Imbro moritur cognatus senex
Horunc', ea ad hos rediebat lege hereditas.
Eò amantem invitum Pamphilum extrudit pater.
Relinquit cum matre hic uxorem : nam senex
Rus abdidit se : huc raro in urbem commeat.      100
PH. Quid adhuc habent infirmitatis nuptiæ ?
PA. Nunc audies. primùm dies complusculos
Bene conveniebat sane inter eas : interim
Miris modis odisse cœpit Sostratam :
Neque lites uilæ inter eas, postulatio      105
Nunquam. PH. quid igitur ? PA. si quando ad eam
   accesserat
Confabulatum, fugere è conspectu illico,
Videre nolle. denique, ubi non quit pati,
Simulat se à matre accersi ad rem divinam, abit.
Ubi illic dies est complures, accersi jubet :      110
Dixere causam tunc nescio quam : iterum jubet :
Nemo remisit. postquam accersunt sæpius,
Ægram esse simulant mulierem. nostra iilico
It visere ad eam : admisit nemo. hoc ubi senex
Rescivit, heri eâ causâ rure huc advenit,      115
Patrem continuò convenit Philumenæ.
Quid egerint inter se, nondum etiam scio :
Nisi sane curæ est, quorsum eventurum hoc siet.
Habes omnem rem : pergam quò cœpi hoc iter.
PH. Et quidem ego. nam constitui quodam ho-
   spite,



*illic complures dies, Sostrata jubet eam accersi. Dixere tunc nescio quam causam : jubet iterum :*
*Nemo remisit. Postquam accersunt sæpius, simulant mulierem esse ægram. Illico nostra it ad*
*eam visere : nemo admisit. Ubi senex rescivit hoc ; hei ea causa advenit huc rure ; continuo con-*
*venit patrem Philumenæ. Nondum etiam scio, quid igerint inter se : nisi sane est mihi curæ,*
*quorsum hoc sit eventurum. Habes omnem rem : pergam que cœpi hoc iter. PH. Et quidem ego,*
*num constituti cum quedam hospite.*

### *ANNOTATIONS.*

**104** *Miris modis odisse cœpit Sostratam.*
This *Parmeno* says barely by Conjecture ;
for as the real Reason of her absenting was
not known, it was ascrib'd to some Misunderstanding that had happened, betwixt
her and her Mother-in-Law. This Suspicion,
considering all Circumstances, was natural
enough, and the Poet has made an excellent Use of it in the Sequel of the Play.

**114** *In visere ad eam.* Criticks mark a
Difference in the Signification of *visere*, and
*videre.* *Visere* they tell us marks a Visit
of Complaisance and Civility ; *videre* of In-

terest, or Business. *Visere, officii est ; videre*
*quærentis.*

**115** *Hoc ubi senex rescivit.* There is no
thoroughly understanding the Genius of the
*Latin* Language, without attending carefully
to the Signification and Force of particular
Words, and understanding the nice Differences of Terms that are commonly called
synonymous. Thus *scire* and *rescire* seem to
be Words of the same Signification, and yet
the Ancients observed a Distinction between
them. Thus *scire* was used in more common Cases, where what we heard, or learnt,



gave

*Par.* I wiſh you good Luck.

*Phil.* Farewel.

*Par.* And farewell to you, good *Philotis.*

ANNOTATIONS.

gave us no Pain. *R ſcire* again was of Things that had been concealed from us, that were ſurprizing, and came unexpected. So *De-natus : Scimus quæ ad nos deferuntur, re-ſcimus*

---

# ACT II, SCENE I.

### ARGUMENT.

Laches *accuſes his Wife* Softrata, *that by her Severity and diſagreeable Temper ſhe had driven her Daughter-in-Law from the Houſe.* Softrata, *on the contrary, maintains, that this Charge is without Foundation.*

LACHES, SOSTRATA.

*Lac.* GOOD Heavens! What a ſtrange Set of Creatures are theſe? What an odd Conſpiracy? That Women ſhould thus all poſſeſs the ſame Inclinations and Averſions! Nor can you meet with ſo much as one, who ſwerves from the natural Diſpoſition of the Sex. Thus, Mothers-in-Law, as it were by Conſent, hate their Daughters-in-Law. Nor is it leſs their Study to croſs their Husbands: their Obſtinacy here is the ſame, To me they ſeem all to have been train'd up in the ſame School of Perverſeneſs : of which School, if there is any ſuch, I dare ſwear my Wife is the Miſtreſs.

*Soſt.* Unhappy that I am, who don't ſo much as know why it is I am thus accuſed.

*Lac.* Ha! You not know why?

*Soſt.* No, as I hope for Mercy, *Laches,* and as it is my Wiſh that we may long live happily together.

*Lac.* Heaven guard us all!

*Soſt.* You'll afterwards be ſenſible how unjuſtly you have accuſed me in this Affair.

*Lac.* I ſay unjuſtly too! Can Words be found ſufficient to expreſs what you deſerve, who thus diſcredit me, yourſelf, and the whole
Family,

ANNOTATIONS.

It will be neceſſary here to let the Reader partly into the Series of the Plot. *Pamphilus,* one Night overcome with Liquor, chanced to meet a Girl in the Street, whom he debauched ; but neither were known to the other, as it happened to be in the dark. It proved however to be the very *Philumena,* who was now his Wife. As ſhe was married ſoon after, the Affair might have been wholly ſmothered, but that his Attachment to *Bacchis* made *Pamphilus* abſtain ſome Months from the conjugal Embrace. Conſcious of this, and finding the Time of Childbed drawing near, ſhe in her Husband's Abſence makes ſome pretence of going home to her Mother, and there ſtays, expecting to be delivered before her Huſband's Return, and that thus all might be kept huſh and quiet. The Situation in which ſhe was, obliged her to avoid all Viſits from her Mother-in-Law; and this was what chiefly gave Riſe to the Suſpicion of a Miſunderſtanding
between

Me eſſe illum conventuram. PA. Di vortant bene
Quod agas. PH. vale. PA. & tu bene vale, Philotium.
PH. *Vale.* PA. *Et tu, Philotium, bene vale.*

| | me eſſe conventuram illum. PA. Dii vortant bene quod agas. |

### ANNOTATIONS.

*ſcimus celata.* And *Aulus Gellius*: Qui fa-
*Etum aliquod occultius aut inopinatum inſpe-* | *ratumque cognoſcit, is dicitur proprie reſcire.* It is thus that *Terence* always uſes it.

---

## ACTUS II. SCENA I.

### ARGUMENTUM.

*Soſtratam uxorem accuſat Laches, quod nurum Philumenam du-
ritie ſua, et morum-incommoditate, domo ejicerit: S.crus contra nihil tale a ſe peccatum eſſe contendit.*

### LACHES, SOSTRATA.

PROH Deûm atque hominum fidem, quod hoc ge-
    nus eſt? quæ hæc eſt conjuratio?
Utin' omnes mulieres eadem æquè ſtudeant nolintque
    omnia?                  [reperias:
Neque declinatam quidquam ab aliarum ingenio ullam
Itaque adeo uno animo omnes ſocrus oderunt nurus.
Viris eſſe advorſas æquè ſtudium eſt: ſimilis pertina-
    cia eſt.                             5
In eodemque omnes mihi videntur ludo doctæ ad ma-
    litiam.
Ei ludo. ſi ullus eſt, magiſtram hanc eſſe ſatis certò ſcio.
So. Me miſeram, quæ nunc, quamobrem accuſer, neſcio.
LA. hem, tu neſcis? So. non, ita me Dii ament, mi
    Laches,..
Itaque unà inter nos agere ætatem liceat. LA. Dii
    mala prohibeant!                   10
So. Meque abs te immeritò eſſe accuſatam, poſt-
    modò reſciſces. LA. ſcio.        [dici poteſt,
Te immeritò? an quidquam pro iſtis factis dignum te

*neſcis? SO. Non, mi Laches, ita Dii ament me, itaque liceat agere ætatem una inter nos. LA.
Dii prohibeant mala! So. Reſciſceſque poſtmodo, me eſſe accuſatum immerito abs te. LA. Scio,
Te immerito? An quidquam dignum te poteſt dici pro iſtis factis.*

ORDO.

LA. PRoh ſd.m
    Deûv: at-
que hominum, quod
genus eſt hoc? quæ
conjuratio eſt hæc?
Utine omnes mulieres,
æque ſtudeant nolint-
que eædem omnia?
neque reperias ullam
quidquam declinatam
ab ingenio aliarum:
Itaque adeo omnes ſo-
crus uno animo ode-
runt nurus. Eſt iis
æque ſtudium eſſe ad-
verſas viris: Perti-
nacia eſt ſimilis. Om-
neſque videntur mibi
doctæ ad malitiam in
eodem ludo. Scio ſa-
tis certo banc eſſe ma-
giſtram ei ludo, ſi eſt
ullus. So. Me miſe-
ram, quæ nunc ne-
ſcio quamobrem ac-
cuſer. LA. Hem, tu

### ANNOTATIONS.

between them. *Laches* proceeds upon this
Suppoſition, and ſeverely chides his Wife;
who, on the contrary, endeavours to juſtify
herſelf.

4 *Itaque adeo uno animo.* This is a general Perſuaſion, prevalent not only in the
Times of our Poet, but ſtill equally received;
and it is certain, that the frequent Animo-
ſities between Mothers and Daughters-in-

Law have given but too great Foundation
for ſuch a Notion. But it is a Fault to be
governed by general Prejudices. Many inſtances of perfect Harmony and a good Underſtanding between the abovementioned
Kind of Relations, occur to our Obſerva-
tion every Day; and theſe ought to have
equal Influence, and make us judge in doubtful Caſes favourably. *Laches* here reviles



his

Family, and lay up Vexation for your Son. You even make Ene mies of our Friends and Relations, thofe who thought your Son worthy of being efpoufed to their Daughter. 'Tis you, forfooth, that have ftarted up to raife all this Difturbance by your Folly.

*Soft.* I ftarted up?

*Lac.* You, I fay, Woman, who take me furely for a Stone, and not a Man. Do you think, becaufe I'm fo often in the Country, that I am a Stranger to your Manner of Life here? But let me tell you, I know better what's done here, than at the Place where I am daily, becaufe your Behaviour at home affects my Character abroad. I heard indeed fometime ago, that *Philumena* had taken an Averfion to you, nor did I wonder at it; nay, I fhould have wondered much more, had fhe not done it. But I did not fufpect that fhe would hate alfo the whole Family for your fake. Could I have forefeen that, fhe fhould rather have ftaid, and you marched off. Do but confider, *Softrata*, how little I deferve to meet with thefe Vexations from you. In Complaifance to you I have retir'd into the Country to look after my Affairs; that I may be the better able to fupport you in your Idlenefs, and expenfive Way of living, not grudging my own Labour, beyond what is even reafonable, or my Age allows. Ought not you in your turn to have taken care, that nothing might happen to vex me?

*Soft.* Truly it happens not thro' me, or by any Fault of mine.

*Lac.* Nay, thro' you alone, *Softrata*: For here was nobody but yourfelf. All the Blame muft therefore fall upon you only. You ought to have taken care of Affairs here, as I had releafed you from all other Cares. Are you not afham'd of yourfelf? For you, an old
Woman

## ANNOTATIONS.

his Wife upon a falfe Suppofition, founded merely in his own Conjectures; becaufe forfooth he had laid it down as a Maxim, that all Step-mothers are invincibly averfe to their Daughters-in-Law. *Terence* here expofes the Folly of giving too eafily into fuch Prejudices. We have a Step-mother, who, far from hating her Daughter-in-Law, loves her tenderly; and the old Man expofes himfelf to Ridicule by his Obftinacy, and unreafonable Abufe of a Woman, who fo little deferved it.

15 *Suos cui liberos committerent.* It is remarkable here, that *Terence* fpeaking of an only Daughter ufes *liberos. Donatus* obferves, that it makes the Sentence more emphatical, and adds Force and Strength to the Accufation. *Multum fonanter, & accufatorio ftrepitu, nec mafculinum genus, nec femininum pofuit: nec unam, fed liberos. Cicero* exprefies himfelf in the fame Language, fpeaking of *Cæfar's* only Daughter. *Si ad jucundiffimos liberos, fi ad clariffimum generum properaret.* Thus *Cajus* de verb. fignif. *Non eft fine liberis, cui vel unus filius, unave filia eft. Terence* himfelf gives another Inftance of this Manner of fpeaking in a former Play; *Andrian,* Act 5. Scene 3. where *Simo* fpeaking of *Pamphilus's* Son, that was born to him by *Glycery* without his Knowledge, fays, *Liberi inventi, invito patre.*

16 *Tu fola uxorere. Exorior* is commonly ufed of Things fudden and unexpected, that ftart up, when leaft apprehended, and create great Difturbance and Mifchief. 'Tis in this Senfe that *Dido* ufes it in the fourth Book of the *Æneis,* hinting at the future Appearance of *Hannibal.*

*Exoriare aliquis noftris ex offibus ultor. Orior* again is faid of Things that happen in a regular Courfe, or fuch as may be reafonably prefum'd from the Concurrence of natural Caufes; as the Rifing of the Sun, or now and then the Appearance of a good Prince. who makes Nations happy. Thus *Horace* fpeaking of *Auguftus,* Epift. Lib. 2. 1. fays,

*Nil oriturum alias, nil ortum tale fatentes.*
21 *Ideo quia, ut vos mihi domi eritis, pro-*
*indq*

Quæ me, & te, & familiam omnem dedecoras, filio
  luctum paras ?           [facis:
Tum autem, ex amicit inimici ut sint nobis affines,
Qui illum decrérunt dignum, suos cui liberos com-
  mitterent.         15
Tu sola exorere, quæ perturbes hæc tuâ imprudentiâ.
So. Egone ? La. tu, inquam, mulier, quæ me om-
  nino lapidem, non hominem, putas.
An, quia ruri crebrò esse soleo, nescire arbitramini,
Quo quisque pacto hic vitam vostrarum exigat ?
Multo meliùs, hic quæ fiunt, quàm illic, ubi sum as-
  sidue, scio :        20
Ideo quia, ut vos mihi domi eritis, proinde ego ero
  famâ foris.      [menam:
Jampridem equidem audivi cepisse odium tui Philu-
Minimeque adeo mirum : &, ni id fecisset, magis
  mirum foret.
Sed non credidi adeo, ut etiam totam hanc odisset do-
  mum.      [foras.
Quod si scissem, illa hîc maneret potiùs, tu hinc isses
At vide, quàm immeritò ægritudo hæc oritur mî abs
  te, Sostrate.      26
Rus habitatum abii, concedens vobis, & rei serviens ;
Sumtus vostros otiumque ut nostra res posset pati,
Meo labori haud parcens, præter æquom atque æta-
  tem meam.
Non te pro his curasse rebus, ne quid ægret esset mihi ?
So. Non meâ operâ, neque pol culpâ evenit. La. imo
  maxumè.
Sola hîc fuisti : in te omnis hæret culpa solâ, Sostrata.
Quæ hîc erant, curares ; cúm ego vos solvi curis cæ-
  teris.

quæ dedecoras me et te, & omnem familiam, paras luctum filio ? Tum autem facis, ut affines ex amicis sint inimici nobis ; qui decrerunt illum dignum, cui committerent suos liberos. Tu sola exorere, quæ perturbes hæc tua imprudentia. So. Egone ? La. Tu, inquam, mulier, quæ omnio putas me lapidem, non hominem. An quia soleo esse crebro ruri, arbitramini me nescire qто pacto quisque vestrarum exigat vitam hic ? Scio multo melius qui fiunt hic, quam illic, ubi sum assiduè : ideo, quia ut vos eritis mihi domi, proinde ego ero fama foris. Jampridem equidem audivi Philumenam cepisse odium tui : minimeque adeò mirum : et ni fecisset id, foret magis mirum. Sed non adeo credidi, ut etiam edisset hanc totam domium. Quod si scissem, illa potius maneret hic, tu isses hinc foras. At vide, Sostrata, quam immeritò hæc ægritudo oritur mihi abs

te. Abii habitatum rus, concedens vobis, et servens rei ; ut nostra res posset patri vestros sumtus etiumque, haud parcens meo labori, præter æquum atque meam ætatem. Nonne opportuit te pro his rebus curasse, ne quid esse ægre mihi ? So. Pol non evenit mea opera, neque culpa. La. Imo maxime. Fuisti sola hic : omnes culpa hæret in te sola, Sostrata. Curares quæ erat hic, cum ego solvi vos cæteris curis.

## ANNOTATIONS.

*inde ego ero fama foris.* I am apt to think, says Madam *Dacier*, that this Passage has not hitherto been well understood ; for *Laebes* does not mean that it was well or ill with him in the Country, according as his Wife and Daughter-in-Law behaved in Town, or that their good or bad Conduct brought him good or bad News : his meaning is, that according as they behaved, he should be esteem'd or despis'd in the World. This is the plain meaning of the Words, and agreeable to Reason and good Sense. For it is certain, that the good or bad Conduct of the Wife is often imputed to the Husband, because he as Head of the Family, ought to govern it, and prevent Disorders. I entirely agree with the *French* Lady, that this is the true Sense of the Passage, but can't allow that she was the first who discovered it ; for 'tis both the obvious Meaning of the Words, and *Casaubon* before her has expresly explained them so. *Honesta curiositatis excusatio* (says he) *nempe quod ab illarum vita, & conversatione domestica sua fama foris penderet ; quæ bona, si vita illarum talis : mala, si et illa.*

3 *Non mea opera, neque pol culpa evenit. Sostrata*

Woman to quarrel with a Girl? I know you'll pretend it was her Fault.

*Soſt.* Truly, Husband, I do not pretend ſo.

*Lac.* I'm glad, as I hope to live, for my Son's ſake. As to you, I know enough of you already. No new Fault can make you appear in a worſe Light.

*Soſt.* How do you know, Husband, but this pretended Averſion is all a Feint, to be the more with her Mother?

*Lac.* How d'ye mean? Is not that Proof enough, that you was not admitted yeſterday when you went to ſee her.

*Soſt.* They told me ſhe was very ill then; that was the Reaſon of my not being admitted.

*Lac.* 'Tis my Opinion, that your odd Behaviour is more her Diſeaſe than any thing elſe: nor do I wonder at it, for there is none of you but will have your Sons to marry, and whoever chances moſt to pleaſe you, muſt be the Perſon. But no ſooner are they married at your Solicitation, than at your Solicitation they muſt turn away their Wives again.

### ANNOTATIONS.

*Soſtrata* was herſelf entirely at a Loſs, as to the Reaſon of her Daughter-in-Law's Abſence, and therefore, without laying the Blame of it on any other, is ſatisfied with barely juſtifying herſelf: Had ſhe accuſed *Philumena*, it would have but ſtrengthened *Laches*'s Suſpicions.

36 *Nam de te quidem, ſatis ſcio,* &c. He rejoiced that his Wife laid no blame upon *Philumena* for his Son's Sake, becauſe he probably knew how much he lov'd her, and how glad he muſt be to find that ſhe was one againſt whom even a Step-mother could make no exception. For, as to you, ſays he, mean-

---

# ACT II. SCENE II.

### ARGUMENT.

Laches, *the Father of* Pamphilus, *talks with* Phidippus, *Father to* Philumena, *about ſending back his Daughter-in-Law.* Phidippus *tells him, that ſhe can't think of living with her Step-Mother, while* Pamphilus *is abſent.*

#### PHIDIPPUS, LACHES, SOSTRATA,

*Phi.* THO', *Philumena*, I know I have a Right to inſiſt upon your ſubmitting to my Will; yet ſway'd by a fatherly Fondneſs, I'll yield to you in this, nor will *any longer* oppoſe your Inclination.

*Lac.* But here comes *Phidippus* very ſeaſonably, I'll preſently know

of

### ANNOTATIONS.

While *Laches* is thus engaged with *Soſtrata*, *Phidippus*, the Father of *Philumena*, is ſeen coming out from his own Houſe, and diſcourſing to his Wife and Daughter within. He as little knew the real Reaſon of *Philumena*'s leaving her Mother-in-Law as the other, and imputes it to the ſame Cauſe. His Character is that of an eaſy good-natured Man, who loved Peace, and would rather give way to his Family than bear the Pain of too violent an Oppoſition. *Laches* commends him for this Temper, but thinks he is

apt

Cum puellâ anùm fufcepiffe inimicitias non pudet ?
Illius dices culpâ factum.  So. haud equidem dico,
  mi Laches.                                              35
La. Gaudeo, ita me Dii ament, nati causâ. nam de
  te quidem,
Satis fcio, peccando detrimenti nil fieri poteft.
So. Quî fcis, an eâ causâ, mi vir, me odiffe adfimu-
  laverit,                              [hoc fat eft,
Ut cum matre unâ plus effet ? La. quid ais ? non figni
Quòd herì nemo voluit vifentem ad eam te intro ad-
  mittere ?                                     40
So. Enim laffam oppidò tum effe aiebant ; eò ad eam
  non admiffa fum             [aliam rem, arbitror :
La. Tuos effe illi mores morbum magis, quàm ullam
Et merito adeo : nam voftrarum nulla eft quin gna-
  tum velit                    [datur.
Ducere uxorem ; & quæ vobis placita eft conditio,
Ubi duxere impulfu voftro, voftro impulfu eafdem exi-
  gunt.                                      45

Non pudet anùm fuf-
cepiffe inimicitias cum
puella ? Dices fac-
tum culpa illius. So.
Equidem haud dico,
mi Laches. La.
Gaudeo, ita Dii a-
ment me, gnati cau-
fa. Nam qùidem fcio
fatis de te, nil detri-
menti poteft fieri pec-
cando. Qui fcis, mi
vir, an adfimulavie-
rit odiffe me ea caufa,
ut effet plùs una cum
matre ? La. Quid
ais ? Non hoc eft fat
figni, quod heri nemo
voluit admittere te
vifentem intro ad
eam ? So. Enim aie-
bant effe tum oppido
laffam : eo non fum
admiffu ad eam. La.
Arbitror tuos mores
effe magis morbum

illi, quàm ullam aliam rem : et merito adeo ; nam eft nulla veftrarum, quid velit gnatum ducere
uxorem, & conditio, quæ eft placita vobis, datur. Ubi veftro impulfu duxere, veftro impulfu exi-
gunt eafdem.

ANNOTATIONS.

(meaning *Softrata*) 'tis a Matter of Indifference, you can appear in neither a better nor
worfe Light.  I know you thoroughly, no
Action of yours can furprize me, nor have
you any thing to lofe with me on that fide.
'Tis thus that *Donatus* explains it, *Hic fenfus
obfcurus* eft : attamen hic dum quantumcun-
que, inquit, fceleris admiferis, id eft, quan-
tu ncunque peccaveris, nihil de tua exiftima-
tione minuitur, nihil de pudore derogatur : eadem es, quæ fuifti, quia pejor fieri non potes.
  44 *Et quæ vobis placita eft conditio, datur.*
Conditio, i. e. uxor.  See the Remarks upon
*Phormis*, Act 4. Scene 1.

---

# ACTUS II.  SCENA II.

## ARGUMENTUM.

*Laches Pamphili pater Phidippum Philumenæ parentem convenit
fuper reditu fuæ nurus, quam certe Phidippus negat apud fo-
crum, abfente Pamphilo, perdurare poffe.*

PHIDIPPUS, LACHES, SOSTRATA

E T S I fcio ego, Philumena, meum jus effe, ut te
  cogam,                                [victus faciam
Quæ ego imperem, facere : ego tamen patrio animo
Ut tibi concedam, neque tuæ libidini advorfabor.
La. Atque eccum Phidippum optumè video. hînc jam
  fcibo, quid fiet.

que adverfabor tuæ libidini. La. Atque eccum video Phidippum optime ; jam fcibo hinc quid
fit.

ORDO.

Ph. E T S I ego
  fcio Philu-
mena, effe mecum jus,
ut cogam te facere,
quæ ego imperem :
ego tamen victus pa-
trio animo, faciam
ut concedam tibi ne-

ANNOTATIONS.

apt to carry it too far, and would therefore
have him alter his Mind, and fend back his
Daughter, which the other will by no means
agree to.

e Scd

of him how the Case stands. Tho' I own myself, *Phidippus*, to be particularly indulgent to all my Family, yet I suffer not my Easiness to go so far as to corrupt their Minds. And were you to take the same Course, I persuade myself it would be more for your Advantage as well as mine. At present I see you are wholly in their power.

*Phi.* There now !

*Lac.* I waited on you yesterday about your Daughter: you sent me away as wise as I came. But it is not right thus to conceal your Grudges, if you are willing that this Alliance continue. If there is any Fault on our side, let me know it: either by clearing ourselves, or excusing it, you shall have full Satisfaction, even according to your own Desire. But if her Illness be the Cause of your keeping her with you, I think you wrong me, *Phidippus*, to doubt whether sufficient care will be taken of her at my House. For as I hope to live, I will not yield this to you, though you be her Father, that you are more anxious about her Health than I: and that on my Son's account, who, I understand, loves her no less than he does himself; nor am I ignorant how much it will vex him, if he comes to hear of this. For this Reason I am so desirous to have her home, before he returns.

*Phi.* I am no Stranger, *Laches*, to your Care and Good-will, and verily believe all to be as you say: and I would have you be persuaded too, that it is my Inclination to make her return again, if by any means I can.

*Lac.* What hinders you? Hark ye, does she make any Complaints of her Husband?

*Phi.* None at all: for when I began to urge it more strongly, and would have forc'd her to return, she solemnly protested, that she could not endure the House in *Pamphilus*'s Absence. Every one has
his

*ANNOTATIONS.*

*¹ Sed non adeo.* There is something particular here in the Use of the Particles, where *sed* comes in after *etsi*, and is of the same import with *tamen*. We find an Instance of it in *Cicero*, Fam. 9. 16. *Nam* etsi *non facile dijudicator amor verus, & fictus, nisi aliquod indicat ejusmodi tempus, ut, quasi aurum igni, sic benevolentia fidelis periculo aliquo perspici possit, cætera sunt signa communia: sed ego uno utor argumento, quamobrem me ex animo, veroque arbitrer diligi.* And *Horace*, Lib. 1. Sat. 10. 64.

——*Fuerit Lucilius, inquam,*
*Comis & urbanus: fuerit limatior idem,*
*Quam rudis, & Græcis intacti carminis*
   *auctor,*
*Quamque poetarum seniorum turba: sed ille*
*Si foret hoc nostrum fato delatus in avum.*
*Detereret sibi multa.*

9 *Heia vero.* These Words, tho' seemingly easy, have yet puzzled Commentators. *Donatus* makes them an Adverb, interrupting Discourse with design to check it. Madam *Dacier* seems to think that they are addressed to his Daughter, and refer to the Conversation that had been between them before. For *Phidippus* thus assailed with Complaints from *Laches*, that he suffered his Daughter to be so long absent from her Husband's House; turns to her, and says, *Heia vero*, i. e. Did not I tell you so, that your Father-in-Law would be here, to complain of your Absence? For my part, I take it to be an Emotion of Surprize mixed with Discontent. *Phidippus*, while he is yet discoursing with his Daughter, is suddenly, and unexpectedly accosted by *Laches*, and in Language too, that he did not much like. The Words seem to answer pretty nearly to our *Look ye there now:* a Phrase often used in Cases of the same Nature.

17 *Id*

Phidippe, etſi ego meis me omnibus ſcio eſſe adprime
    obſequentem ;                                                          5
Sed non adeo, ut mea facilitas corrumpat illorum ani-
    mos.                                                    [voſtram id eſſet.
Quod tu ſi idem faceres, magis in rem & noſtram &
Nunc video in illarum poteſtate eſſe te. PH. heia vero.
LA. Adii tè heri de filià : ut veni, itidem incertum
    amîſti.
Haud ita decet, ſi perpetuam vis eſſe affinitatem hanc
Celare te iras. ſi quid eſt peccatum à nobis, profer : 11
Aut ea refellendo, aut purgando, vobis corrigemus,
Te judice ipſo. ſin ea eſt cauſa retinendi apud vos,
Quia ægra eſt ; te mî injuriam facere arbitror, Phi-
    dippe,
Si metuis, ſatis ut meæ domi curetur diligenter.       15
At, ita me Dii ament, haud tibi hoc concedo, etſi
    illi pater es,                                          [gnati causâ,
Ut tu illam ſalvam magis velis, quàm ego : id adeo
Quem ego intellexi illam haud minus, quàm ſeipſam,
    magnificare.                                        [turum credam,
Neque adeo clam me eſt, quàm eſſe eum graviter la-
Hoc ſi reſcierit. eò domum ſtudeo hæc priùs, quàm
    ille, ut redeat.                                                   20
PH. Laches, & diligentiam veſtram, & benignitatem
Novi : &, quæ dicis, omnia eſſe ut dicis, animum in-
    duco.                                                       [ſtudeo,
Et te hoc mihi cupio credere : illam ad vos redire
Si facere poſſim ullo modo. LA. quæ res te facere id
    prohibet ?
Eho, numquidnam accuſat virum ? PH. minimè :
    nam poſtquam attendi                                        25
Magis, & vi cœpi cogere ut rediret, ſanctè adjurat
Non poſſe apud vos Pamphilo ſe abſente perdurare.

*Phidippe, etſi ego ſcio me eſſe apprime obſequentem omnibus meis, ſed non adeo, ut mea facilitas corrumpat, animos illarum ; quod ſi tu faceres idem, id eſſet magis in rem et noſtram, et veſtram ; nunc, video te eſſe in poteſtate illarum. PH. Heia vero. LA. Adii te heri de filia : amiſiſti itidem incertum, ut veni. Haud decet te ita celare iras, ſi vis hanc affinitatem eſſe perpetuam. Si quid peccatum eſt a nobis, profer : aut refellendo, aut purgando, corrigemus ea vobis, te ipſo judice. Sin ea eſt cauſa retinendi ejus apud vos, quia eſt ægra, arbitrore, Phidippe, facere injuriam mibi, ſi metuis, ut curetur ſatis diligenter meæ domi. At, ita Dii ament me, haud concedo hoc tibi, etſi es pater illi, ut tu magis velis illam eſſe ſalvam, quam ego : id adeo cauſa gnati, quem ego intellexi haud minus magnificare illam, quam ſcipſum. Neque adeo eſt clam me, quam credam eum*

*eſſe laturum graviter, ſi reſcierit hoc. Eo ſtudio, ut hæc redeat domum, priuſquam ille. PH. Laches, novi & diligentiam veſtram, et benignitatem, & animum induco credere omnia, quæ dicis, eſſe ut dicis, et cupio te credere hoc mihi : ſtudeo redire illam ad vos, ſi poſſim facere ullo modo. LA. Quæ reo probibet te facere id ? Eho, numquidnam accuſat virum ? PH. Minime, nam poſtquam attendi magis, et cœpi vi cogere ut rediret, ſanctè adjurat, ſe non poſſe perdurare apud vos, Pamphilo abſente.*

## ANNOTATIONS.

**17** *Id adeo gnati cauſa.* It was neceſſary to add this Circumſtance to gain Credit, and prevent unjuſt Suſpicions. *Honeſte* (ſays *Donatus*) *amori nurus rationem ſubjecit piam. Nam non continuo rectum eſt, nimis amari ſocero nurum, niſi propter filium diligatur. Bene ergo gnati cauſa, incredibile eſt enim patrem non patris pietate ſuperari.*

**25** *Eho, numquidnam accuſat virum ?* There is a particular Emphaſis upon *eho* here. It ſhews *Laches* advancing towards *Phidippus* and holding up his Ear, as if he expected him to whiſper ſome Secret which it had been improper to ſpeak aloud. 'Tis thus, that *Donatus* explains it, and without doubt, he is in the right. " Geſticulatio quædam " ſecretiora quærentis ; ſæpe enim de matri- " tis puellæ parentibus queri ſolent aliquid " ej—

his Failing; I'm naturally of a foft and eafy Temper, and can't refolve to thwart my Family.

*Lac.* Ha! *Soſtrata.*

*Soſt.* Wretch that I am!

*Lac.* Is that your final Refolution?

*Phi.* At prefent it is? but have ye any thing elfe to fay? For I
have fome Bufinefs that calls me directly to the Forum.

*Lac.* I go with you.

## ANNOTATIONS.

" ejufmodi, quod folis ipfis committendum
" eft. *Ebo* igitur eft interjectio ponentis
" aurem propiorem: nam illa quærit, quæ
" folent de maritis puellæ matribus queri."

29 *Hem, Soſtrata.* This arifes from the Anfwer that *Phidippus* had given to *Laches* enquiring, whether *Philᵢmena* made any Complaints of her Hufband. For the old Man fubjoins to his Reply his Daughter's own Words: *fancte adjurat, non poſſe apud vos Pamphilo fe abſᵢnte perdupare.* This, tho' it implies an undoubted Vindication of *Pamphilus,* yet does not undeceive the Spec-tators with regard to the Mother-in-Law, and confirms *Laches* in his Sufpicions: hence turning to his Wife, he fays, *Hem, Soſtrata.*

Nor

---

# ACT II. SCENE III.

### ARGUMENT.

Soſtrata *complains that Hufbands are too apt to fufpect their
Wives without Ground.*

#### SOSTRATA.

*Soſt.* IN truth we Wives are all equally obnoxious to our Hufbands, and very unjuſtly; becaufe of the Faults of a few, who
make the World judge hardly of us all. For, as I hope for Happinefs, I am quite blamelefs, in regard to what my Husband now ac-
cufes me of. But it is not eafy to clear one's felf in this Cafe, fo
general is the Perfuafion that Step-Mothers are all fevere. But fure
it is not fo with me, for I never regarded her otherwife than if fhe
had been my own Daughter, nor can I conceive how this has happened to me. But for many Reafons I expect with Impatience my
Son's Return.

## ANNOTATIONS.

*Phidippus* and *Laches* retire, leaving *Soſtrata* on the Stage by herfelf, who, as might naturally be expected, falls a complaining of her hard Fate, to be thus unjuſtly accufed, without a Profpect of being able to vindicate herfelf. Her Hufband was fo poffefs'd with the Notion, that all Step-Mothers bore an inveterate Hatred to their Daughters-in-Law, that it was in vain to expect he would hearken to Reafon, and *Philumena* herfelf a-voided her fo Induſtrioufly, and fpoke fo myſterioufly, that there was no likelihood of effecting any Thing by her Means, She has no other Solace therefore, but the Re-flection of her own Innocence, and the Ex-pectation that at her Son's Return, all would be cleared up and fet to rights.

a *Inique æque omnes invifæ viris, propter
paucas*

ACT

Aliud fortaffe alii vitii eft : ego fum animo leni natus :
Non poffum advorfari meis. LA. hem, Softrata ! So.
   heu me miferam !
LA. Certumne eft iftuc ? PH. nunc quidem, ut videtur.
   fed numquid vis ?                   30
Nam eft, quod me tranfire ad forum jam oportet.
   LA. eo tecum unà.

*Eft fortaffe aliud vitii alii : ego fum natus leni animo, non poffum adverfari meis. LA. Hem, Softrata. So. Heu me miferam ! LA. Iftucne eft certum ? PH. Nunc quidem ut videtur, fed numquid vis ? Nam*

*eft propter quod oportet me jam tranfire ad forum. LA. Eo una tecum.*

## ANNOTATIONS.

Nor indeed could he poffibly avoid thinking that fhe alone was to blame. For a Daughter-in-Law, who protefts that fhe can't return to her Step-mother's Houfe, while her Hufband is abfent, does fhe not exprefsly give us to underftand, that the Prefence of her Hufband is what alone can render the Houfe fupportable, and make her forget the Chagrins that fhe is daily affaulted with in it ? Whom can this affect, but the Mother-in-Law ? There was no body elfe in the Houfe that could give her Umbrage, for *Laches* himfelf was retired into the Country, and came to Town but feldom. It muft be owned, that Appearances are ftrong againft *Softrata*.

---

# ACTUS II. SCENA III.
## ARGUMENTUM.
*Softrata queritur genus mulierum nimis effe fufpectum viris.*
### SOSTRATA.

EDEPOL næ nos fumus inique æque omnes in-
   vifæ viris,                     [mur malo.
Propter paucas ; quæ omnes faciunt dignæ ut videa-
Nam, ita me Dii ament, quod me accufat nunc vir,
   fum extra noxiam.               [runt, focrus
Sed non facile eft expurgatu : ita animum induxe-
Omnes effe iniquas, haud pol me quidem : nam nun-
   quam fecus                     5
Habui illam, ac fic ex me effet nata : nec, quî hoc mî
   eveniat, fcio.                [domum.
Nifi pol filium multimodis jam expecto, ut redeat

**ORDO.**

So. *Edepol næ nos omnes fumus æque invifæ viris iniquæ, propter paucas ; quæ faciunt ut videamur omnes dignæ malo. Nam ita Dii ament me, in eo propter quod vir nunc accufat me, fum extra noxiam. Sed non eft facile expurgatu ; ita induxerunt animum omnes focrus effe iniquas. Pol*

*haud quidem hoc pertinet ad me: nam nunquam habui illam fecus ac fi effet nata ex me : nec fcio, qui hoc eveniat mibi, nifi pol jam expecto filium multimodis, ut redeat domum.*

## ANNOTATIONS.

*paucas. Apollodorus*, from whofe Original, *Terence* tranflated this Play, feems to have borrowed this Sentiment from *Homer*, who, in one of *Agamemnon*'s Speeches, makes that Hero fay : that a Woman who behaves imprudently, or indifcreetly, difhonours by that the whole Sex, and reflects her Shame upon the moft modeft, wife, and referved.

7 *Multimodis.* For many Reafons, on many Accounts. As a tender affectionate Mother, fhe was impatient to fee her Son; but more efpecially as by his Means fhe hoped to fettle thofe Family Diforders, that had happened in his Abfence.

## ACT III. SCENE I.

### ARGUMENT.

Pamphilus *being returned from* Imbrus, *when he understands that his Wife had left her Mother-in-Law, and returned home, deplores the Unhappiness that always attended his Love.* —

PAMPHILUS, PARMENO, MYRRHINA.

*Pam.* I Believe that never Man met with so many Crosses and Disappointments in Love as I. Unhappy Wretch ! Was it for this I have been so tender and careful of my Life ? Was it for this I was so impatient to return home. How much better had it been for me to pass my Life any where, than to return, and make myself compleatly miserable, by finding Things in this Way ? For it is an undoubted Maxim with all Men, that when any Disaster happens to us, all the Time that passes before we come to the Knowledge of it, is so much clear Gain.

*Par.* Nay, but as it is, you'll the sooner know how to extricate yourself from this Misfortune. Had you not returned, the Breach might have grown much wider. But now, *Pamphilus,* I know that both will be aw'd by your Presence. You'll know the whole Business, reconcile Differences, and make them Friends again. What you represent to yourself as so terrible, is, I verily believe, at bottom a meer Trifle.

*Pam.* Why do you pretend to comfort me ? Is there in the World a Wretch so compleatly miserable? Before I married, I had my Heart
engaged

### ANNOTATIONS.

*Pamphilus* is now arrived, and informed of what had happened in his Absence. As the real Reason of his Wife's leaving the House is unknown, he too imputes it to the same Cause with the rest, some Difference between her and his Mother. This appears to him to be a Misfortune beyond all others, because whatever he resolved on, he foresaw unavoidable Misery to himself. His Character, indeed, is amiable beyond Example. He is fond of, and loves his Wife, and the Thought of parting with her torments him cruelly. He is a no less dutiful Son, and, though urged by such powerful and favourite Passions, can't resolve upon any thing inconsistent with the Respect he owes his Mother. This Distraction and Uncertainty is the Cause of his Complaints in the Beginning of this Scene, and leads him into a long Train of Reflections upon his ill Success and Unhappiness in Love. He was compelled to marry when his Affections were engaged elsewhere, nor did he find it an easy Matter to withdraw them from the Person whom they had taken such deep Root. And now that he had at last settled them upon his Wife, and began to be happy in her Society, and mutual Tenderness, so a new Stroke of adverse Fortune threatens to tear him from her too. *Parmeno* endeavours to sooth him with the Hopes, that it may, perhaps, be no more than a mere Trifle, which he will find it easy to compose and settle. While they are thus discoursing together, by some Hurry and Trepidation heard in the House, *Pamphilus* learns, that his Wife had been out of Order, and impatiently rushes in to know what was the Matter.

[2] *Nemini plura ego acerba.'* *Donatus* has very well observed, that the first Verses of this Scene were too sublime, and the Complaints of *Pamphilus* more suited to Tragedy than Comedy, but for the Addition of *ex amore*; which corrects all, and gives the whole Speech a natural consistent Air. Love inspires the same Sentiments into almost every Breast, it warms forcibly, and while the Heart is beset with it, every Rub or Interruption appears
pears

# ACTUS III. SCENA I.

### ARGUMENTUM.

*Pamphilus reversus ex Imbro, ubi rescivit uxorem, socru relicta, ad matrem abiisse, deplorat suam in amore infelicitatem.*

PAMPHILUS, PARMENO, MYRRHINA.

<table>
<tr><td>

NEMINI ego plura acerba credo esse ex amore
   homini unquam oblata,     [parsi perdere !
Quàm mî. heu me infelicem ! hanccine ego vitam
Haccine causâ ego eram tantopere cupidus redeundi do-
   mum ?     [ætatem,
Cui quanto fuerat præstabilius, ubivis gentium agere
Quàm huc redire ? atque hæc ita esse miserum me re-
   sciscere ?     5
Nam nos omnes, quibus est alicunde aliquis objectus
   labos,     [est, lucro est.
Omne quod est interea tempus, priusquam id rescitum
PAR. At sic, citiùs quî te expedias his ærumnis, re-
   perias.
Si non redisses, hæ iræ factæ essent multo ampliores :
Sed nunc adventum tuum ambas, Pamphile, scio re-
   verituras.     10
Rem cognosces : iram expedies : rursum in gratiam
   restitues.     [ti tuum.
Levia sunt, quæ tu pergravia esse in animum indux-
PAM. Quid consolare me ? an quisquam usquam gen-
   tium est æque miser ?     [amori deditum :
Priusquam hanc uxorem duxi, habebam alibi animum

</td><td>

ORDO.

PAM. EGO cre-
do plu-
ra acerba ex amore
esse oblata nemini un-
quam homini, quam
mihi. Heu me infe-
licem ! ego parsi per-
dere hanccine vitam !
Ego eram tantopere
cupidus redeundi do-
mum haccine causa ?
Cui quanto præstabi-
lius fuerat agere æ-
tatem ubivis gentium,
quam redire huc ? at-
que me miserum re-
sciscere hæc esse ita ?
Nam apud nos omnes,
quibus aliquis labos
est alicunde objectus,
omne tempus quod est
interea, priusquam id
est rescitum, est lucro.
PAR. At sic, repe-
rias citius qui expe-
dias te his ærumnis.
Si non redisses, hæ
iræ essent factæ mul-
to ampliores : sed nunc
dies iram ; restitues e.
pergravia. PAM. Quid
duxi hanc uxorem, habe-

</td></tr>
</table>

*Pamphile, scio ambas reverituras tuum adventum. Cognosces rem ; expedies iram ; restitues e. rursum in gratiam. Levia sunt, quæ tu induxti in animum tuum esse pergravia. PAM. Quid consolare me ? An quisquam usquam gentium est æque miser ? Priusquam duxi hanc uxorem, habebam animum deditum amori alibi :*

### ANNOTATIONS.

pears a Calamity not to be equalled. A Lover therefore will not be surprized to hear *Pamphilus* complaining so warmly, as he will think he had abundant Reason, and probably may have been himself more than once in the same Situation.

6. *Nam nos omnes, quibus,* &c. The Manner of Expression here is somewhat puzzling and perplex'd, for it is not easy to see to what *nos omnes* refers ; nor is there any Word in the Text that governs it. There is evidently an Ellipsis, and something must be supplied by the Mind, to compleat the Sense. Madam *Dacier*, after *Donatus*, makes it a Nominative, and thinks we ought to sup-ply *sic existimare debemus.* This manner of Expression is what Grammarians call *Genus locutionis absolutum.* We have an Example of it in *Virgil*, Æn. 10. 244.

*Crastina lux, mea si non irrita dicta pu-taris,*

*Ingentes Rutulæ spectabis cædis acervos.*

Where we must supply *erit cum,* which makes all even and smooth : Cum *crastina lux* erit, affording an obvious Sense and Construction. This appears probably enough ; I have however, in the *Ordo,* taken a shorter way, by supposing *nos omnes* an Accusative, governed by the Preposition *apud.* This takes away at once all Obscurity, and is

engaged elsewhere: how much I must have suffered in that Affair, any one may easily conceive, without my telling it; yet I never dared to refuse the Match my Father forc'd upon me. Scarce had I weaned myself from *Bacchis*, scarce disengaged my Affections so firmly rooted there, and fixed them on my Wife; when lo, a new Misfortune arises, to tear me from her too. Besides, I shall, no doubt, find either my Wife, or my Mother to blame; and which-ever happens, how can I avoid being miserable? For Duty, *Parmeno*, requires that I bear with the Failings of my Mother. Then I am under a thousand Obligations to my Wife, who bore my ill Usage with so much Temper, nor ever complained to any of the many Wrongs she suffered from me. But something, I know not what extraordinary must have happened, *Parmeno*, to give Occasion to a Quarrel that has lasted so long.

*Par.* Nay, rather something very frivolous, if you were indeed to know the real Case. Quarrels, even the fiercest, do not always argue the greatest Offences. For it often happens, that what would not in the least provoke another, will make a wrathful Man your mortal Enemy. For what Trifles do Children fall out among themselves? And why? Because they have but a weak Understanding to direct them. Women, in this Respect, very much resemble Children; their Understandings are but weak. Perhaps, one chance Word has been the Occasion of all this mighty Disturbance.

*Pam.* Go in, *Parmeno*, and let them know that I am come.

*Par.* Hah! What can this be?

*Pam.* Hush.

## ANNOTATIONS.

besides an Ellipsis very frequent with our Poet.

*Jam in hac re.* What are we to understand here, his Attachment to *Bacchis*, or his Marriage? Perhaps both. Unless you had rather refer it to that fluctuating and wavering State of Mind soon after his Marriage, when a Fondness for his Wife beginning to grow upon him, he found it still difficult to get the better of his Love for *Bacchis*.

21 *Matris ferre injurias.* This is truly worthy a great and good Character, as the Poet is solicitous to make that of *Pamphilus* appear. Cicero pro *A. Cluent.* 6. *Facile intelligo, non modo reticere homines parentum injurias, sed etiam animo æquo ferre oportere. Sed ego ea, quæ ferri possunt, ferenda: quæ taceri, tacenda esse arbitror.*

22 *Tum uxori obnoxius sum.* Obnoxious here seems to import a Tye or Obligation arising from Gratitude. He supposed, that either his Mother or Wife was in fault. If his Mother, Duty obliged him to bear with her; if his Wife, he was under so many Obligations to her, for her prudent and discreet Behaviour in hiding his Faults, that he knew not with what Face to shew himself disgusted with her. This, tho' not the original Signification of the Word, is yet so evidently connected with it, that we can easily discern with what Propriety the Poet has used it in the present Case. For *noxa*, in the Civil Law, signifies any Loss, Injury, or Hurt; so that he is properly obnoxious, who is bound in any of these ways to make Reparation. This was *Pamphilus*'s Case. *Philumena* had borne with Patience his Wrongs and ill Usage; it was therefore but reasonable, that he, in his Turn, should overlook her Faults. What we read in *Gellius* upon the Word *obnoxium*, will give some additional Light to this Criticism. *Gell.* 7. 17. *Quis adeo tam linguæ Latinæ ignarus est, qui nesciat eum dici obnoxium, cui quid ab eo, cui esse obnoxium dicitur, incommodari aut ob- ceri potest, et qui habeat aliquem noxæ, id est, culpæ suæ conscium.*

27 *Non maxumas, quæ maxumæ sunt.* These Words of *Parmeno* are very intricate and perplexed.

Jam in hac re ut taceam, cuivis facile scitu est quàm
    fuerim miser:
Tamen nunquam ausus sum recusare eam, quam m        15
    obtrudit pater.               [vi animum meum
Vix me illinc abstraxi, atque impeditum in eâ expedi-
Vixque huc contuleram; hem, nova res orta est
    porro ab hac quæ me abstrahat.
Tum matrem ex eâ re me aut uxorem in culpâ in-
    venturum arbitror:
Quod cùm ita esse invenero, quid restat, nisi porro
    ut fiam miser?                 20
Nam matris ferre injurias me, Parmeno, pietas jubet:
Tum uxori obnoxius sum: ita olim suo me ingenio
    pertulit,
Tot meas injurias quæ nunquam in ullo patefecit loco.
Sed magnum nescio quid necesse est evenisse, Parmeno.
Unde ira inter eas intercessit, quæ tam permansit diu. 25
PAR. At quidem hercle parvum: si vis vero veram ra-
    tionem exsequi,                 [jurias
Non maxumas, quæ maxumæ sunt interdum iræ, in-
Faciunt; nam sæpe est, quibus in rebus alius ne ira-
    tus quidem est,
Cùm de eadem causâ est iracundus factus inimicissimus.
Pueri inter sese quàm pro levibus noxiis iras gerunt?
Quapropter? quia enim qui eos gubernat animus, in-
    firmum gerunt.                 31
Itidem Illæ mulieres sunt ferme, ut pueri, levi senten-
    tiâ:                       [conciverit.
Fortasse unum aliquod verbam hanc inter eas iram
PAM. Abi, Parmeno, intrò, ac me venisse nuncia.
    PAR. hem, quid hoc est? PAM. tace.

*non faciunt maximas injurias: nam est sæpe in quibus rebus alius ne quidem*
*cundus est factus inimicissimus de eadem causa. Pro quam levibus noxiis pueri ge-*
*Quapropter? Quia enim gerunt infirmum animum, qui animus gubernat col-*
*lieres sunt ferme ut pueri, levi sententia: fortasse unum aliquod verbum conciserit hanc iram intra*
*eas. PAM. Abi, Parmeno, intro, ac nuncia me venisse. PAR. Hem quid hoc est? PAM.*
*Tace.*

## ANNOTATIONS.

perplexed. The natural Order of Construction is thus: *Iræ, quæ sunt maximæ, non*
*faciunt interdum maximas injurias.* Which
seems to be the direct contrary of what *Par-*
*meno* should have said; for *Donatus* observes,
*Injuriæ faciunt iras, non iræ injurias.* Hence
Grammarians contend for an Hypallage, i. e.
an Inversion in the Sense and Order of the
Words, which naturally ought to run thus:
*Non maximas, quæ maximæ sunt interdum in-*
*juriæ, iras faciunt. Injuriæ faciunt iras,* is
here for *efficiunt, gignunt, conciliant.* But

perhaps *faciunt* is here equivalent to *ostendunt,*
*monstrant,* &c. according to which there is
no need of having Recourse to Grammatical
Figures. Madam *Dacier* offers an ingenious
Conjecture, in a Remark upon this Passage,
that as *Parmeno* here pretends to philoso-
phize, and assume a Character that did not
belong to him, the Poet designedly makes
him talk in an obscure, confused unintelli-
gible Manner. And indeed, if we consider
the whole Speech throughout, there is great
Reason to believe that her Conjecture is just.

*Par.* I perceive a Bustle, and running backwards and forwards; let us go up to the Door, a little nearer still. Ha, don't you perceive it?

*Pam.* Hold your prating. O *Jupiter!* I hear a Shriek.

*Par.* You speak yourself, and bid me be silent?

*Myr.* For Heaven's Sake, dear Child, make no Noise.

*Pam.* It seemed to be *Philumena*'s Mother's Voice. I'm ruin'd.

*Par.* How so?

*Pam.* Undone.

*Par.* Why?

*Pam.* Ah! *Parmeno*, you certainly conceal some great Misfortune from me.

*Par.* I heard indeed, your Wife *Philumena* was a little out of order. If that may be it, I can't tell.

*Pam.* I'm undone: Why did you not tell me this before?

*Par.* Because I could not tell you all at once.

*Pam.* What is her Disorder?

*Par.* I don't know.

*Pam.* What? Has she had no Physician?

*Par.* I don't know.

*Pam.* But do I delay going in, that I may learn myself the Truth whatever it is? In what Condition, my dear *Philumena*, shall I now find you? For if your Life is any wise in danger, I sure can never survive you.

*Par.* There is no need for my following him now in, for I perceive they little care to see any of our Family. Yesterday nobody would admit *Sostrata*. Did she happen to grow worse (which I should be sorry for, chiefly for my Master's Sake) they'd immediately say, that *Sostrata*'s Servant must be coming in, and fancy, no doubt, some Omen in it, that boded Danger, and exasperated the Disease. My Mistress of course will be blamed, nor shall I find it easy to clear myself of Suspicion.
ACT

*ANNOTATIONS.*

34 *Abi, Parmeno, intro, ac me venisse nuntia.* This was the Custom of those Times; Husbands returning from abroad, usually sent a Messenger before, to let their Wives know of their Arrival. Thus in *Flautus, Amph.* 1. 1. 40.

*Me a portu præmisit domum, ut hæc nuntiem uxori suæ.*

*Nannius* thinks that this, however usual with the *Romans*, was not the Custom among the *Greeks*, because we meet with no Instance of it in *Plutarch.* But there are so many Testimonies of it from other Writers, as leaves no room to doubt, that this Custom was more sacredly observ'd by the *Greeks*, than even by the *Romans* themselves. The *Roman* Ladies, as enjoying more Liberty than those of *Greece*, frequently went out to meet their Husbands upon their Arrival from any distant Expedition.

37 *Proh Jupiter! Clamorem audivi.* Some Criticks pretend that the Words *Proh Jupiter*, are to be referr'd to *Philumena*, and that *Pamphilus* hearing them, immediately subjoins *clamorem audivi*. But 'tis not likely, that *Pamphilus*, who, when in the next Line he overhears *Myrrhina* speaking, takes instant Notice of it, *matris vox visa est Philumenæ*; would not have been more express, had he heard *Philumena*'s Voice.

41 *Pavitare nescio quid. Pavere* et *timere*, & ad corporis & ad animi-perturbationem, veteres referebant. *Plautus in Bacchidibus*, I. 1. 73. *Nam, ut in navi vectæ es, credo timida es. Ergo pavitare, ægrotare quia sic horruisse visa, ac palpitare venis. Donatus.*

46 *Nam si periclum ullum in te est.* It is worth while to remark here, the Art and

PAR. Trepidari sentio, cursari rursum prorsum. age-
   dum, ad fores. 35
Accede propius. hem, sensistin'? PAM. noli fabularier.
Proh Jupiter! clamorem audivi. PAR. tute loqueris,
   me vetas?      [est Philumenæ.
MY. Tace, obsecro, mea gnata. PAM. matris vox visa
Nullus sum. PAR. qui dum? PAM. perii. PAR. quam-
   obrem? PAM. nescio quod magnum malum
Profectò, Parmeno, me celant. PAR. uxorem Philu-
   menam 40
Pavitare nescio quid, dixerunt: id si fortè est, nescio.
PAM. Interii: cur mihi id non dixti? PAR. quia non
   poteram unà omnia.
PAM. Quid morbi est? PAR. nescio. PAM. quid? ne-
   mon' medicum adduxit? PAR. nescio.
PAM. Cesso hinc ire intrò, ut hoc quamprimùm, quid-
   quid est, certum sciam?
Quònam modo, Philumenà mea, nunc te offendam
   affectam? 45
Nam si periclum ullum in te inest, perisse me unà
   haud dubium est.
PAR. Non usus factò est mihi nunc hunc intiò sequi:
Nam invisos omnes nos esse illis sentio.
Heri nemo voluit Sostratam intro admittere.
Si forte morbus amplior factus siet, 50
Quòd sanè nolim, maxumè heri causá mei;
Servum illicò introisse dicent Sostratæ:
Aliquid tulisse comminiscentur mali,
Capiti atque ætati illorum, morbus qui auctu' sit:
Hera in crimen veniet, ego verò in magnum malum: 55

*dam te affectam? Nam si periculum ullum inest in te, haud dubium est me unà perisse. PAR. Non usus factò est mihi nunc sequi hunc intro: nam sentio nos omnes esse invisos illis. Heri nemo voluit intro admittere Sostratam. Si forte morbus sit factus amplior, quod sane nolim, maxime causa heri mei; illicò dicent servum Sostratæ introisse. Comminiscentur eum tulisse aliquid mali, capiti atque ætati illorum, qui morbus sit auctus: Hera veniet in crimen, ego verò in magnum malum.*

*PAR. Sentio trepidari, cursari rursum prorsum: agedum, accede propius ad foras: hem, sensistin'? PAM. Noli fabulari. Proh Jupiter! Audivi clamorem. PAR. Tute loqueris, & vetas me loqui? MY. Mea gnata, obsecro, tace. PAM. Visa est vox matris Philumenæ. Sum nullus. PAR. Qui cum? PAM. Perii. PAR. Quamobrem? PAM. Profectò, Parmeno, celant me nescio quod magnum malum. PAR. Dixerunt uxorem tuam Philumenam pavitare nescio quid. Si forte est id, nescio. PAM. Interii: cur non dixti id mihi? PAR. Quia non poteram una dicere omnia. PAM. Quid morbi est? PAR. Nescio. PAM. Quid? Nemone adduxit medicum? PAR. Nescio. PA. Cesso ire intro hinc, ut quamprimum sciam hoc certum, quidquid est? Quonam modo, mea Philumena, nunc offendam te affectam?*

## ANNOTATIONS.

and Address of the Poet, who makes *Pamphilus* express himself in Terms so full of Affection for his Wife, at the very time he is going to be a Witness of the Thing in the World most shocking to a Husband. This makes the Contrast still greater, and gives us a higher Idea of the Distress, into which *Pamphilus* must be plunged.

  *54 Capiti atque ætati illorum.* These Words are commonly included in a Parenthesis, and explained as an Imprecation from *Parmeno*, that the Evil he had been speaking of might light upon their own Heads. But this leaves an Obscurity behind it, not

easy to be cleared up: nor would an Imprecation come with any Propriety from *Parmeno*'s Mouth, who had just before said, *si forte morbus amplior factus fiet, quod sane nolim.* I have therefore construu'd it, *comminiscentur eum tulisse aliquid mali capiti atque ætati illorum,* &c. Which is unforc'd, and at once removes all Obscurity.

  *55 Ego vero in magnum malum.* He means that he might be put to the Rack, to oblige him to confess whether by any Drug, Fascination, or Charm, he had contributed to *Philumena*'s Illness. For the *Greeks* were in this respect very superstitious.

# ACT III. SCENE II.

## ARGUMENT.

*Pamphilus comes out sorrowful from* Philumena, *finding that she was just then brought to bed, which he endeavours all in his power to conceal.*

### SOSTRATA, PARMENO, PAMPHILIUS.

*Sost.* ALAS! I have for some time heard I don't know what Noise within here. I greatly fear, lest *Philumena* should be worse. Pray Heaven it be not so! I'll now go see how she does.

*Par.* Hark ye, *Sostrata.*

*Sost.* Hah!

*Par.* You'll be again refused Admittance.

*Sost.* Ha! *Parmeno,* was you here? Wretch that I am! What shall I do?—Shall I not go see my Son's Wife, who lies sick at next Door?

*Par.* Neither see her, nor even so much as send any one to see her; for to love them that hate us, is in my Mind a double Folly; 'tis vain Labour to ourselves, and troublesome to them besides. Then your Son, as soon as he came to Town, went in to see how she was.

*Sost.* How! Is *Pamphilius* come home, say you?

*Par.* He is.

*Sost.* Thank Heaven! That News revives me, and has eased my Heart of all Care.

*Par.* And for this Reason chiefly, I would not have you now go in. For, if *Philumena's* Complaints abate any thing, I know she will tell him, when they are by themselves, all that has pass'd between you, and how this Difference first began. But I see him coming out; how sad he looks!

*Sost.* O my Son!

*Pam.* Mother, your Servant.

*Sost.* I'm glad you're return'd safe. Is *Philumena* in a good way?

*Pam.* She's a little better.

*Sost.* Heaven grant it continue so! But why in Tears then, my Son! Why so dejected?

*Pam.* Nothing at all, Mother.

## ANNOTATIONS.

While *Pamphilus* is gone in to *Philumena,* his Mother *Sostrata,* who had likewise overheard the Noise, is hastening to know the Cause of it. *Parmeno* recalls her, and acquaints her of her Son's Arrival, who was just then gone in, and from whom she would soon learn all she wanted to know. *Pamphilus* soon appears, but with a sorrowful and dejected Air. He dissembles however his real Griefs, and contrives to remove both *Parmeno* and his Mother, that he may be at liberty to vent his Sorrow; and, by repeating to himself this new and unexpected Scene of Woe, let the Audience into the Secret of the Condition in which he had found his Wife.

³ *Quod te Æsculapi, & te, Salus.* She invokes the Goddess of Health along with *Æsculapius,* because in *Greece,* their Statues were commonly placed by one another; so, that to address the one without the other, would have been an open Affront to whichsoever was neglected. *Lucian* speaks of these Statues in his *Hippias.* Within are two Statues of white Marble of ancient Workmanship; the one of the Goddess of Health, the other of *Æsculapius.*

⁸ *Qui amat cui odio ipsus est, bis facere stulte duco.* Nothing is more just than this Observation,

## ACTUS III. SCENA II.

### ARGUMENTUM.

*Pamphilus tristior egreditur à Philumena, deprehenso ejus partu quem modis omnibus celare conatur ac tegere.*

SOSTRATA, PARMENO, PAMPHILUS.

NESCIO quid jamdudum audio hîc tumultuari
    misera?
Male metuo, ne Philumenæ magi' morbus adgravescat:
Quod te, Æsculapi, & te, Salus, ne quid sit hujus, oro:
Nunc ad eam visam. PAR. heus, Sostrata. So. hem.
    PAR. iterum istinc excludêre.
So. Ehem Parmeno; tune hîc eras? perii; quid faciam
    misera? 5
Non visam uxorem Pamphili, cùm in proximo hîc sit
    ægra? [quam.
PAR. Non visas; ne mittas quidem visendi causâ quen-
Nam qui amat cui odio ipsus est, bis facere stultè duco:
Laborem inanem ipsus capit, & illi molestiam affert.
Tum filius tuus introiit videre, ut venit, quid agat. 10
So. Quid ais? an venit Pamphilus? PAR. venit. So.
    Diis gratiam habeo. [de excessit.
Hem, istoc verbo animus mihi rediit, & cura ex cor-
PAR. Jam ea te causâ maxume nunc huc intro re nolo.
Nam si remittent quippiam Philumenæ dolores,
Omnem rem narrabit, scio, continuò sola soli, 15
Quæ inter vos intervenit, unde ortum est initium iræ.
Atque eccum video ipsum egredi. quàm tristis est.
    So. ô mi gnate. [van'
PAM. Mea mater, salve. So. gaudeo venisse salvom: sal-
Philumena est? PAM. meliuscula est. So. utinam istoc
    ita Dii faxint.
Quid tu igitur lacrumas? aut quid est tam tristis?
    PAM. recte, mater. 20

### ORDO.

So. MISERA jamdudum audio nescio quid tumultuari hic; male metui, ne morbus Philumenæ magis aggravescat a quod oro te, Æsculapi, et te, Salus, ne quid hujus sit. Nunc visam ad eam. PA. Heus, Sostrata. So. Hem. PAR. iterum excludere istinc. So. Ehem Parmeno, tunc eras hic? Perii, quid faciam misera? Non visam uxorem Pamphili, cùm sit ægræ hic in proximo? PAR. Non visas, ne quidem mittas quenquam causâ visendi. Nam qui amat cui ipsus est odio, duco eum bis facere stultè: capit ipsui inanem laborem, et affert molestiam illi. Tum filius tuus, ut venit, introiit videre quid agat. So. Quid ais? An Pamphilus venit? PAR. Venit. So. Habeo gratiam Diis. Hem, istoc verbo animus rediit mihi, et cura ex corde excessit. PAR. Jam ea causâ maxime, nolo te nunc introire huc. Nam si dolores Philumenæ remittent quippiam, scio continuò sola, narrabit omnem rem soli, quæ intervenit inter vos, unde initium iræ est ortam. Atque eccum video ipsum egredi, quam tristis est. So. O mi gnate. PAM. Mea mater, salve. So. Gaudeo te venisse salvum: estne Philumena salva? PAM. Meliuscula est. So. Utinam Dii faxint istuc ita. Quid tu igitur lacrymas? aut quid es tam tristis? PAM. Recte, mater.

## ANNOTATIONS.

servation, for Love and Esteem are free, and not to be acquired by Importunity and Zeal. 'Tis one of the wisest Maxims in Life, where we find ourselves not agreeable, never to [ ] with a strong Friendship; because our Endeavours to please will only serve to heighten the Aversion and Disgust. *Plaut. Trin.* III.

*Nullam beneficium esse duco id, quod, nisi fa- cias, non placet.* So. Cicero, *Fam.* V. 5, *Quæ ego si non pro- fundere ac perdere videbor, omnibus meis pi- ribus sustineho. Sin autem ingrata esse sen- team: non committam ut tibi ipsi insanire vi- dear.* 20 *Recte, mater.* Sic dicimus, cum sine
    T 4      vin-

*Soft.* What could that Buftle and Noife we heard mean; tell me, was fhe fuddenly taken ill?

*Pam.* She was.

*Soft.* What's her Diftemper?

*Pam.* A Fever.

*Soft.* A continual one?

*Pam.* So they fay. Pray Mother go in, I'll follow immediately.

*Soft.* I will.

*Pam. to Parmeno)* Do you run and meet the Servants, and help them home with the Baggage.

*Par.* What? Don't they know the Way themfelves?

*Pam.* Do you loiter?

*A N N O T A T I O N S.*

injuria interrogantis aliquid reticemus. Et bene additum *mater*, ut duritia reticentiæ blando nomine molliretur. Alii *recte* fic acci- | piunt, ut intelligant, *nibil eft mali. Donatus.* Our Language has not any Word that fully comes up to its Meaning, and therefore fore

---

## A C T  III.  S C E N E  III.

### A R G U M E N T.

Pamphilus *debates with himfelf, whether he had beft take back his Wife, or divorce her.*

PAMPHILUS.

I Cannot eafily find a proper Beginning, whence to trace the Detail of thofe many furprifing Misfortunes which have befallen me; part of which I have feen with my Eyes, and part my Ears have heard; which made me foon leave the Houfe greatly dejected. For as I haftily rufhed in, full of Fears, expecting to find my Wife complaining of an Illnefs very different from what alas! it proved; when the Maids faw me come in, all overjoyed, cry'd out immediately with one Voice, *He is come,* becaufe I entered fuddenly and unexpected, *nor had they had time to reflect.* But I foon perceived a Change in their Looks, as Chance had brought me upon them at a very unfeafonable Juncture. Meanwhile, one of them haftily runs before to give Notice of my Arrival; I follow her directly, impatient to fee my Wife. When I came in, I foon found out her Diforder; for I followed fo quick, as to allow

                                         no

*A N N O T A T I O N S.*

*Pamphilus* having removed all that were about him, is now at Liberty to open his Mind freely, and let us into the Knowledge of what he had, feen when he went into *Philumena,* and which was the Caufe of that Sorrow and Dejection, which now appeared fo manifeft in his Looks. We have feen before, that he had forc'd a Girl, whom he chanc'd one Night to meet in the Street. It was *Philumena,* who, in confequence of that Embrace, was now in Labour. *Pam-* | *philus,* confcious of having abftained from her fome Months after Marriage, and far from fufpecting her to be the fame he had forc'd in the Street, upon feeing her in Labour, is thrown into the greateft Perplexity, not doubting but fhe had entertained another before him, and was therefore unworthy of his Love. We are not then to wonder at the Concern *Pamphilus* feems to be in. Tho' he has refolved to abandon her, yet it cofts him a hard Struggle; for where Love

So. Quid fuit tumultu? dic mihi: an dolor repente in-
vasit? [So. quotidiana? Pam. ita aiunt
Pam. Ita factum est. So. quid morbi est? Pam. febris
I sodes intro, consequar jam te, mea mater. So. fiat.
Pam. tu pueris curre, Parmeno, obviam, atque iis
onera adjuta.
Par. Quid? non sciunt ipsi viam, domum quâ rede-
ant? Pam. cessas?

*So. Quid tumulti fuit? dic mihi, an dolor repente invasit? Pam. Ita factum est. So. Quid morbi est? Pam. Febris. So. Quotidiana? Pam. Ita aiunt, i sodes intro, mea mater, jam consequar te. So. Fiat. Pam. Tu, Parmeno, curre obviam pueris, atque adjuta onera iis. Pam. Quid? non ipsi sciunt viam, quâ redeant domum? Pam. Cessas?*

## ANNOTATIONS.

fore we are under a Necessity of using Cir-
cumlocution. I have endeavoured in the
Translation to be as near to the Sense and
Force of it as possible, tho' I am sensible
there is still something wanting to convey the
full Idea exhibited by the Latin Word.

## ACTUS III. SCENA III.

### ARGUMENTUM.

*Deliberat Pamphilus, velit uxorem recipere, an repudiare.*

### PAMPHILUS.

NEQUEO mearum rerum initium ullum invenire
idoneum,
Unde exordiar narrare, quæ nec opinanti accidunt,
Partim quæ perspexi his oculis, partim quæ accepi au-
ribus
Quâ me propter exanimatum citius eduxi foras.
Nam modo intro me ut corripui timidus, alio suspi-
cans
Morbo me visurum affectam, ac sensi esse, uxorem: hei
mihi! [simul
Postquam me aspexere ancillæ advenisse, illico omnes
Lætæ exclamant, venit, id quòd derepente aspexerant.
Sed continuò voltum earum sensi immutari omnium,
Quia tam incommodè illis fors obtulerat adventum
meum. 10
Una illarum interea propere præcucurrit, nuncians
Me venisse: ego ejus videndi cupidus rectà consequor.

*ORDO. N Equid invenire ullum idoneum initium mearum rerum, unde exordiar narrare, quæ accidunt nec opinanti, partim quæ perspexi his oculis, partim quæ accepi auribus: quâ propter illius, me, exanimatum feras. Nam ut modo timidus corripui me intro, suspicans me visuram uxorem affectam alio morbo ac sensi esse: hei mihi! Postquam ancillæ aspexere me advenisse, illico omnes simul lætæ exclamant, Venit, id, quòd aspexerant me derepente. Sed continuo sensi voltum earum omnium immutari, quia fors obtulerat meum adventum tam incommode illis. Interea una illarum propere præcucurrit, nunciant me venisse; ego cupidus videndi ejus, recta consequor.*

## ANNOTATIONS.

Love has once firmly taken root, it is not
easy, even upon the greatest Provocation to
... it.

9. *Voltum earum sensi immutari omnium.* It is
certain that from the Countenance we may
often make a Discovery of what passes within

no time for concealing the Business; nor could she complain in any other Voice than what betrayed her Condition. When I saw how it was, *O unpardonable Baseness*, said I; and immediately flung out of the Room all in Tears, struck to the Soul at a Blow so cruel and unexpected. Her Mother followed me, and just as I came to the Door, threw herself at my Feet bathed in Tears. I pitied her heartily. It is indeed the Case, as far as I can judge: We are all elated or depressed, according as Fortune smiles or frowns upon us. Immediately she address'd me in these Words: O my *Pamphilus*, you see now the Reason of her leaving your House. She was forc'd, some time since, by an unknown Villain, and is now fled hither to hide her Shame from you and the World. But when I call to mind the Requests she made, I am unable to refrain from Tears. Whatever Chance or Fortune brought you hither to-day; by that we both conjure you (if with Equity and Justice we may) that you never reveal or discover to any this her Misfortune. If ever you were sensible, dear *Pamphilus*, that she had any Tenderness for you, she now begs that in return you would frankly grant her this Favour. As for taking her back, do in that what is most agreeable to yourself, as you are alone conscious of her Lying-in, and that the Child is none of yours; for I am told you took no notice of her the first two Months after Marriage; so that it is now but seven Months she has liv'd with you as your Wife; nor are you insensible of this, as is evident from the Confusion you are in. Now, *Pamphilus*, if possible, 'tis my Wish and Study, that her Labour be a Secret to her Father and every body else. But if that can't be, and they come to find it out, I'll pretend she miscarried. Every body, I know, will believe what is so likely, that you are the Father; it shall be exposed

*ANNOTATIONS.*

in the Mind, at least so far as to know when it is easy and contented, or when disturb'd and full of Perturbation: *Cicero* has very happily painted this Sympathy and mutual Friendship, if one may so call it, between the Soul and Body, in his third Book *de Oratore. §. 57.* [19] "Omnis enim motus "animi suum quendam a natura habet vul- "tum, et sonum, et gestum: totumque cor- "pus hominis, et ejus omnis vultus, om- "nesque voces, ut nervi in fidibus, ita sonant, "ut a motu animi quaque sunt pulsæ."

[20] *Omnibus nobis, ut res dant sese.* Nothing can be more just and agreeable to Truth, than this Observation. *Homer* is the first that we know of, in whose Writings it is found. Many have adopted it after him, and *Terence* translated it literally from *Apollodorus*, whose very Words *Donatus* has preserv'd to us. *Pamphilus* was deeply struck with the humble Air and Posture of

his Mother-in-Law, who, as a Parent, had rather a Right to claim Respect and Reverence from him. He reflects upon it here with real Concern, and is sensible, that her then unhappy Circumstances alone could have made her stoop to what was so much below her. Nothing can be more just, natural, or reasonable than this Reflection, or more strongly indicate a generous and liberal Turn of Mind.

[21] *Hanc habere orationem metum principia institit.* There is something remarkable in the manner of Expression here used: *principia institit*: immediately she began. *Cicero*, and *Livy*, who seem both to have been great Admirers of *Terence*, and frequently copy him in their Style, have borrow'd from him this word *institit*. The first says *flagitare senatus institit Cornutumi.* And *Livy* *pro se precibus, puellis saltem ut parcerent, orare institit.*

Poſtquam intro adveni, extemplo ejus morbum cog-
novi miſer. [dabat.
Nam neque, ut celari poſſet, tempus ſpatium ullum
Neque voce alia, ac res monebat, ipſa poterat con-
queri. [15
Poſtquam aſpexi; ó facinus indignum, inquam &
corripui illico.
Me inde, lacrumans, incredibili re atque atroci percitus.
Mater conſequitur: jam ut limen exirem, ad genua
accidit, [eſt, ut puto,
Lacrumans miſera: miſeritum eſt. profecto hoc ſic
Omnibus nobis ut res dant ſeſe, ita magni atque hu-
miles ſumus. [20
Hanc habere orationem mecum principio inſtitit:
O mi Pamphile, abs te quamobrem hæc abierit, cau-
ſam vides [improbo:
Nam vitium eſt oblatum virgini olim ab neſcio quo
Nunc huc confugit, te atque alios partum ut celaret
ſuum.
Sed cum orata ejus reminiſcor, nequeo quin lacrumem
eſſe miſer. [25
Quæque fors fortuna eſt, inquit, nobis quæ te hodie
obtulit,
Per eam te obſecramus ambæ, ſi jus, ſi fas eſt, uti
Advorſa ejus per te tecta tacitaque apud omnes ſient;
Si unquam erga te animo eſſe amico ſenſiſti eam, mi
Pamphile;
Sine labore hanc gratiam, te, ut ſibi des pro illa nunc,
rogat. [30
Cæterum de reducenda id facias, quod in rem ſit
tuam. [ſcius.
Parturire eam, neque gravidam eſſe ex te, ſolus con-
Nam aiunt tecum poſt duobus concubuiſſe menſibus:
Tum, poſtquam ad te venit, menſis agitur hic jam
ſeptimus:
Quod te ſcire, ipſa indicat res, nunc ſi poteſt eſt
Pamphile, [35
Maxume volo doque operam, ut clam eveniat partus
patrem, [ſentiant,
Atque adeo omnes, ſed ſi fieri id non poteſt, quin
Dicam abortum eſſe, ſcio nemini aliter ſuſpectum fore,

*Poſtquam intro adveni, extemplo miſer cognovi morbum ejus. Nam neque ſumptus ullum ſpatium dabat ut poſſet celari: neque ipſa poterat conqueri alia voce, ac res monebat. Poſtquam aſpexi; inquam, O facinus indignum: & illico corripui me, lacrumans, percitus re incredibili atque atroci. Mater conſequitur: ut jam exirem limen, miſera accidit ad genua lacrumans: miſeritum eſt. Profecto hoc eſt ſic, ut puto, ſumus magni atque humiles, ita ut res dant ſeſe nobis omnibus. Principio inſtitit habere hanc orationem mecum; O mi Pamphile, vides cauſam, quamobrem hæc abierit abs te. Nam vitium eſt olim oblatum virgini ab neſcio quo improbo: nunc confugit huc ut celaret ſuum partum te, atque alios. Sed cum reminiſcor ejus orata, miſer, nequeo quin lacrumem. Quæcunque fors fortuna eſt, inquit, quæ obtulit te hodie nobis, ambæ obſecramus te per eam, ſi jus, ſi fas eſt, uti adverſa ejus ſint tecta tacitaque apud omnes per te. Si unquam ſenſiſti eam eſſe animo amico erga te, mi Pamphile, nunc rogat, ut ſine labore dei hanc gratiam ſibi pro illa.*

*Cæterum de reducenda facias id, quod ſit in tuam rem, ſolus conſcius eam parturire, neque eſſe gravidam ex te. Nam aiunt eam concubuiſſe tecum duobus menſibus poſt: tum hic jam ſeptimus menſis agitur, poſtquam venit ad te, quod ipſa res indicat te ſcire. Nunc ſi eſt potis, Pamphile, maxime volo, doque operam, ut partui eveniat clam patrem, atque adeo omnes. Sed ſi id non poteſt fieri, quin ſentiant, dicam illis abortum. Scio fore ſuſpectum aliter nemini.*

' pofed immediately; fo that here is no Inconvenience to you, and
' you will hide the Wrongs unworthily offered to this poor Girl. I
' promifed, and am determin'd to be faithful to my Word. As for
' taking her back, that's what I'll never do, nor would it be to my
' Honour, tho' I love her dearly, and the Remembrance of fo agree-
' able a Companion ftill affects me much. It forces Tears from me,
' when I confider what a folitary unjoyous Life I am likely hence-
' forward to be doom'd to. O Fortune, that thou art never con-
' ftant and perfevering in thy Favours. But a former Paffion, which
' I then got the better of by Thought and Reflection, hath taught me
' Experience in the prefent Cafe, and I muft now endeavour to do
' the fame. But I fee *Parmeno* with the Servants; he muft by no
' means be here at this time; for he alone was trufted with the Se-
' cret of my Behaviour to her, when I firft married her. I tremble,
' left fhould he hear her frequent Cries, he may difcover fhe is in la-
' bour. I muft difpatch him hence fomewhere, till *Philumena* is de-
' livered.

A N N O T A T I O N S.

45 *Lacrumæ, quæ poftbac futura eft*, &c.
*Pamphilus* had reafon to fufpect his Wife
of a Crime, which, of all others, was moft
likely to extinguish his Love; yet we find
it was an Attachment he could not break
off without Pain. All this is artfully contriv'd by the Poet, to raife the greater Com-
miferation, and prepare us for receiving with
Joy

---

# A C T  III.  S C E N E  IV.

### A R G U M E N T.

*Sofia relates the Dangers of the Sea he had undergone. Par-
meno is fent to the Tower, to hinder him from hearing* Philumena's *Cries in labour.*

PARMENO, SOSIA, PAMPHILUS.

*Par.* SAY you, that you had a very troublefome Voyage of it?
   *Sof.* Indeed, *Parmeno*, it is not poffible to exprefs the many
Hardfhips that attend being at Sea.
  *Par.* Say you fo?
  *Sof.* O happy *Parmeno*! you little know the Dangers you have
efcap'd by never being at Sea: for not to mention other Hardfhips,
mark only this. I was aboard thirty Days or more, and every Mo-
ment expected to be fwallowed up by the Waves, we were fo con-
tinually affaulted with Storms and contrary Winds all the time.
*Par.*

A N N O T A T I O N S.

*Pamphilus*, we have feen, had fent Parmeno to affift *Sofia*, and the other Servants,
in carrying home his things from the Ship.
They accordingly appear now, and the Poet
very naturally fuppofes, that *Sofia* had been
entertaining *Parmeno* with the Particulars
of their Voyage, which Converfation is continued here for fome time. *Pamphilus*, in
the mean time, who had promifed to conceal *Philumena*'s Misfortune, and is therefore

Quin, quod verisimile est, ex te recte eum natum putent.
Continuo exponetur. hîc tibi nihil est quidquam in-
    commodi : & 40
Illi miserae indignè factam injuriam contexeris.
Pollicitus sum, & servare in eo certum est, quod dixi,
    fidem. [arbitror.
Nam de reducenda, id vero neutiquam honestum esse
Nec faciam : etsi amor me graviter, consuetudoque
    ejus tenet.
Lacrumo, quae posthac futura est vita, cùm in men-
    tem venit, 45
Solitudoque. ô fortuna, ut nunquam perpetuò es bona.
Sed jam prior amor me ad hanc rem exercitatum red-
    didit, [operam dabo.
Quem ego tum consilio missum feci. idem nunc huic
Adest Parmeno cum pueris : hunc minimè est opus
In hac re adesse : nam olim soli credidi. 50
Eâ me abstinuisse in principio, cùm data est.
Vereor, si clamorem ejus hic crebro exaudiat,
Ne parturire intellegat. aliquò mihi est
Hinc ablegandus, dum parit Philumena.

*consilio : idem nunc dabo operam huic. Parmeno cum pueris adest : minimè opus est hunc adesse in hac re : nam olim credidi illi soli, me abstinuisse ea in principio, cum data est. — Vereor, si hic crebro exaudiat clamorem ejus, ne intelligat eam parturire : ablegandus est hinc mihi aliquo, dum Philumena pari:.*

*A N N O T A T I O N S.*

Joy the Discovery, which puts *Pamphilus* in
the possession of that Happiness he so much
desired. This is the great Secret in Dramatic Composition, to he able to move the Passions, and keep them interested and engaged,
during the whole Time of the Representation.

---

A C T U S III. S C E N A IV.
A R G U M E N T U M.

*Narrat Sosia quae adierit maris pericula : servus Parmeno in*
*arcem mittitur, ne parere Philumenam interim audiat.*

PARMENO, SOSIA, PAMPHILUS.

AIN' tu, tibi hoc incommodum evenisse iter?
  So. Non hercle verbis, Parmeno, dici potest
Tantum, quàm re ipsâ navigare incommodum est.
PAR. Itane est? So. ô fortunate, nescis quid mali
Praeterieris, qui nunquam es ingressus mare. 5
Nam alias ut mittam miserias, unam hanc vide :
Dies triginta, aut plus eo, in navi fui,
Cùm interea semper mortem exspectabam, miser :
Ita usque advorsâ tempestate usi sumus.

*ORDO.*
PAR. AIN' tu, hoc iter evenisse incommodum tibi? So. Hercle, Parmeno, tantum non potest dici verbis, quàm re-ipsâ est incommodum navigare. PAR. Itane est? So. O fortunate, nescis quid mali praeterieris, qui nunquam es in-gressus mare. Nam, ut mittam alias miserias, vide hanc unam : fui in navi triginta dies, aut plus eo, cum interea miser semper expectabam mortem : ita usque usi sumus tempestate adversa.

*gressus mare. Nam, ut mittam alias miserias, vide hanc unam : fui in navi triginta dies, aut plus eo, cum interea miser semper expectabam mortem : ita usque usi sumus tempestate adversa.*

*A N N O T A T I O N S.*

fore anxious to remove *Parmeno* out of the
way, lest he might overhear her Cries, contrives to dispatch him to the Tower, under
Pretence of an Appointment he had made
with his *Myconian* Host:

*Par.* Dreadful [...]

*Sof.* I know it to my sorrow. In plain Terms, I'd rather run away, than go again to Sea, if I knew there was any such Design?

*Par.* Indeed, *Sofia*, a very slight Cause made you do formerly what you now only threaten. But I see *Pamphilus* himself standing before the Door. Get ye in, I'll step to him, to see if he wants any thing with me. *(to* Pamphilus*)* What, are you still here, Master?

*Pam.* I wait for you.

*Par.* What's the matter?

*Pam.* You must run to the Tower.

*Par.* Who must?

*Pam.* You.

*Par.* To the Tower! What to do there?

*Pam.* To meet *Callidemides*, my Landlord at *Mycone*, who came over in the same Ship with me.

*Parm.* S'death! I'll swear he has made a Vow, if ever he came home, to walk me off my Legs.

*Pam.* Why do you linger so?

*Par.* What shall I say? Or am I to meet him only?

*Pam.* You must tell him that I can't meet him to-day, according to our Appointment, that he mayn't wait there to no purpose. Fly.

*Par.* But I don't know the Man, were I to see him.

*Pam.* But I'll tell you to know him. He's a huge, red-faced, fizzle-pated, fat, grey-eyed Fellow, with a ghastly Visage.

*Par.* Plague on him. But what if he should not come? Must I wait for him till Night?

*Pam.* Yes, wait: run.

*Par.* I can't, I'm so tir'd.

*Pam.* *(by himself)* He's dispatch'd out of the way. What shall I do in this miserable Situation? I'm quite at a loss how to acquit myself of my Promise to *Myrrhina*, and conceal her Daughter's Lying-in: for I pity the Woman from my Soul. I'll do what I can consistent with my Duty, for Obedience to a Parent ought to take place of Love. But ha! here's *Philippus* and my Father, they're coming this way. I don't know what to say to them.

ACT

## ANNOTATIONS.

17 *In arcem.* This is, no doubt, to be understood of the Fort, or Citadel, that defended the *Piræum.* It was at a considerable Distance from the City, and therefore better suited *Pamphilus*'s Design, which was to keep *Parmeno* at a distance for some time.

19 *Vevisse hunc dicam, si salvus demum redisset,* &c. To comprehend the full Force and Beauty of this, we must reflect on what *Sofia* had been telling *Parmeno*, that they had a dangerous Voyage. It was in this case usual to offer up some Vow to the Gods, provided they escap'd the Perils that threaten'd them; and their first Care, after their Return, was to perform their Vow. *Parmeno* facetiously supposes, that *Pamphilus*, during the Storm, had vowed to walk him to death, if he got home safe.

26 *Crispus.* *Terence* here is accused of an Error, in calling the *Myconian* frizzle-pated; for herein he deviates from *Apollodorus*, who had call'd him bald. This Censure is probably

PAR. Odiosum. So. haud clam me est: denique hercle
    aufugerim
Potiùs, quàm redeam, si eo mi redeundum sciam. 110
PAR. Olim quidem te causæ impellebant leves,
Quod nunc minitare facere, ut faceres, Sosia.
Sed Pamphilum ipsum video stare ante ostium.
Ite intro, ego hunc adibo, si quid me velit. 15
Here, etiam nunc tu hîc stas? PAM. equidem te ex-
    specto. PAR. quid est. [PAM. tibi.
PAM. In arcem transcurso opus est. PAR. cui homini?
PAR. In arcem? quid eò? PAM. Callidemidem hos-
    pitem
Myconium, qui mecum unà advectu'st, conveni.
PAR. Perii. vovisse hunc dicam, si salvus domum 20
Rediisset unquam, ut me ambulando rumperet.
PAM. Quid cessas? PAR. quid vis dicam? an conve-
    niam modò?
PAM. Imo, quod constitui, me hodie conventurum eum,
Non posse, ne frustra illic exspectet: vola.
PAR. At non novi hominis faciem. PAM. at faciam
    ut noveris. 25
Magnus, rubicundus, crispus, crassus, cæsius,
Cadaverosa facie. PAR. Di illum perduint.
Quid, si non veniet? maneamque usque ad vesperum?
PAM. Maneto: curre. PAR. non queo: ita defessu'
    sum.
PAM. Ille abiit. quin agam infelix? prorsus nescio, 30
Quo pacto hoc celem, quod me oravit Myrrhina,
Suæ gnatæ partum: nam me miseret mulieris.
Quòd potero faciam tamen, ut pietatem colam:
Nam me parenti potiùs, quam amori, obsequi
Oportet. at at, eccum Phidippum, & patrem 35
Video: horsum pergunt. quid dicam hisce, incertu'
    sum.

*PAR. Odiosum. So. Haud est clam me: denique hercle potius aufugerim, quàm videam, si sciam esse redeundum, mihi eo. PAM. Olim quidem leves causæ impellebant te id facere, quod nunc minitare facere, Sosia. Sed video ipsum Pamphilum stare ante ostium. Ite intro, ego adibo hunc, si velit me quid. Here, etiam nunc tu stas hîc? PAM. Equidem expecto te. PAR. Quid est? PAM. Opus est transcurso an arcem. PAR. Cui homini? PAM. Tibi. PAR. In arcem? Quid eò? PAM. Conveni Callidemidem hospitem Myconium, qui advectus est una mecum. PAR. Perii, dicam hunc vovisse, si unquam rediisset salvus domum, ut rumperet me ambulando. PAM. Quid cessas? PAR. Quid vis dicam? an conveniam modo? PAM. Imo, me non posse conventurum eum hodie, quod constitui facere, ne frustra expectet illic: vola. PAR. At non novi faciem homi-ris: est magnus, rubicundus, crispus, crassus, cæsius, cadaverosa facie. PAR. Dii perduint i... Quid, si non veniet? maneamne usque ad vesperum? PAM. Maneto: curre. PAR. Non queo, sum ita defessus. PAM. Ille abiit: quid agam infelix? Prorsus nescio quo pacto celem hoc quod Myrrhina oravit me celare, nempe partum suæ gnatæ: nam miseret me mulieris. Faciam quod potero tamen, ut colam pietatem: nam oportet me obsequi potias parenti, quam amori. At, at, video eccum Phidippum & patrem: pergunt horsum. Incertus sum, quid dicam hisce.*

## ANNOTATIONS.

...bably owing to the Greek Proverb, *Myconius calvus.* Whence *Lucilius* says, *Myconi calvus omnis juventus.* But, without doubt, Terence knew all this as well as his Censurers, and perhaps here calls his *Myconian crispus,* to distinguish him the more particularly, as being of a Make so remarkably different from that of most of his Countrymen.

(?) *Cadaverosâ facie.* This has been differently explained by different Commentators. *Turnebus* sums up their various Opinions: *Aliis sublivida est, & personata rubore & livore; aliis pulposa & crassa, quasi carnosa; cùm caro proprie sit, quæ anima caret.* Ego *cadaverosam faciem, fædam & turpem* interpretor. I have in the Translation given it the Turn that comes nearest to our Idiom and Manner, and at the same time seems to express fully the Meaning of the Original.

ACTUS

## ACT III. SCENE V.

### ARGUMENT.

*The old Men are consulting together about sending back Philu-*
*mena. Pamphilus refuses to receive her, which Phidippus*
*takes extremely ill.*

LACHES, PHIDIPPUS, PAMPHILUS.

*Lac.* DID you not but just now say, that she told you, she waited
for my Son's Return?

*Phi.* I did.

*Lac.* They say he's come home, let her return then.

*Pam.* I'm extremely puzzled what Excuse to make to my Father,
for not taking her back.

*Lac.* Who was that I heard speaking here?

*Pam.* But I'm resolved to keep firm to my Purpose.

*Lac.* The very Man we were talking of.

*Pam.* Heaven bless you, Father.

*Lac.* And you, my Son.

*Phi.* I'm glad to see you return'd, *Pamphilus,* and more especially
that you are healthy, and look so well.

*Pam.* I believe you.

*Lac.* Are you just come?

*Pam.* But just now.

*Lac.* Well, say: What has our Cousin *Phania* left us?

*Pam.* Why truly, he was one that minded his Pleasures while
he lived; and such People seldom enrich their Heirs. However, he
left this Commendation behind him; *that while he liv'd, he liv'd well.*

*Lac.* So then, you've brought nothing home with you, but this
single Sentence.

*Pam.* Whatever it is he has left, we are the better for it.

*Lac.* Nay, we are the worse; for I could wish him alive and in
Health.

*Phi.* That you may do safely, for he'll scarce rise again from the
dead: and yet I know which you'd rather have.

*Lac. To Pamphilus.)* *Phidippus,* here, sent for *Philumena* yesterday. *(Aside to Phidippus.)* Say you sent for her?

*Phi. (Aside to Laches.)* Don't punch me so.——I did so.

*Lac.* But now he'll send her home again.

*Phi.* Without doubt. *Pam.*

### ANNOTATIONS.

*Pamphilus* has no sooner rid himself of *Parmeno,* but he is thrown into a new Perplexity, that distresses him greatly: for while he is revolving with himself, how he should be best able to keep his Promise to *Myrrhina,* of concealing her Daughter's Misfortune, the two Fathers, *Phidippus* and *Laches,* come up to him. After the first Salutations, and some Conversation on indifferent Subjects, *Laches* introduces the men-tion of his Wife, pretending, that she had been sent for by her Father, but would now return. *Pamphilus* lets them understand, that he is acquainted with the whole matter, and had determined not to take her back. In spite of all their Importunity, he adheres to his Resolution; but as his Father press'd him hard, and he was at a loss to answer, he thinks it prudent to retire, lest he might, perhaps, betray himself, *Phidippus,* enrag'd
at

## ACTUS III. SCENA IV.

### ARGUMENTUM.

*De reducenda Philumena inter senes agitur. Pamphilus reductu-*
*rum se negat: Fert eam rem indigne Phidippus.*

LACHES, PHIDIPPUS, PAMPHILUS.

DIXTIN' dudum, illam dixisse se exspectare fi-
    lium ? [causam dicam patri,
PH. Factum: LA. venisse aiunt: redeat. PA. quam
Quamobrem non reducam, nescio. LA. quem ego hîc
    audivi loqui ? [persequi.
PA. Certum obfirmare est viam me, quam decrevi
LA. Ipsus est, de quo hoc agebam tecum. PA. salve,
    mi pater. 5
LA. Gnate mi, salve. PH. bene factum te advenisse,
    Pamphile, [PA. creditur.
Et adeo quod maxumum est, salvum atque validum.
LA. Advenis modo ? PA. admodum. LA. cedo: quid
    reliquit Phania [obsequens
Consobrinus noster ? PA. sane hercle homo voluptati
Fuit, dum vixit: & qui sic sunt, haud multum here-
    dem juvant. 10
Sibi vero hanc laudem relinquunt : Vixit, dum vixit,
    bene. [tentiâ ?
LA. Tum tu igitur nihil attulisti huc plus unâ sen-
PA. Quidquid est id quod reliquit, profuit. LA. imo
    obfuit : [optare istuc licet :
Nam illum vivum & salvum vellem. PH. impune
Ille reviviscet jam nunquam. & tamen, utrum malis,
    scio. 15
LA. Heri Philumenam ad se accersi hic jussit. dic jus-
    sisse te. [PH. scilicet.
PH. Noli fodere. jussi. LA. sed eam jam remittet.





### ANNOTATIONS.

at this, as he supposed it unreasonable Obstinacy, marches off too in a Huff.

13 *Imo obfuit.* Terence here gives us a
lively Idea of a covetous old Man; who, as
soon as he understands, that he was like to
be a Gainer by his Relation's Death, then
at length begins to testify his Regret and
Sorrow.

15 *Ille reviviscet jam nunquam.* These
Words come from Phidippus, and we are to
conceive them, as partly suggested by Envy,
which cannot bear the Prosperity of another,
without attempting somehow to depreciate
him, and make him appear unworthy of it.
These almost imperceptible Touches, are
the great Beauty of Dramatick Writing. It
is well worth while to study them particularly, as they serve to make us enter deeply
into the Characters of Men, and shew how
well the Poet has painted after Nature and
real Life.

17 *Noli fodere. jussi.* Laches, un

*Pam.* I know the whole Affair, and how it happened. I was told it immediately upon my Arrival.

*Lac.* Curse on these spiteful Devils, who are so ready with their News.

*Pam.* I am conscious that it has been my Study to give no just Cause of Complaint on your Side; and, were I so inclin'd, could here tell how faithful, loving, and tender a Husband I have been: but I had rather you should hear it from herself; for thus you will the readier Credit what is said, when so favourable a Testimony comes from her, who at present acts so unjustly to me. I call Heaven to witness, that this Separation is through no Fault of mine. But since she thinks herself too considerable to submit to my Mother, as is her Duty, and whose Temper she ought modestly to have conformed to, and since 'tis impossible they can live in good Understanding on any other Terms; I find, *Phidippus*, I must resolve, either to leave my Mother, or *Philumena*. Now Duty obliges me to regard rather my Mother's Quiet.

*Lac.* I'm not displeased, *Pamphilus*, to hear you prefer your Duty to a Parent, to every other Consideration. But take care, my Son, that you suffer not your Resentment to carry you too far.

*Pam.* What Resentment, Father, can bias me against her, who never contradicted me in any thing, and who has so often deserved well of me? I love her, honour her, and passionately desire to keep her; for I have found her of a Temper wonderfully sweet and engaging; and I heartily wish, that she may spend the rest of her Life with a Husband more fortunate than myself, since *cruel* Necessity *thus* tears her from me.

*Phi.* 'Tis in your Power to hinder that.

*Lac.* If you are wise, desire that she be sent back.

*Pam.* That's not my Design, Father; I must consult my Mother's Interest.

*Lac.* Where are you going? Stay, stay, I say: Where are you going?

*Phi.* What Obstinacy is this?

*Lac.*

## ANNOTATIONS.

to let his Son know there had been any Difference between his Wife and Mother; pretend, that *Phidippus* had sent for his Daughter the Day before. He, at the same Time whispers *Phidippus* to second the Artifice, and punches him in the Side, to make him the more sensible of his Desire to have the real Truth disguised, lest it might give Offence to *Pamphilus*. Hence the Reason of the first Part of *Phidippus*'s Reply, which we are to conceive expressed with a low Voice, so as to be heard only to *Laches*. This tho' apparent in the Representation, is not so apt to occur to a Reader, without some Remark to illustrate it.

27 *Sed quando sese esse indignam deputat,* &c. Both the Construction and the Import of the Words in this Sentence are remarkable. For this Reason, some Commentators suppose an Error in the Text, and instead of *cui,* read *quæ,* making the Construction run thus: *sed quando deputat sese esse indignam, quæ concedat matri, meæ.* But as we read immediately after, *cujusque mores toleret,* this plainly implies, that a Relative went before, which referred to *matri.* We must therefore suppose an Ellipsis, and supply *mea matre* to compleat the Sentence, according to which the obvious Construction will be: *sed quando deputat sese esse indignam mea matre,*

PA. Omnem rem scio, ut sit gesta. adveniens audivi omnia: LA. at
Istos invidos Di perdant, qui hæc libenter nunciant.
PA. Ego me scio cavisse, ne ulla merito contumelia 20
Fieri à vobis posset. idque si nunc memorare hîc velim,
Quàm fideli animo & benigno in illam, & clementi fui,
Verè possum; ni te ex ipsâ hæc magi' velim resciscere:
Namque eo pacto maxumè apud te meo erit ingenio fides,
Cùm illa, quæ nunc in me iniqua est, æqua de me dixerit. 25
Neque mea culpâ hoc discidium evenisse, id testor Deos.
Sed quando sese esse indignam deputat matri meæ,
Cui concedat, cujus mores toleret suâ modestiâ;
Neque alio pacto componi potest inter eas gratia;
Segreganda aut mater à me est, Phidippe, aut Philumena. 30
Nunc me pietas matris potiùs commodum suadet sequi.
LA. Pamphile, haud invito ad aures sermo mihi accessit tuus,
Cùm te postputasse omnes res præ parente intellego.
Verùm vide, ne impulsus irâ pravè insistas, Pamphile.
PA. Quibus iris impulsus nunc in illam iniquu' sim? 35
Quæ nunquam quidquam erga me commerita est, pater,
Quod nollem: & sæpe, quod vellem, meritam scio.
Amoque, & laudo, & vehementer desidero:
Nam fuisse erga me miro ingenio, expertu' sum.
Illique exopto, ut relliquam vitam exigat 40
Cum eo viro, me qui sit fortunatior;
Quandoquidem illam à me distrahit necessitas.
PH. Tibi id in manu est, ne fiat. LA. si sanus sies,
Jube illam redire. PA. non est consilium, pater:
Matris, servibo commodis. LA. quò abis? mane; 45
Mane, inquam: quò abis? PH. quæ hæc est pertinacia?



*Quibus iris impulsus sim nunc iniquus in illam? Quæ nunquam commerita est quidquam erga me, pater, quod nollem; & scio esse sæpe meritam quod vellem. Amoque, & laudo, & vehementer desidero eam: nam expertus sum, eam fuisse miro ingenio erga me. Exopteque illi, ut exigat e liquam vitam cum eo viro, qui sit fortunatior me; quandoquidem necessitas distrahit illam à me. PH. Est in manu tibi, ne id fiat. LA. Si sis sanus, jube illam redire. PA. Non est consilium, pater: servibo commodis matris. LA. Quo abis? mane, mane, inquam: quo abis? PH. Quæ est hæc pertinacia?*

## ANNOTATIONS.

matre, cui matri meæ concedat, cujusque mores toleret sua modestia. "But since she thinks "herself too considerable to submit to my "Mother, to whom it is her Duty to yield, "and whose Temper she ought modestly to "conform to."

32 Haud invito ad aures. Madam Dacier observes, that the Poet has framed this Answer of Laches with great Judgment, so as not to be wanting in a due Return to the dutiful Declaration of his Son, nor contradict what he had so earnestly set his Mind



upon

*Lac.* Did I not tell you, *Phidippus*, that he would take this extremely ill? And therefore I was so earnest with you to send back your Daughter.

*Phi.* Why truly I could not have thought he would have been so brutish: Does he imagine that I'll now descend to court him? If he has a mind to take back his Wife, he may: if not, let him return her Portion, and have done.

*Lac.* See there, you must begin to be huffish too!

*Phi.* You seem, *Pamphilus*, to be returned in a very stiff, haughty Mood.

*Lac.* His Anger will soon be over, tho' I can't but say he has some Reason.

*Phi.* Because, forsooth, you have got a little Money, you are mightily elevated upon it.

*Lac.* What! Are you going to fall out with me too?

*Phi.* Let him consider, and resolve me to-day, whether he'll have her, or not; that if he won't, another may.

*Lac.* *Phidippus*, stay, hear me a little——He's gone. What is it to me? In fine, let them even order it among themselves, since neither my Son nor he mind what I say, or pay any Regard to my Advice. I'll carry the Quarrel to my Wife; who is the Occasion of all this Mischief, and discharge my Spleen at her, because it sits heavy upon me.

A N N O T A T I O N S.

upon. He does not entirely commend his Son's Speech, or say, that he had done him a great Pleasure, for fear of encouraging him in the Resolution he had taken of parting from his Wife: he contents himself with saying, he was not displeased with a Speech, wherein he had expressed so high a Regard for his Parents. To translate the Passage thus, *You do me a great Pleasure*, would entirely destroy its Beauty and Justness.

52 *Renumeret dotem huc.* For according to the *Roman* Law, when a Marriage was dissolved, except in the Case of Adultery, the Wife's Father had a Right to redemand her Portion, and there is no doubt, but that the same was the Custom also among the *Greeks*,

<hr>

# ACT IV. SCENE I.

### ARGUMENT.

*Phidippus knows of his Daughter's being brought To-bed, and expostulates with his Wife for concealing it; charging her as the Cause of the Difference between* Pamphilus *and* Philumena.

MYRRHINA, PHIDIPPUS.

*Myr.* I'M undone! What shall I do? Which Way turn myself? What Answer shall I give my Husband? for I fear he heard the Child crying, he run so hastily into his Daughter's Chamber, without
out

A N N O T A T I O N S.

We have seen in the last Scene, that *Phidippus* leaves *Lacbes* in a great Huff, as being offended at the haughty Behaviour of *Pamphilus*. It is no Wonder, if thus disgusted,

LA. Dixin', Phidippe, hanc rem ægrè laturum esse
    eum?
Quamobrem te orabam, filiam ut remitteres.
PH. Non credidi edepol adeo inhumanum fore:
Ita nunc is sibi me supplicaturum putat?     50
Si est, ut velit reducere uxorem, licet:
Sin alio est animo, renumeret dotem huc, eat.
LA. Ecce autem, tu quoque protervè iracundus es.
PH. Percontumax redisti huc nobis, Pamphile.
LA. Decedet jam ira hæc: etsi meritò iratus est.     55
PH. Quia paulum vobis accessit pecuniæ,
Sublati animi sunt.   LA. etiam mecum litigas?
PH. Deliberet, renuncietque hodie mihi,
Velitne, an non; ut alii, si huic non sit, siet.
LA. Phidippe, ades, audi paucis, abiit: quid meâ?     60
Postremò inter se transigant ipsi, ut lubet:
Quando nec gnatus, neque hic mihi quidquam obtem-
        perant:
Quæ dico, parvi pendunt, porto hoc jurgium ad
Uxorem, cujus hæc fiunt consilio omnia.
Atque in eam hoc omne, quòd mihi ægrè est, evo-
    mam.     65

*an non; ut sit alii, si non sit huic. LA. Phidippe, ades, audi paucis. Abiit: quid refert meâ? Postremo ipsi transigant inter se, ut lubet: quando nec gnatus, neque hic obtemperant quidquam mihi: parvi pendunt, quæ dico. Porto hoc jurgium ad uxorem, cujus consilio omnia hæc fiunt: atque evomam omne hoc, quod est ægre mihi, in eam.*

ORDO.

My. PERII, quid a-
gam? quo vertam me? Quid misera
respondebo meo viro? Nam visus est audivisse vocem pueri vagientis? Quamobrem o-
rabam te, ut remit-
teres filiam. Pu. E-
depol non credidi eum
fore adeo inhumá-
num? an is nunc
putat me ita suppli-
caturum sibi? Si est,
ut velit reducere ux-
orem, licet: sin est
alio animo, renume-
ret dotem huc, eat.
LA. Ecce autem, tu
quoque es protervè
iracundus. Huc Re-
disti huc nobis per-
contumax. LA. Hæc
ira jam decidet: etsi
est merito iratus. PH.
Quia paulum pecu-
niæ accessit vobis,
animi sunt sublati.
LA. Litiges etiam
mecum? PH. Deli-
beret, renuncietque
hodie mihi, velitne,

### ANNOTATIONS.

Greeks, as may be gathered from these Words of *Apuleius, Apolog.* p. 547. ed *Delph.* " Nam quodcunque aliud in d tem acceperis, " potes, cum lubuit, ne sis beneficio obstric- " tus, omne, ut acceperis, renumerare, muni- " cipia restituere, domo demigrare, prædiis " cedere. Sola virginitas, cum semel ac- " cepta est, reddi nequitur: sola apud ma- " ritum ex rebus dotalibus remanet."

---

# ACTUS IV. SCENA I.

## ARGUMENTUM.

*Phidippus partum filiæ rescivit, & expostulat cum Myrrhina, quod partum celaverit, & quod auctor sit discidii inter Pamphilum & Philumenam.*

### MYRRHINA, PHIDIPPUS.

PERII, quid agam? quò me vortam? quid viro
    meo respondebo
Misera? nam audivisse vocem pueri visu' est vagientis:

ORDO.

My. PERII,
quid a-
gam? quo vertam
me? Quid misera

### ANNOTATIONS.

gusted, he resolves to use no Constraint with his Daughter, but leave it to her own Choice to stay or return. But what happens in this Scene, gives a very different Turn to his way of thinking. For coming directly home, after he left Laches, it chanced to be soon

out speaking a Word. If he comes to know that she is brought to bed, I can't think what Excuse to form for keeping it a Secret. But the Door opens; I believe he's coming out to me. I'm ruin'd.

*Phi.* My Wife, when she saw me run to my Daughter, slipt out of doors; but here she is. How now, *Myrrhina?* What have you to say for yourself? Hark ye, I speak to you.

*Myr.* To me, Husband?

*Phi.* I your Husband! Do you regard me as a Husband, or even as a Man? For had you ever taken me for either, Woman, you had not thus made me a Tool to your Designs?

*Myr.* What Designs?

*Phi.* Do you ask? Is not your Daughter brought to-bed? Hah, are you silent? Whose Child is it?

*Myr.* Is that a Question for a Father to ask? *(aside.)* I'm undone. Whose do you think, pray, but her Husband's?

*Phi.* I believe it, nor ought a Father to suppose otherwise; but I'm astonished to think what you could mean by concealing it from us all with so much Care, especially as she is safely delivered, and at her full Time. To be so maliciously stubborn as to resolve upon destroying the Child (which you might have known would be a more firm and lasting Bond of Union) rather than suffer a Match to subsist, which you was set against. I indeed thought all along that they were in fault, whereas I now find it to be you.

*Myr.* I'm an unhappy Wretch!

*Phi.* I wish I knew it to be really so: but now I call to mind what you was formerly wont to say, when we first accepted him for our Son-in-Law. You could not, you said, think of your Daughter's being married to a Man who kept a Mistress, and lay out o' Nights.

*Myr.* I'd rather he should suspect any Cause than the true one.

*Phi.*

*ANNOTATIONS.*

after his Daughter was delivered, and he overheard the Child's Cries; upon which, running to *Philumena's* Apartment, he finds how it was. Immediately he runs to his Wife, and expostulates warmly with her, for concealing a thing of that Importance from him; and as it was plainly her Design to have destroyed the Child, he throws the whole Blame of the Separation upon her, who, having taken a Dislike to *Pamphilus,* endeavoured to withdraw her Daughter, and make an irreconcileable Breach between them. This greatly perplexes *Myrrhina,* and makes her doubt how far *Pamphilus* would be able to keep their Secret, as another's Child was like to be bred for his. I have followed the *Cambridge* Edition of our Poet, in making this Scene the Beginning of the fourth Act, tho' others, with seemingly good Reason annex this Scene to the third Act,

and begin the fourth with the following Scene.

[16] *Præsertim cum et recte. Recte* here, is not to be interpreted happily, or well delivered; it respects not the Mother, but the Birth; intimating, that it was a real Child, and no Monster. *Phidippus* adds, *a tempore suo,* which may occasion some difficulty, because of what *Myrrhina* says before to *Pamphilus,* Act 3: S. 3. 34. *Tum, postquam ad te venit, mensis agitur hic jam septimus.* But this probably refers only to their nuptial Commerce, without including the two Months he abstained from her, mentioned in the foregoing Line; a Circumstance that *Phidippus* knew nothing of. But supposing it to be only the seventh Month after Marriage, that was still accounted a timely Birth among the Antients. Digest. Lib. 1. Tit. 5. L. 1. 12. *Verba: Paulus*

*Septimo*

Ita corripuit derepente tacitus sese ad filiam :     [buisse
Quòd si rescierit peperisse, id quà causâ clam me ha-
Dicam, non edepol scio.     5
Sed ostium concrepuit : credo ipsum ad me exire : nulla
     sum.
PH. Uxor, ubi me ad filiam ire sensit, se duxit foras.
  Atque eccam video. quid ais, Myrrhina? heus, tibi di-
     co. MY. mihine, mi vir?     [deputas adeo esse?
PH. Vir ego tuus sum? tu virum me, aut hominem
Nam si utrumvis horum, mulier, unquàm tibi visus
     forem,     10
Non sic ludibrio tuis factis habitus essem. MY. quibus?
  PH. At rogitas?
Peperit filia? hem, taces? ex quo? MY. istuc patrem
     rogare est æquum?     [obsecro?
Perii : ex quo cenes, nisi ex illo, cui data est nuptum,
PH. Credo : neque adeo arbitrari patris est aliter. sed
     demiror,
Quid sit, quamobrem tantopere hunc omnes nos ce-
     lare volueris.     15
Partum ; præsertim cùm & recte, & tempore suo pe-
     pererit.     [perire,
Adcon' pervicaci esse animo, ut puerum præoptares
Ex quo firmiorem inter nos fore amicitiam posthac
     nimicires,     [illo nupta?
Potiùs, quàm advorsum animi tui lubidinem esset cum
Ego etiam illorum esse hanc culpam, credidi, quæ te
     est penes.     20
MY. Misera sum. PH. utinam sciam ita esse istuc. sed
     nunc mihi in mentem venit,
De hac re quod locuta es olim, cùm illum generum
     cepimus :
Nam negabas nuptam posse filiam tuam te pati
Cùm eo, qui meretricem amaret, qui pernoctaret foris.
MY. Quamvis causam hunc suspicari, quàm ipsam ve-
     ram, mavolo.     25

*tacitus corripuit sese sua derepente ad filiam. Quod si rescierit eam peperisse, edepol non scio qua causa dicam me habuisse id clam. Sed ostium concrepuit : credo ipsam exire ad me : sum nulla. PH. Uxor, ubi sensit me ire ad filium, duxit se foras. Atque eccam video. Quid ais, Myrrhina? Heus, dico tibi. MY. Mihine, mi vir? PH. Ego ne sum tuus vir? Tune deputas me esse virum, aut alio hominem? Nam, mulier, si unquam forem istis tibi utrimvis horum, non sic essem habitus ludibrio tuis factis. MY. Quibus? PH. At rogitas? filia peperit? Hem, taces? ex quo? MY. est æquum patrem rogitare istuc? Perii : obsecro ex quo censes, nisi ex illo, cui est data nuptum? PH. Credo, nequid adeo patris est arbitrari aliter. Sed demiror quid sit, quamobrem tantopere vultis celare omnes nos hunc partum : præsertim cum et recte pepererit, & suo tempore. Esse adeone pervicaci animo, ut præoptares puerum perire, ex quo scires posthac fore fir-miorem amicitiam inter nos ; potius ; quam filia esset nupta cum illo adversum libidinem tui animi? Ego etiam credidi hanc esse culpam illorum, quæ est penes te. MY. Sum misera. PH. Utinam sciam istuc esse ita : sed nunc id venit in mentem mihi, quod es olim locuta de hac re, cum cepimus illum generum. Nam negabas te posse pati filiam tuam nuptam cum eo, qui amaret meretricem, qui pernoctaret foris. MY. Mavolo hunc suspicari quamvis causam, quam ipsam veram.*

## ANNOTATIONS.

*Septimo mense nasci perfectum partum, jam receptum est, propter auctoritatem doctissimi viri Hippocratis ; et ideo credendum est, cum qui ex justis nuptiis septimo mense natus est, justum filium esse.*

*21 Utinam sciam ita esse istuc. Hoc quidem sic accipiunt, quasi Philippus dicat, istu* — *penes te culpa est, quam illorum esse credebam ; & utinam quod credo, penes te esse culpam, ita non esse certo sciam. Quia dixit se miseram ; & miseros non nisi innocentes dicimus. Ille enim hoc respondit : inam in hac negotio miseram te, non sci istum reperiam. Sic Sallustius in fragmentis*



Atque

*Phi.* I knew long before you, *Myrrhina*, that he had a Mistress, but I never look'd upon that as a Crime in young Men, for 'tis natural to them all. But the Time will soon come, when he will hate even himself for it. But you shew yourself to be still the same as before, nor could you rest till you had brought away your Daughter, lest what I had done should hold good. The thing itself now plainly shews how you stood affected to the Match.

*Myr.* Do you think me so very wilful, then, that I should act thus towards my own Child, if I though the Marriage for her Good?

*Phi.* Do you pretend to foresee or judge what is for our Advantage? Some one perhaps has told you that he saw him going to, or coming out from his Mistress. What then, if he was discreet, and did it but seldom? Is it not better to dissemble, than pry into Secrets that will naturally beget Misunderstandings and Ill-will? For could he all at once withdraw his Affections from one he had lov'd so many Years, I should not account him a Man, nor likely to prove a constant Husband to my Daughter.

*Myr.* Pray have done with the young Gentleman, and my Faults, as you are pleased to think them. Go, meet him by yourself, and ask whether he is willing to take home his Wife, or no. If he says he is, then send her back; but if he refuses, then 'tis plain I have taken the best Course for my Daughter.

*Phi.* Suppose he will not, and that you knew him to be in fault, *Myrrhina*; I was present, by whose Advice it was proper that these things should have been settled, I am therefore much offended at your presuming thus far without my Leave. I charge you strictly, that the Boy be carried no where out of the House. But what Folly is it, to expect or require Obedience from her? I'll go in myself, and charge the Servants that they suffer it to be carried out no where.

*Myr.*

## A N N O T A T I O N S.

*Atque ea cogentes non coactos; scelestos magis quam miseros distringi.* Et ideo sequitur, *sed nunc mihi in mentem venit.* Argumentum ex antecedentibus dictis & factis.

34. *Id, nunc res indicium hæc facit, quo pacto factum volueris.* The Order of Construction here is not so easily discovered, because the Words may be disposed two ways. For we may take them: *Hæc res nunc id indicium facit:* i. e. *indicat,* as in the *Adelphi,* IV. 4. 7. *Id anus fecit indicium mihi.* Or thus: *Hæc res nunc facit indicium, quo pacto volueris id factum.* This last is what I have followed; and the rather so, because in the most correct Editions and Manuscripts of our Poet, we meet with a Comma after *id,* which confines the Words to this particular Turn.

37. *Nonne ea dissimulare nos magis humanum est, &c.* These Words are somewhat obscure, and have greatly perplex'd Commentators. *Westerhovius* finds fault with *Donatus,* who he tells us explains the Meaning of the Words quite away. His Words are: " *Donatus accipit quasi sensus sit;* " *dare operam nos id scire quamobrem* " *Pamphilus nos oderit. Senso nullo. Id* " *vult Phidippus, eum, qui oderit nos, id* " *per nos nihil dissimulantes scire; q. d.* " *quam dare operam, ut proferatur, atque* " *inimici nostri id sciant, & lætentur.*" But this seems to me too far fetch'd, as being what would scarce ever enter into any one's Mind at the first reading of the Words. *Phidippus* is not here charging his Wife with publishing to the World her Son in Law's Faults, but advises her not to pry with too much Anxiety into his Conduct, or hearken to every idle Story she may hear. I have therefore render'd it; *Is it not better to dissemble, than pry into Secrets that will naturally beget Misunderstandings and Ill-will?*

PH. Multo priùs scivi, quàm tu, illum habere amicam,
  Myrrhina.
Verùm id vitium nunquam decrevi esse ego adolescentiæ:
Nam id omnibus innatum est. at pol jam aderit, se
  quoque etiam cùm oderit.                    [que adhuc,
Sed ut olim te ostendisti eandem esse, nihil cessavisti us-
Ut filiam ab eo abduceres, neu, quod ego egissem,
  esset ratum.                                      30
Id, nunc res indicium hæc facit, quo pacto factum
  volueris.
MY. Adeòn' me esse pervicacem censes, cui mater siem,
Ut eo essem animo, si ex usu esset nostro hoc matri-
  monium?                                  [sit, potes?
PH. Tun' prospicere, aut judicare, nostram in rem quod
Audisti ex aliquo fortasse, qui vidisse eum diceret   35
Exeuntem, aut introeuntem ad amicam. quid tum
  postea,
Si modestè ac raro hoc fecit? nonne ea dissimulare nos
Magis humanum est, quàm dare operam id scire, qui
  nos oderit?
Nam si is posset ab eâ sese derepente avellere,
Quicum tot consuesset annos; non eum hominem du-
  cerem,                                          40
Nec virum sati' firmum gnatæ. MY. mitte adolescen-
  tem, obsecro,
Et quæ me peccasse ais. abi, solum solus conveni:
Roga, velitne uxorem, an non. si est, ut dicat velle se,
Redde: sin est autem, ut nolit, rectè ego consului meæ.
PH. Siquidem ille ipse non volt, & tu sensisti in eo esse,
  Myrrhina,                                        45
Peccatum; aderam, cujus consilio ea par fuerat prospici.
Quamobrem incendor irâ, esse ausam facere hæc te
  injussu meo.
Interdico, ne extulisse extra ædes puerum usquam velis.
Sed ego stultior, meis dictis parere hanc qui postulem.
Ibo intro, atque edicam servis, ne quoquam efferri
  finant.                                          50

*PH. Scivi multo prius, quàm tu, Myrrhina, illum habere amicam. Verùm ego nunquam decrevi id esse vitium adolescentiæ: nam id est innatum omnibus. At pol tempus jam aderit, cùm oderit etiam se quoque ea causâ. Sed ut olim ostendisti te esse eandem, cessavisti nihil usque adhuc, ut abduceres filiam ab eo, neu esset ratum, quòd ego egissem. Hæc res nunc facit indicium, quo pacto volueris id esse factum. MY. Censesne me esse adeo pervicacem, ut essem eo animo erga eam, cui sim mater, si hoc matrimonium esset ex usu nostro? PH. Tune potes prospicere, aut judicare, quid sit in nostram rem? Audisti ex aliquo fortasse, qui diceret se vidisse eum exeuntem, aut introeuntem ad amicam. Quid tum postea; si fecit hoc modestè ac raro? Nonne magis humanimi est, nos dissimulare ea, quam dare operam scire id, ui oderit nos? Nam si is posset derepente avellere seje ab eâ, quicum consuesset tot annos; non ducerem eum hominem, nec virum satis firmum gnatæ. MY. Obse-

*-cro, mitte adolescentem, et quæ ais me peccasse: abi, tu solus conveni illum solum. Roga, velitne ducere uxorem, an non. Si est, ut dicat se velle; redde: sin autem est, ut nolit, ego recte consului meæ. PH. Siquidem ille ipse non vult, et tu, Myrrhina, sensisti peccatum esse in eo: ego aderam, cujus consilio fuerat par eâ prospici. Quamobrem incendor irâ, te esse ausam facere hæc injussu meo. Interdico, ne velit extulisse puerum usquam extra ædes. Sed ego stultior, qui postulem hanc parere meis dictis. Ibo intro, atque edicam servis, ne finant puerum efferri quoquam.

## ANNOTATIONS.

will? For it is a certain and never-failing
Rule, that when Men want to disguise and
conceal their real Characters, they are sure
to hate those who have Penetration enough
to find them out. And as this is true of Men
in general, so it is more especially of such
as pursue unlawful and secret Pleasures,
which they are asham'd should be known to
the World.

44. *Nec virum sati' firmum gnatæ.* Ter-

*Myr.* (*alone.*) I verily believe there is not a Woman living more wretched than I. For how he would take it, were he to know the real thing, I need not be at a loss to apprehend, when he's so impatient and violent at little or nothing : nor do I know how I shall be able to make him change his Mind. This only Misfortune remained after so many others, if I should be forced to bring up a Child whose Father we know nothing of. For when my Daughter was ravished, it was so dark she could not distinguish the Person, nor did she take any thing from him, whereby to know him afterwards : he indeed, when he left her, forc'd a Ring from her Finger. I am afraid too, that *Pamphilus* will no longer keep our Secret, when he hears that another's Child is brought up for his.

### *ANNOTATIONS.*

rence, no doubt, thought that nothing ought to be stronger, or bind the Mind of Man faster, than a long Society, and Commerce. Hence he makes *Phidippus* say, that it would be a suspicious Sign in *Pamphilus* to disengage himself all at once from *Bacchis*, and that a Passion of so long standing requir'd Time and Reflection to get the better of it. This perhaps may be true in the Case of Friendship ; according to what *Cicero* says in his Offices ; *disjungendæ, non disrumpendæ sunt amicitiæ.* But I am apt to think, that in a Commerce of this kind, the contrary ought to hold. When a Man's own Reflections tell him, that he is in the wrong, let him break off immediately ; by dallying he is undone, Bias and Inclination will get the better, blunt the Edge of Reflection, and shake his Resolution. So far we allow to *Terence*, that the Conquest may cost him Pain, but a sudden Turn in this Case is necessary ; for to aim at Victory by slow Degrees, endangers a total Defeat.

57. *Non quita, est.* Anciently the Verb *nequeo*

---

## ACT IV. SCENE II.

### ARGUMENT.

*Sostrata justifies herself to her Son, that she was no Cause of her Daughter-in-Law's leaving the House ; and, that she may be no Impediment to her Return, offers to retire into the Country. Pamphilus endeavours to dissuade her.*

### SOSTRATA, PAMPHILUS.

*Sost.* I'M not ignorant, my Son, that you look upon me to be the Cause of your Wife's leaving the House, however careful you may be to hide your Suspicions. But so may Heaven bless me, so may you in every thing answer my Hopes, as I never knowingly did any thing to deserve her Hatred. And, as I always believed you loved me, so you have confirmed me still more in that Thought ; for your Father has been telling me just now within, in what manner you preferr'd me to your Love. Now I am resolv'd to return the Favour,
that

### *ANNOTATIONS.*

In this Scene, *Pamphilus* is introduc'd in Conversation with his Mother. She had been told by *Laches*, of the Declarations he had made in her favour, and, resolved not to yield to him in point of Generosity, proposes to retire into the Country, and leave him at Liberty to take home his Wife. This Offer, which she thought would be well received, was altogether inconsistent with his Views, as it depriv'd him of a Pretence for separating from *Philumena*, and therefore he earnestly urges her not to think of it.

8 *Itaque obtingant ex te, quæ exopto mihi.* There is a great deal of Tenderness and affectionate

MY. Nullam pol credo mulierem me miseriorem vivere.
Nam ut hic laturus hoc sit, si ipsam rem, ut siet, re-
    sciverit,                    [tam animo iracundo tulit:
Non edepol clam me est; cùm hoc, quod leviu' est,
Nec, quà viâ sententia ejus possit mutari, scio.    54
Hoc mi unum ex plurimis miseriis relliquom fuerat
    malum,                        [pater.
Si, puerum ut tollam, cògit, cujus nos qui sit nescimus
Nam cùm compressa est gnata, forma in tenebris no-
    sci non quita est:            [sit nosci, qui siet:
Neque detractum ei tum quidquam est, qui pòst pos-
Ipse eripuit vi, in digito quem habuit, virgini abiens
    annulum.                      [diutiùs
Simul vereor Pamphilum, ne orata nostra nequeat
Celare, cùm sciet alienum puerum tolli pro suo..    61

*est quita nosci in tenebris. Neque quidquam tum est detractum ei, qui possit nosci, qui siet. Ipse abiens eripuit vi virgini, annulum quem habuit in digito. Simul vereor Pamphilum, ne nequeat diutius celare nostra orata, cum sciet alienum puerum tolli pro suo.*

*MY. Pol credo nullam mulierem vivere miseriorem me. Nam edepol non est clam me, ut hic sit laturus hoc, si resciverit ipsam rem, ut sit; cum tulit tam iracundo animo hoc, quod est levius; nec scio qua via sententia ejus possit mutari: hoc unum malum fuerat reliquum mihi ex plurimis miseriis sis cogit ut tollam puerum cujus nos nescimus qui sit pater. Nam cum gnata est compressa, forma non...*

## ANNOTATIONS.

nequeo had a Passive nequeor. We have a remarkable Example of it in *Sallust, Jug.* 31. *Quidquid sine sanguine civium ulcisci nequitur jure factum sit.* Where not only *nequitur* is passive, but *ulcisci* too is used passively. Several other Examples of the like kind might be cited. *Possum* too had it passive, for we sometimes meet with *poteretur,* and *potestur,* which last Word is usurp'd both by *Lucretius* and *Virgil.*

---

# ACTUS IV. SCENA II.

### ARGUMENTUM.

*Mater expurgat se coram filio, ut nurus abitionem noluerit: neque quominus Philumena ad Pamphilum redeat impedimento sit, rus abire mavult: filius autem dissuadet.*

SOSTRATA, PAMPHILUS.            ORDO.

NON clam me est, gnate mi, tibi me esse suspec-
    tam, uxorem tuam
Propter meos mores hinc abisse: etsi ea dissimulas sedulo.
Verùm ita me Dii ament, itaque obtingant ex te, quæ
    exopta mihi, ut              [illam mei:
Nunquam sciens commerui, meritò ut caperet odium
Teque antequam me amare rebar, ei rei firmasti sidem.

*tingant mihi abs te quæ exopto, ut nunquam sciens commerui, ut odium mei merito caperet illam. Quodque antequam rebar, te amare me, nunc firmasti fidem ei rei.*

*So. GNATE mi, non est clam me, me esse suspectam tibi, tuam uxorem abiisse hinc propter meos mores; etsi sedulo dissimulas. Verum ita Dii ament me; itaque obtingant me; ... caperet illam... firmasti fidem ei rei.*

## ANNOTATIONS.

fectionate Regard in this Form of Swearing. Some Commentators, however, seem not to have thoroughly understood the Force of it, when they tell us, that it means: *So may I obtain from you every thing I wish for:* or, *So may every thing, I wish for from you, happen to me.* The real Meaning is, *So may you in every Thing answer my Hopes; so may I receive from you all that Joy and Consolation, which a Mother hopes for and desires from a Son.*

5 *Teque antequam me amare rebar, &c.* These Words are extremely perplexed, nor is it easy to range them in their natural

that you may see your Dutifulness shall not with me miss of its Reward. My *Pamphilus*, it will be both for your Repose and my Reputation, that I retire hence into the Country with your Father: 'tis my fixed Resolution; that my Presence may be no Obstacle *to your Happiness*, nor any Pretence remain for *Philumena*'s not returning.

*Pam.* Pray, Mother, what sort of a Resolution is this? Shall her Folly drive you from Town into the Country? It must not be: nor will I give our Enemies a Handle to say, that it was done more thro' my Obstinacy, than any real Inclination of yours. Besides, I can't think of your leaving your Friends, Relations, and happy Days, on my account.

*Sost.* Truly, Son, I have but little Relish for these things now; I enjoyed them enough in my Youth, and am grown quite sick of them. 'Tis more my Concern now, that my Age be not a Burthen to any, or cause them to expect my Death with impatience. I find, however little I deserve it, that I am no welcome Guest here; 'tis time therefore to retire: for thus I am apt to think I shall best remove all Cause of Discontent, free myself from Suspicion, and effectually please them too. Let me, pray, avoid this Reproach so generally cast upon our Sex.

*Pam.* How happy am I in every thing else, were it not for this one Affair, having so indulgent a Mother, and so good a Wife!

*Sost.* Pray, *Pamphilus*, can't you bring yourself to submit to one Inconvenience, that may be unavoidable, if every thing else is according to your Wish, and such as I take them to be? Do, my Son, yield to me in this, take her back.

*Pam.* How wretched is my Situation?                               *Sost.*

### ANNOTATIONS.

Order. I have endeavoured in the *Ordo*, by supplying *quod*, to make the Sense easy. *Quodque antequam rebar te amare me, nunc firmasti fidem ei rei*, Some, however, without acknowledging any thing wanting to compleat the Sentence, dispose the Words thus; *Quamque rebar ante, te amare me nunc firmaste fidem ei rei*. Making *quam* here of the same import with *quantopere*, or *quantum*. *You have now made your Love appear as great as I always flattered myself it was.*

19 *Ut ne cui mea longinquitas ætatis obster*, &c. *Sostrata* does all in her power to persuade her Son, that Resentment has no Part in the Resolution she had taken to retire from Town; and she explains herself upon this Head, with all the engaging Sweetness imaginable. In a Word, she suffers nothing to escape her, that could offend either her Husband, Son, or Daughter-in-Law. Yet amidst all this Moderation she takes care to make them sensible, that she thought herself injur'd. The Poet has managed this part of her Character with uncommon Address. *Longinquitas*, here used to denote the Length and Duration of Life, is a Word equally applied by the best Authors, to Place and Time, and therefore comes in very properly here, Liv. VII. 29. *Majora jam hinc bella, et viribus hostium, et longinquitate vel regionem, vel temporum, quibus bellatum est, dicentur.*

25 *Quam fortunatus —— absque una hac foret*, &c. One cannot avoid wondering at the Explication which *Guyetus* offers of these Words. He rejects the following Verse, *hanc matrem habens talem*, and makes *absque hac una foret: where I but without my Mother*. But this evidently contradicts *Pamphilus*'s Intention, and those Sentiments which may naturally be supposed to rise in his Mind on this Occasion. He is affected with the Complaisance his Mother shews him, and at the same time warmly attach'd to *Philumena*. He therefore says, that with so good a Mother, and so amiable a Wife, he must have been the happiest Man in the World, but for this unlucky Accident. This is tender, polite, and wholly in Character.

27 *Non atm intervidem rem.* Madam *Dacier,*

Nam mihi intus tuus pater narravit modò, quo pacto
   me habueris
Præpositam amori tuo. nunc tibi me certum est con-
   trà gratiam
Referre, ut apud me præmium esse positum pietati scias.
Mi Pamphile, hoc et vobis, & meæ commodum fa-
   mæ arbitror :
Ego rus abituram hinc cum tuo me esse certò decrevi
   patre,                        10
Ne mea præsentia obstet, neu causa ulla restet relliqua,
Quin tua Philumena ad te redeat. PA. quæso, quid
   istuc consili est ?
Illius stultitiâ victa, ex urbe tu rus habitatum migres ?
Haud facies : neque sinam, ut qui nobis, mater, ma-
   ledictum velit,
Meâ pertinaciâ esse dicat factum, haud tuâ modestiâ. 15
Tum, tuas amicas te & cognatas deserere, & festos dies,
Meâ causâ, nolo. So. nihil pol jam istæc mihi res vo-
   luptatis ferunt.
Dum ætatis tempus tulit. perfunctâ satis sum : satias
   jam tenet
Studiorum istorum : hæc mihi nunc cura est maxuma,
   ut ne cui mea                   19
Longinquitas ætatis obstet, mortemve exspectet meam.
Hîc video me esse invisam immeritò : tempus est con-
   cedere.                       [omnibus :
Sie optumè, ut ego opinor, omnes causas præcidam
Et me hac suspicione exsolvam, & illis morem gessero.
Sine me, obsecro, hoc effugere, volgus quod male au-
   dit mulierum.
PA. Quàm fortunatus cæteris sum rebus, absque unâ
   hac foret,                      25
Hanc matrem habens talem, illam autem uxorem !
   So. obsecro, mi Pamphile,
Non tute incommodam rem, ut quæque est, in ani-
   mum induces pati,            [existumo ?
Si cætera ita sunt, ut tu vis, itaque ut esse ego illam
Mi gnate, da veniam hanc mihi, reduc illam. PH. væ
   misero mihi !

Nam pater tuus mo-
do narravit mihi in-
tus quo pacto habue-
ris me præpositam
tuo amori : nunc cer-
tum st, me contra
referre gratiam tibi,
ut scias præmium esse
positum tuæ pietati
apud me. Mi Pam-
phili, arbitror hoc
commodum et vobis,
et meæ famæ. Ego
certo decrevi me esse
abituram hinc rus
cum tuo patre, ne meæ
præsentia obstet, neu
ulla causa reliqua
restet, quin tua Phi-
lumena redeat ad te.
PA. Quæso, quid
consilii est istuc ? An
tu victa stultitia il-
lius, migres ex urbe
habitatum rus ? Haud
facies, neque sinar,
mater, ut qui velit
maledictum nobis, di-
cat esse factum mea
pertinacia, haud tua
modestia. Tum nolo
te deserere tuas ami-
cas, et cognatas, et
festos dies, mea causa.
So. Pol istæc res fe-
runt jam nihil volup-
tatis mihi : sum satis
perfuncta, dum tem-
pus ætatis tulit. Sa-
tias istorum studiorum
jam tenet me : hæc
nunc est maxima cu-
ra mihi, ut mea lon-
ginquitas ætatis ne
obstet cui, faciatve
ut exspectet meam
mortem. Video me
esse immerito invisam
hic : est tempus con-
cedere. Sic, ut ego
opinor, optime præ-
cidam omnes causas

omnibus : et exsolvam me hoc suspicione, et gessero morem illis. Obsecro, sine me effugere hoc, quod
vulgus mulierum male audit. PA. Quam fortunatus sam cæteris rebus, foret hæc res absque hac
uca, habens hanc talem matrem, autem illam uxorem! So. Obsecro, mi Pamphile, non tute induces
in animum pati incommodam rem, ut quæque est, si cætera sunt ita, ut tu vis, itaque ut ego existi-
mo illam esse? Mi gnate, da hanc veniam mihi, reduc illam. PA. Væ misero mihi!

## ANNOTATIONS.

*Dacier* finds great Difficulty in this Passage, which none before her had sufficiently explain'd. *Pamphilus* had just said, that he was happy, but for one Thing. His Mother
who was a Stranger to his tender Thoughts, imagines that he complains of his Wife.

*Sof.* And mine too? for this Affair afflicts me no less than it does you, my Son.

ANNOTATIONS.

Temper, becaufe it could not agree with her's. She therefore tells him, that he ought not to fuffer a Thing of that Nature to deftroy his Happinefs in other Refpects, as nothing was more common in a young Wife, than to contract a Diflike to her Mother-in-Law. *Ut quaque uxer eft, non tute inducas in animum te pati rem valde incommodam. Confider the ordinary Character of Women, and you will find it is no great Inconvenience*

---

# ACT IV. SCENE III.

ARGUMENT.

*The Wife and Hufband are reconciled, and lay afide all Animofities. Pamphilus is urged to take home his Wife.*

LACHES, SOSTRATA, PAMPHILUS.

*La.* SO, Wife, I have been ftanding juft by here, and overheard all your Difcourfe with your Son. This is being wife, to bring yourfelf to comply with the Occafion, and do that now, which perhaps you may be obliged to do hereafter.

*Sof.* It may be fo, perhaps.

*Lac.* March, then, into the Country ; there we'll learn to bear with one another.

*Sof.* I hope we fhall.

*Lac.* Go in, then, and get every Thing ready you are to take with you. I'm refolved.

*Sof.* I'll do as you defire.

*Pam.* Father.

*Lac.* What, *Pamphilus !*

*Pam.* My Mother leave the Town ? By no means.

*Lach.* Why fo ?

*Pam.* Becaufe I am not yet refolved what to do in regard to my Wife.

*Lac.* How ! What fhould you do, but take her home again ?

*Pam.* I could like it, and can hardly indeed forbear doing it ; but I will not alter my Defign. I am determined to purfue what promifes faireft, and believe the only Way to prevent Quarrels is not to take her back.

*Lac.*

ANNOTATIONS.

*Laches*, who had overheard all that paft in Converfation between his Wife and Son, here joins them, and urges *Sofrata* to execute her Defign without delay. *Pamphilus* interpofes, and would prevent it, but in vain ; the old Man is inflexible. While they are thus engaged, *Laches* obferves *Phidippus* coming out to them, which breaks off the Converfation.

¹ *Procul hinc ftans. Procul ftans,* ftanding near ; for here *procul* has the Force of *prope,* as often in *Plautus* and *Virgil. Afranius* too fays, *Aufcultavi hinc procul.*

⁴ *Fors fuat pol. Laches's* Speech to his Wife is not very complaifant, efpecially if we confider how much Good-nature appears in all her Behaviour. One is apt to expect in that Cafe, Praifes and Commendations ; whereas

So. Et mihi quidem: nam hæc res non minus me male
   habet, quàm te, gnate mi. 30

*So. Et quidem mi-*
*hi: nam hæc res non*
*habet me minus male,*

*quam te, gnate mi.*

*quam te, gnate mi.*

## ANNOTATIONS.

nience you have to bear, if every thing else
answers your Expectation. Thus Madam
Dacier; but I have chosen in the Translation to give it a more general Turn, and
to consider it as an Interrogation.

---

# ACTUS IV. SCENA III.

### ARGUMENTUM.

*Reconciliantur, & omne bellum inter se componunt vir & uxor:*
*monetur Pamphilus ut uxorem reducat.*

LACHES, SOSTRATA PAMPHILUS.     ORDO.

QUEM cum istoc sermonem habueris, procul hinc
   stans accepi, uxor.    [is flectere;
Istuc est sapere, qui, ubicunque opus sit, animum pos-
Quod sit faciundum post fortasse, idem hoc nunc si fe-
   ceris:    [tu me feres.
So. Fors fuat pol. LA. abi rus ergo hinc: ibi ego te, &
So. Spero ecastor. LA. i ergo intrò, & compone, quæ
   tecum simul
Ferantur. dixi. So. ita, ut jubes, faciam. PA. pater.   5
LA. Quid vis, Pamphile? PA. hinc abire matrem?
   minimè. LA. quid ita istuc vis?
PA. Quia de uxore incertus sum etiam, quid sim fac-
   turus. LA. quid est?
Quid vis facere, nisi reducere? PA. equidem cupio, &
   vix contineor:
Sed non minuam meum consilium. ex usu quod est; id
   persequar.     10
Credo ea gratiâ concordes, si non reducam, fore.

*ORDO.*
*Lac. STANS procul*
*hinc, uxor, accepi*
*sermonem quem ha-*
*bueris cum istoc. Istuc*
*est sapere, qui possis*
*flectere animum, ubi-*
*cunque sit opus, se*
*nunt f. ceris hoc idem*
*quod fortasse sit fac-*
*endum post. So.*
*Fors fuat pol. LA.*
*Abi ergo hinc rus:*
*ibi ego feram te, et*
*tu feres me. So. E-*
*castor, spero. LA. I*
*intro ergo, et compo-*
*ne, quæ ferantur*
*simul tecum: dixi.*
*So. Faciam ita, ut*
*jubes. PA. Pater.*
*LA. Quid vis, Pam-*
*phile? PA. Matrem*
*abire hinc? minime.*

LA. Quid ita vis istuc? PA. Quia sum etiam incertus, quid sim facturus de uxore. LA. Quid
est? Quid vis facere, nisi reducere? PA. Equidem cupio, et vix contineor: sed non minuam
meum consilium: persequar id quod est ex usu. Credo eas fore concordes ea gratia, si non reducam,

## ANNOTATIONS.

whereas her husband bluntly tells her, that
it was wise to do voluntarily, what-other-
wise she must have done by constraint.
Sostrata therefore must be supposed to answer in a Huff, as resenting her Husband's
Harshness and Want of Delicacy; and accordingly in the Translation I have given
her Answer a Turn; that preserves this
Idea: for the English Phrase, by which it
is rendred, is very often used in the like
Circumstances.

9 *Equidem cupio, & vix contineor.* We
are here to call to mind the Character
of *Pamphilus,* who was passionately fond
of his Wife, and who, notwithstanding the
late Discovery he had made, still found
himself strongly inclined to take her back.
He feels in his Breast a violent Struggle
betwixt Love and Shame. Hence his Answer to his Father, so fond, passionate, and
affecting.

*Lac.* You don't know that. But it matters little whether they agree, or not, if your Mother goes into the Country. This Age of ours but ill suits the Tempers of Youth, and therefore we had even best leave you to yourselves. In short, *Pamphilus,* we are now become a Saying, *The old Man, and the old Woman.* But I see *Phidippus* coming out very fortunately; let us go to meet him.

ANNOTATIONS.

14. *Nos. jam fabulæ sumus, senex, atque anus. Donatus* imagines this alludes to the ancient Manner of Writing in Fables, which very often began in these Words: *Senex atque anus.* Thus in *Plautus* we meet with one who begins a Story in these Words: *Fuit*

---

## A C T  IV.  S C E N E  IV.

### ARGUMENT.

Laches *learns that a Son is born to* Pamphilus. *Both the old Men urge him earnestly to take home his Wife. He refuses; his Father charges him with his Passion for* Bacchis.

PHIDIPPUS, LACHES, PAMPHILUS.

*Phi.* INDEED, *Philumena,* I am angry with you too, very much so; for you have behaved very indiscreetly. 'Tis true, you have some Excuse, your Mother forc'd you to it; but she has none at all.

*Lac.* *Phidippus,* 'tis very lucky, my meeting with you now.

*Phi.* What's the Matter?

*Pam.* What Answer shall I make them, or how be able to keep this Secret?

*Lac.* Tell your Daughter, that my Wife is resolved to go into the Country, that she need not now be afraid of returning home.

*Phi.* Ah, your Wife is no way to blame in the Affair, 'tis mine that has been the Occasion of all the Mischief. The Case is altered; she, I find, confounds Matters, *Laches.*

*Pam.* So I am not obliged to take back my Wife, let them make what Disturbance they please.                         *Phi.*

ANNOTATIONS.

While *Pamphilus* and his Father are engaged in Conversation, they see *Phidippus* coming out, and, making up to him, find him in a Disposition very different from that in which he was last time they were together. He had now, as appears from a former Scene, discovered his Daughter's being brought to bed; and, instead of thinking *Pamphilus* in fault, laid all the Blame upon his Wife. *Laches* again is overjoyed to hear he has got a Grandson, and urges his Son more than ever to take back his Wife. But this, instead of being of any weight, is a new Argument against it. For, however he might have been prevailed on to over-look what had happened to *Philumena,* so long as it might be kept secret, yet he could by no means resolve to submit to the Meanness of bringing up another Man's Child. His Obstinacy provokes his Father, who, not knowing the true Reason of it, and imagining it was owing to his old Passion for *Bacchis,* falls upon him with severe and bitter Reproaches, till at length *Pamphilus,* not knowing how to defend himself, withdraws. Upon this the old Men consult between themselves what was best to be done; and, persuaded that they had hit upon the true Reason of his Aversion to *Philumena,* resolve to send for *Bacchis,* and, by Promises or Threats, prevail with her not to entertain *Pamphilus,* or receive his Visits.

1 *Tibi quoque edepol sum iratus, Philumena.* We have seen before how much *Phidippus* was provoked against his Wife. Here

LA. Nescias. verùm tuâ refert nihil, utrum illæ fecerint.
Quando hæc abierit: odiosa hæc eft ætas adolescentulis:
E medio æquom excedere eft. poftremò nos jam fabulæ
Sumus, Pamphile, fenex, atque anus.          15
Sed video Phidippum egredi per tempus. accedamus.

*dere e medio. Poftremò nos jam sumus fabulæ, Pamphile, fenex, atque anus. Sed video Phidip-*
*pum egredi per tempus. Accedamus.*



*Fuit olim quaſi ego sum fenex:* "Pronuntia
"(says Donatus) fenex atque anus quaſi ini-
"tium fabulæ: hæc enim duo nomina,
"ut poſita funt, caput indicant & inceptio-
"nem hujuſmodi fabularum.

---

# ACTUS IV. SCENA IV.

## ARGUMENTUM.

*Natum puerum Laches rescifcit.    Pamphilum ad recipiendam*
*uxorem ambo fenes hortantur.    Ille negat: meretricis amorem*
*incufat pater.*

### PHIDIPPUS, LACHES, PAMPHILUS.

TIBI quoque edepol fum iratus, Philumena,
  Graviter quidem. nam hercle abs te factum eft
    turpiter:
Etfi tibi caufa eft de hâc re: mater te impulit:
Huic vero nulla eft.  LA. opportunè te mihi,
Phidippe, in ipfo tempore oftendis.  PH. quid eft?  5
PA. Quid refpondebo his? aut quo pacto hoc aperiam?
LA. Dic filiæ, rus conceffuram hinc Softratam:
Ne revereatur, minùs jam quo redeat domum.  PH. ah.
Nullam de his rebus culpam commeruit tua:
A Myrrhinâ hæc funt meâ uxore exorta omnia.          10
Mutatio fit: ea nos perturbat, Lache.
PA. Dum ne redùcam, turbent porro, quàm velint.

*tratam conceffuram hinc rus: ne revereatur, quo minus jam redeat domum: PH. Ah, tua uxor*
*commeruit nullam culpam de his rebus: hæc omnia funt exorta a mea uxore Myrrhina: mutatio fit:*
*ea perturbat nos, Lache. PA. Dum ne reducam, turbent porro, quam velint.*

**ORDO.**

PH. *Edepol, Philumena,*
*fum quidem graviter*
*iratus tibi quoque;*
*nam hercle factum eft*
*turpiter obs te? atſi*
*eft caufa tibi de hâc*
*re: Mater impulit*
*te. Vero eft nulla*
*caufa huic. LA.*
*Phidippe, oftendis te*
*mihi opportunè, in ip-*
*fo tempore: PH. Quid*
*fit? PA. Quid ref-*
*pondebo his? aut quo*
*pacto aperiam hoc?*
*LA. Dic filiæ; Sof-*



he is feen coming out, and talking with
*Philumena,* who was within.  He profeffes
himfelf difpleafed with her too, though he
owns her Fault was lefs, and admitted of
fome Excufe from her Mother's Inftigations.

6 *Hoc aperiam?* This is the Reading moft
generally received, though 'tis hard from it
to find any confiftent Meaning to the Words,
unlefs we paraphrafe them with *Wefterho-*
*vius: Quo pacto illud petero indicare fine mag-*
*no Philumenæ detrimento?* But there feems
to be little Propriety in this.  I am therefore apt to think, that inftead of *aperiam,*
we ought to read *operiam,* i. e. *occultabo.*
  VOL. II.

This Conjecture has the Authority of *Da-*
*cier, Rivius,* and Dr. *Bentley* to fupport it.

" *Mutatio fit.* Madam *Dacier* thinks
that thefe Words ought to be given to *Pam-*
*philus,* who, obferving how much *Phidippus's*
Tone was changed from what it had been
before, fecretly mutters to himfelf *mutatio*
*fit.* If we afcribe them to *Phidippus,* as
is done in almoft all the Editions of our
Poet, then *mutatio fit* muft be underftood
*mutato criminis;* as if he had faid, "Culpa
"jam non amplius in tua domo hæret,
"fed in mea. Fit mutatio; a mea enim
"uxore exorta funt omnia, non à tua;

*Phi.* I, *Pamphilus*, could gladly wifh this Alliance of our Families to be, if poffible, perpetual ; but if you are otherwife inclin'd, take the Child however.

*Pam.* He knows of her being brought to-bed ; I'm ruined.

*Lac.* The Child ! What Child ?

*Phi.* We have got a Grandfon born to us ; for my Daughter, when fhe left your Houfe, was, it feems, big with Child, nor did I know any thing of it till to-day.

*Lac.* By *Jupiter*, you bring me very good News. I'm heartily glad the Child is born, and your Daughter well. But what a ftrange, odd-tempered Woman, this Wife of yours muft be ; to conceal a thing of this nature from us fo long ? I can't well exprefs what an ill Look it has.

*Phi.* Truly, *Laches*, I am no lefs difpleafed with it than you.

*Pam.* Altho' before I was fomewhat in fufpenfe about taking back my Wife, yet now I am determined againft it, fince another Man's Child muft follow her.

*Lac.* There is no room left for Choice here, *Pamphilus*.

*Pam.* I'm ruined.

*Lac.* We have often wifhed to fee this Day, when there fhould be one to call you Father. 'Tis come at laft : Heaven be praifed.

*Pam.* I'm undone.

*Lac.* Take home your Wife, and don't *any longer* oppofe my Will.

*Pam.* Had it been her Defire, Father, to continue my Wife, or have Children by me, I very well know, fhe would not have conceal'd from me, what I underftand fhe has. Now, therefore, that find her Inclinations eftranged from me, and that there can be no real Harmony between us, why fhould I take her back ?

*Lac.* The young Woman did as her Mother advifed her : is that to be wondered at ? Do you expect to find a Wife without a Fault ? Have not Men their Failings too ?

*Pam.* Do you *Pamphilus* and *Laches*, confider between yourfelves, which is moft expedient, to leave her, or take her back. I can't anfwer for my Wife's Conduct. In neither Cafe fhall you meet
with

A N N O T A T I O N S.

" idque perturbat nos. Videtur certe fumta
" locutio a fcena, qua toties mutari dicitur,
" quoties perfona princeps mutatur."

16 *Senfit peperiffe : occidi.* This *Pamphi-lus* fays in a low Voice, turning towards the Spectators. He forefaw the Confequence of this Difcovery that *Phidippus* had made. He muft either difclofe the Secret he had fo faithfully promifed to conceal, or fubmit to the redoubled Importunity of his Father, to take back his Wife, and bear a Load of Reproaches for perfifting in a Refufal. No wonder then if he here difcovers fo much Uneafinefs and Perturbation.

25 *Non tibi illud factum minus placet, quam mibi, Laches. Donatus* feems to think, from the Manner of Expreffion here ufed, that there is an Irony implied in this Sentence. The Order of the Words, he fays, muft be, *non minus mibi placet, quam tibi,* and *pla-cet* is here for *difplicet,* as before in the *Andrian, Crito* defcribing how vain it would be for him a Stranger to fue for an Eftate already in the Poffeffion of another well fupported, fays, *Nunc me bofpitem licet fequi, quam bic mibi fit facile atque utile, aliorum
exempla*

PH. Ego, Pamphile, esse inter nos, si fieri potest,
Affinitatem hanc sane perpetuam volo:
Sin est, ut aliter tua siet sententia, 15
Accipias puerum. PA. sensit peperisse: occidi.
LA. Puerum! quem puerum? PH. natus est nobis nepos:
Nam abducta à vobis prægnans fuerat filia;
Neque fuisse prægnantem unguam ante hunc scivi diem
LA. Bene, ita me Dii ament, nuncias: & gaudeo 20
Natum illum, & tibi illam salvam. sed quid mulieris
Uxorem habes? aut quibus moratam moribus?
Nosne hoc celatos tamdiu? nequeo satis,
Quàm hoc mihi videtur factum pravè, proloqui.
PH. Non tibi illud factum minùs placet, quàm mihi.
    Laches. 25
PA. Etiamsi dudum fuerat ambiguum hoc mihi,
Nunc non est, cùm eam consequitur alienus puer.
LA. Nulla tibi, Pamphile, hîc jam consultatio est.
PA. Perii. LA. hunc videre sæpe optabamus diem,
Cùm ex te esset aliquis, qui te appellaret patrem. 30
Evenit: habeo gratiam Dis. PA. nullu' sum.
LA. Reduc uxorem, ac noli advorsari mihi.
PA. Pater, si ex me illa liberos vellet sibi,
Aut se esse mecum nuptam, satis certò scio,
Non clam me haberet, quæ celasse intellego. 35
Nunc, cùm ejus alienum esse a me animum sentiam,
Nec conventurum inter nos posthac arbitror,
Quamobrem reducam? LA. mater quod suasit sua,
Adolescens mulier fecit. mirandúmne id est?
Censen' te posse reperire ullam mulierem, 40
Quæ careat culpâ? an, quia non delinquunt viri?
PH. Vosmet videte jam, Lache, & tu, Pamphile,
Remissan' opu' sit vobis, reductan' domum:
Uxor quid faciat, in manu non est meâ.
Neutrâ in re vobis difficultas à me erit. 45

*PH. Ego, Pamphile, sa e vois hanc affinitatem esse perpetuam inter nos, si potest fieri: sin est, ut tua sententia sit aliter, accipias puerum. PA. Sensit eam peperisse, occidi. LA. Puerum! Quem puerum? PH. Nepos est natus nobis: nam filia fuerat abducta a vobis prægnans; neque unquam scivi ante hunc diem eam fuisse prægnantem. LA. Bene nuncias, ita Dii ament me: et gaudeo puerum esse natum, et illam esse salvam tibi. Sed quid mulieris habes uxorem? aut quibus moribus moratam? Nosne celatos hoc tamdiu? Nequeo satis proloqui, quam pravè hoc actum videtur mihi. PH. Non illud factum minus placet tibi, quam mihi, Laches. PA. Etiamsi hoc fuerat dudum ambiguum mihi, nunc non est, cum alienus puer consequitur eam. LA. Pamphile, est jam nulla consultatio tibi hic. PA. Perii. LA. Sæpe optabamus videre hunc diem, cum esset aliquis ex te, qui appellaret te patrem. Evenit: habeo gratiam Dis. PA. Sum nullus. LA. Reduc uxorem, ac noli adversari mihi. PA. Pater, si illa vellet liberos sibi ex me, aut se esse nuptam metum, scio satis certo, non haberet ea clam me, quæ intelligo eam celavisse. Nunc cum sentio animum ejus esse alienum a me, neque arbitror esse conventurum inter nos posthac, quamobrem reducam? LA. Mulier adolescens fecit, quod mater sua suasit; idne mirandum est? Censen' te posse reperire ullam mulierem, quæ caredt culpa? An quia viri non delinquunt? PH. Vosmet, Lache, et tu, Pamphile, jam videte, sitne opus vobis ea remissa, reductane domum: quid uxor faciat, non est in manu mea. Erit difficultas vobis in neutra re à me.*

ANNOTATIONS.

*exempla commonent.* However uncommon the Expression may be, and however difficult to explain Grammatically, the Sense is evident. 26 *Dudum fuerat ambiguum hoc mihi.* Sub. *reduceremne uxorem, an non reducerem.* So long as he believed her Lying-in might be concealed, and that the Child would be exposed, and no more heard of, he seems to have been in a kind of Uncertainty how to behave in regard to his Wife; but finding now, that by taking her back, he should be obliged to bring up a Child whom he believed to be another's, this fixes his Resolution against it.

with any Hindrance from me. But what shall we do with the Child?

*Lac.* A wife Question truly! Whatever happens, send him his Child, that we may bring it up as ours.

*Pam.* Shall I bring up a Child, whom the Father himself has abandoned?

*Lac.* What was that you said? How! Not bring it up, *Pamphilus!* Shall we rather expose it, pray? What Madness is this? Indeed I can hold my tongue no longer, for you force me to say what I otherwise would not, before your Father-in-Law. Do you think that I am ignorant of the Cause of your Tears? Or whence all this Trouble and Perplexity you are in comes? When you pretended first, that you could not take home your Wife on account of your Mother; she offered to leave the House: and now that you see this Excuse taken away, you have got another, *because a Child is born without your Knowledge.* You mistake, *Pamphilus,* if you fancy I don't know the meaning of all this. How long did I wink at your having a Mistress, in hopes that my Indulgence would at last reclaim you, and bring you to think seriously of Marriage? With what patience did I bear the Expence you was at upon her? I pressed and entreated you to marry, told you it was high time, and by much Persuasion you did. This Obedience was what became you, and you was then in your Duty; but now I find your Mind again runs after your Mistress, and to gratify her, forsooth, you stick at offering no Injuries to your Wife. I see plainly you are relapsed into the old Course of Life.

*Pam.* Me!

*Lac.* You: And 'tis dishonourable and unjust in you, thus to feign false Grounds of Quarrel; that you may live uncontroul'd with your Strumpet, after having removed this Witness *of your Actions* out of the way. And no doubt your Wife has observed as much, for what other Reason was there for her leaving the House?

*Phi.* Certainly he guesses right, for that must be the Reason.

*Pam.* I'll give you my Oath that there is nothing in all this.

*Lac.* Ah, take home your Wife then, or tell me why you should not.

*Pam.* It is not a proper time now.

*Lac.* Take the Child at least: surely he's not in fault. I'll consider of the Mother afterwards.                              *Pam.*

### A N N O T A T I O N S.

48 *Quem ipse neglexit pater, ego alam?* *Donatus* on this Passage takes notice of a Variation in the Reading, which entirely changes the Sense of it. Quem ipsa neglexit, pater: where we have *ipsa* instead of *ipse,* and *pater* is a Vocative. *Shall, I Father, take the care of a Child, whom the Mother herself has abandoned?* Several Criticks, among whom is *Donatus* himself, give the preference to this Reading; but many Reasons may be offered for rejecting it. For what Justice is there in saying, that because a Mother has abandoned her Child, the Father ought to do so too? This were shocking and unnatural. On the contrary, he is under greater Obligations than ever to take care of it, and must alone be in the stead of both Parents to it. Besides, it is probable *Laches* would have said, *That if the Mother abandoned it, it was owing to nothing but the ill Usage she received from him.* The other Reading is certainly the

Sed quid faciemus puero? LA. ridiculè rogas.
Quidquid futurum eft, huic reddas, fuum fcilicet,
Ut alamus noftrum. PA. quem ipfe neglexit pater,
Ego alam? LA. quid dixti? eho, an non alemus,
    Pamphile?
Prodemus, quæfo, potiùs? quæ hæc amentia eft? 50
Enimvero prorfus jam tacere non queo.
Nam cogis ea, quæ nolo, ut præfente hoc loquar.
Ignarum cenfes tuarum lacrumarum effe me?
Aut, quid fit id, quod folicitere ad hunc modum?
Primùm, danc ubi dixti caufam, te propter tuam 55
Matrem non poffe habere hanc uxorèm domi;
Pollicita eft ea, fe conceffuram ex ædibus.     [vides;
Nunc, poftquam, ademtam hanc quoque tibi caufam
Puer quia clam te eft natus, nactus alteram es.
Erras, tui animi fi me effe ignarum putas.     60
Aliquando tandem huc animum ut abducas tuum,
Quàm longum fpatium amandi amicam tibi dedi?
Sumtus, quos fecifti in eam, quàm animo æquo tuli?
Egi atque oravi tecum, uxorem ut duceres:
Tempus dixi effe: impulfu duxifti meo.     65
Quæ tum, obfecutus mihi, fecifti ut decuerat:
Nunc animum rurfum ad meretricem induxti tuum:
Cui tu obfecutus, facis huic adeo injuriam.
Nam in eandem vitam te revolutum denuo
Video effe. PA. mene? LA. teipfum: & facis injuriam,
Confingis falfas caufas ad difcordiam,     71
Ut cum illâ vivas, teftem hanc cùm abs te amoveris.
Senfitque adeo uxor: nam ei caufa alia quæ fuit,
Quamobrem abs te abiret? PH. plane hic divinat:
    nam id eft.     74
PA. Dabo jusjurandum nihil effe iftorum tibi. LA. an,
Reduc uxorem: aut quamobrem non opus fit, cedo.
PA. Non eft nunc tempus. LA. puerum accipias:
    nam is quidem
In culpâ non eft. pòft de matre videro.



*effe tempus: impulfu meo duxifti. Quæ tum fecifti ut decuerat, obfecutus mihi. Nunc induxti tuum animum rurfum ad meretricem: cui tu obfecutus, facis adeo injuriam huic. Nam video te effe denuo revolutum in eandem vitam. PA. Mene? LA. Teipfum: et facis injuriam, confingis falfas caufas ad difcordiam, ut vivas cum illa, eam amoveris hanc teftem abs te. Uxorque adeo fenfit: nam quæ alia caufa fuit ei, quamobrem abiret abs te? PH. Hic plane divinat; nam id eft. PA. Dabo jusjurandum tibi, effe nihil iftorum: LA. Ab, redac uxorem, aut cedo quamobrem non fit opus. PA. Non eft tempus nunc. LA. Accipias puerum; nam is quidem non eft in culpa. Videre de matre poft.*

## *ANNOTATIONS.*

beft; it is full of Paffion, and ftrongly reprefents the wretched Situation to which *Pamphilus* was reduced. There is inded an Objection that may be offered, from a Suppofition, that this were betraying *Philumena's* Misfortune, which he had engaged to keep fecret. But we are to imagine, that he fays this in a low Voice, turning towards the

*Pam.* I'm miserable every Way, nor know I what to do; my Father presses so hard upon me on all Sides. I'll even march off, since my Presence is like to do but little good. I believe they'll hardly bring up the Child without my Consent, especially as my Mother-in-Law will second me in the Thing.

*Lac.* Are you gone, ha, without giving me any distinct Answer? Do you think he's in his Senses? Let him go. Send the Child to me, *Phidippus*, I'll take care to bring it up.

*Phi.* I will. I do'nt wonder that my Wife took this so ill. Women resent strongly, and can't easily away with such Affronts. This is really what provok'd her, for she told it me herself; tho' I was unwilling to say any thing of it to you before him. At first, indeed, I did not believe it; but now the Thing is plain, for I see he is wholly averse to Marriage.

*Lac.* What shall I do in this Case, *Phidippus?* What Advice would you give?

*Phi.* What should you do? I think we had best go first to this Mistress of his. Let us use Intreaties with her, accuse her warmly, or even threaten her, if hereafter she gives him any Entertainment.

*Lac.* I'll take your Advice.——Here, Boy! run to *Bacchis*, this Neighbour of ours, and desire her in my Name to come hither. Do you, *Phidippus*, lend me your Assistance in this Affair.

*Phi.* Ah, I told you before, and repeat it now, *Laches*, 'tis my Desire that this Alliance between us continue, if by any Means it be possible, as I hope it is. But would you have me present when you speak to her?

*Lac.* Yes, but go first and get a Nurse for the Child.

ACT

*ANNOTATIONS.*

the Spectators; as is evident from *Laches's* overhearing only the last Words, *ego alam?* which he spoke probably with a louder Voice, *Quid dixti? Eho! an non alemus, Pamphile?*

89 *Nam ipsa narravit mibi.* In fact *Myrrhina* had said to her Husband, that she could not bear her Daughter should be married to a Man who kept Mistresses, and lay out o'Nights, Act III. S. 6. 23. And *Phidippus* makes no doubt, but his Wife talked thus, because *Philumena* had complained to her upon that Head. Wherefore, finding that the Father too, openly owned the Thing, and charged his Son with it, he no longer questions the Truth of it, and is persuaded, that it must be the Cause of his Wife's Disgust.

103 *Sed visne adesse una?* Madam *Dacier* observes here, that the Poet says, *But do you desire that I should be present?* instead of, *But I suppose you don't desire that I should be present.* And in this *Terence* gives a Proof of his exact Observance of the Rules of Decency and Decorum. For it was not proper that *Phidippus* should converse with one whom he suspected to be the Seducer of his Son-in-Law, as *Donatus* has

well

PH. Omnibus modis miser sum : nec, quid agam scio :
Tot me nunc rebus miserum concludit pater. 80
Abibo hinc, præsens quando promoveo parum.
Nam puerum injussu, credo, non tollet meo,
Præsertim in eâ re cùm sit mihi adjutrix socrus.
LA. Fugis ? hem, nec quidquam certi respondes mihi ?
Num tibi videtur esse apud sese ? sine : 85
Puerum, Phidippe, mihi cedo : ego alam. PH. maxume
Non mirum fecit uxor mea, si hoc ægrè tulit :
Amaræ mulieres sunt, non facilè hæ ferunt.
Propterea hæc ira est : nam ipsa narravit mihi :
Id ego hoc præsente tibi nolueram dicere : 90
Neque illi credebam primò. nunc verò palam est.
Nam omnino abhorrere animum huic video nuptiis.
LA. Quid ergo agam, Phidippé ? quid das consili ?
PH. Quid agas ? meretricem hanc primum adeundam
　　censeo :
Oremus : accusemus gravius : denique 95
Minitemur, si cum illo habuerit rem postea.
LA. Faciam, ut mones. Eho puer, curre ad Bacchidem
　　hanc
Vicinam nostram : huc evoca verbis meis.
Et te oro porro, in hac re adjutor sis mihi. PH. ah,
Jamdudum dixi, idemque nunc dico, Lache, 100
Manere affinitatem hanc inter nos volo,
Si ullo modo est ut possit ; quod spero fore
Sed visne adesse unà, dum istam convenis ?
LA. Imo : vero abi : aliquam puero nutricem para.

*PA. Sum miser omnibus modis : nec scio quid agam : pater nunc concludit me miserum tot rebus. Abibo hinc, quando præsens promovec parum. Nam credo non tollet puerum injussu meo, præsertim cum socrus sit adjutrix mihi in ea re. LA. Fugis? Hem, nec, respondes quidquam certi mihi? Num videtur tibi esse apud sese? Sine: Phidippe, cedo puerum mihi, ego alam. PH. Maxime. Mea uxor non fecit mirum, si tulit hoc ægre: mulieres sunt amaræ, non facilè ferunt. Lac. Hæc ira est propterea, nam ipsa narravit mihi: ego nolueram dicere id tibi, hoc præsente: nam primo credebam illi; nunc vero est palam. Nam video animum huic omnino abhorrere a nuptiis. LA. Quid ergo agam, Phidippe? Quid consilii das? PH. Quid agas? Censeo hanc meretricem primum adeundam : oremus : accusemus gravius : denique minitemur, si postea habueris rem cum illo. LA. Faciam, ut mones: eho puer, curre ad hanc Bacchidem, nostram vicinam : evoca eam huc meis verbis. Et porro oro te, ut sis adjutor mihi in hac re. PH. Ah, jamdudum dixi, Lache, nuncque dico idem, vela hanc affinitatem manere inter nos, si est ut possit ullo modo; quod spero fore. Sed visne me una adesse, dum convenis istam? LA. Imo : vero abi : para aliquam nutricem puero.*

## ANNOTATIONS.

well observed. *Bene servata sunt personis congruentia, nam socerum monere hanc rem tantum decuit, non etiam facere, ut cum pellice filiæ suæ mitius sermocinaretur.* Hence this Verse, as the same Author observes, is pronounced by *Phidippus,* with a cold declining Air; which *Laches* perceiving, hints to him that it would be proper to go and look out a Nurse for the Child. *Melius pronuntiaveris, si renitente & improbante hæc vultu dicere acceperis Phidippum, quasi non oporteat interesse socerum. Ideo mutat sententiam Laches, & relegat eam in provinciam alterius sci...* that Dacier:

## ACT IV. SCENE V.

### ARGUMENT.

Laches, *Father to* Pamphilus, *accosts* Bacchis, *his Son's Mistress, and accuses her of encouraging his Visits. She perseveres in denying it. This Scene opens a way for the Catastrophe.*

BACCHIS, LACHES.

*Bac.* I Dare say it is not for nothing, that *Laches* now desires to speak with me; and I'm very much mistaken, if I don't guess near the Business.

*Lac.* I must take care, left by this Anger, I frustrate my Design, or do what I may have afterwards cause to repent of. I'll accost her. *Bacchis,* your Servant.

*Bac.* Your Servant, *Laches.*

*Lac.* I make no doubt, *Bacchis,* but you wonder what could be my Reason for sending the Boy to desire you to come hither.

*Bac.* Nay, I am even in some pain too, when I reflect on my Manner of Life, left the Profession I follow, should be any Prejudice to me with you; for I can easily justify my Behaviour.

*Lac.* If you speak truth, you have nothing to fear from me, Woman: for I am now of that Age, that to make a false Step were unpardonable, and therefore am so much the more watchful over myself, that I do nothing rashly. For if now, or hereafter, your Behaviour is honourable and becoming; 'twere unjust in me, imprudently to injure one who did not deserve it.

*Bac.* This is extremely good and obliging, and deserves my highest Thanks; for Excuses and Apologies after offering an Injury, give but little Satisfaction. But what's this, pray?

*Lac.* You encourage my Son *Pamphilus*'s Visits.

*Bac.* Ah!                                                  *Lac.*

### ANNOTATIONS.

The two old Men in the last Scene, had agreed to send for *Bacchis*, whom they suspected to be the Cause of *Pamphilus*'s refusing so obstinately to take back his Wife. *Phidippus* meantime goes to look for a Nurse, and *Laches* is left to discourse with *Bacchis*, who here comes upon the Stage, wondering what the old Man could want with her. She, indeed, suspected the matter; and conscious that she had given no Encouragement to *Pamphilus*, was resolved to vindicate him, and if possible to remove every Suspicion he might lie under on her account. Accordingly she enters upon the Task with great Warmth and Friendship, and succeeds so far as to gain Credit with *Laches*; who further requests her to go in to the Women themselves, and use her Endeavours to remove also their Jealousies.

3 *Videndum est, ne minus propter iram hanc impetrem.* *Terence* here discovers great Judgment and Address. He was sensible that it must appear very unlikely for a Father to deal mildly with a Creature, whom he believed to be the Corrupter of his Son, and therefore takes care to inform us of the Reasons of this Conduct, which otherwise would appear out of Character. This is the Remark of *Donatus: Quia non erat verisimile bonum esse patrem meretrici inter turbanti, reddit rationem senex, cur agat mitius, ne videatur personæ modus non esse servatus.*

9 *Nam mores facile tutor.* It may appear somewhat absurd for a Courtezan to talk in this Strain, when they are generally considered as an Assemblage of all kinds of Vice. But this Sentence may regard only her Behaviour in Respect of *Pamphilus* which

# ACTUS IV. SCENA V.

### ARGUMENTUM.

*Laches, Pamphili pater, Bacchidem meretricem alloquitur, il-
lamque accusat, quod ad se recipiat filium : illa constanter negat. In hoc autem scena via munitur ad catastrophen.*

### BACCHIS, LACHES.

NON hoc de nihilo est, quod Laches me nunc
  conventam esse expetit :     [quod velit.
Nec pol me multum fallit, quin, quod suspicor, sit
LA. Videndum est, ne minus propter iram hanc im-
  petrem, quàm possiem,     [satius sit.
Aut ne quid faciam plus, quod pòst me minùs fecisse
Aggrediar. Bacchis, salve.      5
BA. Salve, Laches. LA. Credo edepol te nonnihil
  mirari, Bacchis,
Quid sit, quapropter te huc foras puerum evocare jussi.
BA. Ego pol quoque etiam timida sum, cùm venit in
  mentem, quæ sim,
Ne nomen mihi quæstus obstet. nam mores facile tutor.
LA. Si vera dicis, nihil tibi est à me pericli, mulier : 10
Nam jam ætate eâ sum, ut non siet peccato mihi ig-
  nosci æquom :
Quo magis omnes res cautiús, ne temere faciam accuro.
Nam si facis, facturave es. bonas quod par est facere ;
Inscitum offerre injuriam tibi, immerenti iniquom est.
BA. Est magna eccastor gratia de istac re quam tibi
  habeam.     15
Nam qui post factam injuriam se expurget, parum mi-
  hi prosit.     [Pamphilum. BA. ah.
Sed qui istuc est ? LA. meum receptas filium ad te

*fiet æquum mibi ignosci peccato : quo magis cautius accuro omnes res, ne faciam temere : nam si fa-
cis, facturave es, quod par est bonas facere : iniquum est me inscitum offerre injuriam tibi immerenti. BA. Ecastor est magna gratia quam habeam tibi de istac re. Nam qui expurget se post
injuriam factam, parum prosit mibi. Sed quid istuc est ? LA. Receptas Pamphilum filium meum
ad te. BA. Ah.*

ORDO.

BA. HOC non est de nihilo, quod Laches expetit me nunc esse conventam : nec pol fallit me multum, quin quod velit sit quod suspicor. LA. Videndum est, ne impetrem minus propter hanc iram, quam possiem ; aut ne faciam quid plus, quod post sit satius me minus fecisse. Aggrediar. Bacchis, salve. BA. Salve, Laches. LA. Credo edepol, Bacchis, te nonnihil mirari, quid sit quapropter jussi puerum evocare te huc foras. BA. Ego pol quoque sum etiam timida, cum venit in mentem, quæ sim, ne nomen quæstus obstet mibi : nam facile tutor mores. LA. Si dicis vera, est nibil pericli tibi à me, mulier : nam jam sum ea ætate, ut non ... temere : nam si fa- ... injuriam tibi immue- ... qui expurget se post ...

## ANNOTATIONS.

which she apprehended *Lachis* was now to
question her about. And as in this, she
was conscious of her Innocence, she might
with justice say, *facile tutor mores.*

11 *Ut non fiet peccato mibi ignosci æquom.*
Many learned Men have been mistaken here
upon the Word *peccato*, which they have
joined with *mihi*, supposing it a Dative, and
to correspond to the ἐμοὶ ἁμαρτήσαντι of
*Aristotle.* This Notion is founded upon two
Passages, the one of *Cicero,* the other of
*Quintilian.* That of *Cicero* is in his Oration
against *Rullus. Quæ cum omnibus est diffi-*

*cilis, & magna ratio, tum vero mibi præ-
ter cæteros; cui errato nulla venia ; recte
facto exigua laus, & ab invitis expressa
proponitur. Quintilian* again in his sixth
Book : *Qui vero judicem rapere & in quem
vellet habitum animi posset perducere quo
dicto flendum & irascendum esset, rarius fuit.*
But these two Passages have been very ill
explained, and it is wonderful to think,
that any one could have imagined the *Latin*
would admit of saying *recte factus sum,* for
*recte feci ; erratus sum* for *erravi* : yet this
we must do, if we admit the Opinion of
        these

*Lac.* Hear me out.——Before his Marriage, I bore with your Amour. Have patience; I have not yet done. He is now married. Seek out therefore, while it is yet time, some Lover more to be depended on: for he will not be always of this mind; nor will your Age always retain its Bloom.

*Bac.* Who tells you that?

*Lac.* His Mother-in-Law.

*Bac.* That I encourage his Visits?

*Lac.* You: and she has taken away her Daughter, and for the same Reason would have privately destroyed the Child that is born to him.

*Bac.* Did I know any thing more sacred than an Oath, to gain Credit with you, I'd offer it now, *Laches, to assure you,* that I never had any Commerce with your Son since his Marriage.

*Lac.* There's a good Girl! But do you know what further I want of you?

*Bac.* What, pray?

*Lac.* Go in, to the Women here, and proffer the same Oath to them. Satisfy them, *if possible,* and clear yourself of this Reproach.

*Bac.* I'll do it: tho' I very well know, that no one else of my Occupation would appear before a married-Woman in such a Case. But I am in pain to see your Son suffer from an unjust Report, or undeservedly lie under a Suspicion of Inconstancy, where he ought to be better thought of: for he merits of me every good Office in my power.

*Lac.* What you now say, has made me entirely your Friend, and gain'd my Confidence. For not only they imagined so, but I too believed it. Now, that I find you so different from what we supposed, take care that you continue still the same, and command my Friendship at pleasure. If otherwise——But I forbear, that you may hear nothind unkind from me. This one Advice, however, I give you: try rather what I can do for you, or how serve you, as a Friend, than as an Enemy.

ANNOTATIONS.

these Criticks. The Reason of the Mistake is, that they have not attended to the right Construction of the Words, which ought to be in this Manner. *Non est æquum mihi ignosci peccato. Peccato* is an Ablative absolute, instead of *si peccatum a me fuerit.* It is the same too in *Cicero* and *Quintilian: Cui nulla venia errato,* i. e. *si erratum fuerit. Quo dicto* for *qua re dicta.* This Remark, though of little Consideration, as to the Sense and Meaning, is yet very material in respect of the *Latin* Idiom. *Dacier.*

23 *Aliud si scirem-----sanctius quam jusjurandum.* An Oath among the Ancients, as well as now, was the most solemn Confirmation that could be given to the Truth of a Thing, beyond which no Attempt was made to gain Credit. *Cicero, Off.* III. 31. " Nullum enim vinculum ad astringendam " fidem jurejurando majores arctius esse vo- " luerunt. Id indicant leges in duodecim " tabulis, indicant sacratæ, indicant fœdera " quibus etiam cum hoste devincitur fides; " indicant notiones, animadversionesque Cen- " sorum; qui nulla de re diligentius, quam " de jurejurando judicabant."

30 *Si esset aliæ ex hoc quæstu, haud faceret. Terence* pushes the Honesty of this Courtezan so far, that he finds himself under a Necessity of offering an Apology for the Novelty of her Character, lest the Reader should charge him with offending a-
gainst

La. Sine dicam. uxorem hanc priusquam duxit, vo-
strum amorem pertuli.          [uxorem habet.
Mane: nondum etiam dixi, id, quod volui. hic nunc
Quære alium firmiorem tibi, dum tempus consulendi
          est.                                         20
Nam neque ille hoc animo erit ætatem, neque pol tu
          eadem istac ætate.          [filiam abduxit suam :
Ba. Quis id ait? La. socrus. Ba. mene? L. teipsam. &
Puerumque ob eam rem clàm voluit, natus qui est, ex-
          tinguere.                         [sem fidem,
Ba. aliud si scirem, qui firmare meam apud vos pos-
Sanctius quàm jusjurandum, id pollicerer tibi, Laches,
Me segregatum habuisse, uxorem ut duxit, à me Pam-
          philum.                                       26
La. Lepida es. sed scin', quid volo potiùs sodes facias?
          Ba. quid, cedo?               [idem
La. Eas ad mulieres huc intrò, atque istuc jusjurandum
Polliceare illis : exple animum iis, teque hoc crimine
          expedi.
Ba. Faciam : quod pol, si esset alia ex hoc quæstu,
          haud faceret, sciö ;                     30
Ut de tali causâ nuptæ mulieri se ostenderet.
Sed nolo esse falsâ famâ gnarum suspectum tuum,
Nec leviorem vobis, quibus est minimè æquom, vi-
          derier                         [ut commodem.
Immeritò : nam meritus de me est, quod queam, illi
La. Facilem benevolumque lingua tua jam tibi me
          reddidit.                                     35
Nam non sunt solæ arbitratæ hæ : ego quoque etiam
          credidi.                         [peri ;
Nunc cùm ego te esse præter nostram opinionem com-
Fac eadem ut sis porro : nostrâ utere amicitiâ, ut voles.
Aliter si facis—reprimam me, ne ægre quidquam ex
          me audias.
Verùm hoc te moneo unum ; qualis sim amicus, aut
          quid possim,                                  40
Potiùs quam inimicus, periclum facias.

La. Sine dicam : priusquam duxit hanc uxorem, pertuli vostrum amorem. Manet nondum etiam dixi, id, quod volui. Hic nunc habet uxorem. Quare alium firmiorem tibi, dum est tempus consulendi. Nam neque ille erit illo animo per ætatem, neque pol tu istac eadem ætate. Ba. Quis ait id? La. Socrus. Ba. Mene? La. Teipsam, et abduxit suam filiam : voluitque clàm extinguere puerum, qui est natus, ob eam rem. Ba. Si scirem aliud sanctius quam jusjurandum, qui possem firmare meam filiam apud vos, pollicerer id tibi, Laches, me habuisse Pamphilum segregatum a me, ut duxit uxorem. La. Lepida es. Sed scin' sodes quid volo ut facias potius? Ba. Cedo, quid? La. Ut eas intro huc ad mulieres, atque polliceare istuc idem jusjurandum illis : exple animum iis, expedique te hoc crimine. Ba. Faciam : quod pol si esset alia ex hoc quæstu, scio haud faceret ; ut ostenderet se nuptæ mulieri de tali causa. Sed nolo tuum gnatum esse suspectum falsa fama, ut immerito videri leviorem vobis, quibus est minime æquum : nam est meritus de me, ut commodem illi, quod queam. La. Lingua tua jam reddidit me facilem benevolumque tibi : nam non solum hæ arbitratæ sunt hæc : ego quoque etiam credidi. Nunc cum ego comperi te esse præter nostram opinionem, fac ut sis porro eadem : utere nostra amicitia, ut voles. Si facis aliter—sed reprimam me, ne audias quidquam ægre ex me. Verùm moneo te hoc unum, ut potius facias : periculum qualis sim, aut quid possim amicus, quam inimicus.



ACTUS

## ACT IV. SCENE VI.

### ARGUMENT.

Bacchis *promises the same to* Phidippus, *that she had lately done to* Laches : *that she would go in to* Myrrhina, *and clear herself of the Crime she was charged with.*

PHIDIPPUS, LACHES, BACCHIS.

*Phi. to the Nurse.)* YOU shall want for nothing at my House; every thing needful shall be given in Abundance : but when you have eat and drunk sufficiently yourself, take care that the Child too has enough.

*Lac.* I see my Son's Father-in-Law coming, he brings a Nurse for the Child. *Phidippus, Bacchis* swears solemnly———

*Phi.* Is this she ?

*Lac.* It is.

*Phi.* Truly they have but little Fear of the Gods, nor do the Gods in my opinion, regard them.

*Bac.* Take my Maids here : force the Truth out of them by what Methods you please ; I give you full Power. The Business at present is this : I am, if possible, to make up this Difference between *Pamphilus* and his Wife. If I can accomplish this, I shall not regret the Fame of doing, what others of my Profession would not, *in the like Case, have* done.

*Lac.* We find, *Phidippus*, upon Enquiry, that we have unjustly suspected our Wives in this Affair. Let us now try what we can do by her means here : for if your *Myrrhina* shall find, that she too readily gave Credit to a false Charge, she'll soon drop her Resentment. And if my Son is angry with his Wife, only because she concealed her Labour from him, that's a Trifle, he'll soon be pacified. In short, I can see nothing in all this so bad, as to cause a Separation.

*Phi.* I earnestly wish indeed it may be so.

*Lac.* Examine her ; here she is, she'll satisfy you.                *Phi.*

### ANNOTATIONS.

In this Scene, while *Laches* and *Bacchis* are jointly contriving how to make up Matters between the disagreeing Parties, and remove all Jealousies and Suspicions, *Phidippus* appears with the Nurse. *Laches* informs him of what had passed, and *Bacchis*'s Innocence : which he, not too forward to believe at first, is at last, however, convinced of, and approves of the Project of her going in to satisfy the Women.

¹ *Nihil apud me tibi defieri patiar.* *Phidippus*, as we have said, here returns with the Nurse, to whom he is talking as he comes along. As they are generally a Set of People not easy to be contented, and who are almost ever making new demands, we are to suppose that something of this kind had happened here ; and accordingly, the old Man answers her, that she shall want for nothing.

⁶ *Neque has respicere Deos opinor.* This Phrase is equivocal, and presents us with two different Senses, either of which may be equally drawn from the Words. For they may signify, *Nor do I imagine they have any Reverence for the Gods ;* or, *Nor do I believe the Gods have any Regard for them.* The last Sense bids fairest for the Poet's Meaning, as it expresses a greater Contempt for these Wretches, and forms a kind of Contrast to the first Part of the Sentence. It is worth while to remark here the Difference of Character between *Laches* and *Phidippus.* It was fit that the

Father

# ACTUS IV. SCENA VI.

## ARGUMENTUM.

*Quæ dudum Lacheti, eadem hæc Phidippo Bacchis promittit, se intro abituram ad Myrrhinam, & se a crimine objecto purgaturam.*

PHIDIPPUS, LACHES, BACCHIS.

NIHIL apud me tibi
Defieri patiar, quin, quod opus sit, benigre præ-
   beatur.                             [facito.
Sed cùm tu satura atque ebria eris, puer ut satur sit,
LA. Noster socer, video, venit: puero nutricem adducit.
Phidippe, Bacchis dejerat persanctè. PH. hæccine ca
   est? LA. hæc est.                    5
PH. Nec pol istæ metuunt Deos; neque has respicere
   Deos opinor.
BA. Ancillas dedo: quo lubet cruciatu per me exquire.
Hæc res hîc agitur: me facere, Pamphilo ut redeat uxor,
Oportet: quod si perficio, non pœnitet me famæ,
Solam fecisse id, quod aliæ meretrices facere fugitant.
LA. Phidippe, nostras mulieres suspectas fuisse falsò 11
Nobis re in ipsâ invenimus. porro hanc nunc experia-
   mur.
Nam si compererit crimini tua se uxor credidisse,
Missam iram faciet: sin autem est ob eam rem iratus
   gnatus,
Quòd peperit uxor clàm, id leve est. citò ab eo hæc
   ira abscedet                15
Profectò in hac re nihil mali est, quod sit discidio dig-
   num.               [satis sit, faciet ipsa.
PH. Velim quidem hercle. LA. exquire: adest: quod

*ORDO.*

*PH. PATIAR nibil defieri tibi apud me, quin quod sit opus præbeatur benignè. Quia cum tu eris futura atque ebria, facito ut puer sit satur. LA. Video, noster socer venit, adducit nutricem puero. Phidippe, Bacchis dejerat persanctè. PH. Hæccine est ca? LA. Hæc est. PH. Nec istæ metuunt Deos, neque, opinor Deos respicere has. BA. Dedo ancillas, exquire per me quo cruciatu libet. Hæc res, agitur hic: efficite me facere, ut uxor redeat Pamphilo: quod si perficio, non pœnitet ne famæ, me solam fecisse id quod aliæ meretrices fugitant facere. LA. Phidippe, invenimus in ipsa re, nostras mulieres fuisse falso suspectas nobis. Porro experiamur nunc hanc. Nam si tua uxor compererit se falso credidisse crimini, faciet iram missam: sin autem gnatus est iratus ob eam rem, quod uxor peperit clam, id est leve, hæc ira cito abscedet ab eo. Profectò est nibil mali in hac re, quod sit dignum discidio. PH. Velim quidem hercle. LA. Exquire: adest: ipsa faciet quod sit satis.*

## ANNOTATIONS.

Father of the Wife should appear more passionately enraged against the Courtezan, than the Father of the Husband. The Poet in this shews his perfect Knowledge of Nature, and the Human Passions.

*10 Solam fecisse id, &c.* The Poet foresaw that the Spectators would be apt to wonder at this Behaviour in *Bacchis*, so remote from her real Character, and therefore takes care to make us sensible, that her View was to acquire a Reputation of not resembling those of her Profession. By this he at once saves the Probability, and gives a high Opinion of his Art and Address. This is the Remark of *Donatus* whose Words here are well worth the transcribing. "Multa *Terentius* feliciter ausus "est, arte fretus; nam & socrus bonas, "& meretrices honesti cupidas, præter quam "pervulgatum est, facit. Sed tanta vigi-"lanti causarum & rationum momenta "subjungit, ut ei soli merito videantur om-"nia licere. Nam hoc contra illud est, "quod alibi ait, commune esse jam omni-"bus comicis, bonas matronas facere, mere-"trices verò malas."

*11 Nostra mulieres suspectas fuisse falso.* The Word *suspectas* is equivocal, because

it

*Phi.* Why all this to me, *Laches?* Have you not already heard how I am dispofed ? Let her only fatisfy them.

*Lac.* Pray now, *Bacchis,* do as you promifed me.

*Bac.* Would you then have me to go in to them about this Bufinefs?

*Lac.* Go, remove their Sufpicions, and convince them.

*Bac.* I will, tho' I know my Prefence will not be very agreeable to them to-day ; for a Wife is a fure Enemy to a Miftrefs, efpecially when parted from her Hufband.

*Lac.* But they'll be your Friends, when once they know the Reafon of your coming.

*Phi.* I'll pafs my Word they will, when they come to learn the Bufinefs ; for you'll at once free them of their Error, and yourfelf of all Sufpicion.

*Bac.* Alas ! I am quite afham'd to appear before *Philumena.* *(To her Maids.)* Follow me in, you two.

*Lac.* What could I wifh for more, than what has happened to this Woman, that fhe fhould gain Favour without Lofs to herfelf, and be of fervice to me at the fame time : For if it is fo really, that fhe hath withdrawn herfelf from *Pamphilus,* fhe knows it will tend to her Reputation, Intereft, and Honour. By this too, fhe will greatly oblige my Son, and make us at the fame time her firm Friends.

A N N O T A T I O N S.

It may be confidered as either active or paffive, and therefore renders the Paffage capable of a twofold Interpretation. For it may either mean ; *Our Wives have given into wrong and unjuft Sufpicions with regard to Pamphilus:* Or, *We find that we have unjuftly fufpected our Wives in this Affair.* Good Reafons may be offered to fupport both thefe. For it is plain, that *Phidippus* takes it for granted, that the fuppofed Commerce between *Pamphilus* and *Bacchis* was known to *Myrrhina,* who for that Reafon, as fhe fancied, had taken home her Daughter. But this, though fpecious, does not fo well anfwer the Cafe of *Softrata* ; for which reafon, I prefer the laft Sanfe, as it agrees better with the Conduct of the whole Piece, and flows naturally from what goes before. For

---

# ACT V. SCENE I.

A R G U M E N T.

*By means of a Ring that* Pamphilus *had given to* Bacchis, *it comes to be known, that* Philumena *had been ravifhed by him.*

P A R M E N O, B A C C H I S.

*Par.* BY *Jupiter,* my Mafter feems to make but little account of my Labour, or he would not have thus fent me to the Tower for nothing, where I have loitered away a whole Day to

no

A N N O T A T I O N S.

*Parmeno,* we have feen, had been difpatched to the Tower upon a pretended Errand. Here he is feen returning, and complaining of his Mafter, to fend him fo far in queft

Pa. Quid mihi iſtæc narras ? an quia non tute ipſe du-
dum audiſti,                              [explete animum.
De hac re animus meus ut ſit, Laches ? illis modò
La. Quæſo edepol, Bacchis, quod mihi es pollicita
tute, ut ſerves.                                         20
Ba. Ob eam rem vis ergo introeam ? La. i, atque
exple animum iis, ut credant.            [ſum hodie :
Ba. Eo : etſi ſcio pol iis fore meum conſpectum invi-
Nam nupta meritrici hoſtis eſt, à viro ubi ſegregata eſt.
La. At hæ amicæ erunt, ubi, quamobrem adveneris,
reſciſcent.
Ph. At eaſdem amicas fore tibi promitto, rem ubi cog-
norint :                                                25
Nam illas errore, & te ſimul ſuſpicione exſolves.
Ba. Perii, pudet Philumenæ me. ſequimini me intrò
ambæ.                                    [tellego evenire,
La. Quid eſt, quod mihi malim, quam quod huic in-
Ut gratiam ineat ſi ne ſuo diſpendio, & mihi proſit ?
Nam ſi eſt, ut hæc nunc Pamphilum vere ab ſe ſegre-
garit ;                                                 30
Scit ſibi nobilitatem ex eo, & rem natam, & gloriam
eſſe :                                              [get.
Referet gratiam ei, unâque nos ſibi operâ amicos jun-

Sequimini me intrò ambæ. La. Quid eſt quod malim mihi, quam quod intelligo eveniri huic, ut
ineat gratiam ſine ſuo diſpendio, et proſit mihi ? Nam ſi eſt, ut hæc nunc vere ſegregarit Pamphilum ab ſe, ſcit nobilitatem eſſe ſibi ex eo, es rem natam, et gloriam : referet gratiam ei,
jungit iſte eos amicos ſibi una opera.

### ANNOTATIONS.

For both the old Men had each accuſed their Wives as the Cauſe of the Difference between *Philumena* and *Pamphilus*. The Word *nobis* too pleads ſtrongly for this Turn to the Paſſage, which cannot eaſily be reconcil'd to the other Way of explaining it.

# ACTUS V. SCENA I.

### ARGUMENTUM.

*Per annuli cognitionem, quem Pamphilus dederat Bacchidi, Phi-
lumena ab eo compreſſa oſtenditur.*

PARMENO, BACCHIS.

EDEPOL næ meam herus eſſe operam deputat
parvi preci,                                [diem,
Qui ob rem nullam miſit ; fruſtra ubi totum deſedi

eb nullam rem miſit ubi deſedi totum diem.

### ANNOTATIONS.

queſt of a Man that was not to be found. *Bacchis* in the mean time had been with *Myrrhina* and *Philumena*, and by an Acci-dent that will appear from the next Scene, had found that *Pamphilus* was the Father of the Child in queſtion. Overjoyed at ſo important

no Purpose; waiting, forsooth, for *Callidemides*, his *Myconian* Landlord. There I sat all Day like a Fool, asking every one that came by; Pray, young Man, are you a *Myconian*? No. Is your Name *Callidemides*? No. Have you not a Guest here, one *Pamphilus*? All answered, No. In short, I don't think there is any such Person. At last, I grew perfectly asham'd, and came away. But how's this, that I see *Bacchis* coming out from our Father-in-Law? What Business can she have here?

*Bac.* *Parmeno*, you come very fortunately; run with all speed to *Pamphilus*.

*Par.* For what?

*Bac.* Tell him, I beg he'll come directly.

*Par.* To you?

*Bac.* No, to *Philumena*.

*Par.* What's the Matter?

*Bac.* Nothing that regards you, therefore ask no Questions.

*Par.* Am I to say nothing more to him?

*Bac.* Yes, that *Myrrhina* knew the Ring which he formerly gave me, to have been her Daughter's.

*Par.* I understand you. Is that all!

*Bac.* All: He'll be here immediately, when you tell him of it. But do you linger?

*Par.* No truly, it has not been in my power to linger much to-day, I have been so constantly employed in running and trotting up and down.

*ANNOTATIONS.*

important a Discovery, she hastens out, and, seeing *Parmeno*, dispatches him to *Pamphilus*, to bring him to her immediately, that she may inform him of the good News.

9 *Sed quid Bacchidem?* We are not to wonder, that *Parmeno* appears surprized to see *Bacchis* coming out from *Phidippus*. He was a Stranger to what had lately past, while he was at the Tower, and therefore could not conceive, why she should appear at a House, where it might be justly presumed, she was hated. Here we have an Opportunity of observing the wrong Division of the Scenes in most Editions of this Play of our Poet; for they generally make this the third Scene of the fifth Act, whereas it is undoubtedly the first; it being necessary to suppose such an Interval between this and the last Scene, as is generally allowed between two Acts. For *Bacchis* goes in

# ACT V.    SCENE II.

## ARGUMENT.

Bacchis *here acquaints the Audience, how it came to be known, that* Philumena *had been ravished by* Pamphilus.

BACCHIS.

WHAT Joy has my coming this Day procured to *Pamphilus*? How many Blessings have I brought him? How many Cares have I freed him from? I save his Son upon the Brink of perishing

*ANNOTATIONS.*

In this Scene the whole Plot is unravelled, and every Thing prepared for the happy conclusion of the Play. By the Management of the Poet, *Bacchis* is left alone upon the Stage;

Myconium hospitem dum exspecto in arce Callidemi-
dem.
Itaque ineptus hodie dum illic sedeo, ut quisque venerat,
Accedebam: Adolescens, dic dum, quaeso, es tu My-
conius? 5
Non sum. At Callidemides? Non. Hospitem ecquem
Pamphilum [esse arbitror.
Hic habes? omnes negabant: neque eum quenquam
Denique hercle jam pudebat: abii. sed, quid Bacchidem
Ab nostro affine exeuntem video? quid huic hic est rei?
Ba. Parmeno, opportune te offers: propere curre ad
Pamphilum. 10
Pa. Quid eo? Ba. dic me orare, ut veniat. Pa. ad
te? Ba. imo ad Philumenam.
Pa. Quid rei est? Ba. tua quod nil refert, percontrari
desinas. [illum Myrrhinam
Pa. Nihil aliud dicam? Ba. etiam, cognosse annulum
Gnatae suae fuisse, quem ipsus olim mihi dederat. Pa.
scio.
Tantumne est? Ba. tantum. aderit continuo, hoc ubi
ex te audiverit. 15
Sed cessas? Pa. minime equidem: nam hodie mihi po-
testas haud data est: [diem.
Ita cursando, atque ambulando totum hunc contrivi

*est? Ba. Desinas percontari quod nil refert tua? Pa. Dicam nihil aliud. Ba. Etiam,*
*Myrrhinam cognovisse illum annulum, quem ipse dederat mihi olim, fuisse suae gnatae. Pa.*
*Scio. Tantumne est? Ba. Tantum. Aderit continuo, ubi audiverit hoc ex te. Sed cessas?*
*Pa. Minime equidem, nam hodie potestas haud est data mihi ita contrivi hunc totum diem*
*cursando atque ambulando.*

*dum exspecto in arce Callidemidem Myconium hospitem. Itaque, dum ineptus sedeo illic hodie, ut quisque venerat, accedebam? Adolescens, quaeso, dic dum, es tu Myconius? Non sum. At Callidemides? Non. Habes ecquem hospitem Pamphilum hic? Omnes negabant: neque arbitror eum esse quenquam. Denique hercle jam pudebat: abii: Sed, quid video Bacchidem exeuntem ab nostro affine? Quid rei est huic hic? Ba. Parmeno, offers te opportune: curre propere ad Pamphilum. Pa. Quid eo? Ba. Dic me orare, ut veniat. Pa. Ad te? Ba. Imo ad Philumeniam. Pa. Quid rei...*

## ANNOTATIONS.

in to *Myrrbina* and *Philumena*, enters into
a long Conversation with them, and, by
means of the Ring, makes the important
Discovery above-mentioned. To suppose all
this done, during the time of *Parmeno's* pro-
nouncing eight Lines, were ridiculous and
absurd.

10 *Propere curre. Parmeno's* Character
represents him as one curious to know every
thing, and at the same time indolent and
lazy. *Terence*, to set off this in the stronger
Light, contrives frequently to send him
about, and to raise his Curiosity without satisfying it.

# ACTUS V. SCENA II.

## ARGUMENTUM.

*Bacchis narrat hic quomodo cognitum esset, Philumenam a Pam-*
*philo fuisse compressam.*

### BACCHIS.

QUANTUM obtuli adventu meo laetitiam Pamphilo hodie?
Quot commodas res attuli? quot autem ademi curas?

*commodas attuli? Quot autem curas ademi?*

ORDO.

*Quantum laetitiam obtuli Pamphilo, hodie, meo adventu? Quot res...*

## ANNOTATIONS.

Stage; where she informs the Spectators, | covery, which removes every Obstacle, and
how she came to make this important Dif- | reconciles the several disagreeing Parties.

perishing by this, and their means: I restore a Wife, dear to him,
whom he thought he must cast off for ever; and I have clear'd him
of the Suspicion he lay under with his Father and *Phidippus*. This
same Ring was the means of accomplishing all this. For I remember, that, about ten Months ago, he came running one Evening to
my House; quite out of breath, all alone, and very much in Liquor, with this Ring on his Hand. I was immediately alarmed.
Pray my dear *Pamphilus*, says I, why in such Confusion? Where
had you that Ring? Tell me. He pretended to be thinking of
something else. When I saw that, I began to suspect it must be
something more than ordinary, and urged him earnestly to tell me.
At last, my Gentleman owns, that he had forced a young Woman,
he knew not whom, in the Street, and taken the Ring from her
in the Struggle. *Myrrhina* knew it just now on my Finger, and
ask'd, whence I had it? I tell her all: thence a Discovery was
made, that he was the Person who ravished *Philumena*, and that the
Child, now born, is his. I'm overjoyed, that so much Happiness
accrues to him by my means; tho' others of my Trade would act
very differently, in the like Case, for it is not our Interest to have
our Sparks fond of Matrimony: but I'm determined, Gain shall never be an Inducement to me to do a base thing. While it was allowable in him, I found him always easy, good-natured, and kind.
The Marriage I own happened a little unlucky for me; but I have
the pleasure to think, I have done nothing to deserve such a Misfortune. 'Tis but reasonable I should bear some little Inquietudes from
one who has been so much my Friend.

ACT

## *ANNOTATIONS.*

*Pamphilus*, we have seen, had taken a Ring from *Philumena* when he ravish'd her, and given it to *Bacchis*. She chanced to have it upon her-Finger when she went to *Myrrhina*, who immediately knew it again, and by this means the whole Mystery was brought to light. Nothing could have happened more fortunate for *Pamphilus*. As he was desirous above all things to take back *Philumena*, and was only withheld by the Notion of her having been possessed by another; as soon as that Objection is removed, and he comes to know, that he was the Person who had ravished her, and brought her into her present Circumstances, nothing remained but to receive again into his Bosom, with double Joy, one that was so justly dear to him, and whom he had so very much wrong'd in his own Mind.

<sup></sup> *Confugere anhelantem domum.* It is worth while to observe with what Art and Address *Terence* manages this part of his Sub-

ject. On the one hand, to prevent the Spec-
tators entertaining any disadvantageous Idea of *Philumena*'s Chastity, he was to repre-
sent her as having sustained a real Rape. On the other hand, *Pamphilus* has all along appeared an amiable good-natured Character, and therefore to place him now in an odious Light, would have shocked the Audience extremely, nor at all corresponded with the Poet's Design. To unite all these several Purposes, *Pamphilus* is describ'd, as in a Situation, that left him not Master of him-
self, or his own Actions, and the whole Story is painted with such Circumstances, as plainly shew, that he was under a Necessity of using Force and Compulsion to at-
tain his End. *He flies in great haste home,* like one frighted, and conscious that he had committed a Crime, which it was of the highest importance for him to conceal. *He was, without any Attendant.* Actions of that na-
ture require not Witnesses. *He was breath-*

Gnatum ei restituo, qui penè harum ipsiusque operâ
    periit:                                [rum, reddo:
Uxorem, quam nunquam est ratus pósthac se habitu-
Quâ re suspectus suo patri, & Phidippo fuit, exsolvi.  5
Hic adeo his rebus annulus fuit initium inveniundis.
Nam memini, abhinc menses decem fere ad me nocte
    primâ
Confugere anhelantem domum, sine comite, vini ple-
    num,                               [quam, amabo,
Cum hoc annulo. extimui illico. mi Pamphile, in-
Quid es exanimatus, obsecro? aut unde annulum
    istum nactus?                       10
Dic mihi. ille, alias res agere se simulare. postquam
    video;
Nescio quid suspicarier, magis coepi instare, ut dicat.
Homo se fatetur vi in viâ nescio quam compressisse:
Dicitque sese illi annulum, dum luctat, detraxisse:
Eum hæc cognovit Myrrhina in digito modò me ha-
    bentem:                            15
Rogat, unde sit: narro omnia hæc: inde est cognitio
    facta,                                [hunc natum.
Philumenam esse compressam ab eo, & filium inde
Hæc tot propter me gaudia illi contigissor lætor:
Etsi hoc meretrices alia nolunt: neque enim est in
    rem nostram,
Ut quisquam amator nuptiis lætetur. verùm ecastor  20
Nunquam animum quæsti gratiâ ad malas adducam
    partes.                                [& comi.
Ego, dum illo licitum est, usa sum benigno & lepido,
Incommodè mihi nuptiis evenit, factum fateor.
At pol me fecisse arbitror, ne id meritò mihi eveniret.
Multa ex quo fuerint commoda, ejus incommoda æ-
    quom est ferre.                  25

*Restituo gnatum ei, qui penè periit harum ipsiusque operâ. Reddo uxorem, quam ratus est se nunquam posthac habiturum: quâ re fuit suspectus suo patri et Phidippo, exsolvi eum. Hic annulus adeo fuit initium inveniendis his rebus. Nam memini eum, ferè decem menses abhinc, confugere domum, ad me nocte primâ anhelantem, sine comite, plenum vini, cum hoc annulo. Extimui illico. Mi Pamphile, inquam, amabo, quid es exanimatus, obsecro? aut unde nactus es istum annulum? Dic mihi. Ille coepit simulare se agere alias res. Postquam video id; coepi suspicari nescio quid, instare magis ut dicat. Homo fatetur se compressisse vi nescio quam virginem in via: dicitque sese detraxisse annulum illi, dum luctat: hæc Myrrhina modo cognovit me habentem eum in digito: rogat unde sit. Narro hæc omnia: inde cognitio est facta, Philumenam esse compressam ab eo, et hinc filium*

*esse natum inde. Lætor hæc tot gaudia contigisse illi propter me: etsi aliæ meretrices nolunt hoc; neque enim est in nostram rem, ut quisquam amator lætetur nuptiis. Verùm ecastor, nunquam adducam animum ad malas partes gratia quæsti. Ego, dum licitum est, usa sum illo benigno, et lepido, et comi. Evenit incommodè mihi nuptiis, fateor factum. At pol arbitror me fecisse, ne id eveniret mihi meritò. Æquum est ferre incommoda ejus, ex quo fuerint multa commoda.*

## ANNOTATIONS.

less, as having employed Force against one who resisted all in her power. *He was overcome with Wine:* this gave him Boldness and Courage. Nor are we to suppose a Man of *Pamphilus's* Character would have attempted any thing so ungenerous in other Circumstances: In fine, *he brought a Ring with him.* This he presents to *Bacchis,* as the Spoil he had gained, in consequence of his Victory. *Bacchis* recollecting these Particulars, could no longer doubt of *Pamphilus* being the Ravisher.

Y 2                        ACTUS

## ACT V. SCENE III.

### ARGUMENT.

*Pamphilus is overjoyed at the Discoveries made by the Ring he had formerly given to* Bacchis. *This Scene too contains a high Encomium of his Wife.*

### PAMPHILUS, PARMENO, BACCHIS.

*Pam.* ONCE more, *Parmeno,* take care that you have brought me a clear and distinct Account of these things; and that you don't throw me into a false and momentary Joy.

*Par.* I have.

*Pam.* For certain?

*Par.* For certain.

*Pam.* If so, I'm as happy as a God.

*Par.* You'll find it as I say

*Pam.* Stay a little however; I doubt you tell me one thing, and I think another.

*Par.* Say then.

*Pam.* I think you told me that *Myrrhina* knew her own Ring upon *Bacchis's* Finger.

*Par.* She did.

*Pam.* The same that I formerly gave her; and she desired you to tell me this. Is it not so?

*Par.* It is, I tell you.

*Pam.* Who's happier than I? Who more the Favourite of *Venus?* What Reward shall I give you for this good News? What? What? I don't know.

*Par.* But I know.

*Pam.* What?

*Par.* Why, nothing; for I can see no Advantage either in the Message, or me.

*Pam.* Shall I suffer you to go unrewarded, who have just restored me from Death to Life? Ah! doubtless you think me too ungrateful. But I see *Bacchis* standing before the Door. I believe she waits for me. I'll go to her.

*Bac.* Your Servant, *Pamphilus.*

*Pam.* O *Bacchis,* O my *Bacchis,* my Guardian Goddess!

Bac.

### ANNOTATIONS.

In this Scene *Pamphilus* is seen coming along with *Parmeno,* and all the time in close Conversation. *Bacchis* by mentioning the Circumstance of the Ring, and desiring him to acquaint his Master with it, sent a sufficient Hint to *Pamphilus,* to enable him to comprehend all that had passed. We find that he accordingly does so; but the Discovery is so unexpected, and at the same time so fortunate and agreeable, that he can scarce prevail with himself to believe it true. We find him therefore again and again questioning *Parmeno,* running over minutely every Particular, that he may be satisfied in all Circumstances, and not blindly be led into a false Joy. But when, after due Enquiry, he finds no longer room to question the Truth of what had been told him, he abandons himself to all that Excess of Joy and Transport, which would naturally flow in upon

a

## ACTUS V. SCENA III.

### ARGUMENTUM.

*Pamphilus multo gaudio perfunditur ex cognitione annuli, quem olim dederat Bacchidi. Ejusdemque mirifice laudatur uxor.*

### PAMPHILUS, PARMENO, BACCHIS.

VIDE, mi Parmeno, etiam sodes, ut mi hæc certa
    & clara attuleris:         [falso frui.
Ne me in breve hoc conjicias tempus, gaudio hoc
PAR. Visum est. PAM. certene? PAR. certe. PAM.
    deus sum, si hoc ita est, PAR. verum reperies.
PAM. Manedum, sodes. timeo ne aliud credam, atque
    aliud nuncies.
PAR. Maneo. PAM. sic te dixisse opinor, invenisse
    Myrrhinam,                   5
Bacchidem annulum suum habere. PAR. factum.
    PAM. eum, quem olim ei dedi:
Eaque hoc te mihi nunciare jussit: itane est factum?
    PAR. ita, inquam.
PAM. Quis me est fortunatior, venustatisque adeo ple-
    nior?                     [nescio.
Egon' te pro hoc nuncio quid donem? quid? quid?
PAR. At ego scio. PAM. quid? PAR. nihil enim. 10
Nam neque in nuncio, neque in meipso, tibi quid sit
    boni, scio.                [lucem feceris.
PAM. Egon', qui ab orco mortuum me reducem in
Sinam sine munere à me abire? ah, nimiùm me in-
    gratum putas.
Sed Bacchidem eccam video stare ante ostium:
Me exspectat, credo. adibo. BA. salve, Pamphile. 15
PAM. O Bacchis, ô mea Bacchis, servatrix mea!

*hoc nuncio? Quid? Quid? Nescio. PAR. At ego scio. PAM. Quid? PAR. Enim equidem nihil. Nam neque scio quid boni sit tibi in nuncio, neque in meipso. PAM. Egene finam te abire a me sine munere, qui feceris me mortuum reducem ab orco in lucem? Ah, putas me nimium ingratum. Sed eccam video Bacchidem stare ante ostium: credo, expectat me. BA. Salve, Pamphile. PAM. O Bacchis, ô mea Bacchis, mea servatrix!*



### ANNOTATIONS.

a Mind raised from a State of Despondency, natural to break out into Rhapsodies, and to that very Point of Felicity, it above all things coveted. speak without Coherence or Connexion.

9 *Quid? quid? nescio.* Terence is very happy here, in painting the Transports of Joy, into which *Pamphilus* is thrown, by the good News *Parmeno* had brought him. He expresses his Gratitude to the Messenger, and promises to reward him; but at the same time, his Mind is too full to fix upon any thing. On these Occasions it is

10 *Nihil enim. nam neque in nuncio.* We have here strongly painted the Character of a Servant, curious, inquisitive, and using all the little Artifices he can, to come at the Knowledge of a Secret, he saw so industriously kept from him. For this he would have willingly sacrificed all his Hopes of a Reward. *Magis scire vult, quam munus accipere,* says *Donatus.*

*Bac.* All's well, and I am overjoyed at it.

*Pam.* Your Actions speak it. I see you are still the same charming agreeable Creature; your Presence, Company, Conversation always bring Delight with them, where-ever you go.

*Bac.* And you, I perceive too, possess your wonted Sweetness and Complaisance, there is no one alive more polite and obliging.

*Pam.* Ha! ha, ha, this Speech from you, *Bacchis?*

*Bac.* There was Reason for your being so fond of your Wife, *Pamphilus;* I never, that I remember, saw her before. She's quite a fine Woman.

*Pam.* Tell me sincerely,

*Bac.* As I hope for Happiness I think so, *Pamphilus.*

*Pam.* But say; have you told my Father any thing of all this?

*Bac.* Not a Word.

*Pam.* Nor need you; therefore let all be hush: I would not have it here as in a Comedy, where every thing is known to every body. They whom it most concern'd to know, know already; but they who ought not to know, neither know nor shall know.

*Bac.* Nay, I'll give you a farther Proof how easily it may be concealed. *Myrrhina* told *Phidippus,* that she gave intire Credit to my Oath, and therefore believed you innocent.

*Pam.* Excellent: I hope every thing will succeed according to our Wishes.

*Par.* Pray, Master, mayn't I know what Good it is I have done to day? Or what all this is you are so engaged about?

*Pam.* No.

*Par.* I suspect however. I restore him from Death to Life! How?

*Pam.* You little know, *Parmeno,* what Service you have done me to-day, or from what Troubles you have released me.

Par.

## ANNOTATIONS.

19. *Oblitus, sermo, adventus.* What is most remarkable in this Passage is, the beautiful Assemblage *Pamphilus* here makes, including a most refined and delicate Complement, and the different Significations of *adventus* and *obitus.* *Obitus,* is where we meet one by Chance, as in the Street, or in any publick Company. *Adventus,* is where Persons meet by Design or Appointment. *Pamphilus* therefore says; *You carry Pleasure with you where-ever you go, whether Chance or Design brings you into Company.*

24 *Dic verum.* *Pamphilus* takes a pleasure in hearing *Bacchis* commend *Philumena,* because People of her Character are generally of a nice delicate Taste, and extreme good Judges. The Art of pleasing and rendring themselves agreeable is their chief Study, and Jealousy gives them a wondrous Quickness in discovering every Blemish. Nothing can be conceived more acceptable to a Lover, than to hear his Mistress prais'd even by a Rival.

25 *Dic mihi, harum rerum numquid dixti jam patri?* Neither *Laches* nor *Phidippus* were present when *Myrrhina* challenged the Ring upon *Bacchis's* Finger, so they knew nothing of the matter. Nor was it at all proper they should. *Pamphilus* had a mind to take back his Wife, without letting the World know what had occasioned the Misunderstanding between them.

26 *Placet non fieri. hæc itidem ut in comœdiis.* *Terence* here with reason endeavours to make the most of a Circumstance peculiar to his Play. In Comedy all the World, Spectators and Actors, are generally towards the latter End equally instructed in the whole Train of the Plot, and the

BA. Bene factum, & volup' eft. PAM. factis, ut cre-
dam, facis:
Antiquamque adeo tuam venuftatem obtines,
Ut voluptati obitus, fermo, adventus tuus, quocunque
adveneris,
Semper fies. BA. at tu, ecaftor, morem antiquum at-
que ingenium obtines, 20
Ut unus omnium homo te vivat nunquam quifquam
blandior.
PAM. Ha, ha, hæ! tun' mihi iftuc? BA. recte amafti,
Pamphile, uxorem tuam:
Nam nunquam ante hunc diem meis oculis eam, quod
noffem, videram. [ament, Pamphile.
Perliberalis vifa eft. PAM. dic verum. BA. ita me Dii
PAM. Dic mihi, harum rerum numquid dixit jam
patri? BA. nil. PAM. neque opus eft 25
Adeo mutito: placet non fieri hoc itidem, ut in co-
mœdiis, [fcifcere
Omnia omnes ubi refcifcunt hic, quos par fuerat re-
Sciunt; quos non autem fcite æquom eft, neque re-
fcifcent, neque fcient.
BA. Imo etiam, qui hoc occultari facilius credas, dabo
Myrrhina ita Phidippo dixit, jurijurando meo 30
Se fidem habuiffe, & propterea te fibi purgatum. PAM.
optume eft
Speroque hanc rem effe eventuram nobis ex fententiâ.
PAM. Here, licetne fcire ex te, hodie quid fit quod feci
boni?
Aut quid iftuc, eft, quod vos agitis? PAM. non
licet. PAR. tamen fufpicor.
Egon' hunc ab orco mortuum? quo pacto? PAM. ne-
fcis, Parmeno, 35
Quantum hodie profueris mihi, & ex quantâ ærum-
nâ extraxeris.

*das hoc facilius occultari: Myrrhina ita dixit Phidippo, fe habuiffe fidem meo jurijurando, et propterea te effe purgatum fibi. PAM. Optume eft: fperoque hanc rem effe eventuram nobis ex fententia. PAR. Here, licetne fcire ex te, quid boni fit quod feci hodie? Aut quid iftuc eft, quod vos agitis? PAM. Non licet. PAR. Tamen fufpicor. Egone reduxi hunc mortuum ab orco? Quo pacto? PAM. Nefcis, Parmeno, quantum profueris mihi hodie, et ex quanta ærumna extraxeris.*

## ANNOTATIONS.

the unravelling of it. It would be even a Defect in the Piece, were any Obfcurity left in this part. But Terence raifes him-felf above the common Rules, and contrives to add new Beauties to his Piece by for-faking them. The Reafons which he here gives for concealing from Part of the Actors the principal Incident of the Plot, are fo plaufible, and natural, that no could have followed the beaten Track without of-fending againft Manners and Decency. This bold and uncommon Turn is one of the chief Ornaments of the Play. *Egone hunc ab orco mortuum? Quo pacto? Parmeno* fays this, pondering within himfelf, if poffible to find out what he was fo impatient to know. He therefore repeats what *Pamphilus* had faid,

BA. Bene factum, et volup' eft. PAM. factis, ut credam, facis: adeoque antiquamque tuam venuftatem, ut quocunque adveneris, obitus, fermo, adventus tuus, femper fies voluptati. BA. At tu, ecaftor, obtines morem atque ingenium, ut nunquam quifquam homo te bono omnium vivat blandior te. PAM. Ha, ha, hæ! tune dices iftuc mihi? BA. Recte amafti uxorem tuam, Pamphile: nam nunquam viderám eam meis oculis ante hunc diem, quod noviffem. Eft vifa perliberalis. PAM. Dic verum. BA. Ita Dii ament me, Pamphile. PAM. Dic mihi, num jam dixti quid harum rerum patri? BA. Nil. PAM. Neque eft opus; adeo mutito: non placet hoc fieri itidem, ut in comœdiis, ubi omnes refcifcunt hic: fuerat par refcifcere; illi autem, quos eft æquum non fcire, neque refcifcent, neque fcient. BA. Imo etiam dabo, qui credas hoc facilius occultari:

*Par.* Nay, but I do; nor was it without Design.

*Pam.* I know that well enough.

*Par.* Does *Parmeno* ever let slip an Opportunity of doing what he ought to do?

*Pam.* Follow me in, *Parmeno.*

*Par.* I do, I have done more Good to-day without Design, than I ever did knowingly in my Life. Your Applause.

## ANNOTATIONS.

it was plainly intimated, that the News he had brought him was of the greatest Importance.

38 *An temere quidquam Parmenonem prætereat? Parmeno,* in order to get the Secret

from his Master, affects here to know it already, and vainly boasts as if nothing could escape his Penetration; insinuating, that the agreeable News he had just brought, was not thro' Chance, but by Design. But when

PAR. Imo verò scio, neque hoc imprudens feci. PAM.
ego istuc sati' scio. PAR. an
Temere quidquam Parmenonem prætereat, quod facto
usu' sit?
PAM. Sequere me intrò, Parmeno. PAR. sequor.
equidem plus hodie boni
Feci imprudens, quàm sciens ante hunc diem unquam. Plaudite. 40

CALLIOPIUS RECENSUI.

*quàm sciens ante hunc diem. Plaudite.*

*PAR. Imo verò scio,*
*neque scit hoc impru-*
*dens. PAM. Ego*
*scio istuc satis. PAR.*
*An quidquam*
*prætereat? Parmeno-*
*nem, quod sit usui*
*facto? PAM. Se-*
*quere me intro, Par-*
*meno. PAR. Se-*
*quor. Equidem feci*
*plus boni hodie, im-*
*prudens, quàm un-*

### ANNOTATIONS.

when he finds all his Arts baffled, he turns to the Spectators, and frankly owns his Ig-norance. *Equidem plus hodie boni feci imprudens, quam sciens ante hunc diem unquam.*

INDEX.

**A** Facundia multum posse, pro multum facundia posse; *to prevail by the Force of Eloquence.* Heaut. Prol. 13.

A fratre exire, i. e. e domo fratris; *from my Brother's House.* Phorm. 4. 6. 5.

A parvulo; *from a Child.* Andr. 1. 1. 8. Adelph. 1. 1. 23.

A villa mercenarius, i. e. mercenarius villaticus vel villæ; *for the Preposition* a *with the Ablative is often equivalent to the Genitive of Possession; as* a navi gubernator, *for* gubernator navis. Adelph. 4. 2. 2.

Abs te, pro ex te. Hec. 1. 1. 11.

Absque una foret, pro si absque hac una foret; *if it were not for this one Circumstance.* Hec. 4. 2. 25.

Abducere aliquem sibi convivam; *to carry home one as a Guest.* Eun. 3. 1. 17.

Abhinc triennium, i. e. ante; *about three Years ago.* Andr. 1. 1. 42. Phorm. 5. 7. 23. Hec. 5. 1. 23.

Abhorrere ab re uxoria, i. e. a ducenda uxore; *to be averse to Marriage.* Andr. 5. 1. 10.

Abigere aliquem rus, pro fugare, pellere; *to force one into the Country.* Andr. 3. 4. 38.

Abi hinc in malam rem; *go and be bang'd.* Andr. 2. 1. 19. Eun. 3. 3. 30.

Abire militatum; *to serve in the Army, to go to the Wars.* Heaut. 1. 1. 64.

Abitio, i. e. discessio; *a going abroad, a leaving one's Home.* Heaut. 1. 2. 16. So itiones crebræ. Phorm. 5. 7. 23.

Abligurire patria bona, i. e. suavibus cibis consumere; *to waste an Estate in Luxury, and the Gratification of our Appetites.* Eun. 2. 2. 4.

Abradi, per vim auferri. Phorm. 2. 1. 19.

Absente nobis, pro nobis absentibus. Eun. 4. 3. 7. Sic Plaut. Amph. 2. 2. 191. Nobis præsente.

Absolvere hominem, dimittere; *to discharge, satisfy, pay off.* Adelph. 2. 4. 13. & 18.

Abstergere vulnera, ab abstergeo, non abstergo, metri causâ. Eun. 4. 7. 9.

Absumi cura et sumptu, confici, perdi; *to pine away, to be the Prey of,* &c. Phor. 1. 5. 26.

Abundare amore, i. e. superfluere, eo quod ames; *to be beyond measure fortunate in the Enjoyment of what we love.* Phor. 1. 3. 31.

Abuti operam; *to misemploy, or lose one's Time and Labour.* Andr. Prol. 5.

Accessit haud invito ad aures mihi sermo tuus, i. e. haud invitus sermonem tuum audivi; *I have heard with pleasure the Speech you made.* Hec. 3. 5. 32.

Accedere ad genua; *to beg in a suppliant manner.* Hec. 3. 3. 18.

Accidit in te vere istud verbum; *then might you with justice have applied this Expression to yourself.* Andr. 5. 3. 14.

Accipere conditionem; *to accept of, or submit to a Proposal.* Andr. 1. 1. 52. Aliquem bene et prolixe; *to entertain frankly, and at a great Expence.* Eun. 5. 10. 34. Quid aliorsum atque ego feci; *to take a thing otherwise than I intended.* Ibid. 1. 2. 2. Amorem suum aliter atque est, i. e. aliter de amore suo atque est sentire; *to be mistaken in what regards the Person we love.* Heaut. 2. 2. 23. Omnia magis ad contumeliam; *to be more apt to be affronted.* Adelph. 4. 5. 15. Auribus, audire; *to bear.* Hec. 3. 3. 3.

Accipi indignis modis, i. e. tractari; *to be used ill.* Adelph. 2. 1. 12.

Accurare res cautius, pro curare. Hec. 4. 5. 12.

Actum est; *a proverbial Expression denoting Despair.* Andr. 3. 1. 7. Eun. 1. 1. 9. & 5. 6. 15. Heaut. 3. 1. 47. & 3. 3. 23. Adelph. 3. 2. 27.

Actum agam; *I shall labour in vain.* Adelph. 2. 2. 24.

Actutum, i. e. confestim, celeriter. Adelph. 4. 4. 24.

Ad, comparationem significat. Eun. 2. 3. 69. & 4. 4. 14.

Ad, pro apud. Heaut. 3. 3. 43. Phorm. 4. 2. 8.

Ad ingenium rursus redire; *to come to one's self; to assume his proper Character.* Adelph. 1. 1. 46. Hec. 1. 2. 38.

Ad pauca ut redeam; formula compendio rem narrare volentis. Phorm. 4. 3. 43.

Ad rem redire, i. e. ad negotium, quo de agitur. Adelph. 2. 1. 31. Heaut. 2. 3. 78.

Ad rem (subaudi, faciendam) aliquantum avidior; *inclined to be covetous.* Eun. 1. 2. 51.

Ad restim mihi res rediit; *threatens me with Ruin.* Phorm. 4. 4. 5.

Ad scopulum e tranquillo inferre; *from a State of Security to plunge into Misery.* Phorm. 4. 4. 8.

Ad venandum canes, *pro* venatici; *Hunting-Dogs.* Andr. 1. 1. 30. So *Virg. Æn.* 9. 648. Ad limina custos, *for janitor.*

Adbibere plus paulo; *to be in his Cups.* Heaut. 1. 3. 8.

Addere animum alicui; *to encourage, rouze,* &c. Heaut. 3. 2. 34.

Adductum curare aliquem, i. e. adducere. Andr. 4. 2. 1.

Adduci, impelli, persuaderi. Phorm. 5. 2. 16.

Adeo, res redit, vel rediit, pro ad id, eo. Heaut. 1. 1. 61. Phorm. 1. 2. 5. & 1. 3. 1.

Adhuc, pro ad hoc tempus. Adelph. 4. 4. 11. & 21.

Adigere quem ad insaniam, i. e. concitare, compellere. Eun. 2. 1. 13. Adelph. 1. 2. 31. *To drive one to madness.*

Adimere spem; *to deprive one of hope,* Andr. 2. 1. 5. Metum; *to remove one's Fear.* Andr. 2. 2. 2. Curam argentariam; *to free from a concern how to procure money.* Phorm. 5. 5. 46.

Adjumenti nihil aderat ad pulchritudinem; *there were no ornaments of Dress,* &c. *to set off her Beauty.* Phorm. 1. 2. 56.

Adjungere sibi aliquem beneficio; *to lay one under an Obligation, to gain one's Good-will,* &c. Adelph. 1. 1.

Adjurare sancte; *to protest or swear solemnly.* Hec. 2. 2. 16. Alicui per omnes Deos; *to take all the Gods to witness.* Andr. 4. 2. 11.

Adjutare funus. Phorm. 1. 2. 49. *The same that in* Andr. 1. 1. 83. *is expressed by* una efferre funus. Adjutare, aliis onera, pro alios onera portantes. Hec. 3. 2. 24.

Admittere indigna genere suo, i. e. committere *to behave unworthy of his Birth and Station.* Adelph. 3. 4. 45. Delictum in se; *to be guilty of a Fault.* Ibid. 4. 5. 48. Scelus. Heaut. 5. 2. 3. Culpam, in se. Phorm. 1. 5. 40. Turpe quid in se. Ibid. 2. 2. 68. Noxam. Eun. 5. 2. 14.

Adolescens mulier; *a young Girl,* Phorm. 5. 3. 11. Optama. Andr. 3. 2. 8. Adolescentulus homo. Andr. 5. 4. 7. Adolescentior. Hec. Prol. 11.

Adolescentes liberi, quibus olim studiis instituerentur. Eun. 3. 2. 23.

Adolescentum studia apud veteres diversa. Andr. 1. 1. 28.

Adoptandum dare suui filium suum; *to submit to the Adoption of a Son into another Family.* Adelph. 1. 2. 14. & 3. 5. 17.

Adoriri, aliquem jurgio; *to quarrel, chide, or scold with one.* Adelph. 3. 4. 41.

Adsimulare laetum; *to put on an Appearance of Joy or Content.* Heaut. 5. 1. 13.

Advena anus; *an old Woman, a Foreigner.* [Heaut. 1. 1. 44.

Adveniens, pro quum advenerit. Eun. 2. 2. 3. & 2. 3. 31. Adelph. 1. 2. 11. Phorm. 4. 6. 32.

Adventi, pro adventus. Phorm. 1. 3. 2. Vide Voss. de Anal. l. 2. 17.

Adversari, pro adversum esse alicui. Andr. 1. 1. 37. Eun. 2. 3. 33. Hec. 2. 1. 5.

Advocatum venire alicui; *to be one's Council.* Adelph. 4. 5. 45.

Adversa ærumna; *Adversity.* Phorm. 1. 5. 12.

Ægritudo, si nulla intercedit gaudio; *if no cross Accident happens to interrupt or disturb my Joy.* Andr. 5. 5. 5. Quum eximio tibi abs te immerito; *with... little reason or justice you occasion me this Vexation.* Hec. 3. 1. 26.

Ægritudinem, dic radit it hominibus; *Grief.* Heaut. 1. 2. 4.

Ægritudine praepeditus *blinded by our Grief.* Heaut. 3. 1. Hec.

Ægrotus animus, i. e. amore *captus* æger. Andr. 1. 2. 16. & 3. 2. 27. Heaut. 1. 1. 48.

Æqualis, i. e. qui ejusdem est ætatis. Andr. 2. 6. 20. Eun. 2. 3. 33. Heaut. 2. 3. Adelph. 3. 3. 20.

Æquanimitas, *for favour, good-will, indulgence.* Adelph. Prol. 24. Phorm. Prol.

Æque quidquam nunc quidem; *nothing at all.* Andr. 2. 6. 3.

Æqui bonique facio; *I do... for... propose any thing reasonable.* Heaut. 4. 4. 40. Phorm. 2. 3. 32.

Ætatis longinquitas; i. e. senectus. Hec. 4. 2. 20.

Ætatem agere inter se; *to live together in Peace and Harmony.* Hec. 2. 1.

Ætate exacta; *now that my Course of Life is almost run.* Adelph. 5. 2. 16.

Affectus maledica, i. e. praeditus; ... Confidence. Phorm. 5. 6. 34.

Afficere cura & solicitudine aliquem; *to give one concern and trouble.* Phorm. 2. 3. 31.

Affinitatem alicujus effugere; *to decline* one's *Alliance.* Andr. 1. 5. 13.

Affinit rerum, i. e. particeps. Heaut. 1. 3. 3. *To partake of; to discover a fondness...*

Agere facillime, dicuntur, quibus facile nullo negotio omnia ad vitam degendam ... ditam. Adelph. 3. 5. 16.

Agere, pro loqui. Adelph. 1. 1. 53.

Ager oppositus est pignori ob decem minas; *... have a Piece of Ground mortgaged for thirty Pounds.* Phorm. 3. 3. 156.

Aggravescit morbus; *the Illness increases.* Hec. 3. 2. 2.

Agitare

Aridus, pro, præparco; *stingy, niggardly,*
Heaut. 3. 2. 15.

Arrhaboni relinqui alicui, pro argento, i. e.
pignori. Heaut. 3. 3. 42.

Arrige, aures; *listen, attend.* Andr. 5. 4. 31.

Arti suæ pretium avare, statuere; *to be govern'd by Avarice in fixing a Price on one's
Art.* Hec. Prol. 2. 41.

Artem musicam tractare; *to apply to the poetick Art.* Phorm. Prol. 17.

Ascendere navem; *to embark, to sail.* Adelph.
4. 5. 69.

Asperum vinum; *rough, harsh to the Taste.*
Heaut. 3. 1. 49.

Assentari, cum accusativo. Eun. 2. 2. 22.

Assero illam manu liberali causa; *I claim
her by an Action of Freedom.* Adelph. 2. 1.
40.

Asservare. aliquem; *to keep a watchful eye
over one.* Heaut. 3. 3. 32.

Astringere alicui fidem suam, i. e. promit-
tere; *to plight his Faith.* Eun. 1. 2. 22.

Astu providere; *artfully to provide against.*
And. 1. 3. 3. Phorm. 1. 4. 5.

Asymbolum venire; *to sit at free cost.* Phorm.
2. 1. 25.

Atheniensium Lex de orbis. Phorm. 1. 2. 75.

Athenis, convivia sæpe in subdiali aliquo, &
soli exposito loco instruebantur. Adelph. 4.
2. 46.

Athenis, non solum viri, verum & feminæ
funus prosequebantur, unaque innuptæ virgines. Adelph. 1. 1. 90.

Athenis, de eadem causa bis judicium adipiscier non licebat. Phorm. 2. 2. 59.

At, singulari sensu inservit interrogationi de re
insperata. Hec. 4. 1. 11.

At, interjectio timentis. Phorm. 5. 7. 13.

At at, admirantis & suspicientis. Andr. 1. 1.
98. *paulatim percepti & intellecti mali.* Eun.
4. 5. 1. *malum metuentis.* Ibid. 4. 6. 18.
Phorm. 5. 6. 70.

Atticarum, virginum educatio descripta. Eun.
2. 3. 21.

Attingere aliquem uno digito; *to touch him
with a single finger.* Eun. 4. 6. 2.

Auctum esse damno; *to have an Expence
brought upon one.* Heaut. 3. 4. 15.

Aucupium novum, i. e. nova ratio parandi
victus, & inescandi homines; *a new Fetch,
a new Decoy.* Eun. 2. 2. 16.

Aucta in bene parte esse; *to be in a rich flourishing way.* Heaut. 4. 4. 50.

Audacia affectus, i. e. audax. Phorm. 5. 6.
84.

Auferre quid inultum, i. e. impune. Andr.
3. 5. 4.

Auferent haud sic; *they shan't come off so
easily.* Adelph. 3. 5. 8.

Aufer te hinc; *git you hence.* Phorm. 3. 6.
26. *pollicitationes; have done with your
mighty Promises.* Phorm. 5. 5. 17.

Augere industriam poetæ ad scribendum; *to
encourage the Poet to Industry in writing.*
Adelph. Prol. 25.

Avidior aliquantum ad rem (intellige faciendam.) Eun. 1. 2. 31.

Auribus accipere; *to bear.* Hec. 3. 3. 14.

Auribus lupum teneo; *I have a Wolf by the
Ears.* A Proverb denoting that we are
in danger. Phorm. 3. 2. 21.

Auscultare alicui, obtemperare. Andr. 1. 3. 4.
Heaut. 3. 3. 24.

Auctorem habere quendam facti; *to have
him to copy after as an Example or Prece-
dent.* Andr. Prol. 19.

Auctores id estis mihi, i. e. persuasores.
Adelph. 5. 6. 16.

Auctor his rebus quis fuit? *Who was the
Manager of this Affair?* Adelph. 4. 5. 37.

Auxilium, vitæ ferre; *to save one's Life.*
Andr. 1. 1. 115.

Au, interjectio mentis perturbatæ. Andr. 4.
5. 12. Eun. 4. 3. 14. & 4. 4. 13. Heaut.
5. 3. 12. Adelph. 3. 2. 38. Phorm. 4.
6. 27. & 5. 2. 20.

## B

Babylo, incertæ significationis. Adelph. 5.
5. 17.

Beare aliquem; *to make him happy.* Andr.
1. 1. 79. Eun. 2. 2. 28.

Beatus palam; *evidently happy.* Phorm.
3. 17.

Bellissimum; *the choicest, most delicious.*
Adelph. 4. 2. 51.

Bellua, de homine. Phorm. 4. 4. 11. Eun.
4. 4. 37.

Bene facis, approbantis. Adelph. 4. 4. 10. &
5. 7. 13.

Beneficii immemor; *one forgetful of Favours.*
Andr. 1. 1. 17.

Bene sit tibi, valedicentis, seu bene precantis
in digressu. Phorm. 1. 2. 101.

Benigne præbere; *to give liberally.* Hec. 4.
6. 2.

Benignis dicis; *you are very good.* Phorm.
5. 7. 62.

Blande dicere; *blanda verba loqui, affabilem
esse; to be complaisant, or smooth spoken.*
Adelph. 5. 2. 24.

Bona verba, quæso; *softly, pray.* Andr. 1.
2. 30.

## C

Cadaverosa facie; *with his ghastly Phiz.*
Hec. 3. 4. 27.

Cædere sermones, pro frequenter, & plurimum loqui; *to chat.* Heaut. 2. 2. 1.

Cæterarum rerum sordem, i. e. quantum
ad cæteras res attinet; *equally thoughtless
in your other Concerns.* Adelph. 4. 5. 61.

Calamitas

Convivium

Convivium de die apparare ; *to prepare a re-*
*past in the Morning.* Adelph. 5. 7. 8. Convivium libere agitare antiqua consuetudine ; *to enjoy the same free merry Meet-*
*ings as of old.* Hec. 1. 2. 18.

Convolat populus ; *the People flock together.*
Hec. Prol. 2. 32.

Convortam me domum ; *I'll go home.* Adelph.
2. 4. 22.

Copia, *pro* facultate. Andr. 2. 1. 20. Eun.
Prol. 21. Heaut. Prol. 28. & 2. 2. 87.
Copias alias quærere, *i. e.* aliud consilium,
auxilium. Heaut. 5. 1. 54.

Corporis habitudo ; *plight of Body.* Eun. 2.
2. 11.

Corrigere peccatum ; *to give satisfaction for*
*a Fault.* Adelph. 4. 3. 2.

Corripere sese intro ; *to rush hastily into a*
*House.* Hec. 3. 3. 4. Corripuit sese ad filiam ; *ran hastily into her Daughter's Cham-*
*ber.* Ibid. 4. 1. 3.

Corrumpitur pradium ; *Dinner is spoiled.*
Adelph. 4. 2. 29. Ne corrumpantur pisces
mihi cautio est ; *I must take care that*
*the Fish ben't spoiled.* Adelph. 3. 4. 58.
Corruptela communis liberorum ; *the com-*
*mon Corruptor of our Children.* Adelph. 5.
1. 7.

Crassus, *i. e.* ventricosus. Hec. 3. 4. 26.

Credo. *Ironice.* Eun. 5. 2. 23. Crede hoc
meæ fidei ; *trust me, believe me for once.*
Eun. 5. 2. 59.

Creduas, *pro* credas. Phorm. 5. 7. 4.

Credere, *i. e.* committere. Andr. 1. 5. 38.
Eun. 1. 2. 48. & 3. 1. 12. & 5. 2. 59.

Credidit sibi id negotii dari solum ; *imagined*
*it was his only Task.* Andr. Prol. 2.

Crescendi copiam dare ; *to encourage.* Heaut.
Prol. 28.

Crimine se expedire ; *to clear one's self from*
*Suspicion.* Hec. 4. 5. 29. Hera in crimen
veniet ; *my Mistress will be blam'd.* Hec.
3. 1. 55.

Criminari quem alicui ; *to accuse one Person*
*to another.* Eun. 5. 2. 16.

Crucem in malo quærere ; *to hazard one's*
*Neck.* Phorm. 3. 3. 11.

Cruces, *pro* meretricibus quæ animos amato-
rum excrutiant. Eun. 2. 3. 9.

Cruciatu exquirere quidquam ; *to extort a*
*Confession by the Rack.* Hec. 4. 6. 7.

Cudetur istæc in me faba ; *my bones will pay*
*for all.* Eun. 2. 3. 89.

Cudere argentum ; *to coin, to contrive to get*
*Money.* Heaut. 4. 3. 18.

Culpam in te transferet ; *he'll lay all the*
*Blame upon you.* Andr. 2. 3. 5. Verum ne
post culpam conferas in me ; *but don't*
*afterwards lay the Blame upon me.* Eun.
2. 3. 96. Culpam a me hanc esse procul ;
*that there is no Reproach on my side.*

Adelph. 3. 2. 50. Non mea opera neque culpa evenit ; *it happens not through*
*me, nor by any Fault of mine.* Hec. 2.
1. 31. Quidquid hujus factum est, culpa non factum est mea ; *whatever has*
*happened here in this Affair, is through no*
*Fault of mine.* Eun. 5. 6. 10. In culpa
is non est ; *he's not to blame.* Hec. 4. 4.
78. Culpa est penes te ; *the Fault is*
*wholly yours.* Hec. 4. 1. 20. In te sola
omnis culpa hæret ; *no Creature is to be*
*blam'd but yourself.* Ibid. 2. 1. 32.

Culpam meritum esse illum ; *that he is*
*highly to blame.* Phorm. 5. 7. 25. Nullam de his rebus culpam commeruit tua ;
*your Wife is no way to blame in the Affair.*
Hec. 4. 4. 9. Culpam in se admittere.
Phorm. 1. 5. 40. Culpa est ignoscenda ;
*the Crime is not wholly unpardonable.*
Phorm. 5. 7. 25.

Cum maxime volo ; *I desire of all Things.*
Heaut. 4. 4. 40.

Cupere alicui, *i. e.* bene velle ; *to wish well*
*to one.* Andr. 5. 4. 2.

Cura. Curam argentariam adimere ; *to de-*
*liver one from the Anxiety of procuring*
*Money.* Phorm. 5. 5. 47. Cura ex corde
excessit ; *my Heart is eased of all Care.*
Hec. 3. 2. 12. At cura quotidiana hæc
non augerent animum ; *I should not have*
*suffered under this hourly and perpetual Anxi-*
*ety.* Phorm. 1. 3. 8. Cura sese expedivit ;
*was released from all Care.* Ibid. 5. 3. 4.
Cura confectus ; *over-whelmed with Anxi-*
*ety.* Andr. 2. 1. 5. Cura & solicitudine
aliquem afficere ; *to bring Care and Anxie-*
*ty upon one.* Phorm. 2. 3. 1.

Curare una funus ; *to join with, &c. in pro-*
*viding for the Funeral.* Andr. 1. 1. 81.
Curasti te molliter ; *thou hast car'd for*
*thyself delicately.* Adelph. 4. 8. 1.

Curatura, *pro* cura. Eun. 2. 3. 24.

Curemus æquam uterque partem ; *let each*
*take care of what he ought.* Adelph. 1. 2. 50.

Curriculo percurre ; *run in all haste.* Heaut.
4. 4. 11.

Cursitare sursum deorsum ; *to be running fre-*
*quently up and down.* Eun. 2. 2. 47.

Cursum instituere ; *to be in haste.* Phorm.
5. 5. 8.

Custos, *pro* pædagogo. Phorm. 1. 5. 59.

Cyathos sorbilare ; *to drink off a Glass lei-*
*surely.* Adelph. 4. 2. 52.

### D.

**D**A locum melioribus ; *give place to*
*your Betters.* Phorm. 3. 2. 47.
Dabit hic alicuem turbam denuo ; *he'll raise*
*some new Disturbance again.* Eun. 5. 2.
60.

Dare

P__. 20. Exemplum omnibus curarem ut esses; *I'd take care you should be an Example to all others.* Adelph. 4. 8. 9. Di te malis exemplis perdant; *the God's confound thee for an Example to such Rascals.* Phorm. 4. 4. 7.

Exequias ire alicui; *to be present at one's Funeral.* Phorm. 5. 7. 37.

Exequi, *pro* facere. Andr. 1. 5. 25. Exequi imperium alicujus; *to execute, or fulfil one's Orders.* Heaut. 3. 4. 22. Exequi veram rationem, i. e. recte rem perpendere, rationis verae ductum sequi. Hec. 3. 1. 26.

Exercere, *pro* fatigare. Adelph. 4. 2. 48. Heaut. 1. 1. 64.

Exigere, fabulas; *to damn a Play.* Andr. Prol. 27. Hec. Prol. 2. 7.

Existimatio, *pro* judicio, sententia. Heaut. Prol. 25.

Exit res, i. e. palam fit. Adelph. 4. 4. 16.

Exsolvere quemquam errore, suspicione; *to undeceive one, to free one from a Mistake, to rescue from Suspicion.* Hec. 4. 6. 26.

Exossabitur congrus ubi ego rediero; *when I return, the Conger Eel shall be bon'd.* Adelph. 3. 4. 14.

Expedire se ex turba; *to free one's self from a Perplexity.* Adelph. 4. 4. 5. Expedire se crimine; *to clear one's self from a Charge, or Accusation.* Hec. 4. 5. 29. Expedire se aerumnis; *to extricate one's self from Misery, Misfortune.* Hec. 3. 1. 8.

Expiscari, *pro* diligentissime inquirere & elicere. Phorm. 2. 2. 35.

Explere animum suum; *to satisfy one's self to the full.* Andr. 1. 2. 14. Explere alicujus animum gaudio; *to fill one's Soul with Joy.* Ibid. 2. 2. 2.

Explere voluptatem suam, quam minimo precio (de meretrice;) *to enjoy her at the cheapest Rate.* Hec. 1. 1. 12.

Exporge frontem; *smooth up your Countenance.* Adelph. 5. 1. 53.

Expostulare cum aliquo injuriam; *to expostulate an Injury with one.* Andr. 4. 1. 15.

Expromere apud amicum omnia sua occulta; *to disclose all one's Secrets to a Friend.* Heaut. 3. 3. 14.

Exculpere verum ex aliquo, *pro* extorquere. Eun. 4. 4. 45.

Expuerci ubi miseriam illam ex animo; *when he wanted to rid himself of the Misery of a Croud of Attendants.* Eun. 3. _. 16.

Extrahere se e malis. Phorm. 1. 4. 3. Extrahere aliquem ex aerumna. Hec. 5. 2. _.

Ex usu tuo nemo magis est; *no Man can _ more convenient, or to your wish.* Eun.

5. 10. 29. Ex usu nostro esset si hoc matrimonium; *were this Marriage like to prove well.* Hec. 4. 1. 33.

## F.

Faba istaec in me cudetur; *I shall pay for all.* Eun. 2. 3. 89.

Fabrica, i. e. officina fabrorum. Adelph. 4. 2. 45.

Fabuler ut nunc tibi aperte; *but to be free with you.* Phorm. 4. 3. 49.

Facere, *pro* fingere, inducere; Heaut. Prol. 31. Facere ab orco in lucem reducem mortuum; *to restore one from Death to Life.* Hec. 5. 3. 12. Facere aliquem reducem in patriam; *to bring back one to his native Country.* Heaut. 2. 3. 18. Facere adversum aliquem omnia; *to do against all the Mischief one can.* Phorm. 2. 2. 80. Facere contra _ huic aegre; *wanted in his turn to mortify her.* Eun. 4. 1. 10. Facere alicui ventulum; *to fan one.* Eun. 3. 5. 47. Facere aliquem consilii incertum; *to perplex one, or disturb his Measures.* Phorm. 4. 1. 12. Facere iram missam; *to lay aside Anger.* Hec. 4. 6. 14. Facere aliquem missum; *to dismiss, discharge one,* &c. Andr. 4. 1. 57. Facere sumptum nimium parce; *to be too sparing in Expence,* &c. Ibid. 2. 6. 19. Ex animo facere; *to do a thing from Inclination.* Adelph. 1. 1. 57.

Facies cadaverosa; *a ghastly Phiz.* Hec. 3. 4. 27.

Facile omnes cum valemus, recta consilia aegrotis damus; *we all, when well, find it an easy matter to give good Counsel to the sick.* Andr. 2. 1. 9.

Facile, *pro* liquido & manifesto. Andr. 4. 3. 5.

Facilis & benevolus, quid. Hec. 4. 5. 35.

Facili patre uti; *to find out an easy indulgent Father.* Heaut. 1. 3. 4.

Facilitate nihil homini melius. Adelph. 5. 2. 7.

Facilitas & clementia, ut differunt. Adelph. 5. 2. 4.

Facillime agere; *to be in easy Circumstances of Life.* Adelph. 3. 5. 36.

Facilitatis, i. e. lenitatis & clementiae erga liberos, commoda. Adelph. 5. 2. 17.

Facinus illiberale; *an ungenteel, unhandsome, ungentleman-like Action.* Adelph. 5. 4. 3.

Facinus animadvertendum; *an Action deserving of Censure, Punishment,* &c. Andr. 4. 5. 28.

Faciunt, *pro* ostendunt. Hec. 5. 1. 28.

Factum abs te, i. e. factum tuum. Eun. 1. 2. 24.

Factum velle, *pro* laudare. Hec. 1. 1. _; Adelph. 5. 5. 21.

Frustratae adhuc nos sat tua fides; you have already enough amused us with your fine Promises. Adelph. 4. 4. 12.

Fucum factum mulieri; to deceive an unsuspecting Girl. Eun. 3. 5. 40.

Fugam ornare; to prepare for flight, for an escape. Eun. 4. 4. 6.

Fugiendo miserrimus fui; I harrass'd myself to death in flying. Eun. 5. 2. 8.

Fugitans litium; one that hates Law-Suits. Phorm. 4. 3. 18.

Fugitivum id argentum; that same fugitive Money. Heaut. 4. 2. 11.

Funambulus; a Rope-Dancer. Hec. Prol. 4. The fondness for that Diversion which prevail'd at Rome. Ibid.

Functus officium; one who has acquitted himself of his Duty. Heaut. 3. 3. 19. Adelph. 3. 4. 18.

Fundere verba; to throw away words, to overwhelm with Maxims. Adelph. 4. 3. 7.

Funditus perire; to be ruin'd for ever. Andr. 3. 5. 9.

Fundi calamitas nostri; the Flood that ravages our Fields. Eun. 1. 1. 34.

Furti se alligat; be owns himself a Thief. Eun. 4. 7. 39.

Furum manipulus, pro servorum. Eun. 4. 7. 6.

Futilist servo me, commisisse fortunas me? What! Trust myself and Fortunes to the Management of a wretched Slave! Andr. 3. 5. 3.

### G.

Gallina cecinit; my Hen crow'd. Phorm. 4. 4. 27.

Ganeo, pro scortatore. Heaut. 5. 4. 11.

Gannire, i. e. plorare; to whimper, complain. Adelph. 4. 2. 17.

Gaudere malis alienis; to rejoice at another's Misfortunes. Andr. 4. 1. 2.

Geminabit, nisi caves; he'll give you such another, if you are not more civil. Adelph. 2. 1. 19.

Genius, i. e. naturae deus; Phorm. 1. 1. 10.

Gerunt pueri iras inter se quam pro levibus noxis? for what Trifles do Children fall out among themselves? Hec. 3. 1. 30.

Gladiatores dare; to exhibit a Show of Gladiators. Hec. Prol. 2. 32.

Gladiatorio animo ad me adfectant viam; they make to me with so stern and threatning an Air. Phorm. 5. 6. 71.

Gradu suspenso; with a light soft Pace. Phorm. 5. 5. 27.

Graecorum liberi docebantur, literas, palaestram & musicam. Eun. 3. 2. 24.

Grandis, ad aetatem refertur, non ad corpus. Adelph. 4. 5. 39.

Grandiuscula erat; she was pretty well grown up. Andr. 4. 6. 19.

Gratia, pro causa. Andr. 2. 6. 1. & 3. 4. 8.

Gratiam inire; to gain Favour with one, or his Good-will. Eun. 3. 5. 9. Hec. 4. 6. 19.

Gratiam parem referre; to be even with one, to repay them in kind. Eun. 4. 4. 52.

Gratiis, i. e. sine questu. Adelph. 4. 7. 26.

Graviter ferre; to bear with Impatience, to be heartily vexed. Hec. 2. 2. 19.

Gravius in aliquem quid dicere; to say any thing harsh or severe against one. Andr. 5. 3. 3.

Grex, pro scenicorum turba; Heaut. Prol. 45. Adelph. 3. 3. 8.

Gynaeceum. Phorm. 5. 5. 24.

### H.

Habeas; take her. Andr. 5. 3. 18.

Habere & referre gratiam, ut differunt. Eun. 4. 6. 12.

Habere quid impune; to come off clear, or without Punishment. Eun. 5. 2. 13. Habere cum aliquo orationem; to enter into Conversation with one, to make a Speech to him. Hec. 3. 3. 21. Habere quid eam; to conceal a thing. Ibid. 4. 1. 4. Habere neminem eximium; to suffer none to escape. Ibid. 1. 1. 9. Habere Chrysidem, pro ea ad arbitrium suum frui. Andr. 1. 1. 58. Habere omnes servos solicitos; to keep them all employed, all in a continual Hurry. Heaut. 3. 1. 52.

Habens me male, i. e. aegre ferens. Eun. 4. 2. 6.

Habes, i. e. intelligis. Eun. 3. 1. 11. Habes rem omnem; I have now told you all. Hec. 1. 2. 119. Habes, pro invenisti. Eun. 3. 2. 22.

Habet, i. e. vulneratus est. Andr. 1. 1. 56. Habet hoc male virum; this nettles the Gentleman. Andr. 2. 6. 5.

Habeo quid agam; I know my Cue. Andr. 3. 2. 18.

Habitudo corporis; Plight of Body. Eun. 2. 2. 11.

Habui, pro credidi, duxi. Adelph. 1. 1. 23. Habui, i. e. potui. Andr. 1. 1. 12.

Haerere in parte apud aliquem; to share some part of one's Favours. Eun. 5. 10. 7.

Haud muto factum, i. e. haud paenitet me facti. Andr. 1. 1. 13.

Haud sic auferent; they shant come off so. Adelph. 3. 4. 8.

Hercules servivit Omphalae. Eun. 5. 8. 35.

Hilarem sumamus diem; let us make a chearful Day of it. Adelph. 2. 4.

Hinc illae lacrymae; hence all this Tears. Andr. 1. 1. 99.

Hoccine

Impotenti

Impotenti adeo animo esse ; *to be so little Master of one's self.* Andr. 5. 3. 8.

Imprudens, & ignarus, *ut differunt.* Eun. 1. 2. 56. Imprudens, *i. e.* nihil tale cogitans. Andr. 1. 3. 22. Imprudentia, *pro* ignorantia. Eun. *Prol.* 27.

Impune optare istuc licet ; *that you may safely wish for.* Hec. 3. 5. 14. Impune habere aliquid ; *to escape unpunished.* Eun. 5. 2. 13.

Impuratus ille ; *that Varlet.* Phorm. 4. 3. 64. Impurus, *pro* improbo. Adelph. 2. 1. 29. Impurissimus, *Idem.* Ibid. 2. 4. 17.

In amore est totus, *i. e.* amori. est mancipatus seu immersus. Adelph. 4. 2. 50.

In animum inducere, *i. e.* existimare. Heaut. *Prol.* 49.

In aurem utramvis otiose dormire ; *to be every way easy in one's Mind.* Heaut. 2. 2. 101.

In clientelam & fidem se commendare ; *to put one's self under the Patronage and Protection of another.* Eun. 5. 9. 9.

In commune consulere ; *to be equally concern'd for the good of all Parties.* Andr. 3. 3. 16.

In eodem ludo doctæ ad malitiam ; *brought up in the same School of Perverseness.* Hec. 2. 1. 6.

In ipso articulo ; *in the very critical Article.* Adelph. 2. 2. 21. In ipso tempore ; *in the critical Minute.* Andr. 3. 2. 52.

In jus ambula ; *come before a Magistrate.* Phorm. 5. 6. 53.

In lauta & bene aucta parte esse ; *to be in a thriving or flourishing way.* Heaut. 4. 4. 50.

In manu est tibi ; *'tis in your Power.* Hec. 3. 5. 43.

In manu non est mea quid uxor faciet ; *I can't pretend to answer for my Wife's Behaviour.* Hec. 4. 4. 44.

In manum quid vis tibi dari ? *What would you demand now?* Phorm. 4. 3. 29.

In medio est mater virginis, ipsa virgo ; *both the Girl and her Mother are here ready to satisfy you.* Adelph. 3. 5. 33. In medio est ipsa res ; *the thing itself speaks plain.* Ibid.

In memoria habeo ; *I remember it.* Andr. 1. 1. 13.

In nervum erumpere ; *to be fatal to one, to prove one's Ruin.* Phorm. 2. 1. 11. In nervum ire ; *to go to Jail, to be made a Prisoner.* Ibid. 4. 4. 15.

In oculis aliquem gestare ; *to have one always in our Eye.* Eun. 3. 1. 11.

In ore est omni populo ; *'tis in every body's mouth.* Adelph. 1. 2. 13.

In os laudare ; *to praise one to his Face.* Adelph. 2. 4. 5.

In portu navigare ; *to be secure or out of danger.* Andr. 3. 1. 22.

In præsentia suavia ; *present Pleasures.* Heaut. 5. 2. 9.

In proclivi quod est, id faciam ; *I'll take the Method that most directly offers.* Andr. 4. 2. 18.

In rem si est utrique ; *if it is for their mutual Advantage.* And. 3. 3. 14.

In sinu gestare ; *to love one, to carry him in one's Bosom.* Adelph. 4. 5. 75.

In somnis se illam si amplecti maluit ; *if he had rather she had slept in his Arms.* Andr. 2. 5. 19.

In tempore venire ; *to come seasonably, at the critical Juncture.* Heaut. 2. 2. 123. Andr. 4. 4. 19.

In tranquillo fratri meo amorem esse gaudeo ; *I rejoice in that my Brother Phædria's Mistress is secured to him.* Eun. 5. 9. 8.

In tuto est omnis res ; *all is now safe.* Andr. 2. 4. 3. In vado, *pro* in tuto. Ibid. 5. 2. 4.

In viam redire ; *to take up and amend.* Andr. 1. 2. 16.

In vita alicujus laudem quærere ; *to seek Fame at another's Cost, or Risk.* Heaut. 2. 2. 74.

Incendere aliquem ; *to provoke one.* Phorm. 1. 4. 9. Heaut. 2. 1. 120. Incendor ita merito ; *I am justly angry or offended.* Hec. 4. 1. 47.

Incensam ita tibi dabo ; *I'll so rouze and provoke her.* Phorm. 5. 6. 81.

Inceptio est amentium, haud amantium ; *'tis the Project rather of mad People than Lovers.* Andr. 1. 3. 13.

Inceptare facinus ; *to set about an Enterprize.* Heaut. 3. 3. 39.

Incertus animi ; *wavering, irresolute.* Hec. 1. 2. 46.

Incessit in te nunc nova religio ; *you are become wonderfully scrupulous all of a sudden.* Andr. 4. 4. 9.

Incidere, *pro* in mentem venire. Andr. 2. 2. 22.

Inclementius, *pro* inclementer. Eun. *Prol.* 4.

Incogitans, *pro* temerario. Phorm. 1. 3. 3.

Incommode mihi nuptiis evenit ; *the Marriage was indeed unlucky for me.* Hec. 5. 2. 24.

Incommodum & Infelicitas, *ut differunt.* Eun. 2. 3. 37.

Incurvus & tremulus senex ; *stooping and tottering thro' Age.* Eun. 2. 3. 44.

Incusare coram aliquem aliquid ; *to urge a thing home to one, to charge him Face to Face.* Phorm. 5. 6. 21.

Inde, *pro* ex quibus. Adelph. 1. 1. 22.

Indicium id facio alicui, *pro* indico. Adelph. 4. 4. 7.

Indiligens ne nimium sis vereor ; *but I doubt*

# INDEX.

Intervenire de improviso ; *to rush in upon, unexpectedly.* Adelph. 3. 3. 52.

Intimum aliquem habere ; *to make a Confident of one.* Eun. 1. 2. 27.

Intimus alicujus confiliis ; *trusted with all one's secret Designs.* Andr. 3. 3. 44.

Invenire, incipere, & perficere, *ut differunt.* Eun. 5. 8. 5.

Invenire, *pro* adipisci, & acquirere. Eun. 2. 1. 4.

Inversa verba ; *your double Entendres.* Heaut. 2. 2. 131.

Invitus quod facias, difficile fit ; *what we set about unwillingly becomes difficult.* Heaut. 4. 5. 1.

Invocatus, *i. e.* non vocatus. Eun. 5. 1. 29.

Involare alicui in oculos ; *to scratch one's Eyes out.* Eun. 4. 3. 6. In capillum. Ibid. 5. 2. 20.

Jocularium in malum insciens pene incide ; *I was like to have fallen unawares into a comical kind of Scrape.* Andr. 4. 5. 43.

Ira inter eas intercessit unde, quae permansit tamdiu ; *to give Occasion to a Quarrel that has lasted so long.* Hec. 3. 1. 25.

Irritatus ita sum ; *I'm so provoked, so much out of humour.* Phorm. 1. 5. 10.

Irruere in aedes alienas ; *to break into another Person's House.* Adelph. 1. 2. 8.

Istnaec in me cudetur faba ; *I shall pay for all.* Eun. 2. 3. 89.

Ita fugias ne praeter casam, quod aiunt ; *run so as not to pass your own Gate, as the Saying is.* Phorm. 5. 2. 3.

Ita, *pro* valde, & *pro* talis. Andr. Prol. 11. *pro* ut. Hec. 3. 5. 50.

Ita mihi atque huic sis superstes ; *Heaven grant you to survive us both.* Heaut. 5. 4. 7.

Itiones crebrae & mansiones ; *his frequent Journies, and long stays.* Phorm. 5. 7. 23.

Jubeo, *pro* volo. Andr. 3. 3. 1. Adelph. 3. 4. 15. & 5. 6. 1. Eun. 4. 7. 20.

Judicium cras est mihi ; *my Cause comes on to-morrow.* Eun. 2. 3. 47.

Jugulare aliquem suo gladio ; *to foil one at his own Weapons.* Adelph. 5. 6. 35.

Junget nos una sibi amicos ; *she will at the same Time make us her Friends.* Hec. 4. 6. 32.

Juno, a juvando dicta. Andr. 3. 1. 15.

Jus summum saepe summa est malitia ; *the more Law, oft the less Justice.* Heaut. 4. 4. 48.

Justa servitus, *i. e.* moderata. Andr. 1. 1. 9.

## L.

L Abasch, victus uno verbo ; *be yields, vanquished by a single Word.* Eun. 1. 2. 98.

Labor, *pro* molestia. Andr. 1. 1. 30. & 5. 2. 29.

Laborare de reliqua, *id est,* solicitum esse. Adelph. Prol. 1.

Laborare e dolore, *i. e.* parturitione. Andr. 1. 5. 33.

Labore alieno partem gloriam in se transmovere ; *to appropriate to one's self the Glory acquired by others* Eun. 3. 1. 9.

Laborem inanem capit ; *'tis vain Labour to t mself.* Hec. 3. 2. 9.

Labos, *pro* aegritudine & dolore. Hec. 3. 1. 6.

Lacerare aliquem variis modis ; *to devise various Kinds of Torture for one.* Adelph. 3. 2. 17.

Lachrimae illi illico cadunt ; *immediately the Tears fall from him.* Adelph. 4. 1. 20.

Lacrumo gaudio ; *I weep for Joy.* Adelph. 3. 4. 46.

Lactare aliquem ; *to tantalize one.* Andr. 4. 1. 24. Animum solicitando & pollicitando ; *to seduce by fine Speeches and Promises.* Ibid. 5. 4. 9.

Laedere, *pro* injuria afficere. Eun. Prol. 2.

Laedere nulli os ; *to be inoffensive, to hurt nobody.* Adelph. 5. 2. 10.

Lamentari ; *to mourn, to be dejected.* Andr. 1. 1. 94.

Lana ac tela victum quaeritans ; *living an industrious Life, gaining her livelihood by the Distaff and Loom.* Andr. 1. 1. 48.

Lapis, *de homine ignavo & stupido.* Heaut. 4. 6. 3. Hec. 2. 1. 17.

Largitas subita ; *a sudden and unusual Liberality.* Adelph. 5. 7. 28.

Largitor de te, puer ; *promise for yourself, Boy.* Adelph. 5. 6. 17.

Lascivia & luxuria diffluere ; *to be borne away by Luxury and Debauchery.* Heaut. 5. 1. 72.

Latere tecto abscedere ; *to come off with a whole Skin.* Heaut. 4. 1. 5.

Laterem lavare ; *to labour in vain.* Phorm. 1. 4. 9.

Lavare peccatum precibus ; *to wash away an Offence by Submissions.* Phorm. 5. 6. 80.

Laudare fortunas alicujus ; *to congratulate one on his good Fortune.* Andr. 1. 1. 70.

Lectum est, scilicet, argentum ; *'tis good Coin.* Phorm. 1. 2. 3.

Lege hac, *i. e.* conditione. Eun. 1. 2. 23. Andr. 1. 2. 25.

Lenirent quo mihi illam miseriam ; *to please me, and soften my Chagrin.* Heaut. 1. 1. 75.

Lenitas, *pro* facilitate. Andr. 1. 2. 4.

Lepus tute es, & pulpamentum quaeris, *proverbium usitatum.* Eun. 3. 1. 36.

Libenter vivis, & bene libenter victitas ; *you live at a very free Rate, and feast high.* Eun. 5. 10. 26.

Mali,

Mali, *pro* difficilibus, tenacibus, & parcis. Phorm. 4. 2. 1.

Malum hoc nisi putas ad salutem converti non posse; *unless you think this Misfortune incapable of being redressed.* Andr. 4. 1. 48.

Malum, *pro* interjectione. Eun. 4. 7. 10. Adelph. 4. 2. 5.

Mammam dare; *to suckle.* Adelph. 3. 7. 18.

Mancipium, *pro* puella. Eun. 2. 2. 43.

Manedum, *pro* mane; *stay a little.* Hec. 5. 3. 4.

Manent, *pro* remanent. Eun. 3. 3. 6. Ibid. 3. 5. 33.

Manere, *pro* expectare. Phorm. 4. 1. 4. & 3. 2. 27.

Manibus pedibusque obnixe omnia facere; *to make all the Opposition in one's Power, to leave nothing unessay'd.* Andr. 1. 1. 134.

Manipulus furum; *a Regiment of Black-Guards.* Eun. 4. 7. 6.

Matres filiis in peccato adjutrices solent esse; *Mothers are commonly Advocates for their Son's Faults.* Heaut. 5. 2. 38.

Mansum oportuit; *he ought to have staid at home.* Heaut. 1. 2. 6.

Maturem ut nuptias quantum quam; *to hasten forward the Match as fast as I can.* Andr. 3. 3. 45.

Mavolo, *pro* male. Hec. 4. 1. 25.

Me vide; *mark me, attend to what I say, I engage for it.* Andr. 2. 2. 13.

Me incidente hæc non fiunt; *these things don't happen without my foretelling them.* Adelph. 3. 5. 62.

Mea tu, & amabo, blandimenta mulieres sunt. Eun. 4. 3. 14. Adelph. 3. 1. 2.

Meam paulatim plebem primulum facio; *I begin with the lowest, and strive to gain them by degrees.* Adelph. 5. 4. 10.

Mecastor & ædepol, jurandi formulæ. Hec. 1. 2. 8.

Mecum, *pro* penes me. Eun. 3. 3. 10.

Moderi quas paulo possis parare in animo cupiditatis; *to give way only to Passions that can be gratified at a small Expence.* Phorm. 5. 3. 3.

Medicari cum ego mihi in hac re possim; *when I have it in my Power to remedy myself at once.* Andr. 5. 4. 41.

Meditata mihi sunt omnia mea incommoda; *I have already considered with myself all the Evils that threaten me.* Phorm. 1. 5. 18.

Medium aliquem arripere; *to snatch one up by the Middle.* Adelph. 3. 2. 18.

Megalenses ludi; *Games in honour of* Cybele, *the Mother of the Gods.* Andr. Didasc. &c.

Meliuscula est; *she's somewhat better.* Hec. 3. 2. 19.

Memoria, *pro* dexteritate agendi. Andr. 4. 3. 8.

Memoriter facere, *cognoscere.* Andr. 4. 3. 8. Eun. 5. 3. 6.

Mensis agitur hic jam septimus; *'tis now seven Months.* Hec. 3. 3. 34.

Memtem vobis meliorem dari; *that you may learn more Wisdom.* Adelph. 3. 4. 69.

Mentiri non est meum; *I seldom fail in what I undertake, I'm not given to vain boasting.* Heaut. 3. 2. 38.

Meorum solus sum meus; *I'm myself the only Friend I have at home.* Phorm. 4. 1. 21.

Meretrix, *a merendo sic dicta.* Hec. 4. 3. 29.

Metui a Chryside; *I dreaded some Mischief from this Chrysis.* Andr. 1. 1. 79.

Metuo ut substet; *I doubt whether he can put up this ill Usuage.* Andr. 5. 4. 11.

Mihi sic est usus; *I find my Account in doing so.* Heaut. 1. 1. 28.

Minerva ex capite Jovis nata. Heaut. 5. 4. 13.

Minueris nec tu hæc quæ facis, &c. *nor would I have you hesitate a Moment.* Andr. 2. 3. 18.

Minuere suum consilium; *to alter one's Purpose or Design.* Hec. 4. 3. 10.

Minue vero iram; *moderate your Passion.* Phorm. 2. 2. 88.

Misera sum, *pro* innocens sum. Hec. 4. 1. 21.

Misere cupio, i. e. nimis valde cupio. Adelph. 4. 5. 64. Misere solicita, i. e. valde solicita. Andr. 1. 5. 33.

Miserescat te inopis meis mei; *pity me in this Distress.* Heaut. 5. 4. 3.

Miseria, *pro* molestia. Eun. 3. 1. 16.

Misericordia & pudor, *passivæ.* Andr. 1. 5. 26. & 27.

Missa hæc face; *let these idle Ceremonies alone.* Adelph. 5. 5. 8.

Missum me face; *have done with me, dismiss, discharge me.* Andr. 4. 1. 56. Phorm. 5. 6. 53.

Modeste terre, *pro* moderate. Phorm. 1. 3. 18.

Modesto adeo, adeo venusto vultu; *of a Countenance so full of Modesty and Sweetness,* Andr. 1. 1. 93.

Modo, *pro* præsenti tempore. Adelph. 3. 1. 2. Modo, *pro* jamdudum. Eun. 4. 4. 30. Modo non, i. e. propemodum. Phorm. 1. 2. 18. Modo meo, i. e. mea voluntate. Andr. 1. 1. 126. Modo meo, *pro* arbitrio. Eun. 5. 3. 11. Modus, *pro* moderatione, Andr. 1. 1. 68.

Molestus certe ei fuero; *I shall at least give him some Disturbance.* Andr. 4. 1. 17.

Molir, *pro* magno labore facere. Heaut. 2. 1. 11.

Molliri

Molliri ut neque misericordia neque precibus queas ; *that you can be softened neither by Pity, nor Entreaties.* Phorm. 3. 2. 13.

Molliter te curasti ; *thou hast cared for thyself delicately.* Adelph. 4. 9. 1.

Mollities hæc animi ejicienda ; *I must shake off this Effeminacy and Weakness of Mind.* Eun. 2. 1. 16.

Montes auri pollicens ; *promising him Mountains of Gold.* Phorm. 1. 2. 18.

Morbus me detinuit ; *I was detained by an Illness.* Phorm. 4. 1. 8.

Mordere clanculum, *pro* obtrectare. Eun. 3. 1. 21.

More hominum evenit ; *'tis according to the common Run of human Things.* Andr. 5. 6. 3.

Morem gestum oportuit adolescenti ; *you should have yielded to the young Gentleman.* Adelph. 2. 2. 6.

Mores pudici in pulchro gratiores. Heat. 2. 4. 2.

Moribus quam multa prava ac injusta fiunt ! *How many wrong and unjust Things has Custom introduced !* Heaut. 4. 6. 11.

Mors consecuta est miseram ex ægritudine ; *the poor Mother after much Suffering and Anxiety, died of Grief.* Phorm. 5. 6. 23.

Morum similitudo, amicitiæ mater. Heaut. 2. 3. 13.

Mos gerundus est ; *I find I must yield.* Eun. 1. 2. 108.

Movere, *pro* differre. Andr. 3. 2. 36. *pro* festinare. Eun. 5. 3. 3.

Move ocius te ; *bestir yourself.* Andr. 4. 3. 16.

Moveone ego isthæc ? *Am I the Cause of this Disturbance.* Audr. 5. 4. 18.

Mulier mulieri magis congruit ; *it will come better from one Woman to another.* Phorm. 4. 5. 14.

Mulieres semper adversantur viris ; *Women are always ready to cross their Husbands.* Hec. 2. 1. 5.

Mulierum natura describitur. Heaut. 2. 1. 10. & ingenium. Eun 4. 7. 42.

Multa ex quo fuerint commoda, ejus incommoda æquum est ferre ; *'tis but reasonable to bear some little Inquietudes from one who has been so much my Friend.* Hec. 5. 2. 25.

Multis modis, i. e. vehementer. Hec. 3. 3. 7. Legitur & multimodis. Heaut. 2. 2. 79.

Musica ars, i. e. poetica. Hec. Prol. 2. 15.

Musicum studium, *pro* poetico. Heaut. 3. 2. 23.

Mutuas operas tradunt ; *they help one another by turns.* Phorm. 2. 1. 37.

### N.

N ÆE, *Græce* ναὶ, jurandi particula. Andr. 4. 4. 3. Heaut. 2. 1. 5.

Narrando male, quidvis depravari potest ; *the best Story may be spoil'd in the telling.* Phorm. 4. 4. 16.

Narrare fabulam surdo ; *a Proverb used where no regard is paid to one's Remonstrances.* Heaut. 1. 3. 10.

Nata nunc demum istæc oratio est ; *you have at length then found this Salvo.* Adelph. 5. 1. 19.

Natus huic rei, *pro* ad hanc rem. Adelph. 4. 2. 6.

Navigare incommodum est ; *the being at Sea is attended with many Hardships.* Hec. 3. 4. 3.

Navigo ego in portu ; *I'm out of Danger.* Andr. 3. 1. 22.

Naviter, *pro* strenue & fortiter. Eun. 1. 1. 6.

Ne, *pro* nec nimis, multum, & valde. Andr. Prol. 17. Ne, *pro* non & nedum. Andr. 4. 2. 23. Phorm. 1. 5. 84.

Ne gravere ; *pray don't refuse.* Adelph. 5. 6. 19.

Ne præter casam, ita fugias ; *run so as not to pass your Gate.* Phorm. 5. 1. 3.

Ne quid fit nimis ; *follow nothing too eagerly.* Andr. 1. 1. 34.

Nec qui, *pro* quomodo, qua ratione. Hec. 2. 3. 5.

Nec quid me nunc faciam scio ; *ner can I think what Course to follow.* Andr. 3. 5. 8.

Nec opinantes ; *not aware, not dreaming of the Thing.* Andr. 1. 2. 4.

Negotium, *pro* molestia & cura. Andr. Prol. 2.

Nervos ubi tu intendas tuos ; *in a Case that so well deserves your exerting all your Abilities.* Eun. 2. 3. 20.

Nutiquam, id est, non nimis. Hec. 1. 2. 50. & 3. 3. 43.

Ni, *pro* ne. Eun. 3. 3. 36. *pro* si non. Adelph. 3. 4. 8.

Nil suave meritum est ; *I can see no manner of Temptation for it.* Phorm. 2. 1. 75.

Nil tam difficile est, quin quærendo possit investigari ; *nothing is so difficult but by Industry it may be accomplished.* Heaut. 4. 1. 8.

Nihil nisi sapientis es ; *you're Wisdom itself.* Adelph. 3. 3. 40.

Nihili pendere ; *to undervalue, to despise.* Eun. 1. 2. 14.

Nisi animus me fallit ; *if I am not much mistaken.* Phorm. 4. 5. 8.

Niti, *pro* facere, experiri. Adelph. 3. 4. 51.

Nitor, *pro* pinguedine ; *Plight of Body.* Eun. 2. 2. 11.

Nobilitas, *pro* fama, celebritate. Hec. 4. 6. 31.

Nobilitare

Nobilitare aliquem, *flagitiis*; *to train one on in Crimes.* Eun. 5. 7. 20.

Nobilitatem ex eo sibi natam scit; *she knows it will tend to her Reputation.* Hec. 4. 6. 31.

Nodum in scirpo quæris; *you are hunting for a Knot in a Bulrush.* Andr. 5. 4. 38.

Nollem factum; *I'm heartily sorry for it.* Adelph. 2. 1. 11.

Nolo, volo, &c. *imperiosa verba.* Phorm. 5. 6. 57. Andr. 2. 5. 7.

Non est mentiri meum; *I'm not given to vain boasting.* Heaut. 3. 3. 38.

Non fit sine periclo facinus magnum & memorabile; *no great and memorable Attempt can be undertaken without Danger.* Heaut. 2. 2. 73.

Non justa, justa, quia non prorsus omnino obsequor; *because I don't wholly humour you in every thing, right or wrong.* Adelph. 5. 7. 33.

Non licet hominem esse sæpe ita ut volt; *A Man often can't do as he would.* Heaut. 3. 4. 53.

Non pænitet me famæ; *I shall not regret the Fame.* Hec. 4. 6. 9.

Non possum pati, quin, &c. *I can scarce, I protest, forbear from,* &c. Heaut. 4. 4. 13.

Non rete quia accipitri tenditur; *because the Net is never spread for the Hawk.* Phorm. 2. 1. 16.

Non usus facto est, *there's no occasion, there's no need for,* &c. Hec. 3. 1. 47.

Non usus veniet, spero; *that I hope will never be.* Heaut. 3. 2. 42.

Nostri nosmet plenitet; *we are never contented with our own Condition.* Phorm. 1. 3. 20.

Nova figura oris; *a Countenance of quite a new make.* Eun. 2. 3. 25.

Nox, & amor, vinumque nihil moderabile suadent. Adelph. 3. 4. 24.

Noxa, pro injuriis ac culpis. Hec. 3. 1. 30.

Nugas magnas dicere; *to bring out something very trifling.* Heaut. 3. 4. 8.

Nullum jam dictum, quod non sit dictum prius; *nothing can be said now, but what has been said before.* Eun. *Prol.* 41.

Nullus sum, *pro* perii, actum est. Andr. 3. 4. 20. Hec. 4. 4. 31. Phorm. 1. 4. 1.

Nullus, *pro* non. Andr. 2. 2. 33. Hec. 1. 2. 4.

Numquam, *pro* non. Eun. 5. 8. 62. Adelph. 2. 1. 3. Phorm. 1. 2. 71. Numquam quidquam, *id est*, non. Adelph. 4. 1. 12.

Numquid vis, abiturientium mos. Eun. 2. 3. 49.

Nunquam ita quisquam bene subducta ratione fuit ad vitam; *there is no Man has so well computed the Measures of Life.* Adelph. 5. 2. 1.

VOL. II.

Nupera notitia; *an Acquaintance of but short standing.* Heaut. 1. 1. 1.

Nupta nam meretrici hostis est; *for a Wife is an irreconcileable Enemy to a Mistress.* Hec. 4. 6. 23.

Nupta mulier, *id est*, uxor. Hec. 4. 5. 31.

Nuptias dum nimis sanctas facere student; *in this Formality of Preparation for the Marriage.* Adelph. 5. 5. 1.

Nuptum daturne illa Pamphilo hodie; *Is she to be married to Pamphilus to-day?* Andr. 2. 2. 1.

Nusquam gentium fratrem invenio; *I can find my Brother no where.* Adelph. 4. 2. 1.

## O.

O, Interjectio optantis. Andr. 1. 5. 32. O cœlum, o terra! *Verba vehementer dolentis, & exclamantis.* Adelph. 5. 1. 4.

O festus dies hominis! *O happy Day!* Eun. 3. 5. 12.

Obdere pessulum foribus, *id est*, opponere. Heaut. 2. 2. 37. Ostio. Eun. 3. 5. 55.

Obfirmare me posse; *that I can keep to my Resolution.* Eun. 2. 1. 11.

Obfirma ne tam te, Chreme; *don't be so obstinate, Chremes.* Heaut. 5. 5. 8.

Obfirmare me viam quam decrevi persequi certum est; *I'm resolved to keep firm to my Purpose.* Hec. 3. 5. 4.

Objicere alicui lætitiam nec opinanti; *to give one unexpected Joy.* Heaut. 1. 2. 12.

Obire mortem; *to die.* And. 1. 3. 18.

Oblatum *dicitur*, quod offertur invito. Adelph. 3. 1. 9.

Oblectare se in aliquo; *to take delight in one.* Adelph. 1. 1. 24.

Oblectes ut te me; *that you delight yourself with the Remembrance of me.* Eun. 1. 2. 115.

Obnixe, *id est*, cum conatu. Andr. 1. 1. 134.

Obnoxius tum uxori sum; *then I'm under a thousand Obligations to my Wife.* Hec. 3. 1. 22.

Obnuntiare, & renuntiare, *ut differunt.* Adelph. 4. 2. 8.

Obulus, *pro* exiguo admodum pretio. Andr. 2. 2. 32.

Obsaturabere istius propediem; *you'll soon have enough of him.* Heaut. 4. 7. 29.

Obsecundare in loco; *to direct as Occasion offers.* Adelph. 5. 7. 37.

Obsecundato in loco; *mind your cue.* Heaut. 4. 5. 22.

Obsequi alicui; *to do a Kindness to, to oblige one.* Andr. 1. 1. 156. Ibid. 5. 1.

...ben, be has nick'd me in the very critical Article. Adelph. 2. 2. 21. Oppressisset nox prius; *Night would come on before.* Ibid. 4. 1. 9.

Optare, unum de duobus eligere. Andr. 4. 5. 2.

Optata loquere; *give me a more favourable Answer.* Heaut. 3. 3. 50.

Opus, *pro* agricultura. Eun. 2. 1. 14.

Oratio, index ingenii. Heaut. 2. 4. 4.

Ore quo appellabo patrem? *How can I look my Father in the face?* Heaut. 4. 2. 22.

Ornare fugam; *to provide for Flight, for an Escape.* Eun. 4. 4. 6.

Ornare munus verbis; *to set off a Present with all one's Eloquence.* Eun. 2. 1. 8.

Os durum; *Assurance, Impudence.* Eun. 4. 7. 36. & 5. 1. 22.

Os, nulli laedere; *to live without Offence.* Adelph. 5. 1. 10.

Os sibi distorquere; *to distort his Countenance.* Eun. 4. 4. 3.

Otiose, *pro* secure; *at his Ease, without Fear or Apprehension.* Adelph. 2. 1. 2.

Otium, & cibus quid facit alienus, vide; *do but see the Effects of Idleness, and living at another's Expence.* Eun. 2. 2. 34.

Otium hercle non est mihi auscultandi; *I am not at leisure now to hear you out.* Adelph. 3. 4. 65. Ovem lupo commisisti; *you set the Wolf to guard the Sheep.* Eun. 5. 1. 16.

## P

PAce quod fiat tua, quaeso; *pray, Sir, with your leave.* Eun. 3. 2. 13.

Pace infecta; *without having first made up the Breach.* Eun. 1. 1. 8.

Pacem ut conciliem exeo; *I am come out if possible to make up this Breach.* Heaut. 5. 5. 2.

Pacto eo, *pro* modo; *by that means.* Andr. 1. 1. 22.

Palaestra; *a School for training up Youth in the various Exercises of the Body.* Eun. 3. 2. 34. Pro ganeo, Phorm. 3. 1. 20.

Palam est; *it is out, I make a Discovery of it immediately.* Eun. 1. 2. 24.

Palam ac fieret; *lest it might be divulged.* Adelph. 4. 4. 13.

Palmam in medio omnibus esse positam; *that the Prize of Honour is proposed in common to all.* Phorm. Prol. 18.

Palmam equidem do huic consilio; *this indeed I look upon as my Master-Piece.* Heaut. 4. 2. 31.

Palmarium, quod palma dignum. Eun. 5. 4. 8.

Par pari referre; *to repay in kind.* Eun. 3. 1. 75. Adelph. 1. 1. 48.

Par pari ut respondeas vide; *be sure that you return like for like.* Phorm. 1. 4. 35.

Para puero nutricem; *provide a Nurse for the Child.* Hec. 4. 4. 104.

Parare amicos, odium; *to get Friends, or raise Enemies.* Andr. 1. 1. 41.

Parasitorum descriptio graphica. Eun. 2. 2. 17. & seq.

Paratus, id est, subornatus. Andr. 5. 4. 6.

Parce ac duriter se habere; *to be sober, sparing, and industrious.* Adelph. 5. 1. 20.

Pariter, id est, similiter. Eun. 1. 2. 12.

Pars aequa amoris tecum utinam esset mihi; *I wish we loved one another upon equal Terms.* Eun. 1. 2. 12.

Parsi perdere, id est, continui. Hec. 3. 1. 2.

Partes seni cur poeta dederit; *why the Poet has given to an old Man a Part.* Heaut. Prol. 1.

Partes priores apud aliquem habere; *to have the Preference with one.* Eun. 1. 2. 71.

Partes primas agere; *to be chief in conducting the Plot.* Phorm. Prol. 28.

Partes tuas vicissim est acturus; *he going in his Turn to act your Part.* Phorm. 5. 4. 7.

Partes duras fratris praedicas; *my Brother must have but an indifferent time of it, by your Account.* Eun. 2. 3. 62.

Particeps, pro haerede. Heaut. 1. 1. 98.

Parvi pendere; *to make no account of.* Andr. 3. 2. 46.

Patefacere fenestram ad nequitiam; *to open a Door to Debauchery.* Heaut. 5. 1. 72.

Pater ac dominus hoc interest; *in this lies the Difference between a Father and a Master.* Adelph. 1. 1. 91.

Pater illi es natura; *you are his Father by Nature.* Adelph. 1. 2. 46.

Paternum istuc hand dedisti; *you never learnt that of your Father.* Adelph. 3. 5. 4.

Paternus amicus virginis; *a Relation of the Girl's by the Father's side.* Phorm. 1. 2. 78.

In patinis jamdudum est animus; *my Mind has long ago been set upon my Dishes.* Eun. 4. 7. 46.

Pati, pro durare. Hec. 1. 2. 108.

Patrissas; *you take after your Father.* Adelph. 4. 2. 35.

Patrocinari inopi aetatis; *to take part with Girls under one's Protection.* Phorm. 5. 6. 46.

Patronam te mihi capio; *I desire to have you for my Patroness.* Eun. 5. 2. 48.

Pavitare, pro aegrotare, vel vehementer timere. Hec. 3. 1. 41.

Paulum intellexe, pro multum. Andr. 4. 4. 55.

Paupertas olim militiae causa fuit. Adelph. 3. 4. 21.

Pestis, *pro damno vel pernicie.* Adelph. 2. 1. 35.

Petere cibum e flamma; *to stick at nothing however sordid.* Eun. 3. 2. 38.

Phaleratis dictis ut ducas me; *to think you can make me the Dupe of your fine Speeches.* Phorm. 3. 2. 15.

Phasma Menandri; *a Comedy of Menander, so call'd.* Eun. Prol. 9.

Piget me hoc, *pro hujus,* Phorm. 3. 3. 21.

Pignori oppositus est ager; *I have a little Estate mortgaged.* Phorm. 4. 3. 56.

Piræum, *Athenarus portus.* Eun. 2. 2. 59.

Pistrinum. Andr. 3. 4. 21. Ejus descriptio. Ibid. 1. 2. 23.

Placidum instar ovis reddo; *I make him as meek as a Lamb.* Adelph. 4. 1. 18.

Planissume filia abs te prodita est illi anui; *'tis evident you've betray'd your Child to this old Woman.* Heaut. 3. 4. 26.

Plectar pendens, *id est, feriar.* Phorm. 1. 4. 43.

Plaudite, *quid sibi velit.* Andr. 5. 6. 7.

Plenus rimarum sum; *I'm full of Chinks.* Eun. 1. 2. 25.

Plerique omnes; *almost all Men.* Andr. 1. 1. 28. Eun. 1. 2. 5.

Plumbeus, *de ignavo loquens.* Heaut. 5. 1. 4.

Plus millies audivi; *I have heard it above a thousand times.* Eun. 3. 1. 32.

Plusculâ supellectili opus est; *I must too be provided with a little Houshold Furniture.* Phorm. 4. 3. 60.

Pœnitet, *id est,* parum putat. Heaut. 1. 1. 20.

Pol haud paternum istuc dedisti; *you never learnt that of your Father.* Adelph. 5. 4. 4.

Pollicitando eorum animos lactas? *Do you bewitch them with your fine Promises?* Andr. 5. 4. 9.

Pollinis, fumi, ac savillæ plena; *bedaub'd with Ashes, Meal, and Smoke.* Adelph. 5. 1. 60.

Pompa, *pro comitatu.* Heaut. 4. 4. 17.

Pone pallio apprehendere; *to pull one back by his Cloke.* Phorm. 5. 5. 23.

Porro, conjunctio expletiva. Andr. 1. 5. 43. *pro* præterea, ultra. Hec. 3. 1. 18. & 20. *pro* deinceps. Andr. 3. 4. 17. Eun. 2. 5. 65. *pro* postea, deinde. Eun. 1. 2. 87.

Post principia ego ero; *I'll take my Station in the Rear.* Eun. 4. 7. 11.

Postputavit sibi omnia; *postpon'd every other Consideration.* Adelph. 2. 3. 9.

Posteriores non feram; *I shan't be behind with him.* Adelph. 5. 2. 26.

Posterius iste tuus ipse sentiet; *that Spark of yours will be sensible of it in time.* Adelph. 1. 2. 60.

Posthabui omnes res, ita uti par fuit; *I*

postpon'd *every thing else, as was fit I should.* Phorm. 5. 6. 15.

Postilla, *pro postea.* Andr. 5. 4. 33.

Postulare, *pro optare.* Andr. 4. 1. 20.

Postulatio, *id est,* querela. Hec. 1. 2. 105.

Postules, *pro vel.s.* Eun. 1. 1. 16. Postulo, *pro* jubeo. Andr. 2. 5. 11.

Pote, *pro* potis est, potin' es. Adelph. 2. 3. 11. Andr. 2. 6. 6.

Potentes, dites, fortunati. Adelph. 3. 4. 57.

Potesse, *pro* posse. Eun. 4. 3. 24.

Potiri, cum accusativo. Adelph. 5. 2. 37.

Potissimum, superlativum, *a potis.* Adelph. 3. 1. 9.

Præ manu paululum aliquid dare; *to give some small Matter beforehand.* Adelph. 5. 7. 23.

Præ me hic ego illum contempsi; *here I had him in Contempt in comparison of myself.* Eun. 2. 2. 8.

Præut hujus rabies quæ dabit; *in comparison of the wild Pranks his Madness will drive him to.* Eun. 2. 3. 9.

Præbes te servum haud inliberalem; *you shew yourself to be a very faithful Servant.* Adelph. 5. 3. 5.

Præcidere omnes causas omnibus; *to remove all Causes of Discontent.* Hec. 4. 2. 22.

Præfinito nisi loqui illic haud licebat; *for there I durst not speak, but when, and what he pleased.* Hec. 1. 2. 19.

Prægnans, unde dictum. Hec. 4. 4. 19.

Præmonstrator, *id est,* ductor. Heaut. 5. 1. 2.

Præoptare potius, *id est,* malle. Hec. 4. 1. 17.

Præpediti gaudio aut ægritudine; *byass'd by our Joys, or Griefs.* Heaut. 3. 1. 109.

Præpositam amori tuo; quo pacto me habueris; *in what manner you preferred me to your Love.* Hec. 4. 2. 7.

Præpositam se ire tibi apud me si fidem habeat, ait; *he says, that if he could be sure of having always the first degree of Favour with me.* Eun. 1. 2. 59.

Præsagit mihi animus nescio quid mali; *my Mind presages I don't know what Misfortune.* Heaut. 2. 1. 7.

Præscisse me ante oportuit; *I ought to have been made acquainted with it before-hand.* Andr. 1. 5. 5.

Præscripsti tute ipse, pater, finem his rebus; *you, Father, have fixed the Period of all these Levites.* Andr. 1. 1. 124.

Præsens cum milite isto, absens ut fies; *that when in company with this Soldier, your Heart may be elsewhere.* Eun. 1. 2. 112.

Præsens absensque idem erit; *present or absent he will be the same.* Adelph. 1. 1. 48.

Præsens præsenti eripi cum videbit; *when he shall see her hurried away, and torn from his Sight for ever.* Adelph. 4. 5. 34.

Præsente

Q.

## Q.

Qua, id est, qua ratione; & per annos. Adelph. 4. 5. 59.

Quadrupedem constringito; *bind him Hand and Foot.* Andr. 5. 2. 24.

Quæstum occipere; *to enter upon a Trade, or Method of Gain.* Andr. 1. 1. 55.

Quamvis pretii homo; *a Man of Worth and Consequence.* Andr. 5. 1. 15.

Quantus quantus; nihil tu nisi sapientia es; *you're Wisdom itself.* Adelph. 3. 3. 40.

Quasi jam usquam tibi sint viginti minæ, dum huic obsequare; *as if threescore Pounds were any thing to you in comparison of obliging my Master.* Adelph. 2. 2. 15.

Quatietur foras cum donis; *he'll be kickt out of doors with his Presents.* Eun. 2. 3. 66.

Qui dicit ea quæ vult, ea quæ non vult audiet; *he shall get as good as he brings.* Andr. 5. 4. 17.

Quicum, pro quocum. Adelph. 3. 4. 31. Eun. 4. 4. 31.

Qui, pro quemadmodum. Andr. 1. 3. 5. pro quamobrem; Ibid. 5. 4. 51. pro quare. Adelph. 5. 1. 14. pro quæ. Hec. 4. 3. 1. pro quo, & qua. Eun. 3. 2. 35. & 4. 4. 31. pro unde. Andr. 2. 1. 2. Eun. 3. 2. 35. Hec. 2. 3. 6. pro ut. Andr. 2. 1. 7.

Quidquid præter spem evenit in lucro deputandum; *if things fall out different from what was apprehended, we may account it so much clear Gain.* Phorm. 1. 5. 16.

Quid, pro propter quid. Andr. 1. 4. 7. Eun. 3. 5. 7. pro quare. Adelph. 3. 3. 50.

Quid faciemus puero? *What shall we do with the Child?* Hec. 4. 4. 46.

Quid animi tum credit illi fuisse? *How great do you think must have been his Confusion?* Eun. 5. 7. 14.

Quid cum illis agas qui nec jus nec æquum sciunt? *What can be done with People who know neither Reason, Right, nor Justice?* Heaut. 3. 4. 29.

Quid hoc morbi est? (viz. amor.) *What for a Disease is this?* Eun. 2. 1. 19.

Quid mulieris uxorem habes? *What kind of Woman have you got for your Wife?* Hec. 4. 4. 22.

Quid si animam debet? *What, if he owes more than his Head is worth?* Phorm. 4. 3. 56.

Quid si cælum nunc ruit? *What, if the Sky should fall now?* Heaut. 4. 2. 41.

Quid tu es tristis, quidve alacris? *Why so thoughtful, why in such a flutter?* Eun. 2. 3. 12.

Quid tu Athenas insolens? *What could occasion a thing so unusual as your coming to Athens?* Andr. 5. 4. 4.

Quidquid est; Hec. 3. 3. 13. Ad rem mul-

tiplicem & ambiguam claudendum aptum est hoc loquendi genus. Lucret. Lib. V. V. 577. Virg. Æneidos Lib. II. V. 49.

Quid hnc reditio est? i. e. quid huc redis. Eun. 4. 4. 4.

Quin, pro imo. Andr. 2. 2. 9. Eun. 4. 7. 41. Quin, ex qui & ne compositum, pro ut non. Hec. 1. 2. 75. Quin, pro quinimo, & quo minus. Eun. 5. 2. 3.

Quoad, pro quamdiu & quando. Phorm. 1. 2. 68.

Quo jure, qua injuria, *proverbium; Right or Wrong.* Andr. 1. 3. 9.

Quod, pro quoad. Eun. 2. 1. 9. pro ut. Ibid. 5. 8. 34. pro ad quod, ad quam rem. Adelph. 5. 1. 49. pro quantum. Hec. 4. 5. 34. pro ob quod. Phorm. 1. 5. 33.

Quod cum salute ejus fiat? *Could it be without Prejudice to his Health?* Adelph. 4. 1. 3.

Quoniam id fieri quod vis non potest; velis id quod possis; *since it can't be as you would have it, content yourself with what may be.* Andr. 2. 1. 5.

Quoquo terrarum asportabitur; *wherever she shall be carried.* Phorm. 3. 3. 18.

Quot homines, tot sententiæ; *so many Men, so many Minds.* Phorm. 2. 3. 14.

Quotidianarum harum formarum tædet; *I'm weary of these every day Faces.* Eun. 2. 3. 6.

## R.

Rapere in pejorem partem; *to discredit a Thing, to represent it in a bad Light.* Adelph. Prol. 3.

Raptio, rapina, & raptus, ut differunt. Adelph. 3. 3. 2.

Rastros ad, illæc res vere redit mihi; *that will indeed soon reduce me to the Rake and Harrow.* Heaut. 5. 1. 58.

Rationem veram si vis vero exsequi; *if you were indeed to know the real Case.* Hec. 3. 1. 26. Rationem inire; *to consider with one's self.* Phorm. 2. 1. 30. Rationem eandem illam antiquam obtine; *observe now this your wonted Rule.* Adelph. 5. 1. 26.

Ratiuncula illi erat; *I had a trifle of an Account with him.* Phorm. 1. 1. 2.

Re comprobare beneficium; *to confirm Promises by Deeds.* Andr. 5. 1. 5.

Recta qui prava faciunt, his nunc præmium est; *there is now a Reward for confounding right and wrong.* Phorm. 5. 1. 6.

Reddere, & restituere, ut differunt. Eun. 4. 6. 8. Hec. 3. 1. 21.

Redigam ego vos in gratiam; *I'll make all up between you.* Phorm. 5. 6. 73.

Redigere aliquem ad inopiam; *to beggar one.* Heaut. 5. 1. 56.

Redigere in memoriam alicujus; *to rub up one's Memory.* Phorm. 2. 2. 56.

Redire

Rumpere aliquem ambulando; *to walk one off his Legs.* Hec. 3. 4. 21.

Rursum, quasi retro versum. Adelph. 1. 1. 46.

## S.

SAcrificabant apud veteres celebraturi nuptias. Phorm. 4. 4. 21.

Sacrilegus, *pro* scelerato. Eun. 5. 3. 2. & 13.

Sæva uxor, *id est,* difficilis, aspera, immitis. Phorm. 4. 6. 17.

Sævidicis dictis protelare; *to disconcert one by Rant and Blustering.* Phorm. 1. 4. 16.

Salem qui in te est qui habet; *a Man who is Master of your Wit and Talent of Humour.* Eun. 3. 1. 10.

Saltem; *a Word frequently used in speaking of Things in a desperate way, as* Andr. 2. 1. 13.

Salva res est; *all's safe, or in a fair way.* Eun. 2. 2. 37. Adelph. 4. 5. 9.

Salus ipsa si cupiat servare hanc familiam, non potest; *Providence itself, however desirous, will never be able to save this Family.* Adelph. 4. 7. 43.

Sancte jurare, i. e. religiose. Hec. 1. 1. 3. Adjurare. Ibid. 2. 2. 26. Dejerare persancte. Ibid. 4. 6. 5.

Sandalium, calceamenti genus; *a Slipper.* Eun. 5. 8. 4.

Sane, *pro* multum & valde. Andr. 1. 4. 2. Ibid. 4. 2. 41.

Sapienti sat est dictum; *a Word to the Wise.* Phorm. 3. 3. 8.

Sapientia, *pro* homine sapiente. Adelph. 3. 4. 31.

Sat habeo, *pro* sufficit; *enough.* Andr. 2. 1. 35.

Satagere, rerum suarum; *to have Business enough of his own upon his Hands.* Heaut. 2. 2. 13.

Satias me cepit, *pro* satietas. Eun. 5. 5. 3. Hec. 4. 2. 18.

Satin' sanus es; *are you in your right Senses?* Adelph. 5. 6. 14. Satin' ex sententia? *Is it as you would have it?* Phorm. 1. 5. 26. Satin' salva? *Is all right?* Eun. 5. 6. 8.

Satrapes; provinciæ præfectus, vox Persica. Heaut. 3. 1. 43.

Saxum hoc satis diu jam volo; *this is what I have all along aim'd at.* Eun. 5. 10. 37.

Scelus, *pro* infortunio. Eun. 2. 3. 34. *pro* scelesto, & scelesta. Andr. 3. 4. 1. Eun. 4. 3. 3.

Scilicet; *sometimes used ironically; as* Andr. 1. 2. 14.

Scisti uti foro; *you know how to make the best of your Market.* Phorm. 1. 2. 29.

Scitus puer; *pro* pulchro; *a fine Child.* Andr. 3. 2. 2.

Scrupulum injeci homini; *I have aim'd right, I have touched the Sore.* Adelph. 2. 2. 20. Phorm. 5. 6. 61.



Scrupulus unus mihi restat; *I have yet one Scruple remaining.* Andr. 5. 4. 37.

Sectari lites; *to engage in a Law-Suit.* Phorm. 2. 2. 61.

Secundæ res quum sint, de adversis cogitandum; *in Prosperity we ought to think of Adversity.* Phorm. 1. 5. 11.

Segregatum me habuisse Pamphilum; *that I have had no Commerce with Pamphilus.* Hec. 4. 5. 25.

Senectus est morbus. Phorm. 4. 1. 9. Nimium ad rem attenta. Adelph. 5. 8. 31. Verecundos facit. Phorm. 5. 7. 34.

Senium, *pro* sene. Eun. 2. 3. 10. pro tedio, & molestia. Hec. 4. 2. 19.

Sentiet ipse posterius; *he'll feel it afterwards to his Cost.* Adelph. 1. 2. 59.

Sentire cum aliquo; *to be of the same mind with another.* Andr. 2. 1. 26.

Sepultus sum; *verba plane desperantis, & plus est quam nullus sum.* Phorm. 5. 6. 50.

Sermo, animi index. Heaut. 2. 2. 4.

Sermones cædere; *to chat, to discourse together.* Heaut. 2. 2. 1.

Servus homo causam ne orato; lex Atheniensium. Phorm. 1. 5. 62.

Si mihi pergit ea quæ volt dicere, quæ non vult audiet; *I'll give him as good as he brings.* Andr. 5. 4. 17.

Sic, *pro* leviter. Andr. 1. 2. 4. pro temere. Phorm. 1. 2. 95.

Sic ut quimus, quando ut volumus non licet; *the best we can, since we can't have it to our wish.* Andr. 4. 6. 10.

Similia omnia, omnes congruunt; *they are all of a piece, all hang together.* Phorm. 1. 5. 34.

Simulare, & dissimulare, ut differant. Andr. 3. 4. 9.

Simulare certe hominis est; *it were decent however to seem so.* Adelph. 4. 7. 16.

Simulatio non est mea; *I'm not apt to boast vainly.* Heaut. 4. 4. 34.

Sine Cerere & Libero friget Venus; *without Wine and good Cheer, Love is but cold Entertainment.* Eun. 4. 5. 6.

Singulatim commemorare; *to recount the same.* Phorm. 5. 7. 43.

Sis, *pro* si vis. Adelph. 5. 1. 4. Eun. 2. 3. 19.

Sobrius non es, i. e. sanæ mentis. Andr. 4. 3. 39.

Socors cæterarum rerum; *thoughtless of other Matters.* Adelph. 4. 5. 61.

Socrus omnes sunt iniquæ; *Step-mothers all hate their Daughters-in-Law.* Hec. 2. 1. 4. & 5.

Sollicitatio, & sollicitudo, quid sit. Andr. 1. 5. 26.

Sollicitari, i. e. perturbari; *to be made uneasy; or unhappy.* Andr. 4. 1. 6.

Solidum, *pro* plano & integro. Andr. 4. 1. 25.